Lust,
VIOLENCE,
Sin,
MAGIC

Lust, VIOLENCE, *Sin,* MAGIC

Sixty Years of Esquire Fiction

EDITED BY RUST HILLS, WILL BLYTHE, AND ERIKA MANSOURIAN

Introduction by Terry McDonell

THE ATLANTIC MONTHLY PRESS
NEW YORK

Published simultaneously in Canada
Printed in the United States of America

Library of Congress Cataloging-in-Publication Data

Lust, violence, sin, magic: sixty years of Esquire fiction / edited
by Rust Hills and Will Blythe; introduction by Terry McDonell.
ISBN 0-87113-552-3
1. American fiction—20th century. 2. Short stories, American.
I. Hills, L. Rust. II. Blythe, Will. III. Esquire (New York, N.Y.)
PS648.S5L87 1993   813'.010805—dc20   93-22855

Design by Laura Hough

The Atlantic Monthly Press
841 Broadway
New York, NY 10003

FIRST PRINTING

This book was put together

in the memory and spirit of

Arnold Gingrich, who had the idea.

Contents

SIN

MAGIC

True Fiction:

An Introduction

Culture is memory. We know who we are by telling each other about the way we live; and the stories we write down are more important than the stories we tell each other. This is what is important about the book you are holding in your hands. It is more than an anthology of stories; it is an imagined history of the way we have lived for the last sixty years, a picture of who we were and who we have become.

It is also a history by example of what has happened to fiction over the past sixty years. We have been told many times that American readers get along just fine without reading short stories and that more and more magazines are doing quite well without printing them. This does not hold for *Esquire*, which publishes fiction in every issue and whose readers continue to look to the stories for insight as well as entertainment.

It was that way from the beginning.

Every story that has made its way into *Esquire* has a publishing story behind it. This is where to look for additional understanding of the author of a particular story (not to mention the workings of the magazine), if not the story itself. Such insights are key to defining the role of fiction—especially the short story—within American culture at the time that the piece was originally published.

When *Esquire* was launched in 1933, its founding editor, Arnold Gingrich, determined to run the absolute best writing he could find—both fiction and nonfiction. Gingrich met Ernest Hemingway for the first time that same year in a New York City bookstore that dealt in first editions. Gingrich had arrived to pick up a copy of Hemingway's *Three Stories and Ten Poems*—one of three hundred and fifty copies printed in Paris in 1923. Hemingway was just leaving when Gingrich came in, and the young editor went right up to him, reminding Hemingway that he was a collector of the celebrated writer's work (they had been corresponding in this regard for some months) and pleading with him to contribute to the new magazine. Hemingway agreed to Gingrich's suggestion that he write "some kind of sporting letter covering his different outdoor activities in the course of his travels." When it came to payment, Gingrich said that he hoped to "make up in promptness of payment what it would lack in size," but that he was going to be forced to start rather low, even if it was "as much as I could to start and going up as fast as we make it, if we make it."

"I don't care how much you pay," Hemingway told him, then reconsidered immediately. "Hell, yes, I do care, but the big stuff I can always get by selling stories and you and I are just talking about journalism. Let's say you pay fifty bucks or whatever you pay, you pay me double."

Gingrich said he was planning to pay a hundred.

"Fine," said Hemingway, "that means I get two hundred, and if you find as you go along that you can do better than that, then I get that much more, too, only doubled, and right away, without making me sit up and beg for it."

The two shook hands. That became the only deal Hemingway ever had with the magazine.

Over the next three years, as Hemingway conscientiously met deadlines from wherever he happened to be, the magazine's rate more than doubled. By the late spring of 1936, Hemingway was making five hundred dollars per contribution and thoroughly enjoying his relationship with the magazine. When he saw he couldn't meet an upcoming deadline for the then standard "Letter From . . ." Hemingway sent Gingrich a story he had been working on instead. It was called "The Snows of Kilimanjaro," and it was to be his first short story with the magazine. From Gingrich's point of view, it was extraordinary for two reasons: it was more than twice as long as Hemingway's usual contribution, and it was a masterpiece.

For "The Snows of Kilimanjaro," Gingrich paid Hemingway a thousand dollars, or double his standard double rate. It was the most the magazine had ever paid for any single contribution up to that time, but as Gingrich pointed out in his memoir, *Nothing but People,* it was less than a fourth of what the big magazines like *Cosmopolitan* were paying Hemingway for stories of much less power and importance.

Editors who hear this story about the publication of "The Snows of Kilimanjaro" are immediately struck by the haphazardness by which the great piece came into *Esquire*'s pages, not to mention the dealmaking eccentricities of its author and the charming opportunism of editor Gingrich. Those of us who edit the magazine these days are more inclined to ponder Hemingway's willingness to do the work offered by Gingrich for next to nothing because they were "only talking about journalism."

Straight journalism as Hemingway was referring to it at the time was perhaps as greatly undervalued as it is sometimes overvalued today. In the thirties, the short story ruled, and as the decades moved on and life (and the media) became more complicated, certain adventurous journalists began to adopt the techniques of the short story. Narrative and scene became more important to them, as did believable dialogue and even speculation about what was going on inside a subject's head. (Thanks, Tom!!!)

Much has been made of New Journalism. And *Esquire* is generally thought of as its most important cradle, if not its actual birthplace. This is, of course, true. Along with the Sunday magazine of the *New York Herald Tribune* and, later, *New York* magazine and *Rolling Stone*, *Esquire* ran the work of Norman Mailer, Gay Talese, and Tom Wolfe, among many others who locked onto the new form. These writers have, of course, been claimed as their own by nearly every magazine that ever published the slightest ruminations penned by them, but the fact remains that while working primarily for editors Harold Hayes (at *Esquire*), Clay Felker *(Esquire,* the *Tribune, New York)*, and Jann Wenner *(Rolling Stone)*, they gave journalism a new position of importance above that of the short story—a status that lingers like a literary hangover in publishing circles today.

But even as these great journalists were making their reputations by using the techniques of fiction, *Esquire* was also publishing short story writers who were shaping their own work with more grit and realism. The stories seemed more rooted in reality, even if that reality was imagined. If you looked closely you could see that as our popular fiction in general was becoming more sophisticated and refined, the philosophic differences between what was imagined and what was observed by a particular author were more difficult to recognize. *Esquire* was winning National Magazine awards for its stories, but it is also true that during all of the ping-ponging of techniques between fiction and nonfiction writers, very little attention was being paid to the fiction side of the game. And, in fact, a most important idea was lost: that the best fiction written since *Esquire* began publication in 1933 had almost always answered the who, what, when, where, and why questions associated with solid journalism, but in ways that made it what John Updike called "the subtlest instrument for self-examination and self-display that mankind has invented yet." Updike wrote this in his introduction to *The Esquire Fiction Reader, Volume II* (1986), and went on to explain that fiction "makes sociology look priggish, history problematical, the film media two-dimensional and the *National Enquirer* as silly as last week's cereal box."

How silly not to recognize that questions of what is imagined and what is observed cannot be answered by simply asking what is true and what is not. This is what Tim O'Brien means when he speaks of "story truth" being "truer sometimes than happening truth." And this is also what Ken Kesey meant when he wrote at the beginning of *One Flew over the Cuckoo's Nest* that some things were "true even if they didn't happen."

A young woman in a bar once asked me if my first novel, which she had heard about from the bartender, was fiction or nonfiction. The awesome post-literateness of this comment was picked up by most of the fiction writers I knew at the time as evidence of the precariousness of their place in the culture and hurled back and forth among them as a kind of crybaby mantra. The truth is, in another context—specifically the one outlined above—her question would have been a very good one.

And the answer to that question as applied to the stories that follow can be delivered in one word: both.

From the first issue of *Esquire*, which ran eight short stories, the writers who have contributed fiction threw long shadows. Just to list their names in a row is powerful beyond the recollection of any specific story: Erskine Caldwell, Irwin Shaw, Truman Capote, Philip Roth, Joy Williams, Jayne Anne Phillips, James Salter, Saul Bellow, Reynolds Price, Ernest Hemingway, John Steinbeck, Norman Mailer, Leslie A. Fiedler, Stanley Elkin, Raymond Carver, Gail Godwin, T. Coraghessan Boyle, Herbert Wilner, Tobias Wolff, Tim O'Brien, Thomas McGuane, F. Scott Fitzgerald, James Jones, John Cheever, Flannery O'Connor, Harold Brodkey, Richard Ford, Denis Johnson, John Updike, Vince Passaro, Ethan Canin, John Barth, Bruce Jay Friedman, Barry Targan, Gabriel García Márquez, William Kotzwinkle, Louise Erdrich,

Ray Bradbury, Barry Hannah, Don DeLillo, Mark Richard. It's like listing the 1927 Yankees and then Vince Lombardi's Green Bay Packers and then Lord Buckley and then all of the astronauts and heavyweight champions and Butch Cassidy and the Sundance Kid and maybe even Elvis. And from the magazine's point of view, it's also a remarkable list for the names and stories that have been left out because of length or lack of fit within the confines of this particular organization—great, great writers from Gore Vidal and Peter Matthiessen to Cormac McCarthy and Richard Price. Over the years *Esquire* has published virtually every noted American fiction writer working in the last two-thirds of this century. It is an impossible trivia question to come up with one who has not graced the magazine's pages. There have, in fact, been 2,905 pieces of fiction published in the magazine. Many of the longer ones have never been anthologized by *Esquire*, although many have been made into films, like Truman Capote's "Breakfast at Tiffany's" and Jim Harrison's "Legends of the Fall." The point is that *Esquire* is proud of every story it has ever published, each in its own way underlining the magazine's continuing commitment to fiction.

The organization of stories collected here under the categories of Lust, Violence, Sin, and Magic also reflects a commitment made by each of the writers in his or her unique way to reveal the most difficult shadings of real life and the complexities of the human condition. This sounds very ambitious, and it is. And this is why these stories, taken together, form a safety net for the most difficult truths about the way we live, catching them as they fall from our lives. Some are funny, some are painful to confront. All of them are very real.

Terry McDonell
Esquire Editor in Chief
New York City
May 25, 1993

Lust

ERSKINE CALDWELL

August Afternoon

Erskine Caldwell (1903–1987) was born in Georgia and worked as a cotton picker, stagehand, professional football player, and screenwriter. He is best known for God's Little Acre *and* Tobacco Road. *Written in the early 1930s, these novels were controversial for their raw depiction of human squalor. "August Afternoon" was a literary sensation when it appeared in the inaugural issue of* Esquire *in 1933.*

Vic Glover awoke with the noonday heat ringing in his ears. He had been asleep for only half an hour, and he was getting ready to turn over and go back to sleep when he opened his eyes for a moment and saw Hubert's black head over the top of his bare toes. He stretched his eyelids and held them open as long as he could.

Hubert was standing in the yard, at the edge of the porch, with a pine cone in his hand.

Vic cursed him.

The colored man raked the cone over the tops of Vic's toes and stepped back out of reach.

"What do you mean by standing there tickling me with that dad-burned cone?" Vic shouted at Hubert. "Is that all you can find to do? Why don't you get out in that field and do something to those boll weevils? They're going to eat up every pound of cotton on the place if you don't stop them."

"I surely hated to wake you up, Mr. Vic," Hubert said, "but there's a white man out here looking for something. He won't say what he wants, but he's hanging around for something."

Vic was wide awake by that time. He sat up on the quilt and pulled on his shoes without looking into the yard. The white sand in the yard beat the glare of the sun directly into his eyes and he could see nothing beyond the edge of the porch. Hubert threw the pine cone under the porch and stepped aside.

"He must be looking for trouble," Vic said. "When they come around and don't say anything, and just sit, it's trouble they're looking for."

"There he is, Mr. Vic," Hubert said, nodding his head across the yard. "There he sits up against that water oak."

Vic looked around for Willie. Willie was sitting on the top step at the other end of the porch, directly in front of the stranger. She did not look at Vic.

"You ought to have better sense than to wake me up while I'm taking a nap. This is no time of day to be up. I've got to get a little sleep every now and then."

"Boss," Hubert said, "I wouldn't wake you up at all, not at any time, but Miss Willie just sits there high up on the steps and that white man has been out there whittling on a little stick a pretty long time without saying anything. I've got scared about something happening when he whittles that little stick clear through, and it's just about whittled down to nothing now."

Vic glanced again at Willie, and from her he turned to stare at the stranger sitting under the water oak tree in his front yard.

The piece of wood had been shaved down to paper thinness.

"Boss," Hubert said, "we ain't aiming to have no trouble today, are we?"

"Which way did he come from?" Vic asked.

"I never did see him come, Mr. Vic. I just looked up, and there he was, sitting against that water oak whittling on a little stick. I reckon I must have been sleeping when he came, because when I looked up, there he was."

Vic slid down over the quilt until his legs were hanging over the edge of the porch. Perspiration began to trickle down his neck as soon as he sat up.

"Ask him what he's after, Hubert."

"We ain't aiming to have no trouble today, are we, Mr. Vic?"

"Ask him what he wants, I said."

Hubert went almost halfway to the water oak tree and stopped.

"Mr. Vic says what can he do for you, white-folks."

The man said nothing. He did not even glance up.

Hubert came back to the porch, the whites of his eyes becoming larger with each step.

"What did he say?" Vic asked him.

"He ain't said nothing yet, Mr. Vic. He acts like he don't hear me at all. You'd better go talk to him, Mr. Vic. He won't give me no attention. Appears to me like he's just sitting there looking at Miss Willie on the high step. Maybe if you was to tell her to go in the house and shut the door, he might be persuaded to give some notice to what we say to him."

"Can't see any sense in sending her in the house," Vic said. "I can make him talk. Hand me that stilyerd."

"Mr. Vic, I'm trying to tell you about Miss Willie. Miss Willie's been sitting there on that high step and he's been looking up at her a right long time, Mr. Vic. If you won't object to me saying so, Mr. Vic, I reckon I'd tell Miss Willie to go sit somewhere else, if I was you. Miss Willie ain't got much on today, Mr. Vic. That's what I've been trying to tell you."

"Hand me that stilyerd, I said."

Hubert went to the end of the porch and brought the cotton steelyard to Vic. He stepped back out of the way.

"Boss," Hubert said, "we ain't aiming to have no trouble today, are we?"

Vic was getting ready to jump down into the yard when the man under the water oak reached into his pocket and pulled out another knife. It was about nine inches long, and both sides of the handle were covered with hairy cowhide. There was a springbutton on one end. The man pushed the button with his thumb, and the blade sprang open. He began playing with both knives, throwing them up in the air and catching them on the back of his hands.

Hubert moved to the other side of Vic.

"Mr. Vic," he said, "I ain't intending to mix in your business none, but it looks to me like you got yourself in for a mess of trouble when you went off and brought Miss Willie back here. It looks to me like she's got up for a city girl, more so than a country girl."

Vic cursed him.

"I'm telling you, Mr. Vic, a country girl wouldn't sit on a high step in front of a man, not when she wasn't wearing nothing but that blue wrapper, anyhow."

"Shut up," Vic said, laying the steelyard down on the quilt beside him.

The man under the water oak closed the blade of the small knife and put it into his pocket. The big cowhide-covered knife he flipped into the air and caught easily on the back of his hand.

"What's your name?" he asked Willie.

"Willie."

He flipped the knife again.

"What's yours?" she asked him.

"Floyd."

"Where are you from?"

"Carolina."

He flipped it higher, catching it underhanded.

"What are you doing in Georgia?"

"Don't know," he said. "Just looking around."

Willie giggled, smiling at him.

Floyd got up and walked across the yard to the steps and sat down on the bottom one. He put his arm around his knees and looked up at Willie.

"You're not so bad-looking," he said. "I've seen lots worse looking."

"You're not so bad yourself," Willie giggled, resting her arms on her knees and looking down at him.

"How about a kiss?"

"What would it be to you?"

"Not bad. I reckon I've had lots worse."

"Well, you can't get it sitting down there."

Floyd climbed the steps on his hands and feet and sat down on the next to the top step. He leaned against Willie, putting one arm around her waist and the other over her knees. Willie slid down to the step beside him.

"Boss," Hubert said, his lips twitching, "we ain't going to have no trouble today, are we?"

Vic cursed him.

Willie and Floyd moved down a step without loosening their embrace.

"Who is that yellow-headed sapsucker, anyhow?" Vic said. "I'll be dad-burned if he ain't got a lot of nerve—coming here and fooling with Willie."

"You wouldn't do nothing to cause trouble, would you, Mr. Vic? I surely don't want to have no trouble today, Mr. Vic."

Vic glanced at the nine-inch knife Floyd had, stuck into the step at his feet. It stood on its tip eighteen inches high, while the sun was reflected against the bright blade and made a streak of light on Floyd's pant leg.

"Go over there and take that knife away from him and bring it here," Vic said. "Don't be scared of him."

"Mr. Vic, I surely hate to disappoint you, but if you want that white-folk's knife, you'll just have to get it your own self. I don't aim to have myself all carved up with that thing. Mr. Vic, I surely can't accommodate you this time. If you want that white-folk's knife, you'll just be bound to get it yourself, Mr. Vic."

Vic cursed him.

Hubert backed away until he was at the end of the porch. He kept on looking behind him all the time, looking to be certain of the exact location of the sycamore stump that was between him and the pine grove on the other side of the cotton field.

Vic called to Hubert and told him to come back. Hubert came slowly around the corner of the porch and stood a few feet from the quilt where Vic was sitting. His lips quivered and the whites of his eyes grew larger. Vic motioned for him to come closer, but he would not come an inch farther.

"How old are you?" Floyd asked Willie.

"Fifteen."

Floyd jerked the knife out of the wood and thrust it deeper in the same place.

"How old are you?" she asked him.

"About twenty-seven."

"Are you married?"

"Not now," he said. "How long have you been?"

"About three months," Willie said.

"How do you like it?"

"Pretty good so far."

"How about another kiss?"

"You've just had one."

"I'd like another one now."

"I ought not to let you kiss me again."

"Why not?" Floyd said.

"Men don't like girls who kiss too much."

"I'm not that kind."

"What kind are you?" Willie asked him.

"I'd like to kiss you a lot."

"But after I let you do that, you'd go away."

"No, I won't. I'll stay for something else."

"What?"

"Let's go inside for a drink and I'll tell you."

"We'll have to go to the spring for fresh water."

"Where's the spring?"

"Just across the field in the grove."

"All right," Floyd said, standing up. "Let's go."

He bent down and pulled the knife out of the wood. Willie ran down the steps and across the yard. When Floyd saw that she was not going to wait for him, he ran after her, holding the knives in his pocket with one hand. She led him across the cotton field to the spring in the pine grove. Just before they got there, Floyd caught her by the arm and ran beside her the rest of the way.

"Boss," Hubert said, "we ain't aiming to have no trouble today, are we?"

Vic cursed him.

"I don't want to get messed up with a heap of trouble and maybe get my belly slit open with that big hairy knife. If you ain't got objections, I reckon I'll mosey on home now and cut a little firewood for the cookstove."

"Come back here!" Vic said. "You stay where you are and stop making moves to go off."

"What are we aiming to do, Mr. Vic?"

Vic eased himself off the porch and walked across the yard to the water oak. He looked down at the ground where Floyd had been sitting, and then he looked at the porch steps where Willie had been. The noonday heat beat down through the thin leaves overhead and he could feel his mouth and throat burn with the hot air he breathed.

"Have you got a gun, Hubert?"

"No, sir, boss," Hubert said.

"Why haven't you?" he said. "Right when I need a gun, you haven't got it. Why don't you keep a gun?"

"Mr. Vic, I ain't got no use for a gun. I used to keep one to shoot rabbits and squirrels with, but I got to thinking one day, and I traded it off the first chance I had. I reckoned it was a good thing I traded, too. If I had kept it, you'd be asking for it like you did just now."

Vic went back to the porch and picked up the steelyard and hammered the porch with it. After he had hit the porch four or five times, he dropped it and started out in the direction of the spring. He walked as far as the edge of the shade and stopped. He stood listening for a while.

Willie and Floyd could be heard down near the spring. Floyd said something to Willie, and Willie laughed loudly. There was silence for several minutes, and then Willie laughed again. Vic was getting ready to turn back to the porch when he heard her cry out. It sounded like a scream, but it was not exactly that; it sounded like a shriek, but it was not that, either; it sounded more like someone laughing and crying simultaneously in a high-pitched voice.

"Where did Miss Willie come from, Mr. Vic?" Hubert asked. "Where did you bring her from?"

"Down below here a little way," he said.

Hubert listened to the sounds that were coming from the pine grove.

"Boss," he said after a while, "it appears to me like you didn't go far enough away."

"I went far enough," Vic said. "If I had gone any farther, I'd have been in Florida."

The colored man hunched his shoulders forward several times while he smoothed the white sand with his broad-soled shoes.

"Mr. Vic, if I was you, the next time I'd surely go that far."

"What do you mean, the next time?"

"I was figuring that maybe you wouldn't be keeping her much longer than now, Mr. Vic."

Vic cursed him.

Hubert raised his head several times and attempted to see down into the pine grove over the top of the growing cotton.

"Shut up and mind your own business," Vic said. "I'm going to keep her till the cows come home. Where else do you reckon I'd find a better-looking girl than Willie?"

"Boss, I wasn't thinking of how she looks—I was thinking how she acts."

"She acts that way now because she's not old enough to do different. She won't act that way much longer. She'll get over the way she's doing pretty soon."

Hubert followed Vic across the yard. While Vic went towards the porch, Hubert stopped and leaned against the water oak where he could almost see over the cotton field into the pine grove. Vic went up on the porch and stretched out on the quilt. He took off his shoes and flung them aside.

"I surely God knowed something was going to happen when he whittled that stick down to nothing," Hubert was saying to himself. "White-folks take a long time to whittle a little piece of wood, but after they whittle it down to nothing, they're going to be up and doing."

Presently Vic sat upright on the quilt.

"Listen here, Hubert—"

"Yes, sir, boss."

"You keep your eyes on that stilyerd so it will stay right where it is now, and when they come back up the path from the spring, you wake me up in a hurry. Do you hear?"

"Yes, sir, boss," Hubert said. "Are you aiming to take a little nap now?"

"Yes, I am. And if you don't wake me up when they come back, I'll break your head for you when I do wake up."

Vic lay down again on the quilt and turned over on his side to shut out the blinding glare of the early afternoon sun that was reflected upon the porch from the hard white sand in the yard.

Hubert scratched his head and sat down against the water oak facing the path from the spring. He could hear Vic snoring on the porch above the sounds that came at intervals from the pine grove across the field. He sat staring down the path, singing under his breath. It was a long time until sundown.

[AUTUMN 1933]

IRWIN SHAW

The Eighty-Yard Run

Irwin Shaw (1913–1984) was one of the best friends Esquire *ever had. Beginning with the classic "The Eighty-Yard Run" in the early 1940s, he went on to publish a dozen more stories in the magazine. But perhaps his greatest contribution to* Esquire *was in persuading the owner and editor in chief, Phillip Moffitt, in 1984, to publish a "summer reading issue" of fiction each year, a tradition that has continued since. Among his many books are* The Young Lions, Two Weeks in Another Town, Voices of a Summer Day, Rich Man, Poor Man, *and* Acceptable Losses*

The pass was high and wide and he jumped for it, feeling it slap flatly against his hands, as he shook his hips to throw off the halfback who was diving at him. The center floated by, his hands desperately brushing Darling's knee as Darling picked his feet up high and delicately ran over a blocker and an opposing linesman in a jumble on the ground near the scrimmage line. He had ten yards in the clear and picked up speed, breathing easily, feeling his thigh pads rising and falling against his legs, listening to the sound of cleats behind him, pulling away from them, watching the other backs heading him off toward the sideline, the whole picture, the men closing in on him, the blockers fighting for position, the ground he had to cross, all suddenly clear in his head, for the first time in his life not a meaningless confusion of men, sounds, speed. He smiled a little to himself as he ran, holding the ball lightly in front of him with his two hands, his knees pumping high, his hips twisting in the almost-girlish run of a back in a broken field. The first halfback came at him and he fed him his leg, then swung at the last moment, took the shock of the man's shoulder without breaking stride, ran right through him, his cleats biting securely into the turf. There was only the safety man now, coming warily at him, his arms crooked, hands spread. Darling tucked the ball in, spurted at him, driving hard, hurling himself along, his legs pounding, knees high, all two hundred pounds bunched into controlled attack. He was sure he was going to get past the safety man. Without thought, his arms and legs working beautifully together, he headed right for the safety man, stiff-armed him, feeling blood spurt instantaneously from the man's nose onto his hand, seeing his face go awry, head turned, mouth pulled to one side. He pivoted away, keeping the arm locked, dropping the safety man as he ran easily toward the goal line, with the drumming of cleats diminishing behind him.

How long ago? It was autumn then and the ground was getting hard because the nights were cold and leaves from the maples around the stadium blew across the practice fields in gusts of wind and the girls were beginning to put polo coats over their sweaters when they came to watch practice in the afternoons . . . Fifteen years. Darling walked slowly over the same ground in the spring twilight, in his neat shoes, a man of thirty-five dressed in a double-breasted suit, ten pounds heavier in the fifteen years, but not fat, with the years between 1925 and 1940 showing in his face.

The coach was smiling quietly to himself and the assistant coaches were looking at each other with pleasure the way they always did when one of the second stringers suddenly did something fine, bringing credit to them, making their $2,000 a year a tiny bit more secure.

Darling trotted back, smiling, breathing deeply but easily, feeling wonderful, not tired, though this was the tail end of practice and he'd run eighty yards. The sweat poured off his face and soaked his jersey and he liked the feeling, the warm moistness lubricating his skin like oil. Off in a corner of the field some players were punting and the smack of leather against the ball came pleasantly through the afternoon air. The freshmen were running signals on the next field and the quarterback's sharp voice, the pound of the eleven pairs of cleats, the "Dig, now, *dig!*" of the coaches, the laughter of the players all somehow made him feel happy as he trotted back to midfield, listening to the applause and shouts of the students along the sidelines, knowing that after that run the coach would have to start him Saturday against Illinois.

Fifteen years, Darling thought, remembering the shower after the workout, the hot water steaming off his skin and the deep soapsuds and all the young voices singing with the water streaming down and towels going and managers running in and out and the sharp sweet smell of oil of wintergreen and everybody clapping him on the back as he dressed and Packard, the captain, who took being captain very seriously, coming over to him and shaking his hand and saying. "Darling, you're going to go places in the next two years."

The assistant manager fussed over him, wiping a cut on his leg with alcohol and iodine, the little sting making him realize suddenly how fresh and whole and solid his body felt. The manager slapped a piece of adhesive tape over the cut and Darling noticed the sharp clean white of the tape against the ruddiness of the skin, fresh from the shower.

He dressed slowly, the softness of his shirt and the soft warmth of his wool socks and his flannel trousers a reward against his skin after the harsh pressure of the shoulder harness and thigh and hip pads. He drank three glasses of cold water, the liquid reaching down coldly inside of him, soothing the harsh dry places in his throat and belly left by the sweat and running and shouting of practice.

Fifteen years.

The sun had gone down and the sky was green behind the stadium and he laughed quietly to himself as he looked at the stadium, rearing above the trees, and knew that on Saturday when the seventy thousand voices roared as the team came running out onto the field, part of that enormous salute would be for him. He walked slowly, listening to the gravel crunch satisfactorily under his shoes in the still twilight, feeling his clothes swing lightly against his skin, breathing the thin evening air, feeling the wind move softly in his damp hair, wonderfully cool behind his ears and at the nape of his neck.

Louise was waiting for him at the road, in her car. The top was down and he noticed all over again, as he always did when he saw her, how pretty she was, the rough blond hair and the large, inquiring eyes and the bright mouth, smiling now.

She threw the door open. "Were you good today?" she asked.

"Pretty good," he said. He climbed in, sank luxuriously into the soft leather, stretched his legs far out. He smiled, thinking of the eighty yards. "Pretty damn good."

She looked at him seriously for a moment, then scrambled around, like a little girl, kneeling on the seat next to him, grabbed him, her hands along his ears, and kissed him as he sprawled, head back, on the seat cushion. She let go of him, but kept her head close to his, over his. Darling reached up slowly and rubbed the back of his hand against her cheek, lit softly by a streetlamp a hundred feet away. They looked at each other, smiling.

Louise drove down to the lake and they sat there silently, watching the moon rise behind the hills on the other side. Finally he reached over, pulled her gently to him, kissed her. Her lips grew soft, her body sank into his, tears formed slowly in her eyes. He knew, for the first time, that he could do whatever he wanted with her.

"Tonight," he said. "I'll call for you at seven-thirty. Can you get out?"

She looked at him. She was smiling, but the tears were still full in her eyes. "All right," she said. "I'll get out. How about you? Won't the coach raise hell?"

Darling grinned. "I got the coach in the palm of my hand," he said. "Can you wait till seven-thirty?"

She grinned back at him. "No," she said.

They kissed and she started the car and they went back to town for dinner. He sang on the way home.

Christian Darling, thirty-five years old, sat on the frail spring grass, greener now than it ever would be again on the practice field, looked thoughtfully up at the stadium, a deserted ruin in the twilight. He had started on the first team that Saturday and every Saturday after that for the next two years, but it had never been as satisfactory as it should have been. He never had broken away, the longest run he'd ever made was thirty-five yards, and that in a game that was already won, and then that kid had come up from the third team, Diederich, a blankfaced German kid from Wisconsin, who ran like a bull, ripping lines to pieces Saturday after Saturday, plowing through, never getting hurt, never changing his expression, scoring more points, gaining more ground than all the rest of the team put together, making everybody's All-American, carrying the ball three times out of four, keeping everybody else out of the headlines. Darling was a good blocker and he spent his Saturday afternoons working on the big Swedes and Polacks who played tackle and end for Michigan, Illinois, Purdue, hurling into huge pileups, bobbing his head wildly to elude the great raw hands swinging like meat cleavers at him as he went charging in to open up holes for Diederich coming through like a locomotive behind him. Still, it wasn't so bad. Everybody liked him and he did his job and he was pointed out on the campus and boys always felt important when they introduced their girls to him at their proms, and Louise loved him and watched him faithfully in the games, even in the mud, when your own mother wouldn't know you, and drove him around in her car keeping the top down because she was proud of him and wanted to show everybody that she was Christian Darling's girl. She bought him crazy presents because her father was rich, watches, pipes, humidors, an icebox for beer for his room, curtains, wallets, a fifty-dollar dictionary.

"You'll spend every cent your old man owns," Darling protested once when she showed up at his rooms with seven different packages in her arms and tossed them onto the couch.

"Kiss me," Louise said, "and shut up."

"Do you want to break your poor old man?"

"I don't mind. I want to buy you presents."

"Why?"

"It makes me feel good. Kiss me. I don't know why. Did you know that you're an important figure?"

"Yes," Darling said gravely.

"When I was waiting for you at the library yesterday two girls saw you coming and one of them said to the other, 'That's Christian Darling. He's an important figure.' "

"You're a liar."

"I'm in love with an important figure."

"Still, why the hell did you have to give me a forty-pound dictionary?"

"I wanted to make sure," Louise said, "that you had a token of my esteem. I want to smother you in tokens of my esteem."

Fifteen years ago.

They'd married when they got out of college. There'd been other women for him, but all casual and secret, more for curiosity's sake, and vanity, women who'd thrown themselves at him and flattered him, a pretty mother at a summer camp for boys, an old girl from his home town who'd suddenly blossomed into a coquette, a friend of Louise's who had dogged him grimly for six months and had taken advantage of the two weeks when Louise went home when her mother died. Perhaps Louise had known, but she'd kept quiet, loving him completely, filling his rooms with presents, religiously watching him battling with the big Swedes and Polacks on the line of scrimmage on Saturday afternoons, making plans for marrying him and living with him in New York and going with him there to the nightclubs, the theaters, the good restaurants, being proud of him in advance, tall, white-teethed, smiling, large, yet moving lightly, with an athlete's grace, dressed in evening clothes, approvingly eyed by magnificently dressed and famous women in theater lobbies, with Louise adoringly at his side.

Her father, who manufactured inks, set up a New York office for Darling to manage and presented him with three hundred accounts and they lived on Beekman Place with a view of the river with fifteen thousand dollars a year between them, because everybody was buying everything in those days, including ink. They saw all the shows and went to all the speakeasies and spent their fifteen thousand dollars a year and in the afternoons Louise went to the art galleries and the matinees of the more serious plays that Darling didn't like to sit through and Darling slept with a girl who danced in the chorus of *Rosalie* and with the wife of a man who owned three copper mines. Darling played squash three times a week and remained as solid as a stone barn and Louise never took her eyes off him when they were in the same room together, watching him with a secret, miser's smile, with a trick of coming over to him in the middle of a crowded room and saying gravely, in a low voice, "You're the handsomest man I've ever seen in my whole life. Want a drink?"

Nineteen twenty-nine came to Darling and to his wife and father-in-law, the maker of inks, just as it came to everyone else. The father-in-law waited until 1933 and then blew his brains out and when Darling went to Chicago to see what the books of the firm looked like he found out all that was left were debts and three or four gallons of unbought ink.

"Please, Christian," Louise said, sitting in their neat Beekman Place apartment, with a view of the river and prints of paintings by Dufy and Braque and Picasso on the wall, "please, why do you want to start drinking at two o'clock in the afternoon?"

"I have nothing else to do," Darling said, putting down his glass, emptied of its fourth drink. "Please pass the whiskey."

Louise filled his glass. "Come take a walk with me," she said. "We'll walk along the river."

"I don't want to walk along the river," Darling said, squinting intensely at the prints of paintings by Dufy, Braque and Picasso.

"We'll walk along Fifth Avenue."

"I don't want to walk along Fifth Avenue."

"Maybe," Louise said gently, "you'd like to come with me to some art galleries. There's an exhibition by a man named Klee—"

"I don't want to go to any art galleries. I want to sit here and drink Scotch whiskey," Darling said. "Who the hell hung those goddam pictures up in the wall?"

"I did," Louise said.

"I hate them."

"I'll take them down," Louise said.

"Leave them there. It gives me something to do in the afternoon. I can hate them." Darling took a long swallow. "Is that the way people paint these days?"

"Yes, Christian. Please don't drink any more."

"Do you like painting like that?"

"Yes, dear."

"Really?"

"Really."

Darling looked carefully at the prints once more. "Little Louise Tucker. The middle-western beauty. I like pictures with horses in them. Why should you like pictures like that?"

"I just happen to have gone to a lot of galleries in the last few years . . ."

"Is that what you do in the afternoon?"

"That's what I do in the afternoon," Louise said.

"I drink in the afternoon."

Louise kissed him lightly on the top of his head as he sat there squinting at the pictures on the wall, the glass of whiskey held firmly in his hand. She put on her coat and went out without saying another word. When she came back in the early evening, she had a job on a woman's fashion magazine.

They moved downtown and Louise went out to work every morning and Darling sat home and drank and Louise paid the bills as they came up. She made believe she was going to quit work as soon as Darling found a job, even though she was taking over more responsibility day by day at the magazine, interviewing authors, picking painters for the illustrations and covers, getting actresses to pose for pictures, going out for drinks with the right people, making a thousand new friends whom she loyally introduced to Darling.

"I don't like your hat," Darling said, once, when she came in in the evening and kissed him, her breath rich with Martinis.

"What's the matter with my hat, Baby?" she asked, running her fingers through his hair. "Everybody says it's very smart."

"It's too damned smart," he said. "It's not for you. It's for a rich, sophisticated woman of thirty-five with admirers."

Louise laughed. "I'm practicing to be a rich, sophisticated woman of thirty-five with admirers," she said. He stared soberly at her. "Now, don't look so grim, Baby. It's still the same simple little wife under the hat." She took the hat off, threw it into a corner, sat on his lap. "See? Homebody Number One."

"Your breath could run a train," Darling said, not wanting to be mean, but talking out of boredom, and sudden shock at seeing his wife curiously a stranger in a new hat, with a new expression in her eyes under the little brim, secret, confident, knowing.

Louise tucked her head under his chin so he couldn't smell her breath. "I had to take an author out for cocktails," she said. "He's a boy from the Ozark mountains and he drinks like a fish. He's a Communist."

"What the hell is a Communist from the Ozarks doing writing for a woman's fashion magazine?"

Louise chuckled. "The magazine business is getting all mixed up these days. The publishers want to have a foot in every camp. And anyway, you can't find an author under seventy these days who isn't a Communist."

"I don't think I like you to associate with all those people, Louise," Darling said. "Drinking with them."

"He's a very nice, gentle boy," Louise said. "He reads Ernest Dobson."

"Who's Ernest Dobson?"

Louise patted his arm, stood up, fixed her hair. "He's an English poet."

Darling felt that somehow he had disappointed her. "Am I supposed to know who Ernest Dobson is?"

"No, dear. I'd better go in and take a bath."

After she had gone, Darling went over to the corner where the hat was lying and picked it up. It was nothing, a scrap of straw, a red flower, a veil, meaningless on his big hand, but on his wife's head a signal of something . . . big city, smart and knowing women drinking and dining with men other than their husbands, conversation about things a normal man wouldn't know much about, Frenchmen who painted as though they used their elbows instead of brushes, composers who wrote whole symphonies without a single melody in them, writers who knew all about politics and women who knew all about writers, the movement of the proletariat, Marx, somehow mixed up with five-dollar dinners and the best-looking women in America and fairies who made them laugh and half-sentences immediately understood and secretly hilarious and wives who called their husbands "Baby." He put the hat down, a scrap of straw and a red flower, and a little veil. He drank some whiskey straight and went into the bathroom where his wife was lying deep in her bath, singing to herself and smiling from time to time like a little girl, paddling the water gently with her hands, sending up a slight spicy fragrance from the bath salts she used.

He stood over her, looking down at her. She smiled up at him, her eyes half closed, her body pink and shimmering in the warm, scented water. All over again, with all the old suddenness, he was hit deep inside him with the knowledge of how beautiful she was, how much he needed her.

"I came in here," he said, "to tell you I wish you wouldn't call me 'Baby.' "

She looked up at him from the bath, her eyes quickly full of sorrow, half-understanding what he meant. He knelt and put his arms around her, his sleeves plunged heedlessly in the water, his shirt and jacket soaking wet as he clutched her wordlessly, holding her crazily tight, crushing her breath from her, kissing her desperately, searchingly, regretfully.

He got jobs after that, selling real estate and automobiles, but somehow, although he had a desk with his name on a wooden wedge on it, and he went to the office religiously at nine each morning, he never managed to sell anything and he never made any money.

Louise was made assistant editor and the house was always full of strange men and women who talked fast and got angry on abstract subjects like mural painting, novelists, labor unions. Negro short-story writers drank Louise's liquor, and a lot of Jews, and big solemn men with scarred faces and knotted hands who talked slowly but clearly about picket lines and battles with guns and lead pipe at mine-shaft-heads and in front of factory gates. And Louise moved among them all, confidently, knowing what they were talking about, with opinions that they listened to and argued about just as though she were a man. She knew everybody, condescended to no one, devoured books that Darling had never heard of, walked along the streets of the city, excited, at home, soaking in all the million tides of New York without fear, with constant wonder.

Her friends liked Darling and sometimes he found a man who wanted to get off in the corner and talk about the new boy who played fullback for Princeton, and the decline of the double wingback, or even the state of the stock market, but for the most part he sat on the edge of things, solid and quiet in the high storm of words. "The dialectics of the situation . . . the theater has been given over to expert jugglers . . . Picasso? What man has a right to paint old bones and collect ten thousand dollars for them? . . . I stand firmly behind Trotsky . . . Poe was the last American critic. When he died they put lilies on the grave of American criticism. I don't say this because they panned my last book, but . . ."

Once in a while he caught Louise looking soberly and consideringly at him through the cigarette smoke and the noise and he avoided her eyes and found an excuse to get up and go into the kitchen for more ice or to open another bottle.

"Come on," Cathal Flaherty was saying, standing at the door with a girl, "you've got to come down and see this. It's down on Fourteenth Street, in the old Civic Repertory, and you can only see it on Sunday nights and I guarantee you'll come out of the theater singing." Flaherty was a big young Irishman with a broken nose who was the lawyer for a longshoreman's union, and he had been hanging around the house for six months on and off, roaring and shutting everybody else up when he got in an argument. "It's a new play, *Waiting for Lefty,* it's about taxi drivers."

"Odets," the girl with Flaherty said. "It's by a guy named Odets."

"I never heard of him," Darling said.

"He's a new one," the girl said.

"It's like watching a bombardment," Flaherty said. "I saw it last Sunday night. You've got to see it."

"Come on, Baby," Louise said to Darling, excitement in her eyes already. "We've been sitting in the Sunday *Times* all day, this'll be a great change."

"I see enough taxi drivers every day," Darling said, not because he meant that, but because he didn't like to be around Flaherty, who said things that made Louise laugh a lot and whose judgment she accepted on almost every subject. "Let's go to the movies."

"You've never seen anything like this before," Flaherty said. "He wrote this play with a baseball bat."

"Come on," Louise coaxed. "I bet it's wonderful."

"He has long hair," the girl with Flaherty said. "Odets. I met him at a party. He's an actor. He didn't say a goddam thing all night."

"I don't feel like going down to Fourteenth Street," Darling said, wishing Flaherty and his girl would get out. "It's gloomy."

"Oh, hell!" Louise said loudly. She looked coolly at Darling, as though she'd just been introduced to him and was making up her mind about him, and not very favorably. He saw her looking at him, knowing there was something new and dangerous in her face, and he wanted to say something, but Flaherty was there and his damned girl, and anyway, he didn't know what to say.

"I'm going," Louise said, getting her coat. "I don't think Fourteenth Street is gloomy."

"I'm telling you," Flaherty was saying, helping her on with her coat, "it's the Battle of Gettysburg, in Brooklynese."

"Nobody could get a word out of him," Flaherty's girl was saying as they went through the door. "He just sat there all night."

The door closed. Louise hadn't said good night to him. Darling walked around the room four times, then sprawled out on the sofa, on top of the Sunday

Times. He lay there for five minutes looking at the ceiling, thinking of Flaherty walking down the street talking in that booming voice, between the girls, holding their arms.

Louise had looked wonderful. She'd washed her hair in the afternoon and it had been very soft and light and clung close to her head as she stood there angrily putting her coat on. Louise was getting prettier every year, partly because she knew by now how pretty she was, and made the most of it.

"Nuts," Darling said, standing up. "Oh, nuts."

He put on his coat and went down to the nearest bar and had five drinks off by himself in a corner before his money ran out.

The years since then had been foggy and downhill. Louise had been nice to him, and in a way, loving and kind, and they'd fought only once, when he said he was going to vote for Landon. ("Oh, Christ," she'd said, "doesn't *anything* happen inside your head? Don't you read the papers? The penniless Republican!") She'd been sorry later and apologized as she might to a child. He'd tried hard, had gone grimly to the art galleries, the concert halls, the bookshops, trying to gain on the trail of his wife, but it was no use. He was bored, and none of what he saw or heard or dutifully read made much sense to him and finally he gave it up. He had thought, many nights as he ate dinner alone, knowing that Louise would come home late and drop silently into bed without explanation, of getting a divorce, but he knew the loneliness, the hopelessness, of not seeing her again would be too much to take. So he was good, completely devoted, ready at all times to go anyplace with her, do anything she wanted. He even got a small job, in a broker's office, and paid his own way, bought his own liquor.

Then he'd been offered the job of going from college to college as a tailor's representative. "We want a man," Mr. Rosenberg had said, "who as soon as you look at him, you say 'There's a university man.'" Rosenberg had looked approvingly at Darling's broad shoulders and well-kept waist, at his carefully brushed hair and his honest, wrinkleless face. "Frankly, Mr. Darling, I am willing to make you a proposition. I have inquired about you, you are favorably known on your old campus, I understand you were in the backfield with Alfred Diederich."

Darling nodded. "Whatever happened to him?"

"He is walking around in a cast for seven years now. An iron brace. He played professional football and they broke his neck for him."

Darling smiled. That, at least, had turned out well.

"Our suits are an easy product to sell, Mr. Darling," Rosenberg said. "We have a handsome, custom-made garment. What has Brooks Brothers got that we haven't got? A name. No more."

"I can make fifty, sixty dollars a week," Darling said to Louise that night. "And expenses. I can save some money and then come back to New York and really get started here."

"Yes, Baby," Louise said.

"As it is," Darling said carefully, "I can make it back here once a month, and holidays and the summer. We can see each other often."

"Yes, Baby." He looked at her face, lovelier now at thirty-five than it had ever been before, but fogged over now as it had been for five years with a kind of patient, kindly, remote boredom.

"What do you say?" he asked. "Should I take it?" Deep within him he hoped fiercely, longingly, for her to say, "No, Baby, you stay right here," but she said, as he knew she'd say, "I think you'd better take it."

He nodded. He had to get up and stand with his back to her, looking out the window, because there were things plain on his face that she had never seen in the fifteen years she'd known him. "Fifty dollars is a lot of money," he said, "I never thought I'd ever see fifty dollars again." He laughed. Louise laughed too.

Christian Darling sat on the frail green grass of the practice field. The shadow of the stadium had reached out and covered him. In the distance the lights of the university shone a little mistily in the light haze of evening. Fifteen years. Flaherty even now was calling for his wife, buying her a drink, filling whatever bar they were in with that voice of his and that easy laugh. Darling half-closed his eyes, almost saw the boy fifteen years ago reach for the pass, slip the halfback, go skittering lightly down the field, his knees high and fast and graceful, smiling to himself because he knew he was going to get past the safety man. That was the high point, Darling thought, fifteen years ago, on an autumn afternoon, twenty years old and far from death, with the air coming easily into his lungs, and a deep feeling inside him that he could do anything, knock over anybody, outrun whatever had to be outrun. And the shower after and the three glasses of water and the cool night air on his damp head and Louise sitting hatless in the open car with a smile and the first kiss she ever really meant. The high point, an eighty-yard run in the practice, and a girl's kiss and everything after that a decline. Darling laughed. He had practiced the wrong thing, perhaps. He hadn't practiced for 1929 and New York City and a girl who would turn into a woman. Somewhere, he thought, there must have been a point where she moved up to me, was even with me for a moment, when I could have held her hand, if I'd known, held tight, gone with her. Well, he'd never known. Here he was on a playing field that was fifteen years away and his wife was in another city having dinner with another and better man, speaking with him a different, new language, a language nobody had ever taught him.

Darling stood up, smiled a little, because if he didn't smile he knew the tears would come. He looked around him. This was the spot. O'Connor's pass had come sliding out just to here . . . the high point. Darling put up his hands, felt all over again the flat slap of the ball. He shook his hips to throw off the halfback, cut back inside the center, picked his knees high as he ran gracefully over two men jumbled on the ground at the line of scrimmage, ran easily, gaining speed, for ten yards, holding the ball lightly in his two hands, swung away from the halfback diving at him, ran, swinging his hips in the almost girlish manner of a back in a broken field, tore into the safety man, his shoes drumming heavily on the turf, stiff-armed, elbow locked, pivoted, raced lightly and exultantly for the goal line.

It was only after he had sped over the goal line and slowed to a trot that he saw the boy and girl sitting together on the turf, looking at him wonderingly.

He stopped short, dropping his arms. "I . . ." he said, gasping a little though his condition was fine and the run hadn't winded him, "I . . . Once I played here."

The boy and the girl said nothing. Darling laughed embarrassedly, looked hard at them sitting there, close to each other, shrugged, turned and went toward his hotel, the sweat breaking out on his face and running down into his collar.

[JANUARY 1941]

TRUMAN CAPOTE

Among the Paths to Eden

Born in New Orleans, Truman Capote (1924–1984) found success with his first novel, Other Voices, Other Rooms, which was published when he was just twenty-four. The flamboyant Capote tested many of society's limits with both his life-style and his talent, often lifting gossip about a social event or the mundane facts about a murder into the reaches of art. His most celebrated novel, Breakfast at Tiffany's, was first published, in its entirety, in Esquire. When he died in California in 1984 he left unfinished the novel Answered Prayers, sections of which also appeared in Esquire, along with great controversy about who the real-life models for his fictional characters might be. His other books include In Cold Blood and The Grass Harp and a Tree of Night.

One Saturday in March, an occasion of pleasant winds and sailing clouds, Mr. Ivor Belli bought from a Brooklyn florist a fine mass of jonquils and conveyed them, first by subway, then foot, to an immense cemetery in Queens, a site unvisited by him since he had seen his wife buried there the previous autumn. Sentiment could not be credited with returning him today, for Mrs. Belli, to whom he had been married twenty-seven years, during which time she had produced two now-grown and matrimonially settled daughters, had been a woman of many natures, most of them trying: he had no desire to renew so unsoothing an acquaintance, even in spirit. No; but a hard winter had just passed, and he felt in need of exercise, air, a heart-lifting stroll through the handsome, spring-prophesying weather; of course, rather as an extra dividend, it was nice that he would be able to tell his daughters of a journey to their mother's grave, especially so since it might a little appease the elder girl, who seemed resentful of Mr. Belli's too comfortable acceptance of life as lived alone.

The cemetery was not a reposeful, pretty place; was, in fact, a damned frightening one: acres of fog-colored stone spilled across a sparsely grassed and shadeless plateau. An unhindered view of Manhattan's skyline provided the location with beauty of a stage-prop sort—it loomed beyond the graves like a steep headstone honoring these quiet folk, its used-up and very former citizens: the juxtaposed spectacle made Mr. Belli, who was by profession a tax accountant and therefore equipped to enjoy irony however sadistic, smile, actually chuckle— yet, oh God in heaven, its inferences chilled him, too, deflated the buoyant stride carrying him along the cemetery's rigid, pebbled paths. He slowed until he stopped, thinking: "I ought to have taken Morty to the zoo"; Morty being his grandson, aged three. But it would be churlish not to continue, vengeful: and why waste a bouquet? The combination of thrift and virtue reactivated him; he was breathing hard from hurry when, at last, he stooped to jam the jonquils into a rock urn perched on a rough gray slab engraved with Gothic calligraphy declaring that

SARAH BELLI

1901–1959

had been the

DEVOTED WIFE OF IVOR

BELOVED MOTHER OF IVY AND REBECCA.

Lord, what a relief to know the woman's tongue was finally stilled. But the thought, pacifying as it was, and though supported by visions of his new and silent bachelor's apartment, did not relight the suddenly snuffed-out sense of immortality, of glad-to-be-aliveness, which the day had earlier kindled. He had set forth expecting such good from the air, the walk, the aroma of another spring about to be. Now he wished he had worn a scarf; the sunshine was false, without real warmth, and the wind, it seemed to him, had grown rather wild. As he gave the jonquils a decorative pruning, he regretted he could not delay their doom by supplying them with water; relinquishing the flowers, he turned to leave.

A woman stood in his way. Though there were few other visitors to the cemetery, he had not noticed her before, or heard her approach. She did not step aside. She glanced at the jonquils; presently her eyes, situated behind steel-rimmed glasses, swerved back to Mr. Belli.

"Uh. Relative?"

"My wife," he said, and sighed as though some such noise was obligatory. She sighed, too; a curious sigh that implied gratification. "Gee, I'm sorry."

Mr. Belli's face lengthened. "Well."

"It's a shame."

"Yes."

"I hope it wasn't a long illness. Anything painful."

"No-o-o," he said, shifting from one foot to the other. "In her sleep." Sensing an unsatisfied silence, he added, "Heart condition."

"Gee. That's how I lost my father. Just recently. Kind of gives us something in common. Something," she said, in a tone alarmingly plaintive, "something to talk about."

"—know how you must feel."

"At least they didn't suffer. That's a comfort."

The fuse attached to Mr. Belli's patience shortened. Until now he had kept his gaze appropriately lowered, observing, after his initial glimpse of her, merely the woman's shoes, which were of the sturdy, so-called sensible type often worn by aged women and nurses. "A great comfort," he said, as he executed three tasks: raised his eyes, tipped his hat, took a step forward.

Again the woman held her ground; it was as though she had been employed to detain him. "Could you give me the time? My old clock," she announced, self-consciously tapping some dainty machinery strapped to her wrist, "I got it for graduating high school. That's why it doesn't run so good any more. I mean, it's pretty old. But it makes a nice appearance."

Mr. Belli was obliged to unbutton his topcoat and plow around for a gold watch embedded in a vest pocket. Meanwhile, he scrutinized the lady, really took her apart. She must have been blond as a child, her general coloring suggested so: the clean shine of her Scandinavian skin, her chunky cheeks, flushed with peasant health, and the blueness of her genial eyes—such honest eyes, attractive despite the thin silver spectacles surrounding them; but the hair itself, what could be discerned of it under a drab felt hat, was poorly permanented frizzle of no particular tint. She was a bit taller than Mr. Belli, who was five-foot-eight with the aid of shoe lifts, and she may have weighed more; at any rate he couldn't imagine that she mounted scales too cheerfully. Her hands: kitchen hands; and the nails: not only nibbled ragged, but painted with a pearly lacquer queerly phosphorescent. She wore a plain brown coat and carried a plain black purse. When the student of these components recomposed them he found they assembled themselves into a very decent-looking person whose looks he liked; the nail polish was discouraging; still he felt that here was someone you could trust. As he trusted Esther Jackson, Miss Jackson, his secretary. Indeed, that was who she reminded him of, Miss Jackson; not that the comparison was fair—to Miss Jackson, who possessed, as he had once in the course of a quarrel informed Mrs. Belli, "intellectual elegance and elegance otherwise." Nevertheless, the woman confronting him seemed imbued with that quality of goodwill he appreciated in his secretary, Miss Jackson, Esther (as he'd lately, absentmindedly, called her). Moreover, he guessed them to be about the same age: rather on the right side of forty.

"Noon. Exactly."

"Think of that! Why, you must be famished," she said, and unclasped her purse, peered into it as though it were a picnic hamper crammed with sufficient treats to furnish a smorgasbord. She scooped out a fistful of peanuts. "I practically live on peanuts since Pop—since I haven't anyone to cook for. I must say, even if I do say so, I miss my own cooking; Pop always said I was better than any restaurant he ever went to. But it's no pleasure cooking just for yourself, even when you *can* make pastries light as a leaf. Go on. Have some. They're fresh-roasted."

Mr. Belli accepted; he'd always been childish about peanuts and, as he sat down on his wife's grave to eat them, only hoped his friend had more. A gesture of his hand suggested that she sit beside him; he was surprised to see that the invitation seemed to embarrass her; sudden additions of pink saturated her cheeks, as though he'd asked her to transform Mrs. Belli's bier into a love bed.

"It's okay for you. A relative. But me. Would she like a stranger sitting on her—resting place?"

"Please. Be a guest. Sarah won't mind," he told her, grateful the dead cannot hear, for it both awed and amused him to consider what Sarah, that vivacious scene-maker, that energetic searcher for lipstick traces and stray blond strands, would say if she could see him shelling peanuts on her tomb with a woman not entirely unattractive.

And then, as she assumed a prim perch on the rim of the grave, he noticed her leg. Her left leg; it stuck straight out like a stiff piece of mischief with which she planned to strip passersby. Aware of his interest, she smiled, lifted the leg up and down. "An accident. You know. When I was a kid. I fell off a roller coaster at Coney. Honest. It was in the paper. Nobody knows why I'm alive. The only thing is I can't bend my knee. Otherwise it doesn't make any difference. Except to go dancing. Are you much of a dancer?"

Mr. Belli shook his head; his mouth was full of peanuts.

"So that's something else we have in common. Dancing. I *might* like it. But I don't. I like music, though."

Mr. Belli nodded his agreement.

"And flowers," she added, touching the bouquet of jonquils; then her fingers traveled on and, as though she were reading Braille, brushed across the marble lettering of his name. "Ivor," she said, mispronouncing it. "Ivor Belli. My name is Mary O'Meaghan. But I wish I were Italian. My sister is; well, she married one. And oh, he's full of fun; happy-natured and outgoing, like all Italians. He says my spaghetti's the best he's ever had. Especially the kind I make with seafood sauce. You ought to taste it."

Mr. Belli, having finished the peanuts, swept the hulls off his lap. "You've got a customer. But he's not Italian. Belli sounds like that. Only I'm Jewish."

She frowned, not with disapproval, but as if he had mysteriously daunted her.

"My family came from Russia; I was born there."

This last information restored her enthusiasm, accelerated it. "I don't care what they say in the papers. I'm sure Russians are the same as everybody else. Human. Did you see the Bolshoi Ballet on TV? Now didn't that make you proud to be a Russian?"

He thought: she means well; and was silent.

"Red cabbage soup—hot or cold—with sour cream. Hmnn. See," she said, producing a second helping of peanuts, "you *were* hungry. Poor fellow." She sighed. "How you must miss your wife's cooking."

It was true, he did; and the conversational pressure being applied to his appetite made him realize it. Sarah had set an excellent table: varied, on time, and well flavored. He recalled certain cinnamon-scented feast days. Afternoons of gravy and wine, starchy linen, the "good" silver; followed by a nap. Moreover, Sarah had never asked him to dry a dish (he could hear her calmly humming in the kitchen), had never complained of housework; and she had contrived to make the raising of two girls a smooth series of thought-out, affectionate events; Mr. Belli's contribution to their upbringing had been to be an admiring witness; if his daughters were a credit to him (Ivy living in Bronxville, and married to a dental surgeon; her sister the wife of A. J. Krakower, junior partner in the law firm of Finnegan, Loeb and Krakower), he had Sarah to thank; they were her accomplishment. There was much to be said for Sarah, and he was glad to discover himself thinking so, to find himself remembering not the long hell of hours she had spent honing her tongue on his habits, supposed poker-playing, woman-chasing vices, but gentler episodes: Sarah showing off her self-made hats,

Sarah scattering crumbs on snowy window sills for winter pigeons: a tide of visions that towed to sea the junk of harsher recollections. He felt, was all at once happy to feel, mournful, sorry he had not been sorry sooner; but, though he did genuinely value Sarah suddenly, he could not pretend regret that their life together had terminated, for the current arrangement was, on the whole, preferable by far. However, he wished that, instead of jonquils, he had brought her an orchid, the gala sort she'd always salvaged from her daughters' dates and stored in the icebox until they shriveled.

"—aren't they?" he heard, and wondered who had spoken until, blinking, he recognized Mary O'Meaghan, whose voice had been playing along unlistened to: a shy and lulling voice, a sound strangely small and young to come from so robust a figure.

"I said they must be cute, aren't they?"

"Well," was Mr. Belli's safe reply.

"Be modest. But I'm sure they are. If they favor their father; ha ha, don't take me serious, I'm joking. But, seriously, kids just slay me. I'll trade any kid for any grown-up that ever lived. My sister has five, four boys and a girl. Dot, that's my sister, she's always after me to baby-sit now that I've got the time and don't have to look after Pop every minute. She and Frank, he's my brother-in-law, the one I mentioned, they say Mary, nobody can handle kids like *you*. At the same time have fun. But it's so easy; there's nothing like hot cocoa and a mean pillow fight to make kids sleepy. Ivy," she said, reading aloud the tombstone's dour script. "Ivy and Rebecca. Sweet names. And I'm sure you do your best. But two little girls without a mother."

"No, no," said Mr. Belli, at last caught up. "Ivy's a mother herself. And Becky's expecting."

Her face restyled momentary chagrin into an expression of disbelief. "A grandfather? You?"

Mr. Belli had several vanities: for example, he thought he was *saner* than other people; also, he believed himself to be a walking compass; his digestion, and an ability to read upside down, were other ego-enlarging items. But his reflection in a mirror aroused little inner applause; not that he disliked his appearance; he just knew that it was very so-what. The harvesting of his hair had begun decades ago; now his head was an almost barren field. While his nose had character, his chin, though it made a double effort, had none. His shoulders were broad; but so was the rest of him. Of course he was neat: kept his shoes shined, his laundry laundered, twice a day scraped and talcumed his bluish jowls; but such measures failed to camouflage, actually they emphasized, his middle-class, middle-aged ordinariness. Nonetheless, he did not dismiss Mary O'Meaghan's flattery; after all, an undeserved compliment is often the most potent.

"Hell, I'm fifty-one," he said, subtracting four years. "Can't say I feel it." And he didn't; perhaps it was because the wind had subsided, the warmth of the sun grown more authentic. Whatever the reason, his expectations had reignited, he was again immortal, a man planning ahead.

"Fifty-one. That's nothing. The prime. Is if you take care of yourself. A man your age needs tending to. Watching after."

Surely in a cemetery one was safe from husband stalkers? The question, crossing his mind, paused midway while he examined her cozy and gullible face, tested her gaze for guile. Though reassured, he thought it best to remind her of their surroundings. "Your father. Is he"—Mr. Belli gestured awkwardly—"nearby?"

"Pop? Oh, no. He was very firm; absolutely refused to be buried. So he's at home." A disquieting image gathered in Mr. Belli's head, one that her next words, "His ashes are," did not fully dispel. "Well," she shrugged, "that's how he wanted it. Or—I see—you wondered why *I'm* here? I don't live too far away. It's somewhere to walk, and the view. . . ." They both turned to stare at the skyline where the steeples of certain buildings flew pennants of cloud, and sun-dazzled windows glittered like a million bits of mica. Mary O'Meaghan said, "What a perfect day for a parade!"

Mr. Belli thought, *You're a very nice girl;* then he said it, too, and wished he hadn't, for naturally she asked him why. "Because. Well, that was nice what you said. About parades."

"See? So many things in common! I never miss a parade," she told him triumphantly. "The bugles. I play the bugle myself; used to, when I was at Sacred Heart. You said before—" She lowered her voice, as though approaching a subject that required grave tones. "You indicated you were a music lover. Because I have thousands of old records. Hundreds. Pop was in the business and that was his job. Till he retired. Shellacking records in a record factory. Remember Helen Morgan? She slays me, she really knocks me out."

"*Je*sus Christ," he whispered. Ruby Keeler, Jean Harlow: those had been keen but curable infatuations; but Helen Morgan, albino-pale, a sequinned wraith shimmering beyond Ziegfeld footlights—truly, truly he had loved her.

"Do you believe it? That she drank herself to death? On account of a gangster?"

"It doesn't matter. She was lovely."

"Sometimes, like when I'm alone and sort of fed up, I pretend I'm her. Pretend I'm singing in a night club. It's fun; you know?"

"Yes, I know," said Mr. Belli, whose own favorite fantasy was to imagine the adventures he might have if he were invisible.

"May I ask: would you do me a favor?"

"If I can. Certainly."

She inhaled, held her breath as if she were swimming under a wave of shyness; surfacing, she said: "Would you listen to my imitation? And tell me your honest opinion?" Then she removed her glasses: the silver rims had bitten so deeply their shape was permanently printed on her face. Her eyes, nude and moist and helpless, seemed stunned by freedom; the skimpily lashed lids fluttered like long-captive birds abruptly let loose. "There: everything's soft and smoky. Now you've got to use your imagination. So pretend I'm sitting on a piano— gosh, for*give* me, Mr. Belli."

"Forget it. Okay. You're sitting on a piano."

"I'm sitting on a piano," she said, dreamily drooping her head backward until it assumed a romantic posture. She sucked in her cheeks, parted her lips; at the same moment Mr. Belli bit into his. For it was a tactless visit that glamour made on Mary O'Meaghan's filled-out and rosy face; a visit that should not have been paid at all; it was the wrong address. She waited, as though listening for music to cue her; then, *"Don't ever leave me, now that you're here! Here is where you belong. Everything seems so right when you're near, When you're away it's all wrong"* and Mr. Belli was shocked, for what he was hearing was exactly Helen Morgan's voice, and the voice, with its vulnerable sweetness, refinement, its tender quaver toppling high notes, seemed not to be borrowed, but Mary O'Meaghan's own, a natural expression of some secluded identity. Gradually she abandoned theatrical poses, sat upright singing with her eyes squeezed shut: *"—I'm so dependent, When I need comfort, I always run to you. Don't ever leave me! 'Cause if you do, I'll have no one to run to."* Until too late, neither she nor Mr. Belli noticed the coffin-laden entourage invading their privacy: a black caterpillar composed of sedate Negroes who stared at the white couple as though they had stumbled upon a pair of drunken grave robbers—except one mourner, a dry-eyed little girl who started laughing and couldn't stop; her hiccup-like hilarity resounded long after the procession had disappeared around a distant corner.

"If that kid was mine," said Mr. Belli.

"I feel so ashamed."

"Say, listen. What for? That was beautiful. I mean it; you can sing."

"Thanks," she said; and, as though setting up a barricade against impending tears, clamped on her spectacles.

"Believe me, I was touched. What I'd like is, I'd like an encore."

It was as if she were a child to whom he'd handed a balloon, a unique balloon that kept swelling until it swept her upward, danced her along with just her toes now and then touching ground. She descended to say: "Only not here. Maybe," she began, and once more seemed to be lifted, lilted through the air, "maybe sometime you'll let me cook you dinner. I'll plan it really Russian. And we can play records."

The thought, the apparitional suspicion that had previously passed on tiptoe, returned with a heavier tread, a creature fat and foursquare that Mr. Belli could not evict. "Thank you, Miss O'Meaghan. That's something to look forward to," he said. Rising, he reset his hat, adjusted his coat. "Sitting on cold stone too long, you can catch something."

"When?"

"Why, never. You should *never* sit on cold stone."

"When will you come to dinner?"

Mr. Belli's livelihood rather depended upon his being a skilled inventor of excuses. "Anytime," he answered smoothly. "Except anytime soon. I'm a tax man; you know what happens to us fellows in March. Yes sir," he said, again hoisting out his watch, "back to the grind for me." Still he couldn't—could he?—simply saunter off, leave her sitting on Sarah's grave? He owed her courtesy; for the peanuts, if nothing more, though there was more—perhaps it was due to her that he had remembered Sarah's orchids withering in the icebox. And anyway, she *was* nice, as likable a woman, stranger, as he'd ever met. He thought to take advantage of the weather, but the weather offered none: clouds were fewer, the sun exceedingly visible. "Turned chilly," he observed, rubbing his hands together. "Could be going to rain."

"Mr. Belli. Now I'm going to ask you a very personal question," she said, enunciating each word decisively. "Because I wouldn't want you to think I go about inviting just anybody to dinner. My intentions are—" Her eyes wandered, her voice wavered, as though the forthright manner had been a masquerade she could not sustain. "So I'm going to ask you a very personal question. Have you considered marrying again?"

He hummed, like a radio warming up before it speaks; when he did, it amounted to static: "Oh, at *my* age. Don't even want a dog. Just give me TV. Some beer. Poker once a week. Hell. Who the hell would want me?" he said; and, with a twinge, remembered Rebecca's mother-in-law, Mrs. A. J. Krakower, Sr., Dr. Pauline Krakower, a female dentist (retired) who had been an audacious participant in a certain family plot. Or what about Sarah's best friend, the persistent "Brownie" Pollock? Odd, but as long as Sarah lived he had enjoyed, upon occasion taken advantage of, "Brownie's" admiration; afterwards—finally he had *told* her not to telephone him anymore (and she had shouted: "Everything Sarah ever said, she was right. You fat little *hairy* little bastard"). Then; and then there was Miss Jackson. Despite Sarah's suspicions, her in fact devout conviction, nothing untoward, very untoward, had transpired between him and the pleasant Esther, whose hobby was bowling. But he had always surmised, and in recent months known, that if one day he suggested drinks, dinner, a workout in some bowling-alley . . . He said: "I *was* married. For twenty-seven years. That's enough for any lifetime"; but as he said it, he realized that, in just this moment, he had come to a decision, which was: he *would* ask Esther to dinner, he would take her bowling and buy her an orchid, a gala purple one with a lavender-ribbon bow. And where, he wondered, do couples honeymoon in April? At the latest May. Miami? Bermuda? Bermuda! "No, I've never considered it. Marrying again."

One would have assumed from her attentive posture that Mary O'Meaghan was raptly listening to Mr. Belli—except that her eyes played hooky, roamed as though she were hunting at a party for a different, more promising face. The color had drained from her own face; and with it had gone most of her healthy charm. She coughed.

He coughed. Raising his hat, he said: "It's been very pleasant meeting you, Miss O'Meaghan."

"Same here," she said, and stood up. "Mind if I walk with you to the gate?"

He did, yes; for he wanted to mosey along alone, devouring the tart nourishment of this spring-shiny, parade weather, be alone with his many thoughts of Esther, his hopeful, zestful, live-forever mood. "A pleasure," he said, adjusting his stride to her slower pace and the slight lurch her stiff leg caused.

"But it *did* seem like a sensible idea," she said argumentatively. "And there was old Annie Austin: the living proof. Well, nobody had a *better* idea. I mean, everybody was at me: Get married. From the day Pop died, my sister and everybody was saying: Poor Mary, what's to become of her? A girl that can't type. Take shorthand. With her leg and all; can't even wait on table. What happens to a girl—a *grown* woman—that doesn't know anything, never done anything? Except cook and look after her father. All I heard was: Mary, you've got to get married."

"So. Why fight that? A fine person like you, you ought to be married. You'd make some fellow very happy."

"Sure I would. But *who?*" She flung out her arms, extended a hand toward Manhattan, the country, the continents beyond. "So I've looked; I'm not lazy by nature. But honestly, frankly, how does anybody ever find a husband? If they're not very, very pretty; a terrific dancer. If they're just—oh, ordinary. Like me."

"No, no, not at all," Mr. Belli mumbled. "Not ordinary, no. Couldn't you make something of your talent? Your voice?"

She stopped, stood clasping and unclasping her purse. "Don't poke fun. Please. My life is at stake." And she insisted: "I *am* ordinary. So is old Annie Austin. And she says the place for me to find a husband—a decent, comfortable man—is in the obituary column."

For a man who believed himself a human compass, Mr. Belli had the anxious experience of feeling he had lost his way; with relief he saw the gates of the cemetery a hundred yards ahead. "She does? She says that? Old Annie Austin?"

"Yes. And she's a very practical woman. She feeds six people on fifty-eight dollars and seventy-five cents a week: food, clothes, everything. And the way she explained it, it certainly *sounded* logical. Because the obituaries are full of unmarried men. Widowers. You just go to the funeral and sort of introduce yourself: sympathize. Or the cemetery: come here on a nice day, or go to Woodlawn, there are always widowers walking around. Fellows thinking how much they miss home life and maybe wishing they were married again."

When Mr. Belli understood that she was in earnest, he was appalled; but he was also entertained: and he laughed, jammed his hands in his pockets and threw back his head. She joined him, spilled a laughter that restored her color, that, in skylarking style, made her rock against him. "Even I—" she said, clutching at his arm, "even *I* can see the humor." But it was not a lengthy vision; suddenly solemn, she said: "But that is how Annie met her husbands. Both of them: Mr. Cruikshank, and then Mr. Austin. So it *must* be a practical idea. Don't you think?"

"Oh, I do think."

She shrugged. "But it hasn't worked out too well. Us, for instance. *We* seemed to have such a lot in common."

"One day," he said, quickening his steps. "With a livelier fellow."

"I don't know. I've met some grand people. But it always ends like this. Like us . . ." she said, and left unsaid something more, for a new pilgrim, just entering through the gates of the cemetery, had attached her interest: an alive little man spouting cheery whistlings and with plenty of snap to his walk. Mr. Belli noticed him, too, observed the black band sewn round the sleeve of the visitor's bright green tweed coat, and commented: "Good luck, Miss O'Meaghan. Thanks for the peanuts."

[JULY 1960]

PHILIP ROTH

Very Happy Poems

Philip Roth (1933–   ) published one of his earliest stories, "Expect the Vandals," in <u>Esquire</u>, two years before the publication of <u>Goodbye, Columbus</u>, the collection that was to make his reputation. Over the decades he went on to publish journalism and essays with the magazine, as well as fiction. In February 1990, <u>Esquire</u> ran a condensed version of his short novel <u>Deception</u> as the cover story. The selection for this anthology, "Very Happy Poems," was excerpted from his first novel, <u>When She Was Good</u>; it is rare in his work for being told from a woman's point of view—and is recognized as a tour de force magnificently sustained. His other books include <u>Portnoy's Complaint</u>, <u>The Prague Orgy</u>, <u>The Counterlife</u>, and <u>The Breast</u>.

She grabbed a yellow pad that was on the floor beside the books and ran off with it to the kitchen; she sat down at the table and so excited was she that she simply swept her hand across the table, brushing away the breakfast crumbs. She would attend to them later—they were unimportant. She had never written a poem before (though sick and in bed in Reading she had tried a story), but the idea of poetry had always stirred her. Toward certain poems she had particularly tender feelings. She liked *To His Coy Mistress* and she loved *Ode to a Nightingale; Ode on Melancholy* too. She liked all of Keats, in fact; at least the ones that were anthologized.

She wrote on the pad:

Already with thee! Tender is the night

She liked *Tender Is the Night,* which of course wasn't a poem. She identified with Nicole; in college she had identified with Rosemary. She would have to read it over again. After Faulkner she would read all of Fitzgerald, even the books she had read before. But poetry. What other poems did she like?

She wrote:

Come live with me and be my love,
And we will all the pleasures prove.

Then directly below:

The expense of spirit in a waste of shame
Is lust in action—and till action, lust
Is perjured, murderous. . . .

She could not remember the rest. Those few lines, however, had always filled her with a headlong passion, even though she had to admit never having come precisely to grips with the meaning. Still, the sound.

She went on writing, with recollections of her three years of college, with her heart heaving and sighing appropriately.

Sabrina fair
Listen where thou are sitting
Under the glassy wave—
And I am black but o my soul is white
How sweetly flows
The liquefaction of her clothes
At last he rose, and twitch'd his mantle blue
Tomorrow to fresh woods and pastures new.
I am! Yet what I am none cares or knows
My friends forsake me like a memory lost,
I am the self-consumer of my woes.

And who had written those last lines? Keats again? What was the difference who had written them? She hadn't.

Oh, if she could sculpt, if she could paint, if she could write something! Anything—

The doorbell rang.

A *friend!* She ran to the door, pulling her belt tight around her. All I need is a friend to take my mind off myself and tell me how silly I'm being. A girl friend with whom I can go shopping and have coffee, in whom I can confide.

She opened the door. It was not a friend because she had had little opportunity, what with her job, her night classes, and generally watching out for herself, to make any friends since coming to Chicago. In the doorway was a pleasant-looking fellow of thirty or thirty-five—and simply from the thinness of his hair, the fragile swelling of his brown eyes, the narrowness of his body, the neatness of his clothes, she knew he would have a kind and modest manner. One was supposed to be leery of opening the door all the way in this neighborhood; Paul cautioned her to peer out over the latch first, but she was not sorry now that she had forgotten. You just couldn't distrust everybody and remain human.

His hat in one hand, a briefcase in the other, the fellow asked, "Are you Mrs. Herz?"

"Yes." All at once she was feeling solid and necessary. The "Mrs. Herz" had done it. Libby had, of course, a great talent for spiritual resurrection; when her fortunes finally changed, she knew they would change overnight. She did not really believe in unhappiness and privation and never would; it was an opinion, unfortunately, that did not make life any easier for her.

"I'm Marty Rosen," the young man said. "I wonder if I can come in. I'm from the Jewish Children's League."

Her moods came and went in flashes; now elation faded. Rosen smiled in what seemed to Libby both an easygoing and powerful way; clearly he was not on his first mission for a nonprofit organization. Intimidated, she stepped back and let him in, thinking: one *should* look over the latch first. Not only was she in her bathrobe (which hadn't been dry-cleaned for two years), but she was barefoot. "We didn't think you were coming," Libby said, "until next week. My husband isn't here. I'm sorry—didn't we get the date right? We've been busy, I didn't check the calendar—"

"That's all right," Rosen said. He looked down a moment, and there was nowhere she could possibly stick her feet. Oh, they should at least have laid the rug. So *what* if it was somebody else's! Now the floor stretched off, bare and cold, clear to the walls. "I will be coming around again next week," Rosen said. "I thought I'd drop in this morning for a few minutes, just to say hello."

"If you'd have called, my husband might have been able to be here."

"If we can work it out," Rosen was saying, "we do like to have sort of an informal session anyway, before the formal scheduled meeting."

"Oh, yes," said Libby, and her thoughts turned to her bedroom.

"—see the prospective parents"—he smiled—"in their natural habitat."

"Definitely, yes." The whole world was in conspiracy, even against her pettiest plans. "Let's sit down. Here." She pointed to the sofa. "Let me take your things."

"I hope I didn't wake you."

"God, no," she said, realizing it was almost ten. "I've been up for hours." After these words were out, they didn't seem right either.

With his topcoat over her arm, she went off to the bedroom, though by way of the sofa, where she slid into her slippers as glidingly as she could manage. She walked down the hall, shut the bedroom door, and then, having flung Mr. Rosen's stuff across a chair, she frantically set about whipping the sheets and blankets into some kind of shape. The clock on the half-painted dresser said not ten o'clock, but quarter to eleven. Up for hours! Still in her nightclothes! She yanked at the sheets, hoisted the mattress (which seemed to outweigh her), and caught her fingernail in the springs. She ran to the other side, tugged on the blankets, but alas, too hard—they came slithering over at her and then were on the floor. Oh, Christ! She threw them back on the bed, raced around again—but five whole minutes had elapsed. At the dresser she pulled a comb through her hair, and came back into the living room, having slammed shut the bedroom door behind her. Mr. Rosen was standing before the Utrillo print. Beside him, their books were piled on the floor. "We're getting some bricks and boards for the books." He did not answer. "That's Utrillo," she said.

He did not answer again.

Of course it was Utrillo. Everybody knew Utrillo—that was the trouble. "It's corny, I suppose," said Libby. "My husband doesn't like the Impressionists that much either—but we've had it, I've had it, since college—and we carry it around and I guess we hang it whenever we move—not that we move that much, but, you know."

Turning, he said, "I suppose you like it, well, for sentimental reasons."

"Well . . . I just like it. Yes, sentiment—but aesthetics, of course, too."

She did not know what more to say. They both were smiling. He seemed like a perfectly agreeable man, and there was no reason for her to be giving him so frozen an expression. However, she soon discovered that the smile she wore she was apparently going to have to live with a while longer; the muscles of her face were working on their own.

"Yes," she said. "And—and this is our apartment. Please, sit down. I'll make some coffee."

"It's a very big apartment," he said, coming back to the sofa. "Spacious."

What did he mean—they didn't have enough furniture? "Well, yes—no," replied Libby. "There's this room and then down the hall is the kitchen. And my husband's study—"

Rosen, having already taken his trouser creases in hand, now rose and asked pleasantly, "May I look around?"

Libby did not believe that the idea had simply popped into his head. But he was so smooth-faced and soft-spoken and well-groomed, she was not yet prepared to believe him a sneak. He inclined toward her whenever she spoke, and, though it unnerved her some, she had preferred up till now to think of it as a kind of sympathetic lean.

"Oh, do," Libby said. "You'll have to excuse us, though; we were out to dinner last night. Not that we go out to dinner that much—however, we were out to dinner"—they proceeded down the hall and were in the kitchen—"and," she confessed, "I didn't get around to the dishes. . . . But," she said, cognizant of the sympathetic lean, though doing her best to avoid the sympathetic eyes, "this is the kitchen."

"Nice," he said. "Very nice."

There were the breakfast crumbs on the floor around the table. All she could think to say was, "It needs a paint job, of course."

"Very nice. Uh-huh."

He sounded genuine enough, she supposed. She went on. "We have plenty of hot water, of course, and everything."

"Does the owner live on the premises?"

"Pardon?"

"Does the owner of the building live on the premises?" he asked.

"It's an agency that manages the place," she said nervously.

"I was only wondering." He walked to the rear of the kitchen, crunching toast particles. Out the back window, through which he paused to look, there was no green yard. "There was just"—he lifted a hand to indicate that it was nothing—"a bulb out in the hallway, coming up. I wondered if the owner . . ."

He dwindled off, and again she didn't know what to say. The bulb had been out since their arrival; she had never even questioned it—it came with the house. "You see," Libby said, "there are two Negro families in the building—" *What!* I don't have anything against Negroes! But what if the agency does—why do I keep bringing up Negroes all the time! "And," she said, blindly, "the bulb went out last night, you see. My husband's going to pick one up today. Right now he's teaching. We don't like to bother the agency for little things. You know. . . ." But she could not tell whether he knew or not; he was leaning her way, but what of it? He turned and started back down the hall. Libby shut her eyes. I must stop lying. I must not lie again. He will be able to tell when I lie. They don't want liars for mothers, and they're perfectly right. Tell the truth. You have nothing to be ashamed of.

"My husband is a writer, aside from being a teacher," she said, running down the hall and slithering by Rosen, "and this"—she turned the knob to Paul's room, praying—"is his study."

Thank God. It was orderly; though there was not much that could be disordered. In the entire room—whose two tall winter-stained windows were set no further than ten feet from the apartment building next door—there was only a desk and a desk lamp, a chair and a typewriter, and a wastepaper basket. But the window shades were even and all the papers on the desk piled neatly. God bless Paul.

"My husband works in here." She flipped on the overhead light, but the room seemed to get no brighter; if anything, dingier. Whose fault was it that the sun couldn't come around that way? *They* hadn't constructed the building next door. "He's writing a novel," Libby told Mr. Rosen.

Rosen took quite an interest in that too. "Oh, yes? That must be some undertaking."

"Well, it's not finished yet—it is an undertaking, all right. But he's working on it. He works very hard. However, this," she said quickly, "this, of course, would be the baby's room. Will be the baby's room." She blushed. "Well, when we have a baby this will be—" Even while she spoke she was oppressed by the barren feebleness of the room. Where would a baby sleep? From what window would the lovely, healthy, natural light fall onto a baby's cheek? Where would one get the baby's crib? Catholic Salvage?

"Where will your husband work on his novel then?"

"I"—she wouldn't lie—"I don't know. We haven't talked about it. This has all happened very quickly. Our decision to have a baby."

"Of course."

"Not that we haven't thought about it—you see, it's not a problem. He can work anywhere. The bedroom. Anywhere. I'll discuss it with him tonight, if you like."

Rosen made a self-effacing gesture with his hands. "Oh, look, I don't care. That's all up to you folks." Even if there was something professional about his gentleness, she liked him for trying to put her at her ease. (Though that meant he knew about her nervousness; later he would mull over motives.) She had no real reason to be uneasy or overexcited or ashamed. Marty Rosen wouldn't kill her, wouldn't insult her—he wasn't even that much older than she—and what right, damn it, did he have to come unannounced! *That* was the trouble! What kind of business was this natural habitat business! *They have no right to trick people*—she was thinking, and the next thing she was opening the door to their own bedroom, and there was the bed, and the disheveled linens, and the half-painted dresser, and there were Paul's pajamas on the floor. There, in fact, was Rosen's coat, half on the floor. She closed the door and they went back into the living room.

"Actually," she said, addressing the back of his suit as they moved toward the sofa. "I was trying to write a poem . . ."

"Really? A poem?" He sat down, and then instantly was leaning forward, his arms on his legs and his hands clasped, and he was smiling. It was as though nothing he had seen up until now meant a thing; as though there was an entirely different set of rules called into play when the prospective mother turned out to be a poet. "You write, too, do you?"

"Well," said Libby, "no." Then she did not so much sit down into their one easy chair as capitulate into it. Why had she told Rosen about the poem? What did that explain to anybody—did writing poetry excuse crumbs on the floor? It was the truth, but that was all it was. They may want poets for mothers, she thought, but they sure as hell don't want slobs.

"Well," said Rosen cheerily, "it's a nice-sized apartment." It seemed impossible to disappoint him. "How long have you been here, would you say?"

"Not long," the girl answered. "A few months. Since October."

Rosen was opening his briefcase. "Do you mind if I take down a few things?"

"Oh, no, go right ahead." But her heart moved earthward. "We're going to paint, of course, as soon as—soon." Stop saying of course! "When everything's settled. When I get some time, I'll begin." The remark did not serve to make her any less conscious of her bathrobe and slippers. "You see," she went on, for Rosen had a way of listening even when no one was speaking—"I was working. I worked at the university. However I wasn't feeling well. Paul said I had better quit."

"That's too bad. Are you better now?"

"I'm fine. I feel fine—" she assured him. "I'm not pale, or sick, I just have very white skin—" Even as she spoke the white skin turned red.

Rosen smiled his smile. "I hope it wasn't serious."

"It wasn't anything really. I might have gotten quite sick—" *Why isn't Paul home? What good is he if he isn't here now?* "I had a kidney condition," she explained, starting in again. "It's why the doctors say I shouldn't have a baby. It would be too strong a risk. You see, I'm the one who can't have a baby. Not my husband."

"Well, there are many many couples that can't have babies, believe me."

His remark was probably intended to brace her, but tears nearly came to her eyes when she said, "Isn't that too bad . . ."

He took a paper from his case and pushed out the tip of a ballpoint pen. The click sounded to Libby very official. She pulled herself up straight in her chair and waited for the questions. Rosen asked nothing; he jotted some words on the paper. Libby waited. He glanced up. "Just the number of rooms and so forth," he said.

"Oh, certainly. Go right ahead. I've just been having"—she yawned— "my lazy morning, you know"—she tried to stretch, but stifled the impulse halfway, she by no means wanted for a moment to appear in any way loose or provocative—"not making the bed or anything, just taking the day off, just doing nothing. With a baby, of course, it would be different."

"Oh, yes." His brow furrowed, even as he wrote. "Children are a responsibility."

"There's no doubt about that." And she could not help it—she did not care if that was so much simple ass-kissing. At least, at last, she'd said the right thing. All she had to do was to keep saying the right thing, and get him out of here, and the next time Paul would be home. There were so many Jewish families wanting babies, and so few Jewish babies, and so what if she was obsequious. As long as: one, she didn't lie; and two, she said the right thing. "They are a responsibility," she said. "We certainly know that."

"Your husband's an instructor then, isn't that right, in the college?"

"In English. He teaches English and he teaches Humanities."

"And he's got a Ph.D.?"

He seemed to take it so for granted—wasn't he writing it down already?— that she suffered a moment of temptation. "An M.A. He's working on his Ph.D. Actually, he's just finishing up on it. He'll have it very soon, of course. Don't worry about that. Excuse me—I'm sorry, I don't mean to sound so instructive, I suppose I'm just a little nervous." She smiled, sweetly and spontaneously—a second later she thought that she must have charmed him. At least if he were someone else, if he were Gabe say, he would have been charmed; but this fellow seemed only to become more attentive. "I only meant," Libby said, "that I think

Paul has a splendid career before him. Even if I am his wife." And didn't that have the ring of truth about it? Hadn't her words conveyed all the respect and admiration she had for Paul—and too all the love she still felt for him, and would feel forever? It had been a nice wifely remark uttered in a nice wifely way—why then, wasn't Rosen *moved* by it? Did he not see what a dedicated, doting, loving mother she would be?

"I'm sure he has," Rosen said, and he might just as well have been attesting to a belief in the process of evolution.

But one had to remember that he was here in an official capacity; you couldn't expect him to gush. He must see dozens of families every day and hear dozens of wives attest to their love for their husbands. He could probably even distinguish those who meant it, from those who didn't, from those who were no longer quite so sure. She tried then to stifle her disappointment, though it was clear to her she would probably not be able to get off so solid a remark again.

Rosen had set his paper down now. "And so you just—well, live here," he said, tossing the remark out with a little roll of the hands, "and see your friends, and your husband teaches and writes, and you keep house—"

"As I said, today is just my lazy day—"

"—and have a normal young people's life. That's about it then, would you say?"

"Well—" He seemed to have left something out, though she couldn't put her finger on it. "Yes. I suppose that's it."

He nodded. "And you go to the movies," he said, "and see an occasional play, and have dinner out once in a while, I suppose, and take walks"—his hands went round with each activity mentioned—"and try to put a few dollars in the bank, and have little spats, I suppose—"

She couldn't stand it—she was ready to scream. "We read, of course." Though that wasn't precisely what she felt had been omitted, it was something.

He didn't seem at all to mind having been interrupted. "Are you interested in reading?"

"Well, yes. We read."

He considered further what she had said; or perhaps only waited for her to go on. He said finally, "What kind of books do you like best? Do you like fiction, do you like nonfiction, do you like biographies of famous persons, do you like how-to-do-it books, do you like who-done-its? What kind of books would you say you liked to read?"

"Books." She became flustered. "All kinds."

He leaned back now. "What books have you read recently?" To the question, he gave nothing more nor less than it had ever had before in the history of human conversation and its impasses.

It was her turn now to wave hands at the air. "God, I can't remember. It really slips my mind." She felt the color of her face changing again. "We're always reading something though—and well, Faulkner. Of course I read *The Sound and the Fury* in college, and *Light in August,* but I've been planning to read all of Faulkner, you know, chronologically. To get a sense of development."

His reply was slow in coming; he might have been waiting for her to break down and give the name of one thin little volume that she had read in the last year. "That sounds like a wonderful project, like a very worthwhile project."

In a shabby way she felt relieved.

"And your poetry," he asked, "what kind of poetry do you write?"

"What?"

"Do you write nature poems; do you write, oh, I don't know, rhymes; do you write little jingles? What kind of poetry would you say you write?"

Her eyes widened. "Well, I'm sorry, I don't write poetry," she said, as though he had stumbled into the wrong house.

"Oh, *I'm* sorry," he said, leaning forward to apologize. "I misunderstood."

"Ohhhh," Libby cried. "Oh, just this morning you mean."

Even Rosen seemed relieved. It was the first indication she had that the interview was wearing him down too. "Yes," he said, "this morning. Was that a nature poem, or, I don't know, philosophical? You know, your thoughts and so forth. I don't mean to be a nuisance, Mrs. Herz," he said, spreading his fingers over his foulard tie. "I thought we might talk about your interests. I don't want to pry, and if you—"

"Oh, yes, surely. Poetry, well, certainly," she said in a light voice.

"And this poem this morning, for instance—"

"Oh, that. I didn't know you meant that. That was—mostly my thoughts. I guess just a poem," she said, hating him, "about my thoughts."

"That sounds interesting." He looked down at the floor. "It's very interesting meeting somebody who writes poetry. Speaking for myself, I think, as a matter of fact, that there's entirely too much television and violence these days, that somebody who writes poetry would be an awfully good influence on a child."

"Thank you," Libby said softly. And now she didn't hate him. She closed her eyes—not the two shiny dark ones that Rosen could see. She closed her eyes, and she was back in that garden, and it was dusk, and her husband was with her, and in her arms was a child to whom she would later, by the crib, recite some of her poetry. "I think so too," she said.

"What makes poetry a fascinating subject," she heard Rosen saying, "is that people express all kinds of things in it."

"Oh, yes, it is fascinating. I'm very fond of poetry. I like Keats very much," and she spoke passionately now (as though her vibrancy concerning verse would make up for the books she couldn't remember having read recently). "And I like John Donne a great deal too, though I know he's the vogue, but still I do. And I like Yeats. I don't know a lot of Yeats, that's true, but I like some of him, what I know. I suppose they're mostly anthologized ones," she confessed, "but they're awfully good. 'The worst are full of passionate intensity, the best lack all conviction.' " A second later she said, "I'm afraid I've gotten that backward, or wrong, but I do like that poem, when I have it in front of me."

"Hmmmm," Rosen said, listening even after she had finished. "You seem really to be able to commit them to memory. That must be a satisfaction."

"It is."

"And how about your own poems? I mean would you say they're, oh, I don't know, happy poems or unhappy poems? You know, people write all kinds of poems, happy poems, unhappy poems—what do you consider yours to be?"

"Happy poems," said Libby. "Very happy poems."

At the front door, while Mr. Rosen went around in a tiny circle as he wiggled into his coat, he said, "I suppose you know Rabbi Kuvin."

"Rabbi who?"

He was facing her, fastening buttons. "Bernie Kuvin. He's the rabbi over in the new synagogue. Down by the lake."

Libby urged up into her face what she hoped would be an untroubled look. "No. We don't."

Rosen put on his hat. "I thought you might know him." He looked down and over himself, as though he had something more important on his mind anyway, like whether he was wearing his shoes or not.

And Libby understood. "No, no, we don't go around here to the synagogue. We're New Yorkers, originally that is—we go when we're in New York. We have a rabbi in New York. You're right, though," she said, her voice beginning to reflect the quantity and quality of her hope, or hopelessness. "You're perfectly right"—her eyes teary now—"religion is very important—"

"I don't know. I suppose it's up to the individual couple—"

"Oh no, oh no," Libby said, and she was practically pushing the door shut in his face, and she was weeping, "oh no, you're perfectly right, you're a hundred percent right, religion is very important to a child. But—" she shook and shook her tired head—"but my husband and I don't believe a God damn bit of it!"

And the door was closed, only by inches failing to chop off Rosen's coattails. She did not move away. She merely slid down right in the draft, right on the cold floor, and oh the hell with it. She sat there with her legs outstretched and her head in her hands. She was crying again. What had she done? *Why?* How could she possibly tell Paul? Why did she cry all the time? It was all wrong—*she* was all wrong. If only the bed had been made, if only it hadn't been for that stupid poetry writing— She had really ruined things now.

As far as she could see there was only one thing left to do.

Rushing up Michigan Boulevard in the unreasonable sunlight—unreasonable for this frost-bound city—she realized she was going to be late. She had gone into Saks with no intention of buying anything; she had with her only her ten-dollar bill (accumulated with pennies and nickels, then cashed in and hidden away for just such a crisis), and, besides, she knew better. She had simply not wanted to arrive at the office with fifteen minutes to spare. She did not intend to sit there perspiring and flushing, her body's victim. If you show up so very early, it's probably not too unfair of them to assume that you are weak and needy and pathetically anxious. And she happened to know she wasn't. She had been coping with her problems for some time now, and would, if she had to, continue to cope with them on into the future, until they just resolved themselves. She was by no means, she told herself, the most unhappy person in the world.

As a result, she had taken her time looking at sweaters. She had spent several minutes holding up against her a lovely white cashmere with a little tie at the neck. She had left the store (stopping only half a minute to look at a pair of black velveteen slacks) with the clock showing that it still wasn't one o'clock. And even if it had been, she would prefer not to arrive precisely as the big hand and the small hand came together on the hour. They would surely assume you were a compulsive then—which was another thing no one was simply going to *assume* about her.

But it was twelve minutes past the hour now, and even if she weren't a compulsive, she was nevertheless experiencing some of the more characteristic emotions of one. She clutched at her hat—which she had worn not to be warm, but attractive—and raced up the street. Having misjudged the distance, she was still some fifty numbers south of the building she was after. And it was no good to be this late, no good at all; in a way it was so aggressive of her (or defensive?) and God, she wasn't either! She was . . . what?

She passed a jewelry store; a golden clock in the window said fourteen after. She would miss her appointment. Where would she find the courage to make another? Oh, she *was* pathetically anxious—why hadn't she just gone ahead and been it! Why shopping? Clothes! Life was falling apart and she had to worry about velveteen slacks—and without even the money to buy them! She would miss her appointment. Then what? She could leave Paul. It was a mistake to think that he would ever take it upon himself to leave her. It must be she who says good-bye to him. Go away. To where?

She ran as fast as she could. The doctor had to see her.

The only beard in the room was on a picture of Freud that hung on the wall beside the desk. Dr. Lumin, himself, was clean-shaven and accentless. What he had were steamrolled Midwestern vowels and hefty South Chicago consonants, nothing at all that was European. Not that Libby had hung all her hopes on something as inconsequential as a bushy beard or a foreign intonation; nevertheless neither would by any means have shaken her confidence in his wisdom.

The doctor leaned across his desk and took her hand. He was a short, wide man with oversized head and hands. She had imagined before she met him that he would be tall; though momentarily disappointed, she was no less intimidated. He could have been a pygmy, and her hand when it touched his would have been no warmer. He gave her a nice meaty shake and she thought he looked like a butcher. She knew he wouldn't take any nonsense.

"I'm sorry I'm late." There were so many explanations she didn't give any.

"That's all right." He settled back into his chair. "I have someone coming in at two, so we won't have a full hour. Why don't you sit down?"

There was a straight-backed red-leather chair facing his desk and a brownish leather couch along the wall. She did not know whether she was supposed to know enough to just go over and lie down on the couch and start right in telling her problems. . . . Who had problems anyway? She could not think of one. Except, if she lay down on the couch, should she step out of her shoes first? Her shoulders drooped. "Where?" she asked finally.

"Wherever you like," he said.

"You won't mind," she said in a thin voice, "if I just sit for today."

He extended one of his hands, and said with a mild kind of force, "Why don't you sit." Oh, he was nice; a little crabby, but nice. She kept her shoes on and sat down in the straight chair.

And her heart took up a sturdy, martial rhythm. She looked directly across the desk into a pair of gray and, to her, impenetrable eyes. She had had no intention of becoming evasive in his presence; not when she had suffered so in making the appointment. The room, however, was a good deal brighter than she had thought it would be, and on top of her fear settled a thin icing of shyness.

"I stopped off at Saks on the way up. I didn't mean to keep you."

With one of those meat-cutter's hands he waved her apology aside. "I'm interested—look, how did you get my name? For the record." It was the second time that day that she found herself settled down across from a perfect stranger who felt it necessary to be casual with her. . . . Dr. Lumin leaned back in his swivel chair, so that for a moment it looked as though he'd keep on going, and fall backward, sailing clear through the window, but not him. And go ahead, she thought, fall. *There goes Lumin.* . . . "How did you find out about me?" he asked.

With no lessening of her heartbeat, she blushed. It was like living with an idiot whose behavior was unpredictable from one moment to the next: what would this body of hers do then seconds from now? "I heard your name at a party at the University of Chicago." She figured the last would make it all more dignified, less accidental. Otherwise he might take it as an insult, her coming to him so arbitrarily. "My husband teaches at the university," she said.

"It says here"—the doctor was looking at a card—"Victor Honingfeld." His eyes were two nailheads. Would he turn out to be stupid? Did he read those books on the wall or were they just for public relations? She wished she could get up and go.

"Your secretary asked on the phone," she explained, "and I gave Victor's name. He's a colleague of my husband's. I—he mentioned your name in passing, and I remembered it, and when I thought I might like to—try something, I only knew you, so I called. I didn't mean to say that Victor had recommended you. It was just that I heard it—"

Why go on? Why bother? She had insulted him professionally now, she was sure. He would start off disliking her.

"I think," she said quickly, "I'm becoming very selfish."

Swinging back in his chair, his head framed in the silver light, he didn't answer.

"That's really my only big problem, I suppose," said Libby. "Perhaps it's not even a problem. I suppose you could call it a foible or something along that line. But I thought, if I am *too* selfish, I'd like to talk to somebody. If I'm not, if it turns out it is just some sort of passing thing, circumstances you know, not me, well then I won't worry about it any more. Do you see?"

"Sure," he said, fluttering his eyelashes. He tugged undaintily at one of his fleshy ears and looked down in his lap, waiting. All day people had been waiting on her words. She wished she had been born self-reliant.

"It's been very confusing," she told him. "I suppose moving, a new environment. . . . It's probably a matter of getting used to things. And I'm just being impatient—" Her voice stopped, though not the rhythmic stroking in her breast. She didn't believe she had Lumin's attention. She was boring him. He seemed more interested in his necktie than in her. "Do you want me to lie down?" she asked, her voice quivering with surrender.

His big, raw face—the sharp, bony wedge of nose, the purplish, overdefined lips, those ears, the whole, huge, impressive red thing—tilted up in a patient, skeptical smile. "Look, come on, stop worrying about me. Worry about yourself," he said, almost harshly. "So how long have you been in Chicago, you two?"

She was no longer simply nervous; she was frightened. *You two.* If Paul were to know what she was doing, it would be his final disappointment. "October we came."

"And your husband's a teacher?"

"He teaches English at the university. He also writes."

"What? Books, articles, plays?"

"He's writing a novel now. He's still only a young man."

"And you—what about yourself?"

"I don't write," she said firmly. She was not going to pull her punches this second time. "I don't do anything."

He did not seem astonished. How could he, with that unexpressive butcher's face? He *was* dumb. Of course—it was always a mistake to take your troubles outside your house. You had to figure things out for yourself. *How?* "I was working," she said. "I was secretary to the Dean, and I was going to school, taking some courses at night downtown. But I've had a serious kidney condition."

"Which kind?"

"Nephritis. I almost died."

Lumin moved his head as though he were a clock ticking. "Oh, a nasty thing . . ."

"Yes," she said. "I think it weakened my condition. Because I get colds, and every stray virus, and since it is really dangerous once you've had a kidney infection, Paul said I should quit my job. And the doctor, the medical doctor"— she regretted instantly having made such a distinction—"said perhaps I shouldn't take classes downtown at night, because of the winter. I suppose I started thinking about myself when I started being sick all the time. I was in bed, and I began to think of myself. Of course I'm sure everyone thinks of himself eighty percent of the time. But, truly, I was up to about eighty-five."

She looked to see if he had smiled. Wasn't anybody going to be charmed today? Were people simply going to listen? She wondered if *he* found *her* dull. They tried to mask their responses, one expected that, but on the other hand it might be that she was no longer the delightful, bubbly girl she knew she once had been. Well, that's partly why she was here; to somehow get back to what she was. She wanted now to tell him only the truth. "I did become self-concerned, I think," she said. "Was I happy? was I this? was I that? and so forth, until I was self-absorbed. And it's hung on, in a way. Though I suppose what I need is an interest really, something to take my mind off myself. You simply can't go around all day saying I just had an orange, did that make me happy; I just typed a stencil, did that make me happy; because you only make yourself miserable."

The doctor rocked in his chair; he placed his hands on his belly, where it disappeared into his trousers like half a tent. "I don't know," he mumbled. "What, what does your husband think about all this?"

"I don't understand."

"About your going around all day eating oranges and asking yourself if they make you happy."

"I eat," she said, smiling, lying, "the oranges privately."

"Ah, hah." He nodded.

She found herself laughing, just a little. "Yes."

"So—go ahead. How privately? What privately?" He seemed suddenly to be having a good time.

"It's very involved," Libby said. "Complicated."

"I would imagine," Lumin said, a pleasant light in his eye. "You've got all those pits to worry about." Then he was shooting toward her—he nearly sprang full-grown from his chair. Their faces might as well have been touching, his voice some string she herself had plucked. "Come on, Libby," Lumin said, "what's the trouble?"

For the second time that day, the fiftieth that week, she was at the mercy of her tears. "Everything," she cried. "Every rotten thing. Every rotten, despicable thing. Paul's the trouble—he's just a terrible, terrible trouble to me."

She covered her face and for a full five minutes her forehead shook in the palms of her hands. Secretly she was waiting, but she did not hear Lumin's gruff voice nor feel upon her shoulders anyone's hands. When she finally looked up he was still there.

She pleaded, "Please just psychoanalyze me and straighten me out. I cry so much."

"What about Paul?"

She almost rose from her seat. "He never makes love to me! I get laid once a month!" Some muscle in her—it was her heart—relaxed. Though by no means restored to permanent health, she felt unsprung.

"Well," said Lumin, with authority, "everybody's entitled to get laid more than that. Is this light in your eyes?" He raised an arm and tapped his nail on the bright pane of glass behind him.

"No, no," she said and, for no apparent reason, what she was to say next caused her to sob. "You can see the lake." She tried, however, to put some real effort into pulling herself together. She wanted to stop crying and make sense, but it was the crying that seemed finally to be more to the point than the explanations she began to offer him in the best of faith. "You see, I think I've been in love with somebody else for a very long time. And it isn't Paul's fault. Don't think that. It couldn't be. He's the most honest man, Paul—he's always been terribly good to me. I was a silly college girl, self-concerned and frivolous and unimportant, and brutally typical, and he was the first person I ever wanted to listen to. I used to go on dates, years ago this is, and never listen—just talk. But Paul gave me books to read and he told me thousands of things, and he was—well, he saved me really from being like all those other girls. And he's had the toughest life. Oh, honestly," she said, "my eyeballs are going to fall out of my skull, roll right on out. Between this and being sick . . . I never imagined everything was going to be like this, believe me. . . ." After a while she wiped her face with her fingers. "Is it time? Is it two?"

Lumin seemed not to hear. "What else?"

"I don't know." She drew in to clear her nose. "Paul—" Medical degrees and other official papers hung on either side of Freud's picture. Lumin's first name was Arnold. That little bit of information made her not want to go on. But he was waiting. "I'm not really in love with this old friend," she told him. "He's an old friend, we know him since graduate school. And he's—he's very nice, he's carefree, he's full of sympathy—"

"Isn't Paul?"

"Oh, yes," she said, in what came out like a whine. "Oh, *so* sympathetic.

Dr. Lumin, I don't know what I want. I *don't* love Gabe. I really can't stand him, if you want to know the truth. He's not for me, he's not Paul—he never could be. Now he's living with some woman. She's so vulgar, I don't know what's gotten into him. We had dinner there—nobody said anything, and there was Gabe with that bitch."

"Why is she such a bitch?"

"Oh"—Libby wilted—"she's not that either. Do you want to know the bitch? Me. I was. But I knew it would be awful even before we got there. So, God, that didn't make it any easier."

He did not even have to bother; the next question she asked herself. "I don't *know* why. I just thought: why shouldn't we? We never go out to dinner, we hardly have been able to go out anywhere—and that's because of me too, and my health. Why shouldn't we? Do you see? And besides, I wanted to," she said. "It's as simple as that. I mean, isn't that still simple—to want to? But then I went ahead and behaved worse than anybody, I know I did. Oh, Gabe was all right—even she was all right, in a way. I understand all that. She's not a bitch probably. She's probably just a sexpot, good in bed or something, and why shouldn't Gabe live with her anyway? He's single, he can do whatever he wants to do. *I'm* the one who started the argument. All I do lately is argue with people. And cry. I mean that keeps me pretty busy, you can imagine."

Lumin remained Lumin; he didn't smile. In fact he frowned. "What do you argue about? Who are you arguing with?"

She raised two hands to the ceiling. "Everybody," she said. "Everything."

"Not Paul?"

"Not Paul—that's right, not Paul. *For* Paul," she announced. "Everybody's just frustrating the hell out of him, and it makes me so angry, so *furious!* . . . Oh, I haven't even *begun* to tell you what's happened."

"Well, go on."

"What?" she said helplessly. "Where?"

"Paul. Why is this Paul so frustrated?"

She leaned forward, and her two fists came hammering down on his desk. "If he wasn't, Doctor, *oh, if they would just leave him alone!*" She fell back, breathless. "Isn't it two?"

At last he gave her a smile. "Almost."

"It must be. I'm so tired. I have such lousy resistance. . . ."

"It's a very tiring thing, this kind of talking," Lumin said. "Everybody gets tired."

"Doctor, can I ask you a question?"

"What?"

"What's the matter with me?"

"What do you think's the matter?"

"Please, Dr. Lumin, please don't pull that stuff. Really, that'll drive me nuts."

He shook a finger at her. "C'mon, Libby, don't threaten me." The finger dropped, and she thought she saw through his smile. "It's not my habit to drive people nuts."

She backed away. "I'm nuts already anyway."

For an answer he clasped and unclasped his hands.

"Well, I am," she said. "I'm cracked as the day is long."

He groaned. "What are you talking about. Huh? I'm not saying you should make light of these problems. These are real problems. Absolutely. Certainly. You've got every reason to be upset and want to talk to somebody. But"—he made a sour face—"what's this cracked business? How far does it get us? It doesn't tell us a hell of a lot, wouldn't you agree?"

She had, of course, heard of transference, and she wondered if it could be beginning so soon. She was beaming at him; her first friend in Chicago.

"So . . ." he said peacefully.

"Really, I haven't begun to tell you things."

"Sure, sure."

"When should I come again? I mean," she said, softer, with less bravado, "should I come again?"

"If you want to, of course. How's the day after tomorrow? Same time."

"That's fine. I think that would be perfect. Except—" Her heart, which had stopped its pounding earlier, started up again, like a band leaving the field. "How much will it be then?"

"Same as today—"

"I only brought," she rushed to explain, "ten dollars."

"We'll send a bill then. Don't worry about that."

"It's more than ten, for today?"

"The usual fee is twenty-five dollars."

"An hour?"

"An hour."

She had never in her life passed out; that she didn't this time probably indicated that she never would in her remaining years either. She lost her breath, voice, vision, sense, but managed to stay upright in her chair. "I—don't send a bill to the house."

"I'd rather you wouldn't," Lumin began, a kind of gaseous expression crossing his face, "worry about the money. We can talk about that too."

Libby had stood up. "I think I have to talk about it."

"All right. Sit down. We'll talk."

"It's after two, I think."

"That's all right."

What she meant was, would he charge for overtime? Twenty-five dollars an hour—forty cents a minute. "I can't pay twenty-five dollars." She tried to cry, but couldn't. She felt very dry, very tired.

"Perhaps we can work it out at twenty."

"I can't pay twenty. I can't pay fifteen. I can't pay anything."

"Of course," said Lumin firmly, "you didn't expect it would be for nothing."

"I suppose I did. I don't know—" She got up to go.

"Please sit down. Sit."

She almost crept back into the chair as though it were a lap. "Don't you see, it's all my doctor bills in the first place. Don't you see that?"

He nodded.

"Well, I can't pay!" But she couldn't cry either. *"I can't pay!"*

"Look, Libby, look here. I'm giving you an address. You go home, you give it some thought. It's right here on Michigan Avenue—the Institute. They have excellent people, the fee is less. You'll have an interview—"

"I married Paul," she said, dazed, "this is ridiculous—you're being ridiculous—excuse me, but you're being—"

He was writing something.

She shouted, "I don't want any Institute! *Why can't I have you!"*

He offered her the paper. "You can be interviewed at the Institute," he said, "and see if they'll be able to work you in right away. Come on, now," he said, roughly, "why don't you think about which you might prefer, which might better suit your circumstances—"

She stood up. "You don't even know they'll take me."

"It's research and training, so of course, yes, it depends—"

"I came to *you*, damn it!" She reached for the paper he had written on, and threw it to the floor. "I came to you and I told you all this. You listened. You just sat there, listening. And now I have to go tell somebody else all over again. Everything. I came to you—*I want you!"*

He stood up, showing his burly form, and that alone seemed to strip her of her force, though not her anger. "Of course," he said, "one can't always have everything one wants—"

"I don't want everything! I want *something!"*

He did not move, and she would not be intimidated; she had had enough for one day. Quite enough. "I want you," she said.

"Libby—"

"I'll jump out the window." She pointed over his shoulder. "I swear it."

He remained where he was, blocking her path. And Libby, run down, unwound, empty-minded suddenly, turned and went out his door. *He provoked me,* she thought in the elevator. *He provoked me. Him and that son-of-a-bitch Gabe. They led me on.*

Ten minutes later, in Saks, she bought a sweater; not the white cashmere, but a pale-blue lamb's-wool cardigan that was on sale. It was the first time in years she had spent ten dollars on herself. She left the store, walked a block south, toward the I.C. train, and then turned and ran all the way back to Saks.

Because the sweater had been on sale she had to plead with two floor managers and a buyer before they would give her her money back.

[JANUARY 1962]

JOY WILLIAMS

The Lover

Joy Williams (1944–   ) originally published short stories in Esquire during Gordon Lish's tenure as fiction editor. Williams says that one of these, "Shorelines," about a woman suffering anguish after a miscarriage, was so heavily edited that Arnold Gingrich swore he couldn't understand it at all—Lish had cut out all mentions of the baby. Williams went on to publish more accessible stories, like this selection, "The Lover," and more recently has contributed a pair of articles on ecological matters with such a strong, mocking personal tone that each was collected in the Best American Essays of its year. She's also written two collections of stories, Taking Care and Escapes, and a novel, Breaking and Entering. She lives in the Florida Keys.

The girl is twenty-five. It has not been very long since her divorce but she cannot remember the man who used to be her husband. He was probably nice. She will tell the child this, at any rate. Once he lost a fifty-dollar pair of sunglasses while surf casting off Gay Head and felt badly about it for days. He did like kidneys, that was one thing. He loved kidneys for weekend lunch. She would voyage through the supermarkets, her stomach sweetly sloped, her hair in a twist, searching for fresh kidneys for this young man, her husband. When he kissed her, his kisses, or so she imagined, would have the faint odor of urine. Understandably, she did not want to think about this. It hardly seemed that the same problem would arise again, that is, with another man. Nothing could possibly be gained from such an experience! The child cannot remember him, this man, this daddy, and she cannot remember him. He had been with her when she gave birth to the child. Not beside her, but close by, in the corridor. He had left his work and come to the hospital. As they wheeled her by, he said, "Now you are going to have to learn how to love something, you wicked woman." It is difficult for her to believe he said such a thing.

The girl does not sleep well and recently has acquired the habit of listening all night to the radio. It is a weak, not very good radio and at night she can only get one station. From midnight until four she listens to *Action Line*. People call the station and make comments on the world and their community and they ask questions. Music is played and a brand of beef and beans is advertised. A woman calls up and says, "Could you tell me why the filling in my lemon meringue pie is runny?" These people have obscene materials in their mailboxes. They want to know where they can purchase small flags suitable for waving on Armed Forces Day. There is a man on the air who answers these questions right away. Another woman calls. She says, "Can you get us a report on the progress of the collection of Betty Crocker coupons for the lung machine?" The man can and does. He answers the woman's question. Astonishingly, he complies with her request. The girl thinks such a talent is bleak and wonderful. She thinks this man can help her.

The girl wants to be in love. Her face is thin with the thinness of a failed lover. It is so difficult! Love is concentration, she feels, but she can remember nothing. She tries to recollect two things a day. In the morning with her coffee, she tries to remember and in the evening, with her first bourbon and water, she tries to remember as well. She has been trying to remember the birth of her child now for several days. Nothing returns to her. Life is so intrusive! Everyone was talking. There was too much conversation! The doctor was above her, waiting for the pains. "No, I still can't play tennis," the doctor said. "I haven't been able to play for two months. I have spurs on both heels and it's just about wrecked our marriage. Air conditioning and concrete floors is what does it. Murder on your feet." A few minutes later, the nurse had said, "Isn't it wonderful to work with Teflon? I mean for those arterial repairs? I just love it." The girl wished that they would stop talking. She wished that they would turn the radio on instead and be still. The baby inside her was hard and glossy as an ear of corn. She wanted to say something witty or charming so that they would know she was fine and would stop talking. While she was thinking of something perfectly balanced and amusing to say, the baby was born. They fastened a plastic identification bracelet around her wrist and the baby's wrist. Three days later, after they had come home, her husband sawed off the bracelets with a grapefruit knife. The girl had wanted to make it an occasion. She yelled, "I have a lovely pair of tiny silver scissors that belonged to my grand-mother and you have used a grapefruit knife!" Her husband was flushed and nervous but he smiled at her as he always did. "You are insecure," she said tearfully. "You are insecure because you had mumps when you were eight." Their divorce was one year and two months away. "It was not mumps," he said carefully. "Once I broke my arm while swimming is all."

The girl becomes a lover to a man she met at a dinner party. He calls her up in the morning. He drives over to her apartment. He drives a white convertible which is all rusted out along the rocker panels. They do not make convertibles anymore, the girl thinks with alarm. He asks her to go sailing. They drop the child off at a nursery school on the way to the pier. She is two years old now. Her hair is an odd color, almost gray. It is braided and pinned up under a big hat with mouse ears that she got on a visit to Disney World. She is wearing a striped jersey stuffed into striped shorts. She kisses the girl and she kisses the man and goes into the nursery carrying her lunch in a Wonder Bread bag. In the afternoon, when they return, the girl has difficulty recognizing the child. There are so many children, after all, standing in the rooms, all the same size, all small, quizzical creatures, holding pieces of wooden puzzles in their hands.

It is late at night. A cat seems to be murdering a baby bird in a nest somewhere outside the girl's window. The girl is listening to the child sleep. The child lies in her varnished crib, clutching a bear. The bear has no tongue. Where there should be a small piece of red felt there is nothing. Apparently, the child had eaten it by accident. The crib sheet is in a design of tiny yellow circus animals. The girl enjoys looking at her child but cannot stand the sheet. There is so much going on in the crib, so many colors and patterns. It is so busy in there! The girl goes into the kitchen. On the counter, four palmetto bugs are exploring a pan of coffee cake. The girl goes back to her own bedroom and turns on the radio. There is a great deal of static. The Answer Man on *Action Line* sounds very annoyed. An old gentleman is asking something but the transmission is terrible because the old man refuses to turn off his rock tumbler. He is polishing stones in his rock tumbler like all old men do and he refuses to turn it off while speaking. Finally, the Answer Man hangs up on him. "Good for you," the girl says. The Answer Man clears his throat and says in a singsong way, "The wine of this world has caused only satiety. Our homes suffer from female sadness, embarrassment and confusion. Absence, sterility, mourning, privation and separation abound throughout the land." The girl puts her arms around her knees and begins to rock back and forth on the bed. The child murmurs in sleep. More palmetto bugs skate across the Formica and into the cake. The girl can hear them. A woman's voice comes on the radio now. The girl is shocked. It seems to be her mother's voice. The girl leans toward the radio. There is a terrible weight on her chest. She can scarcely breathe. The voice says, "I put a little pan under the air conditioner outside my window and it catches the condensation from the machine and I use that water to water my ivy. I think anything like that makes one a better person."

The girl has made love to nine men at one time or another. It does not seem like many but at the same time it seems more than necessary. She does not know what to think about them. They were all very nice. She thinks it is wonderful that a woman can make love to a man. When lovemaking, she feels she is behaving reasonably. She is well. The man often shares her bed now. He lies sleeping, on his stomach, his brown arm across her breasts. Sometimes, when the child is restless, the girl brings her into bed with them. The man shifts position, turns on his back. The child lies between them. The three lie, silent and rigid, earnestly conscious. On the radio, the Answer Man is conducting a quiz. He says, "The answer is: the time taken for the fall of the dashpot to clear the piston is four seconds, and what is the question? The answer is: when the end of the pin is five-sixteenths of an inch below the face of the block, and what is the question?"

She and the man travel all over the South in his white convertible. The girl brings dolls and sandals and sugar animals back to the child. Sometimes the child travels with them. She sits beside them, pretending to do something gruesome to her eyes. She pretends to dig out her eyes. The girl ignores this. The child is tanned and sturdy and affectionate although sometimes, when she is being kissed, she goes limp and even cold, as though she has suddenly, foolishly died. In the restaurants they stop at, the child is well-behaved although she takes only butter and ice water. The girl and the man order carefully but do not eat much either. They move the food around on their plates. They take a bite now and then. In less than a month the man has spent many hundreds of dollars on food that they do not eat. *Action Line* says that an adult female consumes seven hundred pounds of dry food in a single year. The girl believes this of course but it has nothing to do with her. Sometimes, she greedily shares a bag of Fig Newtons with the child but she seldom eats with the man. Her stomach is hard, flat, empty. She feels hungry always, dangerous to herself, and in love. They leave large tips on the tables of restaurants and then they reenter the car. The seats are hot from the sun. The child sits on the girl's lap while they travel, while the leather cools. She seems to ask for nothing. She makes clucking, sympathetic sounds when she sees animals smashed flat on the side of the road. When the child is not with them, they travel with the man's friends.

The man has many friends whom he is devoted to. They are clever and well-off; good-natured, generous people, confident in their prolonged affairs. They have known each other for years. This is discomforting to the girl who has known no one for years. The girl fears that each has loved the other at one time or another. These relationships are so complex, the girl cannot understand them! There is such flux, such constancy among them. They are so intimate and so calm. She tries to imagine their embraces. She feels that theirs differ from her own. One afternoon, just before dusk, the girl and man drive a short way into the Everglades. It is very dull. There is no scenery, no prospect. It is not a swamp at all. It is a river, only inches deep! Another couple rides in the back of the car. They have very dark tans and have pale yellow hair. They look almost like brother and sister. He is a lawyer and she is a lawyer. They are drinking gin and tonics, as are the girl and the man. The girl has not met these people before. The woman leans over the back seat and drops another ice cube from the cooler into the girl's drink. She says, "I hear that you have a little daughter." The girl nods. She feels funny, a little frightened. "The child is very *sortable*," the girl's lover says. He is driving the big car very fast and well but there seems to be a knocking in the engine. He wears a long-sleeved shirt buttoned at the wrists. His thick hair needs cutting. The girl loves to look at him. They drive, and on either side of them, across the slim canals or over the damp saw grass, speed airboats. The sound of them is deafening. The tourists aboard wear huge earmuffs. The man turns his head toward her for a moment. "I love you," she says. "Ditto," he says loudly, above the clatter of the airboats. "Double-ditto." He grins at her and she begins to giggle. Then she sobs. She has not cried for many months. There seems something wrong with the way she is doing it. Everyone is astounded. The man drives a few more miles and then pulls into a gas station. The girl feels desperate about this man. She would do the unspeakable for him, the unforgivable, anything. She is lost but not in him. She wants herself lost and never found, in him. "I'll do anything for you," she cries. "Take an aspirin," he says. "Put your head on my shoulder."

The girl is sleeping alone in her apartment. The man has gone on a business trip. He assures her he will come back. He'll always come back, he says. When the girl is quite alone she measures her drink out carefully. Carefully, she drinks twelve ounces of bourbon in two and a half hours. When she is not with the man, she resumes her habit of listening to the radio. Frequently, she hears only the replies of *Action Line*. "Yes," the Answer Man says, "in answer to your question, the difference between rising every morning at six or at eight in the course of forty years amounts to twenty-nine thousand two hundred hours or three years, two hundred twenty-one days and sixteen hours which are equal to eight hours a day for ten years. So that rising at six will be the equivalent of adding ten years to your life." The girl feels, by the Answer Man's tone, that he is a little repulsed by this. She washes her whiskey glass out in the sink. Balloons are drifting around the kitchen. They float out of the kitchen and drift onto the balcony. They float down the hall and bump against the closed door of the child's room. Some of the balloons don't float but slump in the corners of the kitchen like mounds of jelly. These are filled with water. The girl buys many balloons and is always blowing them up for the child. They play a great deal with the balloons, breaking them over the stove or smashing the water-filled ones against the walls of the bathroom. The girl turns off the radio and falls asleep.

The girl touches her lover's face. She runs her fingers across the bones. "Of course I love you," he says. "I want us to have a life together." She is so restless. She moves her hand across his mouth.

There is something she doesn't understand, something she doesn't know how to do. She makes them a drink. She asks for a piece of gum. He hands her a small crumpled stick, still in the wrapper. She is sure that it is not the real thing. The Answer Man has said that Lewis Carroll once invented a substitute for gum. She fears that this is that. She doesn't want this! She swallows it without chewing. "Please," she says. "Please what?" the man replies, a bit impatiently.

Her former husband calls her up. It is autumn and the heat is unusually oppressive. He wants to see the child. He wants to take her away for a week to his lakeside house in the middle of the state. The girl agrees to this. He arrives at the apartment and picks up the child and nuzzles her. He is a little heavier than before. He makes a little more money. He has a different watch, wallet and key ring. "What are you doing these days?" the child's father asks. "I am in love," she says.

The man does not visit the girl for a week. She doesn't leave the apartment. She loses four pounds. She and the child make Jell-O and they eat it for days. The girl remembers that after the baby was born, the only food the hospital gave her was Jell-O. She thinks of all the water boiling in hospitals everywhere for new mothers' Jell-O. The girl sits on the floor and plays endlessly with the child. The child is bored. She dresses and undresses herself. She goes through everything in her small bureau drawer and tries everything on. The girl notices a birthmark on the child's thigh. It is very small and lovely, in the shape, the girl thinks, of a wineglass. A doll's wineglass. The girl thinks about the man constantly but without much exactitude. She does not even have a photograph of him! She looks through old magazines. He must resemble someone! Sometimes, late at night, when she thinks he might come to her, she feels that the Answer Man arrives instead. He is like a moving light, never still. He has the high temperature and metabolism of a bird. On *Action Line*, someone is saying, "And I live by the airport, what is this that hits my house, that showers my roof on takeoff? We can hear it. What is this, I demand to know! My lawn is healthy, my television reception is fine but something is going on without my consent and I am not well, my wife's had a stroke and someone stole my stamp collection and took the orchids off my trees." The girl sips her bourbon and shakes her head. The greediness and wickedness of people, she thinks, their rudeness and lust. "Well," the Answer Man says, "each piece of earth is bad for something. Something is going to get it on it and the land itself is no longer safe. It's weakening. If you dig deep enough to dip your seed, beneath the crust you'll find an emptiness like the sky. No, nothing's compatible to living in the long run. Next caller, please." The girl goes to the telephone and dials hurriedly. It is very late. She whispers, not wanting to wake the child. There is static and humming. "I can't make you out," the Answer Man shouts. "Are you a phonemophobiac?" The girl says more firmly, "I want to know my hour." "Your hour came, dear," he says. "It went when you were sleeping. It came and saw you dreaming and it went back to where it was."

          The girl's lover comes to the apartment. She throws herself into his arms. He looks wonderful. She would do anything for him! The child grabs the pocket of his jacket and swings on it with her full weight. "My friend," the child says to him. "Why yes," the man says with surprise. They drive the child to the nursery and then go out for a wonderful lunch. The girl begins to cry and spills the roll basket on the floor.

    "What is it?" he asks. "What's wrong?" He wearies of her, really. Her moods and palpitations. The girl's face is pale. Death is not so far, she thinks. It is easily arrived at. Love is further than death. She kisses him. She cannot stop. She clings to him, trying to kiss him. "Be calm," he says.

          The girl no longer sees the man. She doesn't know anything about him. She is a gaunt, passive girl, living alone with her child. "I love you," she says to the child. "Mommy loves me," the child murmurs, "and Daddy loves me and Grandma loves me and Granddaddy loves me and my friend loves me." The girl corrects her, "Mommy loves you," she says. The child is growing. In not too long the child will be grown. When is this happening! She wakes the child in the middle of the night. She gives her a glass of juice and together they listen to the radio. A woman is speaking on the radio. She says, "I hope you will not think me vulgar." "Not at all," the Answer Man replies. "He is never at a loss," the girl whispers to the child. The woman says, "My husband can only become excited if he feels that some part of his body is missing." "Yes," the Answer Man says. The girl shakes the sleepy child. "Listen to this," she says. "I want you to know about these things." The unknown woman's voice continues, dimly. "A finger or an eye or a leg. I have to pretend it's not there."

    "Yes," the Answer Man says.

[JULY 1973]

JAYNE ANNE PHILLIPS

Bess

A native of Buckhannon, West Virginia, Jayne Anne Phillips
(1952–   ) graduated from the University of West Virginia in 1974
and promptly hit the road, traveling by slow degrees to the West Coast,
often working along the way as a waitress. In 1976 she entered the Iowa
Writers' Workshop, where she composed many of the stories that ended
up in Black Tickets (1979), her highly regarded short story collection.
Her novel Machine Dreams was published to similar acclaim in 1984
and was followed by another story collection, Fast Lanes, in 1987.
Phillips focuses her fiction on characters who by class or personal history
find themselves living precipitously on the edge of respectable society.
Her characters locate themselves within language, which for Phillips
serves as a "private, secretive means of travel, a way of living your own
life."

You have to imagine: this was sixty,
seventy, eighty years ago, more than the lifetimes allotted most persons. We
could see no other farms from our house, not a habitation or the smoke of
someone's chimney; we could not see the borders of the road anymore but only
the cover of snow, the white fields, and mountains beyond. Winters frightened

me, but it was summers I should have feared. Summers, when the house was large and full, the work out-of-doors so it seemed no work at all, everything done in company—summers all the men were home, the farm was crowded, lively; it seemed nothing could go wrong then.

Our parents joked about their two families, first the six sons, one after the other; then a few years later the four daughters, Warwick, and me. Another daughter after the boy was a bad sign, Pa said; there were enough children. I was the last, youngest of twelve Hampsons, and just thirteen months younger than Warwick. Since we were born on each other's heels, Mam said, we would have to raise each other.

The six elder brothers had all left home at sixteen to homestead somewhere on the land, each going first to live with the brother established before him. They worked mines or cut timber for money to start farms and had an eye for women who were not delicate. Once each spring they were all back to plant garden with Pa, and the sisters talked amongst themselves about each one.

By late June the brothers had brought their families, each a wife and several children. All the rooms in the big house were used, the guesthouse as well, swept and cleaned. There was always enough space because each family lived in two big rooms, one given to parents and youngest baby and the other left for older children to sleep together, all fallen uncovered across a wide cob-stuffed mattress. Within those houses were many children, fifteen, twenty, more. I am speaking now of the summer I was twelve, the summer Warwick got sick and everything changed.

He was nearly thirteen. We slept in the big house in our same room, which was bay-windowed, very large and directly above the parlor, the huge oak tree lifting so close our window it was possible to climb out at night and sit hidden on the branches. Adults on the porch were different from high up, the porch lit in the dark and chairs creaking as the men leaned and rocked, murmuring, drinking homemade beer kept cool in cellar crocks.

Late one night that summer, Warwick woke me, pinched my arms inside my cotton shift and held his hand across my mouth. He walked like a shadow in his white nightclothes, motioning I should follow him to the window. Warwick was quickly through and I was slower, my weight still on the sill as he settled himself, then lifted me over when I grabbed a higher branch, my feet on his chest and shoulders. We climbed into the top branches that grew next the third floor of the house and sat cradled where three branches sloped; Warwick whispered not to move, stay behind the leaves in case they look. We were outside Claude's window, seeing into the dim room.

Claude was youngest of the older brothers and his wife was hugely with child, standing like a white column in the middle of the floor. Her white chemise hung wide round her like a tent and her sleeves were long and belled; she stood, both hands pressed to the small of her back, leaning as though to help the weight at her front. Then I saw Claude kneeling, darker than she because he wasn't wearing clothes. He touched her feet and I thought at first he was helping her take off her shoes, as I helped the young children in the evenings. But he had nothing in his hands and was lifting the thin chemise above her knees, higher to her thighs, then above her hips as she was twisting away but stopped and moved toward him, only holding the cloth bunched to conceal her belly. She pressed his head away from her, the chemise pulled to her waist in back and his one hand there trying to hold her. Then he backed her three steps to the foot of the bed and she half leaned, knees just bent; he knelt down again, his face almost at her feet and his mouth moving like he was biting her along her legs. She held him just away with her hands and he touched over and over the big globed belly, stroking it long and deeply like you would stroke a scared animal. Suddenly he stood quickly and turned her so her belly was against the heaped sheets. She grasped the bed frame with both hands so when he pulled her hips close she was bent prone forward from the waist; now her hands were occupied and he uncovered all of her, pushing the chemise to her shoulders and past her breasts in front; the filmy cloth hid her head and face, falling even off her shoulders so it hung halfway down her arms. She was all naked globes and curves, headless and wide-hipped with the swollen belly big and pale beneath her like a moon; standing that way she looked all dumb and animal like our white mare before she foaled. All this time she was whimpering, Claude looking at her. We saw him, he started to prod himself inside her very slow, tilting his head and listening. . . . I put my cool hands over my eyes then, hearing their sounds until Warwick pulled my arms down and made me look. Claude was tight behind her, pushing in and flinching like he couldn't get out of her, she bawled once. He let her go, stumbling; they staggered onto the bed, she lying on her back away from him with the bunched chemise in her mouth. He pulled her to him and took the cloth from her lips and wiped her face.

This was perhaps twenty minutes of a night in July 1900. I looked at Warwick as though for the first time. When he talked he was so close I could feel the words on my skin distinct from night breeze. "Are you glad you saw," he whispered, his face frightened.

He had been watching them from the tree for several weeks.

In old photographs of Coalton that July 4, the town looks scruffy and blurred. The blue of the sky is not shown in those black-and-white studies. Wooden sidewalks on the two main streets were broad and raised; that day people sat along them as on low benches, their feet in the road, waiting for the parade. We were all asked to stay still as a photographer took pictures of the whole scene from a nearby hillside. There was a prayer blessing the new century and the cornet band assembled. The parade was forming out of sight, by the river; Warwick and Pa had already driven out in the wagon to watch. It would be a big parade; we had word that local merchants had hired part of a circus traveling through Bellington. I ran up the hill to see if I could get a glimpse of them; Mam was calling me to come back and my shoes were blond to the ankles with dust. Below me the crowd began to cheer. The ribboned horses danced with fright and kicked, jerking reins looped over low branches of trees and shivering the leaves. From up the hill I saw dust raised in the woods and heard the crackling of what was crushed. There were five elephants; they came out from the trees along the road and the trainer sat on the massive harnessed head of the first. He sat in a sort of purple chair, swaying side to side with the lumbering swivel of the head. The trainer wore a red cap and jacket; he was dark and smooth on his face and held a boy close his waist. The boy was moving his arms at me and it was Warwick; I was running closer and the trainer beat with his staff on the shoulders of the elephant while the animal's snaky trunk, all alive, ripped small bushes. Warwick waved; I could see him and ran dodging the men until I was alongside. The earth was pounding and the animal was big like a breathing wall, its rough side crusted with dirt and straw. The skin hung loose, draped on the limbs like sacking crossed with many creases. The enormous creature worked, wheezing, and the motion of the lurching walk was like the swing of a colossal gate. Far, far up, I saw Warwick's face; I was yelling, yelling for them to stop, stop and take me up, but they kept on going. Just as the elephants passed, wind lifted the dust and ribbons and hats, the white of the summer skirts swung and billowed. The cheering was a great noise under the trees and birds flew up wild. Coalton was a sea of yellow dust, the flags snapping in that wind and banners strung between the buildings broken, flying.

Warwick got it in his head to walk a wire. Our Pa would not hear of such foolishness, so Warwick took out secretly to the creek every morning and practiced on the sly. He constructed a thickness of barn

boards lengthwise on the ground, propped with nailed supports so he could walk
along an edge. First three boards, then two, then one. He walked barefoot tensing
his long toes and cradled a bamboo fishing pole in his arms for balance. I
followed along silently when I saw him light out for the woods. Standing back
a hundred feet from the creek bed, I saw through dense summer leaves my
brother totter magically just above the groundline; thick ivy concealed the edges
of the boards and made him appear a jerky magician. He often walked naked since
the heat was fierce and his trousers too-large hand-me-downs that obstructed
careful movement. He walked parallel to the creek and slipped often. Periodically
he grew frustrated and jumped cursing into the muddy water. Creek bottom at
that spot was soft mud and the water perhaps five feet deep; he floated belly-up
like a seal and then crawled up the bank mud-streaked to start again. I stood in
the leaves. He was tall and still coltish then, dark from the sun on most of his
body, long-muscled; his legs looked firm and strong and a bit too long for him,
his buttocks were tight and white. It was not his nakedness that moved me to
stay hidden, barely breathing lest he hear the snap of a twig and discover me—it
was the way he touched the long yellow pole, first holding it close, then opening
his arms gently as the pole rolled across his flat still wrists to his hands; another
movement, higher, and the pole balanced like a visible thin line on the tips of
his fingers. It vibrated as though quivering with a sound. Then he clasped it
lightly and the pole turned horizontally with a half rotation; six, seven, eight
quick flashes, turning hard and quick, whistle of air, snap of the light wood
against his palms. Now the pole lifted, airborne a split second and suddenly
standing, earthward end walking Warwick's palm. He moved, watching the sky
and a wavering six feet of yellow needle. The earth stopped in just that moment,
the trees still, Warwick moving, and then as the pole toppled in a smooth arc
to water he followed in a sideways dive. While he was under, out of earshot and
rapturous in the olive water, I ran quick and silent back to the house, through
forest and vines to the clearing, the meadow, the fenced boundaries of the
high-grown yard and the house, the barn where it was shady and cool and I could
sit in the mow to remember his face and the yellow pole come to life. You had
to look straight into the sun to see its airborne end and the sun was a blind white
burn the pole could touch. Like Warwick was prodding the sun in secret, his
whole body a prayer partly evil.

One day of course he saw me watching him, and knew in an instant I had
watched him all along; by then he was actually walking a thick rope strung about
six feet off the ground between two trees. For a week he'd walked only to a
midpoint, as he could not rig the rope so it didn't sag and walking all the way

across required balance on the upward slant. That day he did it; I believe he did it only that once, straight across. I made no sound but as he stood there poised above me his eyes fell upon my face; I had knelt in the forest cover and was watching as he himself had taught me to watch. Perhaps this explains his anger—I see still, again and again, Warwick jumping down from the rope, bending his knees to an impact as dust clouds his feet but losing no balance, no stride, leaping toward me at a run. His arms are still spread, hands palm-down as though for support in the air and then I hear rather than see him because I'm running, terrified—shouting his name in supplication through the woods as he follows, still coming after me wild with rage as I'd never seen anyone. Then I was nearly out of breath and just screaming, stumbling—

It's true I led him to the thicket, but I had no idea where I was going. We never went there, as it was near a rocky outcropping where copperheads bred, and not really a thicket at all but a small apple orchard gone diseased and long dead. The trees were oddly dwarfed and broken, and the ground cover thick with vines. Just as Warwick caught me I looked to see those rows of small dead trees; then we were fighting on the ground, rolling. I fought with him in earnest and scratched his eyes; already he was covered all over with small cuts from running through the briars. This partially explains how quickly he was poisoned but the acute nature of the infection was in his blood itself. Now he would be diagnosed severely allergic and given antibiotics; then we knew nothing of such medicines. The sick were still bled. In the week he was most ill, Warwick was bled twice daily, into a bowl. The doctor theorized, correctly, that the poison had worsened so as to render the patient's blood toxic.

Later Warwick told me, if only I'd stopped yelling—now that chase seems a comical as well as nightmarish picture; he was only a naked enraged boy. But the change I saw in his face, that moment he realized my presence, foretold everything. Whatever we did from then on was attempted escape from the fact of the future.

"**W**arwick? Warwick?"

In the narrow sun porch, which is all windows but for the house wall, he sleeps like a pupa, larva wrapped in a woven spit of gauze and never turning. His legs weeping in the loose bandages, he smells of clear fluid seeped from wounds. The seepage clear as tears, clear as sweat, but sticky on my hands when my own sweat never sticks but drips from my forehead onto his flat stomach where he says it stings like salt.

"Warwick. Mam says to turn you now."

Touching the wide gauze strips in the dark. His ankles propped on rolls of cloth so his legs air and the blisters scab after they break and weep. The loose gauze strips are damp when I unwrap them, just faintly damp; now we don't think he is going to die.

He says, "Are they all asleep inside?"

"Yes. Except Mam woke me."

"Can't you open the windows. Don't flies stop when there's dew?"

"Yes, but the mosquitoes. I can put the netting down but you'll have that dream again."

"Put it down but come inside, then I'll stay awake."

"You shouldn't, you should sleep."

Above him the net is a canopy strung on line, rolled up all the way round now and tied with cord like a bedroll. It floats above him in the dark like a cloud the shape of the bed. We keep it rolled up all the time now since the bandages are off his eyes; he says looking through it makes everyone a ghost and fools him into thinking he's still blind.

Now I stand on a chair to reach the knotted cords, find them by feel, then the netting falls all around him like a skirt.

"All right, Warwick, see me? I just have to unlatch the windows."

Throw the hooks and windows swing outward all along the sun porch walls. The cool comes in, the lilac scent, and now I have to move everywhere in the dark because Mam says I can't use the lamp, have kerosene near the netting—

"I can see you better now," he says from the bed.

I can tell the shadows, shapes of the bed, the medicine table, the chair beside him where I slept the first nights we moved him to the sun porch. Doctor said he'd never seen such a poison, Warwick's eyes swollen shut, his legs too big for pants, soles of his feet oozing in one straight seam like someone cut them with scissors. Mam with him day and night until her hands broke out and swelled; then it was only me, because I don't catch poison, wrapping him in bandages she cut and rolled wearing gloves.

"Let me get the rose water," I whisper.

Inside the tent he sits up to make room. I hold the bowl of rose water and the cloth, crawl in and it's like sitting low in high fields hidden away, except there isn't even sky, no opening at all.

"It's like a coffin, that's what," he'd said when he could talk.

"A coffin is long and thin," I told him, "with a lid."

"Mine has a ceiling," Warwick said.

Inside everything is clean and white and dry; every day we change the white bottom sheet and he isn't allowed any covers. He's sitting up—I still can't see him in the dark, even the netting looks black, so I find him, hand forehead nose throat.

"Can't you see me. There's a moon, I see you fine."

"Then you've turned into a bat. I'll see in a moment, it was light in the kitchen."

"Mam?"

"Mam and three lamps. She's rolling bandages this hour of the night. She doesn't sleep when you don't."

"I can't sleep."

"I know."

He only sleeps in daytime when he can hear people making noise. At night he wakes up in silence, in the narrow black room, in bandages in the tent. For a while when the doctor bled him he was too weak to yell for someone.

He says, "I won't need bandages much longer."

"A little longer," I tell him.

"I should be up walking. I wonder if I can walk, like before I wondered if I could see."

"Of course you can walk, you've only been in bed two weeks, and a few days before upstairs—"

"I don't remember when they moved me here, so don't it seem like always I been here."

Pa and two brothers and Mam moved him, all wearing gloves and their forearms wrapped in gauze I took off them later and burned in the wood stove.

"Isn't always. You had deep sleeps in the fever, you remember wrong." I start at his feet, which are nearly healed, with the sponge and the cool water. Water we took from the rain barrel and scented with torn roses, the petals pounded with a pestle and strained, since the doctor said not to use soap.

The worst week I bathed him at night so he wouldn't get terrified alone. He was delirious and didn't know when he slept or woke. When I touched him with the cloth he made such whispers, such inside sounds; they weren't even words but had a cadence like sentences. If he could feel this heat and the heat of his fever, blind as he was then in bandages, and tied, if he could still think, he'd think he was in hell. I poured the alcohol over him, and the water from the basin, I was bent close his face just when he stopped raving and I thought he had died. He said a word.

"Bessie," he said.

Bless me, I heard. I knelt with my mouth at his ear, in the sweat, in the horrible smell of the poison. "Warwick," I said. He was there, tentative and weak, a boy waking up after sleeping in the blackness three days. "Stay here, Warwick. Warwick."

I heard him say the word again, and it was my name, clearly.

"Bessie," he said.

So I answered him. "Yes, I'm here. Stay here."

Later he told me he slept a hundred years, swallowed in a vast black belly like Jonah, no time anymore, no sense but strange dreams without pictures. He thought he was dead, he said, and the moment he came back he spoke the only word he'd remembered in the dark.

Sixteen years later, when he did die, in the mine—did he say a word again, did he say that word? Trying to come back. The second time, I think he went like a streak. I had the color silver in my mind. A man from Coalton told us about the cave-in. The man rode out on a horse, a bay mare, and he galloped the mare straight across the fields to the porch instead of taking the road. I was sitting on the porch and saw him coming from a ways off. I stood up as he came closer; I knew the news was Warwick, and that whatever had happened was over. I had no words in my mind, just the color silver, everywhere. The fields looked silver too just then, the way the sun slanted. The grass was tall and the mare moved through it up to her chest, like a powerful swimmer. I did not call anyone else until the man arrived and told me, breathless, that Warwick and two others were trapped, probably suffocated, given up for dead. The man, a Mr. Forbes, was surprised at my composure. I simply nodded; the news came to me like an echo. I had not thought of that moment in years—the moment Warwick's fever broke and I heard him speak—but the moment returned in an instant. Having felt it once, that disappearance, even so long before, I was prepared. Memory does not work according to time. I was twelve years old, perceptive, impressionable, in love with Warwick as a brother and sister can be in love. I loved him then as one might love one's twin, without a thought. After that summer I understood too much. I don't mean I was ashamed; I was not. But no love is innocent once it has recognized its own existence.

At eighteen I went away to a finishing school in Lynchburg. The summer I came back, foolishly, I ran away west. I eloped partially because Warwick found fault with anyone who courted me, and made a case against him to Mam. The name of the man I left with is unimportant. I do not really remember his face. He was blond but otherwise he did resemble Warwick—in his movements, his walk, his way of speaking. All told, I was in his company eight weeks. We were traveling, staying in hotels. He'd told me he was in textiles but it seemed actually he gambled at cards and roulette. He had a sickness for the roulette wheel, and other sicknesses. I could not bear to stand beside him in the gambling parlors; I hated the noise and the smoke, the perfumes mingling, the clackings of the wheels like speeded-up clocks and everyone's eyes following numbers. Often I sat in a hotel room with a blur of noise coming through the floor, and imagined the vast space of the barn around me: dark air filling a gold oval, the tall beams, the bird sounds ghostly, like echoes. The hay, ragged heaps that spilled from the mow in pieces and fell apart.

The man who was briefly my husband left me in St. Louis. Warwick came for me; he made a long journey in order to take me home. A baby boy was born the following September. It was decided to keep my elopement and divorce, and the pregnancy itself, secret. Our doctor, a country man and friend of the family, helped us forge a birth certificate stating that Warwick was the baby's father. We invented a name for his mother, a name unknown in those parts, and told that she'd abandoned the baby to us. People lived so far from one another, in isolation, that such deceit was possible. My boy grew up believing I was his aunt and Warwick his father, but Warwick could not abide him. To him, the child was living reminder of my abasement, my betrayal in ever leaving the farm.

The funeral was held at the house. Men from the mine saw to it Warwick was laid out in Coalton, then they brought the box to the farm on a lumber wagon. The lid was kept shut. That was the practice then; if a man died in the mines his coffin was closed for services, nailed shut, even if the man was unmarked.

The day after Warwick's funeral, all the family was leaving back to their homesteads having seen each other in a confused picnic of food and talk and sorrowful conjecture. Half the sorrow was Warwick alive and half was Warwick dead. His dying would make an end of the farm. I would leave now for Bellington, where, in a year, I would meet another man. Mam and Pa would go to live with Claude and his wife. But it was more than losing the farm that puzzled and saddened everyone; no one knew who Warwick was, really. They said it was hard to believe he was inside the coffin, with the lid nailed shut that way. Touch the box, anywhere, with the flat of your hand, I told them. They did, and stopped that talk.

The box was thick pine boards, pale white wood; I felt I could fairly look through it like water into his face, like he was lying in a piece of water on top of the parlor table. Touching the nailed lid you felt first the cool slide of new wood on your palm, and a second later the depth—a heaviness inside like the box was so deep it went clear to the center of the earth, his body contained there like a big caged wind. Something inside, palpable as the different air before flash rains, with clouds blown and air clicking before the crack of downpour.

I treated the box as though it were living, as though it had to accustom itself to the strange air of the house, of the parlor, a room kept for weddings and death. The box was simply there on the table, long and pure like some deeply asleep, dangerous animal. The stiff damask draperies at the parlor windows looked as though they were about to move, gold tassels at the hems suspended and still.

The morning before the service most of the family had been in Coalton, seeing to what is done at a death. I had been alone in the house with the coffin churning what air there was to breathe. I had dressed in best clothes as though for a serious, bleak suitor. The room was just lighted with sunrise, window shades pulled halfway, their cracked sepia lit from behind. One locust began to shrill as I took a first step across the floor; somehow one had gotten into the room. The piercing, fast vibration was very loud in the still morning: suddenly I felt myself smaller, cramped as I bent over Warwick inside his white tent of netting, his whole body afloat below me on the narrow bed, his white shape in the loose bandages seeming to glow in dusk light while beyond the row of open windows hundreds of locusts sang a ferocious pattering. I could scarcely see the parlor anymore. My vision went black for a moment, not black but dark green, like the color of the dusk those July weeks years before.

[AUGUST 1984]

JAMES SALTER

American Express

James Salter (1925–   ) was raised in New York City. He followed
in his father's footsteps and enrolled at West Point. For ten years he
served in the Army Air Corps, writing whenever and however he could.
In 1957, when his first book, <u>The Hunter</u>, was accepted for publication,
Salter left the service. When <u>A Sport and a Pasttime</u> was published in
1967—"one of the most murmurously erotic novels ever written,"
reported James Wolcott in <u>Esquire</u>—it marked, says Salter, "the real
beginning of my career." In the late sixties, he lived in France and wrote
film scripts, among them <u>Downhill Racer</u>. One of his most memorable
novels, the sensuous yet desolate <u>Light Years</u>, appeared in 1975, followed in 1979 by a classic novel of mountain climbing, <u>Solo Faces</u>. The
story presented here, "American Express," was reprinted in the O. Henry
prize anthology, as well as in Salter's collection <u>Dusk</u>, which won the
PEN/Faulkner Award for fiction.

It's hard to think of all the places and
nights, Nicola's like a railway car, deep and gleaming, the crowd at the Un Deux
Trois, Billy's. Unknown brilliant faces jammed at the bar. The dark, dramatic eye
that blazes for a moment and disappears.

In those days they were living in apartments with funny furniture and on

Sundays sleeping until noon. They were in the last rank of the armies of law. Clever junior partners were above them, partners, associates, men in fine suits who had lunch at the Four Seasons. Frank's father went there three or four times a week, or else to the Century Club or the Union, where there were men even older than he. Half of the members can't urinate, he used to say, and the other half can't stop.

Alan on the other hand was from Cleveland, where his father was well known, if not detested. No defendant was too guilty, no case too clear-cut. Once in another part of the state he was defending a murderer, a black man. He knew what the jury was thinking, he knew what he looked like to them. He stood up slowly. It could be they had heard certain things, he began. They may have heard, for instance, that he was a big-time lawyer from the city. They may have heard that he wore $300 suits, that he drove a Cadillac and smoked expensive cigars. He was walking along as if looking for something on the floor. They may have heard that he was Jewish.

He stopped and looked up. Well, he was from the city, he said. He wore $300 suits, he drove a Cadillac, smoked big cigars, and he was Jewish. "Now that we have that settled, let's talk about this case."

Lawyers and sons of lawyers. Days of youth. In the morning in stale darkness the subways shrieked.

"Have you noticed the new girl at the reception desk?"

"What about her?" Frank asked.

They were surrounded by noise like the launch of a rocket. "She's hot," Alan confided.

"How do you know?"

"I know."

"What do you mean, you know?"

"Intuition."

"Intuition?" Frank said.

"What's wrong?"

"That doesn't count."

Which was what made them inseparable, the hours of work, the lyric, the dreams. As it happened, they never knew the girl at the reception desk with her nearsightedness and wild, full hair. They knew various others, they knew Julie, they knew Catherine, they knew Ames. The best, for nearly two years, was Brenda, who had somehow managed to graduate from Marymount and had a walk-through apartment on West Fourth. In a smooth, thin silver frame was the photograph of her father with his two daughters at the Plaza, Brenda, thirteen, with an odd little smile.

"I wish I'd known you then," Frank told her.

Brenda said, "I bet you do."

It was her voice he liked, the city voice, scornful and warm. They were two of a kind, she liked to say, and in a way it was true. They drank in her favorite places, where the owner played the piano and everyone seemed to know her. Still, she counted on him. The city has its incomparable moments—rolling along the wall of the apartment, kissing, bumping like stones. Five in the afternoon, the vanishing light. "No," she was commanding. "No, no, no."

He was kissing her throat. "What are you going to do with that beautiful struma of yours?"

"You won't take me to dinner," she said.

"Sure I will."

"Beautiful what?"

She was like a huge dog, leaping from his arms.

"Come here," he coaxed.

She went into the bathroom and began combing her hair. "Which restaurant are we going to?" she called.

She would give herself, but it was mostly unpredictable. She would do anything her mother hadn't done and would live as her mother lived, in the same kind of apartment, in the same soft chairs. Christmas and the envelopes for the doormen, the snow sweeping past the awning, her children coming home from school. She adored her father. She went on a trip to Hawaii with him and sent back postcards, two or three scorching lines in a large, scrawled hand.

It was summer.

"Anybody here?" Frank called.

He rapped on the door, which was ajar. He was carrying his jacket, it was hot.

"All right," he said in a loud voice, "come out with your hands over your head. Alan, cover the back."

The party, it seemed, was over. He pushed the door open. There was one lamp on, the room was dark.

"Hey, Bren, are we too late?" he called. She appeared mysteriously in the doorway, bare-legged but in heels. "We'd have come earlier but we were working. We couldn't get out of the office. Where is everybody? Where's all the food? Hey, Alan, we're late. There's no food, nothing."

She was leaning against the doorway.

"We tried to get down here," Alan said. "We couldn't get a cab."

Frank had fallen onto the couch. "Bren, don't be mad," he said. "We were working, that's the truth. I should have called. Can you put some music on or something? Is there anything to drink?"

"There's about that much vodka," she finally said.

"Any ice?"

"About two cubes." She pushed off the wall without much enthusiasm. He watched her walk into the kitchen and heard the refrigerator door open.

"So, what do you think, Alan?" he said. "What are you going to do?"

"Me?"

"Where's Louise?" Frank called.

"Asleep," Brenda said.

"Did she really go home?"

"She goes to work in the morning."

"So does Alan."

Brenda came out of the kitchen with the drinks.

"I'm sorry we're late," he said. He was looking in the glass. "Was it a good party?" He stirred the contents with one finger. "This is the ice?"

"Jane Harrah got fired," Brenda said.

"That's too bad. Who is she?"

"She does big campaigns. Ross wants me to take her place."

"Great."

"I'm not sure if I want to," she said lazily.

"Why not?"

"She was sleeping with him."

"And she got fired?"

"Doesn't say much for him, does it?"

"It doesn't say much for her."

"That's just like a man. God."

"What does she look like? Does she look like Louise?"

The smile of the thirteen-year-old came across Brenda's face. "No one looks like Louise," she said. Her voice squeezed the name whose legs Alan dreamed of. "Jane has these thin lips."

"Is that all?"

"Thin-lipped women are always cold."

"Let me see yours," he said.

"Burn up."

"Yours aren't thin. Alan, these aren't thin, are they? Hey, Brenda, don't cover them up."

"Where were you? You weren't really working."

He'd pulled down her hand. "Come on, let them be natural," he said. "They're not thin, they're nice. I just never noticed them before." He leaned back. "Alan, how're you doing? You getting sleepy?"

"I was thinking. How much the city has changed," Alan said.

"In five years?"

"I've been here almost six years."

"Sure, it's changing. They're coming down, we're going up."

Alan was thinking of uncaring Louise, who had left him only a jolting ride home through the endless streets. "I know."

That year they sat in the steam room on limp towels, breathing the eucalyptus and talking about Hardmann Roe. They walked to the showers like champions. Their flesh still had firmness. Their haunches were solid and young.

Hardmann Roe was a small drug company in Connecticut that had strayed slightly out of its field and found itself suing a large manufacturer for infringement of an obscure patent. The case was highly technical with little chance of success. The opposing lawyers had thrown up a barricade of motions and delays and the case had made its way downward, to Frik and Frak, whose offices were near the copying machines, who had time for such things and who pondered it amid the hiss of steam. No one else wanted it and this also made it appealing.

So they worked. They were students again, sitting around in polo shirts with their feet on the desk, throwing off hopeless ideas, crumpling wads of paper, staying late in the library and having the words blur in books.

They stayed on through vacations and weekends, sometimes sleeping in the office and making coffee long before anyone came to work. After a late dinner they were still talking about it, its complexities, where elements somehow fit in, the sequence of letters, articles in journals, meetings, the limits of meaning. Brenda met a handsome Dutchman who worked for a bank. Alan met Hopie. Still there was this infinite forest, the trunks and vines blocking out the light, the roots of distant things joined. With every month that passed they were deeper into it, less certain of where they had been or if it could end. They had become like the old partners whose existence had been slowly sealed off, fewer calls, fewer consultations, lives that had become lunch. It was known they were swallowed up by the case with knowledge of little else. The opposite was true—no one else understood its detail. Three years had passed. The length of time alone made it important. The reputation of the firm, at least in irony, was riding on them.

Two months before the case was to come to trial they quit Weyland, Braun. Frank sat down at the polished table for Sunday lunch. His father was one of the best men in the city. There is a kind of lawyer you trust and who becomes your friend. "What happened?" he wanted to know.

"We're starting our own firm," Frank said.

"What about the case you've been working on? You can't leave them with litigation you've spent years preparing."

"We're not. We're taking it with us," Frank said.

There was a moment of dreadful silence.

"Taking it with you? You can't. You went to one of the best schools, Frank. They'll sue you. You'll ruin yourself."

"We thought of that."

"Listen to me," his father said.

Everyone said that, his mother, his Uncle Cook, friends. It was worse than ruin, it was dishonor. His father said that.

Hardmann Roe never went to trial, as it turned out. Six weeks later there was a settlement. It was for $38 million, a third of it their fee.

His father had been wrong, which was something you could not hope for. They weren't sued either. That was settled, too. In place of ruin there were new offices overlooking Bryant Park, which from above seemed like a garden behind a dark chateau, young clients, opera tickets, dinners in apartments with divorced hostesses, surrendered apartments with books and big tiled kitchens.

The city was divided, as he had said, into those going up and those coming down, those in crowded restaurants and those on the street, those who waited and those who did not, those with three locks on the door and those rising in an elevator from a lobby with silver mirrors and walnut paneling.

And those like Mrs. Christie, who was in the intermediate state though looking assured. She wanted to renegotiate the settlement with her ex-husband. Frank had leafed through the papers. "What do you think?" she asked candidly.

"I think it would be easier for you to get married again."

She was in her fur coat, the dark lining displayed. She gave a little puff of disbelief. "It's not that easy," she said.

He didn't know what it was like, she told him. Not long ago she'd been introduced to someone by a couple she knew very well. "We'll go to dinner," they said, "you'll love him, you're perfect for him, he likes to talk about books."

They arrived at the apartment and the two women immediately went into the kitchen and began cooking. What did she think of him? She'd only had a glimpse, she said, but she liked him very much, his beautiful bald head, his dressing gown. She had begun to plan what she would do with the apartment, which had too much blue in it. The man—Warren was his name—was silent all evening. He'd lost his job, her friend explained in the kitchen. Money was no problem, but he was depressed. "He's had a shock," she said. "He likes you." And in fact he'd asked if he could see her again.

"Why don't you come for tea, tomorrow?" he said.

"I could do that," she said. "Of course. I'll be in the neighborhood," she added.

The next day she arrived at four with a bag filled with books, at least a hundred dollars' worth, which she'd bought as a present. He was in pajamas. There was no tea. He hardly seemed to know who she was or why she was there. She said she remembered she had to meet someone and left the books. Going down in the elevator she felt suddenly sick to her stomach.

"Well," said Frank, "there might be a chance of getting the settlement overturned, Mrs. Christie, but it would mean a lot of expense."

"I see." Her voice was smaller. "Couldn't you do it as one of those things where you got a percentage?"

"Not on this kind of case," he said.

It was dusk. He offered her a drink. She worked her lips, in contemplation, one against the other. "Well, then, what can I do?"

Her life had been made up of disappointments, she told him, looking into her glass, most of them the result of foolishly falling in love. Going out with an older man just because he was wearing a white suit in Nashville, which was where she was from. Agreeing to marry George Christie while they were sailing off the coast of Maine. "I don't know where to get the money," she said, "or how."

She glanced up. She found him looking at her, without haste. The lights were coming on in buildings surrounding the park, in the streets, on homeward-bound cars. They talked as evening fell. They went out to dinner.

At Christmas that year Alan and his wife broke up. "You're kidding," Frank said. He'd moved into a new place with thick towels and fine carpets. In the foyer was a Biedermeier desk, black, tan, and gold. Across the street was a private school.

Alan was staring out the window, which was as cold as the side of a ship. "I don't know what to do," he said in despair. "I don't want to get divorced. I don't want to lose my daughter." Her name was Camille. She was two.

"I know how you feel," Frank said.

"If you had a kid, you'd know."

"Have you seen this?" Frank asked. He held up the alumni magazine. It was the fifteenth anniversary of their graduation. "Know any of these guys?"

Five members of the class had been cited for achievement. Alan recognized two or three of them. "Cummings," he said, "he was a zero—elected to Congress. Oh, God, I don't know what to do."

"Just don't let her take the apartment," Frank said.

Of course, it wasn't that easy. It was easy when it was someone else. Nan Christie had decided to get married. She brought it up one evening.

"I just don't think so," he finally said.

"You love me, don't you?"

"This isn't a good time to ask."

They lay silently. She was staring at something across the room. She was making him feel uncomfortable. "It wouldn't work. It's the attraction of opposites," he said.

"We're not opposites."

"I don't mean just you and me. Women fall in love when they get to know you. Men are just the opposite. When they finally know you they're ready to leave."

She got up without saying anything and began gathering her clothes. He watched her dress in silence. There was nothing interesting about it. The funny thing was that he had meant to go on with her.

"I'll get you a cab," he said.

"I used to think that you were intelligent," she said, half to herself. Exhausted, he was searching for a number. "I don't want a cab. I'm going to walk."

"Across the park?"

"Yes." She had an instant glimpse of herself in the next day's paper. She paused at the door for a moment. "Good-bye," she said coolly.

She wrote him a letter, which he read several times. *Of all the loves I have known, none has touched me so. Of all the men, no one has given me more.* He showed it to Alan, who did not comment.

"Let's go out and have a drink," Frank said toward the end of the day.

They walked up Lexington. Frank looked carefree, the scarf around his neck, the open topcoat, the thinning hair. "Well, you know . . ." he managed to say.

They went into a place called Jacks. Light was gleaming from the dark wood and the lines of glasses on narrow shelves. The young bartender stood with his hands on the edge of the bar. "How are you this evening?" he said with a smile. "Nice to see you again."

"Do you know me?" Frank asked.

"You look familiar." The bartender smiled.

"Do I? What's the name of this place, anyway? Remind me not to come in here again."

There were several other people at the bar. The nearest of them carefully looked away. After a while the manager came over. He had emerged from the brown-curtained back. "Anything wrong, sir?" he asked politely.

Frank looked at him. "No," he said, "everything's fine."

"We've had a big day," Alan explained. "We're just unwinding."

"We have a dining room upstairs," the manager said. Behind him was an iron staircase winding past framed drawings of dogs—borzois they looked like. "We serve from six to eleven every night."

"I bet you do," Frank said. "Look, your bartender doesn't know me."

"He made a mistake," the manager said.

"He doesn't know me and he never will."

"It's nothing, it's nothing," Alan said, waving his hands.

They sat at a table by the window. "I can't stand these out-of-work actors who think they're everybody's friend," Frank commented.

At dinner they talked about Nan Christie. Alan thought of her silk dresses, her devotion. The trouble, he said after a while, was that he never seemed to meet that kind of woman, the ones who sometimes walked by outside Jacks. The women he met were too human, he complained. Ever since his separation he'd been trying to find the right one.

"You shouldn't have any trouble," Frank said. "They're all looking for someone like you."

"They're looking for you."

"They think they are."

Frank paid the check without looking at it. "Once you've been married," Alan was explaining, "you want to be married again."

"I don't trust anyone enough to marry them," Frank said.

"What do you want then?"

"This is all right," Frank said.

Something was missing in him and women had always done anything to find out what it was. They always would. Perhaps it was simpler, Alan thought. Perhaps nothing was missing.

The car, which was a big Renault, a tourer, slowed down and pulled off the autostrada with Brenda asleep in back, her mouth a bit open and the daylight gleaming off her cheekbones. It was near Como, they had just crossed, the border police had glanced in at her.

"Come on, Bren, wake up," they said, "we're stopping for coffee."

She came back from the ladies' room with her hair combed and fresh lipstick on. The boy in the white jacket behind the counter was rinsing spoons.

"Hey, Brenda, I forget. Is it *espresso* or *expresso?*" Frank asked her.

"Espresso," she said.

"How do you know?"

"I'm from New York," she said.

"That's right," he remembered. "The Italians don't have an *x,* do they?"

"They don't have a *j* either," Alan said.

"Why is that?"

"They're such careless people," Brenda said lazily. "They just lost them."

It was like old times. She was divorced from Doop or Boos or whoever. Her two little girls were with her mother. She had that quirky smile.

In Paris, Frank had taken them to the Crazy Horse. In blackness like velvet the music struck up and six girls in unison kicked their legs in the brilliant light. They wore high heels and a little strapping. The nudity that is immortal. He was leaning on one elbow in the darkness. He glanced at Brenda. "Still studying, eh?" she said.

They were over for three weeks, Frank wasn't sure. Maybe they would stay longer, take a house in the South of France or something. Their clients would have to struggle along without them. There comes a time, he said, when you have to get away for a while.

They had breakfast together in hotels with the sound of workmen chipping at the stone of the fountain outside. They listened to the angry woman shouting in the kitchen, drove to little towns and drank every night. They had separate rooms, like staterooms, like passengers on a fading boat.

At noon, the light shifted along the curve of buildings and people were walking far off. A wave of pigeons rose before a trotting dog. The man at the table in front of them had a pair of binoculars and was looking here and there. Two Swedish girls strolled past.

"Now they're turning dark," the man said.

"What is?" said his wife.

"The pigeons."

"Alan," Frank confided.

"What?"

"The pigeons are turning dark."

"That's too bad."

There was silence for a moment.

"Why don't you just take a photograph?" the woman said.

"A photograph?"

"Of those women. You're looking at them so much."

He put down the binoculars.

"You know, the curve is so graceful," she said. "It's what makes this square so perfect."

"Isn't the weather glorious?" Frank said in the same tone of voice.

"And the pigeons," Alan said.

"The pigeons, too."

After a while the couple got up and left. The pigeons leaped up for a running child and hissed overhead. "I see you're still playing games," Brenda said. Frank smiled.

"We ought to get together in New York," she said that evening. They were waiting for Alan to come down. She reached across the table to pick up a magazine. "You've never met my kids, have you?" she said.

"No."

"They're terrific kids." She leafed through the pages, not paying attention to them. Her forearms were tanned. She was not wearing a wedding band. The first act was over or rather the first five minutes. Now came the plot. "Do you remember those nights at Goldie's?" she said.

"Things were different then, weren't they?"

"Not so different."

"What do you mean?"

She wiggled her bare third finger and glanced at him. Just then Alan appeared. He sat down and looked from one of them to the other. "What's wrong?" he asked. "Did I interrupt something?"

When the time came for her to leave she wanted them to drive to Rome. They could spend a couple of days and she would catch the plane. They weren't going that way, Frank said.

"It's only a three-hour drive."

"I know, but we're going the other way," he said.

"For God's sake. Why won't you drive me?"

"Let's do it," Alan said.

"Go ahead. I'll stay here."

"You should have gone into politics," Brenda said. "You have a real gift."

After she was gone the mood of things changed. They were by themselves. They drove through the sleepy country to the north. The green water slapped as darkness fell on Venice. The lights in some palazzos were on. On the curtained upper floors the legs of countesses uncoiled, slithering on the sheets like a serpent.

In Harry's, Frank held up a dense, icy glass and murmured his father's line, "Good night, nurse." He talked to some people at the next table, a German who was manager of a hotel in Düsseldorf and his girlfriend. She'd been looking at him. "Want a taste?" he asked her. It was his second. She drank looking directly at him. "Looks like you finished it," he said.

"Yes, I like to do that."

He smiled. When he was drinking he was strangely calm. In Lugano in the park that time a bird had sat on his shoe.

In the morning across the canal, wide as a river, the buildings of the Giudecca lay in their soft colors, a great sunken barge with roofs and the crowns of hidden trees. The first winds of autumn were blowing, ruffling the water.

Leaving Venice, Frank drove. He couldn't ride in a car unless he was driving. Alan sat back, looking out the window, sunlight falling on the hillsides of antiquity. European days, the silence, the needle floating at a hundred.

In Padua, Alan woke early. The stands were being set up in the market. It was before daylight and cool. A man was laying out boards on the pavement, eight of them like doors to set bags of grain on. He was wearing the jacket from a suit. Searching in the truck he found some small pieces of wood and used them to shim the boards, testing with his foot.

The sky became violet. Under the colonnade the butchers had hung out chickens and roosters, spurred legs bound together. Two men sat trimming artichokes. The blue car of the carabiniere lazed past. The bags of rice and dried beans were set out now, the tops folded back like cuffs. A girl in a tailored coat with a scarf around her head called, *"Signore,"* then arrogantly, *"dica!"*

He saw the world afresh, its pavements and architecture, the names that had lasted for a thousand years. It seemed that his life was being clarified, the sediment was drifting down. Across the street in a jeweler's shop a girl was laying out pieces in the window. She was wearing white gloves and arranging with great care. She glanced up as he stood watching. For a moment their eyes met, separated by the lighted glass. She was holding a lapis lazuli bracelet, the blue of the police car. Emboldened, he formed the silent words, *Quanto costa?* *Trecentosettantemila,* her lips said. It was eight in the morning when he got back to the hotel. A taxi pulled up and rattled the narrow street. A woman dressed for dinner got out and went inside.

The days passed. In Verona the points of steeples and then its domes rose from the mist. The white-coated waiters appeared from the kitchen. *Primi, secondi, dolce.* They stopped in Arezzo. Frank came back to the table. He had some postcards. Alan was trying to write to his daughter once a week. He never knew what to say: where they were and what they'd seen. Giotto—what would that mean to her?

They sat in the car. Frank was wearing a soft tweed jacket. It was like cashmere—he'd been shopping in Missoni and everywhere, Windbreakers, shoes. Schoolgirls in dark skirts were coming through an arch across the street. After a while one came through alone. She stood as if waiting for someone. Alan was studying the map. He felt the engine start. Very slowly they moved forward. The window glided down.

"*Scusi, signorina,*" he heard Frank say.

She turned. She had pure features and her face was without expression, as if a bird had turned to look, a bird that might suddenly fly away.

Which way, Frank asked her, was the *centro,* the center of town? She looked one way and then the other. "There," she said.

"Are you sure?" he said. He turned his head unhurriedly to look more or less in the direction she was pointing.

"*Si,*" she said.

They were going to Siena, Frank said. There was silence. Did she know which road went to Siena?

She pointed the other way.

"Alan, you want to give her a ride?" he asked.

"What are you talking about?"

Two men in white smocks like doctors were working on the wooden doors of the church. They were up on top of some scaffolding. Frank reached back and opened the rear door.

"Do you want to go for a ride?" he asked. He made a little circular motion with his finger.

They drove through the streets in silence. The radio was playing. Nothing was said. Frank glanced at her in the rearview mirror once or twice. It was at the time of a famous murder in Poland, the killing of a priest. Dusk was falling. The lights were coming on in shop windows and evening papers were in the kiosks. The body of the murdered man lay in a long coffin in the upper right corner of the *Corriere Della Sera*. It was in clean clothes like a worker after a terrible accident.

"Would you like an *aperitivo?*" Frank asked over his shoulder.

"*No,*" she said.

They drove back to the church. He got out for a few minutes with her. His hair was very thin, Alan noticed. Strangely, it made him look younger. They stood talking, then she turned and walked down the street.

"What did you say to her?" Alan asked. He was nervous.

"I asked if she wanted a taxi."

"We're headed for trouble."

"There's not going to be any trouble," Frank said.

His room was on the corner. It was large, with a sitting area near the windows. On the wooden floor there were two worn oriental carpets. On a glass cabinet in the bathroom were his hairbrush, lotions, cologne. The towels were a pale green with the name of the hotel in white. She didn't look at any of that. He had given the *portiere* forty thousand lire. In Italy the laws were very strict. It was nearly the same hour of the afternoon. He kneeled to take off her shoes.

He had drawn the curtains, but light came in around them. At one point she seemed to tremble, her body shuddered. "Are you all right?" he said.

She had closed her eyes.

Later, standing, he saw himself in the mirror. He seemed to have thickened around the waist. He turned so that it was less noticeable. He got into bed again but was too hasty. "*Basta,*" she finally said.

They went down later and met Alan in a café. It was hard for him to look at them. He began to talk in a foolish way. What was she studying at school, he asked. For God's sake, Frank said. Well, what did her father do? She didn't understand.

"What work does he do?"

"Furniture," she said.

"He sells it?"

"*Restauro.*"

"In our country, no *restauro,*" Alan explained. He made a gesture. "Throw it away."

"I've got to start running again," Frank decided.

The next day was Saturday. He had the *portiere* call her number and hand him the phone.

"Hello, Eda? It's Frank."

"I know."

"What are you doing?"

He didn't understand her reply.

"We're going to Florence. You want to come to Florence?" he said. There was a silence. "Why don't you come and spend a few days?"

"No," she said.

"Why not?"

In a quieter voice she said, "How do I explain?"

"You can think of something."

At a table across the room children were playing cards while three well-dressed women, their mothers, sat and talked. There were cries of excitement as the cards were thrown down.

"Eda?"

She was still there. *"Sì,"* she said.

In the hills they were burning leaves. The smoke was invisible, but they could smell it as they passed through, like the smell from a restaurant or paper mill. It made Frank suddenly remember childhood and country houses, raking the lawn with his father long ago. The green signs began to say Firenze. It started to rain. The wipers swept silently across the glass. Everything was beautiful and dim.

They had dinner in a restaurant of plain rooms, whitewashed, like vaults in a cellar. She looked very young. She looked like a young dog, the white of her eyes was that pure. She said very little and played with a strip of pink paper that had come off the menu.

In the morning they walked aimlessly. The windows displayed things for women who were older, in their thirties at least, silk dresses, bracelets, scarves. In Fendi's was a beautiful coat, the price beneath in small metal numbers.

"Do you like it?" he asked. "Come on, I'll buy it for you."

He wanted to see the coat in the window, he told them inside.

"For the signorina?"

"Yes."

She seemed uncomprehending. Her face was lost in the fur. He touched her cheek through it.

"You know how much that is?" Alan said. "Four million five hundred thousand."

"Do you like it?" Frank asked her.

She wore it continually. She watched the football matches on television in it, her legs curled beneath her. The room was in disorder, they hadn't been out all day.

"What do you say to leaving here?" Alan asked unexpectedly. The announcers were shouting in Italian. "I thought I'd like to see Spoleto."

"Sure. Where is it?" Frank said. He had his hand on her knee and was rubbing it with the barest movement, as one might a dozing cat.

The countryside was flat and misty. They were leaving the past behind them, unwashed glasses, towels on the bathroom floor. There was a stain on his lapel, Frank noticed in the dining room. He tried to get it off as the headwaiter grated fresh parmesan over each plate. He dipped the corner of his napkin in water and rubbed the spot. The table was near the doorway, visible from the desk. Eda was fixing an earring.

"Cover it with your napkin," Alan told him.

"Here, get this off, will you?" he asked Eda.

She scratched at it quickly with her fingernail.

"What am I going to do without her?" Frank said.

"What do you mean, without her?"

"So this is Spoleto," he said. The spot was gone. "Let's have some more wine." He called the waiter. "*Senta.* Tell him," he said to Eda.

They laughed and talked about old times, the days when they were getting $800 a week and working ten, twelve hours a day. They remembered Weyland and the veins in his nose. The word he always used was *vivid*, testimony a bit too vivid, far too vivid, a rather vivid decor.

They left talking loudly. Eda was close between them in her huge coat. *"Alla rovina,"* the clerk at the front desk muttered as they reached the street, *"alle macerie,"* he said, the girl at the switchboard looked over at him, *"alla polvere."* It was something about rubbish and dust.

The mornings grew cold. In the garden there were leaves piled against the table legs. Alan sat alone in the bar. A waitress, the one with the mole on her lip, came in and began to work the coffee machine. Frank came down. He had an overcoat across his shoulders. In his shirt without a tie he looked like a rich patient in some hospital. He looked like a man who owned a produce business and had been playing cards all night.

"So, what do you think?" Alan said.

Frank sat down. "Beautiful day," he commented. "Maybe we ought to go somewhere."

In the room, perhaps in the entire hotel, their voices were the only sound, irregular and low, like the soft strokes of someone sweeping. One muted sound, then another.

"Where's Eda?"

"She's taking a bath."

"I thought I'd say good-bye to her."

"Why? What's wrong?"

"I think I'm going home."

"What happened?" Frank said.

Alan could see himself in the mirror behind the bar, his sandy hair. He looked pale somehow, nonexistent. "Nothing happened," he said. She had come into the bar and was sitting at the other end of the room. He felt a tightness in his chest. "Europe depresses me."

Frank was looking at him. "Is it Eda?"

"No. I don't know." It seemed terribly quiet. Alan put his hands in his lap. They were trembling.

"Is that all it is? We can share her," Frank said.

"What do you mean?" He was too nervous to say it right. He stole a glance at Eda. She was looking at something outside in the garden.

"Eda," Frank called, "do you want something to drink? *Cosa vuoi?*" He made a motion of glass raised to the mouth. In college he had been a great favorite. Shuford had been shortened to Shuf and then Shoes. He had run in the Penn Relays. His mother could trace her family back for six generations.

"Orange juice," she said.

They sat there talking quietly. That was often the case, Eda had noticed. They talked about business or things in New York.

When they came back to the hotel that night, Frank explained it. She understood in an instant. No. She shook her head. Alan was sitting alone in the bar. He was drinking some kind of sweet liqueur. It wouldn't happen, he knew. It didn't matter anyway. Still, he felt shamed. The hotel above his head, its corridors and quiet rooms, what else were they for?

Frank and Eda came in. He managed to turn to them. She seemed impassive—he could not tell. What was this he was drinking, he finally asked? She didn't understand the question. He saw Frank nod once slightly, as if in agreement. They were like thieves.

In the morning the first light was blue on the window glass. There was the sound of rain. It was leaves blowing in the garden, shifting across the gravel. Alan slipped from the bed to fasten the loose shutter. Below, half-hidden in the hedges, a statue gleamed white. The few parked cars shone faintly. She was asleep, the soft, heavy pillow beneath her head. He was afraid to wake her. "Eda," he whispered, "Eda."

Her eyes opened a bit and closed. She was young and could stay asleep. He was afraid to touch her. She was unhappy, he knew, her bare neck, her hair, things he could not see. It would be a while before they were used to it. He didn't know what to do. Apart from that, it was perfect. It was the most natural thing in the world. He would buy her something himself, something beautiful.

In the bathroom he lingered at the window. He was thinking of the first day they had come to work at Weyland, Braun—he and Frank. They would become inseparable. Autumn in the gardens of the Veneto. It was barely dawn. He would always remember meeting Frank. He couldn't have done these things himself. A young man in a cap suddenly came out of a doorway below. He crossed the driveway and jumped onto a motorbike. The engine started, a faint blur. The headlight appeared and off he went, delivery basket in back. He was going to get the rolls for breakfast. His life was simple. The air was pure and cool. He was part of that great, unchanging order of those who live by wages, whose world is unlit and who do not realize what is above.

[FEBRUARY 1988]

SAUL BELLOW

Something to Remember Me By

"Leaving the Yellow House" was Saul Bellow's (1915–   ) first contribution to Esquire, in January 1958, and the publication of such a long and serious story confirmed the magazine's return to the tradition of literary fiction after a sort of hiatus during the years of World War II. Subsequently Bellow published part of Herzog, perhaps the most important of his novels, in Esquire's pages. He did commentary and journalism for the magazine over the years—on figures as diverse as Khrushchev and FDR—as well as more fiction, including "Something to Remember Me By," which won the National Magazine Award for Fiction for Esquire in 1991. Bellow also won the Nobel Prize for Literature in 1976. His other books include The Adventures of Augie March, Seize the Day, Henderson the Rain King, Him with His Foot in His Mouth, More Die of Heartbreak, and The Theft.

When there is too much going on, more than you can bear, you may choose to assume that nothing in particular is happening, that your life is going round and round like a turntable. Then one day you are aware that what you took to be a turntable, smooth, flat, and even, was in fact a whirlpool, a vortex. My first knowledge of the hidden work of uneventful days goes back to February 1933. The exact date won't matter much to you. I like to think, however, that you, my only child, will want to hear about this hidden work. When you were a small boy you were keen on family history. You will quickly understand that I couldn't tell a child what I am about to tell you now. You don't talk about deaths and vortices to a kid, not nowadays. In my time my parents didn't hesitate to speak of death and the dying. What they seldom mentioned was sex. We've got it the other way around.

My mother died when I was an adolescent. I've often told you that. What I didn't tell you was that I knew she was dying and didn't allow myself to think about it—there's your turntable.

The month was February, as I've said, adding that the exact date wouldn't matter to you. I should confess that I myself avoid fixing it.

Chicago in winter, armored in gray ice, the sky low, the going heavy.

I was a high school senior, an indifferent student, generally unpopular, a background figure in the school. It was only as a high jumper that I performed in public. I had no form at all, a curious last-minute spring or convulsion put me over the bar. But this was what the school turned out to see.

Unwilling to study, I was bookish nevertheless. I was secretive about my family life. The truth is that I didn't want to talk about my mother. Besides, I had no language as yet for the oddity of my peculiar interests.

But let me get on with that significant day in the early part of February.

It began like any other winter school day in Chicago—grimly ordinary. The temperature a few degrees above zero, botanical frost shapes on the window-pane, the snow swept up in heaps, the ice gritty and the streets, block after block, bound together by the iron of the sky. A breakfast of porridge, toast, and tea. Late as usual, I stopped for a moment to look into my mother's sickroom. I bent near and said, "It's Louie, going to school." She seemed to nod. Her eyelids were brown, her face much lighter. I hurried off with my books on a strap over my shoulder.

When I came to the boulevard on the edge of the park, two small men rushed out of a doorway with rifles, wheeled around aiming upward, and fired at pigeons near the rooftop. Several birds fell straight down, and the men scooped up the soft bodies and ran indoors, dark little guys in fluttering white shirts. Depression hunters and their city game. Moments before, the police car had loafed by at ten miles an hour. The men had waited it out.

This had nothing to do with me. I mention it merely because it happened. I stepped around the blood spots and crossed into the park.

To the right of the path, behind the winter lilacs, the crust of the snow was broken. In the dead black night Stephanie and I had necked there, petted, my hands under her raccoon coat, under her sweater, under her skirt, adolescents kissing without restraint. Her coonskin cap had slipped to the back of her head. She opened the musky coat to me to have me closer.

I had to run to reach the school doors before the last bell. I was on notice from the family—no trouble with teachers, no summons from the principal at a time like this. And I did observe the rules, although I despised classwork. But I spent all the money I could lay hands on at Hammersmark's Bookstore. I read *Manhattan Transfer, The Enormous Room,* and *A Portrait of the Artist.* I belonged to the Cercle Français and the Senior Discussion Club. The club's topic for this afternoon was Von Hindenburg's choice of Hitler to form a new government. But I couldn't go to meetings now, I had an after-school job. My father had insisted that I find one.

After classes, on my way to work, I stopped at home to cut myself a slice of bread and a wedge of Wisconsin cheese, and to see whether my mother might be awake. During her last days she was heavily sedated and rarely said anything. The tall, square-shouldered bottle at her bedside was filled with clear red Nembutal. The color of this fluid was always the same, as if it could tolerate no shadow. Now that she could no longer sit up to have it washed, my mother's hair was cut short. This made her face more slender, and her lips were sober. Her breathing was dry and hard, obstructed. The window shade was halfway up. It was scalloped at the bottom and had white fringes. The street ice was dark gray. Snow was piled against the trees. Their trunks had a mineral-black look. Waiting out the winter in their alligator armor they gathered coal soot.

Even when she was awake, my mother couldn't find the breath to speak. She sometimes made signs. Except for the nurse, there was nobody in the house. My father was at business, my sister had a downtown job, my brothers hustled. The eldest, Albert, clerked for a lawyer in the Loop. My brother Len had put me onto a job on the Northwestern commuter trains, and for a while I was a candy butcher, selling chocolate bars and evening papers. When my mother put a stop to this because it kept me too late, I found other work. Just now I was delivering flowers for a shop on North Avenue and riding the streetcars carrying wreaths and bouquets to all parts of the city. Behrens the florist paid me fifty cents for an afternoon; with tips I could earn as much as a dollar. That gave me time to prepare my trigonometry lesson, and, very late at night, after I had seen Stephanie, to read my books. I sat in the kitchen when everyone was sleeping, in deep silence, snowdrifts under the windows, and below, the janitor's shovel rasping on the cement and clanging on the furnace door. I read banned books circulated by my classmates, political pamphlets, read *Prufrock* and *Mauberly.* I also studied arcane books too far out to discuss with anyone.

I read on the streetcars (called trolleys elsewhere). Reading shut out the sights. In fact there *were* no sights—more of the same and then more of the same. Shop fronts, garages, warehouses, narrow brick bungalows.

The city was laid out on a colossal grid, eight blocks to the mile, every fourth street a car line. The days short, the streetlights weak, the soiled snowbanks toward evening became a source of light. I carried my carfare in my mitten, where the coins mixed with lint worn away from the lining. Today I was delivering lilies to an uptown address. They were wrapped and pinned in heavy paper. Behrens, spelling out my errand for me, was pale, a narrow-faced man who wore nose glasses. Amid the flowers, he alone had no color—something like the price he paid for being human. He wasted no words: "This delivery will take an hour each way in this traffic, so it'll be your only one. I carry these people on the books, but make sure you get a signature on the bill."

I couldn't say why it was such a relief to get out of the shop, the damp, warm-earth smell, the dense mosses, the prickling cactuses, the glass iceboxes with orchids, gardenias, and sickbed roses. I preferred the brick boredom of the street, the paving stones and steel rails. I drew down the three peaks of my racing-skater's cap and hauled the clumsy package to Robey Street. When the car came panting up there was room for me on the long seat next to the door. Passengers didn't undo their buttons. They were chilled, guarded, muffled, miserable. I had reading matter with me—the remains of a book, the cover gone, the pages held together by binder's thread and flakes of glue. I carried these fifty or sixty pages in the pocket of my short sheepskin. With the one hand I had free I couldn't manage this mutilated book. And on the Broadway–Clark car, reading was out of the question. I had to protect my lilies from the balancing straphangers and people pushing toward the front.

I got down at Ainslie Street holding high the package, which had the shape of a padded kite. The apartment house I was looking for had a courtyard with iron palings. The usual lobby: a floor sinking in the middle, kernels of tile, gaps stuffed with dirt, and a panel of brass mailboxes with earpiece-mouthpieces. No voice came down when I pushed the button; instead, the lock buzzed, jarred, rattled, and I went from the cold of the outer lobby to the overheated mustiness of the inner one. On the second floor one of the two doors on the landing was open, and overshoes and galoshes and rubbers were heaped along the wall. At once I found myself in a crowd of drinkers. All the lights in the house were on, although it was a good hour before dark. Coats were piled on chairs and sofas. All whiskey in those days was bootleg, of course. Holding the flowers high, I parted the mourners. I was quasiofficial. The message went out, "Let the kid through. Go right on, buddy."

The long passageway was full, too, but the dining room was entirely empty. There, a dead girl lay in her coffin. Over her a cut-glass luster was hanging from a taped, deformed artery of wire pulled through the broken plaster. I hadn't expected to find myself looking down into a coffin.

You saw her as she was, without undertaker's makeup, a girl older than Stephanie, not so plump, thin, fair, her straight hair arranged on her dead shoulders. All buoyancy gone, a weight that counted totally on support, not so much lying as sunk in this gray rectangle. I saw what I took to be the pressure mark of fingers on her cheek. Whether she had been pretty or not was no consideration.

A stout woman (certainly the mother), wearing black, opened the swing door from the kitchen and saw me standing over the corpse. I thought she was displeased when she made a fist signal to come forward and pulled both fists against her bosom as I passed her. She said to put the flowers on the sink, and then she pulled the pins and crackled back the paper. Big arms, thick calves, a bun of hair, her short nose thin and red. It was Behrens's practice to tie the stalks to slender green sticks. There was never any damage.

On the drainboard of the sink was a baked ham with sliced bread around the platter, a jar of French's mustard and wooden tongue depressors to spread it. I saw and I saw and I saw.

I was on my most discreet and polite behavior with the woman. I looked at the floor to spare her my commiserating face. But why should she care at all about my discreetness; how did I come into this except as a messenger and menial? If she wouldn't observe my behavior, whom was I behaving for? All she wanted was to settle the bill and send me on my way. She picked up her purse, holding it to her body as she had held her fists. "What do I owe Behrens?" she asked me.

"He said you could sign for this."

However, she wasn't going to deal in kindness. She said, "No." She said, "I don't want debts following me later on." She gave me a five-dollar bill, she added a tip of fifty cents, and it was I who signed the receipt, as well as I could on the enameled grooves of the sink. I folded the bill small and felt under the sheepskin coat for my watch pocket, ashamed to take money from her within sight of her dead daughter. I wasn't the object of the woman's severity, but her face somewhat frightened me. She leveled the same look at the walls, the door. I didn't figure here, however; this was no death of mine.

As if to take another reading of the girl's plain face, I looked again into the coffin on my way out. And then on the staircase I began to extract the pages from my sheepskin pocket, and in the lobby I hunted for the sentences I had read last night. Yes, here they were:

Nature cannot suffer the human form within her system of laws. When given to her charge, the human being before us is reduced to dust. Ours is the most perfect form to be found on earth. The visible world sustains us until life leaves, and then it must utterly destroy us. Where, then, is the world from which the human form comes?

If you swallowed some food and then died, that morsel of food that would have nourished you in life would hasten your disintegration in death.

This meant that nature didn't make life, it only housed it.

In those days I read many such books. But the one I had read the night before went deeper than the rest. You, my only child, are only too familiar with my lifelong absorption in or craze for further worlds. I used to bore you when I spoke of spirit, or pneuma, and of a continuum between spirit and nature. You were too well educated, respectably rational, to take stock in them. I might add, citing a famous scholar, that what is plausible can do without proof. I am not about to pursue this. However, there would be a gap in what I have to tell if I were to leave out my significant book, and this after all is a narrative, not an argument.

Anyway, I returned my pages to the pocket of my sheepskin, and then I didn't know quite what to do. At 4:00, with no more errands, I was somehow not ready to go home. So I walked through the snow to Argyle Street, where my brother-in-law practiced dentistry, thinking that we might travel home together. I prepared an explanation for turning up at his office. "I was on the North Side delivering flowers, saw a dead girl laid out, realized how close I was, and came here." Why did I need to account for my innocent behavior when it *was* innocent? Perhaps because I was always contemplating illicit things. Because I was always being accused. Because I ran a little truck farm of deceits—but self-examination, once so fascinating to me, has become tiresome.

My brother-in-law's office was a high, second-floor walk-up: PHILIP HADDIS D.D.S. Three bay windows at the rounded corner of the building gave you a full view of the street and of the lake, due east—the jagged flats of ice floating. The office door was open, and when I came through the tiny blind (windowless) waiting room and didn't see Philip at the big, back-tilted dentist's chair, I thought that he might have stepped into his lab. He was a good technician and did most of his own work, which was a big saving. Philip wasn't tall, but he was very big, a burly man. The sleeves of his white coat fitted tightly on his bare, thick forearms. The strength of his arms counted when it came to pulling teeth. Lots of patients were referred to him for extractions.

When he had nothing in particular to do he would sit in the chair himself, studying the *Racing Form* between the bent mantis leg of the drill, the gas flame, and the water spurting round and round in the green glass spit-sink. The cigar smell was always thick. Standing in the center of the dental cabinet was a clock under a glass bell. Four gilt weights rotated at its base. This was a gift from my mother. The view from the middle window was divided by a chain that couldn't have been much smaller than the one that stopped the British fleet on the Hudson. This held the weight of the druggist's sign—a mortar and pestle outlined in electric bulbs. There wasn't much daylight left. At noon it was poured out; by 4:00 it had drained away. From one side the banked snow was growing blue, from the other the shops were shining warmth on it.

The dentist's lab was in a cupboard. Easygoing Philip peed in the sink sometimes. It was a long trek to the toilet at the far end of the building, and the hallway was nothing but two walls—a plaster tunnel and a carpet runner edged with brass tape. Philip hated going to the end of the hall.

There was nobody in the lab, either. Philip might have been taking a cup of coffee at the soda fountain in the drugstore below. It was possible also that he was passing the time with Marchek, the doctor with whom he shared the suite of offices. The connecting door was never locked, and I had occasionally sat in Marchek's swivel chair with a gynecology book, studying the colored illustrations and storing up the Latin names.

Marchek's starred glass pane was dark, and I assumed his office to be empty, but when I went in I saw a naked woman lying on the examining table. She wasn't asleep, she seemed to be resting. Becoming aware that I was there, she stirred, and then without haste, disturbing herself as little as possible, she reached for her clothing heaped on Dr. Marchek's desk. Picking out her slip, she put it on her belly—she didn't spread it. Was she dazed, drugged? No, she simply took her sweet time about everything, she behaved with exciting lassitude. Wires connected her nice wrists to a piece of medical apparatus on a wheeled stand.

The right thing would have been to withdraw, but it was already too late for that. Besides, the woman gave no sign that she cared one way or another. She didn't draw the slip over her breasts, she didn't even bring her thighs together. The covering hairs were parted. There were salt, acid, dark, sweet odors. These were immediately effective; I was strongly excited. There was a gloss on her forehead, an exhausted look about the eyes. I believed that I had guessed what she had been doing, but then the room was half dark, and I preferred to avoid any definite thought. Doubt seemed much better, or equivocation.

I remembered that Philip, in his offhand, lazy way, had mentioned a "research project" going on next door. Dr. Marchek was measuring the reactions of partners in the sexual act. "He takes people from the street, he hooks them up and pretends he's collecting graphs. This is for kicks, the science part is horseshit."

The naked woman, then, was an experimental subject.

I had prepared myself to tell Philip about the dead girl on Ainslie Street, but the coffin, the kitchen, the ham, the flowers were as distant from me now as the ice floes on the lake and the killing cold of the water.

"Where did you come from?" the woman said to me.

"From next door—the dentist's office."

"The doctor was about to unstrap me, and I need to get loose. Maybe you can figure out these wires."

If Marchek should be in the inner room, he wouldn't come in now that he heard voices. As the woman raised both her arms so that I could undo the buckles, her breasts swayed, and when I bent over her the odor of her upper body made me think of the frilled brown papers in a box after the chocolates had been eaten—a sweet after-smell and acrid cardboard mixed. Although I tried hard to stop it, my mother's chest mutilated by cancer surgery passed through my mind. Its gnarled scar tissue. I also called in Stephanie's closed eyes and kissing face—anything to spoil the attraction of this naked young woman. It occurred to me as I undid the clasps that instead of disconnecting her I was hooking myself. We were alone in the darkening office, and I wanted her to reach under the sheepskin and undo my belt for me.

But when her hands were free she wiped the jelly from her wrists and began to dress. She started with her bra, several times lowering her breasts into the cups, and when her arms went backward to fasten the snaps she bent far forward, as if she were passing under a low bough. The cells of my body were like bees, drunker and drunker on sexual honey (I expect that this will change the figure of Grandfather Louie, the old man remembered as this or that but never as a hive of erotic bees).

But I couldn't be blind to the woman's behavior even now. It was very broad, she laid it on. I saw her face in profile, and although it was turned downward there was no mistaking her smile. To use an expression from the Thirties, she was giving me the works. She knew I was about to fall on my face. She buttoned every small button with deliberate slowness, and her blouse had at least twenty such buttons, yet she was still bare from the waist down. Though we were so minor, she and I, a schoolboy and a floozy, we had such major instruments to play. And if we were to go further, whatever happened would never get beyond this room. It would be between the two of us and nobody would ever hear of it. Still, Marchek, that pseudoexperimenter, was probably biding his time in the next room. An old family doctor, he must have been embarrassed and angry. And at any moment, moreover, my brother-in-law Philip might come back.

When the woman slipped down from the leather table she gripped her leg and said she had pulled a muscle. She lifted one heel onto a chair and rubbed her leg, swearing under her breath and looking everywhere with swimming eyes. And then, after she had put on her skirt and fastened her stockings to the garter belt, she pushed her feet into her pumps and limped around the chair, holding it by the arm. She said, "Will you please reach me my coat? Just put it over my shoulders."

She, too, wore a raccoon. As I took it from the hook I wished it had been something else. But Stephanie's coat was newer than this one and twice as heavy. The pelts had dried out, and the fur was thin. The woman was already on her way out, and stopped as I laid the coat over her back. Marchek's office had its own exit to the corridor.

At the top of the staircase, the woman asked me to help her down. I said that I would, of course, but I wanted to look once more for my brother-in-law. As she tied the woolen head scarf under her chin she smiled at me, with an Oriental wrinkling of her eyes.

Not to check in with Philip wouldn't have been right. My hope was that he would be returning, walking down the narrow corridor in his burly, sauntering, careless way. You won't remember your Uncle Philip. He had played college football, and he still had the look of a tackle, with his swelling, compact forearms. (At Soldier Field today he'd be physically insignificant; in his time, however, he was something of a strong man.)

But there was the long strip of carpet down the middle of the wall-valley, and no one was coming to rescue me. I turned back to his office. If only a patient were sitting in the chair and I could see Philip looking into his mouth, I'd be on track again, excused from taking the woman's challenge. One alternative was to tell her that Philip expected me to ride back with him to the Northwest Side. In the empty office I considered this lie, bending my head so that I wouldn't confront the clock with its soundless measured weights revolving. Then I wrote on Philip's memo pad: "Louie, passing by." I left it on the seat of the chair.

The woman had put her arms through the sleeves of the collegiate, rah-rah raccoon and was resting her fur-bundled rear on the banister. She was passing her compact mirror back and forth, and when I came out she gave the compact a snap and dropped it into her purse.

"Still the charley horse?"

"My lower back, too."

We descended, very slow, both feet on each tread. I wondered what she would do if I were to kiss her. Laugh at me, probably. We were no longer between the four walls, where anything might have happened. In the street, space was unlimited. I had no idea how far we were going, how far I would be able to go. Although she was the one claiming to be in pain, it was I who felt sick. She asked me to support her lower back with my hand, and there I discovered what an extraordinary action her hips could perform. At a party I had overheard an older woman saying to another lady, "I know how to make them burn." Hearing this was enough for me.

No special art was necessary with a boy of seventeen, not even so much as being invited to support her with my hand—to feel that intricate, erotic working of her back. I had already *seen* the woman on Marchek's examining table and had also felt the full weight of her when she leaned—when she laid her female substance on me. Moreover, she fully knew my mind. She was the thing I was thinking continually, and how often does thought find its object in circumstances like these—the object *knowing* that it has been found? The woman knew my expectations. She *was,* in the flesh, those expectations. I couldn't have sworn that she was a hooker, a tramp. She might have been an ordinary family girl with a taste for trampishness, acting loose, amusing herself with me, doing a comic sex turn as in those days people sometimes did.

"Where are we headed?"

"If you have to go, I can make it on my own," she said. "It's just Winona Street, the other side of Sheridan Road."

"No, no. I'll walk you there."

She asked whether I was still at school, pointing to the printed pages in my coat pocket.

I observed when we were passing a fruit shop (a boy of my own age emptying bushels of oranges into the lighted window) that, despite the woman's thick-cream color, her eyes were Far Eastern, black.

"You should be about seventeen," she said.

"Just."

She was wearing pumps in the snow and placed each step with care.

"What are you going to be, have you picked your profession?"

I had no use for professions. Utterly none. There were accountants and engineers in the soup lines. In the world slump, professions were useless. You were free, therefore, to make something extraordinary of yourself. I might have said, if I hadn't been excited to the point of sickness, that I didn't ride around the city on the cars to make a buck or to be useful to the family, but to take a reading of this boring, depressed, ugly, endless, rotting city. I couldn't have thought it then, but I now understand that my purpose was to interpret this place. Its power was tremendous. But so was mine. I refused absolutely to believe for a moment that people here were doing what they thought they were doing. Beneath the apparent life of these streets was their real life, beneath each face the real face, beneath each voice and its words the true tone and the real message. Of course, I wasn't about to say such things. It was beyond me at that time to say them. I was, however, a high-toned kid, "La-di-dah," my critical, satirical brother Albert called me. A high purpose in adolescence will expose you to that.

At the moment, a glamorous, sexual girl had me in tow. I couldn't guess where I was being led, nor how far, nor what she would surprise me with, nor the consequences.

"So the dentist is your brother?"

"In-law—my sister's husband. They live with us. You're asking what he's like? He's a good guy. He likes to lock his office on Friday and go to the races. He takes me to the fights. Also, at the back of the drugstore there's a poker game. . . ."

"*He* doesn't go around with books in his pocket."

"Well, no, he doesn't. He says, 'What's the use? There's too much to keep up or catch up with. You could never in a thousand years do it, so why knock yourself out?' My sister wants him to open a Loop office but that would be too much of a strain. I guess he's for inertia. He's not ready to do more than he's already doing."

"So what are you reading—what's it about?"

I didn't propose to discuss anything with her. I wasn't capable of it now. What I had in mind just then was entirely different.

But suppose I had been able to try. One does have a responsibility to answer genuine questions: "You see, miss, this is the visible world. We live in it, we breathe its air and eat its substance. When we die, however, matter goes to matter and then we're annihilated. Now, which world do we really belong to, this world of matter or another world from which matter takes its orders?"

Not many people were willing to talk about such notions. They made even Stephanie impatient. "When you die, that's it. Dead is dead," she would say. She loved a good time. And when I wouldn't take her downtown to the Oriental Theatre she didn't deny herself the company of other boys. She brought back off-color vaudeville jokes. I think the Oriental was part of a national entertainment circuit. Jimmy Savo, Lou Holtz, and Sophie Tucker played there. I was sometimes too solemn for Stephanie. When she gave imitations of Jimmy Savo singing "River, Stay Away from My Door," bringing her knees together and holding herself tight, she didn't break me up, and she was disappointed.

You would have thought that the book or book fragment in my pocket was a talisman from a fairy tale to open castle gates or carry me to mountaintops. Yet when the woman asked me what it was, I was too scattered to tell her. Remember, I still kept my hand as instructed on her lower back, tormented by that sexual grind of her movements. I was discovering what the lady at the party had meant by saying, "I know how to make them burn." So of course I was in no condition to talk to this girl about the Ego and the Will, or about the secrets of the blood. Yes, I believed that higher knowledge was shared out among all human beings. What else was there to hold us together but this force hidden behind daily consciousness? But to be coherent about it now was absolutely out of the question.

"Can't you tell me?" she said.

"I bought this for a nickel from a bargain table."

"That's how you spend your money?"

I assumed her to mean that I didn't spend it on girls.

"And the dentist is a good-natured, lazy guy," she went on. "What has he got to tell you?"

I tried to review the mental record. What did Phil Haddis say? He said that a stiff prick has no conscience. At the moment it was all I could think of. It amused Philip to talk to me. He was a chum. Where Philip was indulgent, my brother Albert, your late uncle, was harsh. He might have taught me something if he had trusted me. He was then a night-school law student clerking for Rowland, the racketeer congressman. He was Rowland's bagman, and Rowland didn't hire him to read law but to make collections. Philip suspected that Albert was skimming, for he dressed sharply. He wore a derby (called, in those days, a Baltimore heater) and a camel's hair and sharp, pointed, mafioso shoes. Toward me, Albert was scornful. He said, "You don't understand fuck-all. You never will."

We were approaching Winona Street, and when we got to her building she'd have no further use for me and send me away. I'd see no more than the flash of the glass and then stare as she let herself in. She was already feeling in her purse for the keys. I was no longer supporting her back, preparing instead to mutter "bye-bye," when she surprised me with a sideward nod, inviting me to enter. I think I had hoped (with sex-polluted hope) that she would leave me in the street. I followed her through another tile lobby and through the inner door. The staircase was fiercely heated by coal-fueled radiators, the skylight was wavering, and the wallpaper had come unstuck and was curling and bulging. I swallowed my breath. I couldn't draw this heat into my lungs.

This had been a deluxe apartment house once, built for bankers, brokers, and well-to-do professionals. Now it was occupied by transients. In the big front room with its French windows there was a crap game. In the next room people were drinking or drowsing on the old chesterfields. The woman led me through what had once been a private bar—some of the fittings were still in place. Then I followed her through the kitchen—I would have gone anywhere, no questions asked. In the kitchen there were no signs of cooking, neither pots nor dishes. The linoleum was shredding, brown fibers standing like hairs. She led me into a narrower corridor, parallel to the main one. "I have what used to be a maid's room," she said. "It's got a nice view of the alley but there is a private bathroom."

And here we were—the place wasn't much to look at. So this was how whores operated—assuming that she was a whore: a bare floor, a narrow cot, a chair by the window, a lopsided clothespress against the wall. I stopped under the light fixture while she passed behind, as if to observe me. Then she gave me a hug and a small kiss on the cheek, more promissory than actual. Her face powder, or perhaps it was her lipstick, had a sort of green-banana fragrance. My heart had never beaten as hard as this.

She said, "Why don't I go into the bathroom awhile and get ready while you undress and lie down in bed. You look like you were brought up neat, so lay your clothes on the chair. You don't want to drop them on the floor."

Shivering (this seemed the one cold room in the house), I began to pull off my things, beginning with the winter-wrinkled boots. The sheepskin I hung over the back of the chair. I pushed my socks into the boots and then my bare feet recoiled from the grit of the floor. I took off everything, as if to disassociate my shirt, my underthings from whatever it was that was about to happen, so that only my body could be guilty. The one thing that couldn't be excepted. When I pulled back the cover and got in I was thinking that the beds in the Bridewell would be like this. There was no pillowcase, my head lay on the ticking. What I saw of the outside was only the utility wires hung between the poles like lines on music paper, only sagging, and the glass insulators like clumps of notes. The woman had said nothing about money. Because she liked me. I couldn't believe my luck—luck with a hint of disaster. I blinded myself to the Bridewell metal cot, not meant for two. I felt also that I couldn't hold out if she kept me waiting long. And what feminine thing was she doing in there—undressing, washing, perfuming, changing?

Abruptly, she came out. She had been waiting, nothing else. She still wore the raccoon coat, even the gloves. Without looking at me she walked very quickly, almost running, and opened the window. As soon as the window shot up it let in a blast of cold air, and I stood up on the bed but it was too late to stop her. She took my clothes from the back of the chair and heaved them out. They fell into the alley. I shouted, "What are you doing!" She still refused to turn her head. As she ran away she was tying the head scarf under her chin and left the door open. I could hear her pumps beating double time in the hallway.

I couldn't run after her, could I, and show myself naked to the people in the flat? She had banked on this. When we came in, she must have given the high sign to the man she worked with, and he had been waiting in the alley. When I ran to look out, my things had already been gathered up. All I saw was the back of somebody with a bundle under his arm hurrying in the walkway between two garages. I might have picked up my boots—those she had left me—and jumped from the first-floor window, but I couldn't chase the man very far, and in a few minutes I would have wound up on Sheridan Road naked and freezing.

I had seen a drunk in his union suit, bleeding from the head after he had been rolled and beaten, staggering and yelling in the street. I didn't even have a shirt and drawers. I was as naked as the woman herself had been in the doctor's office, stripped of everything, including the five dollars I had collected for the flowers. And the sheepskin my mother had bought for me last year. Plus the book, the fragment of an untitled book, author unknown. This may have been the most serious loss of all.

Now I could think on my own about the world I really belonged to, whether it was this one or another.

I pulled down the window, and then I went to shut the door. The room didn't seem lived in, but suppose it had a tenant, and what if he were to storm in now and rough me up? Luckily there was a bolt to the door. I pushed it into its loop and then I ran around the room to see what I could find to wear. In the lopsided clothespress, nothing but wire hangers, and in the bathroom, only a cotton hand towel. I tore the blanket off the bed; if I were to slit it I might pull it over my head like a serape, but it was too thin to do me much good in freezing weather. When I pulled the chair over to the clothespress and stood on it, I found a woman's dress behind the molding, and a quilted bed jacket. In a brown paper bag there was a knitted brown tam. I had to put these things on, I had no choice.

It was now, I reckoned, about 5:00. Philip had no fixed schedule. He didn't hang around the office on the off chance that somebody might turn up with a toothache. After his last appointment he locked up and left. He didn't necessarily set out for home; he was not too keen to return to the house. If I wanted to catch him I'd have to run. In boots, dress, tam, and jacket, I made my way out of the apartment. Nobody took the slightest interest in me. More people (Philip would have called them transients) had crowded in—it was even likely that the man who had snatched up my clothes in the alley had returned, was among them. The heat in the staircase now was stifling, and the wallpaper smelled scorched, as if it were on the point of catching fire. In the street I was struck by a north wind straight from the Pole and the dress and sateen jacket counted for nothing. I was running, though, and had no time to feel it.

Philip would say, "Who was this floozy? Where did she pick you up?" Philip was unexcitable, always mild, amused by me. Anna would badger him with the example of her ambitious brothers—they hustled, they read books. You couldn't fault Philip for being pleased. I anticipated what he'd say—"Did you get in? Then at least you're not going to catch the clap." I depended on Philip now, for I had nothing, not even seven cents for carfare. I could be certain, however, that he wouldn't moralize at me, he'd set about dressing me, he'd scrounge a sweater among his neighborhood acquaintances or take me to the Salvation Army shop on Broadway if that should still be open. He'd go about this in his slow-moving, thick-necked, deliberate way. Not even dancing would speed him up, he spaced out the music to suit him when he did the fox-trot and pressed his cheek to Anna's. He wore a long, calm grin. My private term for this particular expression was Pussy-Veleerum. I saw Philip as fat but strong, strong but cozy, purring but inserting a joking comment. He gave a little suck at the corner of the mouth when he was about to make a swipe at you, and it was then that he was Pussy-Veleerum. A name it never occurred to me to speak aloud.

I sprinted past the windows of the fruit store, the delicatessen, the tailor's shop. I could count on help from Philip. My father, however, was an intolerant, hasty man. Slighter than his sons, handsome, with muscles of white marble (so they seemed to me), laying down the law. It would put him in a rage to see me like this. And it was true that I had failed to consider: my mother dying, the ground frozen, a funeral coming, the dug grave, the packet of sand from the Holy Land to be scattered on the shroud. If I were to turn up in this filthy dress, the old man, breaking under his burdens, would come down on me in a blind, Old Testament rage. I never thought of this as cruelty but as archaic right everlasting. Even Albert, who was already a Loop lawyer, had to put up with these blows—outraged, his eyes swollen and maddened, but he took it. It never occurred to us that my father was cruel, only that we had gone over the limit.

There were no lights in Philip's D.D.S. office. When I jumped up the stairs the door with its blank starred glass was locked. Frosted panes were still rare.

What we had was this star-marred product for toilets and other private windows. Marchek—whom nowadays we would call a voyeur—was also, angrily, gone. I had screwed up his experiment. I tried the doors, thinking that I could spend the night on the leather examining table where the beautiful nude had lain. There also I could make telephone calls. I did have a few friends, although there were none who might help me. I couldn't have known how to explain my predicament to them. They'd think I was putting them on, that it was a practical joke—"This is Louie. A whore robbed me of my clothes and I'm stuck on the North Side without carfare. I'm wearing a dress. I lost my house keys. I can't get home."

I ran down to the drugstore to look for Philip there. He sometimes played five or six hands of poker in the druggist's back room, trying his luck before getting on the streetcar. I knew Kiyar, the druggist, by sight. He had no recollection of me—why should he have? He said, "What can I do for you, young lady?"

Did he really take me for a girl, or a tramp off the street, or a gypsy from one of the storefront fortune-teller camps? Those were now all over town. But not even a gypsy would wear this blue sateen quilted boudoir jacket instead of a coat.

"I wonder, is Phil Haddis the dentist in the back?"

"What do you want with Dr. Haddis, have you got a toothache, or what?"

"I need to see him."

The druggist was a compact little guy, and his full round bald head was painfully sensitive looking. It could pick up any degree of disturbance, I thought. Yet there was a canny glitter coming through his specs, and Kiyar had the mark of a man whose mind never would change once he had made it up. Oddly enough, he had a small mouth, baby lips. He had been on the street—how long? Forty years? In forty years you've seen it all and nobody can tell you a single thing.

"Did Dr. Haddis have an appointment with you? Are you a patient?"

He knew this was a private connection. I was no patient. "No. But if I was out here he'd want to know it. Can I talk to him one minute?"

"He isn't here."

Kiyar had walked behind the grille of the prescription counter. I mustn't lose him. If he went, what would I do next? I said, "This is important, Mr. Kiyar." He waited for me to declare myself. I wasn't about to embarrass Philip by setting off rumors. Kiyar said nothing. He may have been waiting for me to speak up. Declare myself. I assume he took pride in running a tight operation, and gave nothing away. To cut through to the man I said, "I'm in a spot. I left Dr. Haddis a note, before, but when I came back I missed him."

At once I recognized my mistake. Druggists were always being appealed to. All these pills, remedy bottles, bright lights, medicine ads drew wandering screwballs and moochers. They all said they were in bad trouble.

"You can go to the Foster Avenue station."

"The police, you mean."

I had thought of that too. I could always tell them my hard-luck story and they'd keep me until they checked it out and someone would come to fetch me. That would probably be Albert. Albert would love that. He'd say to me, "Well, aren't you the horny little bastard." He'd play up to the cops too, and amuse them.

"I'd freeze before I got to Foster Avenue," was my answer to Kiyar.

"There's always the squad car."

"Well, if Phil Haddis isn't in the back maybe he's still in the neighborhood. He doesn't always go straight home."

"Sometimes he goes over to the fights at Johnny Coulon's. It's a little early for that. You could try the speakeasy down the street, on Kenmore. It's an English basement, side entrance. You'll see a light by the fence. The guy at the slot is called Moose."

He didn't so much as offer a dime from his till. If I had said that I was in a scrape and that Phil was my sister's husband he'd probably have given me carfare. But I hadn't confessed, and there was a penalty for that.

Going out, I crossed my arms over the bed jacket and opened the door with my shoulder. I might as well have been wearing nothing at all. The wind cut at my legs, and I ran. Luckily I didn't have far to go. The iron pipe with the bulb at the end of it was halfway down the block. I saw it as soon as I crossed the street. These illegal drinking parlors were easy to find, they were meant to be. The steps were cement, four or five of them bringing me down to the door. The slot came open even before I knocked and instead of the doorkeeper's eyes I saw his teeth.

"You Moose?"

"Yah. Who?"

"Kiyar sent me."

"Come on."

I felt as though I were falling into a big, warm, paved cellar. There was little to see, almost nothing. A sort of bar was set up, a few hanging fixtures, some tables from an ice cream parlor, wire-backed chairs. If you looked through the window of an English basement your eyes were at ground level. Here the glass was tarred over. There would have been nothing to see anyway: a yard, a wooden porch, a clothesline, wires, a back alley with ash heaps.

"Where did you come from, sister?" said Moose.

But Moose was a nobody here. The bartender, the one who counted, called me over and said, "What is it, sweetheart? You got a message for somebody?"

"Not exactly."

"Oh? You needed a drink so bad that you jumped out of bed and ran straight over—you couldn't stop to dress?"

"No, sir. I'm looking for somebody—Phil Haddis? The dentist?"

"There's only one customer. Is that him?"

It wasn't. My heart sank into river mud.

"It's not a drunk you're looking for?"

"No."

The drunk was on a high stool, thin legs hanging down, arms forward, and his head lay sidewise on the bar. Bottles, glasses, a beer barrel. Behind the barkeeper was a sideboard pried from the wall of an apartment. It had a long mirror—an oval laid on its side. Paper streamers curled down from the pipes.

"Do you know the dentist I'm talking about?"

"I might. Might not," said the barkeeper. He was a sloppy, long-faced giant—something of a kangaroo look about him. That was the long face in combination with the belly. He told me, "This is not a busy time. It's dinner, you know, and we're just a neighborhood speak."

It was no more than a cellar, just as the barman was no more than a Greek, huge and bored. Just as I myself, Louie, was no more than a naked male in a woman's dress. When you had named objects in this elementary way, hardly anything remained in them. The barman, on whom everything now depended, held his bare arms out at full reach and braced on his spread hands. The place smelled of yeast sprinkled with booze. He said, "You live around here?"

"No, about an hour on the streetcar."

"Say more."

"Humboldt Park is my neighborhood."

"Then you got to be a Uke, a Polack, a Scandihoof, or a Jew."

"Jew."

"I know my Chicago. And you didn't set out dressed like that. You'da frozen to death inside of ten minutes. It's for the boudoir, not winter wear. You don't have the shape of a woman, neither. The hips aren't there. Are you covering a pair of knockers? I bet not. So what's the story, are you a morphadite? Let me tell you, you got to give this Depression credit. Without it you'd never find out what kind of funny stuff is going on. But one thing I'll never believe is that you're a young girl and still got her cherry."

"You're right as far as that goes, but the rest of it is that I haven't got a cent, and I need carfare."

"Who took you, a woman?"

"Up in her room when I undressed, she grabbed my things and threw them out the window."

"Left you naked so you couldn't chase her . . . I would have grabbed her and threw her on the bed. I bet you didn't even get in."

Not even, I repeated to myself. Why didn't I push her down while she was still in her coat, as soon as we entered the room—pull up her clothes, as he would have done? Because he was born to, while I was not. I wasn't intended for it.

"So that's what happened. You got taken by a team of pros. She set you up. You were the mark. Jewish fellows aren't supposed to keep company with those bad cunts. But when you get out of your house, into the world, you want action like anybody else. So. And where did you dig up this dress with the fancy big roses? I guess you were standing with your sticker sticking out and were lucky to find anything to put on. Was she a good looker?"

Her breasts, as she lay there, kept their shape. They didn't slip sideward. The inward lines of her legs, thigh swelling toward thigh. The black crumpled hairs. Yes, a beauty, I would say.

Like the druggist, the barman saw the fun of the thing—an adolescent in a fix, the soiled dress, the rayon or sateen bed jacket. It was a lucky thing for me that business was at a standstill. If he had had customers, the barman wouldn't have given me the time of day. "In short, you got mixed up with a whore and she gave you the works."

For that matter, I had no sympathy for myself. I confessed that I had this coming, a high-minded Jewish high school boy, too high-and-mighty to be orthodox and with his eye on a special destiny. Inside the house, an archaic rule; outside, the facts of life. The facts of life were having their turn. Their first effect was ridicule. To throw my duds into the alley was the woman's joke on me. The druggist with his pain-sensitive head was all irony. And now the barman was going to get his fun out of my trouble before he, maybe, gave me the seven cents for carfare. Then I could have a full hour of shame on the streetcar. My mother, with whom I might never speak again, used to say that I had a line of pride straight down the bridge of my nose, a foolish stripe that she could see.

I had no way of anticipating what her death would signify.

The barman, having me in place, was giving me the business. And Moose ("Moosey," the Greek called him) had come away from the door so as not to miss the entertainment. The Greek's kangaroo mouth turned up at the corners.

Presently his hand went up to his head and he rubbed his scalp under the black, spiky hair. Some said they drank olive oil by the glass to keep their hair so rich. "Now, give it to me again, about the dentist," said the barman.

"I came looking for him, but by now he's well on his way home."

He was then on the Broadway–Clark car, reading the Peach edition of the *Evening American*, a broad man with an innocent pout to his face, checking the race results. Anna had him dressed up as a professional man but he let the fittings—shirt, tie, buttons—go their own way. His instep was fat and swelled inside the narrow shoe she picked for him. He wore the fedora correctly. Toward the rest he admitted no obligation.

Anna cooked dinner after work, and when Philip came in my father would begin to ask, "Where's Louie?" "Oh, he's out delivering flowers," they'd tell him. But the old man was nervous about his children after dark, and if they were late he waited up for them, walking—no, trotting—up and down the long apartment. When you tried to slip in he caught you and twisted you tight by the neckband. He was small, neat, slender, a gentleman, but abrupt, not unworldly— he wasn't ignorant of vices, he had lived in Odessa and even longer in St. Petersburg—but he had no patience. The least thing might craze him. Seeing me in this dress, he'd lose his head at once. *I* lost *mine* when that woman showed me her snatch with all the pink layers, when she raised up her arm and asked me to disconnect the wires, when I felt her skin and her fragrance came upward.

"What's your family, what does your dad do?" asked the barman.

"His business is wood fuel for bakers' ovens. It comes by freight car from northern Michigan. Also from Birnamwood, Wisconsin. He has a yard off Lake Street, east of Halsted."

I made an effort to give the particulars. I couldn't afford to be suspected of invention now.

"I know where that is. Now that's a neighborhood just full of hookers and cathouses. You think you can tell your old man what happened to you, that you got picked up by a cutie and she stole your clothes off you?"

The effect of this question was to make me tight in the face, dim in the ears. The whole cellar grew small and distant, toylike but not for play.

"How's your old man to deal with—tough?"

"Hard," I said.

"Slaps the kids around? This time you've got it coming. What's under the dress, a pair of bloomers?"

I shook my head.

"Your behind is bare? Now you know how it feels to go around like a woman."

The Greek's great muscles were dough-colored. You wouldn't have wanted him to take a headlock on you. That's the kind of man the Organization hired, the Capone people were in charge by now. The customers would be like celluloid Kewpie dolls to him. He looked like one of those boxing kangaroos in the movies, and he could do a standing jump over the bar. Yet he enjoyed playing zany. He could curve his long mouth up at the corners like the happy face in a cartoon.

"What were you doing on the North Side?"

"Delivering flowers."

"Hustling after school but with ramming on your brain. You got a lot to learn, buddy boy. Well, enough of that. Now, Moosey, take this flashlight and see if you can scrounge up a sweater or something in the back basement for this down-on-his-luck kid. I'd be surprised if the old janitor hasn't picked the stuff over pretty good. If mice have nested in it, shake out the turds. It'll help on the trip home."

I followed Moose into the hotter half of the cellar. His flashlight picked out the laundry tubs with the hand-operated wringers mounted on them, the padlocked wooden storage bins. "Turn over some of these cardboard boxes. Mostly rags, is my guess. Dump 'em out, that's the easiest."

I emptied a couple of big cartons. Moose passed the light back and forth over the heaps. "Nothing much, like I said."

"Here's a flannel shirt," I said. I wanted to get out. The smell of heated burlap was hard to take. This was the only wearable article. I could have used a pullover or a pair of pants. We returned to the bar. As I was putting on the shirt, which revolted me (I come of finicky people whose fetish is cleanliness), the barman said, "I tell you what, you take this drunk home—this is about time for him, isn't it, Moosey?—he gets plastered here every night. See he gets home and it'll be worth half a buck to you."

"I'll do it," I said. "It all depends how far away he lives. If it's far, I'll be frozen before I get there."

"It isn't far. Winona, west of Sheridan isn't far. I'll give you the directions. This guy is a city-hall payroller. He has no special job, he works direct for the ward committeeman. He's a lush with two little girls to bring up. If he's sober enough he cooks their dinner. Probably they take more care of him than he does of them."

"I'll walk him home, if he can walk."

"First I'll take charge of his money," said the barman. "I don't want my buddy here to be rolled. I don't say you would do it, but I owe this to a customer."

Bristle-faced Moose began to empty the man's pockets—his wallet, some keys, crushed cigarettes, a red bandanna that looked foul, matchbooks, greenbacks, and change. All these were laid out on the bar.

When I look back at past moments I carry with me an apperceptive mass that ripens and perhaps distorts, mixing what is memorable with what may not be worth mentioning. Thus I see the barman with one big hand gathering in the valuables as if they were his winnings, the pot in a poker game. And then I think that if the kangaroo giant had taken this drunk on his back he might have bounded home with him in less time than it would have taken me to support him as far as the corner. But what the barman actually said was, "I got a nice escort for you, Jim."

Moose led the man back and forth to make sure his feet were operating. His swollen eyes now opened and then closed again. "McKern," Moose said, briefing me. "Southwest corner of Winona and Sheridan, the second building on the south side of the street, and it's the second floor."

"You'll be paid when you get back," said the barman.

The freeze was now so hard that the snow underfoot sounded like metal foil. Though McKern may have sobered up in the frozen street, he couldn't move very fast. Since I had to hold on to him I borrowed his gloves. He had a coat with pockets to put his hands in. I tried to keep behind him and get some shelter from the wind. That didn't work. He wasn't up to walking. I had to hold him. Instead of a desirable woman, I had a drunkard in my arms. This disgrace, you see, while my mother was surrendering to death. At about this hour, upstairs neighbors came down and relatives arrived and filled the kitchen and the dining room—a deathwatch. I should have been there, not on the far North Side. When I had earned the carfare, I'd still be an hour from home on a streetcar making four stops to the mile.

Toward the last, I was dragging McKern. I kept the street door open with my back while I pulled him into the dim lobby by the arms.

The little girls had been waiting and came down at once. They held the inner door open while I brought their daddy upstairs with a fireman's carry and laid him on his bed. The children had had plenty of practice at this. They undressed him down to the long johns and then stood silent on either side of the room. This, for them, was how things were. They took deep oddities calmly, as children generally will. I had spread his winter coat over him.

I had little sympathy for McKern, in the circumstances. I believe I can tell you why: He had passed out many times before, and he would pass out again, dozens of times before he died. Drunkeness was common and familiar, and therefore accepted, and drunks could count on acceptance and support and relied on it. Whereas if your troubles were uncommon, unfamiliar, you could count on nothing. There was a convention about drunkenness established in part by drunkards. The founding proposition was that consciousness is terrible. Its lower, impoverished forms are perhaps the worst. Flesh and blood are poor and weak, susceptible to human shock. Here my descendant will hear the voice of Grandfather Louie giving one of his sermons on higher consciousness and interrupting the story he promised to tell. You will hold him to his word, as you have every right to do.

The older girl now spoke to me. She said, "The fellow phoned and said a man was bringing Daddy home, and you'd help with supper if Daddy couldn't cook it."

"Yes. Well? . . ."

"Only you're not a man, you've got a dress on."

"It looks like it, doesn't it. Don't you worry, I'll come to the kitchen with you."

"Are you a lady?"

"What do you mean—what does it look like? All right, I'm a lady."

"You can eat with us."

"Then show me where the kitchen is."

I followed them down the corridor, narrowed by the clutter—boxes of canned groceries, soda biscuits, sardines, pop bottles. When I passed the bathroom, I slipped in for quick relief. The door had neither a hook nor a bolt, the string of the ceiling fixture had snapped off. A tiny night-light was plugged into the baseboard. I thanked God it was so dim. I put up the board while raising my skirt, and when I had begun I heard one of the children behind me. Over my shoulder I saw that it was the younger one, and as I turned my back (*everything* was happening today) I said, "Don't come in here." But she squeezed past and sat on the edge of the tub. She grinned at me. She was expecting her second teeth. Today all females were making sexual fun of me, and even the infants were looking lewd. I stopped, letting the dress fall, and said to her, "What are you laughing about?"

"If you were a girl, you'd of sat down."

The kid wanted me to understand that she knew what she had seen. She pressed her fingers over her mouth, and I turned and went to the kitchen.

There the older girl was lifting the black cast-iron skillet with both hands. On dripping paper, the pork chops were laid out—nearby, a mason jar of grease. I was competent enough at the gas range, which shone with old filth. Loath to touch the pork with my fingers, I forked the meat into the spitting fat. The chops turned my stomach. My thought was, "I'm into it now, up to the ears." The drunk in his bed, the dim secret toilet, the glaring tungsten twist over the gas range, the sputtering droplets stinging the hands. The older girl said, "There's plenty for you. Daddy won't be eating dinner."

"No, not me. I'm not hungry," I said.

All that my upbringing held in horror geysered up, my throat filling with it, my guts griping.

The children sat at the table, an enamel rectangle. Thick plates and glasses, a waxed package of sliced white bread, a milk bottle, a stick of butter, the burning fat clouding the room. The girls sat beneath the smoke, slicing their meat. I brought salt and pepper back from the range. They ate without conversation. My chore (my duty) done, there was nothing to keep me. I said, "I have to go."

I looked in at McKern, who had thrown down the coat and taken off his drawers. The parboiled face, the short nose pointed sharply, the life signs in the throat, the broken look of his neck, the black hair of his belly, the short cylinder between his legs ending in a spiral of loose skin, the white shine of the shins, the tragic expression of his feet. There was a stack of pennies on his bedside table. I helped myself to carfare but had no pocket for the coins. I opened the hall closet feeling quickly for a coat I might borrow, a pair of slacks. Whatever I took, Philip could return to the Greek barman tomorrow. I pulled a trench coat from a hanger, and a pair of trousers. For the third time I put on strangers' clothing— this is no time to mention stripes or checks or make exquisite notations. Escaping, desperate, I struggled into the pants on the landing, tucking in the dress, and pulled on the coat as I jumped down the stairs, knotting tight the belt and sticking the pennies, a fistful of them, into my pocket.

But still I went back to the alley under the woman's window to see if her light was on, and also to look for pages. The thief or pimp perhaps had chucked them away, or maybe they had dropped out when he snatched the sheepskin. The windows were dark. I found nothing on the ground. You may think this obsessive crankiness, a crazy dependency on words, on printed matter. But remember, there were no redeemers in the streets, no guides, no confessors, comforters, enlighteners, communicants to turn to. You had to take teaching wherever you could find it. Under the library dome downtown, in mosaic letters, there was a message from Milton, so moving but perhaps of no utility, perhaps aggravating difficulties: A GOOD BOOK, it said, IS THE PRECIOUS LIFE'S BLOOD OF A MASTER SPIRIT.

These are the plain facts, they have to be uttered. This, remember, is the

New World, and here one of its mysterious cities. I should have hurried directly, to catch a car. Instead I was in a back alley hunting pages that would in any case have blown away.

I went back to Broadway—it was very broad—and waited on a safety island. Then the car came clanging, red, swaying on its trucks, a piece of Iron Age technology, double cane seats framed in brass. Rush hour was long past. I sat by a window, homebound, with flashes of thought like tracer bullets slanting into distant darkness. Like London in wartime. What story would I tell? I wouldn't tell any. I never did. It was assumed anyway that I was lying. While I believed in honor, I did often lie. Is a life without lying conceivable? It was easier to lie than to explain myself. My father had one set of assumptions, I had another. Corresponding premises were not to be found.

I owed five dollars to Behrens. But I knew where my mother secretly hid her savings. Because I looked into all books, I had found the money in her Mahzor, the prayer book for the High Holidays, the days of awe. As yet I hadn't taken anything. She had hoped until this final illness to buy passage to Europe to see her mother and her sister. When she died I would turn the money over to my father, except for ten dollars, five for the florist and the rest for Von Hugel's *Eternal Life* and *The World as Will and Idea*.

The after-dinner neighbors and cousins would be gone when I reached home. My father would be on the lookout for me. It was the rear porch door that was locked after dark. The kitchen door was off the latch. I could climb over the wooden partition. I often did that. Once you got your foot on the doorknob you could pull yourself over the top and drop to the porch without noise. Then I could see into the kitchen and slip in as soon as my patrolling father had left it. The bedroom shared by all three brothers was just off the kitchen. I could borrow my brother Len's cast-off winter coat tomorrow. I knew which closet it hung in. If my father should catch me I could expect hard blows on the top of my head, on my face, on my shoulders. But if my mother had, tonight, just died, he wouldn't hit me.

This was when the measured, reassuring, sleep-inducing turntable of days became a whirlpool, a vortex darkening toward the bottom. I had had only the anonymous pages in the pocket of my sheepskin to interpret it to me. They told me that the truth of the universe was inscribed into our very bones. That the human skeleton was itself a hieroglyph. That everything we had ever known on earth was shown to us in the first days after death. That our experience of the world was desired by the cosmos, and needed by it for its own renewal.

I do not think that these pages, if I hadn't lost them, would have persuaded me forever or made the life I led a different one.

I am writing this account, or statement, in response to an eccentric urge swelling toward me from the earth itself.

Failed my mother! That may mean, will mean, little or nothing to you, my only child, reading this document.

I myself know the power of nonpathos, in these low, devious days.

On the streetcar, heading home, I braced myself, but all my preparations caved in like sand diggings. I got down at the North Avenue stop, avoiding my reflection in the shop windows. After a death, mirrors were immediately covered. I can't say what this pious superstition means. Will the soul of your dead be reflected in a looking glass, or is this custom a check to the vanity of the living?

I ran home, approached by the back alley, made no noise on the wooden backstairs, reached for the top of the partition, placed my foot on the white porcelain doorknob, went over the top without noise, and dropped down on our porch. I didn't follow the plan I had laid for avoiding my father. There were people sitting at the kitchen table. I went straight in. My father rose from his chair and hurried toward me. His fist was ready. I took off my tam or woolen beret and when he hit me on the head the blow filled me with gratitude. If my mother had already died, he would have embraced me instead.

Well, they're all gone now, and I have made my preparations. I haven't left a large estate, and this is why I have written this memoir, a sort of addition to your legacy.

[JULY 1990]

REYNOLDS PRICE

Serious Need

With the exception of three years spent at Oxford as a Rhodes scholar in the late fifties, Reynolds Price (1933–   ) has been a lifelong resident of North Carolina, where he teaches half the year at Duke University. In much of his work, which includes plays, verse, stories, and novels, among them Permanent Errors *(1970),* The Surface of the Earth *(1975),* The Source of Light *(1981), and* Kate Vaiden *(1986), Price has attempted to "isolate in a number of lives the central error of act, will, understanding which, once made, has been permanent, incurable, but whose diagnosis and palliation are the hopes of continuance." His relationship with* Esquire *spans four decades, beginning in 1966 with the acceptance of "Life for Life," and continuing most recently with the publication of "Serious Need," which won the 1990 National Magazine Award for Fiction.*

I was thirty-six years old, with all my original teeth in place, most of my hair, and my best job yet—furniture sales on Oak Park Road, the rich-lady trade with occasional strays from the poor East End. Now that our girl Robin was twelve, Louise, my wife, had gone back to nursing at the county clinic. She worked the day shift; so that wasn't it, not my main reason, not loneliness. And by Lou's lights, which are strong and fair, she was nothing less than a good woman my age who tried hard, wore time well, and hoped for more.

I wasn't too badly destroyed myself, according to her and the mirrors I passed. So I didn't crawl out, wrecked and hungry, to chase fresh tail on the cheap side of town. But honest to Christ I saw my chance after three and a half of what suddenly felt like starved decades that had stalled on a dime. I knew it on sight—a maybe last chance to please my mind, which had spent so long pleasing everybody else that was kin to me or that had two dollars for a sofa down payment.

She came in the store one Saturday afternoon that spring with her mother—a heavyset woman and a tall girl. I thought I had a hazy notion of who they were, a low-rent family from up by the box mill, most of them weasel-eyed and too mean to cross. The mother had one of those flat, raw faces that looks like it's been hit broadside with a board this instant—none of which meant you'd want to fool with her; she had prizefighter arms and wrists.

Both of them stayed near the front door awhile, testing a rocker. Then they headed for me; and before I got my grin rigged up, I saw I was wrong and remembered their name. They were Vaughans; the mother was Irma Vaughan— she'd been in my same class at school, though she quit at fourteen. I remembered the day; she sobbed as she left, three months pregnant (the child was a boy and was now in prison, armed robbery of a laundry).

I said, "Miss Irma, you look fresh as dew on a baby's hand." I had no idea what I meant; words just come to me.

Her face got worse and she stopped in her tracks. "Do I know you?"

"You chased me down one Valentine's Day, when the world was young, and kissed my ear."

For a second I thought she'd haul back and strike, but she hunted around my face and found me. "Jock? Jocky Pittman? I ought to knowed!"

After we laughed and shared a few memories, she said "Here, Jock, you've bettered yourself—good job like this, that old crooked smile. See what I done, my pride and joy." Big as she was, Irma skipped a step back and made a neat curtsy toward the girl. Then she said, "Eileen, this is one smart man. He can do long division like a runaway car. You listen to him."

Eileen looked a lot like Ava Gardner in schoolgirl pictures (Ava grew up half an hour south of us). Like a female creature in serious need that you find back in the deepest woods on a bed of ivy—a head of black curls, dark doe eyes that lift at the ends, and a mouth that can't help almost smiling, night and day. Almost, not quite, not yet anyhow.

I estimated she was near fifteen. So I held my hand out and said, "Here, Irma, you're not old enough to have a girl eighteen."

Irma said, "So right. She's sixteen and what?" She turned to Eileen.

Eileen met my eyes straight on and said, "Sixteen and four months this Wednesday noon." She met my hand with her own soft skin; those eyes found mine and stayed right on me like I had something she'd roamed the world for and had nearly lost hope of.

With all my faults, I know my mind. Ask me the hardest question you got, I'll answer you true before you catch your next full breath. I met those steady hazy eyes, volt for volt; and told myself, *Oh Jocky, you're home.* She felt that right, that custom-made, with two feet of cool air solid between us.

Not for long. Not cool, not two feet apart. That evening my wife and I were trying to watch some TV family story, as true to life but sad to see as a world-belt wrestling match in mud; and Lou said, "Jock, you're dreaming upright. Go take you a nap. I'll make us some fudge."

Robin was off at a friend's for the weekend; the house was quiet enough for a snooze. But I said I was fine, just a touch dog-eared.

Louise could sniff my mind through granite. She came up grinning, took my face in her hands, studied my eyes at point-blank range and said, "I hope you're dreaming of me in there."

Both my eyes went on and shut of their own free will and stayed shut awhile. For a change Louise didn't start on one of her Interpol hunts for the secret locked up in me, but just the feel of her firm hands stayed on my skin, and in two seconds I knew that I'd find Eileen Vaughan someway before midnight, or else I'd keep driving till the rainbow ended in a pot of lead washers.

She was on her porch in an old-time swing with one dim light bulb straight overhead; and she faced the road, though I guessed I was too dark to recognize. I didn't want to drive unusually slow, but I saw enough to know I was dead right, back in the store. A socket to hold this one girl here had been cut deep inside my heart before I was born and was waiting warm.

Her dress was the color of natural violets exposed to black light, that rich and curious anyhow. The rest of the house looked dark behind her (I vaguely knew that there were no more children). Irma was likely playing bingo at her crazy church, the hollering kind. But I drove past to see who might be parked out back. Then I recalled that Irma's husband had died some years ago. Like so many drunks, for some weird reason, he lay down to sleep on the train tracks at night.

And by the time I'd gone a ways onward, turned and pulled to the shoulder out front, I told myself, *Eileen Vaughan's young enough to be your first daughter. You don't know who's got hooks in her or even who she's hoping for now. Go lay your feeble mind on the tracks. It'll be a lot quicker and will hurt just you.*

But what Eileen said when she saw me was, "I guessed it would be you before you turned." Not said like she was the earth's big magnet that drew me in but like the next nice fact of the evening—lightning bugs, the sweet crape myrtles, and Jocky Pittman.

Dark as it was, her eyes got to me, even stronger now. I said, "Miss Vaughan, my actual name is Jackson Pittman. Nobody yet ever called me that—will you be the first?" I reached from the ground up toward her swing and gave her the great ball of deep-red myrtle I'd picked in the dark.

She disappeared down in it awhile. Then her eyes looked out. "Mr. Jackson, reach inside that door and switch off the light. Let's swing in the cool."

The fine and terrible thing is this. It is in the power of one young woman still in her teens to cooperate with your orphan mind; and inside a week, she can have you feeling like you're surrounded by kind ancestors, crown to toe, all waiting to do your smallest wish with tender hands. I've already said I had a good wife that tried the best she understood, and a thoroughly satisfactory child. I hadn't exactly been beat by fate; but like a big part of the married men I knew in Nam, many nights of my life, and a good many days, I felt as hollow as a junked stovepipe. That is, till Eileen Vaughan took me that same mild night, saying she warmed the way I did, on sight at the store that same afternoon, which felt like two lifetimes ago.

From there it went like a gasoline fire. If I could give you one snapshot of her face and mine, close together, you could spell it all out in however much detail you needed. We burned that high in every cell; we taught each other ways and means that even the angels barely know, though for six fast weeks we never moved a step past the three-mile limit from the midst of town. At first, to be sure, it was all at night, on past her house in the heart of a thicket behind the mill.

But by the third week we were wild enough to meet by day, every chance we got. On three afternoons she baby-sat her brother's kids (his trash wife had skipped); but otherwise she'd get out of school and walk a straight line to the old cemetery, where I'd be waiting by my paternal grandfather's plot—he lies among three exhausted wives and nine children, having outlived them all.

On weekdays nobody passed through there except black boys heading to swim in the creek; and they didn't know either me or her, though after a month, when boys passed too near the car more than once, Eileen sat up, buttoned her blouse, and said, "Mr. Jackson, if this is your best, I'll thank you and leave. Don't look for me here, not after today."

I asked what she meant, *If this was my best.* Turned out, she meant the swimming kids. She thought they might be seeing her skin. I'd lived long enough to estimate she had almost as fine a skin as God had produced; and while she was not conceited a bit, every move she made showed how steady she meant to treat herself with respect. "Nobody else has," she said that day.

I asked who she meant.

"Every goddamned man and boy in space." She was still half smiling, but I knew she was mad by the crouch in her eyes.

I laughed and said, "I don't think Eaton's quite the same thing as space."

But she knew her mind like I knew my own. She said, "So long and best of luck," then got out slowly and aimed through trees toward her mother's house, a long mile off. When she vanished she looked like my last hope.

I let her leave, though, and said out loud in my thick skull, *Thanks, kind Lord. You cleared my path.*

He hadn't of course. Or I strowed mess and blocked it again by that weekend—my old path here, a dependable worker, husband, and father. Eileen had left the car on a Tuesday. By that Sunday evening, bright and dry, I was truly starved out. So I crept on toward her house again. It cost me almost all I had to climb those sagging steps and risk a knock. I felt like some untold crossbreed of the world's worst junkie and a child molester of the saddest stripe. The porch light was on and burned my mind.

But knock I did, a single blow, and nobody answered. I waited a long time, in plain sight of slow cars passing behind me, knowing my name. Then I knocked once more and finally begged out plain through the wood, "Eileen, I'm pleading with you. See me." In another few seconds, I heard bare feet.

She'd been asleep. First time I saw her confused like that, a hurt child with a pale, blank mouth. It cut me deep as anything yet; I felt like the cause. But then she surprised me.

She said, "Big *stranger,*" but she still hadn't smiled.

In twenty more minutes we were back in the cemetery, parked by my graves. Eileen wanted to talk about school—how it was nothing she could use in the future; how she planned to quit at the end of this year, then make enough money to own her own soul and go to a secretary school in Raleigh. She saw herself in a clean single room in a nice widow's house with a private door key and kitchen privileges in case she wanted, every week or so, a soft-boiled egg or a slice of dry toast. Everything else good would follow from that.

I listened and nodded long as I could. But once she paused I politely asked her to leave the car with me—till then we'd stayed shut up inside.

She waited to think it carefully through but she finally nodded.

So I came round, opened her door, led her over to Granddad's plot, and read her the tall old moldy stones.

To be sure, she was bored as any teenager faced with death; but she tried to listen. I think she guessed I was up to something entirely new; at first she let me run it my way, just listening and nodding. I told myself the night before that if I could take her that near my kin and still feel like I needed her bones beside me for good—her skin and bones—then I'd tell her plain and ask for her life.

I was reading my own grandmother's stone—HER CHILDREN RISE AND CALL HER BLESSED—when Eileen came up quiet behind me and played an age-old playground trick. She bumped the backs of my knees with hers, and I came near to kneeling on Gran. First I was shamed to be ambushed and sacrilegious (I never knowingly walk on a grave), but all I could hear was high clear laughter.

I had never heard Eileen laugh until then; we'd been so dead-down earnest and grim. But when I finally stood and turned and saw her leaning on a baby's stone, lost in her fun, I still had to wait. I was stunned again. Nothing I'd seen from here to Asia, awake or dreaming, offered what looked like that full an answer to every question my life could ask. Till then I'd known I lacked a good deal; but seeing her there, in possible reach, I suddenly knew my two big hands were empty, and had been all my life. I wondered why; excellent women had tried to fill them—my mother, Lou, and even young Robin. I'd somehow declined every offer they'd made.

Now here was the fourth. I understood no offer was free, least of all from the hands of a girl with eyes like these dark eyes, which no Marine division could stem. If I reached out now and finally took, I estimated I'd feel and cause unmanageable pain. But before I thought another word, my mind made an actual sound like a tight box lid that shuts with a click. I held my ground six yards away; and I said, "Sweet child, run off with me."

I didn't think Eileen heard my words. Her laugh calmed though, and she wiped her eyes. Then she leaned out slowly and set her lips on the family name, cut deep in the stone. When she faced me, even her smile was gone. She said, "You got us a full tank of gas?"

I couldn't speak. But I nodded hard, she came on toward me; and my life bent like a thick iron bar way back in the forge.

[NOVEMBER 1990]

VIOLENCE

ERNEST HEMINGWAY

The Snows of Kilimanjaro

In Esquire's early years Hemingway's name, like Fitzgerald's, was nearly synonymous with the magazine. His work appeared in the very first issue in the autumn of 1933, and for many years Esquire published the best of his work, including a monthly column of "outdoor letters." In what turned out to be a literary jackpot for the magazine, Hemingway missed the August 1936 deadline for his monthly letter and submitted "The Snows of Kilimanjaro" in its place. The story went on to have a profound and enduring effect on the nature of the American short story (see the Introduction). Hemingway (1899–1961) won the Nobel Prize for Literature in 1954, although his early work is generally considered his best—specifically the novels The Sun Also Rises and A Farewell to Arms and the story collections In Our Time, Men Without Women, and Winner Take Nothing.

KILIMANJARO IS A SNOW-COVERED MOUNTAIN 19,710 FEET HIGH, AND IS SAID TO BE THE HIGHEST MOUNTAIN IN AFRICA. ITS WESTERN SUMMIT IS CALLED BY THE MASAI "NGÀJE NGÀI," THE HOUSE OF GOD. CLOSE TO THE WESTERN SUMMIT THERE IS THE DRIED AND FROZEN CARCASS OF A LEOPARD. NO ONE HAS EXPLAINED WHAT THE LEOPARD WAS SEEKING AT THAT ALTITUDE.

"The marvelous thing is that it's pain-less," he said. "That's how you know when it starts."

"Is it really?"

"Absolutely. I'm awfully sorry about the odor though. That must bother you."

"Don't! Please don't."

"Look at them," he said. "Now is it sight or is it scent that brings them like that?"

The cot the man lay on was in the wide shade of a mimosa tree and as he looked out past the shade onto the glare of the plain there were three of the big birds squatted obscenely, while in the sky a dozen more sailed, making quick-moving shadows as they passed.

"They've been there since the day the truck broke down," he said. "Today's the first time any have lit on the ground. I watched the way they sailed very carefully at first in case I ever wanted to use them in a story. That's funny now."

"I wish you wouldn't," she said.

"I'm only talking," he said. "It's much easier if I talk. But I don't want to bother you."

"You know it doesn't bother me," she said. "It's that I've gotten so very nervous not being able to do anything. I think we might make it as easy as we can until the plane comes."

"Or until the plane doesn't come."

"Please tell me what I can do. There must be something I can do."

"You can take the leg off and that might stop it, though I doubt it. Or you can shoot me. You're a good shot now. I taught you to shoot didn't I?"

"Please don't talk that way. Couldn't I read to you?"

"Read what?"

"Anything in the book bag that we haven't read."

"I can't listen to it," he said. "Talking is the easiest. We quarrel and that makes the time pass."

"I don't quarrel. I never want to quarrel. Let's not quarrel anymore. No matter how nervous we get. Maybe they will be back with another truck today. Maybe the plane will come."

"I don't want to move," the man said. "There is no sense in moving now except to make it easier for you."

"That's cowardly."

"Can't you let a man die as comfortably as he can without calling him names? What's the use of slanging me?"

"You're not going to die."

"Don't be silly. I'm dying now. Ask those bastards." He looked over to where the huge, filthy birds sat, their naked heads sunk in the hunched feathers. A fourth planed down, to run quick-legged and then waddle slowly toward the others.

"They are around every camp. You never notice them. You can't die if you don't give up."

"Where did you read that? You're such a bloody fool."

"You might think about someone else."

"For Christ's sake," he said, "That's been my trade." He lay then and was quiet for a while and looked across the heat shimmer of the plain to the edge of the bush. There were a few Tommies that showed minute and white against the yellow and, far off, he saw a herd of zebra, white against the green of the bush. This was a pleasant camp under big trees against a hill, with good water, and, close by, a nearly dry water hole where sandgrouse flighted in the mornings.

"Wouldn't you like me to read?" she asked. She was sitting on a canvas chair beside his cot. "There's a breeze coming up."

"No thanks."

"Maybe the truck will come."

"I don't give a damn about the truck."

"I do."

"You give a damn about so many things that I don't."

"Not so many, Harry."

"What about a drink?"

"It's supposed to be bad for you. It said in Black's to avoid all alcohol. You shouldn't drink."

"Molo!" he shouted.

"Yes Bwana."

"Bring whiskey-soda."

"Yes Bwana."

"You shouldn't," she said. "That's what I mean by giving up. It says it's bad for you. I know it's bad for you."

"No," he said. "It's good for me."

So now it was all over, he thought. So now he would never have a chance to finish it. So this was the way it ended in a bickering over a drink. Since the gangrene started in his right leg he had no pain and with the pain the horror had gone and all he felt now was a great tiredness and anger that this was the end of it. For this, that now was coming, he had very little curiosity. For years it had obsessed him; but now it meant nothing in itself. It was strange how easy being tired enough made it.

Now he would never write the things that he had saved to write until he knew enough to write them well. Well, he would not have to fail at trying to write them either. Maybe you could never write them, and that was why you put them off and delayed the starting. Well he would never know, now.

"I wish we'd never come," the woman said. She was looking at him holding the glass and biting her lip. "You never would have gotten anything like this in Paris. You always said you loved Paris. We could have stayed in Paris or gone anywhere. I'd have gone anywhere. I said I'd go anywhere you wanted. If you wanted to shoot we could have gone shooting in Hungary and been comfortable."

"Your bloody money," he said.

"That's not fair," she said. "It was always yours as much as mine. I left everything and I went wherever you wanted to go and I've done what you wanted to do. But I wish we'd never come here."

"You said you loved it."

"I did when you were all right. But now I hate it. I don't see why that had to happen to your leg. What have we done to have that happen to us?"

"I suppose what I did was to forget to put iodine on it when I first scratched it. Then I didn't pay any attention to it because I never infect. Then, later, when it got bad, it was probably using that weak carbolic solution when the other antiseptics ran out that paralyzed the minute blood vessels and started the gangrene." He looked at her, "What else?"

"I don't mean that."

"If we would have hired a good mechanic instead of a half-baked Kikuyu driver, he would have checked the oil and never burned out that bearing in the truck."

"I don't mean that."

"If you hadn't left your own people, your goddamned old Westbury, Saratoga, Palm Beach people to take me on——"

"Why I loved you. That's not fair. I love you now. I'll always love you. Don't you love me?"

"No," said the man. "I don't think so. I never have."

"Harry, what are you saying? You're out of your head."

"No. I haven't any head to go out of."

"Don't drink that," she said. "Darling, please don't drink that. We have to do everything we can."

"You do it," he said. "I'm tired."

Now in his mind he saw a railway station at Karagatch and he was standing with his pack and that was the headlight of the Simplon-Orient cutting the dark now and he was leaving Thrace then after the retreat. That was one of the things he had saved to write, with, in the morning at breakfast, looking out the window and seeing snow on the mountains in Bulgaria and Nansen's secretary asking the old man if it were snow and the old man looking at it and saying, No, that's not snow. It's too early for snow. And the secretary repeating to the other girls, No, you see. It's not snow and them all saying, It's not snow we were mistaken. But it was the snow all right and he sent them on into it when he evolved exchange of populations. And it was snow they tramped along in until they died that winter.

It was snow too that fell all Christmas week that year up in the Gauertal, that year they lived in the woodcutter's house with the big square porcelain stove that filled half the room, and they slept on mattresses filled with beech leaves, the time the deserter came with his feet bloody in the snow. He said the police were right behind him and they gave him woolen socks and held the gendarmes talking until the tracks had drifted over. In Schruns, on Christmas day, the snow was so bright it hurt your eyes when you looked out from the weinstube and saw everyone coming home from church. That was where they walked up the sleigh-smoothed urine-yellowed road along the river with the steep pine hills, skis heavy on the shoulder, and where they ran that great run down the glacier above the Madlener-haus, the snow as smooth to see as cake frosting and as light as powder and he remembered the noiseless rush the speed made as you dropped down like a bird. They were snowbound a week in the Madlener-haus that time in the blizzard playing cards in the smoke by the lantern light and the stakes were higher all the time as Herr Lent lost more. Finally he lost it all. Everything, the skischule money and all the season's profit and then his capital. He could see him with his long nose, picking up the cards and then opening, "Sans Voir." There was always gambling then. When there was no snow you gambled and when there was too much you gambled. He thought of all the time in his life he had spent gambling. But he had never written a line of that, nor of that cold, bright Christmas day with the mountains showing across the plain that Barker had flown across the lines to bomb the Austrian officers' leave train, machine-gunning them as they scattered and ran. He remembered Barker afterwards coming into the mess and starting to tell about it. And how quiet it got and then somebody saying, "You bloody, murderous bastard." Those were the same Austrians they killed then that he skied with later. No not the same. Hans, that he skied with all that year, had been in the Kaiser-Jägers and when they went hunting hares together up the little valley above the sawmill they had talked of the fighting on Pasubio and of the attack on Pertica and Asalone and he had never written a word of that. Nor of Monte Corno, nor the Siete Communi, nor of Arsiero. How many winters had he lived in the Vorarlberg and the Arlberg? It was four and then he remembered the man who had the fox to sell when they had walked into Bludenz, that time to buy presents, and the cherry pit taste of good kirsch, the fast-slipping rush of running powder-snow on crust, singing "Hi Ho said Rolly!" as you ran down the last stretch to the steep drop, taking it straight, then running the orchard in three turns and out across the ditch and onto the icy road behind the inn. Knocking your bindings loose, kicking the skis free and leaning them up against the wooden wall of the inn, the lamplight coming from the window where inside, in the smoky, new-wine smelling warmth, they were playing the accordion.

"Where did we stay in Paris?" he asked the woman who was sitting by him in a canvas chair, now, in Africa.

"At the Crillon. You know that."

"Why do I know that?"

"That's where we always stayed."

"No. Not always."

"There and at the Pavillion Henri-Quatre in St. Germain. You said you loved it there."

"Love is a dunghill," said Harry. "And I'm the cock that gets on it to crow."

"If you have to go away," she said, "is it absolutely necessary to kill off everything you leave behind? I mean do you have to take away everything? Do you have to kill your horse, and your wife and burn your saddle and your armour?"

"Yes," he said. "Your damned money was my armour. My Swift and my Armour."

"Don't."

"All right. I'll stop that. I don't want to hurt you."

"It's a little bit late now."

"All right then. I'll go on hurting you. It's more amusing. The only thing I ever really liked to do with you I can't do now."

"No, that's not true. You liked to do many things and everything you wanted to do I did."

"Oh for Christ sake stop bragging will you?"

He looked at her and saw her crying.

"Listen," he said. "Do you think that it is fun to do this? I don't know why I'm doing it. It's trying to kill to keep yourself alive I imagine. I was all right when we started talking. I didn't mean to start this, and now I'm crazy as a coot and being as cruel to you as I can be. Don't pay any attention, darling, to what I say. I love you, really. You know I love you. I've never loved anyone else the way I love you." He slipped into the familiar lie he made his bread and butter by.

"You're sweet to me."

"You bitch," he said. "You rich bitch. That's poetry. I'm full of poetry now. Rot and poetry. Rotten poetry."

"Stop it. Harry, why do you have to turn into a devil now?"

"I don't like to leave anything," the man said. "I don't like to leave things behind."

It was evening now and he had been asleep. The sun was gone behind the hill and there was a shadow all across the plain and the small animals were feeding close to camp; quick dropping heads and switching tails, he watched them keeping well out away from the bush now. The birds no longer waited on the ground. They were all perched heavily in a tree. There were many more of them. His personal boy was sitting by the bed.

"Memsahib's gone to shoot," the boy said. "Does Bwana want?"

"Nothing."

She had gone to kill a piece of meat and, knowing how he liked to watch the game, she had gone well away so she would not disturb this little pocket of the plain that he could see. She was always thoughtful, he thought. On anything she knew about, or had read, or that she had ever heard.

It was not her fault that when he went to her he was already over. How could a woman know that you meant nothing that you said; that you spoke only from habit and to be comfortable. After he no longer meant what he said, his lies were more successful with women than when he had told them the truth.

It was not that he lied as that there was no truth to tell. He had had his life and it was over and then he went on living it again with different people and more money, with the best of the same places, and some new ones. You kept from thinking and it was all marvelous. You were equipped with good insides so that you did not go to pieces that way, the way most of them had, and you made an attitude that you cared nothing for the work you used to do, now that you could no longer do it. But, in yourself, you said that you would write about these people; about the very rich; that you were really not of them but a spy in their country; that you would leave it and write of it and for once it would be written by someone who knew what he was writing of. But he would never do it, because each day of not writing, of comfort, of being that which he despised, dulled his ability and softened his will to work so that, finally, he did no work at all. The people he knew now were all much more comfortable when he did not work. Africa was where he had been happiest in the good time of his life so he had come out here to start again. They had made this safari with the minimum of comfort. There was no hardship; but there was no luxury and he had thought that he could get back into training that way. That in some way he could work the fat off his soul the way a fighter went into the mountains to work and train in order to burn it out of his body.

She had liked it. She said she loved it. She loved anything that was exciting, that involved a change of scene, where there were new people and where things were pleasant. And he had felt the illusion of returning strength of will to work. Now if this was how it ended, and he knew it was, he must not turn like some snake biting itself because its back was broken. It wasn't this woman's fault. If it had not been she it would have been another. If he lived by a lie he should try to die by it. He heard a shot beyond the hill.

She shot very well this good, this rich bitch, this kindly caretaker and destroyer of his talent. Nonsense. He had destroyed his talent himself. Why should he blame this woman because she kept him well? He had destroyed his talent by not using it, by betrayals of himself and what he believed in, by drinking so much that he blunted the edge of his perceptions, by laziness, by sloth, and by snobbery, by pride and by prejudice, by hook and by crook. What was this? A catalog of old books? What was his talent anyway? It was a talent all right but instead of using it, he had traded on it. It was never what he had done, but always what he could do. And he had chosen to make his living with something else instead of a pen or a pencil. It was strange too, wasn't it, that when he fell in love with another woman, that woman should always have more money than the last one? But when he no longer was in love, when he was only lying, as to this woman, now, who had the most money of all, who had all the money there was, who had had a husband and children, who had taken lovers and been dissatisfied with them, and who loved him dearly as a writer, as a man, as a companion and as a proud possession; it was strange that when he did not love her at all and was lying, that he should be able to give her more for her money than when he had really loved. We must all be cut out for what we do, he thought. However you make your living is where your talent lies. He had sold vitality, in one form of another, all his life and when your affections are not too involved you give much better value for the money. He had found that out but he would never write that, now, either. No, he would not write that, although it was well worth writing.

Now she came in sight, walking across the open toward the camp. She was wearing jodhpurs and carrying her rifle. The two boys had a Tommie slung and they were coming along behind her. She was still a good-looking woman, he thought, and she had a pleasant body. She had a great talent and appreciation for the bed, she was not pretty, but he liked her face, she read enormously, liked to ride and shoot and, certainly, she drank too much. Her husband had died when she was still a comparatively young woman and for a while she had devoted herself to her two just-grown children, who did not need her and were embarrassed at having her about, to her stable of horses, to books, and to bottles. She liked to read in the evening before dinner and she drank scotch and soda while she read. By dinner she was fairly drunk and after a bottle of wine at dinner she was usually drunk enough to sleep.

That was before the lovers. After she had the lovers she did not drink so much because she did not have to be drunk to sleep. But the lovers bored her. She had been married to a man who had never bored her and these people bored her very much.

Then one of her two children was killed in a plane crash and after that was over she did not want the lovers, and drink being no anaesthetic she had to make another life. Suddenly she had been acutely frightened of being alone. But she wanted someone that she respected with her.

It had begun very simply. She liked what he wrote and she had always envied the life he led. She thought he did exactly what he wanted to. The steps by which she had acquired him and the way in which she had finally fallen in love with him were all part of a regular progression in which she had built herself a new life and he had traded away what remained of his old life. He had traded it for security, for comfort too, there was no denying that, and for what else? He did not know. She would have bought him anything he wanted. He knew that. She was a damned nice woman too. He would as soon be in bed with her as anyone; rather with her, because she was richer, because she was very pleasant and appreciative and because she never made scenes. And now this life that she had built again was coming to a term because he had not used iodine two weeks ago when a thorn had scratched his knee as they moved forward trying to photograph a herd of waterbuck standing, their heads up, peering while their nostrils searched the air, their ears spread wide to hear the first noise that would send them rushing into the bush. They had bolted, too, before he got the picture.

Here she came now.

He turned his head on the cot to look toward her. "Hello," he said.

"I shot a Tommie ram," she told him. "He'll make you good broth and I'll have them mash some potatoes with the Klim. How do you feel?"

"Much better."

"Isn't that lovely. You know I thought perhaps you would. You were sleeping when I left."

"I had a good sleep. Did you walk far?"

"No. Just around behind the hill. I made quite a good shot on the Tommie."

"You shoot marvelously you know."

"I love it. I've loved Africa. Really. If *you're* all right it's the most fun that I've ever had. You don't know the fun it's been to shoot with you. I've loved the country."

"I love it too."

"Darling you don't know how marvelous it is to see you feeling better. I couldn't stand it when you felt that way. You won't talk to me like that again, will you? Promise me?"

"No," he said. "I don't remember what I said."

"You don't have to destroy me. Do you? I'm only a middle-aged woman who loves you and wants to do what you want to do. I've been destroyed two or three times already. You wouldn't want to destroy me again, would you?"

"I'd like to destroy you a few times in bed," he said.

"Yes. That's the good destruction. That's the way we're made to be destroyed. The plane will be here tomorrow."

"How do you know?"

"I'm sure. It's bound to come. The boys have the wood all ready and the grass to make the smudge. I went down and looked at it again today. There's plenty of room to land and we have the smudges ready at both ends."

"What makes you think it will come tomorrow?"

"I'm sure it will. It's overdue now. Then, in town, they will fix up your leg and then we will have some good destruction. Not that dreadful talking kind."

"Should we have a drink? The sun is down."

"Do you think you should?"

"I'm having one."

"We'll have one together. *Molo, letti dui whiskey-soda!*" she called.

"You'd better put on your mosquito boots," he told her.

"I'll wait till I bathe. . . ."

While it grew dark they drank and just before it was dark and there was no longer enough light to shoot, a hyena crossed the open on his way around the hill.

"That bastard crosses there every night," the man said. "Every night for two weeks."

"He's the one makes the noise at night. I don't mind it. They're a filthy animal though."

Drinking together, with no pain now except the discomfort of lying in the one position, the boys lighting a fire, its shadow jumping on the tents, he could feel the return of acquiescence in this life of pleasant surrender. She *was* very good to him. He had been cruel and unjust in the afternoon. She was a fine woman, marvelous really. And just then it occurred to him that he was going to die.

It came with a rush; not as a rush of water nor of wind; but of a sudden evil-smelling emptiness and the odd thing was that the hyena slipped lightly along the edge of it.

"What is it, Harry?" she asked him.

"Nothing," he said. "You had better move over to the other side. To windward."

"Did Molo change the dressing?"

"Yes. I'm just using the boric now."

"How do you feel?"

"A little wobbly."

"I'm going in to bathe," she said. 'I'll be right out. I'll eat with you and then we'll put the cot in."

So, he said to himself, we did well to stop the quarreling. He had never quarreled much with this woman, while with the women that he loved he had quarreled so much they had finally, always, with the corrosion of the quarreling, killed what they had together. He had loved too much, demanded too much, and he wore it all out.

He thought about alone in Constantinople that time, having quarreled in Paris before he had gone out. He had whored the whole time and then, when that was over, and he had failed to kill his loneliness, but only made it worse, he had written her, the first one, the one who left him, a letter telling her how he had never been able to kill it. . . . How when he thought he saw her outside the Regence *one time it made him go all faint and sick inside, and that he would follow a woman who looked like her in some way, along the Boulevard, afraid to see it was not she, afraid to lose the feeling it gave him. How everyone he had slept with had only made him miss her more. How what she had done could never matter since he knew he could not cure himself of loving her. He wrote this letter at the Club, cold sober, and mailed it to New York asking her to write him at the office in Paris. That seemed safe. And that night missing her so much it made him feel hollow sick inside, he wandered up past Taxim's, picked a girl up and took her out to supper. He had gone to a place to dance with her afterward, she danced badly, and left her for a hot Armenian slut, that swung her belly against him so it almost scalded. He took her away from a British gunner subaltern after a row. The gunner asked him outside and they fought in the street on the cobbles in the dark. He'd hit him twice, hard, on the side of the jaw and when he didn't go down he knew he was in for a fight. The gunner hit him in the body, then beside his eye. He swung with his left again and landed and the gunner fell on him and grabbed his coat and tore the sleeve off and he clubbed him twice behind the ear and then smashed him with his right as he pushed him away. When the gunner went down his head hit first and he ran with the girl because they heard the M.P.'s coming. They got into a taxi and drove out to Rimmily Hissa along the Bosphorus, and around, and back in the cool night and went to bed and she felt as overripe as she looked but smooth, rose-petal, syrupy, smooth-bellied, big-breasted and needed no pillow under her, and he left her before she was awake looking blousy enough in the first daylight and turned up at the Pera Palace with a black eye, carrying his coat because one sleeve was missing. That same night he left for Anatolia and he remembered, later on that trip, riding all day through fields of the poppies that they raised for opium and how strange it made you feel finally and all the distances seemed wrong, to where they had made the attack with the newly arrived Constantine officers, that did not know a goddamned thing, and the artillery had fired into the troops and the British observer had cried like a child. That was the day he'd first seen dead men wearing white ballet skirts and upturned shoes with pompons on them. The Turks had come steadily and lumpily and he had seen the skirted men running and the officers shooting into them and running then themselves and he and the British observer had run too until his lungs ached and his mouth was full of the taste of pennies and they stopped behind some rocks and there were the Turks coming as lumpily as ever. Later he had seen the things that he could never think of and later still he had seen much worse. So when he got back to Paris that time he could not talk about it or stand to have it mentioned. And there in the café as he passed was that American poet with a pile of saucers in front of him and a stupid look on his potato face talking about the Dada movement with a Roumanian who said his name was Tristan Tzara, who always wore a monocle and had a headache, and, back at the apartment with his wife that now he loved again, the quarrel all over, the madness all over, glad to be home, the office sent his mail up to the flat. So then the letter in answer to the one he'd written came in on a platter one morning and when he saw the handwriting he went cold all over and tried to slip the letter underneath another. But his wife said, "Who is that letter from, dear?" and that was the end of the beginning of that. He remembered the good times with them all, and the quarrels. They always picked the finest places to have the quarrels. And why had they always quarreled when he was feeling best? He had never written any of that because, at first, he never wanted to hurt anyone and then it seemed as though there was enough to write without it. But he had always thought that he would write it finally. There was so much to write. He had seen the world change; not just the events; although he had seen many of them and had watched the people, but he had seen the subtler change and he could remember how the people were at different times. He had been in it and he had watched it and it was his duty to write of it; but now he never would.*

"How do you feel?" she said. She had come out from the tent now after her bath.

"All right."

"Could you eat now?" He saw Molo behind her with the folding table and the other boy with the dishes.

"I want to write," he said.

"You ought to take some broth to keep your strength up."

"I'm going to die tonight," he said. "I don't need my strength up."

"Don't be melodramatic, Harry, please," she said.

"Why don't you use your nose? I'm rotted half way up my thigh now. What the hell should I fool with broth for? Molo bring whiskey-soda."

"Please take the broth," she said gently.

"All right."

The broth was too hot. He had to hold it in the cup until it cooled enough to take it and then he just got it down without gagging.

"You're a fine woman," he said. "Don't pay any attention to me."

She looked at him with her well-known, well-loved face from *Spur* and *Town and Country*, only a little the worse for drink, only a little the worse for bed, but *Town and Country* never showed those good breasts and those useful thighs and those lightly small-of-back-caressing hands, and as he looked and saw her well-known pleasant smile, he felt death come again. This time there was no rush. It was a puff, as of a wind that makes a candle flicker and the flame go tall.

"They can bring my net out later and hang it from the tree and build the fire up. I'm not going in the tent tonight. It's not worth moving. It's a clear night. There won't be any rain."

So this was how you died, in whispers that you did not hear. Well, there would be no more quarreling. He could promise that. The one experience that he had never had he was not going to spoil now. He probably would. You spoiled everything. But perhaps he wouldn't.

"You can't take dictation, can you?"

"I never learned," she told him.

"That's all right."

There wasn't time, of course, although it seemed as though it telescoped so that you might put it all into one paragraph if you could get it right.

There was a log house, chinked white with mortar, on a hill above the lake. There was a bell on a pole by the door to call the people in to meals. Behind the house were fields and behind the fields was the timber. A line of lombardy poplars ran from the house to the dock. Other poplars ran along the point. A road went up to the hills along the edge of the timber and along that road he picked blackberries. Then that log house was burned down and all the guns that had been on deer foot racks above the open fireplace were burned and afterwards their barrels, with the lead melted in the magazines, and the stocks burned away, lay out on the heap of ashes that were used to make lye for the big iron soap kettles, and you asked Grandfather if you could have them to play with, and he said, no. You see they were his guns still and he never bought any others. Nor did he hunt anymore. The house was rebuilt in the same place out of lumber now and painted white and from its porch you saw the poplars and the lake beyond; but there were never any more guns. The barrels of the guns that had hung on the deer feet on the wall of the log house lay out there on the heap of ashes and no one ever touched them.

In the Black Forest, after the war, we rented a trout stream and there were two ways to walk to it. One was down the valley from Triberg and around the valley road in the shade of the trees that bordered the white road, and then up a side road that went up through the hills past many small farms, with the big Schwartzwald houses, until that road crossed the stream. That was where our fishing began. The other way was to climb steeply up to the edge of the woods and then go across the top of the hills through the pine woods, and then out to the edge of a meadow and down across this meadow to the bridge. There were birches along the stream and it was not big, but narrow, clear and fast, with pools where it had cut under the roots of the birches. At the Hotel in Triberg the proprietor had a fine season. It was very pleasant and we were all great friends. The next year came the inflation and the money he had made the year before was not enough to buy supplies to open the hotel and he hanged himself.

You could dictate that, but you could not dictate the Place Contrescarpe where the flower sellers dyed their flowers in the street and the dye ran over the paving where the autobus started and the old men and the women, always drunk on wine and bad marc; and the children with their noses running in the cold; the smell of dirty sweat and poverty and drunkenness at the Café des Amateurs and the whores at the Bal Musette they lived above. The Concierge who entertained the trooper of the Garde Republicaine in her loge, his horsehair plumed helmet on a chair. The locataire across the hall whose husband was a bicycle racer and her joy that morning at the Cremerie when she had opened L'Auto and seen where he placed third in Paris-Tours, his first big race. She had blushed and laughed and then gone upstairs crying with the yellow sporting paper in her hand. The husband of the woman who ran the Bal Musette drove a taxi and when he, Harry, had to take an early plane the husband knocked upon the door to wake him and they each drank a glass of white wine at the ʒinc of the bar before they started. He knew his neighbors in that quarter then because they all were poor. Around that Place there were two kinds; the drunkards and the sportifs. The drunkards killed their poverty that way; the sportifs took it out in exercise. They were the descendants of the Communards and it was no struggle for them to know their politics. They knew who had shot their fathers, their relatives, their brothers, and their friends when the Versailles troops came in and took the town after the Commune and executed anyone they could catch with calloused hands, or who wore a cap, or carried any other sign he was a working man. And in that poverty, and in that quarter across the street from a Boucherie Chevaline and a wine cooperative he had written the start of all he was to do. There never was another part of Paris that he loved like that, the sprawling trees, the old white plastered houses painted brown below, the long green of the autobus in that round square, the purple flower dye upon the paving, the sudden drop down the hill of the rue Cardinal Lemoine to the River, and the other way the narrow crowded world of the rue Mouffetard. The street that ran up toward the Pantheon and the other that he always took with the bicycle, the only asphalted street in all that quarter, smooth under the tires, with the high narrow houses and the cheap tall hotel where Paul Verlaine had died. There were only two rooms in the apartment where they lived and he had a room on the top floor of that hotel that cost him sixty francs a month where he did his writing, and from it he could see the roofs and chimney pots and all the hills of Paris.

From the apartment you could only see the wood and coal man's place. He sold wine too, bad wine. The golden horse's head outside the Boucherie Chevaline where the carcasses hung yellow gold and red in the open window, and the green painted cooperative where they bought their wine; good wine and cheap. The rest was plaster walls and the windows of the neighbors. The neighbors who, at night, when someone lay drunk in the street, moaning and groaning in that typical French ivresse that you *were propaganded to believe did not exist, would open their windows and then the murmur of talk.*

"Where is the policeman? When you don't want him the bugger is always there. He's sleeping with some concierge. Get the Agent." *Till someone threw a bucket of water from a window and the moaning stopped. "What's that? Water. Ah, that's intelligent." And the windows shutting. Marie, his femme de menage, protesting against the eight-hour day saying, "If a husband works until six he gets only a little drunk on the way home and does not waste too much. If he works only until five he is drunk every night and one has no money. It is the wife of the working man who suffers from this shortening of hours."*

"Wouldn't you like some more broth?" the woman asked him now.

"No thank you very much. It is awfully good."

"Try just a little."

"I would like a whiskey-soda."

"It's not good for you."

"No. It's bad for me. Cole Porter wrote the words and the music. This knowledge that you're going mad for me."

"You know I like you to drink."

"Oh yes. Only it's bad for me."

When she goes, he thought. I'll have all I want. Not all I want but all there is. Ayee he was tired. Too tired. He was going to sleep a little while. He lay still and death was not there. It must have gone around another street. It went in pairs, on bicycles, and moved absolutely silently on the pavements.

No, he had never written about Paris. Not the Paris that he cared about. But what about the rest that he had never written?

What about the ranch and the silvered gray of the sagebrush, the quick, clear water in the irrigation ditches, and the heavy green of the alfalfa. The trail went up into the hills and the cattle in the summer were shy as deer. The bawling and the steady noise and slow moving mass raising a dust as you brought them down in the fall. And behind the mountains, the clear sharpness of the peak in the evening light and, riding down along the trail in the moonlight, bright across the valley. Now he remembered coming down through the timber in the dark holding the horse's tail when you could not see and all the stories that he meant to write.

About the half-wit chore boy who was left at the ranch that time and told not to let anyone get any hay, and that old bastard from the Forks who had beaten the boy when he had worked for him stopping to get some feed. The boy refusing and the old man saying he would beat him again. The boy got the rifle from the kitchen and shot him when he tried to come into the barn and when they came back to the ranch

he'd been dead a week, frozen in the corral, and the dogs had eaten a big part of him.
But what was left you packed on a sled wrapped in a blanket and roped on and you
got the boy to help you haul it, and the two of you took it out over the road on skis,
and sixty miles down to town to turn the boy over. He having no idea that he would
be arrested. Thinking he had done his duty and that you were his friend and he would
be rewarded. He'd helped to haul the old man in so everybody could know how bad
the old man had been and how he'd tried to steal some feed that didn't belong to him,
and when the sheriff put the handcuffs on the boy he couldn't believe it. Then he'd
started to cry. That was one story he had saved to write. He knew at least twenty
good stories from out there and he had never written one. Why?

"You tell them why," he said.

"Why what, dear?"

"Why nothing."

She didn't drink so much, now, since she had him. But if he lived he would never write about her, he knew that now. Nor about any of them. The rich were dull and they drank too much, or they played too much backgammon. They were dull and they were repetitious. He remembered poor Julian and his romantic awe of them and how he had started a story once that began, "The very rich are different from you and me." And how someone had said to Julian, Yes they have more money. But that was not humorous to Julian. He thought they were a special glamorous race and when he found they weren't it wrecked him just as much as any other thing that wrecked him.

He had been contemptuous of those who wrecked. You did not have to like it because you understood it. He could beat anything, he thought, because no thing could hurt him if he did not care.

All right. Now he would not care for death. One thing he had always dreaded was the pain. He could stand pain as well as any man, until it went on too long, and wore him out, but here he had something that had hurt frightfully and just when he had felt it breaking him, the pain had stopped.

He remembered long ago when Williamson, the bombing officer, had been hit
by a stick bomb someone in a German patrol had thrown as he was coming in through
the wire that night and, screaming, had begged everyone to kill him. He was a fat
man, very brave, and a good officer, although addicted to fantastic shows. But that
night he was caught in the wire, with a flare lighting him up and his bowels spilled
out into the wire, so when they brought him in, alive, they had to cut him loose. Shoot
me, Harry. For Christ sake shoot me. They had had an argument one time about our
Lord never sending you anything you could not bear and someone's theory had been
that meant that at a certain time the pain passed you out automatically. But he had

always remembered Williamson that night. Nothing passed out Williamson until he gave him all his morphine tablets that he had always saved to use himself and then they did not work right away.

Still this now, that he had, was very easy; and if it was no worse as it went on there was nothing to worry about. Except that he would rather be in better company.

He thought a little about the company that he would like to have.

No, he thought, when everything you do, you do too long, and do too late, you can't expect to find the people still there. The people all are gone. The party's over and you are with your hostess now.

I'm getting as bored with dying as with everything else, he thought.

"It's a bore," he said out loud.

"What is, my dear?"

"Anything you do too bloody long."

He looked at her face between him and the fire. She was leaning back in the chair and the firelight shone on her pleasantly lined face and he could see that she was sleepy. He heard the hyena make a noise just outside the range of the fire.

"I've been writing," he said. "But I got tired."

"Do you think you will be able to sleep?"

"Pretty sure. Why don't you turn in?"

"I like to sit here with you."

"Do you feel anything strange?" he asked her.

"No. Just a little sleepy."

"I do," he said.

He had just felt death come by again.

"You know the only thing I've never lost is curiosity," he said to her.

"You've never lost anything. You're the most complete man I've ever known."

"Christ," he said. "How little a woman knows. What is that? Your intuition?"

Because, just then, death had come and rested its head on the foot of the cot and he could smell its breath.

"Never believe any of that about a scythe and a skull," he told her. "It can be two bicycle policemen as easily, or be a bird. Or it can have a wide snout like a hyena."

It had moved up on him now, but it had no shape anymore. It simply occupied space.

"Tell it to go away."

It did not go away but moved a little closer.

"You've got a hell of a breath," he told it. "You stinking bastard."

It moved up closer to him still and now he could not speak to it, and when it saw he could not speak it came a little closer, and now he tried to send it away without speaking, but it moved in on him so its weight was all upon his chest, and while it crouched there and he could not move, or speak, he heard the woman say, "Bwana is asleep now. Take the cot up very gently and carry it into the tent."

He could not speak to tell her to make it go away and it crouched now, heavier, so he could not breathe. And then, while they lifted the cot, suddenly it was all right and the weight went from his chest.

It was morning and had been morning for some time and he heard the plane. It showed very tiny and then made a wide circle and the boys ran out and lit the fires, using kerosene, and piled on grass so there were two big smudges at each end of the level place and the morning breeze blew them toward the camp and the plane circled twice more, low this time, and then glided down and leveled off and landed smoothly and, coming walking toward him, was old Compton in slacks, a tweed jacket and a brown felt hat.

"What's the matter, old cock?" Compton said.

"Bad leg," he told him. "Will you have some breakfast?"

"Thanks. I'll just have some tea. It's the Puss Moth you know. I won't be able to take the Memsahib. There's only room for one. Your lorry is on the way."

Helen had taken Compton aside and was speaking to him. Compton came back more cheery than ever.

"We'll get you right in," he said. "I'll be back for the Mem. Now I'm afraid I'll have to stop at Arusha to refuel. We'd better get going."

"What about the tea?"

"I don't really care about it you know."

The boys had picked up the cot and carried it around the green tents and down along the rock and out onto the plain and along past the smudges that were burning brightly now, the grass all consumed, and the wind fanning the fire, to the little plane. It was difficult getting him in, but once in he lay back in the leather seat, and the leg was stuck straight out to one side of the seat where

Compton sat. Compton started the motor and got in. He waved to Helen and to the boys and, as the clatter moved into the old familiar roar, they swung around with Compie watching for warthog holes and roared, bumping, along the stretch between the fires and with the last bump rose and he saw them all standing below, waving, and the camp beside the hill, flattening now, and the plain spreading, clumps of trees, and the bush flattening, while the game trails ran now smoothly to the dry water holes, and there was a new water that he had never known of. The zebra, small rounded backs now, and the wildebeeste, big-headed dots seeming to climb as they moved in long fingers across the plain, now scattering as the shadow came toward them, they were tiny now, and the movement had no gallop, and the plain as far as you could see, gray-yellow now and ahead old Compie's tweed back and the brown felt hat. Then they were over the first hills and the wildebeeste were trailing up them, and then they were over mountains with sudden depths of green-rising forest and the solid bamboo slopes, and then the heavy forest again, sculptured into peaks and hollows until they crossed, and hills sloped down and then another plain, hot now, and purple brown, bumpy, with heat and Compie looking back to see how he was riding. Then there were other mountains dark ahead. And then instead of going on to Arusha they turned left, he evidently figured that they had the gas, and looking down he saw a pink sifting cloud, moving over the ground, and in the air, like the first snow in a blizzard, that comes from nowhere, and he knew the locusts were coming up from the South. Then they began to climb and they were going to the East it seemed, and then it darkened and they were in a storm, the rain so thick it seemed like flying through a waterfall, and then they were out and Compie turned his head and grinned and pointed and there, ahead, all he could see, as wide as all the world, great, high, and unbelievably white in the sun, was the square top of Kilimanjaro. And then he knew that there was where he was going.

Just then the hyena stopped whimpering in the night and started to make a strange, human, almost crying sound. The woman heard it and stirred uneasily. She did not wake. In her dream she was at the house on Long Island and it was the night before her daughter's debut. Somehow her father was there and he had been very rude. Then the noise the hyena made was so loud she woke and for a moment she did not know where she was and she was very afraid. Then she took the flashlight and shone it on the other cot that they had carried in after Harry had gone to sleep. She could see his bulk under the mosquito bar but somehow he had gotten his leg out and it hung down alongside the cot. The dressings had all come down and she could not look at it.

"Molo," she called, "Molo! Molo!"

Then she said, "Harry, Harry!" Then her voice rising, "Harry! Please, Oh Harry!"

There was no answer and she could not hear him breathing.

Outside the tent the hyena made the same strange noise that had awakened her. But she did not hear him for the beating of her heart.

JOHN STEINBECK

A Snake of One's Own

John Steinbeck (1902–68) contributed fiction to the earliest issues of Esquire, *and these stories went on to rank among his most important work in the short story. He wrote about the poor and the dispossessed, about inarticulate men and women "locked in wordlessness," and even the most flawed of his characters were drawn with empathy and humanity. His novels—including* Cannery Row, East of Eden, Of Mice and Men, *and* The Grapes of Wrath—*are among the classics of American fiction.*

It was almost dark when young Dr. Phillips swung his sack to his shoulder and left the tide pool. He climbed up over the rocks and squashed along the street in his rubber boots. The street lights were on by the time he arrived at his little commercial laboratory on the cannery street of Monterey. It was a tight little building, standing partly on piers over by the water and partly on the land. On both sides the big corrugated iron sardine canneries crowded in on it.

Dr. Phillips climbed the wooden steps and opened the door. The white rats in their cages scampered up and down the wire, and the captive cats in their pens mewed for milk. Dr. Phillips turned on the glaring light over the dissection table and dumped his clammy sack on the floor. He walked to the glass cages by the window where the rattlesnakes lived, leaned over and looked in.

The snakes were bunched and resting in the corners of the cage, but every head was clear; the dusty eyes seemed to look at nothing, but as the young man leaned over the cage the forked tongues, black on the ends and pink behind, twittered out and waved slowly up and down. Then the snakes recognized the man and pulled in their tongues.

Dr. Phillips threw off his leather coat and built a fire in the tin stove; he set a kettle of water on the stove and dropped a can of beans into the water. Then he stood staring down at the sack on the floor. He was a slight young man with the mild, preoccupied eyes of one who looks through a microscope a great deal. He wore a short blond beard.

The draft ran breathily up the chimney and a glow of warmth came from the stove. The little waves washed quietly about the piles under the building. Arranged on shelves about the room were tier above tier of museum jars containing the mounted marine specimens the laboratory dealt in.

Dr. Phillips opened a side door and went into his bedroom, a book-lined cell containing an army cot, a reading light and an uncomfortable wooden chair. He pulled off his rubber boots and put on a pair of sheepskin slippers. When he went back to the other room the water in the kettle was already beginning to hum.

He lifted his sack to the table under the white light and emptied out two dozen common starfish. These he laid out side by side on the table. His preoccupied eyes turned to the busy rats in the wire cages. Taking grain from a paper sack he poured it into the feeding troughs. Instantly the rats scrambled down from the wire and fell upon the food. A bottle of milk stood on a glass shelf between a small mounted octopus and a jellyfish. Dr. Phillips lifted down the milk and walked to the cat cage, but before he filled the containers he reached in the cage and gently picked out a big rangy alley tabby. He stroked her for a moment and then dropped her in a small black-painted box, closed the lid and bolted it and then turned on a petcock which admitted gas into the killing chamber. While the short soft struggle went on in the black box he filled the saucers with milk. One of the cats arched against his hand and he smiled and petted her neck.

The box was quiet now. He turned off the gas for the airtight box would be full of gas.

On the stove the pan of water was bubbling furiously about the can of beans. Dr. Phillips lifted out the can with a big pair of forceps, opened the beans and emptied them into a glass dish. While he ate he watched the starfish on the table. From between the rays little drops of milky fluid were exuding. He bolted his beans and when they were gone he put the dish in the sink and stepped to the equipment cupboard. From this he took a microscope and a pile of little glass dishes. He filled the dishes one by one with seawater from a tap and arranged them in a line beside the starfish. He took out his watch and laid it on the table under the pouring white light. The waves washed with little sighs against the piles under the floor. He took an eyedropper from a drawer and bent over the starfish.

At that moment there were quick soft steps on the wooden stairs and a strong knocking at the door. A slight grimace of annoyance crossed the young man's face as he went to open. A tall lean woman stood in the doorway. She was dressed in a severe dark suit—her straight black hair, growing low on a flat forehead, was mussed as though the wind had been blowing it. Her black eyes glittered in the strong light.

She spoke in a soft throaty voice. "May I come in? I want to talk to you."

"I'm very busy just now," he said halfheartedly. "I have to do things at times." But he stood away from the door. The tall woman slipped in.

"I'll be quiet until you can talk to me."

He closed the door and brought the uncomfortable chair from the bedroom. "You see," he apologized, "the process is started and I must get to it." So many people wandered in and asked questions. He had little routines of explanations for the commoner processes. He could say them without thinking. "Sit here. In a few minutes I'll be able to listen to you."

The tall woman leaned over the table. With the eyedropper the young man gathered fluid from between the rays of the starfish and squirted it into a bowl of water, and then he drew some milky fluid and squirted it in the same bowl and stirred the water gently with the eyedropper. He began his little patter of explanation.

"When starfish are sexually mature they release sperm and ova when they are exposed at low tide. By choosing mature specimens and taking them out of the water, I give them a condition of low tide. Now I've mixed the sperm and eggs. Now I put some of the mixture in each one of these ten watch glasses. In ten minutes I will kill those in the first glass with menthol, twenty minutes later I will kill the second group and then a new group every twenty minutes. Then I will have arrested the process in stages, and I will mount the series on microscope slides for biologic study." He paused. "Would you like to look at this first group under the microscope?"

"No, thank you." He turned quickly to her. People always wanted to look through the glass. She was not looking at the table at all, but at him. Her black eyes were on him but they did not seem to see him. He realized why—the irises were as dark as the pupils, there was no color line between the two. Dr. Phillips was piqued at her answer. Although answering questions bored him, a lack of interest in what he was doing irritated him. A desire to arouse her grew in him.

"While I'm waiting the first ten minutes I have something to do. Some people don't like to see it. Maybe you'd better step into that room until I finish."

"No," she said in her soft flat tone. "Do what you wish. I will wait until you can talk to me." Her hands rested side by side on her lap. She was completely at rest. Her eyes were bright but the rest of her was almost in a state of suspended animation. He thought, "Low metabolic rate, almost as low as a frog's, from the looks." The desire to shock her out of her inanition possessed him again.

He brought a little wooden cradle to the table, laid out scalpels and scissors and rigged a big hollow needle to a pressure tube. Then from the killing chamber he brought the limp dead cat and laid it in the cradle and tied its legs to hooks in the sides. He glanced sidewise at the woman. She had not moved. She was still at rest.

The cat grinned up into the light, its pink tongue stuck out between its needle teeth. Dr. Phillips deftly snipped open the skin at the throat; with a scalpel he slit through and found an artery.

With flawless technique he put the needle in the vessel and tied it in with gut. "Embalming fluid," he explained. "Later, I'll inject yellow mass into the venous system and red mass into the arterial system—for blood stream dissection—biology classes."

He looked around at her again. Her dark eyes seemed veiled with dust. She looked without expression at the cat's open throat. Not a drop of blood had escaped. The incision was clean. Dr. Phillips looked at his watch. "Time for the first group." He shook a few crystals of menthol into the first watch glass.

The woman was making him nervous. The rats climbed about on the wire of their cage again and squeaked softly. The waves under the building beat with little shocks on the piles.

The young man shivered. He put a few lumps of coal in the stove and sat down. "Now," he said, "I haven't anything to do for twenty minutes." He noticed how short her chin was between lower lip and point. She seemed to awaken slowly, to come up out of some deep pool of consciousness. Her head raised and her dark dusty eyes moved about the room and then came back to him.

"I was waiting," she said. Her hands remained side by side on her lap. "You have snakes?"

"Why, yes," he said rather loudly. "I have about two dozen rattlesnakes. I milk out the venom and send it to the anti-venom laboratories."

She continued to look at him but her eyes did not center on him, rather they covered him and seemed to see in a big circle all around him. "Have you a male snake, a male rattlesnake?"

"Well it just happens I know I have. I came in one morning and found a big snake in—in coition with a smaller one. That's very rare in captivity. You see, I do know I have a male snake."

"Where is he?"

"Why right in the glass cage by the window there."

Her head swung slowly around but her two quiet hands did not move. She turned back toward him. "May I see?"

He got up and walked to the case by the window. On the sand bottom the knot of rattlesnakes lay entwined, but their heads were clear. The tongues came out and flickered a moment and then waved up and down feeling the air for vibrations. Dr. Phillips nervously turned his head. The woman was standing beside him. He had not heard her get up from the chair. He had heard only the splash of water among the piles and the scampering of the rats on the wire screen.

She said softly, "Which is the male you spoke of?"

He pointed to a thick, dusty gray snake lying by itself in one corner of the cage. "That one. He's nearly five feet long. He comes from Texas. Our Pacific coast snakes are usually smaller. He's been taking all the rats, too. When I want the others to eat I have to take him out."

The woman stared down at the blunt dry head. The forked tongue slipped out and hung quivering for a long moment. "And you're sure he's a male."

"Rattlesnakes are funny," he said glibly. "Nearly every generalization proves wrong. I don't like to say anything definite about rattlesnakes, but— yes—I can assure you he's a male."

Her eyes did not move from the flat head. "Will you sell him to me?"

"Sell him?" he cried. "Sell him to you?"

"You do sell specimens, don't you?"

"Oh—yes. Of course I do. Of course I do."

"How much? Five dollars? Ten?"

"Oh! Not more than five. But do you know anything about rattlesnakes? You might be bitten."

She looked at him for a moment. "I don't intend to take him. I want to leave him here, but—I want him to be mine. I want to come here and look at him and feed him and to know he's mine." She opened a little purse and took out a five-dollar bill. "Here! Now he is mine."

Dr. Phillips began to be afraid. "You could come to look at him without owning him."

"I want him to be mine."

"Oh, Lord!" he cried. "I've forgotten the time." He ran to the table.

"Three minutes over. It won't matter much." He shook menthol crystals into the second watch glass. And then he was drawn back to the cage where the woman still stared at the snake.

She asked, "What does he eat?"

"I feed them white rats, rats from the cage over there."

"Will you put him in the other cage? I want to feed him."

"But he doesn't need food. He's had a rat already this week. Sometimes they don't eat for three or four months. I had one that didn't eat for over a year."

In her low monotone she asked, "Will you sell me a rat?"

He shrugged his shoulders. "I see. You want to watch how rattlesnakes eat. All right. I'll show you. The rat will cost twenty-five cents. It's better than a bullfight if you look at it one way, and it's simply a snake eating his dinner if you look at it another." His tone had become acid. He hated people who made sport of natural processes. He was not a sportsman but a biologist. He could kill a thousand animals for knowledge, but not an insect for pleasure. He'd been over this in his mind before.

She turned her head slowly toward him and the beginning of a smile formed on her thin lips. "I want to feed my snake," she said. "I'll put him in the other cage." She had opened the top of the cage and dipped her hand in before he knew what she was doing. He leaped forward and pulled her back. The lid banged shut.

"Haven't you any sense," he asked fiercely. "Maybe he wouldn't kill you, but he'd make you damned sick in spite of what I could do for you."

"You put him in the other cage then," she said quietly.

Dr. Phillips was shaken. He found that he was avoiding the dark eyes that didn't seem to look at anything.

He felt that it was profoundly wrong to put a rat into the cage, deeply sinful; and he didn't know why. Often he had put rats in the cage when someone or other had wanted to see it, but this desire tonight sickened him. He tried to explain himself out of it.

"It's a good thing to see," he said. "It shows you how a snake can work. It makes you have a respect for a rattlesnake. Then, too, lots of people have dreams about the terror of snakes making the kill. I think because it is a subjective rat. The person is the rat. Once you see it the whole matter is objective. The rat is only a rat and the terror is removed."

He took a long stick equipped with a leather noose from the wall. Opening

the trap he dropped the noose over the big snake's head and tightened the thong.
A piercing dry rattle filled the room.

The thick body writhed and slashed about the handle of the stick as he
lifted the snake out and dropped it in the feeding cage. It stood ready to strike
for a time, but the buzzing gradually ceased. The snake crawled into a corner,
made a big figure eight with its body and lay still.

"You see," the young man explained, "these snakes are quite tame. I've had
them a long time. I suppose I could handle them if I wanted to, but everyone
who does handle rattlesnakes gets bitten sooner or later. I just don't want to take
the chance." He glanced at the woman. He hated to put in the rat. She had moved
over in front of the new cage; her black eyes were on the stony head of the snake
again.

She said, "Put in a rat."

Reluctantly he went to the rat cage. For some reason he was sorry for the
rat, and such a feeling had never come to him before. His eyes went over the mass
of swarming white bodies climbing up the screen toward him. "Which one?" he
thought. "Which one shall it be?" Suddenly he turned angrily to the woman.
"Wouldn't you rather I put in a cat? Then you'd see a real fight. The cat might
even win, but if it lost it might kill the snake. I'll sell you a cat if you like."

She didn't look at him. "Put in a rat," she said. "I want him to eat."

He opened the rat cage and thrust his hand in. His fingers found a tail and
he lifted a plump, red-eyed rat out of the cage. It struggled up to try to bite his
fingers and failing hung spread out and motionless from its tail. He walked
quickly across the room, opened the feeding cage and dropped the rat in on the
sand floor. "Now, watch it," he cried.

The woman did not answer him. Her eyes were on the snake where it lay
still. Its tongue, flicking in and out rapidly, tasted the air of the cage.

The rat landed on its feet, turned around and sniffed at its pink naked tail
and then unconcernedly trotted across the sand, smelling as it went. The room
was silent. Dr. Phillips did not know whether the water sighed among the piles
or whether the woman sighed. Out of the corner of his eye he saw her body
crouch and stiffen.

The snake moved out smoothly, slowly. The tongue flicked in and out.
The motion was so gradual, so smooth that it didn't seem to be motion at all.
In the other end of the cage the rat perked up in a sitting position and began to
lick down the fine white hair on its chest. The snake moved on, keeping always
a deep S curve in its neck.

The silence beat on the young man. He felt the blood drifting up in his body. He said loudly, "See! He keeps the striking curve ready. Rattlesnakes are cautious, almost cowardly animals. The mechanism is so delicate. The snake's dinner is to be got by an operation as deft as a surgeon's job. He takes no chances with his instruments."

The snake had flowed to the middle of the cage by now. The rat looked up, saw the snake and then unconcernedly went back to licking his chest.

"It's the most beautiful thing in the world," the young man said. His veins were throbbing. "It's the most terrible thing in the world."

The snake was close now. Its head lifted a few inches from the sand. The head weaved slowly back and forth, aiming, getting distance, aiming. Dr. Phillips glanced again at the woman. He turned sick. She was weaving too, not much, just a suggestion.

The rat looked up and saw the snake. He dropped to four feet and backed up, then—the stroke.

It was impossible to see, simply a flash. The rat jarred as though under an invisible blow. The snake backed hurriedly into the corner from which he had come, and settled down, his tongue working constantly.

"Perfect!" Dr. Phillips cried. "Right between the shoulder blades. The fangs must almost have reached the heart."

The rat stood still, breathing like a little white bellows. Suddenly he leaped in the air and landed on his side. His legs kicked spasmodically for a second and he was dead.

The woman relaxed, relaxed sleepily.

"Well," the young man demanded, "it was an emotional bath, wasn't it?"

She turned her misty eyes to him. "Will he eat it now?" she asked.

"Of course he'll eat it. He didn't kill for a thrill. He killed it because he was hungry."

The corners of the woman's mouth turned up a trifle again. She looked back at the snake. "I want to see him eat it."

Now the snake came out of his corner again. There was no striking curve in his neck, but he approached the rat gingerly, ready to jump back in case it attacked him. He nudged the body gently with his blunt nose, and drew away.

Satisfied that it was dead, he touched the body all over with his chin, from head to tail. He seemed to measure it and to kiss it. Finally he opened his mouth and unhinged his jaws at the corners.

Dr. Phillips put his will against his head to keep it from turning toward the woman. He thought, "If she's opening her mouth, I'll be sick. I'll be afraid." He succeeded in keeping his eyes away.

The snake fitted his jaws over the rat's head and then with a slow peristaltic pulsing, began to engulf the rat. The jaws gripped and the whole throat crawled up, and the jaws gripped again.

Dr. Phillips turned away and went to his work table. "You've made me miss one of the series," he said bitterly. "The set won't be complete." He put one of the watch glasses under a low-power microscope and looked at it, and then angrily he poured the contents of all the dishes into the sink.

The waves had fallen so that only a wet whisper came up through the floor. The young man lifted a trapdoor at his feet and dropped the starfish down into the black water. He paused at the cat, crucified in the cradle and grinning comically into the light. Its body was puffed with embalming fluid. He shut off the pressure, withdrew the needle and tied the vein.

"Would you like some coffee?" he asked.

"No, thank you. I shall be going pretty soon."

He walked to her where she stood in front of the snake cage. The rat was swallowed, all except an inch of pink tail that stuck out of the snake's mouth like a sardonic tongue. The throat heaved again and the tail disappeared. The jaws snapped back into their sockets, and the big snake crawled heavily to the corner, made a big eight and dropped his head on the sand.

"He's asleep now," the woman said. "I'm going now. But I'll come back and feed my snake every little while. I'll pay for the rats. I want him to have plenty. And sometime—I'll take him away with me." Her eyes came out of their dusty dream for a moment. "Remember, he's mine. Don't take his poison. I want him to have it. Goodnight." She walked swiftly to the door and went out. He heard her footsteps on the stairs, but he could not hear her walk away on the pavement.

Dr. Phillips turned a chair around and sat down in front of the snake cage. He tried to comb out his thought as he looked at the torpid snake. "I've read so much about psychological sex symbols," he thought. "It doesn't seem to explain. Maybe I'm too much alone. Maybe I should kill the snake. If I knew— no, I can't pray to anything."

For weeks he expected her to return. "I will go out and leave her alone here when she comes," he decided. "I won't see the damned thing again."

She never came again. For months he looked for her when he walked about in the town. Several times he ran after some tall woman thinking it might be she. But he never saw her again—ever.

[FEBRUARY 1938]

NORMAN MAILER

The Language of Men

*Norman Mailer's (1923–   ) talent and reputation enhanced Esquire
each time he appeared in its pages over more than thirty years. His
career as a journalist began in Esquire, when the features editor Clay
Felker dispatched him to cover the Democratic Convention of 1960,
where JFK was nominated, an account that appeared as "Superman
Comes to the Supermarket" in the magazine. By then, however, he had
already contributed a substantial amount of fiction: his novel An American Dream was serialized in its entirety—the first time Esquire had ever
serialized a novel. "The Language of Men" is one of Mailer's few
stories, and critics have often suggested that the short form is too
constricting for his expansive talents. A section of his most recent novel,
Harlot's Ghost, was published in Esquire's fiction issue in July 1988.*

In the beginning, Sanford Carter was
ashamed of becoming an Army cook. This was not from snobbery, at least not
from snobbery of the most direct sort. During the two and a half years Carter
had been in the Army he had come to hate cooks more and more. They existed
for him as a symbol of all that was corrupt, overbearing, stupid, and privileged
in Army life. The image which came to mind was a fat cook with an enormous
sandwich in one hand, and a bottle of beer in the other, sweat pouring down a

porcine face, foot on a flour barrel, shouting at the K.P.'s, "Hurry up, you men, I ain't got all day." More than once in those two and a half years, driven to exasperation, Carter had been on the verge of throwing his food into a cook's face as he passed on the serving line. His anger often derived from nothing: the set of a pair of fat lips, the casual heavy thump of the serving spoon into his plate, or the resentful conviction that the cook was not serving him enough. Since life in the Army was in most aspects a marriage, this rage over apparently harmless details was not a sign of unbalance. Every soldier found some particular habit of the Army spouse impossible to support.

Yet Sanford Carter became a cook and, to elaborate the irony, did better as a cook than he had done as anything else. In a few months he rose from a Private to a first cook with the rank of Sergeant, Technician. After the fact, it was easy to understand. He had suffered through all his Army career from an excess of eagerness. He had cared too much, he had wanted to do well, and so he had often been tense at moments when he would better have been relaxed. He was very young, twenty-one, had lived the comparatively gentle life of a middle-class boy, and needed some success in the Army to prove to himself that he was not completely worthless.

In succession, he had failed as a surveyor in Field Artillery, a clerk in an Infantry headquarters, a telephone wireman, and finally a rifleman. When the war ended, and his regiment went to Japan, Carter was still a rifleman; he had been a rifleman for eight months. What was more to the point, he had been in the platoon as long as any of its members; the skilled hard-bitten nucleus of veterans who had run his squad had gone home one by one, and it seemed to him that through seniority he was entitled to at least a corporal's rating. Through seniority he was so entitled, but on no other ground. Whenever responsibility had been handed to him, he had discharged it miserably, tensely, overconscientiously. He had always asked too many questions, he had worried the task too severely, he had conveyed his nervousness to the men he was supposed to lead. Since he was also sensitive enough and proud enough never to curry favor with the noncoms in the platoons, he was in no position to sit in on their occasional discussions about who was to succeed them. In a vacuum of ignorance, he had allowed himself to dream that he would be given a squad to lead, and his hurt was sharp when the squad was given to a replacement who had joined the platoon months after him.

The war was over, Carter had a bride in the States (he had lived with her for only two months), he was lonely, he was obsessed with going home. As one week dragged into the next, and the regiment, the company, and his own platoon continued the same sort of training which they had been doing ever since he had entered the Army, he thought he would snap. There were months to wait until he would be discharged and meanwhile it was intolerable to him to be taught for the fifth time the nomenclature of the machine gun, to stand a retreat parade three evenings a week. He wanted some niche where he could lick his wounds, some Army job with so many hours of work and so many hours of complete freedom, where he could be alone by himself. He hated the Army, the huge Army which had proved to him that he was good at no work, and incapable of succeeding at anything. He wrote long, aching letters to his wife, he talked less and less to the men around him and he was close to violent attacks of anger during the most casual phases of training—during close-order drill or cleaning his rifle for inspection. He knew that if he did not find his niche it was possible that he would crack.

So he took an opening in the kitchen. It promised him nothing except a day of work, and a day of leisure which would be completely at his disposal. He found that he liked it. He was given at first the job of baking the bread for the company, and every other night he worked till early in the morning, kneading and shaping his fifty-pound mix of dough. At two or three he would be done, and for his work there would be the tangible reward of fifty loaves of bread, all fresh from the oven, all clean and smelling of fertile accomplished creativity. He had the rare and therefore intensely satisfying emotion of seeing at the end of an Army chore the product of his labor.

A month after he became a cook the regiment was disbanded, and those men who did not have enough points to go home were sent to other outfits. Carter ended at an ordnance company in another Japanese city. He had by now given up all thought of getting a noncom's rating before he was discharged, and was merely content to work each alternate day. He took his work for granted and so he succeeded at it. He had begun as a baker in the new company kitchen; before long he was the first cook. It all happened quickly. One cook went home on points, another caught a skin disease, a third was transferred from the kitchen after contracting a venereal infection. On the shift which Carter worked there were left only himself and a man who was illiterate. Carter was put nominally in charge, and was soon actively in charge. He looked up each menu in an Army recipe book, collected the items, combined them in the order indicated, and after the proper time had elapsed, took them from the stove. His product tasted neither better nor worse than the product of all other Army cooks. But the mess sergeant was impressed. Carter had filled a gap. The next time ratings were given out Carter jumped at a bound from Private to Sergeant T/4.

On the surface he was happy; beneath the surface he was overjoyed. It took him several weeks to realize how grateful and delighted he felt. The promotion coincided with his assignment to a detachment working in a small seaport up the coast. Carter arrived there to discover that he was in charge of cooking for thirty men, and would act as mess sergeant. There was another cook, and there were four permanent Japanese K.P.'s, all of them good workers. He still cooked every other day, but there was always time between meals to take a break of at least an hour and often two; he shared a room with the other cook and lived in comparative privacy for the first time in several years; the seaport was beautiful; there was only one officer, and he left the men alone; supplies were plentiful due to a clerical error which assigned rations for forty men rather than thirty; and in general everything was fine. The niche had become a sinecure.

This was the happiest period of Carter's life in the Army. He came to like his Japanese K.P.'s. He studied their language, he visited their homes, he gave them gifts of food from time to time. They worshiped him because he was kind to them and generous, because he never shouted, because his good humor bubbled over into games, and made the work of the kitchen seem pleasant. All the while he grew in confidence. He was not a big man, but his body filled out from the heavy work; he was likely to sing a great deal, he cracked jokes with the men on the chow line. The kitchen became his property, it became his domain, and since it was a warm room, filled with sunlight, he came to take pleasure in the very sight of it. Before long his good humor expanded into a series of efforts to improve the food. He began to take little pains and make little extra efforts which would have been impossible if he had been obliged to cook for more than thirty men. In the morning he would serve the men fresh eggs scrambled or fried to their desire in fresh butter. Instead of cooking sixty eggs in one large pot he cooked two eggs at a time in a frying pan, turning them to the taste of each soldier. He baked like a housewife satisfying her young husband; at lunch and dinner there was pie or cake, and often both. He went to great lengths. He taught the K.P.'s how to make the toast come out right. He traded excess food for spices in Japanese stores. He rubbed paprika and garlic on the chickens. He even made pastries to cover such staples as corn beef hash and meat and vegetable stew.

It all seemed to be wasted. In the beginning the men might have noticed these improvements, but after a period they took them for granted. It did not matter how he worked to satisfy them; they trudged through the chow line with their heads down, nodding coolly at him, and they ate without comment. He would hang around the tables after the meal, noticing how much they consumed, and what they discarded; he would wait for compliments, but the soldiers seemed indifferent. They seemed to eat without tasting the food. In their faces he saw mirrored the distaste with which he had once stared at cooks.

The honeymoon was ended. The pleasure he took in the kitchen and himself curdled. He became aware again of his painful desire to please people, to discharge responsibility, to be a man. When he had been a child, tears had come into his eyes at a cross word, and he had lived in an atmosphere where his smallest accomplishment was warmly praised. He was the sort of young man, he often thought bitterly, who was accustomed to the attention and the protection of women. He would have thrown away all he possessed—the love of his wife, the love of his mother, the benefits of his education, the assured financial security of entering his father's business—if he had been able just once to dig a ditch as well as the most ignorant farmer.

Instead, he was back in the painful unprotected days of his first entrance into the Army. Once again the most casual actions became the most painful, the events which were most to be taken for granted grew into the most significant, and the feeding of the men at each meal turned progressively more unbearable.

So Sanford Carter came full circle. If he had once hated the cooks, he now hated the troops. At mealtimes his face soured into the belligerent scowl with which he had once believed cooks to be born. And to himself he muttered the age-old laments of the housewife: how little they appreciated what he did.

Finally there was an explosion. He was approached one day by Corporal Taylor, and he had come to hate Taylor, because Taylor was the natural leader of the detachment and kept the other men endlessly amused with his jokes. Taylor had the ability to present himself as inefficient, shiftless, and incapable, in such a manner as to convey that really the opposite was true. He had the lightest touch, he had the greatest facility, he could charm a geisha in two minutes and obtain anything he wanted from a supply sergeant in five. Carter envied him, envied his grace, his charmed indifference; then grew to hate him.

Taylor teased Carter about the cooking, and he had the knack of knowing where to put the knife. "Hey, Carter," he would shout across the mess hall while breakfast was being served, "you turned my eggs twice, and I asked for them raw." The men would shout with laughter. Somehow Taylor had succeeded in conveying all of the situation, or so it seemed to Carter, insinuating everything, how Carter worked and how it meant nothing, how Carter labored to gain their affection and earned their contempt. Carter would scowl, Carter would answer in a rough voice, "Next time I'll crack them over your head." "You crack 'em, I'll eat 'em," Taylor would pipe back, "but just don't put your fingers in 'em." And there would be another laugh. He hated the sight of Taylor.

It was Taylor who came to him to get the salad oil. About twenty of the soldiers were going to have a fish fry at the geisha house; they had bought the fish at the local market, but they could not buy oil, so Taylor was sent as the deputy to Carter. He was charming to Carter, he complimented him on the meal, he clapped him on the back, he dissolved Carter to warmth, to private delight in the attention, and the thought that he had misjudged Taylor. Then Taylor asked for the oil.

Carter was sick with anger. Twenty men out of the thirty in the detachment were going on the fish fry. It meant only that Carter was considered one of the ten undesirables. It was something he had known, but the proof of knowledge is always more painful than the acquisition of it. If he had been alone his eyes would have clouded. And he was outraged at Taylor's deception. He could imagine Taylor saying ten minutes later, "You should have seen the grease job I gave to Carter. I'm dumb, but man, he's dumber."

Carter was close enough to giving him the oil. He had a sense of what it would mean to refuse Taylor, he was on the very edge of mild acquiescence. But he also had a sense of how he would despise himself afterward.

"No," he said abruptly, his teeth gritted, "you can't have it."

"What do you mean we can't have it?"

"I won't give it to you." Carter could almost feel the rage which Taylor generated at being refused.

"You won't give away a lousy five gallons of oil to a bunch of G.I.'s having a party?"

"I'm sick and tired," Carter began.

"So am I." Taylor walked away.

Carter knew he would pay for it. He left the K.P.'s and went to change his sweat-soaked work shirt, and as he passed the large dormitory in which most of the detachment slept he could hear Taylor's high-pitched voice. Carter did not bother to take off his shirt. He returned instead to the kitchen, and listened to the sound of men going back and forth through the hall and of a man shouting with rage. That was Hobbs, a Southerner, a big man with a big bellowing voice.

There was a formal knock on the kitchen door. Taylor came in. His face was pale and his eyes showed a cold satisfaction. "Carter," he said, "the men want to see you in the big room."

Carter heard his voice answer huskily. "If they want to see me, they can come into the kitchen."

He knew he would conduct himself with more courage in his own kitchen than anywhere else. "I'll be here for a while."

Taylor closed the door, and Carter picked up a writing board to which was clamped the menu for the following day. Then he made a pretense of examining the food supplies in the pantry closet. It was his habit to check the stocks before deciding what to serve the next day, but on this night his eyes ranged thoughtlessly over the canned goods. In a corner were seven five-gallon tins of salad oil, easily enough cooking oil to last a month. Carter came out of the pantry and shut the door behind him.

He kept his head down and pretended to be writing the menu when the soldiers came in. Somehow there were even more of them than he had expected. Out of the twenty men who were going to the party, all but two or three had crowded through the door.

Carter took his time, looked up slowly. "You men want to see me?" he asked flatly.

They were angry. For the first time in his life he faced the hostile expressions of many men. It was the most painful and anxious moment he had ever known.

"Taylor says you won't give us the oil," someone burst out.

"That's right, I won't," said Carter. He tapped his pencil against the scratchboard, tapping it slowly and, he hoped, with an appearance of calm.

"What a stink deal," said Porfirio, a little Cuban whom Carter had always considered his friend.

Hobbs, the big Southerner, stared down at Carter. "Would you mind telling the men why you've decided not to give us the oil?" he asked quietly.

" 'Cause I'm blowed if I'm going to cater to you men. I've catered enough," Carter said. His voice was close to cracking with the outrage he had suppressed for so long, and he knew that if he continued he might cry. "I'm the acting mess sergeant," he said as coldly as he could, "and I decide what goes out of this kitchen." He stared at each one in turn, trying to stare them down, feeling mired in the rut of his own failure. They would never have dared this approach to another mess sergeant.

"What crud," someone muttered.

"You won't give a lousy five-gallon can of oil for a G.I. party," Hobbs said more loudly.

"I won't. That's definite. You men can get out of here."

"Why, you lousy little snot," Hobbs burst out, "how many five-gallon cans of oil have you sold on the black market?"

"I've never sold any." Carter might have been slapped with the flat of a sword. He told himself bitterly, numbly, that this was the reward he received for being perhaps the single honest cook in the whole United States Army. And he

even had time to wonder at the obscure prejudice which had kept him from
selling food for his own profit.

"Man, I've seen you take it out," Hobbs exclaimed. "I've seen you take it
to the market."

"I took food to trade for spices," Carter said hotly.

There was an ugly snicker from the men.

"I don't mind if a cook sells," Hobbs said. "Every man has his own deal
in this Army. But a cook ought to give a little food to a G.I. if he wants it."

"Tell him," someone said.

"It's bull," Taylor screeched. "I've seen Carter take butter, eggs, every
damn thing to the market."

Their faces were red, they circled him.

"I never sold a thing," Carter said doggedly.

"And I'm telling you," Hobbs said, "that you're a two-bit crook. You
been raiding that kitchen, and that's why you don't give to us now."

Carter knew there was only one way he could possibly answer if he hoped
to live among these men again. "That's a goddamn lie," Carter said to Hobbs.
He laid down the scratchboard, he flipped his pencil slowly and deliberately to
one corner of the room, and with his heart aching he lunged toward Hobbs. He
had no hope of beating him. He merely intended to fight until he was pounded
unconscious, advancing the pain and bruises he would collect as collateral for his
self-respect.

To his indescribable relief Porfirio darted between them, held them apart
with the pleased ferocity of a small man breaking up a fight. "Now, stop this!
Now, stop this!" he cried out.

Carter allowed himself to be pushed back, and he knew that he had gained
a point. He even glimpsed a solution with some honor.

He shrugged violently to free himself from Porfirio. He was in a rage, and
yet it was a rage he could have ended at any instant. "All right, you men," he
swore, "I'll give you the oil, but now that we're at it, I'm going to tell you a
thing or two." His face red, his body perspiring, he was in the pantry and out
again with a five-gallon tin. "Here," he said, "you better have a good fish fry,
'cause it's the last good meal you're going to have for quite a while. I'm sick of
trying to please you. You think I have to work—" he was about to say, my
fingers to the bone—"well, I don't. From now on, you'll see what chow in the
Army is supposed to be like." He was almost hysterical. "Take that oil. Have
your fish fry." The fact that they wanted to cook for themselves was the greatest
insult of all. "Tomorrow I'll give you real Army cooking."

His voice was so intense that they backed away from him. "Get out of this kitchen," he said. "None of you has any business here."

They filed out quietly, and they looked a little sheepish.

Carter felt weary, he felt ashamed of himself, he knew he had not meant what he said. But half an hour later, when he left the kitchen and passed the large dormitory, he heard shouts of raucous laughter, and he heard his name mentioned and then more laughter.

He slept badly that night, he was awake at four, he was in the kitchen by five, and stood there white-faced and nervous, waiting for the K.P.'s to arrive. Breakfast that morning landed on the men like a lead bomb. Carter rummaged in the back of the pantry and found a tin of dehydrated eggs covered with dust, memento of a time when fresh eggs were never on the ration list. The K.P.'s looked at him in amazement as he stirred the lumpy powder into a pan of water. While it was still half-dissolved he put it on the fire. While it was still wet, he took it off. The coffee was cold, the toast was burned, the oatmeal stuck to the pot. The men dipped forks into their food, took cautious sips of their coffee, and spoke in whispers. Sullenness drifted like vapors through the kitchen.

At noontime Carter opened cans of meat and vegetable stew. He dumped them into a pan and heated them slightly. He served the stew with burned string beans and dehydrated potatoes which tasted like straw. For dessert the men had a single lukewarm canned peach and cold coffee.

So the meals continued. For three days Carter cooked slop, and suffered even more than the men. When mealtime came he left the chow line to the K.P.'s and sat in his room, perspiring with shame, determined not to yield and sick with the determination.

Carter won. On the fourth day a delegation of men came to see him. They told him that indeed they had appreciated his cooking in the past, they told him that they were sorry they had hurt his feelings, they listened to his remonstrances, they listened to his grievances, and with delight Carter forgave them. That night, for supper, the detachment celebrated. There was roast chicken with stuffing, lemon meringue pie and chocolate cake. The coffee burned their lips. More than half the men made it a point to compliment Carter on the meal.

In the weeks which followed the compliments diminished, but they never stopped completely. Carter became ashamed at last. He realized the men were trying to humor him, and he wished to tell them it was no longer necessary.

Harmony settled over the kitchen. Carter even became friends with Hobbs, the big Southerner. Hobbs approached him one day, and in the manner of a farmer talked obliquely for an hour. He spoke about his father, he spoke about his girlfriends, he alluded indirectly to the night they had almost fought, and finally with the courtesy of a Southerner he said to Carter, "You know, I'm sorry about shooting off my mouth. You were right to want to fight me, and if you're still mad I'll fight you to give you satisfaction, although I just as soon would not."

"No, I don't want to fight with you now," Carter said warmly. They smiled at each other. They were friends.

Carter knew he had gained Hobbs's respect. Hobbs respected him because he had been willing to fight. That made sense to a man like Hobbs. Carter liked him so much at this moment that he wished the friendship to be more intimate.

"You know," he said to Hobbs, "it's a funny thing. You know I really never did sell anything on the black market. Not that I'm proud of it, but I just didn't."

Hobbs frowned. He seemed to be saying that Carter did not have to lie. "I don't hold it against a man," Hobbs said, "if he makes a little money in something that's his own proper work. Hell, I sell gas from the motor pool. It's just I also give gas if one of the G.I.'s wants to take the jeep out for a joy ride, kind of."

"No, but I never did sell anything." Carter had to explain. "If I ever had sold on the black market, I would have given the salad oil without question."

Hobbs frowned again, and Carter realized he still did not believe him. Carter did not want to lose the friendship which was forming. He thought he could save it only by some further admission. "You know," he said again, "remember when Porfirio broke up our fight? I was awful glad when I didn't have to fight you." Carter laughed, expecting Hobbs to laugh with him, but a shadow passed across Hobbs's face.

"Funny way of putting it," Hobbs said.

He was always friendly thereafter, but Carter knew that Hobbs would never consider him a friend. Carter thought about it often, and began to wonder about the things which made him different. He was no longer so worried about becoming a man; he felt that to an extent he had become one. But in his heart he wondered if he would ever learn the language of men.

[APRIL 1953]

LESLIE A. FIEDLER

Nude Croquet

Leslie A. Fiedler (1917–   ) is one of the most provocative critics American literature has ever encountered. His famous essay "Come Back to the Raft, Huck Honey" was later expanded in his book Love and Death in the American Novel, which shocked intellectuals and general readers alike. His one fiction contribution to Esquire, "Nude Croquet," is about shenanigans among the literati at a place much like Yaddo; it raised eyebrows among the Partisan Review crowd when it appeared in Esquire in 1957.

"**D**on't you ever get tired of being right!" Howard snarled ritually, jamming the brakes down hard as the house rose up from a tangle of runty pines and bushes just where Jessie had said it would be. They had been arguing for twenty minutes about the last turn, he with all the desperate passion of a man without a sense of direction.

"Won't you ever learn how to stop a car!" Jessie snapped back automatically; then, counting the crazy turrets castellated and masked with iron filigree, "Seven! Bernie wasn't exaggerating for once." And at last, "I'm so damn tired of being right, I could *puke!*" She stared miserably at the bats sliding down the evening sky over the slate roofs—her face very pale in the last light. "It'll be raining in half an hour," she added. "There goes your swim."

"Don't sound so happy," he answered, cutting the motor and putting an arm around her shoulder. "Look. Let's turn right around and go home. There's no point in this whole—I mean, what do we have in common anymore, Leonard and Bill and I, except our remembered youth—and that's only a reproach. It's just that—I—" He gave up finally, waving his free hand at the grounds before them: the offensive acres of plants and flowers that neither of them could have named, the lily-infested pond barely visible beside the porte cochere, the untidy extravagance of the great house itself.

Jessie shook herself free of his arm and thrust her face forward, viciously, almost into the mirror on the sun visor. "I look so old—so goddamned *old!*" She touched the creases on her cheek that had once been dimples, the vein-riddled crescents under her eyes, the ungenerous mouth that had sunk inward, pulling her nose and chin closer together.

"You *are* old. *We're* old. Forty-three, forty-five—that's not young. What do you want?" Howard turned slowly to look at the face he seldom saw.

"At least my hair's a good color this time." She lifted a lock of it in her bony hand—very red against the white. "But *you* look like a baby. It isn't fair. A spoiled baby!"

He tried to concentrate on her hair, but could not resist glancing a little smugly at his own face in the glass, baby pink and white under the baby yellow curls, luxuriant and untouched by gray. His face had always been plump and never handsome, but its indestructible youthfulness had managed finally to lend it a certain charm.

"A spoiled baby—and I'm the one who spoils you. I must want you to look young. Why the hell do I want that, Howard? I know why *you* like it; it makes other women feel sorry for you, yoked to such a hag! But why do I want it, Howard, *why?*"

"I don't know. You're just a good American girl, I guess." He could hear the sea walloping the rocks, realized that he had been hearing it for a long time: *thump—thump—thump*. Like a man in an empty house, he thought sadly, banging a table, banging a table and shouting into the darkness that—

"Do I really look so old, Howard? *Do* I?" she interrupted. "What would you think if you just met me for the first time?"

He examined her for a moment with his careful painter's eye. "Yes," he answered at length, "you do." He was quite serious; after much devious thought, he always ended up telling the truth, the simplest truth. It was a kind of laziness. "I always tell the truth," he explained, trying to embrace her again. "It's a kind of laziness."

"A bon mot!" she cried bitterly. "Save it! Save it for your friends and their twenty-year-old wives." She tried vainly to light her cigarette at the car lighter in an intended gesture of nonchalance; and he flipped a match with finger and thumb.

"Listen, Jess, I'm not kidding. Let's turn around. It's bound to be gruesome—six men who never loved each other to begin with, and two brand-new wives. Besides, you're upset. We can call up later and say I got lost. Everyone knows I always get lost. Let's keep going to Atlantic City; a man can die without having been in Atlantic City and this may be our only chance. The kid's in camp and—"

She had not even been listening. "I suppose you intend to play the fool again tonight the way you always do. That's the difference between you and an ordinary fool; you always plan it in advance. Which one will you make a pass at tonight? Which twenty-year-old? Which ingenue: Molly or Eva?"

"Ay-vah," he corrected her. "She says it 'Ay-vah' not 'Eva.' It makes Leonard mad when—"

"To hell with Leonard. He's a worse fool than you are. Giving up a girl like Lucille for a—"

"Please, Jess, don't yell at me. Take it up with Leonard. I'm not the one who divorced his wife. I just said—"

"You just *said*. You just sit there preening in the mirror and thinking what-a-good-boy-am-I because you didn't divorce your wife like Leonard or Bill. Many thanks."

"You're welcome."

"Oh, no, you don't divorce her; you only make a fool of her by slobbering over somebody else's twenty-year-old wife, because you're too lazy and too spoiled and too irresponsible even to be the first-class kind of bastard Leonard is. But don't think you just make a fool out of me. You make a worse fool out of yourself. After all, you *are* forty-five—forty-five and foolish and fat, just like in the comic strips." She took the fold of fat over his belt between two fingers and pinched it hard. She was crying. "The shame of it is that it's such a pattern, so stupid, so *expected*. Everyone knows what Howard Place, boy abstractionist, is going to do at a party, and everybody watches and waits for him to do it. Who will it be tonight? Which sleazy bitch or celebrity-happy sophomore from Bennington?"

"All right, then, we'll—"

"All right, then, we'll *what?* You don't even bother to protest anymore, do you? You won't even lie to me."

"Okay, so let's get out of here." Clumsily and in anger, he began to slew the car around.

But Jessie had changed her mood, though her tears were not yet dry. "At least we can still argue. That's a good sign, Howard, isn't it?"

"It sure is." He kissed her tentatively.

"Then don't turn around. How can you be such a fool? Don't you think I want to see the inside of the house, too? I want it to be so vulgar and stupid that—"

"Look, darling—"

"Oh, you poor, helpless bastard, just lie to me a little, that's all. I *love* you, you know." She leaned over to return his kiss—not very hard.

"That's just because I'm going to be in next year's Biennale. You don't want to lose a winner."

"It helps." She kissed him again, and he held her to him almost with passion.

"I love you, too, Jess. God have mercy on us." It was the simplest truth, and yet he was already thinking how Eva (Leonard's wife whom he had seen only once) and Molly (for whom Bill had left Elaine and whom he had not yet met) would be to touch or taste, their flesh not much more subdued by love or time than his fourteen-year-old daughter's.

The drive led them past two tennis courts and wound now beside the pond, around which they could see the white gleam of marble statues, emperors and fauns, athletes and nymphs, carefully mutilated to look like recovered antiques. It had begun to rain, and over Jessie's shoulder he could see drops glistening on a slender, high-breasted Venus who was arched across a shell in the middle of a pool, with her head tossed arrogantly back. "Aphrodite at the gates. It's a good omen." Howard whooped helplessly, abandoned to laughter, while Jessie said, "For pity's sake, what's so funny? Look, it's Bill himself."

It *was* Bill, at the door—unmistakably Bill, playing squire in this place created by his rich wife's grandfather, waving a Martini glass in their direction and yelling what must have been a fond greeting. Three years (was it only three since they had sat in the Piazza del Popolo choking on Camparisoda?) had done something cruel and comical to him. It was not merely that he had grown fat. He looked somehow as if he had been blown up by a kid with a bicycle pump: the skinny, bewildered face still skinny but *inflated*, the once half-starved body ballooned out under the unbleached-linen jacket.

"I'm not rich for nothing," he said. "Imagine it, me rich." He raised a plump arm with visible effort to indicate his domain. "Sixty-two bedrooms—we even have a ghost, but unfortunately on Sundays ghosts don't—" He seemed to remember for the first time the dark-haired girl with the pale eyes who stood beside him. Everything about her was tiny except for her breasts, which, thrust forward by her sway-backed stance, gave her the overweighted air of an eighth-grader who has not yet grown up to her body. "And this is the secret of my success, Molly-o, my wife." A deprecatory grin fought to take shape in the tight, round blank of his face. It was impossible to say if he changed expression when he added with scarcely a pause, "Did you know Irving's dead?"

Molly reached a hand toward Howard first, very brisk and businesslike, though her pale eyes fluttered coyly. They were green, he thought, if they were any color at all.

"Place," she said, greeting him by last name as if she were a man. "Delighted. I recognized you from the picture in *Harper's Bazaar*."

He touched her cheek lightly, ignoring the hand. "Delighted, too. I recognized you from the picture outside Minsky's."

"Pardon?" Molly asked uncertainly. Her lids moved up and down frantically over the ambiguous green.

"Oh, for pity's sake," Jessie exclaimed, "she's only a child." Then, giving her a hug and a large kiss, "I love you, you know. I love all of Bill's wives."

"He only had *two*," Molly answered, moving uneasily in Jessie's embrace. "I mean, I'm the second, that is—"

"I said Irving's dead," Bill tried again. "Irving's dead. Irving's dead." He was constitutionally incapable of shouting, but he pounded Howard's back with a pudgy hand to claim his attention.

"I know he's dead," Howard answered at last. "Irving's been dead for years. I keep telling him so. He never got out from under the influence of Hoffman. But where the hell is he? I haven't seen—"

"No! No!" Bill insisted, dancing up and down in exasperation. "He really died two nights ago. He was supposed to be here tonight with Esther—"

"Sarah, you mean," Jessie interrupted.

"I thought it was—to hell with it. The important thing is, he's dead."

"You mean *dead*," Howard yelled, registering at last. "Irving? Irving Posner? Dead?"

"He died two nights ago," Molly said, "the fourteenth, at seven-thirty P.M. in the arms of his wife, of a heart attack." This at least, she obviously believed, was a solid fact to be hung on to, to be asserted in the midst of references that baffled her and slippery insults. This was what she knew, what she could tell the others.

            In his distress, Howard had not noticed Marvin and Achsa, who were coming toward them out of the house, Marvin as usual carefully not looking at his wife, who followed him fiercely, like a dog on a fresh scent. Molly tried to continue; but Marvin leaned down toward her from his immense height, almost touching her ponytail with his chin.

    "You sound like a newspaper," he said in his flat, unpleasant voice; "the kind of newspaper I never read. You ask me how I know what kind of newspaper it is, if I never read it; I answer I know that you read it, and knowing you I deduce—"

    "Excuse *me*, Mr. Solomon," Molly retorted with schoolgirl iciness, "I wasn't aware that you were eavesdropping." Marvin had withdrawn again to his full height, lifting his dark, melancholy face back into its customary loneliness; and she had to tilt her own head back perilously to glare at him.

    "Why don't you call me Marvin," he said. "That would make me more uncomfortable yet."

    "For the love of Jesus, shut *up*," Achsa cut in. "You're not even drunk." She did not try to engage his eye, shouting instead with all the hopeless rage of one whose worst enemy has remained out of range for twenty years. At that moment, she caught sight of Jessie and, screaming her name, flung herself with equal though opposite passion from her husband toward her friend.

    "Achsa! Achsa! What have you heard from Lucille and Elaine? You never write." Jessie had not so much forgotten Molly as not yet taken her into account.

    "I have no time for writing. I'm working full time again—in the same office with Lucille. You should see her; she looks like a ghost—skin and bones and eyes, that's all. She's back to social psychiatry—what she was doing in Minneapolis—when Leonard was working on his first book, remember, the proletarian one. Proletarian!"

    "For Christ sake, Achsa—Irving is dead. Have a little decency." Howard found he had his arm around Molly, in a gesture of solidarity he had not really thought out.

    "I know," Achsa said. "Thirty-eight years old. A tragedy for the Jewish people. It couldn't be worse if we lost Sholem Asch. I never liked that little twerp Irving and you know it, Howard. Why should I be a hypocrite now? The last time we saw him he was going to *shul*—couldn't even stop to talk. He's a faker,

Howard, admit it. First a Marxist, then a Jungian, then an Orthodox Jew—
what's the use, Howard; dead or alive, he was a fake!"

"How do you do, Achsa? I'm very glad to see you again after all these—"

"Ah, you see Howard's offended because I didn't kiss him. Aren't you?
Isn't that sweet! You always were a *much* sweeter fake than poor Irving." She
pecked him meaninglessly on his nearest cheek, her eyes swinging feverishly
from face to face.

"And you, Marv? How are you?" It was an idiotic thing for Howard to
say out of his complicated feelings, but he could think of nothing else. It was
Marvin who had first taken him to an art museum, Marvin who had made him
read Marx, and now—

"Sufficiently lousy." Marvin inclined his head wearily toward him without
visible affection. "But she's right after all, though God knows how." He avoided
his wife's name, using the simple pronoun in referring to her. "A mountebank,
a bankrupt comedian. At least you've learned to come to terms with your badness
and be popular."

"Thank you, Marvin," Howard answered, scarcely realizing that he imitated Marv's toneless Brooklyn voice as he spoke. "The tribute of your envy is
worth more to me than being chosen for the Biennale." It was the simplest truth
again, and he wished there were some way for Marvin to know it.

"Oh, please come *in* everybody, come in and have a drink. Please. All you
intellectuals I've read about all my life, and you don't know enough to come in
out of the rain." Molly urged and pushed them inside, aided by Howard, to
whom her stupidity and her not-quite-green eyes seemed equally charming. But
what does her voice remind me of, he asked himself, that polite, private-school
New York voice, so unlike the voices of anyone I ever knew or hated or slept
with, the voice (he had it at last) of F.D.R., a Fireside Chat!

A thin stream of blue water rose and fell from the marble basin rimmed
with palms in the entrance hall, and in the shallow pool great, slow, golden carp
hung as if asleep. Howard could see into the immense living room, with its
balcony for musicians and the mirrored walls on either end that reflected back
and forth into a haze of planeless images and ivory Buddhas, the carved oaken
bishop's throne, the twisted iron lamp stands and the faces of Achsa, Marvin,
Jessie, Bill Ward—so improbably there. Rain beat stupidly against the leaded
window panes, and the room was oppressive after the chill, full of smoke and
dead air and rock-and-roll music blaring mercilessly from a pair of speakers in
opposite corners of the ceiling.

"It's too damn hot. I can't stand it!" Achsa screamed and, grabbing a

Cinzano bottle, hurled it through one of the windows at the point where, above a scarlet shield, the motto read: *Ad astra per aspera.*

"Real vermouth," Bill commented, while Molly giggled, obviously feeling that this was more like what she had read about writers and painters in novels, more like a real party at last.

The sound of breaking glass startled the couple on the other side of the room into turning around. They had stood clutched together heedlessly when the others first came in, not really dancing but making little rubbing motions against each other in time to the music. It was Leonard and his new wife, Howard knew even from the backs of their heads, his black and a little grizzled, hers blond, the hair hanging straight to her shoulders. She was very slim and a little taller than Leonard even in her flat ballet slippers; and when she whirled around, her eyes still large and her mouth a little open, a large gold cross swung lazily between her breasts. Leonard had grown a beard and looked handsomer than ever, almost masculine despite his short legs and tiny feet, his soft, girlish body.

"Disgusting!" Achsa said, not troubling to make clear whether she meant the cross, the beard, the public caresses, or all three; and in the confusion of kissing and greeting that followed, no one cared. It was a full ten minutes and a drink later before they could hear each other saying what they had all been unable to stop thinking: "Thirty-eight." "Poor Irving." "Dead."

"Thirty-eight," Jessie managed to make herself heard above the rest. "Thirty-eight! The youngest of us and the first with a reputation—the first one whose name anyone knew but *us*. We're all a little dead now. What are we doing here anyway? Why don't we lie down like good corpses and—"

"What else was there for him to do?" Achsa asked mercilessly. "A painter who couldn't paint anymore. It's better than praying, isn't it, more honest to die!" Irving had been her lover once, Howard was aware, but whatever tenderness she may have felt had long since dissolved in her scorn. "You don't *have* to die of a heart attack. It's an act of cowardice. Look at Marvin. He's had three already, three attacks, but he doesn't die, and what kind of hero is he?"

"You're kidding," Jessie cried out. "For pity's sake, you don't mean to say that—"

But at the same moment Howard was saying, "He wouldn't give you the satisfaction, Achsa." Turning to Marvin, he winked, but looked away again, seeing the sudden terror in Marvin's loosened lip and staring eye. "Old revolutionaries never die," he went on, just to keep talking. "If the last Trotskyite in America conked out from a twinge of the heart, it would be sacrilege or lèse-majesté or something. . . ."

Howard filled his glass again and gulped it down, feeling very sorry for himself. But why *himself?* He could imagine Irving's pinched, dark-bearded face before him, peering out from behind the tortoiseshell glasses as from behind a mask; and playing whatever part he had temporarily chosen, sage or revolutionary or prophet or kindly old uncle with all the furious commitment of a ten-year-old. "I loved him." Perhaps that was it.

"In 1935, he was the most talked about painter in America. A way out of the cubist academy. And for the last five years he never touched a brush—"

"He had the dignity of failure," Marvin said suddenly. "Nothing else matters."

"The dignity of failure," Achsa screamed, closing in on her husband as if she intended to bite him. She, at least, was drunk. "You should be an expert on that, Marv, a real expert. But I don't understand it, not even after twenty-one years of postgraduate study. Just how dignified is it to be the only spokesman of failure, *pure* failure, in a room with a painter who's going to be one of the five Americans in the next Biennale—"

"Four," Jessie corrected her, while Howard winced.

"Plus the winner of the *Prix de Rome* for literature—the only poet in America married to an escapee from a convent!"

For a moment, it seemed as if Eva's mouth was shaping a protest, but she contented herself with pressing it against Leonard's sleeve, snuggling up to him even closer.

"Not to forget our host, the author of *All Buttoned Up*, which not only got the Drama Critics' Circle Award, but even won him as a special bonus Molly-o, complete with the highest-class sanitarium in the marshes of New Jersey." Achsa spilled the rest of her drink on Molly, bowing exaggeratedly in her direction.

"Hardest buck I ever made," Bill said, giggling. He obviously hoped it was a classic remark—and was resolved to find Achsa merely funny.

"And what do *you* have to offer, Marvin, to this distinguished group of repentant Marxists-on-the-make besides the purity of your principles? Twenty-seven years of conversation everyone admires and no one remembers! Twenty-seven years of nail-biting and insomnia—including twenty-one years of *me*. No book. No prize. No new bride. Only me. How do you like me, Marvin? Am I a dignified enough failure for you?"

"You see what I mean," Leonard cut in with his shrill, somewhat fruity voice. He was not addressing the rest of them, really, only Eva, continuing the one dialogue that was important to him. "Conjugal love. Punishing each other for punishing each other. Eating each other, because each one is sure the other's the only true poison. This is what it was like with *me* and—"

"Say Lucille's name and I'll leave this stupid party!" Jessie cried out. "How did she poison you? How? By letting you sit year after year writing poems no one would print, while she worked for twenty-five lousy bucks a week. By letting you weep on her shoulder after each of your 'little affairs' and wipe away your tears until the next one. By—"

"Forgiving is a poison, too, Jessie," Leonard answered mildly. "It's habit-forming. After a while, you get so you—"

"Put down that poisoned toothpick, Leonard! No one hurts my Jessie!" They had not heard Bernie Levine's Cadillac pull up on the cinders outside or seen him and Beatie come through the open front door; but he bounded now from one to the other, the last guest, fat and bald and incredibly ugly, kissing Jessie, lifting Achsa high into the air, thrusting a finger into Bill's middle to see if it was real, patting Eva's behind. "What a *tuchas!* What a *tuchas!* You're a lucky boy, Leonard. What a poet can do with this, I don't know, but a cloak-and-suiter like me! When do we eat? What a dive—my God, the heating bill alone!"

Beatie had been standing behind him through his whole act, grimacing and shaking her head back and forth in her cradled hands to express mock horror; but now she smiled the slow, sweet smile Howard remembered out of her too-big, noble head under its fashionably cropped gray bob.

"Howard, you're just beautiful. And you're famous, my oldest son tells me, my fifteen-year-old, imagine it! He saw it in *Time* magazine. Kiss me already." Pulling her close, Howard saw the tears in her eyes; they had known each other since they were three. "It's terrible, no? And it'll be worse before it's over? What an idea!" She gestured with her head to indicate she meant the whole party. "What can you expect in such a house. No self-respecting ghost would haunt it. Absolutely. Ah, poor Howard—and Jessie! Jessie!"

They embraced warmly, not speaking. "I'm really tired, I didn't realize it. What a summer—my mother-in-law's been with me for three weeks. Why don't we eat? Thanks. Thanks." She waved off Bill, who approached with a glass. "We stopped on the way for a drink. To tell you the truth, for three drinks. That's why we're late."

"Are we ready?" Bill asked, turning to Molly.

"Ready for what?"

"To eat. It's nearly half-past nine."

"*Eat!*" She said the words with exaggerated contempt, and leaning toward Bill, whispered furiously into his ear.

"Urge them?" he asked, scratching his behind in a mild panic. "But what should I urge them to—what do you mean?"

"You don't even remember. And it was going to be the High Point!"

"The High Point?"

"We were going to *swim!*" There were tears in her eyes, darkening the elusive green.

"But it's raining, sweetie," Bill protested, "and it's cold and late and—"

"It's *best* in the rain."

"What? What?" Bernie shouted. "She wants to swim? The young lady wants to swim? So let her swim; it's a constitutional right. I personally will grease her down. I have in the back of my car—"

"*You*'ll swim with me, won't you, Bernie?"

Howard found himself resenting the "Bernie" (he had been coldly "Place"), as he resented the way Molly-o snuggled up to Bernie now, one breast nudging his solar plexus.

"Me? You mean *me* swim? Excuse me, my dear, this is another question entirely. After all I just ate two olives in my last Martini. Otherwise I'd be glad to oblige."

"Really, dear, it's out of the question," Beatie added with a heavily matronly air that even Howard could scarcely abide. "Besides, we have no bathing suits. Bill didn't say anything when he called about—"

"But that's just it. We don't need any bathing suits. It's no fun if it's not spontaneous. We have a lovely private beach, and I thought we would all just slip out of our clothes and— It was going to be so *exciting!* I mean, I remember when I was in college, a bunch of us kids sneaked off to a quarry with a case of beer and— Oh, everybody was so beautiful that night, so free and beautiful in the moonlight!"

"Moonlight!" Howard could not help breaking in, though he did not want to seem to stand against her with the veteran wives and their scared husbands. "Just look at the moonlight!" He pointed through the splintered pane to the sky whose murkiness an occasional lightning flash showed without dispelling.

"It'll be wonderful! We'll be like ghosts in the lightning. *Nude* ghosts." Noo-oo-oo-oode, she said it, lingering dreamily over the vowel of what was for her a magic word. "Nude ghosts."

"And now *listen!*" Howard persisted, hushing them so that they could hear the noise of the sea on the rocks. "It would tear you to pieces."

"Oh, how can you all be so sensible! I wish your precious Irving was here.

At least he *knows* he's a corpse!" And shedding clothes as she ran, she headed out the door into the rain and toward the roar of the ocean. Her brassiere she flung back over her shoulder as she disappeared in a final, theatrical gesture.

"Bravo!" Marvin shouted, clapping his long, thin hands together. "Bravo!"

"What'll I do?" Bill asked, starting to follow her, and then turning irresolutely back.

"You can show me the silent-flush toilets," Beatie answered, taking Bill's arm. "Leave her alone. Don't you know *anything*, even the second time around?"

"Well, I can go wading at least while my wife consoles abandoned husbands in bathrooms." Bernie had taken off his shoes and socks and was heading for the marble fishpond in the entry hall. "This is more my speed. Oy! it's cold!" He jumped out, then, with a shudder, back in again. "Look at me! Free and beautiful! Hoo-hah, I'm F. Scott Fitzgerald!"

But no one even listened. Leonard and Eva were necking again, she utterly abandoned to an inner rhythm of desire, he glancing up occasionally, vaguely troubled, in search of an O.K. from his old friends. Marvin, with no one to talk to, drank in silence, pacing nervously, while Achsa drifted behind him without being aware she followed. Suddenly Howard realized that the darkness before the house to which he had pointed an instant before was blazing with light, through which the slowing rain ran stitches like a sewing machine gone mad. Someone (it must have been Molly-o through all her tears) had switched on a bank of floodlights under the eaves. But why, Howard wondered; and he pressed his face against the window, staring out into the pointless glare.

Molly had apparently not gone swimming at all, but was sitting quite naked on a stone bench just at the verge of the last dune. She was set in absolute profile, her knees drawn up before her, her arms braced behind, and her head thrown back so that her hair fell onto the stone seat. Howard had not realized that it was so long and full, caught up in the ponytail she usually wore. In that excessive light and at that distance, all color was bleached from her body, leaving her perfectly black and white. She appeared no more or less real than the marble Venus, which also stood in Howard's direct line of sight, naked above the lily pads and under the faltering rain. Tintless and eyeless, without motion and with her hair down, Molly was the twin of the statue, another Aphrodite.

Howard knew she was aware of his watching her as surely as he knew his wife was watching his watching; and he turned away with a sigh.

In ten minutes, Molly was back with them again; she had changed into riding breeches and a man's plaid shirt, but was barefoot. "Soup's on," she said grinning, and lifting her arms over her head, she stretched until the shirt was taut from nipple to nipple. She could not have been wearing a brassiere.

She led them into the adjoining dining room where, around a bowl of fresh-blood-colored flowers, tall silver monks held up lighted candles that set the table silver winking and flashing. "That's Oswald," Molly said, tapping one of the monks on his tonsured head. "He's my favorite. Isn't he a darling!"

Dinner began eventlessly enough and was probably excellent, but everyone was too drunk to taste it. Only Eva did not drink, raising to their occasional half-mocking toasts ("The Critics' Circle Award!" "The Biennale!" "The Prix de Rome!") a depressingly white glass of milk. Bernie, who sat beside her, kept pretending to shy from the glass, raising one hand to his eyes as if to shield them from the glare.

"Revolt!" he kept telling her. "That's the last symptom of Momism. Let go of the titty, Eva."

"Ay-vah," Leonard pronounced it for him, irked at the way Bernie kept kneading his wife's arm.

Howard had managed to sit beside Molly; but she had drenched herself with some almost acrid sandalwood perfume after her imaginary swim, and he was actually relieved whenever she rose to go down to the kitchen in pursuit of something forgotten or overlooked. She walked with greater and more perilous dignity each time, until the trip which brought her screaming back with a bloody rag wrapped about the forefinger of her left hand.

"Oh, Bill, I cut it! I *cut* it!" she howled. "I'll bleed to death all because of your silly friends and their silly socialist ideas. Everybody *knows* we have help! What could one person do with a house this size, even for just a summer place. Why did I have to send Ellen and Janet to the movies? So I could chop my finger to pieces? It's snobbery, that's what it is, silly socialist snobbery. They *like* being servants and I like having them and I—oh, Bill—it's all over my shirt—I'm all *bloody*, Bill." Looking down at the red-stained rag she screamed again.

"Really, I— Really, I—" Bill's mouth opened and closed, opened and closed, as if he were trying to say something, though it became clear finally that he was only laughing soundlessly.

"Bill just sent them away to protect them from Bernie," Howard began, feeling somehow that what would surely seem a good joke when they were sober, they might as well laugh at now.

But Molly was crying again. "I can't help it if I need servants, can I? Don't make me send them away again. *Promise!* I'm just stupid, that's *all*. Oh, *Bill!*" She held her wounded finger under his mouth until he made kissing noises in its general direction, glancing all the while at Marvin to see how strongly he disapproved and making indistinct remarks about the superiority of Band-Aids to kisses.

Marvin, on the other hand, looked happy for the first time that night; his long head moving up and down like a horse eating sugar from a child's hand, he began to speak. "Sending servants away, this is more than a symptom of insecurity; it is clearly a symbolic action—but symbolic of what? What is the objection to a maid from people who have sold out their principles, their former friends, their past. To make jokes for hire about everything you believed in once, this is apparently all right, as long as it's in verse." He bowed toward Leonard, showing his crooked yellow teeth in the nearest thing to a smile he could manage. "To sign a loyalty oath to a state with a law against miscegenation in order to keep a job teaching schoolboys to draw vases and plaster casts, this is kosher." He nodded at Howard. "To live off a stupid mother-in-law who believes in 'Art,' but fortunately does not know what it is—who would object? Not our host, who objects to servants or should I say to displaying his servants to former comrades. Do you follow this?"

A chorus of "no's" answered him, though they had all stopped to listen. He was the only one of them able to compel the attention of the others.

"Please, *I* 'd like to say something," Bill said, holding his hand up like a boy in school. He still had the corkscrew in his clenched fist. "Marvin, you don't understand. About the servants, I won't say anything because it's—well, I just won't. And as for my mother-in-law, whatever help she gave me and for whatever reasons, I don't need it anymore. With what I made on *All Buttoned Up*, I'm independent—for five years now I can—never mind. You know how many people have seen *All Buttoned Up*. And sure they go out laughing at Roderick, the revolutionary bum. But the gimmick is all the time I'm laughing at them for being sucked in. I get them coming and going, Marv, don't you see. I—"

"I won't stand for it," Marvin broke in, pounding the table before him with his loose, hairy fist until the glasses rattled. "I warn you, I won't stand for it. I drank your toasts to the Critics' Circle Award and Prix de Rome, but only on the understanding that no one plays games with me. You're petty-bourgeois conformists. You're whores. Okay, these are the facts. Now, I'm not too proud to sit with whores; I'll even let a whore buy me a drink. But only on the condition that he wears his identification ticket: I AM A WHORE—and underneath it, I LIKE IT! or HOW UNHAPPY I AM! This much is optional; but no *principles*, for God's sake! That's my department. You have everything else: money, prizes, new wives, admiring coeds. I don't resent it. Only admit what you are. I warn you, I won't stand for it!"

"What'll you do, Marv?" Howard asked mildly. "Write an article?" He pretended he could not hear Jessie, who whispered at him from across the table, "The man is sick, Howard. For pity's sake, he's sick."

Marvin refused to dignify his challenge with an answer and Bill, nonplused, had sunk back into his seat, his mouth working soundlessly. The rest stared at each other, unwilling or unable to pick up the conversations they had dropped to listen to Marvin, when Eva's voice rang out astonishingly distinct in the hush. It was the first thing they had heard her say. "Do you understand all this, darling?" She blew into Leonard's ear, bit the lobe gently. She had refused to sit anywhere except beside him, despite Molly-o's outraged protest.

"Certainly."

"But it's ridiculous, darling."

"Of course it's ridiculous, but that's not the point. This is a language for unhappy people—a way of pretending that unhappiness is virtue. Once I talked this language, too."

"But now you're happy and sensible, aren't you, Leonard? And lucky, too, because it *pays* to be happy in America, to give up crazy talk about classes and conformity and discuss the New Criticism or transubstantiation or how many angels can dance on the head of a Thomist poet." Marvin glared first at Leonard, then at Eva's crucifix.

"Why do you all *listen* to him, then? Why do you sit there apologizing to him, as if he were a fuehrer or something?" Eva had risen to her feet, brushing a long, blond lock of hair out of her eyes with the back of one hand. She was very red, and her lower lip trembled as if she might break into tears at any moment. "Don't you see, he's not only silly, he's vicious—a diseased man tearing at everything that's healthy. I suppose you all read his asinine article 'Fanny Freud at the Harpsichord,' and snickered over it, and thought how smart he was and how smart you were for knowing it. Well, Leonard doesn't care a hoot for what Mr. Marvin Solomon says about his poetry. After all, Leonard writes it, and Marvin is just a mad dog baying at the—at the—*whatever* it is." Her voice, tremulous throughout, broke, and she retreated behind her glass of milk, again scarlet and trembling.

"Take a tranquilizer," Bernie advised her. "Beatie swears by them."

"Never mind," Howard said. "It is refreshing to find a wife ready to defend her husband. But Leonard needs no defense. Who reads what Marv writes anymore? Not even us. . . ."

He had, of course, read carefully through Marvin's attack on Leonard, as he read (and the rest with him) each rare piece he wrote, his writing obviously blocked now except when malice moved him to snarl at some younger and more successful friend. It had become clear to everyone long since that Marvin would never write the long epic poem on the Wobblies or the immense study of American culture in four volumes that he had talked about all his life. But how to explain this to the girl with her cross and her glass of milk; how to make clear the sense in which Marvin (though only two or three years older) had been the father of them all, the model for the insolence and involution that they had learned from him to think the hallmarks of the revolutionary intellectual. "Bodhisattva" they had called him when they were in high school, and they had quoted his remarks to each other, passing them from hand to hand until they were worn out—their chief inheritance.

Howard knew that Marv clung to the old counters still, the inviable clichés of Marxism, not because he believed in them, but because they had once been tokens of his power to compel love and respect. In a sense, he held them in trust for them all, their onetime papa, now the keeper of the museum of their common past. He felt an obligation to insult Marvin publicly as Marvin in the first place had taught him to do, to respond to Marv's insults as if they mattered. It was the last possible gesture of respect; to have greeted his sallies with silence would have been to reveal pity, and that Marvin could never have stood.

"Never mind," Howard repeated to Eva. "Nobody takes Marv seriously anyway, a man who writes from rage and out of weakness in a magazine no one sees, except the wives and friends of the author he's giving the treatment. What do you call it again, Marvin, that journal for boys who never grew up? *Peter Pan, Boy's Life, Our Sunday Messenger?*"

"*Contempt*," Achsa answered for her husband. "*Contempt*, you clown!"

"Ah yes, *Contempt, or the Fountain of Youth*. No forty-year-old ex-post-Marxist can read it without sobbing to his image in the mirror, 'They're playing our song!' Believe it or not, I think Marvin really knows that an attack from him under such auspices helps a book, and since he's fast becoming a kindly old man—"

"Listen, Howard—"

"Listen, Howard—"

"Listen, Howard—"

Marvin, Achsa and Bernie, all three beginning at precisely the same moment and in precisely the same way, collapsed in laughter, while Jessie groaned aloud. She thinks I'm showing off for Molly-o, Howard told himself; and maybe I am, maybe I am. . . . But Molly was not even listening.

"Quiet, *please*," Bernie announced into the hubbub, pounding his glass with a fork. "Everyone's too melancholy. I'm going to tell a joke!"

"I thought that's what Howard was doing," Jessie said.

"Well, since you all insist, reluctantly I'll do it. It seems that one day Mendel meets his old friend Sidney on the street and says to him, 'Sidney, where've you been? For two weeks I haven't seen you in the office, on the street. . . .' 'I've been on my honeymoon!' 'Don't kid me,' Mendel says. 'You've been married already for—' 'Twenty-five years,' Sidney finishes. 'A second honeymoon. We went back to the identical hotel in Atlantic City, took the identical room—' "

"Wouldn't you say this is a little long, Bernie?" Achsa asked.

"Sh! I guarantee you you'll love it. Where was I? So, Sidney says to Mendel, 'Everything exactly the same. We had the same waiters; we ate at the same table, the same chopped liver, the same chicken soup—' "

"Do you have to recite the whole menu?" Achsa broke in again.

"Look," Leonard said. "There are at least two people here who've listened to this rigamarole three times before. I for one won't sit through it again." He was pale with anger. "If it's an appropriate joke you want, I know one that's shorter at least."

"I can never remember them," Molly said. "I hear some really cute ones, but—"

"This man and his wife were making love," Leonard persisted, "when suddenly he says—"

"Oh, Leonard, not that *nauseating* one," Jessie cried. "It's exactly what I knew you were going to—"

"This is the ghost at the feast, isn't it?" Leonard screamed. "Irving isn't the only victim of heart failure. It's the disease of us all without benefit of doctors: failure of the heart, failure of the genitals, failure of love. This is the critical fact of our lives—the specter that's haunting New Jersey and Westport and Paducah and Brooklyn. But we don't tell, do we? Not in Bill's plays or my poems or Howard's paintings—only in Bernie's crummy jokes. Ha-ha!"

"Please, Leonard darling," Eva implored him.

"I'll be damned if I'll let them sit around for the rest of the night sniffing at you and me." His voice rose even more shrilly. "Well, I broke out of the trap, and so did Bill; that's what they'll never forgive us for. That's why they're sitting there right now cooking up nasty little stories about us that will last through a whole year of parties. Am I right, Bill?"

Bill was sound asleep at the head of the table, his head cradled in his arms, and the corkscrew, symbol of authority, lying beside him.

"Well, *I* know about it anyhow. *I* know what it is to lie side by side with a woman you've made love to so many times you feel sick and silly when you add up the total—and each of you dead to the other. Such things may not happen to you, Achsa and Marvin, or you, Jess and Howard, or you, Beatie and Bernie; for you the honeymoon may last twenty years. You'll just have to take it on faith that it happened to me, to me and Lucille, who—"

"I told you, Howard, if he mentioned my friend's name in the same room with that silly little girl, I'd—" Jessie wove around the table and stood behind her husband's chair, straddle-legged, her fists on her hips.

"What do you want me to do? Hit him? Should I knock him down for you, Jessie, because he offended divorced American womanhood?"

"She may not have been good enough for you, Leonard," Achsa interrupted him impatiently, "but she's so much more of a woman than you'll *ever* be a man that it's a scandal. You and your masculine-protest-type beard that doesn't fool anybody for one minute! She was a splint for your poor feeble masculinity, Leonard, a splint. Don't think that I don't know that before her, you couldn't even—"

"Achsa, what's the point of dragging up all the bedroom gossip you ever heard? All I'm trying to say is—"

"I wasn't the one who started bringing up bedroom gossip, Leonard, but since you began it, I'll just finish. I'm sure this will all be very educational for your new wife, who's been getting your special version of things. I'm sure she'll appreciate knowing that without Lucille you couldn't—"

"Hell's bells, I'm not trying to justify myself against Lucille, Achsa. I'm a bastard, I know."

"You can say that again," Achsa screamed triumphantly, working her way slowly around the table to put an arm around Jessie's waist. "Now tell us exactly what *kind* of a bastard you are. I have a few little anecdotes to contribute that you may have forgotten."

"All I mean is, what else can you do when—"

"You can shut up, Leonard. So much you can always do." Beatie moved as she spoke toward the other two women, finally taking up a position on the other side of Jessie, though not yet touching her—like a last reserve. "We love you still, Leonard, believe it nor not; but don't you see what an offense it is to bring that poor, sweet girl here and sit smooching with her. I wish you a hundred good years with her and a dozen children, but only—"

" 'Poor, sweet girl,' with that ridiculous voodoo charm around her neck. I tell you—"

"Never mind the voodoo charm, Achsa. We all have our idiocies and that's not the worst. Leonard, all I say to you is this: go sit in a corner like a good boy and hold your Eva's hand, but leave us grown-ups alone."

"Beatie, I can talk to *you*. You're no fishwife. What do you *do* Beatie, when you lie side by side with somebody, two people seeing each other naked, knowing each other by heart, as they say, but without love. It's not tolerable, Beatie. What do you *do?*"

"Lie side by side with the dignity of failure. There is no love." Marvin rose at last with the air of one contributing the final wisdom; he spoke more slowly than any of the others and from his greater height, very pale above their heads.

"Marvin, I tell you right now that if you say 'failure' or 'dignity' again tonight, I'll—I'll throw a water pitcher at your head. I'll—I'll—" Beatie put an arm around Achsa now, soothing her, while Jessie on her other side squeezed her waist without a word. "All right," Beatie kept saying over and over, "all right, all right."

Coffee had been set before everyone, and tasting it now, they discovered it had grown cold. The cognac they dutifully swallowed without tasting, but no one was capable of getting any drunker. Suddenly they had nothing more to say, and they looked away from each other in pained silence, like Leonard's perhaps legendary husbands and wives, wondering what dead and irrecoverable passion had left them stranded in an association that, without it, was merely absurd.

"Oh, let's *dance!*" Eva cried at the top of her voice, sensing that only a shout could break so deep a silence. She made her way to the hi-fi set in the mirrored room, fiddling with the knobs until music assailed them again from the corners.

It was as if not their images only, bedraggled and dim-eyed, but the sound, too, was reflected from glass to glass across the immense room. Bernie and Leonard had carried Bill in, sagging between them, to deposit him in the bishop's chair, where he rolled over once and sank back snoring. Jessie, Achsa and Beatie sat side by side on a sofa, leaning their heads together and whispering like conspirators, while Marvin pulled down book after book from the wall shelves, glancing briefly and disapprovingly in each.

Molly-o had flung herself on the floor, gazing meditatively down between her breasts, her back nestled down into a white bearskin rug. "I'm too warm—and too full—and I drank too much," she announced mournfully, unbuttoning two more buttons of her shirt and smoothing her breeches across the hips.

Bill once dropped, Leonard had taken Eva in his arms, and they were moving together again in their slow un-dance off in one corner. No one joined them.

"We have squash courts in the basement," Molly said without much conviction, snuggling even more sensually into the white fur, "and Ping-Pong tables—and sixty-two bedrooms, if anyone is inclined to—"

"The only game that interests me is craps," Bernie said. "If some of you gentlemen—"

"What about Guggenheim?" Marvin asked.

"Guggenheim!" Achsa cried scornfully. "Next it'll be charades."

"I can't play any of those category games," Molly said, looking quite pleased with herself all the same. "I'm too stupid."

"The only thing I ever played in my life," Howard put in from the doorway, where he stood gulping the damp, cold air by way of therapy, "was croquet. I was at Yaddo in '49, and all the time we weren't at the racetrack, we were playing—"

"You mean that stupid game for children with wooden balls?" Achsa asked.

"I never knew a child with— Isn't there some danger of splinters—" Bernie began, whooping with delight.

"Were you at Yaddo, *too?*" Molly-o inquired, slowly easing herself over, then rising to sit on her feet like a Japanese. She looked admiringly at Howard as if she had just discovered his most dazzling distinction. "Bill was there once. Long, long ago in '38."

"That's not so long ago," Howard objected. "It was that year that the Museum of Modern Art bought my—" .

"I was six years old," Molly said, casting her eyes down modestly.

"Oy! Oy! Oy!" Beatie cried out. "It's the only answer. Oy! Oy! Oy! Imagine it, six years old."

"Bill says that in '38, they used to play *nude* croquet!" Molly lingered over the vowel of the magic word again. "You know, at night when the middle-aged prudes were asleep. There were lots of interesting people there that year. I don't remember their—"

"Marianne Moore and T. S. Eliot," Marvin suggested. "They'd look good at nude croquet."

"And Henry James," Jessie added.

"We have a croquet set somewhere, don't we, Bill?" In her mounting excitement, Molly ignored their quips. "Don't we? Don't we?" She ran over, silent on her bare feet, and shook her husband until he opened his eyes, staring at her unseeingly. *"Don't* we have a croquet set? We can play it *nude,* just like you used to do at Yaddo, can't we, Bill? It'll save the whole party! Howard, why don't *you* go down into the basement and look just behind the steps. I'm sure you'll find it, in a big cardboard box that says—"

"Croquet, I'll bet," Howard finished for her, while Bill, blinking sightlessly, repeated, "Nude . . . nude . . . nude . . . ." and fell back again onto the seat snoring.

"Oh, Bill!" Molly sighed, then turning once more to Howard, "Well, we'll just have to play without him!"

"**I**t's raining again," Howard said by way of answer. He had been holding one hand outside the door, cupped under the dripping eaves; and he wiped it off now on Molly's plump cheek. "Wet! It's a bog out there. You'll have to make it water polo."

"Oh, we're not going to play out there, silly. We'll play in here where it's all comfy. Right *here!* Just move some of these chairs back—and turn off that ridiculous music, and we're all set." As she snapped it off Leonard and Eva stood gasping in the sudden silence, like a couple of sea creatures hauled out of their element. "Well, get it, please. Go and get it," she insisted, laying a hand on Howard's arm.

"Howard," Jessie warned him, rising to her feet. "Let's not commit ourselves to anything childish. Really, it's late already and we have a long way to go."

"It's only eleven thirty-seven," Howard answered, consulting his watch. What he would have done if his wife had not intervened he was not sure; but there was nothing to do now but go after the croquet set and see what would happen.

He found himself wishing that it would not be there, but, of course, discovered it immediately (he who could never find anything at home) at the bottom of the steps where Molly had said it would be. He wrestled the clumsy cardboard box up the steep stairs, tearing a chunk of flesh out of the back of one hand on the doorjamb and scarcely feeling it. "It's here," he said triumphantly, casting it down at Molly's feet and sucking the bleeding place. He liked the taste of his blood. "Strip already!"

He had thought he was joking, but before he could laugh or try to stop her, Molly had stripped off her shirt, leaving herself bare to the waist. "Think fast!" she said, tossing the checkered blouse at him and beginning to fumble with the buttons of her riding breeches.

Bill, still asleep, writhed on the oaken chair, calling out in a choked voice, "Please, please, please . . ." and Bernie rushed toward Molly-o in sudden panic, pulling off his jacket to put around her shoulders. "What is this? Minsky's?" he yelled, flushing and paling by turns. "We're not going to go through with this craziness, are we? What are we anyway, high-school children who think you're only living when you take off your clothes? Howard, you tell her—you're an artist, naked women are your bread and butter. A joke is a joke, but I'm forty-four years old—forty-four—an underwear salesman."

"What are you getting so excited about?" Howard calmed him, feeling superior to them all. "Let's be reasonable about this and—"

"Reasonable!" Molly flung Bernie's jacket contemptuously aside, and stepping out of her breeches now, confronted them in a pair of pale green pants (the color of her eyes), covered with tiny red hearts. "Well, what are we waiting for?" Her skin was smooth and tight, unmarred by childbearing and unmarked even by the crease of brassiere or girdle. On shoulder and thigh, breast and belly alike she was tanned the rich brown of one who turns patiently under the sunlamp, reading a fashion magazine and loving nothing more than her own flesh.

"Just because Bill married a nudnick, do I have to play the bohemian in my old age? Nude croquet! I don't know which is worse, the nude or the croquet! Listen, Howard, God knows we've got nothing to show each other by letting down our pants. We're naked enough now, for Christ's sake!"

"Bernie's right," Marvin said, looking directly at Molly, who had gone on undressing and stood now with her underpants hanging delicately from silvered thumb and forefinger; if he saw her, he registered nothing. "It would be more to the point to put on steel masks and lead drawers, to hide in all decency a nakedness we can no longer pretend is exciting or beautiful. All our compromises are hanging out, our withered principles dangling obscenely. We can't even remember to button our flies!"

"My God, what *difference* does it make!" Achsa cried out. "Let's show what we can't hide anyway. Let these children look at what they have to become, what they are already, even if their mirrors aren't ready to tell them yet. I only wish I could take off my *skin,* too." Her dress and slip, her brassiere with the discreet padding, the girdle she wore only to hold up her stockings, she had off in a moment, rolling them into a ball and heaving them at her husband's head. He did not even lift a hand to block them, but bowed as they went past him, smiling obscurely to himself. Achsa was almost completely breastless, skinny and yellow with strange knobby knees and two scars across her flat, flaccid belly.

"You've all gone nuts," Bernie protested. "Nuts! I'm getting out of here before I find myself galloping bare-ass like a kid. What are we doing, grown men and women? Maybe it's kiddie night in the bughouse! Beatie, come on." He had picked up his rumpled, Italian-silk jacket, stuck his panama on the back of his bald head. "Well, come on!"

"I'm not coming, Bernard," Beatie answered quietly, bending over and beginning to unlace the sensible shoes into which her solid, unlovely legs descended. "I'm going to stay."

"You're going to play nude croquet—*nude* croquet? Are you crazy, too?"

"No—only a little drunk. Nude croquet, nude pinochle! Achsa's right, what difference does it make. Listen, Bernie, I manage to get one night in three months away from the kids—away from a house of flu and measles and diaper rashes. Well, this is the night and here I am and so I intend to stay at least till I've done something I'm sorry for. Do you understand? Excuse me, Bernie, but tonight I don't go home early."

"You're not only drunk," he screamed, pulling her by the arm. "You're crazy, plain, ordinary crazy."

"So, I'm crazy. Just let go of me, Bernie. *Let go of me!*" She turned on him, her usually mild gaze now coldly ferocious, staring at him until he dropped his hold, then bent down to pull off her stockings. "Go home, Bernie, and when you get there, wake up little David and tell him his mama says—tell him I say— 'Merry Christmas.' "

Everyone laughed and Molly shouted, "Hooray!"

"I'm giving you one more chance, Beatie." Bernie stood at the door, his nylon shirt dark with sweat, his coat dangling from his hand. "I for one will not—"

"Oh, *go* already," she sobbed. "Go! Can't you see I'm living it up? A real orgy." She flung her head down onto Jessie's lap weeping. She did not even see Bernie when, a moment later, he stuck his head back through the door, glowered around the room and, crying, "To hell with you all!" disappeared for good.

"Why don't *you* go, too?" Achsa asked, whirling on her husband. But

Marvin was already undressing without a word, placing his black shoes, his socks with the garters attached, his pants folded neatly onto a bookshelf which he had cleared by throwing the books on the floor. His limp, usually almost unnoticeable, grew more evident as he stripped.

Beatie meanwhile had staggered to her feet again, her shoes in her hand, and was making her way to the door, yelling, "Wait, Bernie. I'm coming. Wait! What am I doing here?"

"He's gone," Howard said, stopping her and whirling her around. He was one drink past the simplest truth, and so he lied to her without thinking, though he could still see through the window the red gleam of Bernie's Cadillac, in which he must have been sitting in sullen indecision and self-pity. "It'll do him good to spend a few hours imagining you in a game of nude croquet."

"I don't know what got into me," Beatie sobbed. "You don't understand, Howard. He's in trouble, bad trouble, and I should stand by him. What else can a wife do but stick with her husband? It's her duty, isn't it, no matter what? I just don't know what got into me. I—" She dissolved once more into tears, Howard patting her head uncertainly, until all at once she looked up and winked. "It's all a joke, right, Howard? 'Duty,' 'husband,' 'stand by'—a *joke!* That's what's so hard to remember." She sat sprawled on a gilt-and-brocade chair that looked frail and ridiculous under her, her legs spread wide and one hand on her heart. "I'm here and I'll play if it kills me. Jessie, come here and help unbutton me."

"Oh, *good,*" Molly shouted, clapping her hands. "Good for you. You're a real sport!"

"Some sport," Beatie responded ruefully. "Poor Bernie!"

"And what about those two?" Achsa pointed to one corner where Leonard and Eva stood staring at each other mutely, their hands clasped. Then, even as she spoke, they began to undress each other, still without a word, moving in a slow pantomime that converted each unbuckling or tug of a zipper into a caress.

"And you, Jessie?" Howard turned deliberately toward his wife, wondering exactly how angry she was. He had already taken off his shirt and his T-shirt revealed his fat chest, the thick blond prickles which covered it.

"Whatever you say, Howard." She was apparently going to try the tack of patient submission. "If you want me to join in this—"

"Certainly. You're only young once."

She sighed a little; she had never looked so haggard, so ugly. "Tell me, Molly, is there a room on this floor where I could undress? I'm in poor shape for climbing stairs."

"A room! To undress!" Howard protested, feeling the request as somehow an intended rebuke. "But we're all going to be playing in here together in a minute, without a—"

"What harm does it do you, Howard? I'm willing to stand naked side by side with these young things and let you make comparisons, since it amuses you to torture yourself in this way. But getting undressed is a private matter for me. For pity's sake, indulge me a little. You can stay here with your—"

"I'll come with you," Howard volunteered, not quite knowing why.

"There's a room in there," Molly-o said, shrugging her shoulders a little contemptuously so that her breasts bounced. She pointed a tapering, tanned arm toward a door on her right. "A music room we hardly use anymore."

Howard followed Jessie into the darkness, though she had walked off without even looking back in his direction and he knew he would be able to find nothing to say to her. When he reached for the wall switch, Jessie put a hand over it to prevent him; but she had left the door open a little so that in the mitigated gloom he could make out a dozen or so spindly chairs hunched under dust covers around the walls, a love seat also protected from the dust, a piano and, behind it, a harp.

"It's a harp!" Jessie said wonderingly, touching the strings lightly until they responded with a tingling and humming that filled the shadowy room. "Let's go home, Howard. Let's get out of here. You said before—"

"A ghost of a harp. No. It's too late now." He hung his pants on the harp, muting the strings. "Oh, Lord, now that we've decided to stay, I've got to go."

"There's another door on the other side of the room. I imagine that somewhere through there— Can you see all right in the dark? Please, Howard, couldn't we just—"

"No, no, no. I can see fine." But he lurched and stumbled in the darkness, nearly tripping over one of the hooded chairs, and staggered finally into a lighted corridor, flanked by the john.

Coming out again, he almost walked into Molly-o, who flung her arms around his neck and kissed him briskly. Her breasts were astonishingly firm despite their size, the nipples, not brownish or purple but really pink as a child would paint them, hard enough to press uncomfortably into his soft flesh. Jessie's, he thought dimly, had never been like this even when she was quite young. "Oh, *thank* you, Howard," Molly said breathlessly. "You saved the party. I thought we were going to have to sit there and *talk* all night. I had you all wrong. I—"

He grabbed her again, returning the kiss hard, his hands slipping down her back until he held her around the hips. Her mouth fell open all the way under his and he could feel her knees bend, her body sag, though whether from passion or alcohol he could not tell. I'm just doing this to shut her up anyway, he told himself; I'm not even excited. . . .

He jumped suddenly under a resounding smack on his right buttock, and Molly skittered off, smiling at him vaguely over her shoulder. Beatie stood behind him, grinning broadly and quite naked. *"Shmendrick!"* she said. "Big Brother is watching. Do you call this croquet?"

She had not called him *shmendrick,* Howard realized, since they were both fifteen and they had fumbled their way into what was the first affair for both of them, more like friends playing than lovers. Then Beatie had really fallen in love for the first time and—somehow thirty years had gone by! "Thirty years!" he said, perhaps aloud, but Beatie did not respond. He looked incredulously at her body, a girl's body when he had touched it last, now all at once full-blown, the muscle tone gone, the legs mottled blue-black with varicose veins—like someone's mother.

"I was just—" he stuttered. "That is—"

"Never mind," Beatie answered. "Before you lie to me, I believe you. Go find Jessie."

As he turned around confusedly, looking for a way back into the music room, Howard had the impression that the door through which he had come was closed softly, as if Jessie had been watching him, too, and was now withdrawing. But when he entered, she was lying facedown on the love seat, her naked back rising and falling regularly.

"Are you asleep?" he whispered.

"Asleep!" she answered, rolling over. "You bastard, come here." She pulled him to her, winding her arms around him with a ferocity that astonished him. She had not clung to him so desperately in years. "Oh, hold me, Howard, and for God's sake don't say anything. Tight, tight, *tight!"*

When they rejoined the others, they discovered that someone had set the record player going again, and that the overhead lights had been turned off. Only two huge gilded and twisted candlesticks illuminated the big room now, one set before each of the wall-length mirrors; and reflected back and forth, from glass to gleaming body to glass, the points of light were multiplied to thousands. Leather-bound folios, opened to the middle and set spine up, did duty for wickets. The others were already bent over the varicolored balls, mallets in hand. They had begun to scream insults and encouragement at each other, at ease in the friendly dark that camouflaged their bulges and creases and broken veins.

After a while, he could begin to make them out more clearly through the flickering shadows: Leonard, vaguely hermaphroditic, pudgy and white; Eva, her cross falling just where her pancake makeup gave way to the slightly pimpled pallor of her skin (there was the mark of a bite on one small breast); Jessie, whose body was astonishingly younger than her lined, witch's face, but whose gray below betrayed the red splendor of her hair; Achsa, tallow-yellow and without breasts; Beatie, marked with the red griddle of her corseting and verging on shapelessness; Marvin, sallow and unmuscled beneath the lank black hair that covered even his upper arms. He dragged more and more wearily behind him a withered left leg, creased from hip to knee by a puckered and livid scar, testimony to the osteomyelitis that had kept him in bed through most of his childhood. Only Molly pranced and preened, secure in her massaged and sunlamped loveliness. To each of the others nudity was a confession, a humiliation. Yet they laughed louder and louder, though no one knew precisely what he was doing; and the crack of mallet on ball punctuated their chatter.

❶nce in the hubbub, Beatie drew Howard aside into the music room where he and Jessie had undressed. She was crying abandonedly once more, snorting and heaving and dripping tears that seemed somehow ridiculous above the expanse of her nakedness. "What's going to be with me and Bernie, Howard?" she asked, not in hope of an answer, he knew, but because the question had to be spoken aloud. "He's in bad trouble, sicker than anyone knows—under analysis. Don't tell anyone, Howard, not even Jessie. He doesn't want—and I let him go away alone. He couldn't any more take his clothes off in front of these people, than—I don't know—than finish the novel he's been working on secretly since he was in high school."

What did he have to tell her, what wisdom for all his forty-five years? He may have kissed her then, for he had come always to kiss women when he was at a loss with them—another laziness.

All other episodes, however, faded into the confusion of the endless and pointless game, and into the mockery of Marvin which finally became its point. All the rest, varyingly drunk and skillful, slapped an occasional shot through an improvised folio wicket, or successfully cracked an opponent's ball away from a favorable spot; but Marvin, incredibly uncoordinated, could do nothing. Sometimes, his leg buckling under him, he would miss the ball completely, denting the hardwood floor with his mallet or catching it under a Persian rug; sometimes the ball would skid off the edge of his hammer, trickle two or three inches to one side and maddeningly stop. Once the head of his mallet flew off at the end of a particularly wild swing, just missing Molly's eye.

After a while, they were all trailing after him, Achsa leading the pack, like the gallery of a champion golfer, roaring at every stroke, while Marvin said nothing, only more grimly and comically addressed the ball. The real horror, Howard felt, was that Marvin now *wanted* to smack the elusive object before him squarely through the wicket, to win the applause of his mockers. For all that he knew it to be nonsense, Marvin had been somehow persuaded that it *mattered*—reliving, Howard supposed, the ignominy of his childhood, when in the street and to the jeers of his fellows he had failed at caddy or stoopball or kick the can.

Drawing the stick back between his scarred and rickety legs, Marvin delivered a stroke finally with such force and imbalance that he toppled over onto his face. He lay there for a little while motionless, his pale, skinny buttocks twitching, while they all laughed and hooted and cheered. They could not afford to admit that it was anything but a joke.

Only Eva, who had screamed at him earlier, was moved to protest.

"Oh, don't!" she cried, whirling on the rest with tears in her eyes. "Please, *don't!* Can't you see he's like a fallen king—a fallen king!" She took a step toward him, but could not bring herself to touch his pale, sweaty body, and ended covering her eyes with the hand she had reached out toward him in sympathy.

"A fallen king!" Achsa repeated contemptuously, sensing the others were slipping away from her, beginning to feel shame and pity. "Why don't you get up, your majesty, and say a few words about the dignity of failure?" She was hopelessly drunk and the efforts of Jessie and Beatie to quiet her only seemed to infuriate her the more.

"He likes it down there on the floor and in the dark," she continued. "Don't disturb him, my fallen king. He's working out Canto Twenty-four of the Epic, volume three of the Cultural History. Don't laugh so loud. You might wake him and American literature will suffer." She leaned over and tapped her husband lightly on the side of the head with the flat of her mallet. "Get up! Get up, Marvin, and try again. You're holding up the game. Get up!" He rose slowly into a sitting position, very pale and avoiding her eyes. "Maybe you'd like to make a statement," she insisted. "Maybe you'd like to—"

"Give me a hand, Howard," he said. "I guess I'm higher than I thought. I need a—"

"I'll give you a hand," Achsa screamed before Howard could move; and she held out the end of her mallet toward Marvin, who made no move to lay hold of it. "Here, *take* it!" she cried in rage, drawing it back and smashing it full force across his left cheek. "How come you don't say 'Thank you,' Marv? Say 'Thank you' to the nice lady!" She hit him harder this time on the other side of the head; and when he remained silent, harder and harder still, first right, then left, then right. She could hardly breathe. "Why don't you talk to me, Marvin? Why don't you *talk* to me? Say 'Thank you,' Marvin. Why don't you say 'Thank you'?"

Howard, who had stood by paralyzed with the rest, grabbed her under the arms, dragging her backwards with her feet in the air, and hanging on grimly though she leaned over to sink her teeth into the back of his hand.

"Smack her, Howard," Jessie advised him. "For pity's sake, slap her. She's hysterical." But he did not dare shift his hold, for fear of losing his purchase on her damp and squirming flesh.

Meanwhile, Marvin had risen very slowly to his feet, a thin trickle of blood running out of one corner of his mouth and down over his chin. "I—I—" he began twice over. "I—" then sank to his knees, moaning. "Achsa," he yelled in terror. "Achsa, for God's sake, the pills in my pocket—my right— It's another attack, another—" His words burbled away into incoherence; then, grasping his upper left arm in his right hand and lifting his chin into the air, he cried out in agony. His mouth was drawn back, his teeth showing in what may have been a smile, and his wordless cry may have turned again into Achsa's name before he pitched forward on his face again; but Howard could not be sure.

"Let me go! Let me go!" Achsa begged him, kicking and scratching. "What are you doing to him? My Marvin! Let me go!" He finally released his hold at the moment the overhead lights were switched on again, fixing them all in their nudity and helplessness, caught for one everlasting instant as in a flashlight still.

Molly had begun to scream, a single note, high and pure, that seemed as if it would never end; and whirling about, they all stared at her in the hard light, even Bill, startled back to awareness on his bishop's throne. One arm concealing her breasts, the other thrust downward so that her hand hid the meeting of her thighs, Molly-o confronted them in the classic pose of nakedness surprised, as if she knew for the first time what it meant to be really nude.

[SEPTEMBER 1957]

STANLEY ELKIN

I Look Out

for Ed Wolfe

Stanley Elkin (1930–   ) was born in New York City and is now the Merle Kling Professor of Modern Letters at Washington University in St. Louis. Among his novels are Boswell, A Bad Man, The Dick Gibson Show, *and* George Mills, *which won the National Book Critics Circle Award for fiction. His stories and novellas have been collected in* Searches & Seizures, Criers and Kibitzers, Kibitzers and Criers, *and* Van Gogh's Room at Arles.

He was an orphan, and, to himself, he seemed like one, looked like one. His orphan's features were as true of himself as are their pale, pinched faces to the blind. At twenty-seven he was a neat, thin young man in white shirts and light suits with lintless pockets. Something about him suggested the ruthless isolation, the hard self-sufficiency of the orphaned, the peculiar dignity of men seen eating alone in restaurants on national holidays. Yet it was this perhaps which shamed him chiefly, for there was a suggestion, too, that his impregnability was a myth, a smell not of the furnished room which he did not inhabit, but of the three-room apartment on a good street which he did. The very excellence of his taste, conditioned by need and lack, lent to him the odd, maidenly primness of the lonely.

He saved the photographs of strangers and imprisoned them behind clear plastic windows in his wallet. In the sound of his own voice he detected the accent of the night school and the correspondence course, and nothing of the fat, sunny ring of the world's casually afternooned. He strove against himself, a supererogatory enemy, and sought by a kind of helpless abrasion, as one rubs wood, the gleaming self beneath. An orphan's thinness, he thought, was no accident.

Returning from lunch he entered the office building where he worked. It was an old building, squat and gargoyled, brightly patched where sandblasters had once worked and then quit before they had finished. He entered the lobby, which smelled always of disinfectant, and walked past the wide, dirty glass of the cigarette-and-candy counter to the single elevator, as thickly barred as a cell.

The building was an outlaw. Low rents and a downtown address and the landlord's indifference had brought together from the peripheries of business and professionalism a strange band of entrepreneurs and visionaries, men desperately but imaginatively failing: an eye doctor who corrected vision by massage; a radio evangelist; a black-belt judo champion; a self-help organization for crippled veterans; dealers in pornographic books, in paper flowers, in fireworks, in plastic jewelry, in the artificial, in the artfully made, in the imitated, in the copied, in the stolen, the unreal, the perversion, the plastic, the schlock.

On the sixth floor the elevator opened and the young man, Ed Wolfe, stepped out.

He passed the Association for the Indians, passed Plasti-Pens, passed *Coffin & Tombstone,* passed Soldier Toys, passed Prayer-a-Day. He walked by the opened door of C. Morris Brut, Chiropractor, and saw him, alone, standing at a mad attention, framed in the arching golden nimbus of his inverted name on the window, squeezing handballs.

He looked quickly away but Dr. Brut saw him and came toward him, putting the handballs in his shirt pocket, where they bulged awkwardly. He held him by the elbow. Ed Wolfe looked at the yellowing tile beneath his feet, infinitely diamonded, chipped, the floor of a public toilet, and saw Dr. Brut's dusty shoes. He stared sadly at the jagged, broken glass of the mail chute.

"Ed Wolfe, take care of yourself," Dr. Brut said.

"Right."

"Regard your posture in life. A tall man like yourself looks terrible when he slumps. Don't be a *schlump.* It's not good for the organs."

"I'll watch it."

"When the organs get out of line the man begins to die."

"I know."

"You say so. How many guys make promises. Brains in the brainpan. Balls in the strap. The bastards downtown." He meant doctors in hospitals, in clinics, on boards, nonorphans with M.D. degrees and special license plates and respectable patients who had Blue Cross, charts, died in clean hospital rooms. They were the bastards downtown, his personal New Deal, his neighborhood Wall Street banker. A disease cartel. "They won't tell you. The white bread kills you. The cigarettes. The whiskey. The sneakers. The high heels. They won't tell you. Me, *I'll* tell you."

"I appreciate it."

"Wise guy. Punk. I'm a friend. I give a father's advice."

"I'm an orphan."

"I'll adopt you."

"I'm late for work."

"We'll open a clinic. 'C. Morris Brut and Adopted Son.' "

"It's something to think about."

"Poetry," Dr. Brut said and walked back to his office, his posture stiff, awkward, a man in a million who knew how to hold himself.

Ed Wolfe went on to his own office. He walked in. The sad-faced telephone girl was saying, "Cornucopia Finance Corporation." She pulled the wire out of the board and slipped her headset around her neck, where it hung like a delicate horse collar. "Mr. La Meck wants to see you. But don't go in yet. He's talking to somebody."

He went toward his desk at one end of the big main office. Standing, fists on the desk, he turned to the girl. "What happened to my call cards?"

"Mr. La Meck took them," the girl said.

"Give me the carbons," Ed Wolfe said. "I've got to make some calls."

She looked embarrassed. The face went through a weird change, the sadness taking on an impossible burden of shame so that she seemed massively tragic, like a hit-and-run driver. "I'll get them," she said, moving out of the chair heavily. Ed Wolfe thought of Dr. Brut.

He took the carbons and fanned them out on the desk. He picked one in an intense, random gesture like someone drawing a number on a public stage. He dialed rapidly.

As the phone buzzed brokenly in his ear he felt the old excitement. Someone at the other end greeted him sleepily.

"Mr. Flay? This is Ed Wolfe at Cornucopia Finance." (*Can you cope, can you cope?* he hummed to himself.)

"Who?"

"Ed Wolfe. I've got an unpleasant duty," he began pleasantly. "You've skipped two payments."

"I didn't skip nothing. I called the girl. She said it was okay."

"That was three months ago. She meant it was all right to miss a few days. Listen, Mr. Flay, we've got that call recorded, too. Nothing gets by."

"I'm a little short."

"Grow."

"I couldn't help it," the man said. Ed Wolfe didn't like the cringing tone. Petulance and anger he could meet with his own petulance, his own anger. But guilt would have to be met with his own guilt and that, here, was irrelevant.

"Don't con me, Flay. You're a troublemaker. What are you, Flay, a Polish person? Flay isn't a Polish name, but your address . . ."

"What's that?"

"What are you? Are you Polish?"

"What's that to you? What difference does it make?" That was more like it, Ed Wolfe thought warmly.

"That's what you are, Flay. You're a Pole. It's guys like you who give your race a bad name. Half our bugouts are Polish persons."

"Listen. You can't . . ."

He began to shout. *"You* listen. You wanted the car. The refrigerator. The chintzy furniture. The sectional you saw in the funny papers. And we paid for it, right?"

"Listen. The money I owe is one thing, the way . . ."

"We paid for it, right?"

"That doesn't . . ."

"Right? Right?"

"Yes, you . . ."

"Okay. You're in trouble, Warsaw. You're in terrible trouble. It means a lien. A judgment. We've got lawyers. You've got nothing. We'll pull the furniture the hell out of there. The car. Everything."

"Wait," he said. "Listen, my brother-in-law . . ."

Ed Wolfe broke in sharply. "He's got some money?"

"I don't know. A little. I don't know."

"Get it. If you're short, grow. This is America."

"I don't know if he'll let me have it."

"Steal it. This is America. Good-bye."

"Wait a minute. Please."

"That's it. There are other Polish persons on my list. This time it was just a friendly warning. Cornucopia wants its money. Cornucopia. Can you cope? Can you cope? Just a friendly warning, Polish-American. Next time we come with the lawyers and the machine guns. Am I making myself clear?"

"I'll try to get it to you."

Ed Wolfe hung up. He pulled a handkerchief from his drawer and wiped his face. His chest was heaving. He took another call card. The girl came by and stood beside his desk. "Mr. La Meck can see you now," she mourned.

"Later. I'm calling." The number was already ringing.

"Please, Mr. Wolfe."

"Later, I said. In a minute." The girl went away. "Hello. Let me speak with your husband, madam. I am Ed Wolfe of Cornucopia Finance. He can't cope. Your husband can't cope."

The woman said something, made an excuse. "Put him on, goddamn it. We know he's out of work. Nothing gets by. Nothing." There was a hand on the receiver beside his own, the wide male fingers pink and vaguely perfumed, the nails manicured. For a moment he struggled with it fitfully, as though the hand itself were all he had to contend with. He recognized La Meck and let go. La Meck pulled the phone quickly toward his mouth and spoke softly into it, words of apology, some ingenious excuse Ed Wolfe couldn't hear. He put the receiver down beside the phone itself and Ed Wolfe picked it up and returned it to its cradle.

"Ed," La Meck said, "come into the office with me."

Ed Wolfe followed La Meck, his eyes on La Meck's behind.

La Meck stopped at his office door. Looking around he shook his head sadly and Ed Wolfe nodded in agreement. La Meck let Ed Wolfe pass in first. While La Meck stood, Ed Wolfe could discern a kind of sadness in his slouch, but once La Meck was seated behind his desk he seemed restored, once again certain of the world's soundness. "All right," La Meck began. "I won't lie to you."

Lie to me. Lie to me, Ed Wolfe prayed silently.

"You're in here for me to fire you. You're not being laid off. I'm not going to tell you that I think you'd be happier someplace else, that the collection business isn't your game, that profits don't justify our keeping you around. Profits are terrific, and if collection isn't your game it's because you haven't got a game. As far as your being happier someplace else, that's bullshit. You're not supposed to be happy. It isn't in the cards for you. You're a fall-guy type, God bless you, and though I like you personally I've got no use for you in my office."

I'd like to get you on the other end of a telephone someday, Ed Wolfe thought miserably.

"Don't ask me for a reference," La Meck said. "I couldn't give you one."

"No, no," Ed Wolfe said. "I wouldn't ask you for a reference." A helpless civility was all he was capable of. If you're going to suffer, *suffer*, he told himself.

"Look," La Meck said, his tone changing, shifting from brutality to compassion as though there were no difference between the two, "you've got a kind of quality, a real feeling for collection. I'm frank to tell you, when you first came to work for us I figured you wouldn't last. I put you on the phones because I wanted you to see the toughest part first. A lot of people can't do it. You take a guy who's down and bury him deeper. It's heart-wringing work. But you, you were amazing. An artist. You had a real thing for the deadbeat soul, I thought. But we started to get complaints, and I had to warn you. Didn't I warn you? I should have suspected something when the delinquent accounts started to turn over again. It was like rancid butter turning sweet. So I don't say this to knock your technique. Your technique's terrific. With you around we could have laid off the lawyers. But Ed, you're a gangster. A gangster."

That's it, Ed Wolfe thought. *I'm a gangster. Babyface Wolfe at nobody's door.*

"Well," La Meck said, "I guess we owe you some money."

"Two weeks' pay," Ed Wolfe said.

"And two weeks in lieu of notice," La Meck said grandly.

"And a week's pay for my vacation."

"You haven't been here a year," La Meck said.

"It would have been a year in another month. I've earned the vacation."

"What the hell," La Meck said. "A week's pay for vacation."

La Meck figured on a pad and tearing off a sheet handed it to Ed Wolfe. "Does that check with your figures?" he asked.

Ed Wolfe, who had no figures, was amazed to see that his check was so large. Leaving off the deductions he made $92.73 a week. Five $92.73's was evidently $463.65. It was a lot of money. "That seems to be right," he told La Meck.

La Meck gave him a check and Ed Wolfe got up. Already it was as though he had never worked there. When La Meck handed him the check he almost couldn't think what it was for. It was as if there should have been a photographer there to record the ceremony. ORPHAN AWARDED CHECK BY BUSINESSMAN.

"Good-bye, Mr. La Meck," he said. "It has been an interesting association," he added foolishly.

"Good-bye, Ed," La Meck answered, putting his arm around Ed Wolfe's shoulders and leading him to the door. "I'm sorry it had to end this way." He shook Ed Wolfe's hand seriously and looked into his eyes. He had a hard grip.

Quantity and quality, Ed Wolfe thought.

"One thing, Ed. Watch yourself. Your mistake here was that you took the job too seriously. You hated the chiselers."

No, no, I loved them, he thought.

"You've got to watch it. Don't love. Don't hate. That's the secret. Detachment and caution. Look out for Ed Wolfe."

"I'll watch out for him," he said giddily and in a moment he was out of La Meck's office, and the main office, and the elevator, and the building itself, loose in the world, as cautious and as detached as La Meck could want him.

He took the car from the parking lot, handing the attendant the two dollars. The man gave him fifty cents back. "That's right," Ed Wolfe said, "it's only two o'clock." He put the half dollar in his pocket, and, on an impulse, took out his wallet. He had twelve dollars. He counted his change. Eighty-two cents. With his finger, on the dusty dashboard, he added $12.82 to $463.65. He had $476.47. *Does that check with your figures?* he asked himself and drove into the crowded traffic.

Proceeding slowly, past his old building, past garages, past bar and grills, past second-rate hotels, he followed the traffic further downtown. He drove into the deepest part of the city, down and downtown to the bottom, the foundation, the city's navel. He watched the shoppers and tourists and messengers and men with appointments. He was tranquil, serene. It was something he would be content to do forever. He could use his check to buy gas, to take his meals at drive-in restaurants, to pay tolls. It would be a pleasant life, a great life, and he contemplated it thoughtfully. To drive at fifteen or twenty miles an hour through eternity, stopping at stoplights and signs, pulling over to the curb at the sound of sirens and the sight of funerals, obeying all traffic laws, making obedience to them his very code. Ed Wolfe, the Flying Dutchman, the Wandering Jew, the Off and Running Orphan, "Look out for Ed Wolfe," a ghostly wailing down the city's corridors. *What would be bad?* he thought.

In the morning, out of habit, he dressed himself in a white shirt and light suit. Before he went downstairs he saw that his check and his twelve dollars were still in his wallet. Carefully he counted the eighty-two cents that he had placed on the dresser the night before, put the coins in his pocket, and went downstairs to his car.

Something green had been shoved under the wiper blade on the driver's side.

YOUR CAR WILL NEVER BE WORTH MORE THAN IT IS WORTH RIGHT NOW.
WHY WAIT FOR DEPRECIATION TO MAKE YOU AUTOMOTIVELY BANKRUPT?
I WILL BUY THIS CAR AND PAY YOU CASH! I WILL NOT CHEAT YOU!

Ed Wolfe considered his car thoughtfully a moment and got in. He drove that day through the city playing the car radio softly. He heard the news each hour and each half hour. He listened to Arthur Godfrey far away and in another world. He heard Bing Crosby's ancient voice, and thought sadly, *Depreciation.* When his tank was almost empty he thought wearily of having to have it filled and could see himself, bored and discontented behind the bug-stained glass, forced into a patience he did not feel, having to decide whether to take the Green Stamps the attendant tried to extend. *Put money in your purse, Ed Wolfe,* he thought. *Cash!* he thought with passion.

He went to the address on the circular.

He drove up onto the gravel lot but remained in his car. In a moment a man came out of a small wooden shack and walked toward Ed Wolfe's car. If he was appraising it he gave no sign. He stood at the side of the automobile and waited while Ed Wolfe got out.

"Look around," the man said. "No pennants, no strings of electric lights." He saw the advertisement in Ed Wolfe's hand. "I ran the ad off on my brother-in-law's mimeograph. My kid stole the paper from his school."

Ed Wolfe looked at him.

"The place looks like a goddamn parking lot. When the snow starts falling I get rid of the cars and move the Christmas trees right onto it. No overhead. That's the beauty of a volume business."

Ed Wolfe looked pointedly at the nearly empty lot.

"That's right," the man said. "It's slow. I'm giving the policy one more chance. Then I cheat the public just like everybody else. You're just in time. Come on, I'll show you a beautiful car."

"I want to sell my car," Ed Wolfe said.

"Sure, sure," the man said. "You want to trade with me. I give top allowances. I play fair."

"I want you to buy my car."

The man looked at him closely. "What do you want? You want me to go into the office and put on the ten-gallon hat? It's my only overhead so I guess you're entitled to see it. You're paying for it. I put on this big frigging hat, see, and I become Texas Willie Waxelman, the Mad Cowboy. If that's what you want, I can get it in a minute."

It was incredible, Ed Wolfe thought. *There were bastards everywhere who hated other bastards downtown everywhere.* "I don't want to trade my car in," Ed Wolfe said. "I want to sell it. I, too, want to reduce my inventory."

The man smiled sadly. "You want me to buy *your* car. You run in and put on the hat. I'm an automobile *salesman,* kid."

"No, you're not," Ed Wolfe said. "I was with Cornucopia Finance. We handled your paper. You're an automobile *buyer*. Your business is in buying up four- and five-year-old cars like mine from people who need dough fast and then auctioning them off to the trade."

The man turned away and Ed Wolfe followed him. Inside the shack the man said, "I'll give you two hundred."

"I need six hundred," Ed Wolfe said.

"I'll lend you the hat. Hold up a goddamn stagecoach."

"Give me five."

"I'll give you two fifty and we'll part friends."

"Four hundred and fifty."

"Three hundred. Here," the man said, reaching his hand into an opened safe and taking out three sheaves of thick, banded bills. He held the money out to Ed Wolfe. "Go ahead, count it."

Absently Ed Wolfe took the money. The bills were stiff, like money in a teller's drawer, their value as decorous and untapped as a sheet of postage stamps. He held the money, pleased by its weight. "Tens and fives," he said, grinning.

"You bet," the man said, taking the money back. "You want to sell your car?"

"Yes," Ed Wolfe said. "Give me the money," he said hoarsely.

He had been to the bank, had stood in the patient, slow, money-conscious line, had presented his formidable check to the impassive teller, hoping the four hundred and sixty-three dollars and sixty-five cents she counted out would seem his week's salary to the man who waited behind him. *Fool,* he thought, *it will seem two weeks' pay and two weeks in lieu of notice and a week for vacation for the hell of it, the three-week margin of an orphan.*

"Thank you," the teller said, already looking beyond Ed Wolfe to the man behind him.

"Wait," Ed Wolfe said. "Here." He handed her a white withdrawal slip.

She took it impatiently and walked to a file. "You're closing your savings account?" she asked loudly.

"Yes," Ed Wolfe answered, embarrassed.

"I'll have a cashier's check made out for this."

"No, no," Ed Wolfe said desperately. "Give me cash."

"Sir, we make out a cashier's check and cash it for you," the teller explained.

"Oh," Ed Wolfe said. "I see."

When the teller had given him the two hundred fourteen dollars and twenty-three cents, he went to the next window, where he made out a check for $38.91. It was what he had in his checking account.

On Ed Wolfe's kitchen table was a thousand dollars. That day he had spent a dollar and ninety cents. He had twenty-seven dollars and seventy-one cents in his pocket. For expenses. "For attrition," he said aloud. "The cost of living. For streetcars and newspapers and half gallons of milk and loaves of white bread. For the movies. For a cup of coffee." He went to his pantry. He counted the cans and packages, the boxes and bottles. "The three weeks again," he said. "The orphan's nutritional margin." He looked in his icebox. In the freezer he poked around among white packages of frozen meat. He looked brightly into the vegetable tray. A whole lettuce. Five tomatoes. Several slices of cucumber. Browning celery. On another shelf four bananas. Three and a half apples. A cut pineapple. Some grapes, loose and collapsing darkly in a white bowl. A quarter pound of butter. A few eggs. Another egg, broken last week, congealing in a blue dish. Things in plastic bowls, in jars, forgotten, faintly mysterious leftovers, faintly rotten, vaguely futured, equivocal garbage. He closed the door, feeling a draft. "Really," he said, "it's quite cozy." He looked at the thousand dollars on the kitchen table. "It's not enough," he said. "It's not enough," he shouted. "It's not enough to be cautious on. La Meck, you bastard, detachment comes higher, what do you think? You think it's cheap?" He raged against himself. It was the way he used to speak to people on the telephone. "Wake up. Orphan! Jerk! Wake up. It costs to be detached."

He moved solidly through the small apartment and lay down on his bed with his shoes still on, putting his hands behind his head luxuriously. *It's marvelous,* he thought. *Tomorrow I'll buy a trench coat. I'll take my meals in piano bars.* He lighted a cigarette. *I'll never smile again,* he sang, smiling. "All right, Eddie, play it again," he said. "Mistuh Wuf, you don' wan' ta heah dat ol' song no maw. You know whut it do to you. She ain' wuth it, Mistuh Wuf." He nodded. "Again, Eddie." Eddie played his black ass off. "The way I see it, Eddie," he said, taking a long, sad drink of warm Scotch, "there are orphans and there are orphans." The overhead fan chuffed slowly, stirring the potted palmetto leaves.

He sat up in bed, grinding his heels across the sheets. "There are orphans and there are orphans," he said. "I'll move. I'll liquidate. I'll sell out."

He went to the phone and called his landlady and made an appointment to see her.

             It was a time of ruthless parting from his things, but there was no bitterness in it. He was a born salesman, he told himself. A disposer, a natural dumper. He administered severance. As detached as a funeral director, what he had learned was to say good-bye. It was a talent of a sort. And he had never felt quite so interested. He supposed he was doing what he had been meant for, what, perhaps, everyone was meant for. He sold and he sold, each day spinning off, reeling off little pieces of himself, like controlled explosions of the sun. Now his life was a series of speeches, of nearly earnest pitches. What he remembered of the day was what he had said. What others said to him, or even whether they spoke at all, he was unsure of.

Tuesday he told his landlady, "Buy my furniture. It's new. It's good stuff. It's expensive. You can forget about that. Put it out of your mind. I want to sell it. I'll show you bills for over seven hundred dollars. Forget the bills. Consider my character. Consider the man. Only the man. That's how to get your bargains. Examine. Examine. I could tell you about innersprings; I could talk to you of leather. But I won't. I don't. I smoke, but I'm careful. I can show you the ashtrays. You won't find cigarette holes in *my* tables. Examine. I drink. I'm a drinker. I drink. But I hold it. You won't find alcohol stains. May I be frank? I make love. Again, I could show you the bills. But I'm cautious. My sheets are virginal, white.

"Two hundred fifty dollars, landlady. Sit on that sofa. That chair. Buy my furniture. Rent the apartment furnished. Deduct what you pay from your taxes. Collect additional rents. Realize enormous profits. Wallow in gravy. Get it, landlady? Get it? Just two hundred fifty dollars. Don't disclose the figure or my name. I want to remain anonymous."

He took her into his bedroom. "The piece of resistance, landlady. What you're really buying is the bedroom stuff. I'm selling you your own bare floor. What charm. Charm? Elegance. Elegance! I throw in the living-room rug. That I throw in. You have to take that or it's no deal. Give me cash and I move tomorrow."

Wednesday he said, "I heard you buy books. That must be interesting. And sad. It must be very sad. A man who loves books doesn't like to sell them. It would be the last thing. Excuse me. I've got no right to talk to you this way. You buy books and I've got books to sell. There. It's business now. As it should be. My library—" He smiled helplessly. "Excuse me. Such a grand name.

Library." He began again slowly. "My books, my books are in there. Look them over. I'm afraid my taste has been rather eclectic. You see, my education has not been formal. There are over eleven hundred. Of course many are paperbacks. Well, you can see that. I feel as if I'm selling my mind."

The book buyer gave Ed Wolfe one hundred twenty dollars for his mind. On Thursday he wrote a letter:

American Annuity & Life Insurance Company,
Suite 410,
Lipton-Hill Building,
2007 Beverl Street, S.W.,
Boston 19, Massachusetts

Dear Sirs,

I am writing in regard to Policy Number 593-00034-78, a $5,000, twenty-year annuity held by Edward Wolfe of the address below.

Although only four payments having been made, sixteen years remain before the policy matures, I find I must make application for the immediate return of my payments and cancel the policy.

I have read the "In event of cancellation" clause in my policy, and realize that I am entitled to only a flat three percent interest on the "total paid-in amount of the partial amortizement." Your records will show that I have made four payments of $198.45 each. If your figures check with mine this would come to $793.80. Adding three percent interest to this amount ($23.81), your company owes me $817.61.

Your prompt attention to my request would be gratefully appreciated, although I feel, frankly, as though I were selling my future.

On Monday someone came to buy his record collection. "What do you want to hear? I'll put something comfortable on while we talk. What do you like? Here, try this. Go ahead, put it on the machine. By the edges, man. By the edges! I feel as if I'm selling my throat. Never mind about that. Dig the sounds. Orphans up from Orleans singing the news of chain gangs to café society. You can smell the freight trains, man. Recorded during actual performance. You can hear the ice cubes clinkin' in the glasses, the waiters picking up their tips. I have jazz. Folk. Classical. Broadway. Spoken Word. Spoken Word, man! I feel as though I'm selling my ears. The stuff lives in my heart or I wouldn't sell. I have a one-price throat, one-price ears. Sixty dollars for the noise the world makes, man. But remember. I'll be watching. By the edges. Only by the edges!"

On Friday he went to a pawnshop in a Checker Cab.

"You? You buy gold? You buy clothes? You buy Hawaiian guitars? You buy pistols for resale to suicides? I wouldn't have recognized you. Where's the skullcap, the garters around the sleeves? The cigar I wouldn't ask you about. You look like anybody. You look like everybody. I don't know what to say. I'm stuck. I don't know how to deal with you. I was going to tell you something sordid, you know? You know what I mean? Okay, I'll give you facts.

"The fact is, I'm the average man. That's what the fact is. Eleven shirts, 15 neck, 34 sleeve. Six slacks, 32 waist. Five suits at 38 long. Shoes 10-C. A 7½ hat. You know something? Those marginal restaurants where you can never remember whether they'll let you in without a jacket? Well the jackets they lend you in those places always fit me. That's the kind of guy you're dealing with. You can have confidence. Look at the clothes. Feel the material. And there's one thing about me. I'm fastidious. Fastidious. Immaculate. You think I'd be clumsy. A fall guy falls down, right? There's not a mark on the clothes. Inside? Inside it's another story. I don't speak of inside. Inside it's all Band-Aids, plaster, iodine, sticky stuff for burns. But outside—fastidiousness, immaculation, reality! My clothes will fly off your racks. I promise. I feel as if I'm selling my skin. Does that check with your figures?

"So now you know. It's me, Ed Wolfe. Ed Wolfe, the orphan? I lived in the orphanage for sixteen years. They gave me a name. It was a Jewish orphanage so they gave me a Jewish name. Almost. That is they couldn't know for sure themselves so they kept it deliberately vague. I'm a foundling. A lostling. Who needs it, right? Who the hell needs it? I'm at loose ends, pawnbroker. I'm at loose ends out of looser beginnings. I need the money to stay alive. All you can give me.

"Here's a good watch. Here's a bad one. For good times and bad. That's life, right? You can sell them as a package deal. Here are radios, I'll miss the radios. A phonograph. Automatic. Three speeds. Two speakers. The politic bastard shuts itself off. And a pressure cooker. It's valueless to me, frankly. No pressure. I can live only on cold meals. Spartan. Spartan.

"I feel as if I'm selling—this is the last of it, I have no more things—I feel as if I'm selling my things."

On Saturday he called the phone company: "Operator? Let me speak to your supervisor, please.

"Supervisor? Supervisor, I am Ed Wolfe, your subscriber at TErrace 7-3572. There is nothing wrong with the service. The service has been excellent. No one calls, but you can have nothing to do with that. However, I must cancel. I find that I no longer have any need of a telephone. Please connect me with the business office.

"Business office? Business office, this is Ed Wolfe. My telephone number is TErrace 7-3572. I am closing my account with you. When the service was first installed I had to surrender a twenty-five-dollar deposit to your company. It was understood that the deposit was to be refunded when our connection with each other had been terminated. Disconnect me. Deduct what I owe on my current account from my deposit and refund the rest immediately. Business office, I feel as if I'm selling my mouth."

When he had nothing left to sell, when that was finally that, he stayed until he had finished all the food and then moved from his old apartment into a small, thinly furnished room. He took with him a single carton of clothing—the suit, the few shirts, the socks, the pajamas, the underwear and overcoat he did not sell. It was in preparing this carton that he discovered the hangers. There were hundreds of them. His own. Previous tenants'. Hundreds. In each closet on rods, in dark, dark corners was this anonymous residue of all their lives. He unpacked his carton and put the hangers inside. They made a weight. He took them to the pawnshop and demanded a dollar for them. They were worth, he argued, more. In an A&P he got another carton free and went back to repack his clothes.

At the new place the landlord gave him his key.

"You got anything else?" the landlord asked. "I could give you a hand."

"No," he said. "Nothing."

Following the landlord up the deep stairs he was conscious of the $2,479.03 he had packed into the pockets of the suit and shirts and pajamas and overcoat inside the carton. It was like carrying a community of economically viable dolls.

When the landlord left him he opened the carton and gathered all his money together. In fading light he reviewed the figures he had entered in the pages of an old spiral notebook:

Pay	$463.65
Cash	12.82
Car	300.00

Savings 214.23
Checking 38.91
Furniture (& bedding) 250.00
Books 120.00
Insurance 817.61
Records 60.00
Pawned:
Clothes 110.00
2 watches 18.00
2 radios 12.00
Phonograph 35.00
Pressure cooker 6.00
Phone deposit (less bill) 19.81
Hangers 1.00

Total $2,479.03

So, he thought, that was what he was worth. That was the going rate for orphans in a wicked world. Something under $2,500. He took his pencil and lined through all the nouns on his list. He tore the list carefully from top to bottom and crumpled the half which inventoried his ex-possessions. Then he crumpled the other half.

He went to the window and pushed the loose, broken shade. He opened the window and set both lists on the ledge. He made a ring of his forefinger and thumb and flicked the paper balls into the street. "Look out for Ed Wolfe," he said softly.

In six weeks the season changed. The afternoons failed. The steam failed. He was as unafraid of the dark as he had been of the sunlight. He longed for a special grief, to be touched by anguish or terror, but when he saw the others in the street, in the cafeteria, in the theater, in the hallway, on the stairs, at the newsstand, in the basement rushing their fouled linen from basket to machine, he stood, as indifferent to their errand, their appetite, their joy, their greeting, their effort, their curiosity, their grime, as he was to his own. No envy wrenched him, no despair unhoped him, but, gradually, he became restless.

He began to spend, not recklessly so much as indifferently. At first he was able to recall for weeks what he spent on a given day. It was his way of telling time. Now he had difficulty remembering and could tell how much his life was costing only by subtracting what he had left from his original two thousand four hundred seventy-nine dollars and three cents. In eleven weeks he had spent six hundred seventy-seven dollars and thirty-four cents. It was almost three times more than he had planned. He became panicky. He had come to think of his money as his life. Spending it was the abrasion again, the old habit of self-buffing to come to the thing beneath. He could not draw infinitely on his credit. It was limited. Limited. He checked his figures. He had eighteen hundred and one dollars, sixty-nine cents. He warned himself, "Rothschild, child. Rockefeller, feller. Look out, Ed Wolfe. Look out."

He argued with his landlord, won a five-dollar reduction in his rent. He was constantly hungry, wore clothes stingily, realized an odd reassurance in his thin pain, his vague fetidness. He surrendered his dimes, his quarters, his half-dollars in a kind of sober anger. In seven weeks he spent only one hundred thirty dollars, fifty-one cents. He checked his figures. He had sixteen hundred seventy-one dollars, eighteen cents. He had spent almost twice what he had anticipated. "It's all right," he said. "I've reversed the trend. I can catch up." He held the money in his hand. He could smell his soiled underwear. "Nah, nah," he said. "It's not enough."

It was not enough, it was not enough, it was not enough. He had painted himself into a corner. Death by cul-de-sac. He had nothing left to sell, the born salesman. The born champion, long-distance, Ed Wolfe of a salesman, and he lay in his room winded, wounded, wondering where his next pitch was coming from, at one with the ages.

He put on his suit, took his sixteen hundred, seventy-one dollars and eighteen cents, and went down into the street. It was a warm night. He would walk downtown. The ice which just days before had covered the sidewalk was dissolved in slush. In darkness he walked through a thawing, melting world. There was, on the edge of the air, something, the warm, moist odor of the change of the season. He was, despite himself, touched. "I'll take a bus," he threatened. "I'll take a bus and close the windows and ride over the wheel."

He had dinner and some drinks in a hotel. When he finished he was feeling pretty good. He didn't want to go back. He looked at the bills thick in his wallet and went over to the desk clerk. "Where's the action?" he whispered. The clerk looked at him, startled. He went over to the bell captain. "Where's the action?" he asked and gave the man a dollar. He winked. The man stared at him helplessly.

"Sir?" the bell captain said, looking at the dollar.

Ed Wolfe nudged him in his gold buttons. He winked again. "Nice town you got here," he said expansively. "I'm a salesman, you understand, and this is new territory for me. Now if I were in Beantown or Philly or L.A. or Vegas or Big D or Frisco or Cincy, why I'd know what was what. I'd be okay, you know what I mean?" He winked once more. "Keep the buck, kid," he said. "Keep it, keep it," he said, walking off.

In the lobby a man sat in a deep chair, *The Wall Street Journal* opened widely across his face. "Where's the action?" Ed Wolfe said, peering over the top of the paper into the crown of the man's hat.

"What's that?" the man asked.

Ed Wolfe, surprised, saw that the man was a Negro.

"What's that?" the man repeated, vaguely nervous. Embarrassed, Ed Wolfe watched him guiltily, as though he had been caught in an act of bigotry.

"I thought you were someone else," he said lamely. The man smiled and lifted the paper to his face. Ed Wolfe stood before the man's opened paper, conscious of mildly teetering. He felt lousy, awkward, complicatedly irritated and ashamed, the mere act of hurting someone's feelings suddenly the most that could be held against him. It came to him how completely he had failed to make himself felt. "Look out for Ed Wolfe, indeed," he said aloud. The man lowered his paper. "Some of my best friends are Comanches," Ed Wolfe said. "Can I buy you a drink?"

"No," the man said.

"Resistance, eh?" Ed Wolfe said. "That's good. Resistance is good. A deal closed without resistance is no deal. Let me introduce myself. I'm Ed Wolfe. What's your name?"

"Please, I'm not bothering anybody. Leave me alone."

"Why?" Ed Wolfe asked.

The man stared at him and Ed Wolfe sat suddenly down beside him. "I won't press it," he said generously. "Where's the action? Where *is* it? Fold the paper, man. You're playing somebody else's gig." He leaned across the space between them and took the man by the arm. He pulled at him gently, awed by his own boldness. It was the first time since he had shaken hands with La Meck that he had touched anyone physically. What he was risking surprised and puzzled him. In all those months to have touched only two people, to have touched even two people! To feel their life, even, as now, through the unyielding wool of clothing, was disturbing. He was unused to it, frightened and oddly moved. The man, bewildered, looked at Ed Wolfe timidly and allowed himself to be taken toward the cocktail lounge.

They took a table near the bar. There, in the alcoholic dark, within earshot of the easy banter of the regulars, Ed Wolfe seated the Negro and then himself. He looked around the room and listened for a moment. He turned back to the Negro. Smoothly boozy, he pledged the man's health when the girl brought their drinks. He drank stolidly, abstractedly. Coming to life briefly, he indicated the men and women around them, their suntans apparent even in the dark. "Pilots," he said. "All of them. Airline pilots. The girls are all stewardesses and the pilots lay them." He ordered more drinks. He did not like liquor and liberally poured ginger ale into his bourbon. He ordered more drinks and forgot the ginger ale. *"Goyim,"* he said. *"*White *goyim*. American *goyim.*" He stared at the Negro. "These are the people, man. The mothered and fathered people." He leaned across the table. "Little Orphan Annie, what the hell kind of an orphan is that with all her millions and her white American *goyim* friends to bail her out?"

He watched them narrowly, drunkenly. He had seen them before—in good motels, in airports, in bars—and he wondered about them, seeing them, he supposed, as Negroes or children of the poor must have seen him when he had had his car and driven sometimes through slums. They were removed, aloof—he meant it—a different breed. He turned and saw the Negro and could not think for a moment what the man could have been doing there. The Negro slouched in his chair, his great white eyes hooded. "You want to hang around here?" Ed Wolfe asked him.

"It's your party," the man said.

"Then let's go someplace else," Ed Wolfe said. "I get nervous here."

"I know a place," the Negro said.

"You know a place. You're a stranger here."

"No, man," the Negro said. "This is my hometown. I come down here sometimes just to sit in the lobby and read the newspapers. It looks good, you know what I mean? It looks good for the race."

"The Wall Street Journal? You're kidding Ed Wolfe. Watch that."

"No," the Negro said. "Honest."

"I'll be damned," Ed Wolfe said. "I come for the same reasons."

"Yeah," the Negro said. "No shit."

"Sure, the same reasons." He laughed. "Let's get out of here." He tried to stand, but fell back again in his chair. "Hey, help me up," he said loudly. The Negro got up and came around to Ed Wolfe's side of the table. Leaning over, he raised him to his feet. Some of the others in the room looked at them curiously. "It's all right," Ed Wolfe said. "He's my man. I take him with me everywhere. It looks good for the race." With their arms around each other's shoulders they stumbled out of the room and through the lobby.

In the street Ed Wolfe leaned against the building and the Negro hailed a cab, the dark left hand shooting up boldly, the long black body stretching forward, raised on tiptoes, the head turned sharply along the left shoulder. Ed Wolfe knew he had never done it before. The Negro came up beside Ed Wolfe and guided him toward the curb. Holding the door open he shoved him into the cab with his left hand. Ed Wolfe lurched against the cushioned seat awkwardly. The Negro gave the driver an address and the cab moved off. Ed Wolfe reached for the window handle and rolled it down rapidly. He shoved his head out the window of the taxi and smiled and waved at the people along the curb.

"Hey, man. Close the window," the Negro said after a moment. "Close the window. The cops, the cops."

Ed Wolfe laid his head along the edge of the taxi window and looked up at the Negro who was leaning over him and smiling and seemed trying to tell him something.

"Where we going, man?" he asked.

"We're there," the Negro said, sliding along the seat toward the door.

"One ninety-five," the driver said.

"It's your party," Ed Wolfe told the Negro, waving away responsibility.

The Negro looked disappointed, but reached into his pocket to pull out his wallet.

Did he see what I had on me? Ed Wolfe wondered anxiously. *Jerk, drunk, you'll be rolled. They'll cut your throat and then they'll leave your skin in an alley. Be careful.*

"Come on, Ed," the Negro said. He took him by the arm and got him out of the taxi.

Fake. Fake, Ed Wolfe thought. *Murderer. Nigger. Razor man.*

The Negro pulled Ed Wolfe toward a doorway. "You'll meet my friends," he said.

"Yeah, yeah," Ed Wolfe said. "I've heard so much about them."

"Hold it a second," the Negro said. He went up to the window and pressed his ear against the opaque glass.

Ed Wolfe watched him without making a move.

"Here's the place," the Negro said proudly.

"Sure," Ed Wolfe said. "Sure it is."

"Come on, man," the Negro urged him.

"I'm coming, I'm coming," Ed Wolfe mumbled, "but my head is bending low."

The Negro took out a ring of keys, selected one, and put it in the door. Ed Wolfe followed him through.

"Hey, Oliver," somebody called. "Hey, baby, it's Oliver. Oliver looks good. He looks *good.*"

"Hello, Mopiani," the Negro said to a short black man.

"How is stuff, Oliver?" Mopiani said to him.

"How's the market?" a man next to Mopiani asked, with a laugh.

"Ain't no mahket, baby. It's a *sto',*" somebody else said.

A woman stopped, looked at Ed Wolfe for a moment, and asked: "Who's the ofay, Oliver?"

"That's Oliver's broker, baby."

"Oliver's broker looks good," Mopiani said. "He looks *good.*"

"This is my friend, Mr. Ed Wolfe," Oliver told them.

"Hey, there," Mopiani said.

"Charmed," Ed Wolfe said.

"How's it going, man," a Negro said indifferently.

"Delighted," Ed Wolfe said.

He let Oliver lead him to a table.

"I'll get the drinks, Ed," Oliver said, leaving him.

Ed Wolfe looked at the room glumly. People were drinking steadily, gaily. They kept their bottles under their chairs in paper bags. Ed Wolfe watched a man take a bag from beneath his chair, raise it, and twist the open end of the bag carefully around the neck of the bottle so that it resembled a bottle of champagne swaddled in its toweling. The man poured into his glass grandly. At the dark far end of the room some musicians were playing and three or four couples danced dreamily in front of them. He watched the musicians closely and was vaguely reminded of the airline pilots.

In a few minutes Oliver returned with a paper bag and some glasses. A girl was with him. "Mary Roberta, Ed Wolfe," he said, very pleased. Ed Wolfe stood up clumsily and the girl nodded.

"No more ice," Oliver explained.

"What the hell," Ed Wolfe said.

Mary Roberta sat down and Oliver pushed her chair up to the table. She sat with her hands in her lap and Oliver pushed her as though she were a cripple.

"Real nice little place here, Ollie," Ed Wolfe said.

"Oh, it's just the club," Oliver said.

"Real nice," Ed Wolfe said.

Oliver opened the bottle and poured liquor in their glasses and put the paper bag under his chair. Oliver raised his glass. Ed Wolfe touched it lamely with his own and leaned back, drinking. When he put it down empty, Oliver filled it again from the paper bag. He drank sluggishly, like one falling asleep, and listened, numbed, to Oliver and the girl. His glass never seemed to be empty anymore. He drank steadily but the liquor seemed to remain at the same level in the glass. He was conscious that someone else had joined them at the table. "Oliver's broker looks good," he heard somebody say. Mopiani. Warm and drowsy and gently detached, he listened, feeling as he had in barbershops, having his hair cut, conscious of the barber, unseen behind him, touching his hair and scalp with his warm fingers. "You see Bert? He looks good," Mopiani was saying.

With great effort Ed Wolfe shifted in his chair, turning to the girl.

"Thought you were giving out on us, Ed," Oliver said. "That's it. That's it."

The girl sat with her hands folded in her lap.

"Mary Roberta," Ed Wolfe said.

"Uh huh," the girl said.

"Mary Roberta."

"Yes," the girl said. "That's right."

"You want to dance?" Ed Wolfe asked.

"All right," she said. "I guess so."

"That's it, that's it," Oliver said. "Stir yourself."

He got up clumsily, cautiously, like one standing in a stalled Ferris wheel, and went around behind her chair, pulling it far back from the table with the girl in it. He took her warm, bare arm and moved toward the dancers. Mopiani passed them with a bottle. "Looks good, looks good," Mopiani said approvingly. He pulled her against him to let Mopiani pass, tightening the grip of his pale hand on her brown arm. A muscle leaped beneath the girl's smooth skin, filling his palm. At the edge of the dance floor Ed Wolfe leaned forward into the girl's arms and they moved slowly, thickly across the floor. He held the girl close, conscious of her weight, the life beneath her body, just under her skin. Sick, he remembered a jumping bean he had held once in his palm, awed and frightened by the invisible life, jerking and hysterical, inside the stony shell. The girl moved with him in the music, Ed Wolfe astonished by the burden of her life. He stumbled away from her deliberately. Grinning, he moved ungently back against her. "Look out for Ed Wolfe," he crooned.

The girl stiffened and held him away from her, dancing self-consciously. Ed Wolfe, brooding, tried to concentrate on the lost rhythm. They danced in silence for a while.

"What do you do?" she asked him finally.

"I'm a salesman," he told her gloomily.

"Door to door?"

"Floor to ceiling. Wall to wall."

"Too much," she said.

"I'm a pusher," he said, suddenly angry. She looked frightened. "But I'm not hooked myself. It's a weakness in my character. I can't get hooked. Ach, what would you *goyim* know about it?"

"Take it easy," she said. "What's the matter with you? Do you want to sit down?"

"I can't push sitting down," he said.

"Hey," she said, "don't talk so loud."

"Boy," he said, "you black Protestants. What's that song you people sing?"

"Come on," she said.

"Sometimes I feel like a motherless child," he sang roughly. The other dancers watched him nervously. "That's our national anthem, man," he said to a couple that had stopped dancing to look at him. "That's our song, sweethearts," he said, looking around him. "All right, mine then. I'm an orphan."

"Oh, come on," the girl said, exasperated, "an orphan. A grown man."

He pulled away from her. The band stopped playing. "Hell," he said loudly, "from the beginning. Orphan. Bachelor. Widower. Only child. All my names scorn me. I'm a survivor. I'm a goddamned survivor, that's what." The other couples crowded around him now. People got up from their tables. He could see them, on tiptoes, stretching their necks over the heads of the dancers. *No,* he thought. *No, no. Detachment and caution. The La Meck Plan. They'll kill you. They'll kill you and kill you.* He edged away from them, moving carefully backward against the bandstand. People pushed forward onto the dance floor to watch him. He could hear their questions, could see heads darting from behind backs and suddenly appearing over shoulders as they strained to get a look at him.

He grabbed Mary Roberta's hand, pulling her to him fiercely. He pulled and pushed her up onto the bandstand and then climbed up beside her. The trumpet player, bewildered, made room for him. "Tell you what I'm going to do," he shouted over their heads. "Tell you what I'm going to do."

Everyone was listening to him now.

"Tell you what I'm going to do," he began again.

Quietly they waited for him to go on.

"I don't *know* what I'm going to do," he shouted. "I don't *know* what I'm going to do. Isn't that a hell of a note?

"Isn't it?" he demanded.

"Brothers and sisters," he shouted, "and as an only child bachelor orphan I use the term playfully you understand. Brothers and sisters, I tell you what I'm *not* going to do. I'm no consumer. Nobody's death can make me that. I won't consume. I mean it's a question of identity, right? Closer, come up closer, buddies. You don't want to miss any of this."

"Oliver's broker looks good up there. Mary Roberta looks good. She looks good," Mopiani said below him.

"Right, Mopiani. She looks good, she looks *good*," Ed Wolfe called loudly. "So I tell you what I'm going to do. What am I bid? What am I bid for this fine strong wench? Daughter of a chief, masters. Dear dark daughter of a dead dinge chief. Look at those arms. Those arms, those arms. What am I bid?"

They looked at him, astonished.

"What am I bid?" he demanded. "Reluctant, masters? Reluctant masters, masters? Say, what's the matter with you darkies? Come on, what am I bid?" He turned to the girl. "No one wants you, honey," he said. "Folks, folks, I'd buy her myself, but I've already told you. I'm not a consumer. Please forgive me, miss."

He heard them shifting uncomfortably.

"Look," he said patiently, "the management has asked me to remind you that this is a living human being. This is the real thing, the genuine article, the goods. Oh, I told them I wasn't the right man for this mob. As an orphan I have no conviction about the product. Now you should have seen me in my old job. I could be rough. Rough. I hurt people. Can you imagine? I actually caused them pain. I mean, what the hell, I was an orphan. I *could* hurt people. An orphan doesn't have to bother with love. An orphan's like a nigger in that respect. Emancipated. But you people are another problem entirely. That's why I came here tonight. There are parents among you. I can feel it. There's even a sense of parents behind those parents. My God, don't any of you folks ever die? So what's holding us up? We're not making any money. Come on, what am I bid?"

"Shut up, mister." The voice was raised hollowly someplace in the back of the crowd.

Ed Wolfe could not see the owner of the voice.

"He's not in," Ed Wolfe said.

"Shut up. What right you got to come down here and speak to us like that?"

"He's not in, I tell you. I'm his brother."

"You're a guest. A guest got no call to talk like that."

"He's out. I'm his father. He didn't tell me and I don't know when he'll be back."

"You can't make fun of us," the voice said.

"He isn't here. I'm his son."

"Bring that girl down off that stage!"

"Speaking," Ed Wolfe said.

"Let go of that girl!" someone called angrily.

The girl moved closer to him.

"She's mine," Ed Wolfe said. "I danced with her."

"Get her down from there!"

"Okay," he said giddily. "Okay. All right." He let go of the girl's hand and pulled out his wallet. The girl did not move. He took out the bills and dropped the wallet to the floor.

"Damned drunk!" someone shouted.

"That white man's crazy," someone else said.

"Here," Ed Wolfe said. "There's over sixteen hundred dollars here," he yelled, waving the money. It was, for him, like holding so much paper. "I'll start the bidding. I hear over sixteen hundred dollars once. I hear over sixteen hundred dollars twice. I hear it three times. Sold! A deal's a deal," he cried, flinging the money high over their heads. He saw them reach helplessly, noiselessly toward the bills, heard distinctly the sound of paper tearing.

He faced the girl. "Good-bye," he said.

She reached forward, taking his hand.

"Good-bye," he said again. "I'm leaving."

She held his hand, squeezing it. He looked down at the luxuriant brown hand, seeing beneath it the fine articulation of bones, the rich sudden rush of muscle. Inside her own he saw, indifferently, his own pale hand, lifeless and serene, still and infinitely free.

[SEPTEMBER 1962]

RAYMOND CARVER

Neighbors

When <u>Esquire</u> published Raymond Carver's "Neighbors" in 1971, it was the first time his fiction had appeared in a major national magazine. Born in Clatskanie, Oregon, Carver (1938–1988) was educated at Chico State College and Humboldt State University in California. At the Iowa Writers' Workshop in the mid-sixties, Carver was often forced by the clamor of his domestic life to write in laundromats and the family car. Later he found employment as a janitor, sawmill worker, delivery man, salesman, and textbook editor, experiences that often made their way into his powerful narratives about "rumpled men and ragged women [who] break your heart," as Stanley Elkin put it. Carver's characters usually suffered from a vaguely articulated sense that something was wrong with their lives, that they had somehow become tainted by failure. He wrote accomplished poetry and essays, but his central achievement was in the short story, as is evident in <u>Will You Please Be Quiet Please</u> (1976), <u>What We Talk About When We Talk About Love</u> (1982), <u>Cathedral</u> (1983), and his new and selected stories, <u>Where I'm Calling From</u> (1988).

Bill and Arlene Miller were a happy couple. But now and then they felt they alone among their circle had been passed by somehow, leaving Bill to attend to his bookkeeping duties and Arlene occupied with secretarial chores. They talked about it sometimes, mostly in comparison with the lives of their neighbors, Harriet and Jim Stone. It seemed to the Millers that the Stones lived a fuller and brighter life, one very different from their own. The Stones were always going out for dinner, or entertaining at home, or traveling about the country somewhere in connection with Jim's work.

The Stones lived across the hall from the Millers. Jim was a salesman for a machine-parts firm and often managed to combine business with a pleasure trip, and on this occasion the Stones would be away for ten days, first to Cheyenne, then on to St. Louis to visit relatives. In their absence, the Millers would look after the Stones' apartment, feed Kitty and water the plants.

Bill and Jim shook hands beside the car. Harriet and Arlene held each other by the elbows and kissed lightly on the lips.

"Have fun," Bill said to Harriet.

"We will," said Harriet. "You kids have fun too."

Arlene nodded.

Jim winked at her. " 'Bye, Arlene. Take good care of the old man."

"I will," Arlene said.

"Have fun," Bill said.

"You bet," Jim said, clipping Bill lightly on the arm. "And thanks again, you guys."

The Stones waved as they drove away, and the Millers waved too.

"Well, I wish it was us," Bill said.

"God knows, we could use a vacation," Arlene said. She took his arm and put it around her waist as they climbed the stairs to their apartment.

After dinner Arlene said, "Don't forget. Kitty gets liver flavoring the first night." She stood in the kitchen doorway folding the handmade tablecloth that Harriet had bought for her last year in Santa Fe.

Bill took a deep breath as he entered the Stones' apartment. The air was already heavy and it was always vaguely sweet. The sunburst clock over the television said half-past eight. He remembered when Harriet had come home with the clock, how she crossed the hall to show it to Arlene, cradling the brass case in her arms and talking to it through the tissue paper as if it were an infant.

Kitty rubbed her face against his slippers and then turned onto her side, but jumped up quickly as Bill moved to the kitchen and selected one of the stacked cans from the gleaming drainboard. Leaving the cat to pick at her food, he headed for the bathroom. He looked at himself in the mirror and then closed his eyes and then opened them. He opened the medicine chest. He found a container of pills and read the label: *Harriet Stone. One each day as directed,* and slipped it into his pocket. He went back to the kitchen, drew a pitcher of water and returned to the living room. He finished watering, set the pitcher on the rug and opened the liquor cabinet. He reached in back for the bottle of Chivas Regal. He took two drinks from the bottle, wiped his lips on his sleeve and replaced the bottle in the cabinet.

Kitty was on the couch sleeping. He flipped the lights, slowly closing and checking the door. He had the feeling he had left something.

"What kept you?" Arlene said. She sat with her legs turned under her, watching television.

"Nothing. Playing with Kitty," he said, and went over to her and touched her breasts.

"Let's go to bed, honey," he said.

The next day Bill took only ten of the twenty minutes' break allotted for the afternoon, and left at fifteen minutes before five.

He parked the car in the lot just as Arlene hopped down from the bus. He waited until she entered the building, then ran up the stairs to catch her as she stepped out of the elevator.

"Bill! God, you scared me. You're early," she said.

He shrugged. "Nothing to do at work," he said.

She let him use her key to open the door. He looked at the door across the hall before following her inside.

"Let's go to bed," he said.

"Now?" She laughed. "What's gotten into you?"

"Nothing. Take your dress off." He grabbed for her awkwardly, and she said, "Good God, Bill."

He unfastened his belt.

Later they sent out for Chinese food, and when it arrived they ate hungrily, without speaking, and listened to records.

"Let's not forget to feed Kitty," she said.

"I was just thinking about that," he said. "I'll go right over."

He selected a can of fish for the cat, then filled the pitcher and went to water. When he returned to the kitchen the cat was scratching in her box. She looked at him steadily for a minute before she turned back to the litter. He opened all the cupboards and examined the canned goods, the cereals, the packaged foods, the cocktail and wine glasses, the china, the pots and pans. He opened the refrigerator. He sniffed some celery, took two bites of cheddar cheese and chewed on an apple as he walked into the bedroom. The bed seemed enormous, with a fluffy white bedspread draped to the floor. He pulled out a nightstand drawer, found a half-empty package of cigarettes and stuffed them into his pocket. Then he stepped to the closet and was opening it when the knock sounded at the front door.

He stopped by the bathroom and flushed the toilet on his way.

"What's been keeping you?" Arlene said. "You've been over here more than an hour."

"Have I really?" he said.

"Yes, you have," she said.

"I had to go to the toilet," he said.

"You have your own toilet," she said.

"I couldn't wait," he said.

That night they made love again.

In the morning he had Arlene call in for him. He showered, dressed and made a light breakfast. He tried to start a book. He went out for a walk and felt better, but after a while, hands still in his pockets, he returned to the apartment. He stopped at the Stones' door on the chance he might hear the cat moving about. Then he let himself in at his own door and went to the kitchen for the key.

Inside it seemed cooler than his apartment, and darker too. He wondered if the plants had something to do with the temperature of the air. He looked out the window, and then he moved slowly through each room considering everything that fell under his gaze, carefully, one object at a time. He saw ashtrays, items of furniture, kitchen utensils, the clock. He saw everything. At last he entered the bedroom, and the cat appeared at his feet. He stroked her once, carried her into the bathroom and shut the door.

He lay down on the bed and stared at the ceiling. He lay for a while with his eyes closed, and then he moved his hand into his pants. He tried to recall what day it was. He tried to remember when the Stones were due back, and then he wondered if they would ever return. He could not remember their faces or the way they talked and dressed. He sighed, and then with effort rolled off the bed to lean over the dresser and look at himself in the mirror.

He opened the closet and selected a Hawaiian shirt. He looked until he found Bermudas, neatly pressed and hanging over a pair of brown twill slacks. He shed his own clothes and slipped into the shorts and the shirt. He looked in the mirror again. He went to the living room and poured himself a drink and sipped it on his way back to the bedroom. He put on a dark suit, a blue shirt, a blue and white tie, black wing-tip shoes. The glass was empty and he went for another drink.

In the bedroom again he sat on a chair, crossed his legs and smiled, observing himself in the mirror. The telephone rang twice and fell silent. He finished the drink and took off the suit. He rummaged the top drawers until he found a pair of panties and a brassiere. He stepped into the panties and fastened the brassiere, then looked through the closet for an outfit. He put on a black-and-white checkered skirt which was too snug and which he was afraid to zipper, and a burgundy blouse that buttoned up the front. He considered her shoes, but understood they would not fit. For a long time he looked out the living-room window from behind the curtain. Then he returned to the bedroom and put everything away.

He was not hungry. She did not eat much either, but they looked at each other shyly and smiled. She got up from the table and checked that the key was on the shelf, then quickly cleared the dishes.

He stood in the kitchen doorway and smoked a cigarette and watched her pick up the key.

"Make yourself comfortable while I go across the hall," she said. "Read the paper or something." She closed her fingers over the key. He was, she said, looking tired.

He tried to concentrate on the news. He read the paper and turned on the television. Finally he went across the hall. The door was locked.

"It's me. Are you still there, honey?" he called.

After a time the lock released and Arlene stepped outside and shut the door. "Was I gone so long?" she said.

"Well you were," he said.

"Was I?" she said. "I guess I must have been playing with Kitty."

He studied her, and she looked away, her hand still resting on the doorknob.

"It's funny," she said. "You know, to go in someone's place like that."

He nodded, took her hand from the knob and guided her toward their own door. He let them into their apartment. "It is funny," he said. He noticed white lint clinging to the back of her sweater, and the color was high in her cheeks. He began kissing her on the neck and hair and she turned and kissed him back.

"Oh, damn," she said. "Damn, damn," girlishly clapping her hands. "I just remembered. I really and truly forgot to do what I went over there for. I didn't feed Kitty or do any watering." She looked at him. "Isn't that stupid?"

"I don't think so," he said. "Just a minute, I'll get my cigarettes and go back with you."

She waited until he had closed and locked their door, and then she took his arm at the muscle and said, "I guess I should tell you. I found some pictures."

He stopped in the middle of the hall. "What kind of pictures?"

"You can see for yourself," she said, and watched him.

"No kidding." He grinned. "Where?"

"In a drawer," she said.

"No kidding," he said.

And then she said, "Maybe they won't come back," and was at once astonished at her words.

"It could happen," he said. "Anything could happen."

"Or maybe they'll come back and," but she did not finish.

They held hands for the short walk across the hall, and when he spoke she could barely hear his voice.

"The key," he said. "Give it to me."

"What?" she said. She gazed at the door.

"The key," he said, "you have the key."

"My God," she said, "I left the key inside."

He tried the knob. It remained locked. Then she tried the knob, but it would not turn. Her lips were parted, and her breathing was hard, expectant. He opened his arms and she moved into them.

"Don't worry," he said into her ear. "For God's sake, don't worry." They stayed there. They held each other. They leaned into the door as if against a wind, and braced themselves.

[JUNE 1971]

GAIL GODWIN

A Sorrowful

Woman

Gail Godwin (1937–   ) is well known as the author of long and compelling novels like The Perfectionist, A Mother and Two Daughters, Glass People, *and* The Odd Woman. *But her compressed, terse tale "A Sorrowful Woman," reprinted here from the August 1971 issue of* Esquire, *expressed the anguish of a woman's life in so succinct a form that it became one of the literary touchstones of the women's movement. Godwin lives in Woodstock, New York.*

One winter evening she looked at them: the husband durable, receptive, gentle; the child a tender golden three. The sight of them made her so sad and sick she did not want to see them ever again.

She told her husband these thoughts. He was attuned to her; he understood such things. He said he understood. What would she like him to do? "If you could put the boy to bed and read him the story about the monkey who ate too many bananas, I would be grateful." "Of course," he said. "Why, that's a pleasure." And he sent her off to bed.

The next night it happened again. Putting the warm dishes away in the cupboard, she turned and saw the child's gray eyes approving her movements. In the next room was the man, his chin sunk in the open collar of his favorite wool shirt. He was dozing after her good supper. The shirt was the gray of the child's trusting gaze. She began yelping without tears, retching in between. The man woke in alarm and carried her in his arms to bed. The boy followed them up the stairs, saying, "It's all right, Mommy," but this made her scream. "Mommy is sick," the father said, "go and wait for me in your room."

The husband undressed her, abandoning her only long enough to root beneath the eiderdown for her flannel gown. She stood naked except for her bra, which hung by one strap down the side of her body; she had not the impetus to shrug it off. She looked down at the right nipple, shriveled with chill, and thought, How absurd, a vertical bra. "If only there were instant sleep," she said, hiccuping, and the husband bundled her into the gown and went out and came back with a sleeping draught guaranteed swift. She was to drink a little glass of cognac followed by a big glass of dark liquid and afterwards there was just time to say Thank you and could you get him a clean pair of pajamas out of the laundry, it came back today.

The next day was Sunday and the husband brought her breakfast in bed and let her sleep until it grew dark again. He took the child for a walk, and when they returned, red-cheeked and boisterous, the father made supper. She heard them laughing in the kitchen. He brought her up a tray of buttered toast, celery sticks and black bean soup. "I am the luckiest woman," she said, crying real tears. "Nonsense," he said. "You need a rest from us," and went to prepare the sleeping draught, find the child's pajamas, select the story for the night.

She got up on Monday and moved about the house till noon. The boy, delighted to have her back, pretended he was a vicious tiger and followed her from room to room, growling and scratching. Whenever she came close, he would growl and scratch at her. One of his sharp little claws ripped her flesh, just above the wrist, and together they paused to watch a thin red line materialize on the inside of her pale arm and spill over in little beads. "Go away," she said. She got herself upstairs and locked the door. She called the husband's office and said, "I've locked myself away from him. I'm afraid." The husband told her in his richest voice to lie down, take it easy, and he was already on the phone to call one of the baby-sitters they often employed. Shortly after, she heard the girl let herself in, heard the girl coaxing the frightened child to come and play.

After supper several nights later, she hit the child. She had known she was going to do it when the father would see. "I'm sorry," she said, collapsing on the floor. The weeping child had run to hide. "What has happened to me, I'm not myself anymore." The man picked her tenderly from the floor and looked at her with much concern. "Would it help if we got, you know, a girl in? We could fix the room downstairs. I want you to feel freer," he said, understanding these things. "We have the money for a girl. I want you to think about it."

And now the sleeping draught was a nightly thing, she did not have to ask.

He went down to the kitchen to mix it, he set it nightly beside her bed. The little glass and the big one, amber and deep rich brown, the flannel gown and the eiderdown.

The man put out the word and found the perfect girl. She was young, dynamic and not pretty. "Don't bother with the room, I'll fix it up myself." Laughing, she employed her thousand energies. She painted the room white, fed the child lunch, read edifying books, raced the boy to the mailbox, hung her own watercolors on the fresh-painted walls, made spinach soufflé, cleaned a spot from the mother's coat, made them all laugh, danced in stocking feet to music in the white room after reading the child to sleep. She knitted dresses for herself and played chess with the husband. She washed and set the mother's soft ash-blond hair and gave her neck rubs, offered to.

The woman now spent her winter afternoons in the big bedroom. She made a fire in the hearth and put on slacks and an old sweater she had loved at school, and sat in the big chair and stared out the window at snow-ridden branches, or went away into long novels about other people moving through other winters.

The girl brought the child in twice a day, once in the late afternoon when he would tell of his day, all of it tumbling out quickly because there was not much time, and before he went to bed. Often now, the man took his wife to dinner. He made a courtship ceremony of it, inviting her beforehand so she could get used to the idea. They dressed and were beautiful together again and went out into the frosty night. Over candlelight he would say, "I think you are better, you know." "Perhaps I am," she would murmur. "You look . . . like a cloistered queen," he said once, his voice breaking curiously.

One afternoon the girl brought the child into the bedroom. "We've been out playing in the park. He found something he wants to give you, a surprise." The little boy approached her, smiling mysteriously. He placed his cupped hands in hers and left a live dry thing that spat brown juice in her palm and leapt away. She screamed and wrung her hands to be rid of the brown juice. "Oh, it was only a grasshopper," said the girl. Nimbly she crept to the edge of a curtain, did a quick knee bend and reclaimed the creature, led the boy competently from the room.

"The girl upsets me," said the woman to her husband. He sat frowning on the side of the bed he had not entered for so long. "I'm sorry, but there it is." The husband stroked his creased brow and said he was sorry too. He really did not know what they would do without that treasure of a girl. "Why don't you stay here with me in bed," the woman said.

Next morning she fired the girl, who cried and said, "I loved the little boy, what will become of him now?" But the mother turned away her face and the girl took down the watercolors from the walls, sheathed the records she had danced to and went away.

"I don't know what we'll do. It's all my fault, I know. I'm such a burden, I know that."

"Let me think. I'll think of something." (Still understanding these things.)

"I know you will. You always do," she said.

With great care he rearranged his life. He got up hours early, did the shopping, cooked the breakfast, took the boy to nursery school. "We will manage," he said, "until you're better, however long that is." He did his work, collected the boy from the school, came home and made the supper, washed the dishes, got the child to bed. He managed everything. One evening, just as she was on the verge of swallowing her draught, there was a timid knock on her door. The little boy came in wearing his pajamas. "Daddy has fallen asleep on my bed and I can't get in. There's not room."

Very sedately she left her bed and went to the child's room. Things were much changed. Books were rearranged, toys. He'd done some new drawings. She came as a visitor to her son's room, wakened the father and helped him to bed. "Ah, he shouldn't have bothered you," said the man, leaning on his wife. "I've told him not to." He dropped into his own bed and fell asleep with a moan. Meticulously she undressed him. She folded and hung his clothes. She covered his body with the bedclothes. She flicked off the light that shone in his face.

The next day she moved her things into the girl's white room. She put her hairbrush on the dresser; she put a note pad and pen beside the bed. She stocked the little room with cigarettes, books, bread and cheese. She didn't need much.

At first the husband was dismayed. But he was receptive to her needs. He understood these things. "Perhaps the best thing is for you to follow it through," he said. "I want to be big enough to contain whatever you must do."

All day long she stayed in the white room. She was a young queen, a virgin in a tower; she was the previous inhabitant, the girl with all the energies. She tried these personalities on like costumes, then discarded them. The room had a new view of streets she'd never seen that way before. The sun hit the room in late afternoon and she took to brushing her hair in the sun. One day she decided to write a poem. "Perhaps a sonnet." She took up her pen and pad and began working from words that had lately lain in her mind. She had choices for the sonnet, ABAB or ABBA for a start. She pondered these possibilities until she tottered into a larger choice: she did not have to write a sonnet. Her poem could be six, eight, ten, thirteen lines, it could be any number of lines, and it did not even have to rhyme.

She put down the pen on top of the pad.

In the evenings, very briefly, she saw the two of them. They knocked on her door, a big knock and a little, and she would call Come in, and the husband would smile though he looked a bit tired, yet somehow this tiredness suited him. He would put her sleeping draught on the bedside table and say, "The boy and I have done all right today," and the child would kiss her. One night she tasted for the first time the power of his baby spit.

"I don't think I can see him anymore," she whispered sadly to the man. And the husband turned away, but recovered admirably and said, "Of course, I see."

So the husband came alone. "I have explained to the boy," he said. "And we are doing fine. We are managing." He squeezed his wife's pale arm and put the two glasses on her table. After he had gone, she sat looking at the arm.

"I'm afraid it's come to that," she said. "Just push the notes under the door; I'll read them. And don't forget to leave the draught outside."

The man sat for a long time with his head in his hands. Then he rose and went away from her. She heard him in the kitchen where he mixed the draught in batches now to last a week at a time, storing it in a corner of the cupboard. She heard him come back, leave the big glass and the little one outside on the floor.

Outside her window the snow was melting from the branches, there were more people on the streets. She brushed her hair a lot and seldom read anymore. She sat in her window and brushed her hair for hours, and saw a boy fall off his new bicycle again and again, a dog chasing a squirrel, an old woman peek slyly over her shoulder and then extract a parcel from a garbage can.

In the evening she read the notes they slipped under her door. The child could not write, so he drew and sometimes painted his. The notes were painstaking at first; the man and boy offering the final strength of their day to her. But sometimes, when they seemed to have had a bad day, there were only hurried scrawls.

One night, when the husband's note had been extremely short, loving but short, and there had been nothing from the boy, she stole out of her room as she often did to get more supplies, but crept upstairs instead and stood outside their doors, listening to the regular breathing of the man and boy asleep. She hurried back to her room and drank the draught.

She woke earlier now. It was spring, there were birds. She listened for sounds of the man and the boy eating breakfast; she listened for the roar of the motor when they drove away. One beautiful noon, she went out to look at her kitchen in the daylight. Things were changed. He had bought some new dish towels. Had the old ones worn out? The canisters seemed closer to the sink. She inspected the cupboard and saw new things among the old. She got out flour, baking powder, salt, milk (he bought a different brand of butter), and baked a loaf of bread and left it cooling on the table.

The force of the two joyful notes slipped under her door that evening pressed her into the corner of the little room; she had hardly space to breathe. As soon as possible, she drank the draught.

Now the days were too short. She was always busy. She woke with the first bird. Worked till the sun set. No time for hair brushing. Her fingers raced the hours.

Finally, in the nick of time, it was finished one late afternoon. Her veins pumped and her forehead sparkled. She went to the cupboard, took what was hers, closed herself into the little white room and brushed her hair for a while.

The man and boy came home and found: five loaves of warm bread, a roast stuffed turkey, a glazed ham, three pies of different fillings, eight molds of the boy's favorite custard, two weeks' supply of fresh-laundered sheets and shirts and towels, two hand-knitted sweaters (both of the same gray color), a sheath of marvelous watercolor beasts accompanied by mad and fanciful stories nobody could ever make up again, and a tablet full of love sonnets addressed to the man. The house smelled redolently of renewal and spring. The man ran to the little room, could not contain himself to knock, flung back the door.

"Look, Mommy is sleeping," said the boy. "She's tired from doing all our things again." He dawdled in a stream of the last sun for that day and watched his father roll tenderly back her eyelids, lay his ear softly to her breast, test the delicate bones of her wrist. The father put down his face into her fresh-washed hair.

"Can we eat the turkey for supper?" the boy asked.

[AUGUST 1971]

T. CORAGHESSAN BOYLE

Heart of a Champion

T. Coraghessan Boyle (1948–   ) has written four novels, including most recently The Road to Wellville, and has collected three books of short stories, including Greasy Lake, but perhaps no story of his is more memorable than "Heart of a Champion," the tale of Lassie in lust, which became a model of the New Fiction in its use of figures from popular culture as protagonists. Boyle was raised in Peekskill, New York.

Here are the corn fields and the wheat fields winking gold and goldbrown and yellowbrown in midday sun. Up the grassy slope we go, to the barn redder than red against sky bluer than blue, across the smooth stretch of the barnyard with its pecking chickens, and then right on up to the screen door at the back of the house. The door swings open, a black hole in the sun, and Timmy emerges with his cornsilk hair. He is dressed in crisp overalls, striped T-shirt, stubby blue Keds. There must be a breeze—and we are not disappointed—his clean fine cup-cut hair waves and settles as he scuffs across the barnyard to the edge of the field. The boy stops there to gaze out over the wheat-manes, eyes unsquinted despite the sun, eyes blue as tinted lenses. Then he brings three fingers to his lips in a neat triangle and whistles long and low, sloping up sharp to cut off at the peak. A moment passes: he whistles again. And then we see it—out there at the far corner of the field—the ripple, the dashing furrow, the blur of the streaking dog, white chest, flashing feet.

They are in the woods now. The boy whistling, hands in pockets, kicking along with his short darling strides, the dog beside him wagging the white tip of her tail, an all-clear flag. They pass beneath an arching black-barked oak. It creaks, and suddenly begins to fling itself down on them: immense, brutal: a panzer strike. The boy's eyes startle and then there's the leap, the smart snout clutching his trousers, the thunder-blast of the trunk, the dust and spinning leaves. "Golly, Lassie, I didn't even see it," says the boy, sitting safe in a mound of moss. The collie looks up at him—the svelte snout, the deep gold logician's eyes—and laps at his face.

Now they are down by the river. The water is brown with angry suppurations, spiked with branches, fence posts, tires, and logs. It rushes like the sides of boxcars, chews deep and insidious at the bank under Timmy's feet. The roar is like a jetport—little wonder the boy cannot hear the dog's warning bark. We watch the crack appear, widen to a ditch, then the halves splitting—snatch of red earth, writhe of worm—the poise and pitch, and Timmy crushing down with it. Just a flash—but already he is way downstream, his head like a plastic jug, dashed and bobbed, spinning toward the nasty mouth of the falls. But there is the dog—fast as a flashcube—bursting along the bank, all white and gold, blended in motion, hair sleeked with the wind of it . . . yet what can she hope to do? The current surges on, lengths ahead, sure bet to win the race to the falls. Timmy sweeps closer, sweeps closer, the falls loud as a hundred timpani now, the war drums of the Sioux, Africa gone bloodlust mad! The dog forges ahead, lashing over the wet earth like a whipcrack, straining every ganglion, until at last she draws abreast of the boy. Then she is in the air, then the foaming yellow water. Her paws churning like pistons, whiskers chuffing with exertion—oh, the roar!—and there, she's got him, her sure jaws clamping down on the shirt collar, her eyes fixed on the slip of rock at falls' edge. The black brink of the falls, the white paws digging at the rock—and they are safe. The dog sniffs at the inert little form, nudges the boy's side until she manages to roll him over. She clears his tongue and begins mouth-to-mouth.

Night: the barnyard still, a bulb burning over the screen door. Inside, the family sits at dinner, the table heaped with pork chops, mashed potatoes, applesauce and peas, home-baked bread, a pitcher of immaculate milk. Mom and Dad, good-humored and sympathetic, poised at attention, forks in mid-swoop, while Timmy tells his story.

"So then Lassie grabbed me by the collar and, golly, I guess I blanked out because I don't remember anything more till I woke up on the rock—"

"Well, I'll be," says Mom.

"You're lucky you've got such a good dog, son," says Dad, gazing down at the collie where she lies serenely, snout over paw, tail wapping the floor. She is combed and washed and fluffed, her lashes mascaraed and curled, chest and paws white as soap. She looks up humbly. But then her ears leap, her neck jerks around—and she's up at the door, head cocked, alert. A high yipping yowl, like a stuttering fire whistle, shudders through the room. And then another. The dog whines.

"Darn," says Dad. "I thought we were rid of those coyotes. Next thing you know they'll be after the chickens again."

The moon blanches the yard, leans black shadows on trees, the barn. Upstairs in the house, Timmy lies sleeping in the pale light, his hair gorgeously mussed, his breathing gentle. The collie lies on the throw rug beside the bed, her eyes open. Suddenly she rises and slips to the window, silent as shadow, and looks down the long elegant snout to the barnyard below, where the coyote slinks from shade to shade, a limp pullet dangling from his jaws. He is stunted, scabious, syphilitic, his forepaw trap-twisted, eyes running. The collie whimpers softly from the window. The coyote stops in mid-trot, frozen in a cold shard of light, ears high on his head—then drops the chicken at his feet, leers up at the window and begins a crooning, sad-faced song.

The screen door slaps behind Timmy as he bolts from the house, Lassie at his heels. Mom's head pops forth on the rebound. "Timmy!" The boy stops as if jerked by a rope, turns to face her. "You be home before lunch, hear?"

"Sure, Mom," the boy says, already spinning off, the dog at his side.

In the woods, Timmy steps on a rattler and the dog bites its head off. "Gosh," he says. "Good girl, Lassie." Then he stumbles and flips over an embankment, rolls down the brushy incline and over a sudden precipice, whirling out into the breathtaking blue space, a sky diver. He thumps down on a narrow ledge twenty feet below—and immediately scrambles to his feet, peering timorously down the sheer wall to the heap of bleached bones at its base. Small stones break loose, shoot out like asteroids. Dirt-slides begin. But Lassie yarps reassuringly from above, sprints back to the barn for winch and cable, hoists the boy to safety.

On their way back for lunch Timmy leads them through a still and leaf-darkened copse. But notice that birds and crickets have left off their cheeping. How puzzling! Suddenly, around a bend in the path before them, the coyote appears. Nose to the ground, intent. All at once he jerks to a halt, flinches as if struck, hackles rising, tail dipping between his legs. The collie, too, stops short, yards away, her chest proud and shaggy and white. The coyote cowers, bunches like a cat, glares. Timmy's face sags with alarm. The coyote lifts his lip. But the collie prances up and stretches her nose out to him, her eyes liquid. She is balsamed and perfumed; her full chest tapers to sleek haunches and sculpted legs. The coyote is puny, runted, half her size, his coat a discarded doormat. She circles him now, sniffing. She whimpers, he growls, throaty and tough—and stands stiff while she licks at his whiskers, noses his rear, the bald black scrotum. Timmy is horror-struck as the coyote slips behind her, his black lips tight with anticipation.

"What was she doing, Dad?" Timmy asks over his milk, good hot soup, and sandwich.

"The sky was blue today, son," Dad says. "The barn was red."

Late afternoon: the sun mellow, orange. Purpling clots of shadow hang from the branches, ravel out from tree trunks. Bees and wasps and flies saw away at the wet full-bellied air. Timmy and the dog are far out beyond the north pasture, out by the old Indian burial ground, where the boy stoops to search for arrowheads. The collie is pacing the crest above, whimpering voluptuously, pausing from time to time to stare out across the forest, eyes distant and moonstruck. Behind her, storm clouds, dark exploding brains, spread over the horizon.

We observe the wind kicking up: leaves flapping like wash, saplings quivering. It darkens quickly now, clouds scudding low and smoky over treetops, blotting the sun from view. Lassie's white is whiter than ever, highlighted against the heavy horizon, wind-whipped hair foaming around her. Still, she does not look down at the boy as he digs.

The first fat random drops, a flash, the volcanic blast of thunder. Timmy glances over his shoulder at the noise just in time to see the scorched pine plummeting toward the constellated freckles in the center of his forehead. Now the collie turns—too late!—the *swoosh-whack* of the tree, the trembling needles. She is there in an instant, tearing at the green welter, struggling through to his side. The boy lies unconscious in the muddying earth, hair cunningly arranged, a thin scratch painted on his cheek. The trunk lies across his back, the tail of a brontosaurus. The rain falls.

Lassie tugs doggedly at a knob in the trunk, her pretty paws slipping in the wet—but it's no use—it would take a block and tackle, a crane, a corps of engineers to shift that stubborn bulk. She falters, licks at the boy's ear, whimpers. See the troubled look in Lassie's eye as she hesitates, uncertain, priorities warring: stand guard—or dash for help? Her decision is sure and swift—eyes firm with purpose, she's off like shrapnel, already up the hill, shooting past dripping trees, over river, cleaving high wet banks of wheat.

A moment later she dashes through the puddled and rain-screened barnyard, barking right on up to the back door, where she pauses to scratch daintily, her voice high-pitched, insistent. Mom swings open the door and Lassie pads in, toenails clacking on the shiny linoleum.

"What is it, girl? What's the matter? Where's Timmy?"

"Yarf! Yarfata-yarf-yarf!"

"Oh, my! Dad! Dad, come quickly!"

Dad rushes in, face stolid and reassuring. "What is it, dear? . . . Why, Lassie!"

"Oh, Dad, Timmy's trapped under a pine tree out by the old Indian burial ground—"

"Arpit-arp."

"—a mile and a half past the north pasture."

Dad is quick, firm, decisive. "Lassie, you get back up there and stand watch over Timmy. Mom and I will go for Doc Walker. Hurry now!"

The dog hesitates at the door: "Rarfarrar-ra!"

"Right!" says Dad. "Mom, fetch the chain saw."

See the woods again. See the mud-running burial ground, the fallen pine, and there: Timmy! He lies in a puddle, eyes closed, breathing slow. The hiss of the rain is nasty as static. See it work: scattering leaves, digging trenches, inciting streams to swallow their banks. It lies deep now in the low areas, and in the mid areas, and in the high areas. Now see the dam, some indeterminate distance off, the yellow water, like urine, churning over its lip, the ugly earthen belly distended, bloated with the pressure. Rain-drops pock the surface like a plague.

Now see the pine once more . . . and . . . what is it? There! The coyote! Sniffing, furtive, the malicious eyes, the crouch, the slink. He stiffens when he spots the boy—but then he slouches closer, a rubbery dangle drooling from between his mismeshed teeth. Closer. Right over the prone figure now, stooping, head dipping between shoulders, irises caught in the corners of his eyes: wary, sly, predatory: a vulture slavering over fallen life.

But wait! Here comes Lassie! Sprinting out of the wheat field, bounding rock to rock across the crazed river, her limbs contourless with speed and purpose.

The jolting front seat of the Ford. Dad, Mom, the Doctor, all dressed in slickers and flap-brimmed hats, sitting shoulder to shoulder behind the clapping wipers, their jaws set with determination, eyes aflicker with downright gumption.

The coyote's jaws, serrated grinders, work at the bones of Timmy's hand. The boy's eyelids flutter with the pain, and he lifts his head feebly—but slaps it down again, flat, lifeless, in the mud. Now see Lassie blaze over the hill, show-dog indignation aflame in her eyes. The scrag of a coyote looks up at her, drooling blood, choking down choice bits of flesh. He looks up from eyes that go back thirty million years. Looks up unmoved, uncringing, the ghastly snout and murderous eyes less a physical than a philo-sophical challenge. See the collie's expression alter in mid-bound—the counte-nance of offended A.K.C. morality giving way, dissolving. She skids to a halt, drops her tail and approaches him, a buttery gaze in her golden eyes. She licks the blood from his vile lips.

The dam. Impossibly swollen, the rain festering the yellow surface, a hundred new streams rampaging in, the pressure of those millions of gallons hard-punching millions more. There! The first gap, the water flashing out, a boil splattering. The dam shudders, splinters, blasts to pieces like crockery. The roar is devastating.

The two animals start at the terrible rumbling. Still working their gummy jaws, they dash up the far side of the hill. See the white-tipped tail retreating side by side with the hacked and tick-crawling one—both tails like banners as the animals disappear into the trees at the top of the rise. Now look back to the rain, the fallen pine in the crotch of the valley, the spot of the boy's head. Oh, the sound of it, the wall of water at the far end of the valley, smashing through the little declivity, a God-sized fist prickling with shattered trunks and boulders, grinding along, a planet dislodged. And see Timmy: eyes closed, hair plastered, arm like meatmarket leftovers.

But now see Mom and Dad and the Doctor struggling over the rise, the torrent seething closer, booming and howling. Dad launches himself in full charge down the hillside—but the water is already sweeping over the fallen pine, lifting it like paper. There is a confusion, a quick clip of a typhoon at sea—is that a flash of golden hair?—and it is over. The valley fills to the top of the rise, the water ribbed and rushing.

But we have stopped looking. For we go sweeping up and out of the dismal rain, back to magnificent wheat fields in midday sun. There is a boy cupping his hands to his mouth and he is calling: "Laahh-sie! Laahh-sie!"

Then we see what we must see—way out there at the end of the field—the ripple, the dashing furrow, the blur of the streaking dog, white chest, flashing feet.

[JANUARY 1975]

HERBERT WILNER

The

Quarterback

Speaks to His

God

Herbert Wilner (1925–1977) was a dedicated teacher in the well-known writing program at San Francisco State. He published a startling collection of stories, Dovisch in the Wilderness, in 1968 and a novel, All the Little Heroes, in 1966. "The Quarterback Speaks to His God," also the title of a collection of Wilner's stories, was published posthumously in Esquire; in the clinical details of the protagonist's heart disease it is poignantly autobiographical.

Bobby Kraft, the heroic old pro, lies in his bed in the grip of medicines relieving his ailing heart. Sometimes he tells his doctor your pills beat my ass, and the doctor says it's still Kraft's choice: medicine or open heart surgery. Kraft shuts up.

He wasn't five years out of pro football, retired at thirty-six after fourteen years, when he got the rare viral blood infection. Whatever they were, the damn things ate through his heart like termites, leaving him with pericarditis, valve dysfunction, murmurs, arrhythmia, and finally, congestive failure. The physiology has been explained to him, but he prefers not to understand it. Fascinated in the past by his strained ligaments, sprained ankles, torn cartilage, tendinitis, he now feels betrayed by his heart's disease.

"You want to hear it?" Dr. Felton once asked, offering the earpieces of the stethoscope.

Kraft recoiled.

"You don't want to hear the sound of your own heart?"

Sitting on the examining table, Kraft was as tall as the short doctor, whose mustache hid a crooked mouth.

"Why should I?" Kraft said. "Would you smile in the mirror after your teeth got knocked out?"

This morning in bed, as with almost every third morning of the past two years, Kraft begins to endure the therapeutic power of his drugs. He takes diuretics: Edecrin, or Lasix, or Dyazide, or combinations. They make him piss and piss, relieving for a day or two the worst effects of the congesting fluids that swamp his lungs and gut. He's been told the washout dumps potassium, an unfortunate consequence. The depletions cramp his muscles, give him headaches, sometimes trigger arrhythmias. They always drive him into depressions as deep as comas. He blames himself.

"It has nothing to do with willpower," Dr. Felton explained, "If you ran five miles in Death Valley in August, you'd get about the same results as you do from a very successful diuresis."

To replenish some of his losses, Kraft stuffs himself with bananas, drinks orange juice by the pint, and takes two tablespoons a day of potassium chloride solution. To prevent and arrest the arrhythmia, he takes quinidine, eight pills a day, two hundred milligrams per pill. To strengthen the enlarged and weakened muscle of his heart wall, he takes digoxin. Together they make him nauseous, gassy, and distressed. He takes antinausea pills and chews antacids as though they were Life Savers. Some nights he takes Valium to fall asleep. If one doesn't work, he takes two.

"I can't believe it's me," he protests to his wife, Elfi. "I never took pills, I wouldn't even touch aspirins. There were guys on coke, amphetamines, Novocain. I wouldn't touch anything. Now look at me. I'm living in a drugstore."

His blurred eyes sweep the squads of large and small dark labeled bottles massed on his chest of drawers. His wife offers little sympathy.

"Again and again the same thing with you," she'll answer in her German accent. "So go have the surgery already, you coward ox."

Coward? Him? Bobby Kraft?

"I have to keep recommending against surgery," said Dr. Felton, named by the team physician as the best cardiologist in the city for Kraft's problems. "I'm not certain it can provide the help worth the risk. Meanwhile, we buy time. Every month these hotshot surgeons get better at their work. Our equipment for telling us precisely what's wrong with your heart gets better. In the meantime, since you don't need to work for a living, wait it out. Sit in the sun. Read. Watch television. Talk about the old games. Wait."

What does coward have to do with it?

This morning, in his bed, three hours after the double dose of Lasix with a Dyazide thrown in, Kraft has been to the toilet bowl fourteen times. His breathing is easier, his gut is relieved; and now he has to survive the payments of his good results.

He's dry as a stone, exhausted, and has a headache. The base of his skull feels kicked. The muscles of his neck are wrenched and pulled, as if they'd been wound on a spindle. His hips ache. So do his shoulder joints. His calves are heavy. They're tightening into cramps. His ankles feel as though tissue is dissolving in them, flaking off into small crystals, eroding gradually by bumping each other in slight, swirling collisions before they dissolve altogether in a bath of serum. His ankles feel absent.

He's cold. Under the turned up electric blanket, he has chills. His heart feels soaked.

He wants to stay awake, but he can't help sleeping. By the sixth of his returns from the bowl, he was collapsing into the bed. Falling asleep was more like fainting, like going under, like his knee surgery—some imperfect form of death. He needs to stay awake. His will is all that's left him for proving himself, but his will is shot by the depression he can't control.

By tomorrow he'll be mostly out of bed. He'll have reduced the Lasix to one pill, no Dyazide, piss just a little, and by the day after, with luck guarding against salt in his food, he'll have balanced out. He'll sit on the deck in his shorts when the sun starts to burn a little at noon. He'll squeeze the rubber ball in his right hand. He'll take a shower afterwards and oil himself down to rub the flaking off. He'll look at himself in the full-length mirror and stare at the part of his chest where the injured heart is supposed to be. He'll see little difference from what he saw five years ago when he was still playing. The shoulders sloping and wide, a little less full but not bony, the chest a little less deep but still broad and tapered, the right arm still flat-muscled and whip-hanging, same as it was ten years ago when he could throw a football sixty yards with better than fair accuracy. What he'll see in the mirror can infuriate him.

He once got angry enough to put on his sweat suit, go through the gate at the back fence and start to run in the foot-wide level dirt beside the creek bed in the shade of the laurels. After five cautious strides, he lengthened into ten hard ones. Then he was on his knees gasping for air, his heart arrhythmic, his throat congested. He couldn't move for five minutes. By the next day he'd gained six pounds. He told Elfi what he'd done.

"Imbecile!" She called the doctor. Kraft, his ankles swollen, was into heart failure. It was touch and go about sending him to the hospital for intravenous diuretics and relief oxygen.

It took a month to recover, he never made another effort to run, but he knew even today, that after all this pissing and depression, exhaustion and failure, when he balanced out the day after tomorrow and he was on the deck and the sun hit, nothing could keep the impulse out of his legs. He'd want to run. He'd feel the running in his legs. And he'd settle for a few belittling house chores, then all day imagine he'd have a go at screwing Elfi. But at night he didn't dare try.

When she gets home from her day with the retards, she fixes her Campari on ice, throws the dinner together, at which, as always, she pecks like a bird and he shovels what he can, making faces to advertise his nausea, rubbing his abdomen to soothe his distress and belching to release the gas. After dinner he'll report his day, shooting her combative looks to challenge the boredom glazing her face. They move to the living room. Standing, he towers over her. He's six foot two inches and she's tiny. His hand, large even for his size, would cover the top of her skull the way an ordinary man's might encapsulate an egg. She stretches full length on the couch; he slouches in the club chair. She wears a tweed skirt and buttoned blouse, he's in his pajamas and terry-cloth robe. He still has a headache. His voice drones monotonously in his own ears, but he's obsessed with accounting for his symptoms as though they were football statistics. When he at last finishes, she sits up and nods.

"So all in all today is a little better. Nothing with the bad rhythm."

He gets sullen, then angry. No one has ever annoyed him as effectively as she. He'd married her six years ago, just before his retirement, as he'd always planned. He knew the stewardesses, models, second-rate actresses, and just plain hotel whores would no longer do. He'd need children, a son. And this tiny woman's German accent and malicious tongue had knocked him out. And sometimes he caught her reciting prayers in French (she said for religion it was the perfect language), which seemed to him—a man without religion—unexplainably peculiar and right.

Now, offended by her flint heart (calling *this* a better day!), he goes to the den for TV. He has another den with shelves full of his history—plaques, cups, trophies, photos (one with the President of the United States), footballs, medals, albums, videotapes—but he no longer enters this room. After an hour, she comes in after him. She wants to purr. He wants to be left alone. His headache is worse, his chest tingles. She recounts events of her day, one of the two during the week when she drives to the city and consults at a school for what she calls learning-problem children. He doesn't even pretend to listen. She sulks.

Words go back and forth. He didn't think he could do it, but he tells her. In roundabout fashion, the TV jabbering, he finally makes her understand his latest attack of anxiety: the feel of his not feeling it. His prick.

She looks amazed, as if she were still not understanding him, then her eyes widen and she taps herself on the temple.

"You I don't understand," she sputters. "To me your head is something for doctors. Every day I worry sick about your heart, and you give me this big soap opera about your prick. Coward. You should go for the surgery. Every week you get worse, whatever that Dr. Felton says. You let all those oxes fall on you and knock you black and blue, then a little cutting with a knife, and you shiver. When they took away your football, they broke your baby's heart. So now, sew it up again. Let a surgeon do it. You don't know how. You think your heart can get better by itself? In you, Bobby, never."

When it suits her, she exaggerates her mispronunciation of his name. "*Beaub*ee. *Beaub*ee. What kind of name is this for a grown man your size, Beaubee?"

He heads to the bedroom to slam the door behind him. After ten minutes, the door opens cautiously. She sits at the edge of the bed near his feet. She strokes the part of the blanket covering his feet, puts her cheek to it, then straightens, stands, says it to him.

"I love you better than my own life. I swear it. How else could I stay with you?"

He hardly hears her. His attention concentrates on the first signs of his arrhythmia. He tells her, "It's beginning." She says she'll fetch the quinidine. She carries his low-sodium milk for him to drink it with. He glances at her woefully through what used to be ice-blue eyes fixed in his head like crystals. He stares at the pills before he swallows them. He can identify any of them by color, shape and size. He doesn't trust her. She can't nurse, she always panics.

His heart is fluttering, subsiding, fluttering. Finally it levels off at the irregularity of the slightly felt extra beat which Felton has told him is an auricular fibrillation. Elfi finds an excuse to leave the room. He sits up in bed, his eyes closed, his thick back rammed against the sliding pillows, his head arched over them, the crown drilling into the headboard.

The flurries have advanced to a continuously altering input of extra beats. They are light and rapid, like the scurryings under his breastbone of a tiny creature with scrawny limbs. After ten minutes, the superfluous beats intensify and ride over the regular heartbeats.

There's chaos in his heart. Following a wild will of its own, it has nothing to do with him, nor can he do anything with it. Moderate pain begins in his upper left arm, and though the doctor has assured him it's nothing significant, and he knows it will last only through the arrhythmia, Kraft begins to sweat.

The heart goes wilder. He rubs his chest, runs his hands across the protruding bones of his cheeks and jaw. Ten minutes later the heart begins to yank as well as thump. It feels as if the heart's apex is stitched into tissues near the bottom of his chest, and the yanking of the bulk of the heart will tear the threads loose. Again and again he tries to will himself into the cool accommodation he can't command. Then at last it seems that for a few minutes the force of the intrusive beats is diminishing. He dares to hope it's now the beginning of the end of the episode.

Immediately a new sequence of light and differently irregular flurries resumes. The thumpings are now also on his back. He turns to his right side, flicks the control for the television, tries to lose himself with it, hears Elfi come in. She whispers, "Still?" and leaves again.

The thumpings deepen. They are really pounding. The headache is drilled in his forehead. It throbs. He thinks the heart is making sounds that can be heard in the room. He claws his long fingers into the tough flesh over the heart. It goes on for another hour. He waits, and waits. Then, indeed, in moments, they fade into the flutter with which they began. After a while the flutter is hard to pick out, slips under the regular beating of his heart and gives way at last to an occasional extra beat which pokes at his chest with the feel of a mild bubbling of thick pudding at a slow boil. Then that's gone.

His heart has had its day's event.

Kraft tells himself: nothing's worth this. He's told it to himself often. He tells himself he'll see Felton tomorrow. He'll insist on the surgery.

Afraid of surgery? Coward? She wasn't even in his life when he had his knee done after being blindsided in Chicago. He came out of the anesthesia on a cloud. The bandage on his leg went from thigh to ankle, but the girl who came to visit him—stewardess, model, the cocktail waitress—he couldn't remember now, she was the one whose eyes changed colors—she had to fight him off because he kept rubbing his hand under her skirt up the soft inside of her thigh. She ended on his bed on top of him. He was almost instantaneous. He had to throw her off, remembering his leg, his career. But was it really that Felton runt who was keeping him from surgery?

In despair now, could he really arrange for the surgery tomorrow? Not on a knee, but on his opened heart?

Bobby Kraft's heart?

"That's crap," he once said to a young reporter. "Any quarterback can throw. We all start from there. Some of us do it a little better. That's not what it's all about. Throwing ain't passing, sonny, and passing ain't all of quarterbacking anyway."

"You mean picking your plays. Using your head. Reading defenses?"

"That's important. It's not all of it."

"What's the mystique?" the youth asked shyly, fearful of ignorance. "Not in your arm, not in your head. I know you all have guts or wouldn't play in such a violent game. If it's a special gift, where do you keep it?"

"In your goddamn chest, sonny. Where the blood comes." He smiled and stared icily at the reporter until the young man turned away.

Actually, Kraft worked hard mastering the technical side of his skills. If he needed to, for instance, if the wind wasn't strong against him, he could hang the ball out fifty yards without putting too much arc in it. It should've been a heavy ball to catch for a receiver running better than ten yards to the second. But Kraft, in any practice, could get it out there inches ahead of the outstretched arms and have the forward end of the ball, as it was coming down, begin to point up slightly over its spiraling axis. That way it fell with almost no weight at all. The streaking receiver could palm it in one hand, as if he were snatching a fruit from a tree he ran by. It took Kraft years to get it right and do it in games.

There were ways of taking the ball from the center, places on it for each of his fingers, ways of wrist-cradling the ball before he threw if he had to break his pocket, and there was the rhythm set up between his right arm and the planting of his feet before he released the ball through the picket of huge, upraised arms.

He watched the films. He studied the game book. He worked with the coaches and his receivers for any coming Sunday. What the other team did every other time they played you, and what they did all season was something you had to remember. You also had to be free of it. You had to yield to the life of the particular game, build it, master it, improvise. And always you not only had to stand up to their cries of "Kill Kraft," you had to make them eat it. The sonsabitches!

That's what Kraft did most of the week waiting for his Sunday game. He worked the "sonsabitches" into a heat. Then he slid outside himself and watched it. It was like looking at a fire he'd taken out of his chest to hold before eyes. Tense all week, his eyes grew colder and colder as they gazed at the flame. By game time he was thoroughly impersonal.

Sunday on the field in the game, though he weighed 203, he looked between plays somewhat on the slender side, like someone who could get busted like a stick by most of those he played among. He stood out of the huddle a long time before he entered it through the horseshoe's slot to call the play. Outside the huddle, except in the last minutes when they might be fighting the clock, his pose was invariable. His right foot was anchored with the toe toward the opening for him in his huddle about nine feet away, the left angled toward where the referee had placed the ball. It threw his torso on a rakish slant toward the enormous opposing linemen, as though he'd tight-rigged himself against a headland. He kept the knuckles of his right hand high on his right ass, the fingers limp. His left hand hung motionless on his left side. Under his helmet, his head turned slowly and his eyes darted. He wasn't seeing anything that would matter. They'd change it all around when he got behind the center. He was emptying himself for his concentration. It was on the three strides back to the huddle that he picked his play and barked it to them in a toneless, commanding fierceness just short of rage.

Then the glory began for Kraft. What happened, what he lived for never got into the papers; it wasn't seen on television. What he saw was only part of what he knew. He would watch the free safety or the outside linebackers for giveaway cues on the blitz. He might detect from jumping linemen some of the signs of looping. The split second before he had the ball he might spot assignment against his receivers and automatically register the little habits and capacities of the defending sonsabitches. He could "feel" the defenses.

But none of it really began until, after barking the cadence of his signals, he actually did have the ball in his hand. Then, for the fraction of a second before he gave it away to a runner, or for the maximum three seconds in the pocket before he passed, there was nothing but grunting and roaring and cursing, the crashing of helmets and pads, the oofs of air going out of brutish men and the whisk of legs in tight pants cutting air like a scythe in tall grass and the soft suck of cleats in the grassy sod, and the actual vibration of the earth itself stampeded by that tonnage of sometimes gigantic, always fast, cruel, lethal bodies. And if Kraft kept the ball, if he dropped his three paces back into his protective pocket, he'd inch forward before he released it and turn his shoulders or his hips to slip past the bodies clashing at his sides. He would always sense and sometimes never see the spot to which he had to throw the ball through the nests of the raised arms of men two to five inches taller than himself and twice as broad and sixty, eighty pounds heavier. One of their swinging arms could, if he didn't see it coming, knock him off his feet as though he were a matchstick. He was often on his back or side, a pile of the sonsabitches taking every gouge and kick and swipe at him they could get away with. That was the sweetness for him.

To have his ass beaten and not even know it. To have that rush inside him mounting all through the game, and getting himself more and more under control as he heated up, regarding himself without awareness of it, his heart given to the fury, and his mind to a sly and joyous watching of his heart, storing up images that went beyond the choral roaring of any huge crowd and that he would feed on through the week waiting for the next game, aching through the week but never knowing in the game any particular blow that would make him hurt. Not after the first time he got belted. They said he had rubber in his joints, springs in his ass, and a whip for an arm.

The combination of his fierce combativeness and laid-back detachment infuriated the sonsabitches he played against. They hated him; it made them lose their heads. It was all the advantage Kraft ever needed. His own teammates, of course, went crazy with the game. They wound themselves up for it in the hours before it, and some of them didn't come down until the day after, regardless of who won.

Kraft depended on their lunacy. He loved them for needing it. And he loved them most during the game because no one ever thought of him as being like them. He was too distant. Too cunning. Too cold. But on the sideline, among them, waiting for his defensive team to get him back into the game, he might run his tongue over his lips, taste the salty blood he didn't know was there, and swallow. Then he'd rub his tongue across his gums and over the inside of a cheek, and an expression of wonder might flicker across his face, as if he were a boy with his first lick at the new candy, tasting the sweetness of his gratified desires, not on his tongue but in his own heart.

Three more months passed with Kraft delivered up to the cycles of his illness and medicines and waiting and brooding. Then he was sitting in his sweat socks and trunks at the side of the pool one late afternoon. He gazed vacantly at the water. His chest had caved a little; and his long head seemed larger, his wide neck thicker. Elfi had been reading on a mat near the fence under the shade of a laurel.

"So how long are you going to live like this?" she asked. Immediately he thought she was talking sex. "Two more years? Five? Ten?" She crossed her arms over her slender, fragile chest. "Maybe even fifteen, hah? But sooner or later you'll beg them for the surgery. On your knees. So why do you wait? Look how you lose all the time you could be better in."

His answer was pat.

"I told you. They can cut up my gut. They can monkey with my head. They can cut off my right arm even, how's that? But they're not going to cut up my heart. That's all. They're not putting plastic valves in my heart."

"Again with this plastic. Listen, I am reading a lot about it. There are times they can put in a valve from a sheep, or a pig."

He looked at her in amazement. He stood up. She came to his collarbone; he cast a shade over all of her.

"Sheep and pig!"

He looked like he might slam her, then he turned away and headed for the glass door to the bedroom.

"Your heart," she said. "You have such a special heart?"

When he turned she looked up at him and backed off a step.

"Yeah, it's special. My heart's me." He stabbed his chest with the long thumb of his right hand.

"You think I don't understand that? With my own heart I understand that. But this is the country where surgeons make miracles. You are lucky. It happens to you here, where you are such a famous ox. And here they have the surgeon who's also so famous. For him, what you have is a—is a—a blister."

He glared. She backed off another step. He turned and dove suddenly into the pool, touched bottom, came up slowly and thought he could live a long time in a chilly, blue, chlorinated water in which he would, suspended, always hold his breath. He rose slowly, broke the water at the nearer wall, hoisted himself at the coping and emerged from the water, with his back and shoulders glistening. He was breathless, but he moved on to the bedroom. He didn't double over until he had closed the glass door behind him. While he waited for his throat to empty and his chest to fill, he hurt. He got dizzy. Bent, he moved to the bed and fell on it. He stretched out.

He napped, or thought he did. When he woke, or his mind cleared, words filled him. He clasped his hands behind his neck, closed his eyes and tried to shut the words out. He got off the bed and stood before the full-length mirror. He put his hands to his thighs, bent his weight forward, clamped the heels of his hands together, dropped his left palm to make a nest for the ball the center would snap. Numbers barked in his head. When he heard the hup-hup he moved back the two swift steps, planted his feet, brought his right arm high behind his head, the elbow at his ear, then released the shoulder and snapped the wrist. He did it twice more. He was grinning. When he started it the fourth time, he was into arrhythmia.

Kraft consults Dr. Felton. Felton examines him, sits, glances at him, gazes at the ceiling, puts the tips of his index fingers to a pyramid point on his mustache and says, "I'm still opposed, but I'll call him." He means the heart surgeon, Dr. Gottfried. They arrange for Kraft to take preliminary tests. He has already had some of them, but the heart catheterization will be new. A week later Kraft enters the hospital.

An hour after he's in his room, a parade of doctors begin the listening and thumping on Kraft's chest and back. A bearded doctor in his early thirties who will assist in the morning's catheterization briefs him on what to expect. He speaks rapidly.

"You'll be awake, of course. You'll find it a painless procedure. We'll use a local on your arm where we insert the catheter. When it touches a wall of the heart, you might have a little flurry of heartbeats. Don't worry about it. Somewhere in the process we'll ask you to exercise a little. We need some measurements of the heart under physical stress. You won't have to do more than you can. Toward the end we'll inject a purple dye. We get very precise films that way. You'll probably get some burning sensations while the dye circulates. A couple of minutes or so. Otherwise you'll be quite comfortable. Do you have any questions?"

Kraft has a hundred and asks none.

The doctor starts out of the room, stops, comes back a little haltingly. He has his pen in his hand and his prescription pad out.

"Mr. Kraft, I have a nephew. He'd get a big kick out of . . ."

Kraft takes the extended pad and pen. "What's his name?"

"Oh, just sign yours."

He writes: "For the doc and his nephew for good luck from Bobby Kraft." He returns the items. He feels dead.

In the morning they move him on a gurney to a thick-walled room in the basement. He's asked to slide onto an X-ray table. They cover him with a sheet. He raises himself on his elbows to see people busy at tasks he can't understand. There are two women and two men. All of them wear white. One of the women sits before a console full of knobs and meters on a table near his feet. Above and behind his head is a machine he'll know later is a fluoroscope. In a corner of the room there's a concrete alcove, the kind X-ray technicians hide behind. One of the men keeps popping in and out of its opening on his way to and from the fluoroscope. The ceiling is full of beams and grids on which X-ray equipment slides back and forth and is lowered and raised. The other man plays with it, and with film plates he slides under the table. A nurse attaches EKG bands to his ankles.

The two doctors come in. They are already masked, rubber-gloved and dressed in green. The bearded one introduces the other, who has graying hair and brown eyes. A nurse fits Kraft's right arm into a metal rest draped with towels. "I'm going to tie your wrist," she says. She ties it and tucks the towels over his hand and wrist and over his shoulder and biceps. She washes the inside of his shaved arm with alcohol, rubbing hard at the crook of his elbow. The bearded doctor ties his arm tightly with a rubber strap, just above the elbow, then feels with his fingers in the crook of the elbow for the raised vessels. He swabs the skin with the yellow Xylocaine and waits. The other doctor asks the nurse at the console if she is ready. She says, "Not yet." He looks at Kraft, and Kraft looks up at the rails and grids.

In a few minutes the bearded doctor injects the anesthetic into several spots high on the inside of Kraft's forearm. It takes ten more minutes before the woman at the console is ready. She gets up twice to check with the man in the alcove. The older doctor goes there once. When the woman finally signals she's ready, Dr. Kahl says, "OK." Kraft looks. The older doctor stands alongside Kahl. The scalpel goes quickly into Kraft's flesh in a short cut. He doesn't feel it. Kahl removes the scalpel, and a little blood seeps. The doctor switches instruments and goes quickly into the small wound. Blood spurts. It comes in a few pumps about six inches over Kraft's arm, a thick, rich red blood. Kraft is astonished. Then the blood stops. The towels are soaked with it.

"I'm putting the cath in."

The older doctor nods. He turns toward the fluoroscope. Kraft watches again. The catheter is black and silky and no thicker than a cocktail straw. Still Kraft feels nothing. Kahl's brow creases. He's manipulating the black, slender thing with his rubbered fingers. He rolls his thumb along it as he moves it. Kraft waits to feel something. There is no feeling. He can't see where the loose end of the catheter is coming from. He turns his head away and takes a deep breath. He takes another deep one. He wants to relax. He wants to know how the hell he got into all this. What really happened to him? When? What for?

"You're in," the older doctor says.

The thing is in his heart.

It couldn't have taken more than ten seconds. They are in his heart with a black silky tube and he can't feel it.

"Hold it," the nurse at the console says. She begins calling out numbers.

"How are you feeling?" Dr. Kahl asks. Kraft nods.

"You feeling all right?" the older doctor repeats, walking toward the fluoroscope.

"Yeah."

They go on and on. He feels nothing. He hears the older doctor instructing the younger one: "Try the ventricle. . . . Hold it. . . . What's your reading now? . . . There's the flutter. . . . Don't worry about that, Mr. Kraft. . . . Watch the pulmonary artery. . . . He's irritable in there. . . . Withdraw! . . . Fine, you're through the cusps. . . . Try the mitral. . . . You're on the wall again. . . . How are you feeling, Mr. Kraft?"

Kraft nods. He licks his lips. He tries not to listen to them. When the flutter goes off in his chest, he thinks it will start an arrhythmia. It doesn't. It feels like a hummingbird hovering in his chest for a second. Something catches it. Occasionally the other doctor comes beside Kahl and plays for a moment with the catheter while he watches the fluoroscope. The bearded doctor chats sometimes, saying he's sorry Kraft has to lie so flat for so long, it must be uncomfortable. Does he use many pillows at home? Would he like to raise up for a while?

The arm hurts where the catheter enters it. Kraft feels a firm growing lump under the flesh, as if a golf ball is being forced into the wound. Kraft concentrates on the pain. He thinks of grass.

"How much longer?" he asks.

"We're more than halfway."

In a while the nurse tells him they are going to have him do the exercises now. Something presses against his feet. The brown-eyed doctor talks.

"We have an apparatus here with bicycle pedals. Just push on them as you would on a bike. We'll adjust the pedals to keep making you push with more force. If it gets to be too much work, tell us. We want you to exert yourself, but not tire yourself."

What's he talking about, Kraft asks himself. He begins to pump. There's no resistance. He pumps faster, harder.

"That's fine. Keep it going. You're doing real fine."

He gets a rhythm to it quickly, thrusting his legs as rapidly as he can. He expects to get winded, but he doesn't. He's doing fine. He almost enjoys it. He concentrates. He feels the pain in his arm and pumps harder, faster. He imagines he's racing. For a moment it gets more difficult to pump. He presses harder, feels his calves stretch and harden. He gets his rhythm back. They encourage him. He licks his lips and clasps the edge of the table with his left hand and drives his legs. He forgets about any race. He knows he's doing well with this exercise. It will show on their computation. They'll tell him his heart is getting better. The resistance to his pumping gets stronger. He pumps harder.

"That was very good. We're taking the apparatus away now. You feel all right?"

"Fine."

Kraft closes his eyes. There's the pain in his arm again. His forearm is going to pop. It's too strong a pain now. They are moving in the room. He grinds his teeth.

"We're going to inject the dye now," the older doctor says.

Kraft turns his head and sees the metal cylinder of the syringe catch glinting light for a moment in Kahl's raised hand. He sees the rubbered thumb move; a blackish fluid spurts from the needle's tip. The needle goes toward his arm—into the wound or the catheter, he can't tell. He turns away.

"You'll feel some heat in your head very soon. That's just the effect of the dye. It'll wear off. You'll feel heat at the sphincter too. Are you all right?"

Kraft nods. He turns away. Why do they keep asking him? He sees the man from the alcove hurrying with X-ray plates that he slides into the slot under the table just below Kraft's shoulder blades. He hurries back to the alcove. The doctors call instructions. The voice from the alcove calls some words back and numbers. Kraft closes his eyes and tries to think of something to think of. He thinks if Elfi could—then Kraft feels the rush. It comes in way over the pain in his arm. It raises him off the table. He feels the heat racing through him. A terrific pounding at his forehead. It doesn't go away. He tries to think of the pain in his arm, but he feels the heat rushing through him in a rising fever. Then it hits his asshole and he rises off the table again. It burns tremendously. They have lit a candle in his asshole and the burned flesh is going to drop through.

"Wow!"

"That's all right. It'll go away soon."

It does, but not the headache. It burns and throbs in his forehead. He hears metal dropping under the table. The man runs out and removes film plates. Someone else inserts others. They call numbers. The plates fall again. They repeat the process. He closes his eyes. The rush is fading, but the headache remains, throbbing.

"How you doing?"

"All right. My head aches."

"It'll pass."

"How was the exercise part?"

"You did fine. We'll be through soon. How's the arm?"

"Hurts."

"No problem. More Novocain."

"No. Leave it."

They hurry again. Words are exchanged about the films. Someone leaves the room. Someone enters it later. Kraft keeps his eyes closed. The ache is still in his forehead, but he thinks he might sleep.

"Well, that's it," the bearded Kahl says. Kraft looks toward him, then down at his arm. The wound is stitched. He hasn't felt it. The doctor covers it with a gauze pad and two strips of tape. The catheter's gone. Kraft sees no sign of it. They wash his arm of blood and get him onto the gurney. He hears someone say, "I think we got good results." The older doctor tells Kraft they'll know some things tomorrow. "It looks good."

Back in his room Elfi is waiting for him. He gets into bed, and they leave. She throws herself on him. She's breathless. Her cheeks are streaked, her eyes are red. She's been crying. She's almost crying now.

"I don't want to talk about it now," he says when she begins to speak.

"I don't want to hear it. That's the truth. Listen, I'm going home. Beaubee, I'm not good here."

She rushes from the room. He contemplates the increasing pain in his arm. It reaches into his biceps now. He keeps thinking about his heart. They had their black tube in *his* heart. The sonsabitches.

On the next day, just before lunch, reading a magazine in the chair in his room, he sees Dr. Gottfried for the first time. With him, in his white coat, is the gray-haired doctor from the catheterization. Dr. Gottfried is in the short-sleeved green shirt and the green baggy cotton

trousers of the operating room. He has scuffed sneakers, and the stethoscope—
like a metal and rubber noose—hangs from his neck. He looks tired. He has the
sad eyes of a spaniel. And yet the man—in build neither here nor there, just a
man—introduced by his colleague, stares and stares at Kraft before he moves or
speaks, like a man before a fight. He keeps looking into Kraft's eyes, as if through
his patient's eyes he could find the as yet untested condition of his true heart. He
keeps on staring; Kraft stares back. Then the great famous doctor nods; a corner
of his mouth flickers. He has apparently seen what he has needed to—and judged.
He leans over Kraft and listens with the stethoscope to Kraft's chest. He could
not have heard more than three heartbeats when he removes the earpieces, steps
back, and speaks.

"Under it all, you've got a strong heart. I can tell by the snap."

Kraft, the heroic old pro, begins to smile. He beams. The doctor speaks
in a slow, subdued voice; Kraft's smile fades.

"There's no real rush with your situation. However, the sooner the better,
and there's a canceled procedure two weeks from today. We can do you then.
I'll operate. Right now I want to study more of the material in your folder.
We've got several base lines. I'll be back soon. Dr. Pritchett will fill you in and
answer any questions you have. He knows more than anyone in the world about
pulmonary valve disease."

Leaving, Dr. Gottfried moves without a sound, his head tilted and the
shoulder on that side sagging. When he closes the door, Kraft turns on Dr.
Pritchett.

"What operation? He said my heart's good. You said you got good results
on that catheter. The fat one yesterday said he got good results on his machine."

The doctor explains. The "good" results meant they were finding what
they needed to know. They are all agreed now the linings of the heart should
be removed. A simple procedure for Dr. Gottfried—"he's the best you could
find"—even if the endocardium is scarred enough to be adhesive. They are also
agreed about the pulmonary valve. It will be removed and replaced by an artificial
device made of a flexible steel alloy. "Dr. Gottfried will just pop it right in."
We're not, however, certain of the aortic valve. "Dr. Gottfried will make that
decision during surgery." Positive results are expected. There's the strong
probability of the heart restored to ninety percent efficiency and a good possibility of total cure. Of course, you'll be on daily anticoagulant medicines for the
rest of your life. No big affair. The important point, as Dr. Gottfried said, is the
heart is essentially strong. Surgery, done now, while Kraft is young and before
the heart is irreparably weakened, is the determining factor. Of course, as in any
surgery, there's risk.

"Have I made it clear? Can I answer any questions, Mr. Kraft? I know we get too technical at times."

"I'm not stupid."

"No one implied you were."

Emptying with dread, Kraft slips his hands under the blanket to hide their trembling. "Will I still need pissing pills after the operation?"

"Diuretics? No. I wouldn't think so."

"No more arrhythmia?"

"We can't be sure of that. Sometimes the—"

"Then what kind of total cure, man?"

"I can't explain all the physics and chemistry of the heart rhythm, Mr. Kraft. If you'd continue to have the arrhythmia, it would be benign. A mechanical thing. We have medicine to control it."

"You said I did great with the exercises."

"Yes. We got the results we needed."

Dr. Gottfried returns, still in his operating clothes, holding the manila folder, looking now a little bored as well as fatigued, his voice slow, quiet.

"Any questions for me?"

"The risk? Dr. What's-his-name here said . . ."

"There's ten percent mortality risk. That covers all open heart surgery. A lot of it relates to heart disease more advanced than yours, where general health isn't as good as yours. There's risk, however, for you too. You know that."

Kraft nods. He suddenly detests this man he needs, who'll have the power of life over him. He closes his eyes.

"As I said, there's no emergency. But I can fit you in two weeks from now. You could have it over with. Decide in a day or two. I'd appreciate that. Talk it over with your wife. With Dr. Felton. Let us know through him."

Home again, Kraft, on his medicines, pissed, grew depressed, endured his headaches and lassitude, the arrhythmias, the miscellaneous pains, his sense of dissolution, the nausea; and, as before, continued to blame himself as well as feel betrayed. He submitted, and he waited. He never looked in the mirror anymore. While he shaved, he never saw himself. Sometimes he felt tearful. On the few days that he came around, he no longer went out to the sun and the pool but stayed indoors. He called no one, but answered the phone on his better days and kept up his end of the bullshit with old buddies and some writers who still remembered. No one but Elfi knew his despair.

When he passed the closed door to the den of his heroic history, his trophy room, he wasn't even aware that he kept himself from going in. The door might as well have been the wall. What he kept seeing now was behind his eyes: The face of Dr. Gottfried. It flashed like a blurred, tired, boneless, powerful shape, producing a quality before which Kraft felt weak. He began to exalt the quality and despise the man and groped for a way by which he could begin to tell Elfi.

One night, in bed with her, a week after he'd made the decision to go for the surgery, which was now less than a week away, with the lights out and her figure illumined only by a small glow of clouded moonlight entering through the cracked drapes, he thought her asleep and ventured to loop his hand over her head where he could easily reach her outside shoulder. He touched it gently. It was the first time since his discovery of his impotence that he'd touched her in bed.

Immediately she moved across the space, nestled her head in his armpit, and pressed against his side. He resisted his desire to pull away. He was truly pleased by the way she fit.

"Every day now I pray," she said. "Oh, not for you, don't worry. You are going to be fine. I swear it, how much I believe that. You don't need me to pray for you. I need it. I do it for myself. Selfishly. Entirely."

He spoke of what was on his mind. "That surgeon's freaking me."

"You couldn't find anyone better. I have the utmost confidence. To me that is what you call a man. You should see in his clinic. What the patients say about him. The eyes they have when they look at him. He walks through like a god. And I tell you something else. He has a vast understanding."

He moved his hand from her arm. "It's *my* heart, not yours." His voice fell to despair. "It's a man thing. You can't understand. A sonofabitch puts his hand in Bobby Kraft's heart. He pops in some goddamned metal valve. He's flaky. He freaks me."

"I tell you, I feel sorry for you. Too bad. For any man I feel sorry who doesn't know who are his real enemies. Not to know that, that's your freak. That's the terrible thing can happen to a man in his life. Not to know who his enemies are."

"That's what *he* is," Kraft declaimed in the darkness. "He's my enemy. If there's one thing I've always known, that's it. The sonsabitches. Now Gottfried is. And there ain't no game. I don't even get to play."

"You baby. Play. Play. It's because all your life you played a game for a boy. That's why you can't know. Precisely. I always knew that."

He pulled away from her. He got out of bed and loomed over her threateningly.

"Go on back home, Kraut. I don't need you for the operation. To hell with the operation. I'll call it off. How's that?"

"Here is home, with you. Try and make me leave. I am not a man. I don't need enemies."

He got out of bed to get away. The bitch. She'd caught him at a time when there was nothing left of him.

Kraft enters the hospital trying to imagine it's a stadium. The act lasts as long as his first smell of the antiseptics and the rubbery sound of a wheeled gurney. He tastes old metal in his mouth. He refuses the tranquilizers they keep pushing at him. He wants wakefulness. Elfi keeps visiting and fleeing.

He has nothing to say to her. She wants his buddies to come, she says he needs them. He says if one of them comes, that's it. He clears out of the hospital, period. He wants to talk, but he can't imagine a proper listener. For two years he endured what he never could have believed would've befallen him. There was no way to understand it, and this has left him now with loose ends. He can't think of any arrangement of his mind that could gather them. They simply fall out.

It occurs to him he doesn't know enough people who are dead.

It occurs to him he isn't sick enough.

He thinks he will be all right. He thinks he will be able to brag about it afterwards. Then he sees his heart and Gottfried's hand, and he wants the man there at once to ask him what right he thinks he has.

It occurs to him he never really liked football. It was just an excuse for something else.

It occurs to him he just made that up. It can't be so.

He wonders if he has ever really slept *with* Elfi. With any woman.

He laments his development of a double chin.

Sleep is a measure of defeat. Before games he never slept well.

Here, even at night, he keeps trying not to sleep. Most of the time he doesn't. He asks one of the doctors if it will matter in the outcome that he isn't sleeping now. The doctor says, Nope.

On the morning of the surgery, a nurse comes in. She sneaks up on him. She jabs a needle in his arm before he can say: What are you doing? She leaves before he can say: What the hell'd you do? I told you I ain't taking anything will make me sleep. He begins to fight the fuzzy flaking in his head. He thinks he will talk to himself to keep awake and get it said. Say what?

Say it's only me here to go alone if there's no one going with me when he comes down like that from my apple to my gut to open where my heart is with a band of blood just before the saw goes off and rips from the apple to the gut down the middle of the bone while they pull the ribs wide the way mine under the center's balls when I made the signals to my blood and was from the time it ever was until they saw the goddamned Bobby Kraft slip a shoulder and fake it once and fade back and let it go uncorked up there the way it spirals against the blue of it, the point of it, leather brown spiraling on the jolted blue to the banging on me that was no use to them. You sonsabitches. Cause the ball's gone and hearing the roar of them with Jeffer getting it on his tips on the zig and in and streak that was going all the way cause I read the free safe blitz and called it on the line and faded against his looping where Copper picked him up and I let it go before the rest caved me with their hands pulling my ribs now and cranking on some ratchet bar to keep me spread and oh my God his rubbered hand on. Gottfried down with his knife in my heart's like a jelly sack the way he cuts through it with my blood in a plastic tube with the flow of it into some machine that cleans it for going back into me with blades like wipers on cars in the rain when I played in mud to my ankles and in the snows and over ninety in the Coliseum like in hell before the roar my God. Keep this my heart or let me die you sonsabitches. Pray for me again Elfi that I didn't love you the way such a little thing you are, and it was to do and I couldn't, but what could you know of me and what I had to and what it was for me, born to be a thing in the lot and the park, and in the school too with all of them calling me cold as ice bastard, and I wasn't any of that or how would I come to them in the pros out of a dink pussy college and be as good as any of them and better than most of all those that run the show on the field that are Quarterbacks. Godbacks goddammit. The way he's supposed to, this Gottfried with that stare and not any loser. Me? A loser? Because I cry in the dread I feel now of the what?

[OCTOBER 1978]

TOBIAS WOLFF

Soldier's Joy

Tobias Wolff (1945–   ) grew up in Washington State, Utah,
Florida, and Washington, D.C. He chronicled this nomadic childhood in
his memoir This Boy's Life, *an excerpt of which appeared in* Esquire *in*
1989. After failing to finish high school, he joined the army and saw
action in Vietnam. Later he attended Oxford University and Stanford.
Notwithstanding the success of This Boy's Life, *Wolff has established*
a reputation primarily on the basis of his short stories, collected in In the
Garden of the North American Martyrs *(1981) and* Back in the World
(1985). His novella The Barracks Thief *won the PEN/Faulkner Award*
for fiction in 1985.

On Friday Hooper was named driver of
the guard for the third night that week. He had recently been broken in rank
again, this time from corporal to Pfc, and the first sergeant had decided to keep
Hooper's evenings busy so that he would not have leisure to brood. That was
what the first sergeant told Hooper when Hooper came to the orderly room to
complain.

"It's for your own good," the first sergeant said. "Not that I expect you
to thank me." He moved the book he'd been reading to one side of his desk and
leaned back. "Hooper, I have a theory about you," he said. "Want to hear it?"

"I'm all ears, Top," Hooper said.

The first sergeant put his boots up on the desk and stared out the window to his left. It was getting on toward 5:00. Work details had begun to return from the rifle range and the post laundry and the brigade commander's house, where Hooper and several other men were excavating a swimming pool without aid of machinery. As the trucks let them out they gathered on the barracks steps and under the live oak beside the mess hall, their voices a steady murmur in the orderly room where Hooper stood waiting for the first sergeant to speak.

"You resent me," the first sergeant said. "You think you should be sitting here. You don't know that's what you think because you've totally sublimated your resentment, but that's what it is all right, and that's why you and me are developing a definite conflict profile. It's like you have to keep fucking up to prove to yourself that you don't really care. That's my theory. You follow me?"

"Top, I'm way ahead of you," Hooper said. "That's night school talking."

The first sergeant continued to look out the window. "I don't know," he said. "I don't know what you're doing in my army. You've put your twenty years in. You could retire to Mexico and buy a peso factory. Live like a dictator. So what are you doing in my army, Hooper?"

Hooper looked down at the desk. He cleared his throat but said nothing.

"Give it some thought," the first sergeant said. He stood and walked Hooper to the door. "I'm not hostile," he said. "I'm prepared to be supportive. Just think nice thoughts about Mexico, okay? Okay, Hooper?"

Hooper called Mickey and told her he wouldn't be coming by that night after all. She reminded him that this was the third time in one week, and said that she wasn't getting any younger.

"What am I supposed to do?" Hooper asked. "Go AWOL?"

"I cried three times today," Mickey said. "I just broke down and cried, and you know what? I don't even know why. I just feel bad all the time anymore."

"What did you do last night?" Hooper asked. When Mickey didn't answer, he said, "Did Briggs come over?"

"I've been inside all day," Mickey said. "Just sitting here. I'm going out of my tree." Then, in the same weary voice, she said, "Touch it, Hoop."

"I have to get going," Hooper said.

"Not yet. Wait. I'm going into the bedroom. I'm going to pick up the phone in there. Hang on, Hoop. Think of the bedroom. Think of me lying on the bed. Wait, baby."

There were men passing by the phone booth. Hooper watched them and tried not to think of Mickey's bedroom, but now he could think of nothing else. Mickey's husband was a supply sergeant with a taste for quality. The walls of the bedroom were knotty pine he'd derailed en route to some colonel's office. The brass lamps beside the bed were made from howitzer casings. The sheets were parachute silk. Sometimes, lying on those sheets, Hooper thought of the men who had drifted to earth below them. He was no great lover, as the women he went with usually got around to telling him, but in Mickey's bedroom Hooper had turned in his saddest performances, and always when he was most aware that everything around him was stolen. He wasn't exactly sure why he kept going back. It was just something he did, again and again.

"Okay," Mickey said. "I'm here."

"There's a guy waiting to use the phone," Hooper told her.

"Hoop, I'm on the bed. I'm taking off my shoes."

Hooper could see her perfectly. He lit a cigarette and opened the door of the booth to let the smoke out.

"Hoop?" she said.

"I told you, there's a guy waiting."

"Turn around, then."

"You don't need me," Hooper said. "All you need is the telephone. Why don't you call Briggs? That's what you're going to do after I hang up."

"I probably will," she said. "Listen, Hoop, I'm not really on the bed. I was just pulling your chain. I thought it would make me feel better but it didn't."

"I knew it," Hooper said. "You're watching the tube, right?"

"Somebody just won a saw," Mickey said.

"A saw?"

"Yeah, they drove up to this man's house and dumped a truckload of logs in his yard and gave him a chain saw. This was his fantasy. You should see how happy he is, Hoop. I'd give anything to be that happy."

"Maybe I can swing by later tonight," Hooper said. "Just for a minute."

"I don't know," Mickey said. "Better give me a ring first."

After Mickey hung up Hooper tried to call his wife, but there was no answer. He stood there and listened to the phone ringing. Finally he put the receiver down and stepped outside the booth, just as they began to sound retreat over the company loudspeaker. With the men around him Hooper came to attention and saluted. The record was scratchy, but, as always, the music caused Hooper's mind to go abruptly and perfectly still. The stillness spread down through his body. He held his salute until the last note died away, then broke off smartly and walked down the street toward the mess hall.

The officer of the day was Captain King
from Headquarters Company. Captain King had also been officer of the day on
Monday and Tuesday nights, and Hooper was glad to see him again because
Captain King was too lazy to do his own job or to make sure the guards were
doing theirs. He stayed in the guardhouse and left everything up to Hooper.

Captain King had gray hair and a long grayish face. He was a West Point
graduate with twenty-eight years of service behind him, just trying to make it
through another two years so he could retire at three-quarters pay. All his
classmates were generals or at least bird colonels, but he himself had been held
back for good reasons, many of which he admitted to Hooper their first night
together. It puzzled Hooper at first, this officer telling him about his failures to
perform, his nervous breakdowns and Valium habit, but finally Hooper understood: Captain King regarded him, a Pfc with twenty-one years' service, as a
comrade in dereliction, a disaster like himself with no room left for judgment
against anyone.

The evening was hot and muggy. Little black bats swooped overhead as
Captain King made his way along the rank of men drawn up before the guardhouse steps. He objected to the alignment of someone's belt buckle. He asked
questions about the chain of command but gave no sign whether the answers he
received were right or wrong. He inspected a couple of rifles and pretended to
find something amiss with each of them, though it was clear that he hardly knew
one end from the other, and when he reached the end of the line he began to
deliver a speech. He said that he had never seen such sorry troops in his life. He
asked how they expected to stand up to a determined enemy. On and on he went.
Captain King had delivered the same speech on Monday and Tuesday, and when
Hooper recognized it he lit another cigarette and sat down on the running board
of the truck he'd been leaning against.

The sky was gray. It had a damp, heavy look and it felt heavy too, hanging
close overhead, nervous with rumblings and small flashes in the distance. Just
sitting there made Hooper sweat. Beyond the guardhouse a stream of cars rushed
along the road to town. From the officers' club farther up the road came the
muffled beat of rock music, which was almost lost, like every other sound of the
evening, in the purr of crickets that rose up everywhere and thickened the air like
heat.

When Captain King had finished talking he turned the men over to Hooper for transportation to their posts. Two of them, both privates, were from Hooper's company, and these he allowed to ride with him in the cab of the truck while everybody else slid around in back. One was a cook named Porchoff, known as Porkchop. The other was a radio operator named Trac, who had managed to airlift himself out of Saigon during the fall of the city by hanging from the skids of a helicopter. That was the story Hooper had heard, anyway, and he had no reason to doubt it; he'd seen the slopes pull that trick plenty of times, though few of them were as young as Trac must have been then—nine or ten at the most. When Hooper tried to picture his son Wesley at the same age doing that, hanging over a burning city by his fingertips, he had to smile.

But Trac didn't talk about it. There was nothing about him to suggest his past except perhaps the deep, sickle-shaped scar above his right eye. To Hooper there was something familiar about this scar. One night, watching Trac play the video game in the company rec room, he was overcome with the certainty that he had seen Trac before somewhere—astride a water buffalo in some reeking paddy or running alongside Hooper's APC with a bunch of other kids all begging money, holding up melons or a bag full of weed or a starving monkey on a stick.

Though Hooper had the windows open, the cab of the truck smelled strongly of after-shave. Hooper noticed that Trac was wearing orange Walkman earphones under his helmet liner. They were against regulation, but Hooper said nothing. As long as Trac had his ears plugged, he wouldn't be listening for trespassers and end up blowing his rifle off at some squirrel cracking open an acorn. Of all the guards, only Porchoff and Trac would be carrying ammunition, because they had been assigned to the battalion communications center, where there was a tie-in terminal to the division mainframe computer. The theory was that an intruder who knew his stuff could get his hands on highly classified material. That was how it had been explained to Hooper. Hooper thought it was a load of crap. The Russians knew everything anyway.

Hooper let out the first two men at the PX and the next two at the parking lot outside the main officers' club, where lately several cars had been vandalized. As they pulled away, Porchoff leaned over Trac and grabbed Hooper's sleeve. "You used to be a corporal," he said.

Hooper shook Porchoff's hand loose. He said, "I'm driving a truck, in case you didn't notice."

"How come you got busted?"

"None of your business."

"I'm just asking," Porchoff said. "So what happened, anyway?"

"Cool it, Porkchop," said Trac. "The man doesn't want to talk about it, okay?"

"Cool it yourself, fuckface," Porchoff said. He looked at Trac. "Was I addressing you?"

Trac said, "Man, you must've been eating some of your own food."

"I don't believe I was addressing you," Porchoff said. "In fact, I don't believe that you and me have been properly introduced. That's another thing I don't like about the Army, the way people you haven't been introduced to feel perfectly free to get right into your face and unload whatever shit they've got in their brains. It happens all the time. But I never heard anyone say 'Cool it' before. You're a real phrasemaker, fuckface."

"That's enough," Hooper said.

Porchoff leaned back and said, "That's enough," in a falsetto voice. A few moments later he started humming to himself.

Hooper dropped off the rest of the guards and turned up the hill toward the communications center. There were oleander bushes along the gravel drive, with white blossoms going gray in the dusky light. Gravel sprayed up under the tires and rattled against the floorboards of the truck. Porchoff stopped humming. "I've got a cramp," he said.

Hooper pulled up next to the gate and turned off the engine. He looked over at Porchoff. "Now what's your problem?" he said.

"I've got a cramp," Porchoff repeated.

"For Christ's sake," Hooper said. "Why didn't you say something before?"

"I did. I went on sick call, but the doctor couldn't find it. It keeps moving around. It's here now." Porchoff touched his neck. "I swear to God."

"Keep track of it," Hooper told him. "You can go on sick call again in the morning."

"You don't believe me," Porchoff said.

The three of them got out of the truck. Hooper counted out the ammunition to Porchoff and Trac and watched as they loaded their clips. "That ammo's strictly for show," he said. "Forget I even gave it to you. If you run into a problem, which you won't, use the phone in the guard shack. You can work out your own shifts." Hooper opened the gate and locked the two men inside. They stood watching him, faces in shadow, black rifle barrels poking over their shoulders. "Listen," Hooper said, "nobody's going to break in here, understand?"

Trac nodded. Porchoff just looked at him.

"Okay," Hooper said. "I'll drop by later. Me and the captain." Hooper knew that Captain King wasn't about to go anywhere, but Trac and Porchoff didn't know that. Hooper behaved better when he thought he was being watched and he supposed that the same was true of other people.

Hooper climbed back inside the truck and started the engine. He gave the V sign to the men at the gate. Trac gave the sign back and turned away. Porchoff didn't move. He stayed where he was, fingers laced through the wire. He looked about ready to cry. "Damn," Hooper said, and he hit the gas. Gravel clattered in the wheel wells. When Hooper reached the main road a light rain began to fall, but it stopped before he'd even turned the wipers on.

Hooper and Captain King sat on adjacent bunks in the guardhouse, which was empty except for them and a bat that was flitting back and forth among the dim rafters. As on Monday and Tuesday nights, Captain King had brought along an ice chest filled with little bottles of Perrier water. From time to time he tried pressing one on Hooper, but Hooper declined. His refusals made Captain King apologetic. "It's not a class thing," Captain King said, looking at the bottle in his hand. "I don't drink this stuff because I went to the Point or anything like that." He leaned down and put the bottle between his bare feet. "I'm allergic to alcohol," he said. "Otherwise I'd probably be an alcoholic. Why not? I'm everything else." He smiled at Hooper.

Hooper lay back and clasped his hands behind his head and stared up at the mattress above him. "I'm not much of a drinker myself," he said. He knew that Captain King wanted him to explain why he refused the Perrier water, but there was really no reason in particular. Hooper just didn't like the idea.

"I drank eggnog one Christmas when I was a kid, and it almost killed me," Captain King said. "My arms and legs swelled up to twice their normal size. The doctors couldn't get my glasses off because my skin was all puffed up around them. You know the way a tree will grow around a rock. It was like that. A few months later I tried beer at some kid's graduation party and the same thing happened. Pretty strange, eh?"

"Yes, sir," Hooper said.

"I used to think it was all for the best. I have an addictive personality, and you can bet your bottom dollar I would have been a problem drinker. No question about it. But now I wonder. If I'd had one big weakness like that, maybe I wouldn't have had all these little pissant weaknesses I ended up with. I know that sounds like bull-pucky, but look at Alexander the Great. Alexander the Great was a boozer. Did you know that?"

"No, sir," Hooper said.

"Well he was. Read your history. So was Churchill. Churchill drank a bottle of Cognac a day. And of course Grant. You know what Lincoln said when someone complained about Grant's drinking?"

"Yes, sir. I've heard the story."

"He said, 'Find out what brand he uses so I can ship a case to the rest of my generals.' Is that the way you heard it?"

"Yes, sir."

Captain King nodded. "I'm all in," he said. He stretched out and assumed exactly the position Hooper was in. It made Hooper uncomfortable. He sat up and put his feet on the floor.

"Married?" Captain King asked.

"Yes, sir."

"Kids?"

"Yes, sir. One. Wesley."

"Oh my God, a boy," Captain King said. "They're nothing but trouble, take my word for it. They're programmed to hate you. It has to be like that, otherwise they'd spend their whole lives moping around the house, but just the same it's no fun when it starts. I have two, and neither of them can stand me. Haven't been home in years. Breaks my heart. Of course, I was a worse father than most. How old is your boy?"

"Sixteen or seventeen," Hooper said. He put his hands on his knees and looked at the floor. "Seventeen. He lives with my wife's sister in San Diego."

Captain King turned his head and looked at Hooper. "Sounds like you're not much of a dad yourself."

Hooper began to lace his boots up.

"I'm not criticizing," Captain King said. "At least you were smart enough to get someone else to do the job." He yawned. "I'm whipped," he said. "You need me for anything? You want me to make the rounds with you?"

"I'll take care of things, sir," Hooper said.

"Fair enough." Captain King closed his eyes. "If you need me, just shout."

Hooper went outside and lit a cigarette. It was almost midnight, well past the time appointed for inspecting the guards. As he walked toward the truck mosquitoes droned around his head. A breeze was rustling the treetops, but on the ground the air was hot and still.

Hooper took his time making the rounds. He visited all the guards except

Porchoff and Trac and found everything in order. There were no problems. Finally he started down the road toward the communications center, but when he reached the turnoff he kept his eyes dead ahead and drove past. Warm, fragrant air rushed into his face from the open window. The road ahead was empty. Hooper leaned back and mashed the accelerator. The engine roared. He was moving now, really moving, past darkened barracks and bare flagpoles and bushes whose flowers blazed up in the glare of the headlights. Hooper grinned. He felt no pleasure, but he grinned and pushed the truck as hard as it would go.

Hooper slowed down when he left the post. He was AWOL now. Even if he couldn't find it in him to care much about that, he saw no point in calling attention to himself.

Drunk drivers were jerking their cars back and forth between lanes. Every half mile or so a police car with flashing lights had someone stopped by the roadside. Other police cars sat idling behind billboards. Hooper stayed in the right lane and drove slowly until he reached his turn, then he gunned the engine again and raced down the pitted street that led to Mickey's house. He passed a bunch of kids sitting on the hood of a car with cans of beer in their hands. The car door was open, and Hooper had to swerve to miss it. As he went by he heard a blast of music.

When he reached Mickey's block Hooper turned off the engine. The truck coasted silently down the street, and again Hooper became aware of the sound of crickets. He stopped on the shoulder across from Mickey's house and sat listening. The thick pulsing sound seemed to grow louder every moment. Hooper drifted into memory, his cigarette dangling unsmoked, burning its way toward his fingers. At the same instant that he felt the heat of the ember against his skin Hooper was startled by another pain, the pain of finding himself where he was. It left him breathless for a moment. Then he roused himself and got out of the truck.

The windows were dark. Mickey's Buick was parked in the driveway beside another car that Hooper didn't recognize. It didn't belong to her husband and it didn't belong to Briggs. Hooper glanced around at the other houses, then walked across the street and ducked under the hanging leaves of the willow tree in Mickey's front yard. He knelt there, holding his breath to hear better, but there was no sound but the sound of the crickets and the rushing of the big air conditioner Mickey's husband had taken from a helicopter hangar. Hooper saw no purpose in staying under the tree, so he got up and walked over to the house.

He looked around again, then went into a crouch and began to work his way along the wall. He rounded the corner of the house and was starting up the side toward Mickey's bedroom when a circle of light burst around his head and a woman's voice said, "Thou shalt not commit adultery."

Hooper closed his eyes. There was a long silence. Then the woman said, "Come here."

She was standing in the driveway of the house next door. When Hooper came up to her she stuck a pistol in his face and told him to raise his hands. "A soldier," she said, moving the beam of light up and down his uniform. "All right, put your hands down." She snapped the light off and stood watching Hooper in the flickering blue glow that came from the open door behind her. Hooper heard a dog bark twice and a man say, "Remember—nothing is too good for your dog. It's 'Ruff ruff' at the sign of the double R." The dog barked twice again.

"I want to know what you think you're doing," the woman said.

Hooper said, "I'm not exactly sure." He saw her more clearly now. She was thin and tall. She wore glasses with harlequin frames, and she had on a white dress of the kind girls called formals when Hooper was in high school—tight around the waist and flaring stiffly at the hip, breasts held in hard-looking cups. Shadows darkened the hollows of her cheeks. Under the flounces of the dress her feet were big and bare.

"I know what you're doing," she said. She pointed the pistol, an Army .45, at Mickey's house. "You're sniffing around that whore over there."

Someone came to the door behind the woman. A deep voice called out, "Is it him?"

"Stay inside, Dads," the woman answered. "It's nobody."

"It's him!" the man shouted. "Don't let him talk you out of it again! Do it while you've got the chance, sweetie pie."

"What do you want with that whore?" the woman asked Hooper. Before he could answer, she said, "I could shoot you and nobody would say boo. I'm within my rights."

Hooper nodded.

"I don't see the attraction," she said. "But then, I'm not a man." She made a laughing sound. "You know something? I almost did it. I almost shot you. I was that close, but then I saw the uniform." She shook her head. "Shame on you. Where is your pride?"

"Don't let him talk," said the man in the doorway. He came down the steps, a tall white-haired man in striped pajamas. "There you are, you sonofabitch," he said. "I'll dance on your grave."

"It isn't him, Dads," the woman said sadly. "It's someone else."

"So he says," the man snapped. He started down the driveway, hopping from foot to foot over the gravel. The woman handed him the flashlight and he turned it on in Hooper's face, then moved the beam slowly down to his boots. "Sweetie pie, it's a soldier," he said.

"I told you it wasn't him," the woman said.

"But this is a terrible mistake," the man said. "Sir, I'm at a loss for words."

"Forget it," Hooper told him. "No hard feelings."

"You are too kind," the man said. He reached out and shook Hooper's hand. "You're alive," he said. "That's what counts." He nodded toward the house. "Come have a drink."

"He has to go," the woman said. "He was looking for something and he found it."

"That's right," Hooper told him. "I was just on my way back to base."

The man gave a slight bow with his head. "To base with you, then. Good night, sir."

Hooper and the woman watched him make his way back to the house. When he was inside, the woman turned to Hooper and said, "If I told him what you were doing over there it would break his heart. But I won't tell him. There've been disappointments enough in his life already, and God only knows what's next. He's got to have something left." She drew herself up and gave Hooper a hard look. "Why are you still here?" she asked angrily. "Go back to your post."

Captain King was still asleep when Hooper returned to the guardhouse. His thumb was in his mouth and he made little noises as he sucked it. Hooper lay in the next bunk with his eyes open. He was still awake at 4:00 in the morning when the telephone began to ring.

It was Trac calling from the communications center. He said that Porchoff was threatening to shoot himself, and threatening to shoot Trac if Trac tried to stop him. "This dude is mental," Trac said. "You get me out of here, and I mean now."

"We'll be right there," Hooper said. "Just give him lots of room. Don't try to grab his rifle or anything."

"Fat fucking chance," Trac said. "Man, you know what he called me? He called me a gook. I hope he wastes himself. I don't need no assholes with loaded guns declaring war on me, man."

"Just hold tight," Hooper told him. He hung up and went to wake Captain King, because this was a mess and he wanted it to be Captain King's mess and Captain King's balls that got busted if anything went wrong. He walked over to Captain King and stood looking down at him. Captain King's thumb had slipped out of his mouth, but he was still making sucking noises and pursing his lips. Hooper decided not to wake him after all. Captain King would probably refuse to come anyway, but if he did come he would screw things up for sure. Just the sight of him was enough to make somebody start shooting.

A light rain had begun to fall. The road was empty except for one jeep going the other way. Hooper waved at the two men in front as they went past, and they both waved back. Hooper felt a surge of friendliness toward them. He followed their lights in his mirror until they vanished behind him.

Hooper parked the truck halfway up the drive and walked the rest of the distance. The rain was falling harder now, tapping steadily on the shoulders of his poncho. Sweet, almost unbreathable smells rose from the earth. He walked slowly, gravel crunching under his boots. When he reached the gate a voice to his left said, "Shit, man, you took your time." Trac stepped out of the shadows and waited as Hooper tried to get the key into the lock. "Come on, man," Trac said. He knelt with his back to the fence and swung the barrel of his rifle from side to side.

"Got it," Hooper said. He took the lock off and Trac pushed open the gate. "The truck's down there," Hooper told him. "Just around the turn."

Trac stood close to Hooper, breathing quick, shallow breaths and shifting from foot to foot. His face was dark under the hood of his glistening poncho. "You want this?" he asked. He held out his rifle.

Hooper looked at it. He shook his head. "Where's Porchoff?"

"Around back," Trac said. "There's some picnic benches out there."

"All right," Hooper said. "I'll take care of it. Wait in the truck."

"Shit, man, I feel like shit," Trac said. "I'll back you up, man."

"It's okay," Hooper told him. "I can handle it."

"I never cut out on anybody before," Trac said. He shifted back and forth.

"You aren't cutting out," Hooper said. "Nothing's going to happen."

Trac started down the drive. When he disappeared around the turn, Hooper kept watching to make sure he didn't double back. A stiff breeze began to blow, shaking the trees, sending raindrops rattling down through the leaves. Thunder rumbled far away.

Hooper turned and walked through the gate into the compound. The forms of shrubs and pines were dark and indefinite in the slanting rain. Hooper followed the fence to the right, squinting into the shadows. When he saw Porchoff, hunched over the picnic table, he stopped and called out to him, "Hey, Porchoff! It's me—Hooper."

Porchoff raised his head.

"It's just me," Hooper said, following his own voice toward Porchoff, showing his empty hands. He saw the rifle lying on the table in front of Porchoff. "It's just me," he repeated, monotonously as he could. He stopped beside another picnic table ten feet or so from the one where Porchoff sat, and lowered himself onto the bench. He looked over at Porchoff. Neither of them spoke for a while. Then Hooper said, "Okay, Porchoff, let's talk about it. Trac tells me you've got some kind of attitude problem."

Porchoff didn't answer. Raindrops streamed down his helmet onto his shoulders and dripped steadily past his face. His uniform was soggy and dark, plastered to his skin. He stared at Hooper and said nothing. Now and then his shoulders jerked.

"Are you gay?" Hooper asked.

Porchoff shook his head.

"Well then, what? You on acid or something? You can tell me, Porchoff. It doesn't matter."

"I don't do drugs," Porchoff said. It was the first time he'd spoken. His voice was calm.

"Good," Hooper said. "I mean, at least I know I'm talking to you, and not to some fucking chemical. Now, listen up, Porchoff—I don't want you turning that rifle on me. Understand?"

Porchoff looked down at the rifle, then back at Hooper. He said, "You leave me alone and I'll leave you alone."

"I've already had someone throw down on me once tonight," Hooper said. "I'd just as soon leave it at that." He reached under his poncho and took out his cigarette case. He held it up for Porchoff to see.

"I don't use tobacco," Porchoff said.

"Well, I do," Hooper said. He shook out a cigarette and bent to light it. "Hey," he said. "All right. One match." He put the case back in his pocket and cupped the cigarette under the picnic table to keep it dry. The rain was falling lightly now in fine fitful gusts like spray. The clouds had gone the color of ash. Misty gray light was spreading through the sky. Hooper saw that Porchoff's shoulders twitched constantly now, and that his lips were blue and trembling. "Put your poncho on," Hooper told him.

Porchoff shook his head.

"You trying to catch pneumonia?" Hooper asked. He smiled at Porchoff. "Go ahead, boy. Put your poncho on."

Porchoff bent over and covered his face with his hands. Hooper realized that he was crying. He smoked his cigarette and waited for Porchoff to stop, but Porchoff kept crying and finally Hooper grew impatient. He said, "What's all this crap about you shooting yourself?"

Porchoff rubbed at his eyes with the heels of his hands. "Why shouldn't I?" he asked.

"Why shouldn't you? What do you mean, why shouldn't you?"

"Why shouldn't I shoot myself? Give me a reason."

"This is baloney," Hooper said. "You don't run around asking why shouldn't I shoot myself. That's decadent, Porchoff. Now, do me a favor and put your poncho on."

Porchoff sat shivering for a moment. Then he took his poncho off his belt, unrolled it, and began to pull it over his head. Hooper considered making a grab for the rifle but held back. There was no need, he was home free now. People who were going to blow themselves away didn't come in out of the rain.

"You know what they call me?" Porchoff said.

"Who's 'they,' Porchoff?"

"Everyone."

"No. What does everyone call you?"

"Porkchop. *Porkchop.*"

"Come on," Hooper said. "What's the harm in that? Everyone gets called something."

"But that's my *name,*" Porchoff said. "That's *me.* It's got so even when people use my real name I hear 'Porkchop.' All I can think of is this big piece of meat. And that's what they're seeing too. You can say they aren't, but I know they are."

Hooper recognized some truth in this, a lot of truth in fact, because when he himself said, "Porkchop," that was what he saw: a pork chop.

"I hurt all the time," Porchoff said, "but no one believes me. Not even the doctors. You don't believe me, either."

"I believe you," Hooper said.

Porchoff blinked. "Sure," he said.

"I believe you," Hooper repeated. He kept his eyes on the rifle. Porchoff wasn't going to waste himself, but the rifle still made Hooper uncomfortable. He was about to ask Porchoff to give it to him, but decided to wait a little while.

The moment was wrong somehow. Hooper pushed back the hood of his poncho and took off his fatigue cap. He glanced up at the pale clouds.

"I don't have any buddies," Porchoff said.

"No wonder," Hooper said. "Calling people gooks, making threats. Let's face it, Porchoff, your personality needs some upgrading."

"But they won't give me a chance," Porchoff said. "All I ever do is cook food. I put it on their plates and they make some crack and walk on by. It's like I'm not even there. So what am I supposed to act like?"

Hooper was still gazing up at the clouds, feeling the soft rain on his face. Birds were starting to sing in the woods beyond the fence. He said, "I don't know, Porchoff. It's just part of this rut we're all in." Hooper lowered his head and looked over at Porchoff, who sat hunched inside his poncho, shaking as little tremors passed through him. "Any day now," Hooper said, "everything's going to change."

"My dad was in the National Guard back in Ohio," Porchoff said. "He's always talking about the great experiences he and his buddies used to have, camping out and so on. Nothing like that ever happens to me." Porchoff looked down at the table, then looked up and said, "How about you? What was your best time?"

"My best time," Hooper said. The question made him feel tired. He thought of telling Porchoff some sort of lie, but the effort of making things up was beyond him and the memory Porchoff wanted was close at hand. For Hooper, it was closer than the memory of home. In truth it was a kind of home. It was where he went to be back with his friends again, and his old self. It was where Hooper drifted when he was too low to care how much lower he'd be when he drifted back, and lost it all again. He felt for his cigarettes. "Vietnam," he said.

Porchoff just looked at him.

"We didn't know it then," Hooper said. "We used to talk about how when we got back in the world we were going to do this and we were going to do that. Back in the world we were going to have it made. But ever since then it's been nothing but confusion." Hooper took the cigarette case from his pocket but didn't open it. He leaned forward on the table.

"Everything was clear," he said. "You learned what you had to know and you forgot the rest. All this chickenshit. This clutter. You didn't spend every living minute of the day thinking about your own sorry-ass little self. Am I getting laid enough. What's wrong with my kid. Should I insulate the fucking

house. That's what does it to you, Porchoff. Thinking about yourself. That's
what kills you in the end."

Porchoff had not moved. In the gray light Hooper could see Porchoff's
fingers spread before him on the tabletop, white and still as if they had been
drawn there in chalk. His face was the same color.

"You think you've got problems, Porchoff, but they wouldn't last five
minutes in the field. There's nothing wrong with you that a little search-and-
destroy wouldn't cure." Hooper paused, smiling to himself, already deep in the
memory. He tried to bring it back for Porchoff, tried to put it into words so that
Porchoff could see it, too, the beauty of that life, the faith so deep that in time
you were not different men anymore but one man.

But the words came hard. Hooper saw that Porchoff did not understand,
and then he realized that what he was trying to describe was not only faith but
love, and that it couldn't be done. Still smiling, he said, "You'll see, Porchoff.
You'll get your chance."

Porchoff stared at Hooper. "You're crazy," he said.

"We're all going to get another chance," Hooper said. "I can feel it
coming. Otherwise I'd take my walking papers and hat up. You'll see, Porchoff.
All you need is a little contact. The rest of us, too. Get us out of this rut."

Porchoff shook his head and murmured, "You're really crazy."

"Let's call it a day," Hooper said. He stood and held out his hand. "Give
me the rifle."

"No," Porchoff said. He pulled the rifle closer. "Not to you."

"There's no one here but me," Hooper said.

"Go get Captain King."

"Captain King is asleep."

"Then wake him up."

"No," Hooper said. "I'm not going to tell you again, Porchoff, give me
the rifle." Hooper walked toward him but stopped when Porchoff picked up the
weapon and pointed it at his chest. "Leave me alone," Porchoff said.

"Relax," Hooper told him. "I'm not going to hurt you." He held out his
hand again.

Porchoff licked his lips. "No," he said. "Not you."

Behind Hooper a voice called out, "Hey! Porkchop! Drop it!"

Porchoff sat bolt upright. "Jesus," he said.

"It's Trac," Hooper said. "Put the rifle down, Porchoff—now!"

"Drop it!" Trac shouted.

"Oh Jesus," Porchoff said and stumbled to his feet with the rifle still in his hands. Then his head flapped and his helmet flew off and he toppled backward over the bench. Hooper's heart leaped as the shock of the blast hit him. Then the sound went through him and beyond him into the trees and the sky, echoing on in the distance like thunder. Afterward there was silence. Hooper took a step forward, then sank to his knees and lowered his forehead to the wet grass. He spread his fingers through the grass beside his head. The rain fell around him with a soft whispering sound. A blue jay squawked. Another bird called out, and then the trees grew loud with song.

Hooper heard the swish of boots through the grass behind him. He pushed himself up and sat back on his heels and drew a deep breath.

"You okay?" Trac said.

Hooper nodded.

Trac walked on to where Porchoff lay. He said something in Vietnamese, then looked back at Hooper and shook his head.

Hooper tried to stand but went to his knees again.

"You need a hand?" Trac asked.

"I guess so," Hooper said.

Trac came over to Hooper. He slung his rifle and bent down and the two men gripped each other's wrists. Trac's skin was dry and smooth, his bones as small as a child's. This close, he looked more familiar than ever. "Go for it," Trac said. He tensed as Hooper pulled himself to his feet and for a moment afterward they stood facing each other, swaying slightly, hands still locked on one another's wrists. "All right," Hooper said. Each of them slowly loosened his grip.

In a soft voice, almost a whisper, Trac said, "They gonna put me away?"

"No," Hooper said. He walked over to Porchoff and looked down at him. He immediately turned away and saw that Trac was still swaying, and that his eyes were glassy. "Better get off those legs," Hooper said. Trac looked at him dreamily, then unslung his rifle and leaned it against the picnic table farthest from Porchoff. He sat down and took his helmet off and rested his head on his crossed forearms.

The clouds had darkened. The wind was picking up again, carrying with it the whine of distant engines. Hooper fumbled a cigarette out of his case and smoked it down, staring toward the woods, feeling the rain stream down his face and neck. When the cigarette went out Hooper dropped it, then picked it up again and field-stripped it, crumbling the tobacco around his feet so that no trace of it remained. He put his cap back on and raised the hood of his poncho. "How's it going?" he said to Trac.

Trac looked up. He began to rub his forehead, pushing his fingers in little circles above his eyes.

Hooper sat down across from him. "We don't have a whole lot of time," he said.

Trac nodded. He put his helmet on and looked over at Hooper, the scar on his brow livid where he had rubbed it.

"All right, son," Hooper said. "Let's get our story together."

[OCTOBER 1985]

TIM O'BRIEN

The

Things They

Carried

When he graduated from Minnesota's Macalester College in 1968, Tim O'Brien (1946–   ) was drafted into the U.S. Army and ran head-long into perhaps the central moral question for men of his generation: whether to serve in Vietnam. After considering the possibility of fleeing the country, O'Brien decided to serve as a soldier, and he received the Purple Heart for a shrapnel wound he suffered during combat. Back in the States, he turned away from a career in journalism to pursue his fiction. His first novel, Going After Cacciato, won a National Book Award in 1978. "The Things They Carried" is the title story from an innovative collection that appeared in 1990 and that addresses not only the war and its victims but the dimensions of storytelling itself. "Story truth," O'Brien has said, "is truer sometimes than happening truth."

First Lieutenant Jimmy Cross carried letters from a girl named Martha, a junior at Mount Sebastian College in New Jersey. They were not love letters, but Lieutenant Cross was hoping, so he kept them folded in plastic at the bottom of his rucksack. In the late afternoon, after a day's march, he would dig his foxhole, wash his hands under a canteen, unwrap the letters, hold them with the tips of his fingers, and spend the last hour of light pretending. He would imagine romantic camping trips into the White Mountains in New Hampshire. He would sometimes taste the envelope flaps, knowing her tongue had been there. More than anything, he wanted Martha to love him as he loved her, but the letters were mostly chatty, elusive on the matter of love. She was a virgin, he was almost sure. She was an English major at Mount Sebastian, and she wrote beautifully about her professors and roommates and midterm exams, about her respect for Chaucer and her great affection for Virginia Woolf. She often quoted lines of poetry; she never mentioned the war, except to say, Jimmy, take care of yourself. The letters weighed ten ounces. They were signed "Love, Martha," but Lieutenant Cross understood that Love was only a way of signing and did not mean what he sometimes pretended it meant. At dusk, he would carefully return the letters to his rucksack. Slowly, a bit distracted, he would get up and move among his men, checking the perimeter, then at full dark he would return to his hole and watch the night and wonder if Martha was a virgin.

The things they carried were largely determined by necessity. Among the necessities or near-necessities were P-38 can openers, pocket knives, heat tabs, wristwatches, dog tags, mosquito repellent, chewing gum, candy, cigarettes, salt tablets, packets of Kool-Aid, lighters, matches, sewing kits, Military Payment Certificates, C rations, and two or three canteens of water. Together, these items weighed between fifteen and twenty pounds, depending upon a man's habits or rate of metabolism. Henry Dobbins, who was a big man, carried extra rations; he was especially fond of canned peaches in heavy syrup over pound cake. Dave Jensen, who practiced field hygiene, carried a toothbrush, dental floss, and several hotel-size bars of soap he'd stolen on R&R in Sydney, Australia. Ted Lavender, who was scared, carried tranquilizers until he was shot in the head outside the village of Than Khe in mid-April. By necessity, and because it was SOP, they all carried steel helmets that weighed five pounds including the liner and camouflage cover. They carried the standard fatigue jackets and trousers. Very few carried underwear. On their feet they carried jungle boots—2.1 pounds—and Dave Jensen carried three pairs of socks and a can of Dr. Scholl's foot powder as a precaution against trench foot. Until he was shot, Ted Lavender carried six or seven ounces of premium dope, which for him was a necessity. Mitchell Sanders, the RTO, carried condoms. Norman Bowker carried a diary. Rat Kiley carried comic books. Kiowa, a devout Baptist, carried an illustrated New Testament that had been presented to him by his father, who taught Sunday school in Oklahoma City, Oklahoma. As a hedge against bad times, however, Kiowa also carried his grandmother's distrust of the white man, his grandfather's old hunting hatchet. Necessity dictated. Because the land was mined and booby-trapped, it was SOP for each man to carry a steel-centered, nylon-covered flak jacket, which weighed 6.7 pounds, but which on hot days seemed much heavier. Because you could die so quickly, each man carried at least one large compress bandage, usually in the helmet band for easy access. Because the nights were cold, and because the monsoons were wet, each carried a green plastic poncho that could be used as a raincoat or groundsheet or makeshift tent. With its quilted liner, the poncho weighed almost two pounds, but it was worth every ounce. In April, for instance, when Ted Lavender was shot, they used his poncho to wrap him up, then to carry him across the paddy, then to lift him into the chopper that took him away.

They were called legs or grunts.

To carry something was to "hump" it, as when Lieutenant Jimmy Cross humped his love for Martha up the hills and through the swamps. In its intransitive form, "to hump" meant "to walk," or "to march," but it implied burdens far beyond the intransitive.

Almost everyone humped photographs. In his wallet, Lieutenant Cross carried two photographs of Martha. The first was a Kodachrome snapshot signed "Love," though he knew better. She stood against a brick wall. Her eyes were gray and neutral, her lips slightly open as she stared straight-on at the camera. At night, sometimes, Lieutenant Cross wondered who had taken the picture, because he knew she had boyfriends, because he loved her so much, and because he could see the shadow of the picture taker spreading out against the brick wall. The second photograph had been clipped from the 1968 Mount Sebastian year-book. It was an action shot—women's volleyball—and Martha was bent horizontal to the floor, reaching, the palms of her hands in sharp focus, the tongue taut, the expression frank and competitive. There was no visible sweat. She wore white gym shorts. Her legs, he thought, were almost certainly the legs of a virgin, dry and without hair, the left knee cocked and carrying her entire weight, which was just over one hundred pounds. Lieutenant Cross remembered touching that left knee. A dark theater, he remembered, and the movie was *Bonnie and Clyde*, and Martha wore a tweed skirt, and during the final scene, when he touched her knee, she turned and looked at him in a sad, sober way that made him pull his hand back, but he would always remember the feel of the tweed skirt and the knee beneath it and the sound of the gunfire that killed Bonnie and Clyde, how embarrassing it was, how slow and oppressive. He remembered kissing her good night at the dorm door. Right then, he thought, he should've done something brave. He should've carried her up the stairs to her room and tied her to the bed and touched that left knee all night long. He should've risked it. Whenever he looked at the photographs, he thought of new things he should've done.

What they carried was partly a function of rank, partly of field specialty.

As a first lieutenant and platoon leader, Jimmy Cross carried a compass, maps, code books, binoculars, and a .45-caliber pistol that weighed 2.9 pounds fully loaded. He carried a strobe light and the responsibility for the lives of his men.

As an RTO, Mitchell Sanders carried the PRC-25 radio, a killer, twenty-six pounds with its battery.

As a medic, Rat Kiley carried a canvas satchel filled with morphine and plasma and malaria tablets and surgical tape and comic books and all the things a medic must carry, including M&Ms for especially bad wounds, for a total weight of nearly twenty pounds.

As a big man, therefore a machine gunner, Henry Dobbins carried the M-60, which weighed twenty-three pounds unloaded, but which was almost always loaded. In addition, Dobbins carried between ten and fifteen pounds of ammunition draped in belts across his chest and shoulders.

As PFCs or Spec 4s, most of them were common grunts and carried the standard M-16 gas-operated assault rifle. The weapon weighed 7.5 pounds unloaded, 8.2 pounds with its full twenty-round magazine. Depending on numerous factors, such as topography and psychology, the riflemen carried anywhere from twelve to twenty magazines, usually in cloth bandoliers, adding on another 8.4 pounds at minimum, fourteen pounds at maximum. When it was available, they also carried M-16 maintenance gear—rods and steel brushes and swabs and tubes of LSA oil—all of which weighed about a pound. Among the grunts, some carried the M-79 grenade launcher, 5.9 pounds unloaded, a reasonably light weapon except for the ammunition, which was heavy. A single round weighed ten ounces. The typical load was twenty-five rounds. But Ted Lavender, who was scared, carried thirty-four rounds when he was shot and killed outside Than Khe, and he went down under an exceptional burden, more than twenty pounds of ammunition, plus the flak jacket and helmet and rations and water and toilet paper and tranquilizers and all the rest, plus the unweighed fear. He was dead weight. There was no twitching or flopping. Kiowa, who saw it happen, said it was like watching a rock fall, or a big sandbag or something—just boom, then down—not like the movies where the dead guy rolls around and does fancy spins and goes ass over teakettle—not like that, Kiowa said, the poor bastard just flat-fuck fell. Boom. Down. Nothing else. It was a bright morning in mid-April. Lieutenant Cross felt the pain. He blamed himself. They stripped off Lavender's canteens and ammo, all the heavy things, and Rat Kiley said the obvious, the guy's dead, and Mitchell Sanders used his radio to report one U.S. KIA and to request a chopper. Then they wrapped Lavender in his poncho. They carried him out to a dry paddy, established security, and sat smoking the dead man's dope until the chopper came. Lieutenant Cross kept to himself. He pictured Martha's smooth young face, thinking he loved her more than anything, more than his men, and now Ted Lavender was dead because he loved her so much and could not stop thinking about her. When the dust-off arrived, they carried Lavender aboard. Afterward they burned Than Khe. They marched until dusk, then dug their holes, and that night Kiowa kept explaining how you had to be there, how fast it was, how the poor guy just dropped like so much concrete. Boom-down, he said. Like cement.

In addition to the three standard weapons—the M-60, M-16, and M-79—they carried whatever presented itself, or whatever seemed appropriate as a means of killing or staying alive. They carried catch-as-catch-can. At various times, in various situations, they carried M-14s and CAR-15s and Swedish Ks and grease guns and captured AK-47s and Chi-Coms and RPGs and Simonov carbines and black-market Uzis and .38-caliber Smith & Wesson handguns and 66-mm LAWs and shotguns and silencers and blackjacks and bayonets and C-4 plastic explosives. Lee Strunk carried a slingshot; a weapon of last resort, he called it. Mitchell Sanders carried brass knuckles. Kiowa carried his grandfather's feathered hatchet. Every third or fourth man carried a Claymore antipersonnel mine—3.5 pounds with its firing device. They all carried fragmentation grenades—fourteen ounces each. They all carried at least one M-18 colored smoke grenade—twenty-four ounces. Some carried CS or teargas grenades. Some carried white-phosphorus grenades. They carried all they could bear, and then some, including a silent awe for the terrible power of the things they carried.

In the first week of April, before Lavender died, Lieutenant Jimmy Cross received a good-luck charm from Martha. It was a simple pebble, an ounce at most. Smooth to the touch, it was a milky-white color with flecks of orange and violet, oval-shaped, like a miniature egg. In the accompanying letter, Martha wrote that she had found the pebble on the Jersey shoreline, precisely where the land touched water at high tide, where things came together but also separated. It was this separate-but-together quality, she wrote, that had inspired her to pick up the pebble and to carry it in her breast pocket for several days, where it seemed weightless, and then to send it through the mail, by air, as a token of her truest feelings for him. Lieutenant Cross found this romantic. But he wondered what her truest feelings were, exactly, and what she meant by separate-but-together. He wondered how the tides and waves had come into play on that afternoon along the Jersey shoreline when Martha saw the pebble and bent down to rescue it from geology. He imagined bare feet. Martha was a poet, with the poet's sensibilities, and her feet would be brown and bare, the toenails unpainted, the eyes chilly and somber like the ocean in March, and though it was painful, he wondered who had been with her that afternoon. He imagined a pair of shadows moving along the strip of sand where things came together but also separated. It was phantom jealousy, he knew, but he couldn't help himself. He loved her so much. On the march, through the hot days of early April, he carried the pebble in his mouth, turning it with his tongue, tasting sea salts and moisture. His mind wandered. He had difficulty keeping his attention on the war. On occasion he would yell at his men to spread out the column, to keep their eyes open, but then he would slip away into daydreams, just pretending, walking barefoot along the Jersey shore, with Martha, carrying nothing. He would feel himself rising. Sun and waves and gentle winds, all love and lightness.

What they carried varied by mission.

When a mission took them to the mountains, they carried mosquito netting, machetes, canvas tarps, and extra bug juice.

If a mission seemed especially hazardous, or if it involved a place they knew to be bad, they carried everything they could. In certain heavily mined AOs, where the land was dense with Toe Poppers and Bouncing Betties, they took turns humping a twenty-eight-pound mine detector. With its headphones and big sensing plate, the equipment was a stress on the lower back and shoulders, awkward to handle, often useless because of the shrapnel in the earth, but they carried it anyway, partly for safety, partly for the illusion of safety.

On ambush, or other night missions, they carried peculiar little odds and ends. Kiowa always took along his New Testament and a pair of moccasins for silence. Dave Jensen carried night-sight vitamins high in carotene. Lee Strunk carried his slingshot; ammo, he claimed, would never be a problem. Rat Kiley carried brandy and M&Ms. Until he was shot, Ted Lavender carried the starlight scope, which weighed 6.3 pounds with its aluminum carrying case. Henry Dobbins carried his girlfriend's panty hose wrapped around his neck as a comforter. They all carried ghosts. When dark came, they would move out single file across the meadows and paddies to their ambush coordinates, where they would quietly set up the Claymores and lie down and spend the night waiting.

Other missions were more complicated and required special equipment. In mid-April, it was their mission to search out and destroy the elaborate tunnel complexes in the Than Khe area south of Chu Lai. To blow the tunnels, they carried one-pound blocks of pentrite high explosives, four blocks to a man, sixty-eight pounds in all. They carried wiring, detonators, and battery-powered clackers. Dave Jensen carried earplugs. Most often, before blowing the tunnels, they were ordered by higher command to search them, which was considered bad news, but by and large they just shrugged and carried out orders. Because he was a big man, Henry Dobbins was excused from tunnel duty. The others would draw numbers. Before Lavender died there were seventeen men in the platoon, and whoever drew the number seventeen would strip off his gear and crawl in headfirst with a flashlight and Lieutenant Cross's .45-caliber pistol. The rest of them would fan out as security. They would sit down or kneel, not facing the hole, listening to the ground beneath them, imagining cobwebs and ghosts, whatever was down there—the tunnel walls squeezing in—how the flashlight seemed impossibly heavy in the hand and how it was tunnel vision in the very strictest sense, compression in all ways, even time, and how you had to wiggle in—ass and elbows—a swallowed-up feeling—and how you found yourself worrying about odd things—will your flashlight go dead? Do rats carry rabies? If you screamed, how far would the sound carry? Would your buddies hear it? Would they have the courage to drag you out? In some respects, though not many, the waiting was worse than the tunnel itself. Imagination was a killer.

On April 16, when Lee Strunk drew the number seventeen, he laughed and muttered something and went down quickly. The morning was hot and very still. Not good, Kiowa said. He looked at the tunnel opening, then out across a dry paddy toward the village of Than Khe. Nothing moved. No clouds or birds or people. As they waited, the men smoked and drank Kool-Aid, not talking much, feeling sympathy for Lee Strunk but also feeling the luck of the draw. You win some, you lose some, said Mitchell Sanders, and sometimes you settle for a rain check. It was a tired line and no one laughed.

Henry Dobbins ate a tropical chocolate bar. Ted Lavender popped a tranquilizer and went off to pee.

After five minutes, Lieutenant Jimmy Cross moved to the tunnel, leaned down, and examined the darkness. Trouble, he thought—a cave-in maybe. And then suddenly, without willing it, he was thinking about Martha. The stresses and fractures, the quick collapse, the two of them buried alive under all that weight. Dense, crushing love. Kneeling, watching the hole, he tried to concentrate on Lee Strunk and the war, all the dangers, but his love was too much for him, he felt paralyzed, he wanted to sleep inside her lungs and breathe her blood and be smothered. He wanted her to be a virgin and not a virgin, all at once. He wanted to know her. Intimate secrets—why poetry? Why so sad? Why that grayness in her eyes? Why so alone? Not lonely, just alone—riding her bike across campus or sitting off by herself in the cafeteria. Even dancing, she danced alone—and it was the aloneness that filled him with love. He remembered telling her that one evening. How she nodded and looked away. And how, later, when he kissed her, she received the kiss without returning it, her eyes wide open, not afraid, not a virgin's eyes, just flat and uninvolved.

Lieutenant Cross gazed at the tunnel. But he was not there. He was buried with Martha under the white sand at the Jersey shore. They were pressed together, and the pebble in his mouth was her tongue. He was smiling. Vaguely, he was aware of how quiet the day was, the sullen paddies, yet he could not bring himself to worry about matters of security. He was beyond that. He was just a kid at war, in love. He was twenty-two years old. He couldn't help it.

A few moments later Lee Strunk crawled out of the tunnel. He came up grinning, filthy but alive. Lieutenant Cross nodded and closed his eyes while the others clapped Strunk on the back and made jokes about rising from the dead.

Worms, Rat Kiley said. Right out of the grave. Fuckin' zombie.

The men laughed. They all felt great relief.

Spook City, said Mitchell Sanders.

Lee Strunk made a funny ghost sound, a kind of moaning, yet very happy, and right then, when Strunk made that high happy moaning sound, when he went *Ahhooooo*, right then Ted Lavender was shot in the head on his way back from peeing. He lay with his mouth open. The teeth were broken. There was a swollen black bruise under his left eye. The cheekbone was gone. Oh shit, Rat Kiley said, the guy's dead. The guy's dead, he kept saying, which seemed profound—the guy's dead. I mean really.

The things they carried were determined to some extent by superstition. Lieutenant Cross carried his good-luck pebble. Dave Jensen carried a rabbit's foot. Norman Bowker, otherwise a very gentle person, carried a thumb that had been presented to him as a gift by Mitchell Sanders. The thumb was dark brown, rubbery to the touch, and weighed four ounces at most. It had been cut from a VC corpse, a boy of fifteen or sixteen. They'd found him at the bottom of an irrigation ditch, badly burned, flies in his mouth and eyes. The boy wore black shorts and sandals. At the time of his death he had been carrying a pouch of rice, a rifle, and three magazines of ammunition.

You want my opinion, Mitchell Sanders said, there's a definite moral here.

He put his hand on the dead boy's wrist. He was quiet for a time, as if counting a pulse, then he patted the stomach, almost affectionately, and used Kiowa's hunting hatchet to remove the thumb.

Henry Dobbins asked what the moral was.

Moral?

You know. *Moral.*

Sanders wrapped the thumb in toilet paper and handed it across to Norman Bowker. There was no blood. Smiling, he kicked the boy's head, watched the flies scatter, and said, It's like with that old TV show—Paladin. Have gun, will travel.

Henry Dobbins thought about it.

Yeah, well, he finally said. I don't see no moral.

There it *is,* man.

Fuck off.

They carried USO stationery and pencils and pens. They carried Sterno, safety pins, trip flares, signal flares, spools of wire, razor blades, chewing tobacco, liberated joss sticks and statuettes of the smiling Buddha, candles, grease pencils, *The Stars and Stripes*, fingernail clippers, Psy Ops leaflets, bush hats, bolos, and much more. Twice a week, when the resupply choppers came in, they carried hot chow in green Mermite cans and large canvas bags filled with iced beer and soda pop. They carried plastic water containers, each with a two-gallon capacity. Mitchell Sanders carried a set of starched tiger fatigues for special occasions. Henry Dobbins carried Black Flag insecticide. Dave Jensen carried empty sandbags that could be filled at night for added protection. Lee Strunk carried tanning lotion. Some things they carried in common. Taking turns, they carried the big PRC-77 scrambler radio, which weighed thirty pounds with its battery. They shared the weight of memory. They took up what others could no longer bear. Often, they carried each other, the wounded or weak. They carried infections. They carried chess sets, basketballs, Vietnamese–English dictionaries, insignia of rank, Bronze Stars and Purple Hearts, plastic cards imprinted with the Code of Conduct. They carried diseases, among them malaria and dysentery. They carried lice and ringworm and leeches and paddy algae and various rots and molds. They carried the land itself— Vietnam, the place, the soil—a powdery orange-red dust that covered their boots and fatigues and faces. They carried the sky. The whole atmosphere, they carried it, the humidity, the monsoons, the stink of fungus and decay, all of it, they carried gravity. They moved like mules. By daylight they took sniper fire, at night they were mortared, but it was not battle, it was just the endless march, village to village, without purpose, nothing won or lost. They marched for the sake of the march. They plodded along slowly, dumbly, leaning forward against the heat, unthinking, all blood and bone, simple grunts, soldiering with their legs, toiling up the hills and down into the paddies and across the rivers and up again and down, just humping, one step and then the next and then another, but no volition, no will, because it was automatic, it was anatomy, and the war was entirely a matter of posture and carriage, the hump was everything, a kind of inertia, a kind of emptiness, a dullness of desire and intellect and conscience and hope and human sensibility. Their principles were in their feet. Their calculations were biological. They had no sense of strategy or mission. They searched the villages without knowing what to look for, not caring, kicking over jars of rice, frisking children and old men, blowing tunnels, sometimes setting fires and sometimes not, then forming up and moving on to the next village, then other villages, where it would always be the same. They carried their own lives. The pressures were enormous. In the heat of early afternoon, they would remove their helmets and flak jackets, walking bare, which was dangerous but which helped ease the strain. They would often discard things along the route of march. Purely for comfort, they would throw away rations, blow their Claymores and grenades, no matter, because by nightfall the resupply choppers would arrive with more of the same, then a day or two later still more, fresh watermelons and crates of ammunition and sunglasses and woolen sweaters—the resources were stunning—sparklers for the Fourth of July, colored eggs for Easter. It was the great American war chest—the fruits of science, the smokestacks, the canneries, the arsenals at Hartford, the Minnesota forests, the machine shops, the vast fields of corn and wheat—they carried like freight trains; they carried it on their backs and shoulders—and for all the ambiguities of Vietnam, all the mysteries and unknowns, there was at least the single abiding certainty that they would never be at a loss for things to carry.

After the chopper took Lavender away, Lieutenant Jimmy Cross led his men into the village of Than Khe. They burned everything. They shot chickens and dogs, they trashed the village well, they called in artillery and watched the wreckage, then they marched for several hours through the hot afternoon, and then at dusk, while Kiowa explained how Lavender died, Lieutenant Cross found himself trembling.

He tried not to cry. With his entrenching tool, which weighed five pounds, he began digging a hole in the earth.

He felt shame. He hated himself. He had loved Martha more than his men, and as a consequence Lavender was now dead, and this was something he would have to carry like a stone in his stomach for the rest of the war.

All he could do was dig. He used his entrenching tool like an ax, slashing, feeling both love and hate, and then later, when it was full dark, he sat at the bottom of his foxhole and wept. It went on for a long while. In part, he was grieving for Ted Lavender, but mostly it was for Martha, and for himself, because she belonged to another world, which was not quite real, and because she was a junior at Mount Sebastian College in New Jersey, a poet and a virgin and uninvolved, and because he realized she did not love him and never would.

Like cement, Kiowa whispered in the dark. I swear to God—boom-down. Not a word.

I've heard this, said Norman Bowker.

A pisser, you know? Still zipping himself up. Zapped while zipping.

All right, fine. That's enough.

Yeah, but you had to see it, the guy just—

I *heard*, man. Cement. So why not shut the fuck *up?*

Kiowa shook his head sadly and glanced over at the hole where Lieutenant Jimmy Cross sat watching the night. The air was thick and wet. A warm, dense fog had settled over the paddies and there was the stillness that precedes rain.

After a time Kiowa sighed.

One thing for sure, he said. The Lieutenant's in some deep hurt. I mean that crying jag—the way he was carrying on—it wasn't fake or anything, it was real heavy-duty hurt. The man cares.

Sure, Norman Bowker said.

Say what you want, the man does care.

We all got problems.

Not Lavender.

No, I guess not, Bowker said. Do me a favor, though.

Shut up?

That's a smart Indian. Shut up.

Shrugging, Kiowa pulled off his boots. He wanted to say more, just to lighten up his sleep, but instead he opened his New Testament and arranged it beneath his head as a pillow. The fog made things seem hollow and unattached. He tried not to think about Ted Lavender, but then he was thinking how fast it was, no drama, down and dead, and how it was hard to feel anything except surprise. It seemed unchristian. He wished he could find some great sadness, or even anger, but the emotion wasn't there and he couldn't make it happen. Mostly he felt pleased to be alive. He liked the smell of the New Testament under his cheek, the leather and ink and paper and glue, whatever the chemicals were. He liked hearing the sounds of night. Even his fatigue, it felt fine, the stiff muscles and the prickly awareness of his own body, a floating feeling. He enjoyed not being dead. Lying there, Kiowa admired Lieutenant Jimmy Cross's capacity for grief. He wanted to share the man's pain, he wanted to care as Jimmy Cross cared. And yet when he closed his eyes, all he could think was Boom-down, and all he could feel was the pleasure of having his boots off and the fog curling in around him and the damp soil and the Bible smells and the plush comfort of night.

After a moment Norman Bowker sat up in the dark.

What the hell, he said. You want to talk, *talk*. Tell it to me.

Forget it.

No, man, go on. One thing I hate, it's a silent Indian.

For the most part they carried themselves with poise, a kind of dignity. Now and then, however, there were times of panic, when they squealed or wanted to squeal but couldn't, when they twitched and made moaning sounds and covered their heads and said Dear Jesus and flopped around on the earth and fired their weapons blindly and cringed and sobbed and begged for the noise to stop and went wild and made stupid promises to themselves and to God and to their mothers and fathers, hoping not to die. In different ways, it happened to all of them. Afterward, when the firing ended, they would blink and peek up. They would touch their bodies, feeling shame, then quickly hiding it. They would force themselves to stand. As if in slow motion, frame by frame, the world would take on the old logic—absolute silence, then the wind, then sunlight, then voices. It was the burden of being alive. Awkwardly, the men would reassemble themselves, first in private, then in groups, becoming soldiers again. They would repair the leaks in their eyes. They would repair the leaks in their eyes. They would check for casualties, call in dust-offs, light cigarettes, try to smile, clear their throats and spit and begin cleaning their weapons. After a time someone would shake his head and say, No lie, I almost shit my pants, and someone else would laugh, which meant it was bad, yes, but the guy had obviously not shit his pants, it wasn't that bad, and in any case nobody would ever do such a thing and then go ahead and talk about it. They would squint into the dense, oppressive sunlight. For a few moments, perhaps, they would fall silent, lighting a joint and tracking its passage from man to man, inhaling, holding in the humiliation. Scary stuff, one of them might say. But then someone else would grin or flick his eyebrows and say, Roger-dodger, almost cut me a new asshole, *almost.*

There were numerous such poses. Some carried themselves with a sort of wistful resignation, others with pride or stiff soldierly discipline or good humor or macho zeal. They were afraid of dying but they were even more afraid to show it.

They found jokes to tell.

They used a hard vocabulary to contain the terrible softness. *Greased,* they'd say. *Offed, lit up, zapped while zipping.* It wasn't cruelty, just stage presence. They were actors and the war came at them in 3-D. When someone died, it wasn't quite dying, because in a curious way it seemed scripted, and because they had their lines mostly memorized, irony mixed with tragedy, and because they called it by other names, as if to encyst and destroy the reality of death itself. They kicked corpses. They cut off thumbs. They talked grunt lingo. They told stories about Ted Lavender's supply of tranquilizers, how the poor guy didn't feel a thing, how incredibly tranquil he was.

There's a moral here, said Mitchell Sanders.

They were waiting for Lavender's chopper, smoking the dead man's dope.

The moral's pretty obvious, Sanders said, and winked. Stay away from drugs. No joke, they'll ruin your day every time.

Cute, said Henry Dobbins.

Mind-blower, get it? Talk about wiggy—nothing left, just blood and brains.

They made themselves laugh.

There it is, they'd say, over and over, as if the repetition itself were an act of poise, a balance between crazy and almost crazy, knowing without going. There it is, which meant be cool, let it ride, because oh yeah, man, you can't change what can't be changed, there it is, there it absolutely and positively and fucking well *is*.

They were tough.

They carried all the emotional baggage of men who might die. Grief, terror, love, longing—these were intangibles, but the intangibles had their own mass and specific gravity, they had tangible weight. They carried shameful memories. They carried the common secret of cowardice barely restrained, the instinct to run or freeze or hide, and in many respects this was the heaviest burden of all, for it could never be put down, it required perfect balance and perfect posture. They carried their reputations. They carried the soldier's greatest fear, which was the fear of blushing. Men killed, and died, because they were embarrassed not to. It was what had brought them to the war in the first place, nothing positive, no dreams of glory or honor, just to avoid the blush of dishonor. They died so as not to die of embarrassment. They crawled into tunnels and walked point and advanced under fire. Each morning, despite the unknowns, they made their legs move. They endured. They kept humping. They did not submit to the obvious alternative, which was simply to close the eyes and fall. So easy, really. Go limp and tumble to the ground and let the muscles unwind and not speak and not budge until your buddies picked you up and lifted you into the chopper that would roar and dip its nose and carry you off to the world. A mere matter of falling, yet no one ever fell. It was not courage, exactly; the object was not valor. Rather, they were too frightened to be cowards.

By and large they carried these things inside, maintaining the masks of composure. They sneered at sick call. They spoke bitterly about guys who had found release by shooting off their own toes or fingers. Pussies, they'd say. Candyasses. It was fierce, mocking talk, with only a trace of envy or awe, but even so, the image played itself out behind their eyes.

They imagined the muzzle against flesh. They imagined the quick, sweet pain, then the evacuation to Japan, then a hospital with warm beds and cute geisha nurses.

They dreamed of freedom birds.

At night, on guard, staring into the dark, they were carried away by jumbo jets. They felt the rush of takeoff. *Gone!* they yelled. And then velocity, wings and engines, a smiling stewardess—but it was more than a plane, it was a real bird, a big sleek silver bird with feathers and talons and high screeching. They were flying. The weights fell off, there was nothing to fear. They laughed and held on tight, feeling the cold slap of wind and altitude, soaring, thinking *It's over, I'm gone!*—they were naked, they were light and free—it was all lightness, bright and fast and buoyant, light as light, a helium buzz in the brain, a giddy bubbling in the lungs as they were taken up over the clouds and the war, beyond duty, beyond gravity and mortification and global entanglements—*Sin loi!* they yelled, *I'm sorry, motherfuckers, but I'm out of it, I'm goofed, I'm on a space cruise, I'm gone!*—and it was a restful, disencumbered sensation, just riding the light waves, sailing that big silver freedom bird over the mountains and oceans, over America, over the farms and great sleeping cities and cemeteries and highways and the Golden Arches of McDonald's. It was flight, a kind of fleeing, a kind of falling, falling higher and higher, spinning off the edge of the earth and beyond the sun and through the vast, silent vacuum where there were no burdens and where everything weighed exactly nothing. *Gone!* they screamed, *I'm sorry but I'm gone!* And so at night, not quite dreaming, they gave themselves over to lightness, they were carried, they were purely borne.

On the morning after Ted Lavender died, First Lieutenant Jimmy Cross crouched at the bottom of his foxhole and burned Martha's letters. Then he burned the two photographs. There was a steady rain falling, which made it difficult, but he used heat tabs and Sterno to build a small fire, screening it with his body, holding the photographs over the tight blue flame with the tips of his fingers.

He realized it was only a gesture. Stupid, he thought. Sentimental, too, but mostly just stupid.

Lavender was dead. You couldn't burn the blame.

Besides, the letters were in his head. And even now, without photographs, Lieutenant Cross could see Martha playing volleyball in her white gym shorts and yellow T-shirt. He could see her moving in the rain.

When the fire died out, Lieutenant Cross pulled his poncho over his shoulders and ate breakfast from a can.

There was no great mystery, he decided.

In those burned letters Martha had never mentioned the war, except to say, Jimmy, take care of yourself. She wasn't involved. She signed the letters "Love," but it wasn't love, and all the fine lines and technicalities did not matter.

The morning came up wet and blurry. Everything seemed part of everything else, the fog and Martha and the deepening rain.

It was a war, after all.

Half smiling, Lieutenant Jimmy Cross took out his maps. He shook his head hard, as if to clear it, then bent forward and began planning the day's march. In ten minutes, or maybe twenty, he would rouse the men and they would pack up and head west, where the maps showed the country to be green and inviting. They would do what they had always done. The rain might add some weight, but otherwise it would be one more day layered upon all the other days.

He was realistic about it. There was that new hardness in his stomach.

No more fantasies, he told himself.

Henceforth, when he thought about Martha, it would be only to think that she belonged elsewhere. He would shut down the daydreams. This was not Mount Sebastian, it was another world, where there were no pretty poems or midterm exams, a place where men died because of carelessness and gross stupidity. Kiowa was right. Boom-down, and you were dead, never partly dead.

Briefly, in the rain, Lieutenant Cross saw Martha's gray eyes gazing back at him.

He understood.

It was very sad, he thought. The things men carried inside. The things men did or felt they had to do.

He almost nodded at her, but didn't.

Instead he went back to his maps. He was now determined to perform his duties firmly and without negligence. It wouldn't help Lavender, he knew that, but from this point on he would comport himself as a soldier. He would dispose of his good-luck pebble. Swallow it, maybe, or use Lee Strunk's slingshot, or just drop it along the trail. On the march he would impose strict field discipline. He would be careful to send out flank security, to prevent straggling or bunching up, to keep his troops moving at the proper pace and at the proper interval. He would insist on clean weapons. He would confiscate the remainder of Lavender's dope. Later in the day, perhaps, he would call the men together and speak to them plainly. He would accept the blame for what had happened to Ted Lavender. He would be a man about it. He would look them in the eyes, keeping his chin level, and he would issue the new SOPs in a calm, impersonal tone of voice, an officer's voice, leaving no room for argument or discussion. Commencing immediately, he'd tell them, they would no longer abandon equipment along the route of march. They would police up their acts. They would get their shit together, and keep it together, and maintain it neatly and in good working order.

He would not tolerate laxity. He would show strength, distancing himself.

Among the men there would be grumbling, of course, and maybe worse, because their days would seem longer and their loads heavier, but Lieutenant

Cross reminded himself that his obligation was not to be loved but to lead. He would dispense with love; it was not now a factor. And if anyone quarreled or complained, he would simply tighten his lips and arrange his shoulders in the correct command posture. He might give a curt little nod. Or he might not. He might just shrug and say Carry on, then they would saddle up and form into a column and move out toward the villages west of Than Khe.

[AUGUST 1986]

THOMAS MCGUANE

Flight

Now the Fishing columnist for Esquire, Thomas McGuane (1939–) first published fiction in the magazine in 1978, with an excerpt from his one of his novels, Panama, a "joco-splenetic" (McGuane's word) tale of love, drugs, and memory loss, a cautionary note about the consequences of swerving from the fast lane to the breakdown lane. "I write fiction in the hope of astounding myself," McGuane has said, adding that he is "seldom successful." Most other readers have been easier to please, and his novels, in particular Ninety-two in the Shade, have greatly influenced new generations of both readers and writers. While McGuane has compared the process of writing short stories to having one's head shrunk, he has nonetheless worked memorably in the form, as is clearly apparent in "Flight," which originally appeared in Esquire's 1986 summer fiction issue and was later collected in To Skin a Cat.

During bird season, dogs circle each other in my kitchen, shell vests hang in the mud room, all drains are clogged with feathers, and hunters work up hangover remedies at the icebox. As a diurnal man, I gloat at these presences, estimating who will and will not shoot well.

This year was slightly different in that Dan Ashaway arrived seriously ill. Yet this morning, he was nearly the only clear-eyed man in the kitchen. He helped make the vast breakfast of grouse hash, eggs, juice, and coffee. Most of the others, who were miserable, loaded dogs and made a penitentially early start. I pushed away some dishes and lit a breakfast cigar. Dan refilled our coffee and sat down. We've hunted birds together for years. I live here and Dan flies in from Philadelphia. Anyway, this seemed like the moment.

"How bad off are you?" I asked.

"I'm afraid I'm not going to get well," said Dan, directly, shrugging and dropping his hands to the arms of his chair. That was that. "Let's get started."

We took Dan's dogs at his insistence. They jumped into the aluminum boxes on the back of the truck when he said, "Load." Betty, a liver-and-white female, and Sally, a small bitch with a banded face; these were—I should say *are*—two dead-broke pointers who found birds and retrieved without much handling. Dan didn't even own a whistle.

As we drove toward Roundup, the entire pressure of my thoughts was of how remarkable it was to be alive. It seemed a strange and merry realization.

The dogs rode so quietly I had occasion to remember when Betty was a pup and yodeled in her box, drawing stares in all towns. Since then she had quieted down and grown solid at her job. She and Sally had hunted everywhere from Albany, Georgia, to Wilsall, Montana. Sally was born broke but Betty had the better nose.

We drove between two ranges of desertic mountains, low ranges without snow or evergreens. Section fences climbed very infrequently and disappeared over the top or into blue sky. There was one little band of cattle trailed by a cowboy and a dog, the only signs of life. Dan was pressing 16-gauge shells into the elastic loops of his cartridge belt. He was wearing blue policeman's suspenders and a brown felt hat—a businessman's worn-out Dobbs.

We watched a harrier course the ground under a bluff, sharp-tailed grouse jumping in his wake. The harrier missed a half-dozen, wheeled on one wing tip, and nailed a bird in a pop of down and feathers. As we resumed driving, the hawk was hooded over its prey, stripping meat from the breast.

Every time the dirt road climbed to a new vantage point, the country changed. For a long time, a green creek in a tunnel of willows was alongside us; then it went off under a bridge and we climbed away to the north. When we came out of the low ground, there seemed no end to the country before us: a great wide prairie with contours as unquestionable as the sea. There were buttes pried up from its surface and yawning coulees with streaks of brush where the springs were. We had to abandon logic to stop and leave the truck behind. Dan beamed and said, "Here's the spot for a big nap." The remark frightened me.

"Have we crossed the stagecoach road?" Dan asked.

"Couple miles back."

"Where did we jump all those sage hens in 1965?"

"Right where the stagecoach road passed the old hotel."

Dan had awarded himself a little English 16-gauge for graduating from the Wharton School of Business that year. It was in the gun rack behind our heads now, the bluing gone and its hinge pin shot loose.

"It's a wonder we found anything," said Dan from afar, "with the kind of run-off dog we had. Señor Jack. You had to preach religion to Señor Jack every hundred yards or he'd leave us. Remember? It's a wonder we fed that common bastard."

Señor Jack was a dog with no talent, loyalty, or affection, a dog we swore would drive us to racket sports. Dan gave him away in Georgia.

"He found the sage hens."

"But when we got on the back side of the Snowies, remember? He went right through all those sharptails like a train. We should have had deer rifles. A real wonder dog. I wonder where he is. I wonder what he's doing. Well, it's all an illusion, a very beautiful illusion, a miracle which is taking place before our very eyes. 1965. I'll be damned."

The stagecoach road came in around from the east again, and we stopped: two modest ruts heading into the hills. We released the dogs and followed the road around for half an hour. It took us past an old buffalo wallow filled with water. Some teal got up into the wind and wheeled off over the prairie.

About a mile later the dogs went on point. It was hard to say who struck game and who backed. Sally cat-walked a little, relocated, and stopped; then Betty honored her point. So we knew we had moving birds and got up on them fast. The dogs stayed staunch and the long covey rise went off like something tearing. I killed a going-away and Dan made a clean left and right. It was nice to be reminded of his strong heads-up shooting. I always crawled all over my gun and lost some quickness. It came of too much waterfowling when I was young. Dan had never really been out of the uplands and had speed to show for it.

Betty and Sally picked up the birds; they came back with eyes crinkled, grouse in their mouths. They dropped the birds and Dan caught Sally with a finger through her collar. Betty went back for the last bird. She was the better marking dog.

We shot another brace in a ravine. The dogs pointed shoulder to shoulder and the birds towered. We retrieved those, walked up a single, and headed for a hillside spring with a bar of bright buckbrush, where we nooned up with the dogs. The pretty bitches put their noses in the cold water and lifted their heads to smile when they got out of breath drinking. Then they pitched down for a rest. We broke the guns open and set them out of the way. I laid a piece of paper down and arranged some sandwiches and tangy apples from my own tree. We stretched out on one elbow, ate with a free hand, looked off over the prairie, to me the most beautiful thing in the world. I wish I could see all the grasslands, while we still have them. Then I couldn't stand it.

"What do you mean you're not going to get better?"

"It's true, old pal. It's quite final. But listen, today I'm not thinking about it. So let's not start."

I was a little sore at myself. We've all got to go, I thought. It's like waiting for an alarm to go off when it's too dark to read the dial. Looking at Dan's great chest straining his policeman's suspenders, it was fairly unimaginable that anything predictable could turn him to dust. I was quite wrong about that, too.

A solitary antelope buck stopped to look at us from a great distance. Dan put his hat on the barrels of his gun and decoyed the foolish animal to thirty yards before it snorted and ran off. We had sometimes found antelope blinds the Indians had built, usually not far from the eagle traps, clever things made by vital hands. There were old cartridge cases next to the spring, lying in the dirt, .45-70s; maybe a fight, maybe an old rancher hunting antelope with a cavalry rifle. Who knows. A trembling mirage appeared to the south, blue and banded with hills and distance. All around us the prairie creaked with life. I tried to picture the Indians, the soldiers. I kind of could. Were they gone or were they not?

"I don't know if I want to shoot a limit."

"Let's find them first," I said. I would have plenty of time to think about that remark later.

Dan thought and then said, "That's interesting. We'll find them and decide if we want to limit out or let it stand." The pointers got up, stretched their backs, glanced at us, wagged once, and lay down again next to the spring. After a minute, a smile shot over his face. The dogs had been watching for that and we were all on our feet and moving.

"This is it," Dan said, to the dogs or to me; I was never sure which. Betty and Sally cracked off, casting into the wind, Betty making the bigger race, Sally filling in with meticulous ground work. I could sense Dan's pleasure in these fast and beautiful bracemates.

"When you hunt these girls," he said, "you've got to step up their rations with hamburger, eggs, bacon drippings, you know, mixed in with that kibble. On real hot days, you put electrolytes in their drinking water. Betty comes into heat in April and October; Sally, March and September. Sally runs a little fever with her heat and shouldn't be hunted in hot weather for the first week and a half. I always let them stay in the house. I put them in a roading harness by August 1 to get them in shape. They've both been roaded horseback. Have you followed me very closely?"

I began to feel dazed and heavy. Maybe life wasn't something you lost at the end of a long fight. But I let myself off and thought, these things can go on and on.

Sally pitched over the top of a coulee. Betty went in and up the other side. There was a shadow that crossed the deep grass at the head of the draw. Sally locked up on point just at the rim and Dan waved Betty in. She came in from the other side, hit the scent, sank into running slink, and pointed.

Dan smiled at me and said, "Wish me luck." He closed his gun, walked over the rim, and sank from sight. I sat on the ground until I heard the report. After a bit the covey started to get up, eight dusky birds that went off on a climbing course. I whistled my dogs in and started for the truck.

[AUGUST 1986]

Sin

F. SCOTT FITZGERALD

An Alcoholic Case

As the exemplar of the Lost Generation of writers in the 1920s, F. Scott Fitzgerald (1896–1940) both defined and reported on a legendary period of literary history in his Jazz Age stories. When Fitzgerald first came to prominence with the publication of This Side of Paradise early in that decade he said, "An author ought to write for the youth of his generation, for the critics of the next, and the schoolmasters of ever afterward." In addition to his stories, Fitzgerald is known primarily for two of his five novels, The Great Gatsby and Tender Is the Night. His work, like Hemingway's, appeared in the earliest issues of Esquire. While Hemingway was writing "The Snows of Kilimanjaro" for the magazine, Fitzgerald submitted a series of articles called "The Crack-up," a chronicle of his painful journey into mental and emotional despair that attempted to explain his inability to write "stories about young love." In fact, in the original printing of "The Snows of Kilimanjaro" Hemingway referred to Fitzgerald as "poor Scott," pointedly marking the two writers' intersecting paths, as one rose to literary success while the other fell from it.

"Let—go—that—oh-h-h! Please, now, will you? *Don't* start drinking again! Come on—give me the bottle. I told you

I'd stay awake givin it to you. Come on. If you do like that a-way—then what are goin to be like when you go home. Come on—leave it with me—I'll leave half in the bottle. Pul-lease. You know what Dr. Carter says—I'll stay awake and give it to you, or else fix some of it in the bottle—come on—like I told you, I'm too tired to be fightin' you all night. . . . All right, drink your fool self to death."

"Would you like some beer?" he asked.

"No, I don't want any beer. Oh, to think that I have to look at you drunk again. My God!"

"Then I'll drink the Coca-Cola."

The girl sat down panting on the bed.

"Don't you believe in anything?" she demanded.

"Nothing you believe in—please—it'll spill."

She had no business there, she thought, no business trying to help him. Again they struggled, but after this time he sat with his head in his hands awhile, before he turned around once more.

"Once more you try to get it I'll throw it down," she said quickly. "I will—on the tiles in the bathroom."

"Then I'll step on the broken glass—or you'll step on it."

"Then let go—oh you promised—"

Suddenly she dropped it like a torpedo, sliding underneath her hand and slithering with a flash of red and black and the words: SIR GALAHAD, DISTILLED LOUISVILLE GIN.

It was on the floor in pieces and everything was silent for a while and she read Gone with the Wind about things so lovely that had happened long ago. She began to worry that he would have to go into the bathroom and might cut his feet, and looked up from time to time to see if he would go in. She was very sleepy—the last time she looked up he was crying and he looked like an old Jewish man she had nursed once in California; he had had to go to the bathroom many times. On this case she was unhappy all the time but she thought:

"I guess if I hadn't liked him I wouldn't have stayed on the case."

With a sudden resurgence of conscience she got up and put a chair in front of the bathroom door. She had wanted to sleep because he had got her up early that morning to get a paper with the Yale–Harvard game in it and she hadn't been home all day. That afternoon a relative of his had come in to see him and she had waited outside in the hall where there was a draft with no sweater to put over her uniform.

As well as she could she arranged him for sleeping, put a robe over his shoulders as he sat slumped over his chiffonier, and one on his knees. She sat

down in the rocker but she was no longer sleepy; there was plenty to enter on
the chart and treading lightly about she found a pencil and put it down:

Pulse 120

Respiration 25

Temp 98—98.4—98.2

Remarks—

—She could make so many:

Tried to get bottle of gin. Threw it away and broke it.

She corrected it to read:

In the struggle it dropped and was broken. Patient was generally difficult.

She started to add as part of her report: *I never want to go on an alcoholic
case again,* but that wasn't in the picture. She knew she could wake herself at
seven and clean up everything before his niece awakened. It was all part of the
game. But when she sat down in the chair she looked at his face, white and
exhausted, and counted his breathing again, wondering why it had all happened.
He had been so nice today, drawn her a whole strip of his cartoon just for the
fun and given it to her. She was going to have it framed and hang it in her room.
She felt again his thin wrists wrestling against her wrist and remembered the
awful things he had said, and she thought too of what the doctor had said to him
yesterday:

"You're too good a man to do this to yourself."

She was tired and didn't want to clean up the glass on the bathroom floor,
because as soon as he breathed evenly she wanted to get him over to the bed.
But she decided finally to clean up the glass first; on her knees, searching a last
piece of it, she thought:

—This isn't what I ought to be doing. And this isn't what *he* ought to be
doing.

Resentfully she stood up and regarded him. Through the thin delicate
profile of his nose came a light snore, sighing, remote, inconsolable. The doctor
had shaken his head in a certain way, and she knew that really it was a case that
was beyond her. Besides, on her card at the agency was written, on the advice
of her elders, "No Alcoholics."

She had done her whole duty, but all she could think of was that when she
was struggling about the room with him with that gin bottle there had been a
pause when he asked her if she had hurt her elbow against a door and that she
had answered: "You don't know how people talk about you, no matter how you
think of yourself—" when she knew he had a long time ceased to care about such
things.

The glass was all collected—as she got out a broom to make sure, she realized that the glass, in its fragments, was less than a window through which they had seen each other for a moment. He did not know about her sisters, and Bill Markoe whom she had almost married, and she did not know what had brought him to this pitch, when there was a picture on his bureau of his young wife and his two sons and him, all trim and handsome as he must have been five years ago. It was so utterly senseless—as she put a bandage on her finger where she had cut it while picking up the glass she made up her mind she would never take an alcoholic case again.

II

Some Halloween jokester had split the side windows of the bus and she shifted back to the Negro section in the rear for fear the glass might fall out. She had her patient's check but no way to cash it at this time of night; there was a quarter and a penny in her purse.

Two nurses she knew were waiting in the hall of Mrs. Hixson's Agency.

"What kind of case have you been on?"

"Alcoholic," she said.

"Oh yes—Gretta Hawks told me about it—you were on with that cartoonist who lives at the Forest Park Inn."

"Yes, I was."

"I hear he's pretty fresh."

"He's never done anything to bother me," she lied. "You can't treat them as if they were committed—"

"Oh, don't get bothered—I just heard that around town—oh, you know—they want you to play around with them—"

"Oh, be quiet," she said, surprised at her own rising resentment.

In a moment Mrs. Hixson came out and, asking the other two to wait, signaled her into the office.

"I don't like to put young girls on such cases," she began. "I got your call from the hotel."

"Oh, it wasn't bad, Mrs. Hixson. He didn't know what he was doing, and he didn't hurt me in any way. I was thinking much more of my reputation with you. He was really nice all day yesterday. He drew me—"

"I didn't want to send you on that case." Mrs. Hixson thumbed through the registration cards. "You take TB cases, don't you? Yes. I see you do. Now here's one—"

The phone rang in a continuous chime. The nurse listened as Mrs. Hixson's voice said precisely:

"I will do what I can—that is simply up to the doctor. . . . That is beyond my jurisdiction. . . . Oh, hello, Hattie, no, I can't now. Look, have you got any nurse that's good with alcoholics? There's somebody up at the Forest Park Inn who needs somebody. Call back, will you?"

She put down the receiver. "Suppose you wait outside. What sort of man is this, anyhow? Did he act indecently?"

"He held my hand away," she said, "so I couldn't give him an injection."

"Oh, an invalid he-man," Mrs. Hixson grumbled. "They belong in sanitaria. I've got a case coming along in two minutes that you can get a little rest on. It's an old woman—"

The phone rang again. "Oh, hello, Hattie. . . . Well, how about that big Svensen girl? She ought to be able to take care of any alcoholics. . . . How about Josephine Markham? Doesn't she live in your apartment house? . . . Get her to the phone." Then after a moment, "Jo, would you care to take the case of a well-known cartoonist, or artist, whatever they call themselves, at Forest Park Inn? . . . No, I don't know, but Doctor Carter is in charge and will be around about ten o'clock."

There was a long pause; from time to time Mrs. Hixson spoke:

"I see. . . . Of course, I understand your point of view. Yes, but this isn't supposed to be dangerous—just a little difficult. I never like to send girls to a hotel because I know what riff-raff you're liable to run into. . . . No, I'll find somebody. Even at this hour. Never mind and thanks. Tell Hattie I hope the hat matches the negligee. . . ."

Mrs. Nixon hung up the receiver and made notations on the pad before her. She was a very efficient woman. She had been a nurse and had gone through the worst of it, had been a proud, realistic, overworked probationer, suffered the abuse of smart interns and the insolence of her first patients who thought that she was something to be taken into camp immediately for premature commitment to the service of old age. She swung around suddenly from the desk.

"What kind of cases do you want? I told you I have a nice old woman—"

The nurse's brown eyes were alight with a mixture of thoughts—the movie she had just seen about Pasteur and the book they had all read about Florence Nightingale when they were student nurses. And their pride, swinging across the streets in the cold weather at Philadelphia General, as proud of their new capes as debutantes in their furs going in to balls at the hotels.

"I—I think I would like to try the case again," she said amid a cacophony of telephone bells. "I'd just as soon go back if you can't find anybody else."

"But one minute you say you'll never go on an alcoholic case again and the next minute you say you want to go back to one."

"I think I overestimated how difficult it was. Really, I think I could help him."

"That's up to you. But if he tried to grab your wrists."

"But he couldn't," the nurse said. "Look at my wrists: I played basketball at Waynesboro High for two years. I'm quite able to take care of him."

Mrs. Hixson looked at her for a long minute. "Well, all right," she said. "But just remember that nothing they say when they're drunk is what they mean when they're sober—I've been all through that; arrange with one of the servants that you can call on him, because you never can tell—some alcoholics are pleasant and some of them are not, but all of them can be rotten."

"I'll remember," the nurse said.

It was an oddly clear night when she went out, with slanting particles of thin sleet making white of a blue-black sky. The bus was the same that had taken her into town but there seemed to be more windows broken now and the bus driver was irritated and talked about what terrible things he would do if he caught any kids. She knew he was just talking about the annoyance in general, just as she had been thinking about the annoyance of an alcoholic. When she came up to the suite and found him all helpless and distraught she would despise him and be sorry for him.

Getting off the bus she went down the long steps to the hotel, feeling a little exalted by the chill in the air. She was going to take care of him because nobody else would, and because the best people of her profession had been interested in taking care of the cases that nobody else wanted.

She knocked at his study door, knowing just what she was going to say.

He answered it himself. He was in dinner clothes even to a derby hat—but minus his studs and tie.

"Oh, hello," he said casually. "Glad you're back. I woke up a while ago and decided I'd go out. Did you get a night nurse?"

"I'm the night nurse too," she said. "I decided to stay on twenty-hour duty."

He broke into a genial, indifferent smile.

"I saw you were gone, but something told me you'd come back. Please find my studs. They ought to be either in a little tortoiseshell box or—"

He shook himself a little more into his clothes, and hoisted the cuffs up inside his coat sleeves.

"I thought you had quit me," he said casually.

"I thought I had, too."

"If you look on that table," he said, "you'll find a whole strip of cartoons that I drew you."

"Who are you going to see?" she asked.

"It's the President's secretary," he said. "I had an awful time trying to get ready. I was about to give up when you came in. Will you order me some sherry?"

"One glass," she agreed wearily.

From the bathroom he called presently:

"Oh, nurse, nurse, Light of my Life, where is another stud?"

"I'll put it in."

In the bathroom she saw the pallor and the fever on his face and smelled the mixed peppermint and gin on his breath.

"You'll come up soon?" she asked. "Dr. Carter's coming at ten."

"What nonsense! You're coming down with me."

"Me?" she exclaimed. "In a sweater and skirt? Imagine!"

"Then I won't go."

"All right then, go to bed. That's where you belong anyhow. Can't you see these people tomorrow?"

"No, of course not."

"Of course not!"

She went behind him and reaching over his shoulder tied his tie—his shirt was already thumbed out of press where he had put in the studs, and she suggested:

"Won't you put on another one, if you've got to meet some people you like?"

"All right, but I want to do it myself."

"Why can't you let me help you?" she demanded in exasperation. "Why can't you let me help you with your clothes? What's a nurse for—what good am I doing?"

He sat down suddenly on the toilet seat.

"All right—go on."

"Now don't grab my wrist," she said, and then, "Excuse me."

"Don't worry. It didn't hurt. You'll see in a minute."

She had the coat, vest and stiff shirt off him but before she could pull his undershirt over his head he dragged at his cigarette, delaying her.

"Now watch this," he said. "One—two—three."

She pulled up the undershirt; simultaneously he thrust the crimson-gray point of the cigarette like a dagger against his heart. It crushed out against a copper plate on his left rib about the size of a silver dollar, and he said "ouch!" as a stray spark fluttered down against his stomach.

Now was the time to be hard-boiled, she thought. She knew there were three medals from the war in his jewel box, but she had risked many things herself: tuberculosis among them and one time something worse, though she had not known it and had never quite forgiven the doctor for not telling her.

"You've had a hard time with that, I guess," she said lightly as she sponged him. "Won't it ever heal?"

"Never. That's a copper plate."

"Well, it's no excuse for what you're doing to yourself."

He bent his great brown eyes on her, shrewd—aloof, confused. He signaled to her in one second, his Will to Die, and for all her training and experience she knew she could never do anything constructive with him. He stood up, steadying himself on the wash basin and fixing his eye on some place just ahead.

"Now, if I'm going to stay here you're not going to get at that liquor," she said.

Suddenly she knew he wasn't looking for that. He was looking at the corner where she had thrown the bottle this afternoon. She stared at his handsome face, weak and defiant—afraid to turn even halfway because she knew that death was in that corner where he was looking. She knew death—she had heard it, smelt its unmistakable odor, but she had never seen it before it entered into anyone, and she knew this man saw it in the corner of his bathroom; that it was standing there looking at him while he spit from a feeble cough and rubbed the result into the braid of his trousers. It shone there . . . crackling for a moment as evidence of the last gesture he ever made.

She tried to express it next day to Mrs. Hixson:

"It's not like anything you can beat—no matter how hard you try. This one could have twisted my wrists until he strained them and that wouldn't matter so much to me. It's just that you can't really help them and it's so discouraging— it's all for nothing."

[FEBRUARY 1937]

JAMES JONES

Two Legs for the Two of Us

James Jones's (1921–1977) early short story, "Two Legs for the Two of Us," published in September 1951, expresses the same sense of camaraderie-in-arms as his famous first novel of World War II, From Here to Eternity, but in a less romantic, more mordant way. (Jones was a sergeant in World War II and boxed as a welterweight while in the service.) Jones moved to Paris in 1958 and in the 1960s and 1970s often wrote for Esquire. The magazine also published parts of his later novels, The Thin Red Line and Whistle (which was completed in 1978 by Willie Morris). Jones returned to the United States in 1975.

"No," said the big man in the dark blue suit, and his voice was hoarse with drunkenness. "I cant stay. I've got some friends out in the car."

"Well, why didnt you bring them in with you, George?" the woman said in mock disgust. "Dont let them sit out in the cold."

George grinned fuzzily. "To hell with them. I just stopped by for a minute. You wouldnt like them anyway."

"Why, of course I'd like them, if they're your friends. Go on and call them."

"No. You wouldn't like them. Let the bastards sit. I just wanted to talk to you, Sandy." George looked vaguely around the gayness of the kitchen with its red-and-white checkered motif. "Jesus, I love this place. We done a good job on it, Sandy, you know it? I used to think about it a lot. I still do."

But the woman was already at the kitchen door and she did not hear. "Hey out there!" she called. "Come on in and have a drink."

There was a murmur of words from the car she could not understand and she opened the screen door and went outside to the car in the steaming cold winter night. A man and woman were in the front seat, the man behind the wheel. Another woman was in the back seat by herself. She was smoothing her skirt.

Sandy put her head up to the car window. "George is drunk," she said. "Why dont you go on home and leave him here and let me take care of him?"

"No," the man said.

"He's been here before."

"No," the man said sharply. "He's with us."

Sandy put her hand on the door handle. "He shouldnt be drinking," she said. "In his condition."

The man laughed. "Liquor never bothers me," he said.

"Poor George. I feel so sorry for him I could cry."

"No, you couldn't," the man said contemptuously. "I know you. Besides, it aint your sympathy he wants." He thumped the thigh of his left leg with his fist. It made a sound like a gloved fist striking a heavy bag. "I pawned one myself," he said.

Sandy moved as if he had struck her. She stepped back, putting her hand to her mouth, then turned back toward the house.

George was standing in the door. "Tom's a old buddy of mine," he grinned. "He was in the hospital with me for ten months out in Utah." He opened the screen.

Sandy stepped inside with slumped shoulders. "Why didnt you tell me? I said something terrible. Please tell him to come in, George, he wont come now unless you tell him."

"No. Let them sit. We got a couple of pigs from Greencastle with us." He grinned down at her belligerently through the dark circles and loose lips of an extended bat.

"Ask them all in, for a drink. I'm no Carrie Nation, George. Tell them to come in. Please, George. Tell them."

"All right. By god I will. I wasnt going to, but I will. I just wanted to see you, Sandy."

"Why dont you stay here tonight, George?" Sandy said. "Let them go on and I'll put you to bed."

George searched her face incredulously. "You really want me to stay?"

"Yes. You need to sober up, George."

"Oh." George laughed suddenly. "Liquor never bothers me. No sir by god. I aint runnin out on Tom. Tom's my buddy." He stepped back to the door. "Hey, you bastards!" he bellered. "You comin in here an have a drink? or I got to come out and drag you in?" Sandy stood behind him, watching him, the big bulk of shoulder, the hair growing softly on the back of his neck.

There was a laugh from the car and the door slammed. The tall curly-haired Tom came in, swinging his left side in a peculiar rhythm. After him came the two women, one tall and blond, the other short and dark. They both smiled shyly as they entered. They both were young.

"Oh," said the short one. "This is pretty."

"It's awful pretty," the blond one said, looking around.

"You goddamn right its pretty," George said belligerently. "And its built for utility. Look at them cupboards."

George introduced the girls by their first names, like a barker in a sideshow naming the attractions. "An this here's Tom Hornney," he said, "and when I say Hornney, I mean Hornney." George laughed and Tom grinned and the two girls tittered nervously.

"I want you all to meet Miss Sandy Thomas," George said, as if daring them.

"Sure," Tom said. "I know all about you. I use to read your letters out in Utah."

George looked at Sandy sheepishly. "A man gets so he cant believe it himself. He gets so he's got to show it to somebody. That's the way it is in the army."

Sandy smiled at him stiffly, her eyes seeming not to see. "How do you want your drinks? Soda or Coke?"

"They want Coke with theirs," Tom pointed to the girls. "They dont know how to drink."

"This is really a beautiful place," the blond one said.

"Oh my yes," the short one said. "I wish I ever had a place like this here." Sandy looked up from the drinks and smiled, warmly. "Thank you."

"I really love your place," the blond one said. "Where did you get those funny spotted glasses? I seen some like them in a Woolworth's once."

George, laughing over something with Tom, turned to the blond one. "Shut up, for god sake. You talk too much. You're supposed to be seen."

"Or felt," Tom said.

"I was only being polite," the blond one said.

"Well dont," George said. "You dont know how."

"Well," said the blond one. "I like that."

"Those are antiques, dear," Sandy said to her. "I bought them off an old woman down in the country. Woolworth has reproductions of them now."

"You mean them are *genuine* antiques?" the short one said.

Sandy nodded, handing around the drinks.

"For god sake, shut up," George said. "Them's genuine antiques and they cost ten bucks apiece, so shut up. Talk about something interesting."

The short one made a little face at George. She turned to Sandy and whispered delicately.

"Surely," Sandy said. "I'll show you."

"See what I mean?" Tom laughed. "I said they couldnt hold their liquor."

Sandy led the girls out of the kitchen. From the next room their voices came back, exclaiming delicately over the furnishings.

"How long were you in the army?" Sandy asked when they came back.

"Five years," Tom said, grinning and shaking his curly head. "My first wife left me three months after I got drafted."

"Oh?" Sandy said.

"Yeah. I guess she couldnt take the idea of not getting any for so long. It looked like a long war."

"War is hard on the women too," Sandy said.

"Sure," Tom said. "I dont see how they stand it. I'm glad I was a man in this war."

"Take it easy," George growled.

Tom grinned at him and turned back to Sandy. "I been married four times in five years. My last wife left me day before yesterday. She told me she was leaving and I said, Okay, baby. That's fine. Only remember there won't be nobody here when you come back. If I wanted, I could call her up right now and tell her and she'd start back tonight."

"Why dont you?" Sandy said. "I've got a phone."

Tom laughed. "What the hell. I'm doin all right. Come here, baby," he said to the blond one, and patted his right leg. She came over, smiling, on his left side and started to sit on his lap.

"No," Tom said. "Go around to the other side. You cant sit on that one."

The blond one obeyed and walked around his chair. She sat down smiling on his right thigh and Tom put his arm clear around her waist. "I'm doin all right, baby, ain't I? Who wants to get married?"

George was watching him, and now he laughed. "I been married myself," he said, not looking at Sandy.

"Sure," Tom grinned. "Don't tell me. I was out in Utah when you got the rings back, remember? Ha!" He turned his liquorbright eyes on Sandy. "It was just like Robert Taylor in the movies. He took them out in the snow and threw them away with a curse. Went right out the ward door and into the snowing night.

"One ring, engagement, platinum, two-carat diamond," Tom said, as if giving the nomenclature of a new weapon. "One ring, wedding, platinum, diamond circlet.—I told him he should of hocked them."

"No," Sandy said. "He should have kept them, then he could have used them over and over, every other night."

"I'll say," Tom said. "I'll never forget the first time me and George went on pass in Salt Lake City. He sure could of used them then."

"Aint you drinkin, Sandy?" George said.

"You know I dont drink."

"You used to. Some."

"That was only on special occasions," Sandy said, looking at him. "That was a long time ago. I've quit that now," she said.

George looked away, at Tom, who had his hand up under the blond one's armpit, snuggled in. "Now this heres a very fine thing," Tom said, nodding at her. "She's not persnickity like the broads in Salt Lake."

"I didn't really like it then," Sandy said.

"I know," George said.

"George picked him up a gal in a bar in Salt Lake that first night," Tom said. "She looked a lot like you, honey," he said to the blond one. The blond one tittered and put her hand beneath his ear.

"This gal," Tom continued, "she thought George was wonderful; he was wearing his ribbons. She asked him all about the limp and how he got wounded. She thought he was the nuts till she found out what it was made him limp." Tom paused to laugh.

"Then she got dressed and took off; we seen her later with a marine." He looked at George and they both laughed. George went around the table and sat down beside the short one.

"You ought to have a drink with us, Sandy," George said. "You're the host."

"I dont feel much like being formal," Sandy said.

Tom laughed. "Me neither."

"Do you want something to eat?" Sandy asked him. "I might eat something."

"Sure," Tom said. "I'll eat anything. I'm an old eater from way back. I really eat it. You got any cheese and crackers?"

Sandy went to one of the cupboards. "You fix another drink, George."

"Thats it," Tom said. "Eat and drink. There's only one think can turn my stommick," he said to the blond one. "You know whats the only think can turn my stommick?"

"Yes," said the blond one apprehensively, glancing at Sandy. "I know."

"I'll tell you the only thing can turn my stommick."

"Now, honey," the blond one said.

George turned around from the bottles on the countertop, pausing dramatically like an orator.

"Same thing that can turn my stommick."

He and Tom laughed uproariously, and he passed the drinks and sat down. The blond one and the short one tittered and glanced nervously at Sandy.

Tom thumped George's right leg with his fist and the sound it made was solid, heavy, the sound his own had made out in the car.

"You goddam old cripple, you."

"Thats all right," George said. "You cant run so goddam fast yourself."

"The hell I cant." Tom reached for his drink and misjudged it, spilling some on the tablecloth and on the blond girl's skirt.

"Now see what you did?" she said. "Damn it."

Tom laughed. "Take it easy, baby. If you never get nothing worse than whiskey spilled on your skirt, you'll be all right. Whiskey'll wash out."

George watched dully as the spot spread on the red-and-white checked tablecloth, then he lurched to his feet toward the sink where the dishrag always was.

Sandy pushed him back into his chair. "Its all right, George. I'll change it tomorrow."

George breathed heavily. "Watch yourself, you," he said to Tom. "Goddam you, be careful."

"What the hell. I dint do it on purpose."

"Thats all right, just watch yourself."

"Okay, Sergeant," Tom said. "Okay, halfchick."

George laughed suddenly, munching a slab of cheese between two crackers, spraying crumbs.

"Dont call me none of your family names."

"We really use to have some times," he said to Sandy. "You know what this crazy bastard use to do? After we got our leather, we use to stand out in the corridor and watch the guys with a leg off going down the hall on crutches. Tom would look at them and say to me, Pore feller. He's lost a leg. And I'd say, Why that's terrible, ain't it?"

Sandy was looking at him, watching him, her sandwich untouched in her hand. Under her gaze George's eyebrows suddenly went up, bent in the middle.

"We use to go to town," he said, grinning at her. "We really had some times. You ought to seen their faces when we'd go up to the room from the bar. You ought to see them when we'd take our pants off." He laughed viciously. "One broad even fainted on me. They didnt like it." His gaze wavered, then fell to his drink. "I guess you cant blame them though."

"Why?" Sandy said. "Why did you do it, George?"

"Hell," he said, looking up. *"Why?* Dont you know *why?"*

Sandy shook her head slowly, her eyes unmoving on his face. "No," she said. "I dont know why. I guess I never will know why," she said.

Tom was pinching the blond one's bottom. "That tickles mine," he said. "You know what tickles mine?"

"No," she said, "what?"

Tom whispered in her ear and she giggled and slapped him lightly.

"No," George said. "I guess you wont. You aint never been in the army, have you?"

"No," Sandy said. "I havent."

"You ought to try it," George said. "Fix us one more drink and we'll be goin."

"All right, George. But I wish you'd stay."

George spread his hands and looked down at himself. "Who?" he said. "Me?"

"Yes," Sandy said. "You really do need to sober up."

"Oh," George said. "Sober up. Liquor never bothers me. Listen, Sandy. I wanted to talk to you, Sandy."

Under the red-and-white checked tablecloth George put his hand on Sandy's bare knee below her skirt. His hand cupped it awkwardly, but softly, very softly.

"I'll get your drink," Sandy said, pushing back her chair. George watched her get up and go to the countertop where the bottles were.

"Come here, you," George said to the short dark one. He jerked her toward him so roughly her head snapped back. He kissed her heavily, his left hand behind her head holding her neck rigid, his right hand on her upper arm, stroking heavily, pinching slightly.

Sandy set the drink in front of him. "Here's your drink you wanted, George," she said, still holding the tabled glass. "George, here's your drink."

"Okay," George said. "Drink up, you all, and lets get out of this."

The short one was rubbing her neck with her hand, her face twisted breathlessly. She smiled apologetically at Sandy. "You got a wonderful home here, Miss Thomas," she said.

George lurched to his feet. "All right. All right. Outside." He shooed them out the door, Tom grinning, his hand hidden under the blond one's arm. Then he stood in the doorway looking back.

"Well, so long. And thanks for the liquor."

"All right, George. Why dont you stop drinking, George?"

"Why?" George said. "You ask me why."

"I hate to see you ruin yourself."

George laughed. "Well now thanks. That sure is nice of you, Sandy girl. But liquor never bothers me." He looked around the gayness of the kitchen. "Listen. I'm sorry about the tablecloth. Sorry. I shouldnt of done it, I guess. I shouldnt of come here with them."

"No, George. You shouldnt."

"You know what I love about you, Sandy girl? You're always so goddam stinking right."

"I just do what I have to," Sandy said.

"Sandy," George said. "You dont know what it was like, Sandy."

"No," she said. "I guess I dont."

"You goddam right you dont. And you never will. You'll never be . . ."

"I cant help the way I'm made."

"Yes? Well I cant neither. The only thing for us to do is turn it over to the United Nations. Its their job, let them figure it out."

Tom Hornney came back to the door. "Come on, for Christ sake. Are you comin or aint you?"

"Yes goddam it I'm comin. I'm comin and I'm goin." George limped swingingly over to the countertop and grabbed a bottle.

Tom stepped inside the door. "Listen, lady," he said. "What the hells a leg? The thing a man wants you dames will never give him. We're just on a little vacation now. I got a trucking business in Terre Haute. Had it before the war. There's good money in long-distance hauling, and me and George is goin to get our share. We got six trucks and three more spotted, and I know this racket, see? I know how to get the contracks, all the ways. An I got the pull. And me and George is full-time partners. What the hells a leg?"

George set down the bottle and came back, his right leg hitting the floor heavy and without resilience. "Tom and me is buddies, and right or wrong what we do we do together."

"I think thats fine, George," she said.

"Yeah? Well then, its all right then, aint it?"

"Listen, lady," Tom said. "Someday he'll build another house'll make this place look sick, see? To hell with the respectability if you got the money. So what the hells a leg?"

"Shut up," George said. "Let's go. Shut up. Shut up, or I'll mash you down."

"Yeah?" Tom grinned. "I'll take your leg off and beat you to death with it, Mack."

George threw back his head, laughing. "Fall in, you bum. Lets go."

"George," Sandy said. She went to the countertop and came back with a nearly full bottle. "Take it with you."

"Not me. I got mine in the car. And I got the money to buy more. Whiskey never bothers me. Fall in, Tom, goddam you."

Tom slapped him on the back. "Right," he said. And he started to sing.

They went out of the house into the steaming chill February night. They went arm in arm and limping. And they were singing.

> "Si-n-n-g glorious, glorious,
> One keg of beer for the four of us,
> Glory be to God there's no more of us,
> 'Cause . . ."

Their voices faded and died as the motor started. Tom honked the horn once, derisively.

Sandy Thomas stood in the door, watching the headlights move away, feeling the need inside, holding the bottle in her hand, moisture overflowing her eyes unnoticed, looking backward into a past the world had not seen fit to let alone. Tomorrow she would change the tablecloth, the red-and-white checkered tablecloth.

[SEPTEMBER 1951]

JOHN CHEEVER

The Death of Justina

John Cheever (1912–1982) was born in Quincy, Massachusetts, but spent most of his life in the Westchester, New York, community that he fictionalized in his five novels and over one hundred stories. His luminous declensions of fear and disappointment, suburban and urban dread, and intimations of redemption established his reputation as one of the most important writers of the late twentieth century. For The Wapshot Chronicle he received a National Book Award; his collected stories received the Pulitzer Prize.

So help me God, it gets more and more preposterous, it corresponds less and less to what I remember and what I expect, as if the force of life were centrifugal and threw one further and further away from one's purest memories and ambitions; and I can barely recall the old house where I was raised, where in midwinter Parma violets bloomed in a cold frame near the kitchen door and down the long corridor, past the seven views of Rome—up two steps and down three—one entered the library where all the books were in order, the lamps were bright, where there was a fire and a dozen bottles of good bourbon, locked in a cabinet with a veneer like tortoise shell whose silver key my father wore on his watch chain. Just let me give you one example and if you disbelieve me look honestly into your own past and see if you can't find a comparable experience. On Saturday the doctor told me to stop smoking and drinking and I did. I won't go into the commonplace symptoms of withdrawal, but I would like to point out that, standing at my window in the evening, watching the brilliant afterlight and the spread of darkness, I felt, through the lack of these humble stimulants, the force of some primitive memory in which the coming of night with its stars and its moon was apocalyptic. I thought suddenly of the neglected graves of my three brothers on the mountainside and that death is a loneliness much crueler than any loneliness hinted at in life. The soul (I thought) does not leave the body, but lingers with it through every degrading stage of decomposition and neglect, through heat, through cold, through the long winter nights when no one comes with a wreath or a plant and no one says a prayer. This unpleasant premonition was followed by anxiety. We were going out for dinner and I thought that the oil burner would explode in our absence and burn the house. The cook would get drunk and attack my daughter with a carving knife, or my wife and I would be killed in a collision on the main highway, leaving our children bewildered orphans with nothing in life to look forward to but sadness. I was able to observe, along with these foolish and terrifying anxieties, a definite impairment to my discretionary poles. I felt as if I were being lowered by ropes into the atmosphere of my childhood. I told my wife—when she passed through the living room—that I had stopped smoking and drinking but she didn't seem to care and who would reward me for my privations? Who cared about the bitter taste in my mouth and that my head seemed to be leaving my shoulders? It seemed to me that men had honored one another with medals, statuary and cups for much less and that abstinence is a social matter. When I abstain from sin it is more often a fear of scandal than a private resolve to improve on the purity of my heart, but here was a call for abstinence without the worldly enforcement of society, and death is not the threat that scandal is. When it was time for us to go out I was so light-headed that I had to ask my wife to drive the car. On Sunday I sneaked seven cigarettes in various hiding places and drank two Martinis in the downstairs coat closet. At breakfast on Monday my English muffin stared up at me from the plate. I mean I *saw* a face there in the rough, toasted surface. The moment of recognition was fleeting, but it was deep, and I wondered who it had been. Was it a friend, an aunt, a sailor, a ski instructor, a bartender or a conductor on a train? The smile faded off the muffin, but it had been there for a second—the sense of a person, a life, a pure force of gentleness and censure, and I am convinced that the muffin had contained the presence of some spirit. As you can see, I was nervous.

On Monday my wife's old cousin, Justina, came to visit her. Justina was a lively guest, although she must have been crowding eighty. On Tuesday my wife gave her a lunch party. The last guest left at three and a few minutes later, Cousin Justina, sitting on the living-room sofa with a glass of brandy, breathed her last. My wife called me at the office and I said that I would be right out. I was clearing my desk when my boss, MacPherson, came in.

"Spare me a minute," he asked. "I've been bird-dogging all over the place, trying to track you down. Pierson had to leave early and I want you to write the last Elixircol commercial."

"Oh, I can't, Mac," I said. "My wife just called. Cousin Justina is dead."

"You write that commercial," he said. His smile was satanic. "Pierson had to leave early because his grandmother fell off a stepladder."

Now I don't like fictional accounts of office life. It seems to me that if you're going to write fiction you should write about mountain-climbing and tempests at sea and I will go over my predicament with MacPherson briefly, aggravated as it was by his refusal to respect and honor the death of dear old Justina. It was like MacPherson. It was a good example of the way I've been treated. He is, I might say, a tall, splendidly groomed man of about sixty who changes his shirt three times a day, romances his secretary every afternoon between two and two-thirty and makes the habit of continuously chewing gum seem hygienic and elegant. I write his speeches for him and it has not been a happy arrangement for me. If the speeches are successful, MacPherson takes all the credit. I can see that his presence, his tailor and his fine voice are all a part of the performance, but it makes me angry never to be given credit for what was said. On the other hand, if the speeches are unsuccessful—if his presence and his voice can't carry the hour—his threatening and sarcastic manner is surgical and I am obliged to contain myself in the role of a man who can do no good in spite of the piles of congratulatory mail that my eloquence sometimes brings in. I must pretend, I must, like an actor, study and improve on my pretension, to have nothing to do with his triumphs and I must bow my head gracefully in shame when we have both failed. I am forced to appear grateful for injuries, to lie, to smile falsely and to play out a role as asinine and as unrelated to the facts as a minor prince in an operetta, but if I speak the truth it will be my wife and my children who will pay in hardships for my outspokenness. Now he refused to respect or even to admit the solemn fact of a death in our family and if I couldn't rebel it seemed as if I could at least hint at it.

The commercial he wanted me to write was for a tonic called Elixircol and was to be spoken on television by an actress who was neither young nor beautiful, but who had an appearance of ready abandon and who was anyhow the mistress of one of the sponsor's uncles. *Are you growing old?* I wrote. *Are you falling out of love with your image in the looking glass? Does your face in the morning seem rucked and seamed with alcoholic and sexual excesses and does the rest of you appear to be a grayish-pink lump, covered all over with brindle hair? Walking in the autumn woods, do you feel that subtle distance has come between you and the smell of wood smoke? Have you drafted your obituary? Are you easily winded? Do you wear a girdle? Is your sense of smell fading, is your interest in gardening waning, is your fear of heights increasing and are your sexual drives as ravening and intense as ever and does your wife look more and more to you like a stranger with sunken cheeks who has wandered into your bedroom by mistake? If this or any of this is true you need Elixircol, the true juice of youth.* The small economy size (business with the bottle) costs seventy-five dollars and the giant family bottle comes at two hundred and fifty. It's a lot of scratch, God knows, but these are inflationary times and who can put a price on youth? If you don't have the cash, borrow it from your neighborhood loan shark or hold up the local bank. The odds are three to one that with a ten-cent water pistol and a slip of paper you can shake ten thousand out of any fainthearted teller. Everybody's doing it. (Music up and out.)

I sent this into MacPherson via Ralphie, the messenger boy, and took the 4:16 home, traveling through a landscape of utter desolation.

Now my journey is a digression and has no real connection to Justina's death, but what followed could only have happened in my country and in my time and since I was an American traveling across an American landscape, the trip may be part of the sum. There are some Americans who, although their fathers emigrated from the old world three centuries ago, never seem to have quite completed the voyage, and I am one of these. I stand, figuratively, with one wet foot on Plymouth Rock, looking with some delicacy, not into a formidable and challenging wilderness but onto a half-finished civilization embracing glass towers, oil derricks, suburban continents and abandoned movie houses and wondering why, in this most prosperous, equitable and accomplished world— where even the cleaning women practice the Chopin preludes in their spare time—everyone should seem to be so disappointed?

At Proxmire Manor I was the only passenger to get off the random, meandering and profitless local that carried its shabby lights off into the dusk like some game-legged watchman or beadle, making his appointed rounds. I went around to the front of the station to wait for my wife and to enjoy the traveler's fine sense of crises. Above me on the hill was my home and the homes of my friends, all lighted and smelling of fragrant wood smoke like the temples in a sacred grove, dedicated to monogamy, feckless childhood and domestic bliss, but

so like a dream that I felt the lack of viscera with much more than poignance—
the absence of that inner dynamism we respond to in some European landscapes.
In short, I was disappointed. It was my country, my beloved country and there
have been mornings when I could have kissed the earth that covers its many
provinces and states. There was a hint of bliss—romantic and domestic bliss. I
seemed to hear the jingle bells of the sleigh that would carry me to grandmother's
house, although in fact grandmother spent the last years of her life working as
a hostess on an ocean liner and was lost in the tragic sinking of the S.S. *Lorelei*
and I was responding to a memory that I had not experienced. But the hill of
light rose like an answer to some primitive dream of homecoming. On one of
the highest lawns I saw the remains of a snowman who still smoked a pipe and
wore a scarf and a cap, but whose form was wasting away and whose anthracite
eyes stared out at the view with terrifying bitterness. I sensed some disappointing
greenness of spirit in the scene, although I knew in my bones, no less, how like
yesterday it was that my father left the old world to found a new; and I thought
of the forces that had brought stamina to the image: the cruel towns of Calabria
with their cruel princes, the badlands northwest of Dublin, ghettos, despots,
whorehouses, bread lines, the graves of children. Intolerable hunger, corruption,
persecution and despair had generated these faint and mellow lights and wasn't
it all a part of the great migration that is the life of man?

My wife's cheeks were wet with tears when I kissed her. She was distressed,
of course, and really quite sad. She had been attached to Justina. She drove me
home where Justina was still sitting on the sofa. I would like to spare you the
unpleasant details, but I will say that both her mouth and her eyes were wide
open. I went into the pantry to telephone Dr. Hunter. His line was busy. I poured
myself a drink—the first since Sunday—and lighted a cigarette. When I called
the doctor again he answered and I told him what had happened. "Well, I'm
awfully sorry to hear about it, Moses," he said. "I can't get over until after six
and there isn't much that I can do. This sort of thing has come up before and
I'll tell you all I know. You see you live in a B zone—two-acre lots, no
commercial enterprises, and so forth. A couple of years ago some stranger bought
the old Plewett mansion and it turned out that he was planning to operate it as
a funeral home. We didn't have any zoning provision at the time that would
protect us and one was rushed through the village council at midnight and they
overdid it. It seems that you not only can't have a funeral home in zone B—you
can't bury anything there and you can't die there. Of course it's absurd, but we
all make mistakes, don't we?

"Now there are two things you can do. I've had to deal with this before.

You can take the old lady and put her into the car and drive her over to Chestnut Street where zone C begins. The boundary is just beyond the traffic light by the high school. As soon as you get her over to zone C, it's all right. You can just say she died in the car. You can do that or if this seems distasteful you can call the mayor and ask him to make an exception to the zoning laws. But I can't write you out a death certificate until you get her out of that neighborhood and of course no undertaker will touch her until you get a death certificate."

"I don't understand," I said, and I didn't, but then the possibility that there was some truth in what he had just told me broke against me or over me like a wave, exciting mostly indignation. "I've never heard such a lot of damned foolishness in my life," I said. "Do you mean to tell me that I can't die in one neighborhood and that I can't fall in love in another and that I can't eat . . ."

"Listen. Calm down, Moses. I'm not telling you anything but the facts and I have a lot of patients waiting. I don't have the time to listen to you fulminate. If you want to move her, call me as soon as you get her over to the traffic light. Otherwise, I'd advise you to get in touch with the mayor or someone on the village council." He cut the connection. I was outraged, but this did not change the fact that Justina was still sitting on the sofa. I poured a fresh drink and lit another cigarette.

Justina seemed to be waiting for me and to be changing from an inert into a demanding figure. I tried to imagine carrying her out to the station wagon, but I couldn't complete the task in my imagination and I was sure that I couldn't complete it in fact. I then called the mayor, but this position in our village is mostly honorary and as I might have known he was in his New York law office and was not expected home until seven. I could cover her, I thought; that would be a decent thing to do, and I went up the back stairs to the linen closet and got a sheet. It was getting dark when I came back into the living room, but this was no merciful twilight. Dusk seemed to be playing directly into her hands and she had gained power and stature with the dark. I covered her with the sheet and turned on a lamp at the other end of the room, but the rectitude of the place with its old furniture, flowers, paintings, etc. was demolished by her monumental shape. The next thing to worry about was the children, who would be home in a few minutes. Their knowledge of death, excepting their dreams and intuitions of which I know nothing, is zero and the bold figure in the parlor was bound to be traumatic. When I heard them coming up the walk I went out and told them what had happened and sent them up to their rooms. At seven I drove over to the mayor's.

He had not come home, but he was expected at any minute and I talked with his wife. She gave me a drink. By this time I was chain-smoking. When the mayor came in we went into a little office or library where he took up a position behind a desk, putting me in the low chair of a supplicant.

"Of course I sympathize with you, Moses," he said, settling back in his chair. "It's an awful thing to have happened, but the trouble is that we can't give you a zoning exception without a majority vote of the village council and all the members of the council happen to be out of town. Pete's in California and Jack's in Paris and Larry won't be back from Stowe until the end of the week."

I was sarcastic. "Then I suppose Cousin Justina will have to gracefully decompose in my parlor until Jack comes back from Paris."

"Oh, no," he said, "oh, *no*. Jack won't be back from Paris for another month, but I think you might wait until Larry comes from Stowe. Then we'd have a majority, assuming of course that they would agree to your appeal."

"For Christ's sake," I snarled.

"Yes, yes," he said, "it is difficult, but after all you must realize that this is the world you live in and the importance of zoning can't be overestimated. Why, if a single member of the council could give out zoning exceptions, I could give you permission right now to open a saloon in your garage, put up neon lights, hire an orchestra and destroy the neighborhood and all the human and commercial values we've worked so hard to protect."

"I don't want to open a saloon in my garage," I howled. "I don't want to hire an orchestra. I just want to bury Justina."

"I know, Moses, I know," he said. "I understand that. But it's just that it happened in the wrong zone and if I make an exception for you I'll have to make an exception for everyone, and this kind of morbidity, when it gets out of hand, can be very depressing. People don't like to live in a neighborhood where this sort of thing goes on all the time."

"Listen to me," I said. "You give me an exception and you give it to me now or I'm going home and dig a hole in my garden and bury Justina myself."

"But you can't do that, Moses. You can't bury anything in zone B. You can't even bury a cat."

"You're mistaken," I said. "I can and I will. I can't function as a doctor and I can't function as an undertaker, but I can dig a hole in the ground and if you don't give me my exception, that's what I'm going to do."

I got out of the low chair before I finished speaking and started for the door.

"Come back, Moses, come back," he said. "Please come back. Look, I'll give you an exception if you'll promise not to tell anyone. It's breaking the law, it's a forgery, but I'll do it if you promise to keep it a secret."

I promised to keep it a secret, he gave me the documents and I used his telephone to make the arrangements. Justina was removed a few minutes after I got home, but that night I had the strangest dream.

I dreamed that I was in a crowded supermarket. It must have been night because the windows were dark. The ceiling was paved with fluorescent light—brilliant, cheerful, but, considering our prehistoric memories, a harsh link in the chain of light that binds us to the past. Music was playing and there must have been at least a thousand shoppers pushing their wagons among the long corridors of comestibles and victuals. Now is there—or isn't there—something about the posture we assume when we push a wagon that unsexes us? Can it be done with gallantry? I bring this up because the multitude of shoppers seemed that evening, as they pushed their wagons, penitential and unsexed. There were all kinds, this being my beloved country. There were Italians, Finns, Jews, Negroes, Shropshiremen, Cubans—anyone who had heeded the voice of liberty—and they were dressed with that sumptuary abandon that European caricaturists record with such bitter disgust. Yes, there were grandmothers in shorts, big-butted women in knitted pants, and men wearing such an assortment of clothing that it looked as if they had dressed hurriedly in a burning building. But this, as I say, is my own country and in my opinion the caricaturist who vilifies the old lady in shorts vilifies himself. I am a native and I was wearing buckskin jump boots, chino pants cut so tight that my sexual organs were discernible and a rayon acetate pajama top printed with representations of the *Pinta*, the *Nina* and the *Santa Maria* in full sail. The scene was strange—the strangeness of a dream where we see familiar objects in an unfamiliar light, but as I looked more closely I saw that there were some irregularities. Nothing was labeled. Nothing was identified or known. The cans and boxes were all bare. The frozen-food bins were full of brown parcels, but they were such odd shapes that you couldn't tell if they contained a frozen turkey or a Chinese dinner. All the goods at the vegetable and the bakery counters were concealed in brown bags and even the books for sale had no titles. In spite of the fact that the contents of nothing was known, my companions of the dream—my thousands of bizarrely dressed compatriots—were deliberating gravely over these mysterious containers as if the choices they made were critical. Like any dreamer, I was omniscient—I was with them and I was withdrawn—and stepping above the scene for a minute I noticed the men at the check-out counters. They were brutes. Now sometimes in a crowd, in a bar or a street, you will see a face so full-blown in its obdurate resistance to the appeals of love, reason and decency—so lewd, so brutish and unregenerate—that you turn away. Men like these were stationed at the only way out and as the shoppers approached them they tore their packages open—I still couldn't see what they contained—but in every case the customer, at the sight of what he had chosen, showed all the symptoms of the deepest guilt; that force that brings us to our knees. Once their choice had been opened, to their shame they were pushed—in some cases kicked—toward the door and beyond the door I saw dark water and heard a terrible noise of moaning and crying in the air. They waited at the door in groups to be taken away in some conveyance that I couldn't see. As I watched, thousands and thousands pushed their wagons through the market, made their careful and mysterious choices and were reviled and taken away. What could be the meaning of this?

We buried Justina in the rain the next afternoon. The dead are not, God knows, a minority, but in Proxmire Manor their unexalted kingdom is on the outskirts, rather like a dump, where they are transported furtively as knaves and scoundrels and where they lie in an atmosphere of perfect neglect. Justina's life had been exemplary, but by ending it she seemed to have disgraced us all. The priest was a friend and a cheerful sight, but the undertaker and his helpers, hiding behind their limousines, were not, and aren't they at the root of most of our troubles with their claim that death is a violet-flavored kiss? How can a people who do not mean to understand death hope to understand love and who will sound the alarm?

I went from the cemetery back to my office.

The commercial was on my desk and MacPherson had written across it in large letters in grease pencil: "Very funny, you broken-down bore. Do again."

I was tired but unrepentant and didn't seem able to force myself into a practical posture of usefulness and obedience. I did another commercial.

Don't lose your loved ones because of excessive radioactivity. Don't be a wallflower at the dance because of strontium 90 in your bones. Don't be a victim of fallout. When the tart on 36th Street gives you the big eye, does your body stride off in one direction and your imagination in another? Does your mind follow her up the stairs and taste her wares in revolting detail while your flesh goes off to Brooks Brothers or the foreign-exchange desk of the Chase Manhattan Bank? Haven't you noticed the size of the ferns, the lushness of the grass, the bitterness of the string beans and the brilliant markings on the new breeds of butterflies? You have been inhaling lethal atomic waste for the last twenty-five years and only Elixircol can save you.

I gave this copy to Ralphie and waited perhaps ten minutes, when it was returned, marked again with grease pencil. "Do," he wrote, "or you'll be dead."

I felt very tired. I returned to the typewriter, put another piece of paper into the machine and wrote: *The Lord is my Shepherd, therefore can I lack nothing. He shall feed me in a green pasture and lead me forth beside the waters of comfort. He shall convert my soul and bring me forth in the paths of righteousness for his Name's sake. Yea, though I walk through the valley of the shadow of death I will fear no evil for thou art with me; thy rod and thy staff comfort me. Thou shalt prepare a table for me in the presence of them that trouble me; thou hast anointed my head with oil and my cup shall be full. Surely thy loving kindness and thy mercy shall follow me all the days of my life and I will dwell in the house of the Lord forever.* I gave this to Ralphie and went home.

[NOVEMBER 1960]

FLANNERY O'CONNOR

Parker's Back

*Flannery O'Connor's "Parker's Back" was published posthumously in
Esquire in 1965. Her death at the age of thirty-nine was a premature
loss of one of our most gifted contemporary writers. O'Connor (1925–
1964) led a fiercely religious and sheltered life in Milledgeville, Georgia,
where she wrote two novels, Wise Blood and The Violent Bear It Away,
and two short story collections, Everything That Rises Must Converge
and A Good Man Is Hard to Find.*

Parker's wife was sitting on the front
porch floor, snapping beans. Parker was sitting on the step, some distance away,
watching her sullenly. She was plain, plain. The skin on her face was thin and
drawn as tight as the skin on an onion and her eyes were gray and sharp like the
points of two ice picks. Parker understood why he had married her—he couldn't
have got her any other way—but he couldn't understand why he stayed with her
now. She was pregnant and pregnant women were not his favorite kind. Nevertheless he stayed as if she had him conjured. He was puzzled and ashamed of
himself.

The house they rented sat alone save for a single tall pecan tree on a high
embankment overlooking a highway. At intervals a car would shoot past below
and his wife's eyes would swerve suspiciously after the sound of it and then come

back to rest on the newspaper full of beans in her lap. One of the things she did not approve of was automobiles. In addition to her other bad qualities, she was forever sniffing up sin. She did not smoke, dip, drink whiskey, use bad language or paint her face, and God knew some paint would have improved it, Parker thought. Her being against color, it was the more remarkable she had married him. Sometimes he supposed that she had married him because she meant to save him. At other times he had a suspicion that she actually liked everything she said she didn't. He could account for her one way or another; it was himself he could not understand.

She turned her head in his direction and said, "It's no reason you can't work for a man. It don't have to be a woman."

"Aw, shut your mouth for a change," Parker muttered.

If he had been certain she was jealous of the woman he worked for he would have been pleased, but more likely she was concerned with the sin that would result if he and the woman took a liking to each other. He had told her that the woman was a hefty young blonde; in fact she was nearly seventy years old and too dried up to have an interest in anything except getting as much work out of him as she could. Not that an old woman didn't sometimes get an interest in a young man, particularly if he was as attractive as Parker felt he was, but this old woman looked at him the same way she looked at her old tractor—as if she had to put up with it because it was all she had. The tractor had broken down the second day Parker was on it and she had set him at once to cutting bushes, saying out of the side of her mouth to the nigger, "Everything he touches, he breaks." She also asked him to wear his shirt when he worked; Parker had removed it even though the day was not sultry; he put it back on reluctantly.

This ugly woman Parker married was his first wife. He had had other women but he had planned never to get himself tied up legally. He had first seen her one morning when his truck broke down on the highway. He had managed to pull it off the road into a neatly swept yard on which sat a peeling two-room house. He got out and opened the hood of the truck and began to study the motor. Parker had an extra sense that told him when there was a woman nearby watching him. After he had leaned over the motor a few minutes, his neck began to prickle. He cast his eye over the empty yard and porch of the house. A woman he could not see was either nearby beyond a clump of honeysuckle or in the house, watching him out the window.

Suddenly Parker began to jump up and down and fling his hand about as if he had mashed it in the machinery. He doubled over and held his hand close to his chest. "Goddamnit!" he hollered. "Jesus Christ in hell! Jesus God Almightydamn! Goddamnit to hell!" he went on, flinging out the same few oaths over and over as loud as he could.

Without warning a terrible bristly claw slammed the side of his face and he fell backward on the hood of the truck. "You don't talk no filth here!" a voice close to him shrilled.

Parker's vision was so blurred that for an instant he thought he had been attacked by some creature from above, a giant hawk-eyed angel wielding a hoary weapon. As his sight cleared, he saw before him a tall rawboned girl with a broom.

"I hurt my hand," he said. "I *hurt* my hand." He was so incensed that he forgot that he hadn't hurt his hand. "My hand may be broke," he growled, although his voice was still unsteady.

"Lemme see it," the girl demanded.

Parker stuck out his hand and she came closer and looked at it. There was no mark on the palm and she took the hand and turned it over. Her own hand was dry and hot and rough and Parker felt himself jolted back to life by her touch. He looked more closely at her. I don't want nothing to do with this one, he thought.

The girl's sharp eyes peered at the back of the stubby reddish hand she held. There emblazoned in red and blue was a tattooed eagle perched on a cannon. Parker's sleeve was rolled to the elbow. Above the eagle a serpent was coiled about a shield and in the spaces between the eagle and the serpent there were hearts, some with arrows through them. Above the serpent there was a spread hand of cards. Every space on the skin of Parker's arm, from wrist to elbow, was covered in some loud design. The girl gazed at this with an almost stupefied smile of shock, as if she had accidentally grasped a poisonous snake; she dropped the hand.

"I got most of my other ones in foreign parts," Parker said. "These here I mostly got in the United States. I got my first one when I was only fifteen years old."

"Don't tell me," the girl said. "I don't like it. I ain't got any use for it."

"You ought to see the ones you can't see," Parker said and winked.

Two circles of red appeared like little apples on the girl's cheeks and softened her appearance. Parker was intrigued. He did not for a minute think that she didn't like the tattoos. He had never yet met a woman who was not attracted to them.

Parker was fourteen when he saw a man in a fair, tattooed from head to foot. Except for his loins, which were girded with a panther hide, the man's skin was patterned in what seemed from Parker's distance—he was near the back of the tent, standing on a bench—a single intricate design of brilliant color. The man, who was small and sturdy, moved about on the platform, flexing his muscles so that the arabesque of men and beasts and flowers on his skin appeared to have a subtle motion of its own. Parker was filled with emotion, lifted up as some people are when the flag passes. He was a boy whose mouth habitually hung open. He was heavy and earnest, as ordinary as a loaf of bread. When the show was over, he had remained standing on the bench, staring where the tattooed man had been, until the tent was almost empty.

Parker had never before felt the least motion of wonder in himself. Until he saw the man at the fair, it did not enter his head that there was anything out of the ordinary about the fact that he existed. Even then it did not enter his head, but a peculiar unease settled in him. It was as if a blind boy had been turned so gently in a different direction that he did not know his destination had been changed.

He had his first tattoo sometime after—the eagle perched on the cannon. It was done by a local artist. It hurt very little, just enough to make it appear to Parker to be worth doing. This was peculiar too, for before he had thought that only what did not hurt was worth doing. The next year he quit school because he was sixteen and could. He went to the trade school for a while, and then he quit the trade school and worked for six months in a garage. The only reason he worked at all was to pay for more tattoos. His mother worked in a laundry and could support him, but she would not pay for any tattoo except her name on a heart, which he had put on, grumbling. However, her name was Betty Jean and nobody had to know it was his mother. He found out that the tattoos were attractive to the kind of girls he liked but who had never liked him before. He began to drink beer and get in fights. His mother wept over what was becoming of him. One night she dragged him off to a revival with her, not telling him where they were going. When he saw the big lighted church, he jerked out of her grasp and ran. The next day he lied about his age and joined the Navy.

Parker was large for the tight sailor's pants but the silly white cap, sitting low on his forehead, made his face by contrast look thoughtful and almost intense. After a month or two in the Navy, his mouth ceased to hang open. His features hardened into the features of a man. He stayed in the Navy five years and seemed a natural part of the gray mechanical ship, except for his eyes, which were the same pale slate color as the ocean and reflected the immense spaces around him as if they were a microcosm of the mysterious sea. In port Parker wandered about comparing the run-down places he was in to Birmingham, Alabama. Everywhere he went he picked up more tattoos.

He had stopped having lifeless ones like anchors and crossed rifles. He had a tiger and a panther on each shoulder, a cobra coiled about a torch on his chest, hawks over his thighs, Elizabeth II and Philip over where his stomach and liver were, respectively. He did not care much what the subject was so long as it was colorful; on his abdomen he had a few obscenities but only because that seemed the proper place for them. Parker would be satisfied with each tattoo about a month, then something about it that had attracted him would wear off. Whenever a decent-sized mirror was available, he would get in front of it and study his overall look. The effect was not of one intricate arabesque of colors but of something haphazard and botched. A huge dissatisfaction would come over him and he would go off and find another tattooist and have another space filled up. The front of Parker was almost completely covered but there were no tattoos on his back. He had no desire for one anywhere he could not readily see it himself. As the space on the front of him for tattoos decreased, his dissatisfaction grew and became general.

After one of his furloughs, he didn't go back to the Navy but remained away without official leave, drunk, in a rooming house in a city he did not know. His dissatisfaction, from being chronic and latent, had suddenly become acute and raged in him. It was as if the panther and the lion and the serpents and the eagles and the hawks had penetrated his skin and lived inside him in a raging warfare. The Navy caught up with him, put him in the brig for nine months and then gave him a dishonorable discharge.

After that Parker decided that country air was the only kind fit to breathe. He rented the shack on the embankment and bought the old truck and took various jobs which he kept as long as it suited him. At the time he met his future wife, he was buying apples by the bushel and selling them for the same price by the pound to isolated homesteaders on backcountry roads.

"All that there," the girl said, pointing to his arm, "is no better than what a fool Indian would do. It's a heap of vanity." She seemed to have found the word she wanted. "Vanity of vanities," she said.

Well what the hell do I care what she thinks of it? Parker asked himself, but he was plainly bewildered. "I reckon you like one of these better than another anyway," he said, dallying until he thought of something that would impress her. He thrust the arm back at her. "Which you like best?"

"None of them," she said, "but the chicken is not as bad as the rest."

"What chicken?" Parker almost yelled at her.

She pointed to the eagle.

"That's an eagle," Parker said. "What fool would waste their time having a chicken put on themself?"

"What fool would have any of it?" the girl said and turned away. She went slowly back to the house and left him there to get going. Parker remained for almost five minutes, looking agape at the dark door she had entered.

The next day he returned with a bushel of apples. He was not one to be outdone by anything that looked like her. He liked women with meat on them, so you didn't feel their muscles, much less their old bones. When he arrived, she was sitting on the top step and the yard was full of children, all as thin and poor as herself; Parker remembered it was Saturday. He hated to be making up to a woman when there were children around, but it was fortunate he had brought the bushel of apples off the truck. As the children approached him to see what he carried, he gave each child an apple and told it to get lost; in that way he cleared out the whole crowd.

The girl did nothing to acknowledge his presence. He might have been a stray pig or goat that had wandered into the yard and she too tired to take up the broom and send it off. He set the bushel of apples down next to her on the step. He sat down on a lower step.

"Hep yourself," he said, nodding at the basket; then he lapsed into silence.

She took an apple quickly as if the basket might disappear if she didn't make haste. Hungry people made Parker nervous. He had always had plenty to eat himself. He grew very uncomfortable. He reasoned he had nothing to say so why should he say it? He could not think now why he had come or why he didn't go before he wasted another bushel of apples on the crowd of children. He supposed they were her brothers and sisters.

She chewed the apple slowly but with a kind of relish of concentration, bent slightly but looking out ahead. The view from the porch stretched off across a long incline studded with ironweed and across the highway to a vast vista of hills and one small mountain. Long views depressed Parker. You look out into space like that and you begin to feel as if someone were after you, the Navy or the Government or Religion.

"Who them children belong to, you?" he said at length.

"I ain't married yet," she said. "They belong to momma." She said it as if it were only a matter of time before she would be married.

Who in God's name would marry her? Parker thought.

A large barefooted woman with a wide gap-toothed face appeared in the door behind Parker. She had apparently been there for several minutes.

"Good evening," Parker said.

The woman crossed the porch and picked up what was left of the bushel of apples. "We thank you," she said and returned with it into the house.

"That your old woman?" Parker muttered.

The girl nodded. Parker knew a lot of sharp things he could have said, like "You got my sympathy," but he was gloomily silent. He just sat there, looking at the view. He thought he must be coming down with something.

"If I pick up some peaches tomorrow I'll bring you some," he said.

"I'll be much obliged to you," the girl said.

Parker had no intention of taking any basket of peaches back there, but the next day he found himself doing it. He and the girl had almost nothing to say to each other. One thing he did say was, "I ain't got any tattoo on my back."

"What you got on it?" the girl said.

"My shirt," Parker said. "Haw."

"Haw haw," the girl said politely.

Parker thought he was losing his mind. He could not believe for a minute that he was attracted to a woman like this. She showed not the least interest in anything but what he brought until he appeared the third time with two cantaloupes. "What's your name?" she asked.

"O.E. Parker," he said.

"What does the O.E. stand for?"

"You can just call me O.E.," Parker said. "Or Parker. Don't nobody call me by my name."

"What's it stand for?" she persisted.

"Never mind," Parker said. "What's yours?"

"I'll tell you when you tell me what them letters are the short of," she said. There was just a hint of flirtatiousness in her tone and it went rapidly to Parker's head. He had never revealed the name to any man or woman, only to the files of the Navy and the Government, and it was on his baptismal record which he got at the age of a month; his mother was a Methodist. When the name leaked out of the Navy files, Parker narrowly missed killing the man who used it.

"You'll go blab it around," he said.

"I'll swear I'll never tell nobody," she said. "On God's holy word I swear it."

Parker sat for a few minutes in silence. Then he reached for the girl's neck, drew her ear close to his mouth and revealed the name in a low voice.

"Obadiah," she whispered. Her face slowly brightened as if the name came as a sign to her. "Obadiah," she said.

The name still stank in Parker's estimation.

"Obadiah Elihue," she said in a reverent voice.

"If you call me that aloud, I'll bust your head open," Parker said. "What's yours?"

"Sarah Ruth Cates," she said.

"Glad to meet you, Sarah Ruth," Parker said.

Sarah Ruth's father was a Straight Gospel preacher but he was away, spreading it in Florida. Her mother did not seem to mind Parker's attention to the girl so long as he brought a basket of something with him when he came. As for Sarah Ruth herself, it was plain to Parker after he had visited three times that she was crazy about him. She liked him even though she insisted that pictures on the skin were vanity of vanities and even after hearing him curse, and even after she had asked him if he was saved and he replied that he didn't see it was anything in particular to save him from. After that, inspired, Parker had said, "I'd be saved enough if you was to kiss me."

She scowled. "That ain't being saved," she said.

Not long after that she agreed to take a ride in his truck. Parker parked it on a deserted road and suggested to her that they lie down together in the back of it.

"Not until after we're married," she said—just like that.

"Oh, that ain't necessary," Parker said and as he reached for her, she thrust him away with such force that the door of the truck came off and he found himself flat on the ground. He made up his mind then and there to have nothing further to do with her.

They were married in the County Ordinary's office because Sarah Ruth thought churches were idolatrous. Parker had no opinion about that one way or the other. The Ordinary's office was lined with cardboard file boxes and record books with dusty yellow slips of paper hanging on out of them. The Ordinary was an old woman with red hair who had held office for forty years and looked as dusty as her books. She married them from behind the iron grille of a standup desk and when she finished, she said with a flourish, "Three dollars and fifty cents and till death do you part," and yanked some forms out of a machine.

Marriage did not change Sarah Ruth a jot and it made Parker gloomier than ever. Every morning he decided he had had enough and would not return that night; every night he returned. Whenever Parker couldn't stand the way he felt, he would have another tattoo, but the only surface left on him now was his back. To see a tattoo on his own back he would have to get two mirrors and stand between them in just the correct position and this seemed to Parker a good way to make an idiot of himself. Sarah Ruth, who, if she had had sense, could have enjoyed a tattoo on his back, would not even look at the ones he had elsewhere. When he attempted to point out especial details of them, she would shut her eyes tight and turn her back as well. Except in total darkness, she preferred Parker dressed and with his sleeves rolled down.

"At the judgment seat of God, Jesus is going to say to you, 'What you been doing all your life besides have pictures drawn all over you?' " she said.

"You don't fool me none," Parker said. "You're just afraid that hefty girl I work for'll like me so much she'll say, 'Come on, Mr. Parker, let's you and me. . . .' "

"You're tempting sin," she said, "and at the judgment seat of God you'll have to answer for that too. You ought to go back to selling the fruits of the earth."

Parker did nothing much when he was at home but listen to what the judgment seat of God would be like for him if he didn't change his ways. When he could, he broke in with tales of the hefty girl he worked for. " 'Mr. Parker,' " he said she said, " 'I hired you for your brains.' " (She had added, "So why don't you use them?")

"And you should have seen her face the first time she saw me without my shirt," he said. " 'Mr. Parker,' she said, 'you're a walking panner-rammer!' " This had, in fact, been her remark but it had been delivered out of one side of her mouth.

Dissatisfaction began to grow so great in Parker that there was no containing it outside of a tattoo. It had to be his back. There was no help for it. A dim half-formed inspiration began to work in his mind. He visualized having a tattoo put there that Sarah Ruth would not be able to resist—a religious subject. He thought of an open book with HOLY BIBLE tattooed under it and an actual verse printed on the page. This seemed just the thing for a while; then he began to hear her say, "Ain't I already got a real Bible! What you think I want to read the same verse over and over for when I can read it all?" He needed something better even than the Bible! He thought about it so much that he began to lose sleep. He was already losing flesh—Sarah Ruth just threw the food in the pot and let it boil. Not knowing for certain why he continued to stay with a woman who was both ugly and pregnant and no cook made him generally nervous and irritable, and he developed a little tic in the side of his face.

Once or twice he found himself turning around abruptly as if someone were trailing him. He had had a granddaddy who had ended in the state mental hospital, although not until he was seventy-five, but as urgent as it might be for him to get a tattoo, it was just as urgent that he get exactly the right one to bring Sarah Ruth to heel. As he continued to worry over it, his eyes took on a hollow, preoccupied expression. The old woman he worked for told him that if he couldn't keep his mind on what he was doing, she knew where she could find a fourteen-year-old colored boy who could. Parker was too preoccupied even to be offended. At any time previous, he would have left her then and there, saying dryly, "Well, you go ahead on and get him then."

Two or three mornings later he was baling hay with the old woman's sorry baler and her broken-down tractor in a large field, cleared save for one enormous old tree standing in the middle of it. The old woman was the kind who would not cut down a large old tree just because it was a large old tree. She had pointed it out to Parker as if he didn't have eyes and told him to be careful not to hit it as the machine picked up hay near it. Parker began at the outside of the field and made circles inward toward it. He had to get off the tractor every now and then and untangle the baling cord or kick a rock out of the way. The old woman had told him to carry the rocks to the edge of the field, which he did when she was there watching. When he thought he could make it, he ran over them. As he circled the field his mind was on a suitable design for his back. The sun, the size of a golf ball, began to switch regularly from in front to behind him, but he appeared to see it both places as if he had eyes in the back of his head. All at once he saw the tree reaching out to grasp him. A ferocious thud propelled him into the air, and he heard himself yelling in an unbelievably loud voice, "*God above!*"

He landed on his back while the tractor crashed upside down into the tree and burst into flames. The first thing Parker saw were his shoes, quickly being eaten by the fire; one was caught under the tractor, the other was some distance away, burning by itself. He was not in them. He could feel the hot breath of the burning tree on his face. He scrambled backward, still sitting, his eyes cavernous, and if he had known how to cross himself he would have done it.

His truck was on a dirt road at the edge of the field. He moved toward it, still sitting, still backward, but faster and faster; halfway to it he got up and began a kind of forward-bent run from which he collapsed on his knees twice. His legs felt like two old rusted rain gutters. He reached the truck finally and took off in it, zigzagging up the road. He drove past his house on the embankment and straight for the city, fifty miles distant.

Parker did not allow himself to think on the way to the city. He only knew that there had been a great change in his life, a leap forward into a worse unknown, and that there was nothing he could do about it. It was for all intents accomplished.

The artist had two large cluttered rooms over a chiropodist's office on a back street. Parker, still barefooted, burst silently in on him at a little after three in the afternoon. The artist, who was about Parker's own age—twenty-eight— but thin and bald, was behind a small drawing table, tracing a design in green ink. He looked up with an annoyed glance and did not seem to recognize Parker in the hollow-eyed creature before him.

"Let me see the book you got with all the pictures of God in it," Parker said breathlessly. "The religious one."

The artist continued to look at him with his intellectual, superior stare. "I don't put tattoos on drunks," he said.

"You know me!" Parker cried indignantly. "I'm O.E. Parker! You done work for me before and I always paid!"

The artist looked at him another moment as if he were not altogether sure. "You've fallen off some," he said. "You must have been in jail."

"Married," Parker said.

"Oh," said the artist. With the aid of mirrors the artist had tattooed on the top of his head a miniature owl, perfect in every detail. It was about the size of a half-dollar and served him as a showpiece. There were cheaper artists in town but Parker had never wanted anything but the best. The artist went over to a cabinet in the back of the room and began to look over some art books. "Who are you interested in?" he said. "Saints, angels, Christs or what?"

"God," Parker said.

"Father, Son or Spirit?"

"Just God," Parker said impatiently. "Christ, I don't care. Just so it's God."

The artist returned with a book. He moved some papers off another table and put the book down on it and told Parker to sit down and see what he liked. "The up-to-date ones are in the back," he said.

Parker sat down with the book and wet his thumb. He began to go through it, beginning at the back where the up-to-date pictures were. Some of them he recognized—the Good Shepherd, Forbid Them Not, The Smiling Jesus, Jesus the Physician's Friend, but he kept turning rapidly backward and the pictures became less and less reassuring. One showed a gaunt green dead face streaked with blood. One was yellow with sagging purple eyes. Parker's heart began to beat faster and faster until it appeared to be roaring inside him like a great generator. He flipped the pages quickly, feeling that when he reached the one ordained, a sign would come. He continued to flip through until he had almost reached the front of the book. On one of the pages a pair of eyes glanced at him swiftly. Parker sped on, then stopped. His heart too appeared to cut off; there was absolute silence. It said as plainly as if silence were a language itself, *Go back*.

Parker returned to the picture—the haloed head of a flat stern Byzantine Christ with all-demanding eyes. He sat there trembling; his heart began slowly to beat again as if it were being brought to life by a subtle power.

"You found what you want?" the artist asked.

Parker's throat was too dry to speak. He got up and thrust the book at the artist, opened at the picture.

"That'll cost you plenty," the artist said. "You don't want all those little blocks though, just the outline and some better features."

"Just like it is," Parker said, "just like it is or nothing."

"It's your funeral," the artist said, "but I don't do that kind of work for nothing."

"How much?" Parker asked.

"It'll take maybe two days' work."

"How much?" Parker said.

"On time or cash?" the artist asked. Parker's other jobs had been on time, but he had paid.

"Ten down and ten for every day it takes," the artist said.

Parker drew ten one-dollar bills out of his wallet; he had three left in.

"You come back in the morning," the artist said, putting the money in his own pocket. "First I'll have to trace that out of the book."

"No, no!" Parker said. "Trace it now or gimme my money back," and his eyes blared as if he were ready for a fight.

The artist agreed. Anyone stupid enough to want a Christ on his back, he reasoned, would be just as likely as not to change his mind the next minute, but once the work was begun he could hardly do so.

While he worked on the tracing, he told Parker to go wash his back at the sink with the special soap he used there. Parker did it and returned to pace back and forth across the room, nervously flexing his shoulders. He wanted to go look at the picture again but at the same time he did not want to. The artist got up finally and had Parker lie down on the table. He swabbed his back with ethyl chloride and then began to outline the head on it with his iodine pencil. Another hour passed before he took up his electric instrument. Parker felt no particular pain. In Japan he had had a tattoo of the Buddha done on his upper arm with ivory needles; in Burma, a little brown root of a man had made a peacock on each of his knees using thin pointed sticks, two feet long; amateurs had worked on him with pins and soot. Parker was usually so relaxed and easy under the hand of the artist that he often went to sleep, but this time he remained awake, every muscle taut.

At midnight the artist said he was ready to quit. He propped one mirror, four feet square, on a table by the wall and took a smaller mirror off the lavatory wall and put it in Parker's hands. Parker stood with his back to the one on the table and moved the other until he saw a flashing burst of color reflected from his back. It was almost completely covered with little red and blue and ivory and saffron squares; from them he made out the lineaments of the face—a mouth, the beginnings of heavy brows, a straight nose, but the face was empty; the eyes had not yet been put in. The impression for the moment was almost as if the artist had tricked him and done the Physician's Friend.

"It don't have eyes," Parker cried out.

"That'll come," the artist said, "in due time. We have another day to go on it yet."

Parker spent the night on a cot at the Haven of Light Christian Mission. He found these the best places to stay in the city because they were free and included a meal of sorts. He got the last available cot and because he was still barefooted, he accepted a pair of secondhand shoes which, in his confusion, he put on to go to bed; he was still shocked from all that had happened to him. All night he lay awake in the long dormitory of cots with lumpy figures on them. The only light was from a phosphorescent cross glowing at the end of the room. The tree reached out to grasp him again, then burst into flame; the shoe burned quietly by itself; the eyes in the book said to him distinctly *Go back* and at the same time did not utter a sound. He wished that he were not in this city, not in this Haven of Light Mission, not in a bed by himself. He longed miserably for Sarah Ruth. Her sharp tongue and ice-pick eyes were the only comfort he could bring to mind. He decided he was losing it. Her eyes appeared soft and dilatory compared with the eyes in the book, for even though he could not summon up the exact look of those eyes, he could still feel their penetration. He felt as though, under their gaze, he was as transparent as the wing of a fly.

The tattooist had told him not to come until ten in the morning, but when he arrived at that hour, Parker was sitting in the dark hallway on the floor, waiting for him. He had decided upon getting up that, once the tattoo was on him, he would not look at it, that all his sensations of the day and night before were those of a crazy man and that he would return to doing things according to his own sound judgment.

The artist began where he left off. "One thing I want to know," he said presently as he worked over Parker's back, "why do you want this on you? Have you gone and got religion? Are you saved?" he asked in a mocking voice.

Parker's voice felt salty and dry. "Naw," he said, "I ain't got no use for none of that. A man can't save his self from whatever it is he don't deserve none of my sympathy." These words seemed to leave his mouth like wraiths and to evaporate at once as if he had never uttered them.

"Then why. . . ."

"I married this woman that's saved," Parker said. "I never should have done it. I ought to leave her. She's done gone and got pregnant."

"That's too bad," the artist said. "Then it's her making you have this tattoo."

"Naw," Parker said, "she don't know nothing about it. It's a surprise for her."

"You think she'll like it and lay off you a while?"

"She can't hep herself," Parker said. "She can't say she don't like the looks of God." He decided he had told the artist enough of his business. Artists were all right in their place but he didn't like them poking their noses into the affairs of regular people. "I didn't get no sleep last night," he said. "I think I'll get some now."

That closed the mouth of the artist but it did not bring him any sleep. He lay there, imagining how Sarah Ruth would be struck speechless by the face on his back and every now and then this would be interrupted by a vision of the tree of fire and his empty shoe burning beneath it.

The artist worked steadily until nearly four o'clock, not stopping to have lunch, hardly pausing with the electric instrument except to wipe the dripping dye off Parker's back as he went along. Finally he finished. "You can get up and look at it now," he said.

Parker sat up, but he remained on the edge of the table.

The artist was pleased with his work and wanted Parker to look at it at once. Instead Parker continued to sit on the edge of the table, bent forward slightly but with a vacant look. "What ails you?" the artist said. "Go look at it."

"Ain't nothing ail me," Parker said in a sudden belligerent voice. "That tattoo ain't going nowhere. It'll be there when I get there." He reached for his shirt and began gingerly to put it on.

The artist took him roughly by the arm and propelled him between the two mirrors. "Now *look*," he said, angry at having his work ignored.

Parker looked, turned white and moved away. The eyes in the reflected face continued to look at him—still, straight, all-demanding, enclosed in silence.

"It was your idea, remember," the artist said. "I would have advised something else."

Parker said nothing. He put on his shirt and went out the door while the artist shouted, "I'll expect all of my money!"

Parker headed toward a package shop on the corner. He bought a pint of whiskey and took it into a nearby alley and drank it all in five minutes. Then he moved on to a pool hall nearby which he frequented when he came to the city.

It was a well-lighted barnlike place with a bar up one side and gambling machines on the other and pool tables in the back. As soon as Parker entered, a large man in a red-and-black checkered shirt hailed him by slapping him on the back and yelling, "Yeyyyyyy boy! O.E. Parker!"

Parker was not yet ready to be struck on the back. "Lay off," he said, "I got a fresh tattoo there."

"What you got this time?" the man asked and then yelled to a few at the machine, "O.E.'s got him another tattoo."

"Nothing special this time," Parker said and slunk over to a machine that was not being used.

"Come on," the big man said, "let's have a look at O.E.'s tattoo," and while Parker squirmed in their hands, they pulled up his shirt. Parker felt all the hands drop away instantly and his shirt fell again like a veil over the face. There was a silence in the poolroom which seemed to Parker to grow from the circle around him until it extended to the foundations under the building and upward through the beams in the roof.

Finally someone said, "Christ!" Then they all broke into noise at once. Parker turned around, an uncertain grin on his face.

"Leave it to O.E.!" the man in the checkered shirt said. "That boy's a real card!"

"Maybe he's gone and got religion," someone yelled.

"Not on your life," Parker said.

"O.E.'s got religion and is witnessing for Jesus, ain't you, O.E.?" a little man with a piece of cigar in his mouth said wryly. "An o-riginal way to do it if I ever saw one."

"Leave it to Parker to think of a new one!" the fat man said.

"Yyeeeeeeyyyyyyyy boy!" someone yelled and they all began to whistle and curse in compliment until Parker said, "Aaa shut up."

"What'd you do it for?" somebody asked.

"For laughs," Parker said. "What's it to you?"

"Why ain't you laughing then?" somebody yelled.

Parker lunged into the midst of them and like a whirlwind on a summer's day there began a fight that raged amid overturned tables and swinging fists until two of them grabbed him and ran to the door with him and threw him out. Then a calm descended on the pool hall as nerve-shattering as if the long barnlike room were the ship from which Jonah had been cast into the sea.

Parker sat for a long time on the ground in the alley behind the pool hall, examining his soul. He saw it as a spiderweb of facts and lies that was not at all important to him but which appeared to be necessary in spite of his opinion. The eyes that were now forever on his back were eyes to be obeyed. He was as certain of it as he had ever been of anything. Throughout his life, grumbling and sometimes cursing, often afraid, once in rapture, Parker had obeyed whatever instinct of this kind had come to him—in rapture when his spirit had lifted at the sight of the tattooed man at the fair, afraid when he had joined the Navy, grumbling when he had married Sarah Ruth.

The thought of her brought him slowly to his feet. She would know what he had to do. She would clear up the rest of it, and she would at least be pleased. His truck was still parked in front of the building where the artist had his place, but it was not far away. He got in it and drove out of the city and into the country night. His head was almost clear of liquor and he observed that his dissatisfaction was gone, but he felt not quite like himself. It was as if he were himself but a stranger to himself, driving into a new country though everything he saw was familiar to him, even at night.

He arrived finally at the house on the embankment, pulled the truck under the pecan tree and got out. He made as much noise as possible to assert that he was still in charge here, that his leaving her for a night without word meant nothing except it was the way he did things. He slammed the car door, stamped up the two steps and across the porch and rattled the doorknob. It did not respond to his touch. "Sarah Ruth!" he yelled. "Let me in."

There was no lock on the door and she had evidently placed the back of a chair against the knob. He began to beat on the door and rattle the knob.

He heard the bedsprings creak and bent down and put his head to the keyhole, but it was stopped up with paper. "Let me in!" he hollered, bamming on the door again. "What you got me locked out for?"

A sharp voice close to the door said, "Who's there?"

"Me," Parker said. "O.E."

He waited a moment.

"Me," he said impatiently. "O.E."

Still no sound from inside.

He tried once more. "O.E.," he said, bamming the door two or three more times. "O.E. Parker. You know me."

There was a silence. Then the voice said slowly, "I don't know no O.E."

"Quit fooling," Parker pleaded. "You ain't got any business doing me this way. It's me, old O.E., I'm back. You ain't afraid of me."

"Who's there?" the same unfeeling voice said.

Parker turned his head as if he expected someone behind him to give him the answer. The sky had lightened slightly and there were two or three streaks of yellow floating above the horizon. Then as he stood there, a tree of light burst over the skyline.

Parker fell back against the door as if he had been pinned there by a lance.

"Who's there?" the voice from inside said and there was a quality about it now that seemed final. The knob rattled and the voice said peremptorily, "Who's there, I ast you?"

Parker bent down and put his mouth near the stuffed keyhole. "Obadiah," he whispered and all at once he felt the light pouring through him, turning his spiderweb soul into a perfect arabesque of colors, a garden of trees and birds and beasts.

"Obadiah Elihue!" he whispered.

The door opened and he stumbled in. Sarah Ruth loomed there, hands on her hips. She began at once, "That was no hefty blond woman you was working for and you'll have to pay her every penny on her tractor you busted up. She don't keep insurance on it. She came here and her and me had us a long talk and I . . ."

Trembling, Parker set about lighting the kerosene lamp.

"What's the matter with you, wasting that kerosene this near daylight?" she demanded. "I ain't got to look at you."

A yellow glow enveloped them. Parker put the match down and began to unbutton his shirt.

"And you ain't going to have none of me this near morning," she said.

"Shut your mouth," he said quietly. "Look at this and then I don't want to hear no more out of you." He removed the shirt and turned his back to her.

"Another picture," Sarah Ruth growled. "I might have known you was off after putting some more trash on yourself."

Parker's knees went hollow under him. He wheeled around and cried, "Look at it! Don't just say that! *Look* at it!"

"I done looked," she said.

"Don't you know who it is?" he cried in anguish.

"No, who is it?" Sarah Ruth said. "It ain't anybody I know."

"It's Him," Parker said.

"Him who?"

"God!" Parker cried.

"God? God don't look like that!"

"What do you know how he looks?" Parker moaned. "You ain't seen him."

"He don't *look*," Sarah Ruth said. "He's a spirit. No man shall see his face."

"Aw listen," Parker groaned, "this is just a picture of Him."

"Idolatry!" Sarah Ruth screamed. "Idolatry. Inflaming yourself with idols under every green tree! I can put up with lies and vanity but I don't want no idolator in this house!" and she grabbed up the broom and thrashed him across the shoulders with it.

Parker was too stunned to resist. He sat there and let her beat him until she had nearly knocked him senseless and large welts had formed on the face of the tattooed Christ. Then he staggered up and made for the door.

She stamped the broom two or three times on the floor and went to the window and shook it out to get the taint of him off it. Still gripping it, she looked toward the pecan tree and her eyes hardened still more. There he was—who called himself Obadiah Elihue—leaning against the tree, crying like a baby.

[APRIL 1965]

HAROLD BRODKEY

His Son, in His Arms, in Light,

Aloft

A strong supporter of Harold Brodkey (1930–   ) over the years,
Esquire published in 1975 one of his most remarkable stories, "His Son,
in His Arms, in Light, Aloft," which was collected in Stories in an
Almost Classical Mode (1988). In the story, Brodkey's signature
method of "momentism" (his coinage) is on display—an instant-by-
instant narration of emotional and mental life, and of the tricky intersec-
tion between memory and the present, uncircumscribed by standard
theories of personality. Raised in the Midwest and educated at Harvard,
Brodkey recently published his long-anticipated novel The Runaway
Soul.

My father is chasing me.

My God, I feel it up and down my spine, the thumping on the turf, the approach of his hands, his giant hands, the huge ramming increment of his breath as he draws near: a widening effort. I feel it up and down my spine and in my mouth and belly—Daddy is so swift: who ever heard of such swiftness? Just as in stories. . . .

I can't escape him, can't fend him off, his arms, his rapidity, his will. His interest in me.

I am being lifted into the air—and even as I pant and stare blurredly, limply, mindlessly, a map appears, of the dark ground where I ran: as I hang limply and rise anyway on the fattened bar of my father's arm, I see that there's the grass, there's the path, there's a bed of flowers.

I straighten up. There are the lighted windows of our house, some distance away. My father's face, full of noises, is near: it looms: his hidden face: is that you, old money-maker? My butt is folded on the trapeze of his arm. My father is as big as an automobile.

In the oddly shrewd-hearted torpor of being carried home in the dark, a tourist, in my father's arms, I feel myself attached by my heated-by-running dampness to him: we are attached, there are binding oval stains of warmth.

In most social talk, most politeness, most literature, most religion, it is as if violence didn't exist—except as sin, something far away. This is flattering to women. It is also conducive to grace— because the heaviness of fear, the shadowy henchmen selves that fear attaches to us, that fear sees in others, is banished.

Where am I in the web of jealousy that trembles at every human movement?

What detectives we have to be.

What if I am wrong? What if I remember incorrectly? It does not matter. This is fiction—a game—of pleasures, of truth and error, as at the sensual beginning of a sensual life.

My father, Charley, as I knew him, is invisible in any photograph I have of him. The man I hugged or ran toward or ran from is not in any photograph: a photograph shows someone of whom I think: *Oh, was he like that?*

But in certain memories, *he* appears, a figure, a presence, and I think, *I know him.*

It is embarrassing to me that I am part of what is unsayable in any account of his life.

When Momma's or my sister's excesses, of mood, or of shopping, angered or sickened Daddy, you can smell him then from two feet away: he has a dry, achy little stink of a rapidly fading interest in his life with us. At these times, the women in a spasm of wit turn to me; they comb my hair, clean my face, pat my bottom or my shoulder, and send me off; they bid me to go cheer up Daddy.

Sometimes it takes no more than a tug at his newspaper: the sight of me is enough; or I climb on his lap, mimic his depression; or I stand on his lap, press his head against my chest. . . . His face is immense, porous, complex with stubble, bits of talcum on it, unlikely colors, unlikely features, a bald brow with a curved square of lamplight in it. About his head there is a nimbus of sturdy wickedness, of unlikelihood. If his mood does not change, something tumbles and goes dead in me.

Perhaps it is more a nervous breakdown than heartbreak: I have failed him: his love for me is very limited: I must die now. I go somewhere and shudder and collapse—a corner of the dining room, the back stoop or deck: I lie there, empty, grief-stricken, literally unable to move—I have forgotten my limbs. If a memory of them comes to me, the memory is meaningless. . . .

Momma will then stalk in to wherever Daddy is and say to him, "Charley, you can be mad at me, I'm used to it, but just go take a look and see what you've done to the child. . . ."

My uselessness toward him sickens me. Anyone who fails toward him might as well be struck down, abandoned, eaten.

Perhaps it is an animal state: I-have-nothing-left, I-have-no-place-in-this-world.

Well, this is his house. Momma tells me in various ways to love him. Also, he is entrancing—he is so big, so thunderish, so smelly, and has the most extraordinary habits, reading newspapers, for instance, and wiggling his shoe: his shoe is gross: kick someone with that and they'd fall into next week.

Some memories huddle in a grainy light. What it is is a number of similar events bunching themselves, superimposing themselves, to make a false memory, a collage, a mental artifact. Within the boundaries of one such memory one plunges from year to year, is small and helpless, is a little older: one remembers it all but it is nothing that happened, that clutch of happenings, of associations, those gifts and ghosts of a meaning.

I can, if I concentrate, whiten the light—or yellow-whiten it, actually—and when the graininess goes, it is suddenly one afternoon.

I could not live without the pride and belonging-to-himness of being that man's consolation. He had the disposal of the rights to the out-of-doors—he was the other, the other-not-a-woman: he was my strength, literally, my strength if I should cry out.

Flies and swarms of the danger of being unfathered beset me when I bored my father: it was as if I were covered with flies on the animal plain where some ravening wild dog would leap up, bite and grip my muzzle, and begin to bring about my death.

I had no protection: I was subject now to the appetite of whatever inhabited the dark.

A child collapses in a sudden burst of there-is-nothing-here, and that is added onto nothingness, the nothing of being only a child concentrating on there being nothing there, no hope, no ambition: there is a despair but one without magnificence except in the face of its completeness: *I am a child and am without strength of my own.*

I have—in my grief—somehow managed to get to the back deck: I am sitting in the early evening light; I am oblivious to the light. I did and didn't hear his footsteps, the rumble, the house thunder dimly (behind and beneath me), the thunder of his-coming-to-rescue-me. . . . I did and didn't hear him call my name.

I spoke only the gaping emptiness of grief—that tongue—I understood I had no right to the speech of fathers and sons.

My father came out on the porch. I remember how stirred he was, how beside himself that I was so unhappy, that a child, a child he liked, should suffer so. He laid aside his own mood—his disgust with life, with money, with the excesses of the women—and he took on a broad-winged, malely flustering, broad-winged optimism—he was at the center of a great beating (of the heart, a man's heart, of a man's gestures, will, concern), dust clouds rising, a beating determination to persuade me that the nature of life, of *my* life, was other than I'd thought, other than whatever had defeated me—he was about to tell me there was no need to feel defeated, he was about to tell me that I was a good, or even a wonderful, child.

He kneeled—a mountain of shirt-front and trousers; a mountain that poured, clambered down, folded itself, re-formed itself: a disorderly massiveness, near to me, fabric-hung-and-draped: Sinai. He said, "Here, here, what is this—what is a child like you doing being so sad?" And: "Look at me. . . . It's all right. . . . Everything is all right. . . ." The misstatements of consolation are lies about the absolute that require faith—and no memory: the truth of consolation can be investigated if one is a proper child—that is to say, affectionate—only in a nonskeptical way.

"It's not all right!"

"It is—it is." It was and wasn't a lie: it had to do with power—and limitations: my limitations and his power: he could make it all right for me, everything, provided my everything was small enough and within his comprehension.

Sometimes he would say, "Son—" He would say it heavily—"Don't be sad—I don't want you to be sad—I don't like it when you're sad—"

I can't look into his near and, to me, factually incredible face—incredible because so large (as at the beginning of a love affair): I mean as a *face:* it is the focus of so many emotions and wonderments: he could have been a fool or was—it was possibly the face of a fool, someone self-centered, smug, an operator, semi-criminal, an intelligent psychoanalyst; it was certainly a mortal face—but what did the idea or word mean to me then—*mortal?*

There was a face; it was as large as my chest; there were eyes, inhumanly big, humid—what could they mean? How could I read them? How do you read eyes? I did not know about comparisons: how much more affectionate he was than other men, or less, how much better than common experience or how much worse in this area of being fathered my experience was with him: I cannot say even now: it is a statistical matter, after all, a matter of averages: but who at the present date can phrase the proper questions for the poll? And who will understand the hesitations, the blank looks, the odd expressions on the faces of the answerers?

The odds are he was a—median—father. He himself had usually a conviction he did pretty well: sometimes he despaired—of himself: but blamed me: my love: or something: or himself as a father: he wasn't good at managing stages between strong, clear states of feeling. Perhaps no one is.

Anyway, I knew no such terms as *median* then: I did not understand much about those parts of his emotions which extended past the rather clear area where my emotions were so often amazed. I chose, in some ways, to regard him seriously: in other ways, I had no choice—he was what was given to me.

I cannot look at him, as I said: I cannot see anything: if I look at him without seeing him, my blindness insults him: I don't want to hurt him at all:

I want nothing: I am lost and have surrendered and am really dead and am waiting without hope.

He knows how to rescue people. Whatever he doesn't know, one of the things he knows in the haste and jumble of his heart, among the blither of tastes in his mouth and opinions and sympathies in his mind and so on, is the making yourself into someone who will help someone who is wounded. The dispersed and unlikely parts of him come together for a while in a clucking and focused arch of abiding concern. Oh how he plows ahead; oh how he believes in rescue! He puts—he *shoves*—he works an arm behind my shoulders, another under my legs: his arms, his powers shove at me, twist, lift and jerk me until I am cradled in the air, in his arms: "You don't have to be unhappy—you haven't hurt anyone—don't be sad—you're a *nice* boy. . . ."

I can't quite hear him, I can't quite believe him. I can't be *good*—the confidence game is to believe him, is to be a good child who trusts him—we will both smile then, he and I. But if I hear him, I have to believe him still. I am set up that way. He is so big; he is the possessor of so many grandeurs. If I believe him, hope and pleasure will start up again—suddenly—the blankness in me will be relieved, broken by these—meanings—that it seems he and I share in some big, attaching way.

In his pride he does not allow me to suffer: I belong to him.

He is rising, jerkily, to his feet and holding me at the same time. I do not have to stir to save myself—I only have to believe him. He rocks me into a sad-edged relief and an achingly melancholy delight with the peculiar lurch as he stands erect of establishing his balance and rectifying the way he holds me, so he can go on holding me, holding me aloft, against his chest: I am airborne: I liked to have that man hold me—in the air: I knew it was worth a great deal, the embrace, the gift of altitude. I am not exposed on the animal plain. I am not helpless.

The heat his body gives off! It is the heat of a man sweating with regret. His heartbeat, his burning, his physical force: ah, there is a large rent in the nothingness: the mournful apparition of his regret, the proof of his loyalty wake me: I have a twin, a massive twin, mighty company: Daddy's grief is at my grief: my nothingness is echoed in him (if he is going to have to live without me): the rescue was not quite a secular thing. The evening forms itself, a classroom, a brigade of shadows, of phenomena—the tinted air slides: there are shadowy skaters everywhere; shadowy cloaked people step out from behind things which are then hidden behind their cloaks. An alteration in the air proceeds from openings in the ground, from leaks in the sunlight which is being disengaged, like a stubborn hand, or is being stroked shut like my eyelids when I refuse to sleep: the dark rubs and bubbles noiselessly—and seeps—into the landscape. In the rubbed distortion of my inner air, twilight soothes: there are two of us breathing in close proximity here (he is telling me that grownups sometimes have things on their minds, he is saying mysterious things which I don't comprehend); I don't want to look at him: it takes two of my eyes to see one of his—and then I mostly see myself in his eye: he is even more unseeable from here, this holder: my head falls against his neck: "I know what you like—you'd like to go stand on the wall—would you like to see the sunset?" Did I nod? I think I did: I nodded gravely: but perhaps he did not need an answer since he thought he knew me well.

We are moving, this elephant and I, we are lumbering, down some steps, across grassy, uneven ground—the spoiled child in his father's arms—behind our house was a little park—we moved across the grass of the little park. There are sun's rays on the dome of the moorish bandstand. The evening is moist, fugitive, momentarily sneaking, half welcomed in this hour of crime. My father's neck. The stubble. The skin where the stubble stops. Exhaustion has me: I am a creature of failure, a locus of childishness, an empty skull: I am this being-young. We overrun the world, he and I, with his legs, with our eyes, with our alliance. We move on in a ghostly torrent of our being like this.

My father has the smell and feel of wanting to be my father. Guilt and innocence stream and re-stream in him. His face, I see now in memory, held an untiring surprise: as if some grammar of deed and purpose—of comparatively easy tenderness—startled him again and again, startled him continuously for a while. He said, "I guess we'll just have to cheer you up—we'll have to show you life isn't so bad—I guess we weren't any too careful of a little boy's feelings, were we?" I wonder if all comfort is alike.

A man's love is, after all, a fairly spectacular thing.

He said—his voice came from above me—he spoke out into the air, the twilight—"We'll make it all right—just you wait and see. . . ."

He said, "This is what you like," and he placed me on the wall that ran along the edge of the park, the edge of a bluff, a wall too high for me to see over, and which I was forbidden to climb: he placed me on the stubbed stone mountains and grouting of the wall-top. He put his arm around my middle: I leaned against him: and faced outward into the salt of the danger of the height, of the view (we were at least one hundred and fifty feet, we were, therefore, hundreds of feet in the air); I was flicked at by narrow, abrasive bands of wind, evening wind, veined with sunset's sun-crispness, strongly touched with coolness.

The wind would push at my eyelids, my nose, my lips. I heard a buzzing in my ears which signaled how high, how alone we were: this view of a river valley at night and of parts of four counties was audible. I looked into the hollow in front of me, a grand hole, an immense, bellying deep sheet or vast sock. There were numinous fragments in it—birds in what sunlight was left, bits of smoke faintly lit by distant light or mist, hovering inexplicably here and there: rays of yellow light, high up, touching a few high clouds.

It had a floor on which were creeks (and the big river), a little dim, a little glary at this hour, rail lines, roads, highways, houses, silos, bridges, trees, fields, everything more than half hidden in the enlarging dark: there was the shrinking glitter of far-off noises, bearded and stippled with huge and spreading shadows of my ignorance: it was panorama as a personal privilege. The sun at the end of the large, sunset-swollen sky was a glowing and urgent orange; around it were the spreading petals of pink and stratospheric gold: on the ground were occasional magenta flarings; oh it makes you stare and gasp; a fine, astral (not a crayon) red rode in a broad, magnificent band across the middlewestern sky: below us, for miles, shadowiness tightened as we watched (it seemed); above us, tinted clouds spread across the vast shadowing sky: there were funereal lights and sinkings everywhere. I stand on the wall and lean against Daddy, only somewhat awed and abstracted: the view does not own me as it usually does: I am partly in the hands of the jolting—amusement—the conceit—of having been resurrected—by my father.

I understood that he was proffering me oblivion plus pleasure, the end of a sorrow to be henceforth remembered as Happiness. This was to be my privilege. This amazing man is going to rescue me from any anomaly or barb or sting in my existence: he is going to confer happiness on me: as a matter of fact, he has already begun.

"Just you trust me—you keep right on being cheered up—look at that sunset—that's some sunset, wouldn't you say?—everything is going to be just fine and dandy—you trust me—you'll see—just you wait and see. . . ."

Did he mean to be a swindler? He wasn't clear-minded—he often said, "I mean well." He did not think other people meant well.

I don't feel it would be right to adopt an Oedipal theory to explain what happened between him and me: only a sense of what he was like as a man, what certain moments were like, and what was said.

It is hard in language to get the full, irregular, heavy sound of a man.

He liked to have us "all dressed and nice when I come home from work," have us wait for him in attitudes of serene all-is-well contentment. As elegant as a Spanish prince I sat on the couch toying with an oversized model truck—what a confusion of social pretensions, technologies, class disorder there was in that. My sister would sit in a chair, knees together, hair brushed: she'd doze off if Daddy was late. Aren't we happy! Actually, we often are.

One day he came in plungingly, excited to be home and to have us as an audience rather than outsiders who didn't know their lines and who often laughed at him as part of their struggle to improve their parts in his scenes. We were waiting to have him approve of our tableau—he usually said something about what a nice family we looked like or how well we looked or what a pretty group or some such thing—and we didn't realize he was the tableau tonight. We held our positions, but we stared at him in a kind of mindless what-should-we-do-besides-sit-here-and-be-happy-and-nice? Impatiently he said, "I have a surprise for you, Charlotte—Abe Last has a heart after all." My father said something on that order: or "—a conscience after all"; and then he walked across the carpet, a man somewhat jerky with success—a man redolent of vaudeville, of grotesque and sentimental movies (he liked grotesquerie, prettiness, sentiment). As he walked, he pulled banded packs of currency out of his pockets, two or three in each hand. "There," he said, dropping one, then three in Momma's dressed-up lap. "There," he said, dropping another two: he uttered a "there" for each subsequent pack. "Oh, let me!" my sister cried and ran over to look—and then she grabbed two packs and said, "Oh, Daddy, how much *is* this?"

It was eight or ten thousand dollars, he said. Momma said, "Charley, what if someone sees—we could be robbed—why do you take chances like this?"

Daddy harrumphed and said, "You have no sense of fun—if you ask me, you're afraid to be happy. I'll put it in the bank tomorrow—if I can find an honest banker—here, young lady, put that money down: you don't want to prove your mother right, do you?"

Then he said, "I know one person around here who knows how to enjoy himself—" and he lifted me up, held me in his arms.

He said, "We're going outside, this young man and I."

"What should I do with this money!"

"Put it under your mattress—make a salad out of it: you're always the one who worries about money," he said in a voice solid with authority and masculinity, totally pieced out with various self-satisfactions—as if he had gained a kingdom and the assurance of appearing as glorious in the histories of his time; I put my head back and smiled at the superb animal, at the rosy—and cowardly—panther leaping; and then I glanced over his shoulder and tilted my head and looked sympathetically at Momma.

My sister shouted. "I know how to enjoy myself—I'll come too! . . ."

"Yes, yes," said Daddy, who was *never* averse to enlarging spheres of happiness and areas of sentiment. He held her hand and held me on his arm.

"Let him walk," my sister said. And: "He's getting bigger—you'll make a sissy out of him, Daddy. . . ."

Daddy said, "Shut up and enjoy the light—it's as beautiful as Paris and in our own backyard."

Out of folly, or a wish to steal his attention, or greed, my sister kept on: she asked if she could get something with some of the money; he dodged her question; and she kept on; and he grew peevish, so peevish, he returned to the house and accused Momma of having never taught her daughter not to be greedy—he sprawled, impetuous, displeased, semifrantic in a chair: "I can't enjoy myself—there is no way a man can live in this house with all of you—I swear to God this will kill me soon. . . ."

Momma said to him, "I can't believe in the things you believe in—I'm not a girl anymore: when I play the fool, it isn't convincing—you get angry with me when I try. You shouldn't get angry with her—you've spoiled her more than I have—and how do you expect her to act when you show her all that money— how do you think money affects people?"

I looked at him to see what the answer was, to see what he would answer. He said, "Charlotte, try being a rose and not a thorn."

At all times, and in all places, there is always the possibility that I will start to speak or will be looking at something and I will feel his face covering mine, as in a kiss and as a mask, turned both ways like that: and I am inside him, his presence, his thoughts, his language: *I* am languageless then for a moment, an automaton of repetition, a bagged piece of an imaginary river of descent.

I can't invent everything for myself: some always has to be what I already know: some of me always has to be him.

When he picked me up, my consciousness fitted itself to that position: I remember it—clearly. He could punish me—and did—by refusing to lift me, by denying me that union with him. Of course, the union was not one-sided: I was his innocence—as long as I was not an accusation, that is. I censored him—in that when he felt himself being, consciously, a father, he held back part of his other life, of his whole self: his shadows, his impressions, his adventures would not readily fit into me—what a gross and absurd rape that would have been.

So he was *careful*—he *walked on eggs*—there was an odd courtesy of his withdrawal behind his secrets, his secret sorrows and horrors, behind the curtain of what-is-suitable-for-a-child.

Sometimes he becomes simply a set of limits, of walls, inside which there is the caroming and echoing of my astounding sensibility amplified by being his son and in his arms and aloft; and he lays his sensibility aside or models his on mine, on my joy, takes his emotional coloring from me, like a mirror or a twin: his incomprehensible life, with its strengths, ordeals, triumphs, crimes, horrors, his sadness and disgust, is enveloped and momentarily assuaged by my direct and indirect childish consolation. My gaze, my enjoying him, my willingness to be him, my joy at it, supported the baroque tower of his necessary but limited and maybe dishonest optimism.

⬤ne time he and Momma fought over money and he left: he packed a bag and went. Oh it was sad and heavy at home. I started to be upset, but then I retreated into an impenetrable stupidity: not knowing was better than being despairing. I was put to bed and I did fall asleep: I woke in the middle of the night; he had returned and was sitting on my bed—in the dark—a huge shadow in the shadows. He was stroking my forehead. When he saw my eyes open, he said in a sentimental, heavy voice, "I could never leave *you*—"

He didn't really mean it: I was an excuse: but he did mean it—the meaning and not-meaning were like the rise and fall of a wave in me, in the dark outside of me, between the two of us, between him and me (at other moments he would think of other truths, other than the one of he-couldn't-leave-me sometimes). He bent over sentimentally, painedly, not nicely, and he began to hug me; he put his head down, on my chest; my small heartbeat vanished into the near, sizable, anguished, angular, emotion-swollen one that was his. I kept advancing swiftly into wakefulness, my consciousness came rushing and widening blurredly, embracing the dark, his presence, his embrace. It's Daddy, it's Daddy—it's dark still—wakefulness rushed into the dark grave or grove of his hugely extended presence. His affection. My arms stumbled: there was no adequate embrace in me—I couldn't lift *him*—I had no adequacy yet except that of my charm or what-have-you, except things the grown-ups gave me—not things: traits, qualities. I mean my hugging his head was nothing until he said, "Ah, you love me. . . . You're all right. . . ."

Momma said: "They are as close as two peas in a pod—they are just alike—that child and Charley. That child is God to Charley. . . ."

He didn't always love me.

In the middle of the night that time, he picked me up after a while, he wrapped me in a blanket, held me close, took me downstairs in the dark; we went outside, into the night; it was dark and chilly but there was a moon—I thought he would take me to the wall but he just stood on our back deck. He grew tired of loving me; he grew abstracted and forgot me: the love that had just a moment before been so intently and tightly clasping and nestling went away, and I found myself released, into the cool night air, the floating damp, the silence, with the darkened houses around us.

I saw the silver moon, heard my father's breath, felt the itchiness of the woolen blanket on my hands, noticed its wool smell. I did this alone and I waited. Then when he didn't come back, I grew sleepy and put my head down against his neck: he was nowhere near me. Alone in his arms, I slept.

Over and over a moment seems to recur, something seems to return in its entirety, a name seems to be accurate: and we say it always happens like this. But we are wrong, of course.

I was a weird choice as someone for him to love.

So different from him in the way I was surprised by things.

I am a child with this mind. I am a child he has often rescued.

Our attachment to each other manifests itself in sudden swoops and grabs and rubs of attention, of being entertained, by each other, at the present moment. I ask you, how is it possible it's going to last?

          Sometimes when we are entertained by each other, we are bold about it, but just as frequently, it seems embarrassing, and we turn our faces aside.

         His recollections of horror are more certain than mine. His suspicions are more terrible. There are darknesses in me I'm afraid of, but the ones in him don't frighten me but are like the dark in the yard, a dark a child like me might sneak into (and has)—a dark full of unseen shadowy almost-glowing presences—the fear, the danger—are desirable—difficult—with the call-to-be-brave: the childish bravura of *I must endure this* (knowing I can run away if I choose).

The child touches with his pursed, jutting, ignorant lips the large, handsome, odd, humid face of his father who can run away too. More dangerously.

He gave away a car of his that he was about to trade in on a new one: he gave it to a man in financial trouble; he did it after seeing a movie about crazy people being loving and gentle with each other and everyone else: Momma said to Daddy, "You can't do anything you want—you can't listen to your feelings— you have a family. . . ."

After seeing a movie in which a child cheered up an old man, he took me to visit an old man who probably was a distant relative, and who hated me at sight, my high coloring, the noise I might make, my father's affection for me: "Will he sit still? I can't stand noise. Charley, listen, I'm in bad shape—I think I have cancer and they won't tell me—"

"Nothing can kill a tough old bird like you, Ike. . . ."

The old man wanted all of Charley's attention—and strength—while he talked about how the small threads and thicker ropes that tied him to life were being cruelly tampered with.

Daddy patted me afterward, but oddly he was bored and disappointed in me as if I'd failed at something.

He could not seem to keep it straight about my value to him or to the world in general; he lived at the center of his own intellectual shortcomings and his moral price: he needed it to be true, as an essential fact, that goodness—or innocence—was in him or was protected by him, and that, therefore, he was a good *man* and superior to other men, and did not deserve—certain common masculine fates—horrors—tests of his courage—certain pains. It was necessary to him to have it be true that he knew what real goodness was and had it in his life.

Perhaps that was because he didn't believe in God, and because he felt (with a certain self-love) that people, out in the world, didn't appreciate him and were needlessly difficult—"unloving": he said it often—and because it was true he was shocked and guilty and even enraged when he was "forced" into being unloving himself, or when he caught sight in himself of such a thing as cruelty, or cruel nosiness, or physical cowardice—God, how he hated being a coward— or hatred, physical hatred, even for me, if I was coy or evasive or disinterested or tired of him: it tore him apart literally—bits of madness, in varying degrees, would grip him as in a Greek play: I see his mouth, his salmon-colored mouth, showing various degrees of sarcasm—sarcasm mounting into bitterness and even a ferocity without tears that always suggested to me, as a child, that he was near tears but had forgotten in his ferocity that he was about to cry.

Or he would catch sight of some evidence, momentarily inescapable—in contradictory or foolish statements of his or in unkept promises that it was clear he had never meant to keep, had never made any effort to keep—that he was a fraud; and sometimes he would laugh because he was a fraud—a good-hearted fraud, he believed—or he would be sullen or angry, a fraud caught either by the tricks of language so that in expressing affection absentmindedly he had expressed too much; or caught by greed and self-concern: he hated the evidence that he was mutable as hell: that he loved sporadically and egotistically, and often with rage and vengeance, and that madness I mentioned earlier: he couldn't stand those things: he usually forgot them; but sometimes when he was being tender, or noble, or self-sacrificing, he would sigh and be very sad—maybe because the good stuff was temporary. I don't know. Or sad that he did it only when he had the time and was in the mood. Sometimes he forgot such things and was superbly confident—or was that a bluff?

I don't know. I really can't speak for him.

I look at my hand and then at his; it is not really conceivable to me that both are hands: mine is a sort of a hand. He tells me over and over that I must not upset him—he tells me of my power over him—I don't know how to take such a fact—is it a fact? I stare at him. I gasp

with the ache of life stirring in me—again: again: *again*—I ache with tentative
and complete and then again tentative belief.

For a long time piety was anything at all sitting still or moving slowly and
not rushing at me or away from me but letting me look at it or be near it without
there being any issue of safety-about-to-be-lost.

This world is evasive.

But someone who lets you observe him is not evasive, is not hurtful, at that
moment: it is like in sleep where *the other* waits—the Master of Dreams—and
there are doors, doorways opening into farther rooms where there is an altered
light, and which I enter to find—what? That someone is gone? That the room
is empty? Or perhaps I find a vista, of rooms, of archways, and a window, and
a peach tree in flower—a tree with peach-colored flowers in the solitude of night.

I am dying of grief, Daddy. I am wait-
ing here, limp with abandonment, with exhaustion: perhaps I'd better believe in
God. . . .

My father's virtues, those I dreamed
about, those I saw when I was awake, those I understood and misunderstood,
were, as I felt them, in dreams or wakefulness, when I was a child, like a broad
highway opening into a small dusty town that was myself; and down that road
came bishops and slogans, Chinese processions, hasidim in a dance, the nation's
honor and glory *in its young people,* baseball players, singers who sang "with
their whole hearts," automobiles and automobile grilles, and grave or comic bits
of instruction. This man is attached to me and makes me light up with festal
affluence and oddity; he says, "I think you love me."

He was right.

He would move his head—his giant
face—and you could observe in his eyes the small town which was me in its
temporary sophistication, a small town giving proof on every side of its arrogance and its prosperity and its puzzled contentment.

He also instructed me in hatred: he didn't mean to, not openly: but I saw
and picked up the curious buzzing of his puckered distastes, a nastiness of
dismissal that he had: a fetor of let-them-all-kill-each-other. He hated lots of
people, whole races: he hated ugly women.

He conferred an odd inverted splendor on awfulness—because *he* knew about it: he went into it every day. He told me not to want that, not to want to know about that: he told me to go on being just the way I was—"a nice boy."

When he said something was unbearable, he meant it; he meant he could not bear it.

In my memories of this time of my life, it seems to be summer all the time, even when the ground is white: I suppose it seems like summer because I was never cold.

Ah: I wanted to see. . . .

My father, when he was low (in spirit) would make rounds, inside his head, checking on his consciousness, to see if it was safe from inroads by *"the unbearable"*: he found an all-is-well in a quiet emptiness. . . .

In an uninvadedness, he found the weary complacency and self-importance of All is Well.

(The woman liked invasions—up to a point).

One day he came home, mysterious, exalted, hatted and suited, roseate, handsome, a little sweaty—it really was summer that day. He was exalted—as I said—but nervous toward me—anxious with promises.

And he was, oh, somewhat angry, justified, toward the world, toward me, not exactly as a threat (in case I didn't respond) but as a jumble.

He woke me from a nap, an uneasy nap, lifted me out of bed, me, a child who had not expected to see him that afternoon—I was not particularly happy that day, not particularly pleased with him, not pleased with him at all, really.

He dressed me himself. At first he kept his hat on. After a while, he took it off. When I was dressed, he said, "You're pretty sour today," and he put his hat back on.

He hustled me down the stairs; he held my wrist in his enormous palm—immediate and gigantic to me and blankly suggestive of a meaning I could do nothing about except stare at blankly from time to time in my childish life.

We went outside into the devastating heat and glare, the blathering, humming afternoon light of a midwestern summer day: a familiar furnace.

We walked along the street, past the large, silent houses, set, each one, in hard, pure light. You could not look directly at anything, the glare, the reflections were too strong.

Then he lifted me in his arms—aloft.

He was carrying me to help me because the heat was bad—and worse near the sidewalk which reflected it upward into my face—and because my legs were short and I was struggling, because he was in a hurry and because he liked carrying me, and because I was sour and blackmailed him with my unhappiness, and he was being kind with a certain—limited—mixture of exasperation-turning-into-a-degree-of-mortal-love.

Or it was another time, really early in the morning, when the air was partly asleep, partly adance, but in veils, trembling with heavy moisture. Here and there, the air broke into a string of beads of pastel colors, pink, pale green, small rainbows, really small, and very narrow. Daddy walked rapidly. I bounced in his arms. My eyesight was unfocused—it bounced too. Things were more than merely present: they pressed against me: they had the aliveness of myth, of the beginning of an adventure when nothing is explained as yet.

All at once we were at the edge of a bankless river of yellow light. To be truthful, it was like a big, wooden beam of fresh, unweathered wood: but we entered it: and then it turned into light, cooler light than in the hot humming afternoon but full of bits of heat that stuck to me and then were blown away, a semi-heat, not really friendly, yet reassuring: and very dimly sweaty; and it grew, it spread: this light turned into a knitted cap of light, fuzzy, warm, woven, itchy: it was pulled over my head, my hair, my forehead, my eyes, my nose, my mouth.

So I turned my face away from the sun—I turned it so it was pressed against my father's neck mostly—and then I knew, in a childish way, knew from the heat (of his neck, of his shirt collar), knew by childish deduction, that his face was unprotected from the luminousness all around us: and I looked; and it was so: his face, for the moment unembarrassedly, was caught in that light. In an accidental glory.

[AUGUST 1975]

RICHARD FORD

Rock Springs

Edna and I had started down from Kalispell heading for Tampa–St. Pete, where I still had some friends from the old glory days who wouldn't turn me in to the police. I had managed to scrape with the law in Kalispell over several bad checks—which is a prison crime in Montana. And I knew Edna was already looking at her cards and thinking about a move, since it wasn't the first time I'd been in law scrapes in my life. She herself had already had her own troubles, losing her kids and keeping her ex-husband,

Danny, from breaking in her house and stealing her things while she was at work, which was really why I had moved in in the first place, that and needing to give my little daughter, Cheryl, a better shake in things.

I don't know what was between Edna and me, just beached by the same tides when you got down to it. Though love has been built on frailer ground than that, as I well know. And when I came in the house that afternoon, I just asked her if she wanted to go to Florida with me, leave things where they sat, and she said, "Why not? My datebook's not that full."

Edna and I had been a pair eight months, more or less man and wife, some of which time I had been out of work, and some when I'd worked at the dog track as a lead-out and could help with the rent and talk sense to Danny when he came around. Danny was afraid of me because Edna had told him I'd been in prison in Florida for killing a man once, though that wasn't true. I had once been in jail in Tallahassee for stealing tires and had gotten into a fight on the county farm where a man had lost his eye. But I hadn't done the hurting, and Edna just wanted the story worse than it was so Danny wouldn't act crazy and make her have to take her kids back, since she had made a good adjustment to not having them, and I already had Cheryl with me. I'm not a violent person and would never put a man's eye out, much less kill someone. My former wife, Helen, would come all the way from Waikiki Beach to testify to that. We never had violence, and I believe in crossing the street to stay out of trouble's way. Though Danny didn't know that.

But we were half down through Wyoming, going toward I-80 and feeling good about things, when the oil light flashed on in the car I'd stolen, a sign I knew to be a bad one.

I'd gotten us a good car, a cranberry Mercedes I'd stolen out of an ophthalmologist's lot in Whitefish, Montana. I stole it because I thought it would be comfortable over a long haul, because I thought it got good mileage, which it didn't, and because I'd never had a good car in my life, just old Chevy junkers and used trucks back from when I was a kid swamping citrus with Cubans.

The car made us all high that day. I ran the windows up and down, and Edna told us some jokes and made faces. She could be lively. Her features would light up like a beacon and you could see her beauty, which wasn't ordinary. It all made me giddy, and I drove clean down to Bozeman, then straight on through the park to Jackson Hole. I rented us the bridal suite in the Quality Court in Jackson and left Cheryl and her little dog, Duke, sleeping while Edna and I drove to a rib barn and drank beer and laughed till after midnight.

It felt like a whole new beginning for us, bad memories left behind and a new horizon to build on. I got so worked up, I had a tattoo done on my arm that said FAMOUS TIMES, and Edna bought a Bailey hat with an Indian feather band and a little turquoise-and-silver bracelet for Cheryl, and we made love on the seat of the car in the Quality Court parking lot just as the sun was burning up on the Snake River, and everything seemed then like the end of the rainbow.

It was that very enthusiasm, in fact, that made me keep the car one day longer instead of driving it into the river and stealing another one, like I should have done and *had* done before.

Where the car went bad there wasn't a town in sight or even a house, just some low mountains maybe fifty miles away or maybe a hundred, a barbed-wire fence in both directions, hardpan prairie, and some hawks sailing through the evening air seizing insects.

I got out to look at the motor, and Edna got out with Cheryl and the dog to let them have a pee by the car. I checked the water and checked the oil stick, and both of them said perfect.

"What's that light mean, Earl?" Edna said. She had come and stood by the car with her hat on. She was just sizing things up for herself.

"We shouldn't run it," I said. "Something's not right in the oil."

She looked around at Cheryl and Little Duke, who were peeing on the hardtop side by side like two little dolls, then out at the mountains, which were becoming black and lost in the distance. "What're we doing?" she said. She wasn't worried yet, but she wanted to know what I was thinking about.

"Let me try it again," I said.

"That's a good idea," she said, and we all got back in the car.

When I turned the motor over, it started right away and the red light stayed off and there weren't any noises to make you think something was wrong. I let it idle a minute, then pushed the accelerator down and watched the red bulb. But there wasn't any light on, and I started wondering if maybe I hadn't dreamed I saw it, or that it had been the sun catching an angle off the window chrome, or maybe I was scared of something and didn't know it.

"What's the matter with it, Daddy?" Cheryl said from the back seat. I looked back at her, and she had on her turquoise bracelet and Edna's hat set back on the back of her head and that little black-and-white Heinz dog on her lap. She looked like a little cowgirl in the movies.

"Nothing, honey, everything's fine now," I said.

"Little Duke tinkled where I tinkled," Cheryl said, and laughed.

"You're two of a kind," Edna said, not looking back. Edna was usually good with Cheryl, but I knew she was tired now. We hadn't had much sleep, and she had a tendency to get cranky when she didn't sleep. "We oughta ditch this damn car first chance we get," she said.

"What's the first chance we got?" I said, because I knew she'd been at the map.

"Rock Springs, Wyoming," Edna said with conviction. "Thirty miles down this road."

She pointed out ahead. I had wanted all along to drive the car into Florida like a big success story. But I knew Edna was right about it, that we shouldn't take crazy chances. I had kept thinking of it as my car and not the ophthalmologist's, and that was how you got caught in these things.

"Then my belief is we ought to go to Rock Springs and negotiate ourselves a new car," I said. I wanted to stay upbeat, like everything was panning out right.

"That's a great idea," Edna said, and she leaned over and kissed me hard on the mouth.

"That's a great idea," Cheryl said. "Let's pull on out of here right now."

The sunset that day I remember as being the prettiest I'd ever seen. Just as it touched the rim of the horizon, it all at once fired the air into jewels and red sequins the precise likes of which I had never seen before and haven't seen since. The West has it all over everywhere for sunsets, even Florida, where it's supposedly flat but where half the time trees block your view.

"It's cocktail hour," Edna said after we'd driven awhile. "We ought to have a drink and celebrate something." She felt better thinking we were going to get rid of the car. It certainly had dark troubles and was something you'd want to put behind you.

Edna had out a whiskey bottle and some plastic cups and was measuring levels on the glove-box lid. She liked drinking, and she liked drinking in the car, which was something you got used to in Montana, where it wasn't against the law, where, though, strangely enough, a bad check would land you in Deer Lodge Prison for a year.

"Did I ever tell you I once had a monkey?" Edna said, setting my drink on the dashboard where I could reach it when I was ready. Her spirits were already picked up. She was like that, up one minute and down the next.

"I don't think you ever did tell me that," I said. "Where were you then?"

"Missoula," she said. She put her bare feet on the dash and rested the cup on her breasts. "I was waitressing at the Amvets. It was before I met you. Some guy came in one day with a monkey. A spider monkey. And I said, just to be joking, 'I'll roll you for that monkey.' And the guy said, 'Just one roll?' And I said, 'Sure.' He put the monkey down on the bar, picked up the cup, and rolled out boxcars. I picked it up and rolled out three fives. And I just stood there looking at the guy. He was just some guy passing through, I guess a vet. He got a strange look on his face—I'm sure not as strange as the one I had—but he looked kind of sad and surprised and satisfied all at once. I said, 'We can roll again.' But he said, 'No, I never roll twice for anything.' And he sat and drank a beer and talked about one thing and another for a while, about nuclear war and building a stronghold somewhere up in the Bitterroot, whatever it was, while I just watched the monkey, wondering what I was going to do with it when the guy left. And pretty soon he got up and said, 'Well, goodbye, Chipper'; that was this monkey's name, of course. And then he left before I could say anything. And the monkey just sat on the bar all that night. I don't know what made me think of that, Earl. Just something weird. I'm letting my mind wander."

"That's perfectly fine," I said. I took a drink of my drink. "I'd never own a monkey," I said after a minute. "They're too nasty. I'm sure Cheryl would like a monkey, though, wouldn't you, honey?" Cheryl was down on the seat playing with Little Duke. She used to talk about monkeys all the time then. "What'd you ever do with that monkey?" I said, watching the speedometer. We were having to go slower now because the red light kept fluttering on. And all I could do to keep it off was go slower. We were going maybe thirty-five and it was an hour before dark, and I was hoping Rock Springs wasn't far away.

"You really want to know?" Edna said. She gave me a quick, sharp glance, then looked back at the empty desert as if she was brooding over it.

"Sure," I said. I was still upbeat. I figured *I* could worry about breaking down and let other people be happy for a change.

"I kept it a week," she said. She seemed gloomy all of a sudden, as if she saw some aspect of the story she had never seen before. "I took it home and back and forth to the Amvets on my shifts. And it didn't cause any trouble. I fixed a chair up for it to sit on, back of the bar, and people liked it. It made a nice little clicking noise. We changed its name to Mary because the bartender figured out it was a girl. Though I was never really comfortable with it at home. I felt like it watched me too much. Then one day a guy came in, some guy who'd been in Vietnam, still wore a fatigue coat. And he said to me, 'Don't you know that a monkey'll kill you? It's got more strength in its fingers than you got in your whole body.' He said people had been killed in Vietnam by monkeys, bunches of them marauding while you were asleep, killing you and covering you with leaves. I didn't believe a word of it, except that when I got home and got undressed I started looking over across the room at Mary on her chair in the dark watching me. And I got the creeps. And after a while I got up and went out to the car, got a length of clothesline wire, and came back in and wired her to the doorknob through her little silver collar, and went back and tried to sleep. And I guess I must've slept the sleep of the dead—though I don't remember it— because when I got up I found Mary had tipped off her chair back and hanged herself on the wire line. I'd made it too short."

Edna seemed badly affected by that story and slid low in the seat so she couldn't see out over the dash. "Isn't that a shameful story, Earl, what happened to that poor little monkey?"

"I see a town! I see a town!" Cheryl started yelling from the back seat, and right up Little Duke started yapping and the whole car fell into a racket. And sure enough she had seen something I hadn't which was Rock Springs, Wyoming, at the bottom of a long hill, a little glowing jewel in the desert with I-80 running on the north side and the black desert spread out behind.

"That's it, honey," I said. "That's where we're going. You saw it first."

"We're hungry," Cheryl said. "Little Duke wants some fish, and I want spaghetti." She put her arms around my neck and hugged me.

"Then you'll just get it," I said. "You can have anything you want. And so can Edna and so can Little Duke." I looked over at Edna, smiling, but she was staring at me with eyes that were fierce with anger. "What's wrong?" I said.

"Don't you care anything about that awful thing that happened to me?" she said. Her mouth was drawn tight, and her eyes kept cutting back at Cheryl and Little Duke, as if they had been tormenting her.

"Of course I do," I said. "I thought that was an awful thing." I didn't want her to be unhappy. We were almost there, and pretty soon we could sit down and have a real meal without thinking somebody might be hurting us.

"You want to know what I did with that monkey?" Edna said.

"Sure I do," I said.

She said, "I put her in a green garbage bag, put it in the trunk of my car, drove to the dump, and threw her in the trash." She was staring at me darkly, as if the story meant something to her that was real important but that only she could see and that the rest of the world was a fool for.

"Well, that's horrible," I said. "But I don't see what else you could do. You didn't mean to kill it. You'd have done it differently if you had. And then you had to get rid of it, and I don't know what else you could have done. Throwing it away might seem unsympathetic to somebody, probably, but not to me. Sometimes that's all you can do, and you can't worry about what somebody else thinks." I tried to smile at her, but the red light was staying on if I pushed the accelerator at all, and I was trying to gauge if we could coast to Rock Springs before the car gave out completely. I looked at Edna again. "What else can I say?" I said.

"Nothing," she said, and stared back at the dark highway. "I should've known that's what you'd think. You've got a character that leaves something out, Earl. I've known that a long time."

"And yet here you are," I said. "And you're not doing so bad. Things could be a lot worse. At least we're all together here."

"Things could always be worse," Edna said. "You could go to the electric chair tomorrow."

"That's right," I said. "And somewhere somebody probably will. Only it won't be you."

"I'm hungry," said Cheryl. "When're we gonna eat? Let's find a motel. I'm tired of this. Little Duke's tired of it too."

Where the car stopped rolling was some distance from the town, though you could see the clear outline of the interstate in the dark with Rock Springs lighting up the sky behind. You could hear the big tractors hitting the spacers in the overpass, revving up for the climb to the mountains.

I shut off the lights.

"What're we going to do now?" Edna said irritably, giving me a bitter look.

"I'm figuring it," I said. "It won't be hard, whatever it is. You won't have to do anything."

"I'd hope not," she said, and looked the other way.

Across the road and across a dry wash a hundred yards was what looked like a huge mobile-home town, with a factory or a refinery of some kind lit up behind it and in full swing. There were lights on in a lot of the mobile homes, and there were cars moving along an access road that ended near the freeway overpass a mile the other way. The lights in the mobile homes seemed friendly to me, and I knew right then what I should do.

"Get out," I said, and opened my door.

"Are we walking?" Edna said.

"We're pushing," I said.

"I'm not pushing," Edna said, and reached up and locked her door.

"All right," I said. "Then you just steer."

"You pushing us to Rock Springs, are you, Earl? It doesn't look like it's more than about three miles," Edna said.

"I'll push," Cheryl said from the back.

"No, hon. Daddy'll push. You just get out with Little Duke and move out of the way."

Edna gave me a threatening look, just as if I'd tried to hit her. But when I got out she slid into my seat and took the wheel, staring angrily ahead straight into the cottonwood scrub.

"Edna can't drive that car," Cheryl said from out in the dark. "She'll run it in the ditch."

"Yes, she can, hon. Edna can drive it as good as I can. Probably better."

"No, she can't," Cheryl said. "No, she can't either." And I thought she was about to cry, but she didn't.

I told Edna to keep the ignition on so it wouldn't lock up and to steer into the cottonwoods with the parking lights on so she could see. And when I started, she steered it straight off into the trees, and I kept pushing until we were twenty yards into the cover and the tires sank in the soft sand and nothing at all could be seen from the road.

"Now where are we?" she said, sitting at the wheel. Her voice was tired and hard, and I knew she could have put a good meal to use. She had a sweet nature, and I recognized that this wasn't her fault but mine. Only I wished she could be more hopeful.

"You stay right here, and I'll go over to that trailer park and call us a cab," I said.

"What cab?" Edna said, her mouth wrinkled as if she'd never heard anything like that in her life.

"There'll be cabs," I said, and tried to smile at her. "There's cabs everywhere."

"What're you going to tell him when he gets here? Our stolen car broke down and we need a ride to where we can steal another one? That'll be a big hit, Earl."

"I'll talk," I said. "You just listen to the radio for ten minutes and then walk on out to the shoulder like nothing was suspicious. And you and Cheryl act nice. She doesn't need to know about this car."

"Like we're not suspicious enough already, right?" Edna looked up at me out of the lighted car. "You don't think right, did you know that, Earl? You think the world's stupid and you're smart. But that's not how it is. I feel sorry for you. You might've *been* something, but things just went crazy someplace."

I had a thought about poor Danny. He was a vet and crazy as a shit-house mouse, and I was glad he wasn't in for all this. "Just get the baby in the car," I said, trying to be patient. "I'm hungry like you are."

"I'm tired of this," Edna said. "I wish I'd stayed in Montana."

"Then you can go back in the morning," I said. "I'll buy the ticket and put you on the bus. But not till then."

"Just get on with it, Earl," she said, slumping down in the seat, turning off the parking lights with one foot and the radio on with the other.

The mobile-home community was as big as any I'd ever seen. It was attached in some way to the plant that was lighted up behind it, because I could see a car once in a while leave one of the trailer streets, turn in the direction of the plant, then go slowly into it. Everything in the plant was white, and you could see that all the trailers were painted white and looked exactly alike. A deep hum came out of the plant, and I thought as I got closer that it wouldn't be a location I'd ever want to work in.

I went right to the first trailer where there was a light and knocked on the metal door. Kids' toys were lying in the gravel around the little wood steps, and I could hear talking on TV that suddenly went off. I heard a woman's voice talking, and then the door opened wide.

A large Negro woman with a wide, friendly face stood in the doorway. She smiled at me and moved forward as if she was going to come out, but she stopped at the top step. There was a little Negro boy behind her peeping out from behind her legs, watching me with his eyes half closed. The trailer had that feeling that no one else was inside, which was a feeling I knew something about.

"I'm sorry to intrude," I said. "But I've run up on a little bad luck tonight. My name's Earl Middleton."

The woman looked at me, then out into the night toward the freeway as if what I had said was something she was going to be able to see. "What kind of bad luck?" she said, looking down at me again.

"My car broke down out on the highway," I said. "I can't fix it myself, and I wondered if I could use your phone to call for help."

The woman smiled down at me knowingly. "We can't live without cars, can we?"

"That's the honest truth," I said.

"They're like our hearts," she said firmly, her face shining in the little bulb light that burned beside the door. "Where's your car situated?"

I turned and looked over into the dark, but I couldn't see anything because of where we'd put it. "It's over there," I said. "You can't see it in the dark."

"Who all's with you now?" the woman said. "Have you got your wife with you?"

"She's with my little girl and our dog in the car," I said. "My daughter's asleep or I would have brought them."

"They shouldn't be left in the dark by themselves," the woman said, and frowned. "There's too much unsavoriness out there."

"The best I can do is hurry back," I said. I tried to look sincere, since everything except Cheryl being asleep and Edna being my wife was the truth. The truth is meant to serve you if you'll let it, and I wanted it to serve me. "I'll pay for the phone call," I said. "If you'll bring the phone to the door I'll call from right here."

The woman looked at me again as if she was searching for a truth of her own, then back out into the night. She was maybe in her sixties, but I couldn't say for sure. "You're not going to rob me, are you, Mr. Middleton?" she said, and smiled like it was a joke between us.

"Not tonight," I said, and smiled a genuine smile. "I'm not up to it tonight. Maybe another time."

"Then I guess Terrel and I can let you use our phone with Daddy not here, can't we, Terrel? This is my grandson, Terrel Junior, Mr. Middleton." She put her hand on the boy's head and looked down at him. "Terrel won't talk. Though if he did he'd tell you to use our phone. He's a sweet boy." She opened the screen for me to come in.

The trailer was a big one with a new rug and a new couch and a living room that expanded to give the space of a real house. Something good and sweet was cooking in the kitchen, and the trailer felt like it was somebody's comfortable new home instead of just temporary. I've lived in trailers, but they were just snailbacks with one room and no toilet, and they always felt cramped and unhappy—though I've thought maybe it might've been me that was unhappy in them.

There was a big Sony TV and a lot of kids' toys scattered on the floor. I recognized a Greyhound bus I'd gotten for Cheryl. The phone was beside a new leather recliner, and the Negro woman pointed for me to sit down and call and gave me the phone book. Terrel began fingering his toys, and the woman sat on the couch while I called, watching me and smiling.

There were three listings for cab companies, all with one number different. I called the numbers in order and didn't get an answer until the last one, which answered with the name of the second company. I said I was on the highway beyond the interstate and that my wife and family needed to be taken to town and I would arrange for a tow later. While I was giving the location, I looked up the name of a tow service to tell the driver in case he asked.

When I hung up, the Negro woman was sitting looking at me with the same look she had been staring with into the dark, a look that seemed to want truth. She was smiling, though. Something pleased her and I reminded her of it.

"This is a very nice home," I said, resting in the recliner, which felt like the driver's seat of the Mercedes and where I'd have been happy to stay.

"This isn't *our* house, Mr. Middleton," the Negro woman said. "The company owns these. They give them to us for nothing. We have our own home in Rockford, Illinois."

"That's wonderful," I said.

"It's never wonderful when you have to be away from home, Mr. Middleton, though we're only here three months, and it'll be easier when Terrel Junior begins his special school. You see, our son was killed in the war, and his wife ran off without Terrel Junior. Though you shouldn't worry. He can't understand us. His little feelings can't be hurt." The woman folded her hands in her lap and smiled in a satisfied way. She was an attractive woman and had on a blue-and-pink floral dress that made her seem bigger than she could've been, just the right woman to sit on the couch she was sitting on. She was good nature's picture, and I was glad she could be, with her little brain-damaged boy, living in a place where no one in his right mind would want to live a minute. "Where do *you* live, Mr. Middleton?" she said politely, smiling in the same sympathetic way.

"My family and I are in transit," I said. "I'm an ophthalmologist, and we're moving back to Florida, where I'm from. I'm setting up practice in some little town where it's warm year-round. I haven't decided where."

"Florida's a wonderful place," the woman said. "I think Terrel would like it there."

"Could I ask you something?" I said.

"You certainly may," the woman said. Terrel had begun pushing his Greyhound across the front of the TV screen, making a scratch that no one watching the set could miss. "Stop that, Terrell Junior," the woman said quietly. But Terrel kept pushing his bus on the glass, and she smiled at me again as if we both understood something sad. Except I knew Cheryl would never damage a television set. She had respect for nice things, and I was sorry for the lady that Terrel didn't. "What did you want to ask?" the woman said.

"What goes on in that plant or whatever it is back there beyond these trailers, where all the lights are on?"

"Gold," the woman said, and smiled.

"It's what?" I said.

"Gold," the Negro woman said, smiling as she had for almost all the time I'd been there. "It's a gold mine."

"They're mining gold back there?" I said, pointing.

"Every night and every day," she said, smiling in a pleased way.

"Does your husband work there?" I said.

"He's the assayer," she said. "He controls the quality. He works three months a year, and we live the rest of the time at home in Rockford. We've waited a long time for this. We've been happy to have our grandson, but I won't say I'll be sorry to have him go. We're ready to start our lives over." She smiled broadly at me and then at Terrel, who was giving her a spiteful look from the floor. "You said you had a daughter," the Negro woman said. "And what's her name?"

"Irma Cheryl," I said. "She's named for my mother."

"That's nice," she said. "And she's healthy, too. I can see it in your face." She looked at Terrel Junior with pity.

"I guess I'm lucky," I said.

"So far you are," she said. "But children bring you grief, the same way they bring you joy. We were unhappy for a long time before my husband got his job in the gold mine. Now, when Terrel starts to school, we'll be kids again." She stood up. "You might miss your cab, Mr. Middleton," she said, walking toward the door, though not to be forcing me out. She was too polite. "If *we* can't see your car, the cab surely won't be able to."

"That's true," I said, and got up off the recliner, where I'd been so comfortable. "None of us have eaten yet, and your food makes me know how hungry we probably all are."

"There are fine restaurants in town, and you'll find them," the Negro woman said. "I'm sorry you didn't meet my husband. He's a wonderful man. He's everything to me."

"Tell him I appreciate the phone," I said. "You saved me."

"You weren't hard to save," the woman said. "Saving people is what we were all put on earth to do. I just passed you on to whatever's coming to you."

"Let's hope it's good," I said, stepping back into the dark.

"I'll be hoping, Mr. Middleton. Terrel and I will both be hoping."

I waved to her as I walked out into the darkness toward the car where it was hidden in the night.

The cab had already arrived when I got there. I could see its little red and green roof lights all the way across the dry wash, and it made me worry that Edna was already saying something to get us in trouble, something about the car or where we'd come from, something that would cast suspicion on us. I thought, then, how I never planned things well enough. There was always a gap between my plan and what happened, and I only responded to things as they came along and hoped I wouldn't get in trouble. I was an offender in the law's eyes. But I always *thought* differently, as if I weren't an offender and had no intention of being one, which was the truth. But as I read on a napkin once, between the idea and the act a whole kingdom lies. And I had a hard time with my acts, which were oftentimes offender's acts, and my ideas, which were as good as the gold they mined there where the bright lights were blazing.

"We're waiting for you, Daddy," Cheryl said when I crossed the road. "The taxicab's already here."

"I see, hon," I said, and gave Cheryl a big hug. The cabdriver was sitting in the driver's seat having a smoke with the lights on inside. Edna was leaning against the back of the cab between the taillights, wearing her Bailey hat. "What'd you tell him?" I said when I got close.

"Nothin'," she said. "What's there to tell?"

"Did he see the car?"

She glanced over in the direction of the trees where we had hid the Mercedes. Nothing was visible in the darkness, though I could hear Little Duke combing around in the underbrush tracking something, his little collar tinkling. "Where're we going?" she said. "I'm so hungry I could pass out."

"Edna's in a terrible mood," Cheryl said. "She already snapped at me."

"We're tired, honey," I said. "So try to be nicer."

"She's never nice," Cheryl said.

"Run go get Little Duke," I said. "And hurry back."

"I guess *my* questions come last here, right?" Edna said.

I put my arm around her. "That's not true," I said.

"Did you find somebody over there in the trailers you'd rather stay with? You were gone long enough."

"That's not a thing to say," I said. "I was just trying to make things look right, so we don't get put in jail."

"So *you* don't, you mean," Edna said and laughed a little laugh I didn't like hearing.

"That's right. So I don't," I said. "I'd be the one in Dutch." I stared out at the big, lighted assemblage of white buildings and white lights beyond the trailer community, plumes of white smoke escaping up into the heartless Wyoming sky, the whole company of buildings looking like some unbelievable castle, humming away in a distorted dream. "You know what all those buildings are there?" I said to Edna, who hadn't moved and who didn't really seem to care if she ever moved anymore ever.

"No. But I can't say it matters, 'cause it isn't a motel and it isn't a restaurant," she said.

"It's a gold mine," I said, staring at the gold mine, which, I knew now from walking to the trailer, was a greater distance from us than it seemed, though it seemed huge and near, up against the cold sky. I thought there should've been a wall around it with guards instead of just the lights and no fence. It seemed as if anyone could go in and take what they wanted, just the way I had gone up to that woman's trailer and used the telephone, though that obviously wasn't true.

Edna began to laugh then. Not the mean laugh I didn't like, but a laugh that had something caring behind it, a full laugh that enjoyed a joke, a laugh she was laughing the first time I laid eyes on her, in Missoula in the Eastgate bar in 1979, a laugh we used to laugh together when Cheryl was still with her mother and I was working steady at the track and not stealing cars or passing bogus checks to merchants. A better time all around. And for some reason it made me laugh just hearing her, and we both stood there behind the cab in the dark, laughing at the gold mine in the desert, me with my arm around her and Cheryl out rustling up Little Duke and the cabdriver smoking in the cab and our stolen Mercedes-Benz, which I'd had such hopes for in Florida, stuck up to its axle in sand, where I'd never get to see it again.

"I always wondered what a gold mine would look like when I saw it," Edna said, still laughing, wiping a tear from her eye.

"Me too," I said. "I was always curious about it."

"We're a couple of fools, ain't we, Earl?" she said, unable to quit laughing completely. "We're two of a kind."

"It might be a good sign, though," I said.

"How could it be?" she said. "It's not our gold mine. There aren't any drive-up windows." She was still laughing.

"We've seen it," I said, pointing. "That's it right there. It may mean we're getting closer. Some people never see it at all."

"In a pig's eye, Earl," she said. "You and me see it in a pig's eye."

And she turned and got into the cab to go.

The cabdriver didn't ask anything about our car or where it was, to mean he'd noticed something queer. All of which made me feel like we had made a clean break from the car and couldn't be connected with it until it was too late, if ever. The driver told us a lot about Rock Springs while he drove, that because of the gold mine a lot of people had moved there in just six months, people from all over, including New York, and that most of them lived out in the trailers. Prostitutes from New York City, who he called "B-girls," had come into town, he said, on the prosperity tide, and Cadillacs with New York plates cruised the little streets every night, full of Negroes with big hats who ran the women. He told us that everybody who got in his cab now wanted to know where the women were, and when he got our call he almost didn't come because some of the trailers were brothels operated by the mine for engineers and computer people away from home. He said he got tired of running back and forth out there just for vile business. He said that *60 Minutes* had even done a program about Rock Springs and that a blowup had resulted in Cheyenne, though nothing could be done unless the prosperity left town. "It's prosperity's fruit," the driver said. "I'd rather be poor, which is lucky for me."

He said all the motels were sky-high, but since we were a family he could show us a nice one that was affordable. But I told him we wanted a first-rate place where they took animals, and the money didn't matter because we had had a hard day and wanted to finish on a high note. I also knew that it was in the little nowhere places that the police look for you and find you. People I'd known were always being arrested in cheap hotels and tourist courts with names you'd never heard of before. Never in Holiday Inns or Travelodges.

I asked him to drive us to the middle of town and back out again so Cheryl could see the train station, and while we were there I saw a pink Cadillac with New York plates and a TV aerial being driven slowly by a Negro in a big hat down a narrow street where there were just bars and a Chinese restaurant. It was an odd sight, nothing you could ever expect.

"There's your pure criminal element," the cabdriver said, and seemed sad. "I'm sorry for people like you to see a thing like that. We've got a nice town here, but there're some that want to ruin it for everybody. There used to be a way to deal with trash and criminals, but those days are gone forever."

"You said it," Edna said.

"You shouldn't let it get *you* down," I said to the cabdriver. "There's more of you than them. And there always will be. You're the best advertisement this town has. I know Cheryl will remember you and not *that* man, won't you, honey?" But Cheryl was asleep by then, holding Little Duke in her arms on the taxi seat.

The driver took us to the Ramada Inn on the interstate, not far from where we'd broken down. I had a small pain of regret as we drove under the Ramada awning that we hadn't driven up in a cranberry-colored Mercedes but instead in a beat-up old Chrysler taxi driven by an old man full of complaints. Though I knew it was for the best. We were better off without that car, better, really, in any other car but that one, where the signs had turned bad.

I registered under another name and paid for the room in cash so there wouldn't be any questions. On the line where it said "Representing" I wrote "ophthalmologist" and put "M.D." after the name. It had a nice look to it, even though it wasn't my name.

When we got to the room, which was in the back where I'd asked for it, I put Cheryl on one of the beds and Little Duke beside her so they'd sleep. She'd missed dinner, but it only meant she'd be hungry in the morning, when she could have anything she wanted. A few missed meals don't make a kid bad. I'd missed a lot of them myself and haven't turned out completely bad.

"Let's have some fried chicken," I said to Edna when she came out of the bathroom. "They have good fried chicken at the Ramadas, and I noticed the buffet was still up. Cheryl can stay right here, where it's safe, till we're back."

"I guess I'm not hungry anymore," Edna said. She stood at the window staring out into the dark. I could see out the window past her some yellowish foggy glow in the sky. For a moment I thought it was the gold mine out in the distance lighting the night, though it was only the interstate.

"We could order up," I said. "Whatever you want. There's a menu on the phone book. You could just have a salad."

"You go ahead," she said. "I've lost my hungry spirit." She sat on the bed beside Cheryl and Little Duke and looked at them in a sweet way and put her hand on Cheryl's cheek just as if she'd had a fever. "Sweet little girl," she said. "Everybody loves you."

"What do you want to do?" I said. "I'd like to eat. Maybe *I'll* order up some chicken."

"Why don't you do that?" she said. "It's your favorite." And she smiled at me from the bed.

I sat on the other bed and dialed room service. I asked for chicken, garden salad, potato, and a roll, plus a piece of hot apple pie and ice tea. I realized I hadn't eaten all day. When I put down the phone I saw that Edna was watching me, not in a hateful way or a loving way, just in a way that seemed to say she didn't understand something and was going to ask me about it.

"When did watching me get so entertaining?" I said, and smiled at her. I was trying to be friendly. I knew how tired she must be. It was after nine o'clock.

"I was just thinking how much I hated being in a motel without a car that was mine to drive. Isn't that funny? I started feeling like that last night when that purple car wasn't mine. That purple car just gave me the willies, I guess, Earl."

"One of those cars *outside* is yours," I said. "Just stand right there and pick it out."

"I know," she said. "But that's different, isn't it?" She reached and got her blue Bailey hat, put it on her head, and set it way back like Dale Evans. She looked sweet. "I used to like to go to motels, you know," she said. "There's something secret about them and free—I was never paying, of course. But you felt safe from everything and free to do what you wanted because you'd made the decision to be there and paid that price, and all the rest was the good part. Fucking and everything, you know." She smiled at me in a good-natured way.

"Isn't that the way this is?" I said. I was sitting on the bed, watching her, not knowing what to expect her to say next.

"I don't guess it is, Earl," she said, and stared out the window. "I'm thirty-two and I'm going to have to give up on motels. I can't keep that fantasy going anymore."

"Don't you like this place?" I said, and looked around at the room. I appreciated the modern paintings and the lowboy bureau and the big TV. It seemed like a plenty nice enough place to me, considering where we'd been already.

"No, I don't," Edna said with real conviction. "There's no use in my getting mad at you about it. It isn't your fault. You do the best you can for everybody. But every trip teaches you something. And I've learned I need to give up on motels before some bad thing happens to me. I'm sorry."

"What does that mean?" I said, because I really didn't know what she had in mind to do, though I should've guessed.

"I guess I'll take that ticket you mentioned," she said, and got up and faced the window. "Tomorrow's soon enough. We haven't got a car to take me anyhow."

"Well, that's a fine thing," I said, sitting on the bed, feeling like I was in a shock. I wanted to say something to her, to argue with her, but I couldn't think what to say that seemed right. I didn't want to be mad at her, but it made me mad.

"You've got a right to be mad at me, Earl," she said, "but I don't think you can really blame me." She turned around and faced me and sat on the windowsill, her hands on her knees. Someone knocked on the door. I just yelled for them to set the tray down and put it on the bill.

"I guess I *do* blame you," I said. I was angry. I thought about how I could have disappeared into that trailer community and hadn't, had come back to keep things going, had tried to take control of things for everybody when they looked bad.

"Don't. I wish you wouldn't," Edna said, and smiled at me like she wanted me to hug her. "Anybody ought to have their choice in things if they can. Don't you believe that, Earl? Here I am out here in the desert where I don't know anything, in a stolen car, in a motel room under an assumed name, with no money of my own, a kid that's not mine, and the law after me. And I have a choice to get out of all of it by getting on a bus. What would you do? I know exactly what you'd do."

"You think you do," I said. But I didn't want to get into an argument about it and tell her all I could've done and didn't do. Because it wouldn't have done any good. When you get to the point of arguing, you're past the point of changing anybody's mind, even though it's supposed to be the other way, and maybe for some classes of people it is, just never mine.

Edna smiled at me and came across the room and put her arms around me where I was sitting on the bed. Cheryl rolled over and looked at us and smiled, then closed her eyes, and the room was quiet. I was beginning to think of Rock Springs in a way I knew I would always think of it, a lowdown city full of crimes and whores and disappointments, a place where a woman left me, instead of a place where I got things on the straight track once and for all, a place I saw a gold mine.

"Eat your chicken, Earl," Edna said. "Then we can go to bed. I'm tired, but I'd like to make love to you anyway. None of this is a matter of not loving you, you know that."

Sometime late in the night, after Edna was asleep, I got up and walked outside into the parking lot. It could've been anytime because there was still the light from the interstate frosting the low sky and the big red Ramada sign humming motionlessly in the night and no light at all in the east to indicate it might be morning. The lot was full of cars all nosed in, most of them with suitcases strapped to their roofs and their trunks weighed down with belongings the people were taking someplace, to a new home or a vacation resort in the mountains. I had laid in bed a long time after Edna was asleep, watching the Atlanta Braves on cable television, trying to get my mind off how I'd feel when I saw that bus pull away the next day, and how I'd feel when I turned around and there stood Cheryl and Little Duke and no one to see about them but me alone, and that the first thing I had to do was get hold of some automobile and get the plates switched, then get them some breakfast and get us all on the road to Florida, all in the space of probably two hours, since that Mercedes would certainly look less hid in the daytime than the night, and word travels fast. I've always taken care of Cheryl myself as long as I've had her with me. None of the women ever did; most of them didn't even seem to like her, though they took care of me in a way so that I could take care of her. And I knew that once Edna left, all that was going to get harder. Though what I wanted most to do was not think about it just for a little while, try to let my mind go limp so it could be strong for the rest of what there was. I thought that the difference between a successful life and an unsuccessful one, between me at that moment and all the people who owned the cars that were nosed into their proper places in the lot, maybe between me and that woman out in the trailers by the gold mine, was how well you were able to put things like this out of your mind and not be bothered by them, and maybe, too, by how many troubles like this one you had to face in a lifetime. Through luck or design they had all faced fewer troubles, and by their own characters, they forgot them faster. And that's what I wanted for me. Fewer troubles, fewer memories of trouble.

I walked over to a car, a Pontiac with Ohio tags, one of the ones with bundles and suitcases strapped to the top and a lot more in the trunk, by the way it was riding. I looked inside the driver's window. There were maps and paperback books and sunglasses and the little plastic holders for cans that hang on the window wells. And in the back there were kids' toys and some pillows and a cat box with a cat sitting in it staring up at me like I was the face of the moon. It all looked familiar to me, the very same things I would have in my car if I had a car. Nothing seemed surprising, nothing different. Though I had a funny sensation at that moment and turned and looked up at the windows along the back of the Ramada Inn. All were dark except two. Mine and another one. And I wondered, because it seemed funny, what would you think a man was doing if you saw him in the middle of the night looking in the windows of cars in the parking lot of the Ramada Inn? Would you think he was trying to get his head cleared? Would you think he was trying to get ready for a day when trouble would come down on him? Would you think his girlfriend was leaving him? Would you think he had a daughter? Would you think he was anybody like you?

[FEBRUARY 1982]

DENIS JOHNSON

Steady Hands at Seattle General

The son of a U.S. diplomat, Denis Johnson (1949–   ) grew up largely in the Philippines and Japan, along with the occasional posting to Washington, D.C. He studied poetry at the Iowa Writers' Workshop and has produced several striking volumes of poetry, among them The Incognito Lounge and The Veil. A fan of Bob Dylan's music, Johnson composes fiction that shares with Dylan's songs a propensity for the surreal and the apocalyptic, as is clearly the case with the novels Angels (1983), Fiskadoro (1985), The Stars at Noon (1986), and Resuscitation of a Hanged Man (1990), as well as with the story collection Jesus's Son (1992), in which "Steady Hands at Seattle General" was collected after it appeared in Esquire in 1989. Johnson often accepts nonfiction assignments for the magazine, and has filed dispatches from the civil war in Liberia and the Persian Gulf conflict.

Inside of two days I was shaving myself, and I even shaved a couple of new arrivals, because the drugs they injected me with had an amazing effect. I called it amazing because only hours before, they'd wheeled me through corridors in which I hallucinated a soft, summery rain. In the hospital rooms on either side, objects—vases, ashtrays, beds—had looked wet and scary, hardly bothering to cover up their true meanings.

They ran a few syringefuls into me, and I felt like I'd turned from a light. Styrofoam thing into a person. I held up my hands before my eyes. The hands were as still as a sculpture's.

I shaved my roommate, Bill. "Don't get tricky with my mustache," he said.

"Okay so far?"

"So far."

"I'll do the other side."

"That would make sense, partner."

Just below one cheekbone, Bill had a small blemish where a bullet had entered his face, and in the other cheek a slightly larger scar where the slug had gone on its way.

"When you were shot right through your face like that, did the bullet go on to do anything interesting?"

"How would I know? I didn't take notes. Even if it goes on through, you still feel like you just got shot in the head."

"What about this little scar here, through your sideburn?"

"I don't know. Maybe I was born with that one. I never saw it before."

"Someday people are going to read about you in a story or a poem. Will you describe yourself for those people?"

"Oh, I don't know. I'm a fat piece of shit, I guess."

"No. I'm serious."

"You're not going to write about me."

"Hey, I'm a writer."

"Well then, just tell them I'm overweight."

"He's overweight."

"I been shot twice."

"Twice?"

"Once by each wife, for a total of three bullets, making four holes, three ins and one out."

"And you're still alive."

"Are you going to change any of this for your poem?"

"No. It's going in word for word."

"That's too bad, because asking me if I'm alive makes you look kind of stupid. Obviously, I am."

"Well, maybe I mean alive in a deeper sense. You could be talking and still not be alive in a deeper sense."

"It don't get no deeper than the kind of shit we're in right now."

"What do you mean? It's great here. They even give you cigarettes."

"I didn't get any yet."

"Here you go."

"Hey. Thanks."

"Pay me back when they give you yours."

"Maybe."

"What did you say when she shot you?"

"I said, 'You shot me!' "

"Both times? Both wives?"

"The first time I didn't say anything, because she shot me in the mouth."

"So you couldn't talk."

"I was knocked out cold is the reason I couldn't talk. And I still remember the dream I had while I was knocked out that time."

"What was the dream?"

"How could I tell you about it? It was a dream. It didn't make any fucking sense, man. But I do remember it."

"You can't describe it even a little bit?"

"I really don't know what the description would be. I'm sorry."

"Anything. Anything at all."

"Well, for one thing, the dream is something that keeps coming back over and over. I mean when I'm awake. Every time I remember my first wife, I remember that she pulled the trigger on me, and then, here comes that dream. . . .

"And the dream wasn't—there wasn't anything sad about it. But when I remember it, I get like, *'Fuck, man, she really, she shot me. And here's that dream.' "*

"Did you ever see that Elvis Presley movie, *Follow That Dream?*"

"*Follow That Dream.* Yeah, I did. I was just going to mention that."

"Okay. You're all done. Look in the mirror."

"Right."

"What do you see?"

"How did I get so fat when I never eat?"

"Is that all?"

"Well, I don't know. I just got here."

"What about your life?"

"Hah! That's a good one."

"What about your past?"

"What about it?"

"When you look back, what do you see?"

"Wrecked cars."

"Any people in them?"

"Yes."

"Who?"

"People who are just meat now, man."

"Is that really how it is?"

"How do I know how it is? I just got here. And it stinks."

"Are you kidding? They're pumping Haldol by the quart. It's a playpen."

"I hope so. Because I been in places where all they do is wrap you in a wet sheet and let you bite down on a little rubber toy for puppies."

"I could see living here two weeks out of every month."

"Well, I'm older than you are. You can take a couple more rides on this wheel and still get out with all your arms and legs stuck on right. Not me."

"Hey. You're doing fine."

"Talk into here."

"Talk into your bullet hole?"

"Talk into my bullet hole. Tell me I'm fine."

[MARCH 1989]

JOHN UPDIKE

The Rumor

Frank and Sharon Whittier had come from the Cincinnati area and, with an inheritance of hers and a sum borrowed from his father, had opened a small art gallery on the fourth floor of a narrow building on West Fifty-seventh Street. They had known each other as children; their families had been in the same country-club set. They had married in 1971, when Frank was freshly graduated from Oberlin and Vietnam-vulnerable and Sharon was only nineteen, a sophomore at Antioch majoring in dance. By the time, six years later, they arrived in New York, they had two small children; the birth of a third led them to give up their apartment and the city struggle and move to a house in Hastings, a low stucco house with a wide-eaved Wright-style roof and a view, through massive beeches at the bottom of the yard, of the leaden, ongliding Hudson. They were happy, surely. They had dry midwestern taste, and by sticking to representational painters and abstract sculptors they managed to survive the uglier Eighties styles—faux graffiti, neo-German expressionism, cathode-ray prole play, ecological-protest trash art—and bring their quiet, chaste string of fourth-floor rooms into the calm lagoon of Nineties eclectic revivalism and subdued recession chic. They prospered; their youngest child turned twelve, their oldest was filling out college applications.

When Sharon first heard the rumor that Frank had left her for a young homosexual with whom he was having an affair, she had to laugh, for, far from having left her, there he was, right in the lamplit study with her, ripping pages out of *ARTnews*.

"I don't think so, Avis," she said to the graphic artist on the other end of the line. "He's right here with me. Would you like to say hello?" The easy refutation was made additionally sweet by the fact that, some years before, there had been a brief (Sharon thought) romantic flare-up between her husband and this caller, an overanimated redhead with protuberant cheeks and chin. Avis was a second-wave appropriationist who made color Xeroxes of masterpieces out of art books and then signed them in an ink mixed of her own blood and urine. How could she, who had actually slept with Frank, be imagining this grotesque thing?

The voice on the phone gushed as if relieved and pleased. "I know, it's wildly absurd, but I heard it from two sources, with absolutely solemn assurances."

"Who were these sources?"

"I'm not sure they'd like you to know. But it was Ed Jaffrey and then that boy who's been living with Walton Forney, what does he call himself, one of those single names like Madonna—Jojo!"

"Well, then," Sharon began.

"But I've heard it from still others," Avis insisted. "All over town—it's in the air. Couldn't you and Frank *do* something about it, if it's not true?"

" 'If,' " Sharon protested, and her thrust of impatience carried, when she put down the receiver, into her conversation with Frank. "Avis says you're supposed to have run off with your homosexual lover."

"I don't have a homosexual lover," Frank said, too calmly, ripping an auction ad out of the magazine.

"She says all New York says you do."

"Well, what are you going to believe, all New York or your own experience? Here I sit, faithful to a fault, straight as a die, whatever that means. We made love just two nights ago."

It seemed possibly revealing to her that he so distinctly remembered, as if heterosexual performance were a duty he checked off. He was—had always been, for over twenty years—a slim blond man several inches under six feet tall, with a narrow head he liked to keep trim, even during those years when long hair was in fashion, milky-blue eyes set at a slight tilt, such as you see on certain taut Slavic or Norwegian faces, and a small, precise mouth he kept pursed over teeth a shade too prominent and yellow. He was reluctant to smile, as if giving something away, and was vain of his flat belly and lithe collegiate condition. He weighed himself every morning on the bathroom scale, and if he weighed a pound more than yesterday, he skipped lunch. In this, and in his general attention to his own person, he was as quietly fanatic as—it for the first time occurred to her—a woman.

"You know I've never liked the queer side of this business," he went on. "I've just gotten used to it. I don't even think anymore, who's gay and who isn't."

"Avis was *ju*bilant," Sharon said. "How could she think it?"

It took him a moment to focus on the question and realize that his answer was important to her. He became nettled. "Ask *her* how," he said. "Our brief and regrettable relationship, if that's what interests you, seemed satisfactory to me at least. What troubles and amazes me, if I may say so, is how *you* can be taking this ridiculous rumor so seriously."

"I'm *not*, Frank," she insisted, then backtracked. "But why would such a rumor come out of thin air? Doesn't there have to be *something?* Since we moved up here, we're not together so much, naturally, some days when I can't come into town you're gone sixteen hours. . . ."

"But *Shar*on," he said, like a teacher restoring discipline, removing his reading glasses from his almond-shaped eyes, with their stubby fair lashes. "Don't you *know* me? Ever since after that dance when you were sixteen, that time by the lake? . . ."

She didn't want to reminisce. Their early sex had been difficult for her; she had submitted to his advances out of a larger, more social, rather idealistic attraction. She knew that together they would have the strength to get out of Cincinnati and, singly or married to others, they would stay. "Well," she said, enjoying this sensation, despite the chill the rumor had awakened in her, of descending to a deeper level of intimacy than usual, "how well do you know even your own spouse? People are fooled all the time. Peggy Jacobson, for instance, when Henry ran off with that physical therapist, couldn't believe, even when the evidence was right there in front of her—"

"I'm *deeply* insulted," Frank interrupted, his mouth tense in that way he had when making a joke but not wanting to show his teeth. "My masculinity is insulted." But he couldn't deny himself a downward glance into his magazine; his tidy white hand jerked, as if wanting to tear out yet another item that might be useful to their business. Intimacy had always made him nervous. She kept at it, rather hopelessly. "Avis said two separate people had solemnly assured her."

"Who, exactly?"

When she told him, he said, exactly as she had done, "Well, then." He added, "You know how gays are. Malicious. Mischievous. They have all that time and money on their hands."

"You sound jealous." Something about the way he was arguing with her strengthened Sharon's suspicion that, outrageous as the rumor was—indeed, *because* it was outrageous—it was true.

          In the days that followed, now that she was alert to the rumor's vaporous presence, she imagined it everywhere—on the poised young faces of their staff, in the delicate negotiatory accents of their artists' agents, in the heartier tones of their repeat customers, even in the gruff, self-occupied ramblings of the artists themselves. People seemed startled when she and Frank entered a room together: The desk receptionist and the security guard in their gallery halted their daily morning banter, and the waiters in their pet restaurant, over on Fifty-ninth, appeared especially effusive and attentive. Handshakes lasted a second too long, women embraced her with an extra squeeze, she felt herself ensnared in a soft net of unspoken pity.

Frank sensed her discomfort and took a certain malicious pleasure in it, enacting all the while his perfect innocence. He composed himself to appear, from her angle, aloof above the rumor. Dealing professionally in so much absurdity— the art world's frantic attention-getting, studied grotesqueries—he merely intensified the fastidious dryness that had sustained their gallery through wave after wave of changing fashion, and that had, like a rocket's heat-resistant skin, insulated their launch, their escape from the comfortable riverine smugness of semisouthern, puritanical Cincinnati to this metropolis of dreadful freedom. The rumor amused him, and it amused him, too, to notice how she helplessly watched to see if in the metropolitan throngs his eyes now followed young men as once they had noticed and followed young women. She observed his gestures—always a bit excessively graceful and precise—distrustfully, and listened for the buttery, reedy tone of voice that might signal an invisible sex change.

That even in some small fraction of her she was willing to believe the rumor justified a certain maliciousness on his part. He couldn't help teasing her—glancing over at her, say, when an especially magnetic young waiter served them, or at home, in their bedroom, pushing more brusquely than was his style at her increasing sexual unwillingness. More than once, at last away from the countless knowing eyes of their New York milieu, in the privacy of their Hastings upstairs, beneath the wide midwestern eaves, she burst into tears and struck out at him, his infuriating, impervious apparent blamelessness. He was like one of those photo-realist nudes, merciless in every detail and yet subtly, defiantly not there, not human. "You're distant," she accused him. "You've always been."

"I don't mean to be. You didn't used to mind my manner. You thought it was quietly masterful."

"I was a teenage girl. I deferred to you."

"It worked out," he pointed out, lifting his hands in an effete, disclaiming way from his sides, to take in their room, their expensive house, their joint career. "What is it that bothers you, Sharon? The idea of losing me? Or the insult to your female pride? The people who started this ridiculous rumor don't even *see* women. Women to them are just background noise."

"It's *not* ridiculous—if it were, why does it keep on and on, even though we're seen together all the time?"

For, ostensibly to quiet her and to quench the rumor, he had all but ceased to go to the city alone, and took her with him even though it meant some neglect of the house and their sons.

Frank asked, "Who *says* it keeps on all the time? I've *never* heard it, never once, except from you. Who's mentioned it lately?"

"Nobody."

"Well, then." He smiled, his lips not quite parting on his curved teeth, tawny like a beaver's.

"You bastard!" Sharon burst out. "You have some stinking little secret!"

"I don't," he serenely half-lied.

The rumor had no factual basis. But was there, Frank asked himself, some truth to it after all? Not circumstantial truth, but some higher, inner truth? As a young man, slight of build, with artistic interests, had he not been fearful of being mistaken for a homosexual? Had he not responded to homosexual overtures as they arose, in bars and locker rooms, with a disproportionate terror and repugnance? Had not his early marriage, and then, ten years later, his flurry of adulterous womanizing, been an escape of sorts, into safe, socially approved terrain? When he fantasized, or saw a pornographic movie, was not the male organ the hero of the occasion for him, at the center of every scene? Were not those slavish, lapping starlets his robotlike delegates, with glazed eyes and undisturbed coiffures venturing where he did not dare? Did he not, perhaps, envy women their privilege of worshiping the phallus? But, Frank asked himself, in fairness, arguing both sides of the case, can homosexual strands be entirely disentangled from heterosexual in that pink muck of carnal excitement, of dream made flesh, of return to the presexual womb?

More broadly, had he not felt more comfortable with his father than with his mother? Was not this in itself a sinister reversal of the usual biology? His father had been a genteel Fourth Street lawyer, of no particular effectuality save that most of his clients were from the same social class, with the same accents and comfortably narrowed aspirations, here on this plateau by the swelling Ohio. Darker and taller than Frank, with the same long teeth and primly set mouth, his father had had the lawyer's gift of silence, of judicious withholding, and in his son's scattered memories of times together—a trip downtown on the trolley to buy Frank his first suit, each summer's one or two excursions to see the Reds play at old Crosley Field—the man said little. This prim reserve, letting so much go unstated and unacknowledged, was a relief after the daily shower of words and affection and advice Frank received from his mother. As an adult he was attracted, he had noticed, to stoical men, taller than he and nursing an unexpressed sadness; his favorite college roommate had been of this saturnine type, and his pet tennis partner in Hastings, and artists he especially favored and encouraged—dour, weathered landscapists and virtually illiterate sculptors, welded solid into their crafts and stubborn obsessions. With these men he became a catering, wifely, subtly agitated presence that Sharon would scarcely recognize.

Frank's mother, once a fluffy belle from Louisville, had been gaudy, strident, sardonic, volatile, needy, demanding, loving; from her he had inherited his "artistic" side, as well as his pretty blondness, but he was not especially grateful. Less—as was proposed by a famous formula he didn't know as a boy—would have been more. His mother had given him an impression of women as complex, brightly colored traps, attractive but treacherous, their petals apt to harden in an instant into knives. A certain wistful pallor, indeed, a limp helplessness, had drawn him to Sharon and, after the initial dazzlement of the Avises of the world faded and fizzled, always drew him back. Other women asked more than he could provide; he was aware of other, bigger, warmer men they had had. But with Sharon he had been a rescuing knight, slaying the dragon of the winding Ohio. Yet what more devastatingly, and less forgivably, confirmed the rumor's essential truth than her willingness, she who knew him best and owed him most, to entertain it? Her instinct had been to believe Avis even though, far from run off, he was sitting there right in front of her eyes.

He was unreal to her, he could not help but conclude: all those years of uxorious cohabitation, those nights of lovemaking and days of homemaking ungratefully absorbed and now suddenly dismissed because of an apparition, a shadow of gossip. On the other hand, now that the rumor existed, Frank had become more real in the eyes of José, the younger, daintier of the two security guards, whose daily greetings had edged beyond the perfunctory; a certain mischievous dance in the boy's sable eyes animated their employer-employee courtesies. And Jennifer, too, the severely beautiful receptionist, with her rather Sixties-reminiscent bangs and shawls and serapes, now treated him more relaxedly, even offhandedly, as if he had somehow dropped out of her calculations. She assumed with him a comradely slanginess—"The boss was in earlier but she went out to exchange something at Bergdorf's"—as if both he and she were in roughly parallel ironic bondage to "the boss." Frank's heart felt a reflex loyalty to Sharon, a single sharp beat, but then he too relaxed, as if his phantom male lover and the weightless, scandal-veiled life that lived with him in some glowing apartment had bestowed at last what the city had withheld from the overworked, child-burdened married couple who had arrived fourteen years ago—a halo of glamour, of debonair uncaring.

In Hastings, when he and his wife attended a suburban party, the effect was less flattering. The other couples, he imagined, were slightly unsettled by the Whittiers' stubbornly appearing together and became disjointed in their presence, the men drifting off in distaste, the women turning supernormal and laying up a chinkless wall of conversation about children's college applications, local zoning, and Wall Street layoffs. The women, it seemed to Frank, edged, with an instinctive animal movement, a few inches closer to Sharon and touched her with a deft, protective flicking on the shoulder or forearm, to express solidarity and sympathy.

Wes Robertson, Frank's favorite tennis partner, came over to him and grunted, "How's it going?"

"*Fine,*" Frank said, staring up at Wes with what he hoped weren't unduly starry eyes. Wes, who had recently turned fifty, had an old motorcycle-accident scar on one side of his chin, a small pale rose of discoloration that seemed to concentrate the man's self-careless manliness. Frank gave him more of an answer than he might have wanted: "In the art game we're feeling the slowdown like everybody else, but the Japanese are keeping the roof from caving in. The trouble with the Japanese, though, is, from the standpoint of a marginal gallery like ours, they aren't adventurous—they want blue chips, they want guaranteed value, they can't grasp that in art, value has to be subjective to an extent. Look at their own stuff—it's all standardized. Who the hell can tell a Hiroshige from a Hokusai? When you think about it, their whole society, their whole success, really, is based on everybody being alike, everybody agreeing. The notion of art as a struggle, a gamble, as the dynamic embodiment of an existential problem, they just don't get it." He was talking too much, he knew, but he couldn't help it; Wes's scowling presence, his melancholy scarred face, and his stringy alcoholic body, which nevertheless could still whip a backhand right across the forecourt, perversely excited Frank, made him want to flirt.

Wes grimaced and contemplated Frank glumly. "Be around for a game Sunday?" Meaning, had he really run off?

"Of course. Why wouldn't I be?" This was teasing the issue, and Frank tried to sober up, to rein in. He felt a flush on his face and a stammer coming on. He asked, "The usual time? Ten forty-five, more or less?"

Wes nodded. "Sure."

Frank chattered on: "Let's try to get court five this time. Those brats having their lessons on court two drove me crazy last time. We spent all our time retrieving their damn balls. And listening to their moronic chatter."

Wes didn't grant this attempt at evocation of past liaisons even a word, just continued his melancholy, stoical nodding. This was one of the things, it occurred to Frank, that he liked about men: their relational minimalism, their gender-based realization that the cupboard of life, emotionally speaking, was pretty near bare. There wasn't that tireless, irksome, bright-eyed *hope* women kept fluttering at you.

Once, years ago, on a stag golfing trip to Bermuda, he and Wes had shared a room with two single beds, and Wes had fallen asleep within a minute and started snoring, keeping Frank awake for much of the night. Contemplating the unconscious male body on its moonlit bed, Frank had been struck by the tragic dignity of this supine form, like a stone knight eroding on a tomb—the snoring profile in motionless gray silhouette, the massive, scarred warrior weight helpless as Wes's breathing struggled from phase to phase of the sleep cycle, from deep to REM to a near-wakefulness that brought a few merciful minutes of silence. The next morning, Wes said Frank should have reached over and poked him in the side; that's what his wife did. But he wasn't his wife, Frank thought, though in the course of that night's ordeal, he had felt his heart make many curious motions, among them the heaving, all-but-impossible effort women's hearts make in overcoming men's heavy grayness and achieving—a rainbow born of drizzle—love.

At the opening of Ned Forschheimer's show—Forschheimer, a shy, rude, stubborn, and now elderly painter of tea-colored, wintry Connecticut landscapes, was one of Frank's pets, unfashionable yet sneakily salable—none other than Walton Forney came up to Frank, his round face lit by white wine and odd, unquenchable self-delight, and said, "Say, Frank, old boy. Methinks I owe you an apology. It was Charlie Whit*field*, who used to run that framing shop down on Eighth Street, who left his wife suddenly, with some little Guatemalan boy he was putting through CCNY on the side. They took off for Mexico and left the missus sitting with the shop mortgaged up to its attic and about a hundred prints of wild ducks left unframed. The thing that must have confused me, Charlie came from Ohio, too—Columbus or Cleveland, one of those. It was—what do they call it—a Freudian slip, an understandable confusion. Avis Wasserman told me Sharon wasn't all that thrilled to get the word a while ago, and you must have wondered yourself what the hell was up."

"We ignored it," Frank said, in a voice firmer and less catering than his usual one. "We rose above it." Walton was a number of inches shorter than Frank, with yet a bigger head; his gleaming, thin-skinned face, bearing smooth jowls that had climbed into his sideburns, was shadowed blue here and there, like the moon. His bruised and powdered look somehow went with his small, spaced teeth and the horizontal red tracks his glasses had left in the fat in front of his ears.

The man gazed at Frank with a gleaming, sagging lower lip, his near-sighted little eyes trying to assess the damage, the depth of the grudge. "Well, mea culpa, mea culpa, I guess, though I *didn't* tell Jojo and that *poisonous* Ed Jaffrey to go blabbing it all over town."

"Well, thanks for telling me, Wally, I guess." Depending on which man he was standing with, Frank felt large and straight and sonorous or, as with Wes, gracile and flighty. Sharon, scenting blood amid the vacuous burble of the party, pushed herself through the crowd and joined the two men. To deny Walton the pleasure, Frank quickly told her, "Wally just confessed to me he started the rumor because Charlie Whitfield downtown, who did run off with somebody, came from Ohio, too. Toledo, as I remember."

"Oh, that rumor," Sharon said, blinking once, as if her party mascara were sticking. "I'd forgotten it. Who could believe it, of Frank?"

"Everybody, evidently," Frank said. It was possible, given the strange, willful ways of women, that she had forgotten it, even while Frank had been brooding over its possible justice. If the rumor were truly dispersed—and Walton would undoubtedly tell the story of his Freudian slip around town as a self-promoting joke on himself—Frank would feel diminished. He would lose that small sadistic power to make her watch him watching waiters in restaurants, and to bring her into town as his chaperon. He would feel emasculated if she no longer thought he had a secret. Yet that night, at the party, Walton Forney's Jojo had come up to him. He had seemed, despite an earring the size of a faucet washer and a stripe of bleach in the center of his hair, unexpectedly intelligent and low-key, offering, not in so many words, a kind of apology, and praising the tea-colored landscapes being offered for sale. "I've been thinking, in my own work, of going, you know, more traditional. You get this feeling of, like, a dead end with abstraction." The boy had a bony, rueful face, with a silvery line of a scar under one eye, and seemed uncertain in manner, hesitantly murmurous, as if at a point in life where he needed direction. That fat fool Forney could certainly not provide that, and it pleased Frank to imagine that Jojo was beginning to realize it.

The car as he and Sharon drove home together along the Hudson felt close; the heater fan blew oppressively, parchingly. "*You* were willing to believe it at first," he reminded her.

"Well, Avis seemed so definite. But you convinced me."

"How?"

She placed her hand high on his thigh and dug her fingers in, annoyingly, infuriatingly. "You know," she said, in a lower register, meant to be sexy, but almost inaudible with the noise of the heater fan.

"That could be mere performance," he warned her. "Women are fooled that way all the time."

"Who says?"

"Everybody. Books. Proust. People aren't that simple."

"They're simple enough," Sharon said, in a neutral, defensive tone, removing her presumptuous hand.

"If you say so," he said, somewhat stoically, his mind drifting. That silvery line of a scar under Jojo's left eye . . . lean long muscles snugly wrapped in white skin . . . lofts . . . Hellenic fellowship, exercise machines . . . direct negotiations, a simple transaction among equals. The rumor might be dead in the world, but in him it had come alive.

[JUNE 1991]

VINCE PASSARO

My Mother's Lover

*Vince Passaro (1956–   ) grew up as an only child in Great Neck,
Long Island, in the apartment described in "My Mother's Lover." When
he was eighteen, his mother died, and soon afterward he left for Manhattan to attend Columbia University. He's lived in the city ever since. The
fiction he wrote in college he describes as "labored and sentimental and
awful. . . . I knew I would turn thirty before I would be much good." He
made his first appearance in Esquire at the age of thirty-five.*

I want to tell the truth about my
mother but what's the truth? She married late and badly and died when I was
eighteen and her youth is the hope of my imagination. I can barely see her as
young—by the time I was old enough to distinguish her, to take in her life as
something separate from mine, she was weary and ill and sadder than I knew how
to admit, not living exactly but going on. She had me; I was what she lived for.
We shared a small apartment with my grandmother, who sat in the corner most
of the day, watching television, looking out the window, with the passing seasons
more cranky, dissatisfied, and confused. It was an atmosphere of Irish fixity and
quiet, crammed with heavy furniture and lace doilies on which sat an occupying
army of figurines, small glass jars, delicate immovable objects from the past.

My mother was divorced, which was quite a sin in those days, a life-ending scandal. Our home's permanent, cloistered mourning didn't have so much to do with death as with celibacy and shame. I found things hidden in drawers: photographs, old jewelry, and notes and *Playbills*, evidence of my mother's freedom, her working days in New York. She had gone out in those days, to plays and restaurants and parties; she'd known whole rosters of people whose names could bring to her face a look of sly and wistful pleasure. Such people, it seemed to me, might have been among the powers that saved her. But I never really knew; when she talked about those times, which was rarely, she only talked about the other people, never herself. She lied, I think—she lied mainly by not saying things.

She talked a lot about Phil Schatz, her old boss, or at least she talked about him more than she did anyone else. Especially when I was younger, probably too young in her sense of it to *understand things,* she told me what a good dresser he was, how smart, how loud and funny, and how notoriously bad-tempered too—he kept everyone in the office afraid of him with his bellowing sarcasm. She had a special relationship with Phil Schatz. He never shouted at her that way. He respected her, she was bright and pretty and efficient and sharp-tongued herself, she could give as good as she got.

He liked to take her to restaurants for lunch. She began as his secretary but later became a kind of assistant, which meant he could invite her out to discuss business. What they usually did instead was eavesdrop on the people sitting near them. The people became characters; bits of stolen conversation became stories. And I formed an image of it, *my* story: my mother and her boss in close, silent, exchanging looks. My mother at twenty-two, her face near his face. His dark confidence, his foul language, his dirty jokes and booze. My mother, wool and silk, table linen and silver, a body beside his body in restaurants, amused, shocked, listening. My mother and an important, dangerous man.

Phil Schatz was handsome to the degree he was important. His face, with its rough features, might have been considered hawkish or vulgar-looking had it not also shown so much of his intelligence and confidence and success. He wore beautiful suits, or Peggy thought he did; she was no real judge. Walking out of the office with him, onto Forty-fifth Street and into the cold dampish evening, with the streetlights just on and people rushing along in the December early darkness with their bundles and bags, Peggy had what she thought of as "that Christmas feeling," a kind of electrical buzz, as if someone had given her a shot of something without her knowing. The year was 1948, when most of the boys were back from the war and housing was still so short. She was happy. She liked her job, she liked her life commuting from Darien and the big house on Relahan Road, where she and her sister and mother had moved from Brooklyn one year before, so her mother could take care of Auntie Murray, who was feeble now and confined to her room on the third floor. She liked Phil Schatz for asking her out to drinks, and she even liked the damp brisk air, a sharp reminder of the holiday and just-arriving winter. Phil took her to the Brass Rail. Sitting in one of the high leather banquettes, with a Manhattan on the rocks, she had a wonderful feeling about herself—she was twenty-two and slender, in her nicest dress (a gray wool houndstooth from Best's, with a collar and big black buttons down the front), she had green eyes and nice legs—she was filled with a sense of herself that was dramatic. Phil's hand touching hers on the table, his leg brushing hers underneath, they were real but they weren't, too; in some way they were just thoughts, extensions of her momentary electric vanity. There was desire in the way she felt, and anger too, a bit of spitfire revolution. She missed the 6:05 and the 6:30, would probably miss the 7:05 as well, and she was surprised by how little she cared.

A couple walked by the table—the man was big and the woman small, she wobbled a bit on her heels in the rug—and took the table behind Peggy's side of the banquette. Phil eyed the woman, he did it quickly but Peggy saw it, and then the waitress came and he ordered another round, their third. The first two drinks had made her feel wonderfully confident or powerful or at least safe. She liked Manhattans because of the spiced sweetness of the vermouth and the obscene red cherries, which rolled down to her mouth as she finished the drink, soaked in booze, lascivious. The swizzle sticks at the Brass Rail had little brass bells at the top, and she flicked hers with her nail from time to time, making it go tinkle-tinkle. "Tinkle-tinkle," she said, like a funny little alarm.

Not long after the drinks came, Peggy realized that the man and woman in the booth behind her were talking about going to a hotel together, their voices carried along the wall and around the banquette with a spooky clarity. Phil, a connoisseur of eavesdropping, a devoted voyeur, responded like a starving miner who'd found his mother lode. He pushed his head forward over the table and aimed his right ear over Peggy's shoulder. His face was a Medici in profile—long sharp nose, pointed lips, broad pale cheeks, high forehead. It shone with a kind of smirking greed, or not greed exactly, but avidness, a look she'd seen him get in the office, when he was winning something. For Peggy, an Irish girl raised in Brooklyn, sharp as a tack but less worldly than she seemed, this was the sexiest moment she'd ever had—Phil's head, the smell of his aftershave, the conspiracy in his small, dirty smile. She wanted to put her hands on his head and rub it, like a ball. Really she just wanted to put her hands *on him*, see what he felt like. She had drunk enough and was happy enough that there seemed to be no time at all between the realizing of things and the experiencing of them, something she usually had a lot of.

"What's the name of this place again?" asked the woman behind her.

"The Wellington," the man said. "Room four-twenty-eight." It was like a sergeant's voice, unpleasant and commanding. Peggy couldn't imagine going to a hotel with a man with a voice like that.

"The *Well*ington," Phil said, his voice low and phlegmy. "Jesus, what a romantic guy." The name didn't mean anything to Peggy, it was just a place she'd seen on one of the cross streets.

"The door'll be open," the man was saying. "Just breeze through the lobby, you know. Get on the elevator and ask for the fourth floor. Look like you know what's what and nobody'll bother you."

"Sounds like you've done this before," the woman said, laughing a little, a note in her voice, Peggy thought, less of protest than of come-on.

Phil wagged his head at Peggy and whispered, "Hey, no way, you're the *first*, baby." Peggy smiled but she was shocked too—at the way men lie and at the way they were *amused* at how they lie.

From behind, like an echo, the man said, "No, no, not at all—I just know my way around, that's all," and she and Phil almost broke out laughing, they barely kept it in, squirming in their seats, and there was Phil's knee again. The snuffled laughs and shifting around felt good, it felt like a high school kind of moment that Peggy could understand. Phil's knee was driving a wedge under her right thigh, which was crossed over the left. She knew that if she uncrossed her legs his knee would be almost in her crotch. Her shock was still there, she was aware of it the way you are aware of an oven, go near it and you feel the heat. She had pretended she knew what went on in the world, but really she had only known what she'd hoped and suspected. Like many of the Irish she'd grown up around, she had a keen appreciation for other people's sins and a grave fear of her own.

"And what're we going to do up there, play checkers?" the woman asked. The man laughed.

"We'll have a couple of drinks," he said. "Put on the radio and dance in our stocking feet."

"Drinks!" Phil said. "Stocking feet!"

When the couple left, Peggy saw the man place a proprietary hand under the woman's elbow—he was wearing a black, chalk-striped suit and brown shoes. He moved past with a swift muscularity, maneuvering the woman toward the coat check. He was a good-looking, broad-backed, dark-haired man. "Guinea," Phil said, answering a question no one had asked. Peggy had a sudden vision of the hotel room, the bed, the sheets, for some reason the man's long, broad feet, his brown shoes toppled on the floor below. A little inward shudder, a tremor. As the couple passed along the last row of tables, Phil turned to watch them, eyebrows raised, and there was something intense and awful in the pleasure he took in them; the word *agony* came into Peggy's mind. The woman was short and a bit round, a brunette. She looked like one of the girls from the secretarial pool—Peggy had developed a strong sense of the social distinction between girls in the pool and executive assistants. The man took the coats from the coat-check girl, his movements large and precise, and his face sported a look of grim satisfaction. Peggy watched him pull on his gloves. He looked twitchy, nervous, and too strong; he looked dishonest; he looked like a tyrant.

"You're staring," Phil said. He put two fingers almost tentatively under her chin, turning her face toward his. "Don't be so shocked," he said.

"I'm hungry," Peggy said.

"We'll get dinner," Phil said. The words planted a seed of panic in her; she didn't dare look at her watch. What happened to all that courage, all that pleasure in herself, the world, that wild, flushed, boozed-up vanity? The waitress came with another round. Phil asked for menus. Then he lifted his full glass and looked at it. "Here's to our drinks," he finally said. "Like our good friends, may there be many more."

Peggy raised her glass. "I'll drink to the laundry coming in," she said.

"What's that?" Phil asked.

"I said, 'I'll drink to the laundry coming home.' "

"I don't get it," Phil said.

"It's an expression," Peggy said. "Indicating, I guess, a willingness to celebrate any occasion."

"An Irish expression?" Phil said.

Peggy sipped her drink, her lips not quite in the liquor, just drawing it in across the top. At first it was cold and sweet, and then she felt the bite of it, going down. "Uh-huh," she said.

"Haven't you heard," Phil said, "that Jews don't drink?" His face usually had a thick, rubbery quality that made it volatile and communicative, a vibrating landscape of emotions, but right now it was slack.

"Yes," Peggy said.

"Why is that?" Phil said.

"I don't know," Peggy said. "Maybe the same reason they don't eat pork, they know it's bad."

"I'm a Jew," Phil said. "I drink, I eat pork, I guess that makes me bad."

"You're not bad," Peggy said. "You just don't feel very Jewish."

"Oh, I feel Jewish all right," Phil said. "You should see me at Tripler's, too frightened to buy a suit. Being Jewish right now—" he just left it there. Peggy said nothing. "What it is," he said finally, "is that you never forget. You buy a suit, you have a drink, you go to a play, whatever you do, you cooperate with the larger world, the la-la life, the gentiles, and you think, Why am I alive? Why me, why am I not dead?"

"Oh, that's crazy," Peggy said.

"It's not crazy," Phil said. "Not a bit."

Actually, Peggy knew it wasn't crazy.

"You get through it, but it's not crazy," Phil said. "And you think—this is the unbearable part—just to keep going you think, Okay, I don't care about the Jews. No matter what happened, *I'll* go on. Just living this life, doing all the same things. I don't care. If I cared I wouldn't be here. I'm not a Jew, not anymore."

Peggy traced lines on the tablecloth with the tip of the swizzle stick, holding it tight so that the bell made only a muffled, small *tink-tink-tink* as she scrolled. She said, "You can't figure out these things, why one person dies now and somebody else later, why lightning strikes one house and not another house, why you missed your seat on the *Titanic*, or whatever. The hairs on your head are numbered, but it's not a number you're ever going to know."

"I'm going to know it soon," he said, "the way things are going. The number's going to be three." The waitress came and Phil said: "We have to get something to eat, have you looked at that menu? A little girl like yourself, you drink this much without eating and you'll go into a coma." Peggy glanced at it and shook her head.

"You order," she said.

He ordered steaks and while he and Peggy waited for them the hostess came by with another couple and seated them at the table behind Peggy. Peggy caught only a glimpse of them.

"Another pair," Phil said.

"Maybe they're married," Peggy said.

"Not likely," Phil said.

So that's all there was, then—couples coupling. This shard of an island and people getting tight and screwing on it, in cheap hotels. There were no more houses on Relahan Road, no more of those pleasant gray-haired men on the train who struck up conversations with her and ended up taking out their wallets and showing her pictures of their sons in uniform, their daughters' weddings. They were all gone now, and nothing was left but this vulgar section of Manhattan, where broad-backed, dark-haired men put their hands on women. And the women did it back. It stunned her.

                      It was sometime after 10:00 when they finished dinner and left the bar, stepping out through the brass doors into a soft new padding of snow, a good two inches or more. Peggy's heart just sank away. What would it be in Connecticut now, six, seven? A blizzard?

"Look at that!" Phil said, childishly, full of pleasure. He meant the beauty and surprise of it—the theater lights along Seventh Avenue, the people wading slowly through the whiteness. A couple of cabs swished by, their hailing lights off, and after that, no traffic at all. In that still moment, everything looked like a fine photograph of itself, misty, mysterious, oddly lit. It was a Dickens-Christmas world, a ruddy-cheeked-children world, a chestnut-steaming window-frosted world that Peggy knew was a cheap lie. Phil gave Peggy his arm.

"I have to call home," Peggy said.

"Don't be nervous now," Phil said in a low, sweet voice. It sounded as if he were talking to a horse. They found a phone booth, Peggy stepped in and Phil crowded in after, kind of lodged himself in and pushed the door shut. People stared going by, amused. Peggy dialed the operator. She was really much shorter than Phil—she was aware of him as a breathing brown wool coat, snowflakes melting on his chest. The operator said the call would be thirty cents. Peggy had two dimes in her change purse. "Do you have a dime?" she asked Phil. He pulled his glove off, reached into his coat pocket and took out a handful of change, at least a couple of dollars' worth, almost enough change to equal the money Peggy carried with her every day. On an impulse, she snapped up half of it.

"Hey!" Phil said, pulling his hand back, too late. "I thought you only needed a dime!" Peggy had the phone between her shoulder and her ear; she raised an eyebrow at him.

"All's fair in love and war," she said. She put two quarters in the quarter slot on the telephone and dumped the rest of the change in her purse.

"Twenty cents credit," the operator said.

"Which is this, love or war?" Phil said.

The phone rang twice and Peggy's mother answered.

"Hello, Ma," Peggy said.

"It's eleven o'clock!" her mother said. There was a slight fraying edge to her voice that surprised Peggy, a hint of hysteria. "The lamb chops were ruined and I spilled the pan all over the floor and I had to use vinegar to get up the fat. Where are you?"

"I'm in New York, Ma," Peggy said. "Mr. Schatz took me to dinner. It's snowing."

"Of course it's snowing!" her mother said. "There's terrible snow up here."

"Listen, Ma, the trains might be slow or there might not be any. Don't worry about me."

"What are you going to do if there aren't any trains?" Kitty said.

"I don't know, we'll think of something," Peggy said.

"We'll think of something?" Kitty said. "Peggy, that man has to go home to his family. Where will you stay? You haven't a scrap of clothes or a nightgown or a bar of soap."

"Don't worry, Ma," Peggy said.

"You could take the subway out to Brooklyn and stay with Lily," Kitty said. "Oh, I'll feel terrible calling her at this hour."

"I've got to go," Peggy said.

She hung up and turned her body into Phil's. She thought her knees were going to give out; she needed some air. "Back up!" she ordered, and to her surprise, he did. She thought, No, I won't be sick, not here; she imagined the staring faces of all the handsome men and women of no belief on Seventh Avenue as they observed her bent over double outside the phone booth and spewing. And there was the image of her mother calling cousin Lily in Brooklyn, calling at 11:00 at night, to ask if her daughter could stay there because she was drunk and stranded in New York and loose with a married Jewish man, her boss. Peggy felt like a murderer, waking from forgetful sleep back to the nightmare of her own soul. She could not bear the thought of herself, could not bear it, could not bear it. Of all the things her sisters had done, her cousins had done, anyone in her circle of friends had done, no one had ever done anything like what she was about to do, at least not as far as she knew. They walked. Her red shoes passed through the white snow like a living stain.

"Let's go to a hotel, Peg," Phil Schatz said.

Peggy said nothing.

"Let's go to the goddamned Wellington," Phil said. She felt him slip and catch himself in the new snow.

"No, Phil."

"We could have a couple of highballs and dunz in our stogging feed. Goddamn door would be open. Wide as the pearly gates. We'd invite everybody. What do you say?"

"No, Phil."

"Let me tell you about places like the Wellington on scenic West Forty-fourth Street in Manhattan. Veneer furniture. Shitty foam mattress on a squeaking rotten bed. Overpriced, too. Snotty bellhops who pimp on the side. You could find happiness in a place like that. Call down for booze. Disappear for weeks at a time. Let me tell you, Peg, I feel very special about you."

"Please, Phil."

"I'm sorry," he said. He stopped and turned to her. "I'm sorry for speaking to you that way. I admit it, I was talking about doing dirty, rotten things. Dirty, rotten things that have kept life interesting from time immemorial. Men, women, the whole nine yards. Of course, you're a Catholic, and Catholics don't believe in stuff like that."

"It's not that we don't believe in them," Peggy said. "It's that we try not to do them."

"What happens when you *do* do them?" Phil said.

"We're sorry," Peggy said.

The snow was falling lightly and blowing off the awnings and car roofs in long, unpredictable gusts of wind. Peggy felt as if she and Phil were small figures in a swirling, gray movie scene, a majestic and sad long shot, angling in from overhead, two people trudging along beneath the streetlights, snow blowing like white curtains, the wind a large, strong hand jostling them, whiteness like a final, delicate truth lacing their hats and the shoulders of their coats.

And in a quiet and inaccessible part of Peggy's mind, she was thinking of her mother, waiting three or four hours without word, and of the trains, pushing gently through large drifts, or perhaps not, perhaps unable to push through, running as far north as Rye or New Rochelle or Greenwich. Or not running at all, resting in the long dark tunnels that descended slowly northward and came aboveground again at the foot of the hill that sloped into Harlem. What amazed her was a capacity, something she seemed to be acquiring just now, tonight, to live with these images of herself and the world. This, tonight, her slow walk down Forty-sixth Street, the drinks and dinner, listening to the uninspired seduction at the table behind her, struck Peggy as uncharacteristic in the extreme, or so she felt, but here she was doing those things, so perhaps they weren't; perhaps she was lying to herself, had always lied to herself, about what kind of person she was; perhaps adulthood meant the end of goodness, or made a lie out of the good child in her. They were walking toward Grand Central, so it was possible she would go home now, but even if there was a train, and she got on it, it would be too late; she knew what she had done and what she had failed to do. All this, the cold wind, the snow whipping against her skin like tacks, herself and a man beneath the silkened light of the swaying lampposts, her tumbling sense of timelessness and freedom, constituted the person she had become, and everything else, what she called her iron Irish virtues, were really just the fantasies of a zealous, impure Catholic girl.

"I'm so tired, Phil," she said. She stopped.

"Are you going to faint or what?" Phil said. He was her boss again, sympathetic but commanding. His arm around hers locked into place and gripped her. He was putting her under arrest. She started crying, she just wanted to cry and cry. She felt as if she'd lost everything she'd ever owned in some terrible snowy fire. Smoke rose from the steam holes behind him, everything wavered through her tears. She stepped into the big expanse of his fine wool. He held her there.

"Eleven-thirty-five is the last train," she said finally. "If there is one. What time is it now?"

"Eleven-thirty," he said.

"Oh, well," she said. "Oh well oh well oh well."

"Where are the matches?" Peggy said.

She was sitting in a low orange chair. Phil had taken his jacket off and was lying on one of the beds. "I don't know," he said. "A gentleman would get up and light your cigarette, although a gentleman might notice, as I do, that you don't have a cigarette to light."

Peggy was looking for a match because she couldn't quite remember the name of this hotel and it would be on the cover of the book. It wasn't the Wellington, she had made sure it wasn't the Wellington. They had been on the East Side by then anyway. She had had to wait in the hotel coffee shop while Phil checked into a room. He was gone long enough for a fellow in a gray hat to begin staring at her, until the counterman, a Greek, had come over and given the man a check and said, "Time to go, my friend," and the man had left. She had been grateful for that. She didn't tell Phil about it. It was over now, they had the room.

She found the matches; they were on the light table beside her. The name of the hotel was the San Dominico, that was right, like the Italian church on Third Avenue in Brooklyn.

"When I was a kid," she said, "the Italian funerals went by, sometimes three or four cars filled just with flowers, then the hearse, then thirty cars in the funeral parade, all big, dark, expensive cars. I thought the Italians must be fine people, they had such beautiful funerals."

"The Italians *are* fine people," Phil said, rising. He picked up the phone, tucked it under his ear. "I'm going to call room service." With the phone on his shoulder he looked as if he could get anything he wanted—the man lived to order other people around. Peggy took a cigarette out of the pack on the table; Phil reached into his pocket, took out a pack of matches, lit one, and held it toward her, all the while managing to keep the receiver snug against his ear. That's the kind of thing men can do, she thought, or some can, without even thinking about it.

"You had matches all the time," Peggy said.

"I told you I was a gentleman," he said. Then he held his finger to his lips to shush her. "Yeah," he said into the phone. "Room five-eleven. Yeah. Would you please send up a pack of L&M's, a bottle of Canadian Club, two glasses and some ice, and anything else?" He looked at Peggy.

"Orange juice," Peggy said.

"And orange juice," Phil said.

"And cinnamon toast," Peggy said.

"And some cinnamon toast," Phil said. "Two orders of that, it sounds good. Anything else?" Peggy shook her head. "That'll be it. Yeah. Okay." He hung up.

"Whenever we had a nickle to spend," Peggy said, "the other kids would buy candy or potato sticks but I would buy a pickle. I loved pickles."

"You loved pickles," Phil said. "With your nickels."

"And Italian funerals," Peggy said.

"Italians are fine fucking people," Phil said.

When room service came Phil kept the boy behind the door, took the tray from him, and paid him without letting him into the room; men, doing the dance of civilization and power; Phil would keep her modest in the eyes of the world, preserving from brash bellhop eyes her fallen soul. He brought the tray in and they sat on either side of the writing table and ate toast. Phil had a whiskey. Peggy drank the juice.

"We need *more* cinnamon toast," Peggy said.

"Do you want me to call down for more?" Phil said. "They charged me a buck for that, can you believe it? A buck for toast?"

"No, no more," Peggy said. "It's so late. *Sooooo* late."

They were quiet then. It lasted long enough for it to mean the next thing would be important. Finally, Phil stood. Seeing him do that made Peggy afraid. She would not show him that. She stood too.

"I should go," Phil said. She thought about her sister, the touring car they'd owned together, the trips they'd taken, two young women, alone, people thought they were crazy but they went everywhere, no fear. This is the thing they hadn't been afraid of. One-thirty in the morning, some man. They had never been afraid of it because it was outside the realm of possibility.

"What did you say?" Peggy said. She had lost the train of things.

"I said I should go," Phil said.

"You don't sound very convinced," Peggy said.

"I'm not," Phil said.

"It's all right, Phil," Peggy said. "You can stay." How difficult it was for her to say that—it was the price she was willing to pay for not being left alone now, drunk, in this place. That's what her morality and her sense of shame were bartered away for, not for any surging rush, not for any irresistible passion, but to avoid a certain kind of unacceptable solitude, the prospect of strangeness and panic. She stood there thinking about that for a while, for what seemed like quite a long while, really, many minutes, although it wasn't and she knew it wasn't, but it was a little while anyway, and everything was quiet. And then she did a peculiar thing. She took her dress off. She had been standing by the bed, and she was very, very tired, and taking her dress off seemed the natural thing to do, in the bedroom, ready to go to sleep, standing by the bed. To her, there was an enormous chasm of time between when she'd said to Phil, "You can stay," and when she took her dress off. In her mind, the two weren't related at all. She lay down in her slip and stockings and that felt good, and then Phil was lying down beside her.

She was a Republican—that's what she found herself thinking—she had never been able to stand Roosevelt, thought he was an elitist and a phony; she was a Republican for the same reason she suspected Phil was a Republican, because that was the *class* thing to be, something that set her apart from the rowdy, thoughtless, unsophisticated Brooklyn Irish in her, her family. She was a Republican and now look at her, in a hotel room with a Jew. Phil was remarkably light, getting into the bed. She would have figured a man like that, all rough talk, pugnacious, high-strung, would be more clumsy, bring more mass and momentum to the thing, charge right in there, but he lay down with the delicacy of a child. And then she had to laugh. How the hell should she know who should lie down like what?

"What are you smiling about there?" Phil said. She was lying on her back, looking at the ceiling, and he was on his side with his arm across her, his hand sunken in between her hip and her ribs on the far side of her, gripping her the way you would if you were about to shake someone lightly awake.

"*I'm* very experienced," Peggy said. "*I'm* wise in the ways of the world, though I may not look it." She laughed again, more like a cough than a laugh, her shoulders rose and fell. Phil's hand went gripping up her side, over her arm and onto her shoulders, as if with their little jump just then they had spoken up to get his attentions. Peggy closed her eyes and saw a crowd, hundreds and hundreds of people in wool coats going by, and banks of telephone booths, and long lines of people waiting to use them. There were such long lines during the war, and her mother had stood in most of them. One time she had waited an hour or more on a cigarette line, she didn't smoke but her daughters did, and cigarettes were short, except when she made it to the front and the man offered her two cartons, she'd said, "Oh, that's not my daughters' brand," and left without buying any. Everyone howled over that one.

Phil was kissing her neck. "I want a cigarette," Peggy said. His face was rough on her skin, his head like a little baby squirming on her shoulder. She thought about Christmas—a woman lying like this, naked and dazed in a strange place, holding the blind sucking infant. "Phil, the cigarettes," she said. He reached behind him to the nightstand and grabbed the pack and matches and handed them to her. He nuzzled all around toward the back of her neck, under her hair. She put a cigarette in her mouth with her free hand, the other one she had to wriggle out from under him to light the match. She ended up turning toward him then, presenting her chest, hugging him, really, and it felt awfully good to be against him. She reached her arms around his head and lighted the match and it glared beyond the line of his skull like a bomb going off over a distant, blank horizon. His large head—it made her think of the earth. Phil brought his head around, under her chin, across her chest, to the other side of her neck; she blew smoke above him. Lips and hands, his leg finally up where it had been trying to go all night, between her legs, solid and warm there. With his weight on her and his legs twined with hers, she finally understood the architecture of the act. She had always secretly fretted about this, imagining her wedding night, as if making love would be a test of her engineering capacities, of which she had none.

"Practice," she whispered.

"What?" Phil said.

"This is practice," she said. She raised herself slightly, stabbed the cigarette out in the ashtray, and lay back down. She held his head, she loved his round head. He kissed her. Her eyes closed; she felt herself falling into soft warm air, falling and falling. Phil started to pull at her slip, and she had a moment's panic, a rush of terrible guilt, it made her heart race. But it passed; her awareness moved from the largeness of sin to the kingdom of mercy, as if it were coming up for air, seeing the world for the first time, like a baby. And she felt something else too, something as big as the planet. She felt as if she understood the dumb earth, she knew what it was doing. To her it was a lone, determined soul—ignorant, wary and slow, spinning in vast silence around the single light that guides it.

That's all I can say. What I knew of her later, her deepening sadness, her avoidance of men, and her devotion to her mother, it might have begun that day or later. She admired Phil Schatz, I know that much, so if she felt badly afterward, she felt badly about herself and not him. My mother probably recognized by instinct that Phil Schatz was too certain of himself, too reliable, too likely to succeed on a grand scale for her to ever cling to. Despite her Republicanism, the grand scale was not the scale she cared for. She had an orthodox reaction to false gods and tyrants and a keen appreciation of the Fall, and she gave her love eventually to a much weaker man, a more obviously vulnerable and kinder man—*a guinea salesman*, Phil Schatz would have called him, though he was more than that. He was my father. I was a year and a half old when they split up. She never looked at a man after that, as far as I know, though she was only thirty-one. She stayed with her mother, went to mass every Sunday, and raised me. The minute I was grown, she died.

[JULY 1992]

ETHAN CANIN

Accountant

*Now a medical intern in San Francisco, Ethan Canin (1960–   )
grew up primarily in California. While in high school, he took a writing
class from the romance novelist Danielle Steel. After college, he attended
the Iowa Writers' Workshop and then entered Harvard Medical School.
His collection of lyrical and moving short stories, <u>Emperor of the Air</u>,
was published in 1988 and won the Houghton Mifflin Literary Fellowship. A novel, <u>Blue River</u>, appeared in 1991. According to Canin,
"Accountant" in all likelihood marks his last literary output until he
finishes his medical training.*

I am an accountant, that calling of exac-
titude and scruple, and my crime was small. I have worked diligently, and I do
not mind saying that in the conscientious embrace of the ledger I have done well
for myself over the years, yet now I must also say that due to a flaw in my
character I have allowed one small trespass against my honor. I try to forget it.
Although now I do little more than try to forget it, I find myself considering and
reconsidering this flaw, and then this trespass, although in truth if I am to look
at them both, this flaw is so large that it cannot properly be called a flaw but my
character itself, and this trespass was devious. I have a wife and three children.
My name is Abba Roth.

I say this as background, that is all. I make no excuses for myself, nor have I ever. The facts are as follows: We live in San Rafael, California, and I work at Farmer, Priebe & Emond, the San Francisco firm where I have worked since the last days of the Eisenhower administration. At one time or another we have owned a Shetland pony, dug a swimming pool, leased a summer cottage at Lake Tahoe, and given generously to the Israel General Fund, although all that we still do is lease the cottage. My wife's name is Scheherazade and she will not answer to Sherri, her childhood appellation, anymore. We have two daughters, Naomi and Rachel, and a son, whose name is Abba, after his great-grandfather, although I know this name is no longer in fashion.

Recently a man I have known all my life called me at my office, and this was how this incident began. His name is Eugene Peters. We grew up together in Daly City, California, a suburb of San Francisco that, like accounting, has become the object of some scorn by particular segments of society. A popular song has been written on the theme that all the homes in Daly City are identical, although this happens not to be correct. In reality there were any number of different architectural plans used in the neighborhood where Mr. Peters and I grew up, although by coincidence he and I did in fact grow up in houses that happened to be from the same one. The plans, of course, had been reflected on an axis so that each house became the mirror image of the other—each contained a living room, with the kitchen set in a side bay, two bedrooms off a short hallway, a basement downstairs, and on the garage side of the front yard a palm that in our childhoods grew from a seedling to the height of the roof. His room abutted from the left of the upstairs hall, as mine did, in our own house, from the right; their bathroom from the right of the same hall and ours from the left, et cetera, so that it sometimes struck me as odd when the floors and walls in his house were covered with furnishings belonging to his parents and not to my own. We rode bicycles and later drove in his Buick Century; later still, we double-dated, and we played on the baseball team together. I played third base and Eugene, whose father had gone to Notre Dame with the coach of our team, played shortstop. I know it is commonly assumed that a shortstop has better range than a third baseman, but in this case I can attest that such was not the case. In those days, Eugene and I spent nearly all of our afternoons together after school. He had a sister, as did I, and his father was never at home, as was mine, and so in a funny way in our identical houses it might have seemed for a while that our families were interchangeable. We washed his car together, we learned to ice-skate and for a time spent our afternoons in the frosty, round rink, trying to catch the skates of girls in earmuffs who glided past us snapping their gum.

We learned to roll cigarettes that burned evenly and to drink whiskey without coughing.

However, there came a time when our lives diverged. After high school I was able to benefit from the discipline my father had bestowed upon us even in his general absence and go to the state university, where I began to pursue a degree in accounting. At this point our separation became clear to us both. Mr. Peters had taken a job in an auto-parts dealership, stocking inventory at the time I was learning the indifference curves and just beginning to understand where the intersection of supply and demand could be found for an inelastic commodity, such as city water. He found new friends at the auto warehouse and I began to live my life with no friends at all. I attended school in the day, answered telephones in a hospital in the evening, and studied at night. Whenever I saw him at that time he teased me for still living at home, although he well knew why I did.

To clarify: It became apparent that we had diverged because he was interested in the present and I was interested in the future. I do not mind saying that accounting did not come easily for me and I was studying strenuously. However, I did not waver from my commitment to it. In fact, I came with time to see that it contained a natural eloquence, unbent by human will, and that it was a more profound language than the common man might have assumed. Indeed, at times I felt it was capable of explaining not only outlays and receipts but much of the natural world. It was only rarely, late at night with my books of tax law and microeconomics, that I occasionally indulged the small daydream that I might leave my studies and instead become a professor of music history at a small college. However, I rarely indulged this thought. Indeed, I came with time to cherish my daydream for the principal reason that it challenged and therefore reinforced my resolve to make something of myself. Sitting at the window in the library, where the septate leaves of a Japanese maple brushed the glass, I would look up from Samuelson and allow my mind to wander to the first movement of Berlioz's *Requiem,* or to the second movement of Beethoven's Seventh Symphony, wherein the strings, though barely moving, weep for humankind. Then, deliberately, I would snap back to the Samuelson text and redouble the efforts that had brought me near, I do not mind saying, to the top of my class of accounting students.

Again, I say this as background. Once a week I spent the whole night awake with my books, and I took no time away except Sunday mornings, when I ate breakfast with my family, and Saturday nights, when I allowed myself a date if I could find one or a movie if I could not. Needless to say, this regimen produced a commendable record at my graduation, which Mr. Peters attended, although he did not dress correctly.

He wore a baseball cap, and I could not help noticing—and I do not mind saying this with some satisfaction—that while I was graduating with honors in business accounting, my friend seemed to want nothing more than to stock gaskets and price piston rings until the short hair at his temples turned gray.

However, shortly after I graduated and took a job with Farmer, Priebe & Emond, Mr. Peters approached me and asked for a $1,000 investment in a concern he claimed to be starting that was going to manufacture magnetic oil plugs. At the time he approached me, we hadn't spoken since my commencement exercises. He came to my office, again in a baseball cap. The idea was simple, he said: The magnetic plug would collect the flecks of engine metal that ordinarily circulated in the dirty oil and caused abrasion damage to the pistons and cylinders. Engine life would therefore be extended.

I was unsure whether any of the managing partners had seen him enter my office in a billed cap, and it goes without saying that I felt some discomfort at having him there. I was still new at the firm. To be frank, the idea seemed like a good one, but since I had just spent four years in school all day, at work all evening, and at my desk half the night while he was idling his days at a warehouse and his evenings at bars, I asked him instead whether he had ever considered the flexibility of consumer demand for his product. I asked him this instead of giving him the money. He left our offices still trying to give the pitiful impression that he had understood my question, and I went back to my job, where in six months I had made my first advancement.

However, the fact is that three years later his company employed twelve men, was doing $2.3 million in gross sales, and was rumored to be considering a public offering. Mr. Peters had been profiled in the business section of the newspaper, and in that photograph he wore the same baseball cap he had worn at my commencement and in my office. Indeed, the cap seemed to have become a sort of symbol for him, although I do not know of what. The magnetic oil plugs had been picked up by at least two major auto-parts chains and I saw them for sale everywhere I went. I changed the supermarket where I shopped because one day I found the oil plugs for sale there. My friend's company had also begun manufacturing an auto emergency kit that sold well to women and accounted for a good deal of his profits. He was diversifying. Though we didn't speak anymore, I saw him driving a blue Chrysler New Yorker and heard through our old friends that he had bought a sixteen-room house in Hillsborough and a villa at Lake Tahoe with boat bays. By now several of our high school classmates worked for him.

I myself was not making a bad salary at the time. In fact, I was doing quite well, and I do not mind saying that if not for the success of my friend I would have considered myself perfectly fortunate in my business advancement. Mr. Emond, the elder partner at my firm, had taken an interest in me, and by working late and servicing extra accounts I had elicited a promise from him that I would be made partner within five years.

At this point, I decided to marry. At the time I was seeing two girls, LeAnne and Scheherazade. LeAnne was the assistant in the office of my dentist, and one morning while she was placing the light-blue paper bib around my neck for a teeth cleaning, I asked her outright to have dinner with me. I fell in love with her immediately. On one of our early evenings together, at a moderately expensive Greek restaurant, a man at the next table suffered a coronary, and without hesitation LeAnne moved aside the furniture and laid him down while she kept her hand on his pulse until the ambulance arrived. That kind of level-headedness attracted me. On another occasion a skirt she had purchased at a department store ripped along a seam and LeAnne took it back, where she had to speak not just with a salesclerk but with the manager of the entire operation. Though he tried to intimidate her, saying she had purchased it on sale, LeAnne persisted and gained the return of her money. I don't mind saying that this kind of respect for the value of a dollar won my heart as well.

At the same time, I was seeing Scheherazade. In my situation I felt that I needed some objectivity, and this was what Scheherazade became for me. As I found myself falling further in love with LeAnne, I went on more dates with Scheherazade. During the course of one evening with her we came upon the scene of an auto accident, and instead of getting out to help, as LeAnne might have done, Scheherazade pressed me to drive on and nearly fainted from the sight as we passed. I became more convinced of my love for LeAnne. Furthermore, when we dined out Scheherazade ordered smoked-salmon appetizers and baked desserts that she left mostly untouched on her plate. Of course, I had enough money to pay for the whole menu had she chosen to order it, but still this represented a certain difference between her and LeAnne.

In fact, there was only one incident that made me consider Scheherazade more seriously. As I did with LeAnne as well, Scheherazade and I occasionally went to the symphony. At the concerts I was always proud to be seen with LeAnne, for she wore elegant though simple dresses and spoke with a level eye to whomever we met. Scheherazade sometimes came in sleeveless gowns and heels that had been embedded with glitter, her lips made up in sienna-colored lipstick and her hair tossed over her head and stuck with a pearl-headed stickpin. In general I preferred going with LeAnne. As I have said, my small dream was to become a professor of music, and it was not insignificant that LeAnne always read the back notes to the program. She always knew something of the composer's life for our discussions after the concerts, whereas Scheherazade, who often appeared to be dreaming during the performance, often did not even know who had written the evening's music.

One night, however, during an intermission after we had heard Berlioz's *Romeo and Juliet*, Scheherazade waited on the open-air balcony while I purchased soft drinks for us at the bar. When I came out I found her leaning against the railing, and in the lights of the city square below I could see that she was weeping. Full streams of tears were on her cheeks. I asked her what was wrong and she only shook her head. I tried to think about what might have occurred in her life. As I stood there with the two soft drinks I asked her if her mother's health was still good. I asked if there had been an embarrassment at work or with one of her friends. I asked her about her brother, who had recently moved to New York. I asked her if she needed money. Finally, I left her alone. I moved to the balcony rail and reviewed some pension documentation that I had been working on that morning. Suddenly it occurred to me that she was crying over the music. I am not embarrassed to say that this touched a part of me quite deeply, and I felt grateful to have finally understood. I myself have never cried at anything, not at a movie or at a play or at a concert, and I don't see why it should have pleased me that Scheherazade had. But it did. It was a small thing, but I didn't think LeAnne would have done it.

In the spring after I was promised the partnership in my firm, I decided to ask LeAnne to marry me. I placed a deposit hold on a one-and-a-half-carat diamond ring and began to plan my proposal. The days were growing longer, and often in the evenings we took walks in the pale-green hills south of San Francisco. Behind me on those paths the determined sound of her breath filled me with the sense that the future was ours. A culmination was building, and one evening in those hills I realized that such would be the place to propose. The next night we walked up a new trail and in the distance I saw a small, level plot of ground that looked out over all of San Francisco Bay and the foothills across it to the east. I pretended to twist my ankle and prevailed on LeAnne to turn around before she saw the vista, but I decided that at this spot in two weeks' time I would ask her to be my bride.

However, as soon as I made this decision I began to see her in another light.

Suddenly her practical nature became a sort of shrewishness. Her steady de-meanor became a source of irritation and an indication that in certain situations she might become unbending. By this point I had added to my holding deposit on the ring and was well along toward its purchase. Sometimes I looked at LeAnne and it was as if a demon had taken hold of my soul. I saw her pettiness and the unchangeable tenacity of her perceptions. I began to regard her thriftiness as penury and her practical nature as mannish. One night at a concert she remarked that ticket prices were certainly going to increase next season, and suddenly I found myself thinking back on the night Scheherazade had wept on the balcony.

Now, I have always considered myself a practical man. That is what an accountant is paid for. He is not paid to encourage foundless business schemes nor to weep at public concerts. When an accountant considers a decision, he extrapolates to outcomes and weighs the assets and liabilities. However, two weeks later when I made the final payment on the ring I found myself offering it to Scheherazade and not to LeAnne, and seven months later in the ballroom at the Clift Hotel, Scheherazade and I were dancing at our wedding.

I must add that our marriage has now lasted nearly three decades, and even as our passion has subsided it has been replaced by a spring of tenderness and gratitude at which I drink now as reverently as a pilgrim. I have never said this before, however, and I do not like to say it now, but I must also add that on the day of our wedding I felt gloomy. When the rabbi signaled past the congregation for my bride to approach, my heart leaped in panic, and when he gestured to the cantor at the blessing, I felt doomed. This is a secret I have carried forth into the twenty-nine years of our life together. During this time, by the way, careful conversation has divined that a similar feeling was present in the hearts of several of my fellow accountants during their own nuptials.

It has not escaped my attention that perhaps Scheherazade sensed my gloom, and it was for this reason that she began spending my money like a bandit. In one year, unable to settle on a pattern for our living-room drapes, she installed three separate sets. Our living room, I should add, is large, and so are its windows. Of course, I could afford ten sets of drapes, but that is not the point.

I did not mention the money to her, because it was my duty to provide and that is what I was doing. In fact, I spent little for myself. This, as everyone knows, is a value instilled in childhood, and I have my own mother to thank for it. When the soles of my shoes wore through, I repaired them with vinyl glue, as my mother used to do with my father's, and when my barber began charging sophisticated rates for his haircuts, I went elsewhere. However, though I had intended to reduce our monthly expenditures by such practices, I soon understood that I would not be able to.

It was as though the more I tried to economize, the more she tried to waste. I began servicing extra accounts during my lunch hour, while at auction one day Scheherazade purchased a small etching by Goya, in front of which I found her standing when I returned home from the office. It was only a few inches tall, depicting a farmhouse and several chickens, yet she had placed it in the center of our living-room wall. Over the course of months I saw that she was capable of standing before it for a half-hour at a stretch, and I must concede that at times like this I felt no closer to understanding my wife than I would have been to a Pygmy. The following year she purchased a terra-cotta figurine from the Han Dynasty, smaller than my thumb, which she set on our mantel and which now and then I found her holding in her hands, late at night, when I ventured downstairs for seltzer water.

Nonetheless, I soon grew accustomed to our charge-account balances, and in the decade before our children were born, we reached an equilibrium in our marriage. Indeed, these were the first times in which I can say that I was blissfully content. Thursday evenings at the symphony we stood outdoors on the octagonal balcony at intermission, and while Scheherazade gazed dreamily over the square, I pursued in my mind some of the tax shelters and bankruptcy manipulations that had become a standard part of my practice. Such evenings were the embodiment of happiness for me. I felt I was about to be made partner and had again heard news to that effect from Mr. Emond. My salary was as high as I had ever hoped to earn, and with stock options I could look forward to being a reasonably wealthy man in a decade.

Mr. Peters, however, had in the meantime expanded his auto-parts business into four factories in three states and had opened a chain of retail outlets. Furthermore, he had for some reason seized on the idea of baseball as a theme for his advertisements, which began to appear in the newspaper. I do not see what the connection is between automobile parts and our national pastime, but a smiling portrait of Eugene Peters wearing his baseball cap began to appear in the corner of these announcements, accompanied by slogans like Doubleheader Sale or All-Star Prices.

One evening, while watching the seven o'clock news, I was startled to see that he had begun purchasing television commercials also, and that he himself narrated them. Again, he wore the baseball cap. Needless to add, I soon found them on my car radio as well when I drove to work in the morning, although I cannot say with certainty whether he was the narrator of these. It does not take a professional psychologist to observe that he was probably attempting to compensate for his two seasons of high school play, which were stellar neither at bat nor in the field. Within a short space of time, a number of retired professional players began making cameo appearances at the end of these ads. These were minor players, such as the backup catcher for the World Champion 1954 Giants and a utility infielder from the team of 1962, and I will not bother with their names. However, I suppose it meant he was hobnobbing with these retired athletes, and I do not know why, but this thought irritated me. Though I had no desire to know of his successes, I found myself reading certain items in the business pages. The $1,000 he had once asked me for might well have been a small fortune by now, and I myself might have been hobnobbing with these players, but by a simple act of will I was able to put this from my mind.

At home Scheherazade became pregnant with Naomi. I will remember the day I learned I was to become a father because my wife called me at work, which she rarely did, and because when I came home that day I found that she had purchased for herself an ermine stole. I do not mind saying that the sight of the ermine hanging in our closet when I went to hang my own raincoat was more than I ordinarily would have tolerated, but Scheherazade had just announced that a baby was forthcoming and I felt in no position to object. In June Naomi was born.

It was about this time that Mr. Peters entered our lives again. We received a letter inviting us to dinner, which I accepted, although the letter had been written by his secretary. I had Naomi's college education to plan for now and was ready to consider and yet remain prudent about any business offer he might make. Naomi's money was in government bonds. Sensing that he would be asking me for another investment, I prudently calculated what I could afford to risk on a venture such as his. I arrived at a sum that, I do not mind saying, would have pleased him.

Mr. Peters and Scheherazade and I met at the Squire Restaurant in the Fairmont Hotel, where we ate an elaborate dinner that included a bottle of Burgundy dating from the Second World War and a bottle of port dating from the First. Although needless to say I would not have ordered these vintages myself, I nonetheless attempted to pay for them at the end of the meal. Mr. Peters, however, had evidently made a prior arrangement with the waiter. I have gone over in my mind several times what occurred that evening. I had a reasonably pleasant time and I think he did, too. However, at the end of our meal

Scheherazade without hesitation ordered two different desserts, eating only one of them, and partially. Mr. Peters did not seem to mind, and he even joked about it. However, he made no business offers.

         In short succession Rachel and Abba were born. I had not yet been made partner at the firm because the position of Mr. Emond had been temporarily weakened, yet my own standing was still strong and I was earning in two months what my father used to earn in a year. I had developed a technique that was quite successful in recruiting new clients. I would take them to a meal at a nearby restaurant that had arrangements with the firm, where I would talk about professional sports or, if I could discern a leaning, the current political situation. I would not mention any business proposal until the table had been cleared. At this point, the maître d' would approach, recognize me by name, and offer us a digestif as his guest. This, as I said, was by arrangement, and though I always asked for Grand Marnier, I was brought Scotch whisky instead in a snifter, which it was my standard practice to then drain in a single draft. The whisky could be counted on in the course of seconds to bring about a temporary, garrulous ease that I exploited by leaning toward the potential client and saying in an offhand way that came easily after the cocktail, "Say, I bet they sock you at tax time."

Every partner at the firm had such a method, in one form or another, that produced results, and over the experience of numerous years I found that my particular entreaty worked quite well with the genre of client with whom I had most contact, specifically attorneys and physicians and the not infrequent movie or television actor—members of the professions, in other words, that required a certain ease with the public. Of course, I could vary my approach. Meeting, as we sometimes did, with the financial staff of corporations, I would certainly not try the entreaty of being "socked at tax time." In those situations, of course, Mr. Farmer or Mr. Priebe or Mr. Emond was present alongside, and the entreaty was a formal one, made in advance of the meeting, carefully considered against competing bids and factually represented in documents.

In summary, I was able to do well at the firm, where I earned a good salary and good bonuses and was well on my way to a partnership, although I suppose I should mention another incident that occurred several years ago. At the time, the firm still went by the name Priebe & Emond, as Paul Farmer had not yet been made a principal. One morning before most of the other accountants were at their desks and none of the secretaries had yet arrived, Mr. Priebe appeared in my doorway and asked in a low voice whether I was free to see him in his office. There, we sat in the two padded chairs next to his window, which looked out over the Bay Bridge to the north and the shipyards to the east. Noticing that I was interested in the view, he chatted for several minutes about the enormous tonnage of concrete contained within the bridge's bulwarks; then he abruptly turned to the wall and asked me if I knew anything of what had been recently occurring in the savings-and-loan industry. Being familiar with the trade journals, I replied that I knew something of what was occurring then. It is important to note that this meeting between Mr. Priebe and myself occurred at least two years before the savings-and-loan affair became known to the public. Mr. Priebe then looked me in the eye and asked me what I would think of an accountant who knowingly doctored books to protect the partners in a government-backed savings institution. I understood that I was under consideration for a partnership at the firm and knew immediately that this was a test of my moral principles. "I would not approve," I responded.

"I didn't think you would," said Mr. Priebe, nodding, and then he rose to shake my hand, signaling that our meeting was over. Two days later, Mr. Emond entered my office during the lunch hour and told me that he had heard what had happened and was proud of my response. I myself was as well, of course, and I continued my regular duties with increasing expectation of a promotion. However, within a month it was Mr. Farmer who had received the partnership.

It is fruitless for me to speculate about what had occurred, although I did notice that prior to his promotion Mr. Farmer had become more secretive about his work and was now often already in the office when I arrived in the morning. That is all I will say about this matter.

Without omitting anything of importance, I have skipped to the year when Naomi was fifteen, Rachel thirteen, and Abba nine. To my astonishment the children had grown up each with a distinct personality. Naomi was dark in all her features, in her hair and skin and the cast of her eyes, and dark in her character as well. In our garden she sat in the plum tree's deep shade, and at the table she ate without speaking. She had found a natural kinship with my wife that at times pleased me, for Naomi was my favorite, but I must say that at other times I felt the two of them were in collusion against me. They often went shopping together and sometimes returned with several twine-handled bags that they refused to open for me, laughing darkly to each other while they brought them upstairs to the bedrooms. At home Naomi often sat by herself. The brooding postures she assumed and the reticence with which she expressed her affections made her occasional demonstrations of love exquisite morsels that I pined for. Sometimes while I worked at my desk upstairs she would enter my study, walk up behind me, and without saying anything place a hand on each of my shoulders. If I spoke she withdrew them, so that often I did my work silently, scrutinizing the account books of physicians and attorneys while in the corner of my vision the dark fingers of my daughter lay unmoving. We hardly ever spoke. I believe she knew she was my favorite and for a reason I do not understand, this excited in her a sense of injustice. Her tastes, like my wife's, were extravagant.

Rachel, on the other hand, was everything Naomi was not. She had blond hair and pale, warm skin that rushed to color when she was excited, which was often. Whereas Naomi at the age of thirteen had worn small pearl earrings, Rachel wore boys' sneakers and dressed in the same dungarees for a week. Rachel sat in the open, sunlit portion of our yard and practiced her field hockey in our living room. When I returned from work she hugged me around the legs and begged for a ride on my feet, which I more often than not gave her, holding her by her pale arms and lifting her small sneakers across the Afghani carpet atop my oxfords, which I did not mind shining again later. On Sundays Rachel dusted the windowsills without being asked and emptied the small inlaid wastebasket in my study. I often found my pencils sharpened and the clips and erasers arranged in rows in my desk, and I made sure to thank Rachel whenever this occurred. Rachel, I believe, knew that Naomi was my favorite, though it is odd to think that in Naomi this situation produced forlornness and brooding, while in Rachel it created only exuberance.

As for Abba, he was a son and his childhood passed without the trouble and wondering I had found with my daughters. I bought him baseball gloves and football cleats and felt certain this was enough to pass him forward through his boyhood. He had an even disposition. He spoke softly and in general took easily to the world. He had no problems with his friends or with his teachers, and he seemed to have missed his sisters' propensity to spend my money. Indeed, if it were not for Scheherazade's intervention, I believe he might never have bought a thing for himself.

As I said, this was not true for my daughters. When Naomi was sixteen, for example, she decided she wanted a horse. Her high school offered an equestrian course and against my wishes she had learned to ride. One night soon after, she brought up the idea of owning a horse, and in response I could not help snorting, much like a horse myself. My own father was a wristwatch salesman and I told Naomi that the descendants of such people did not own horses. Some of them *shod* horses, I said, but none owned them. Naomi furrowed her dark brow. I thought the matter was ended, but several days later Scheherazade turned over in bed and mentioned that Naomi was at a brooding age and perhaps I ought to consider her request.

We bought the horse from a young man who lived in a mansion in Woodside. He wore riding breeches that looked as if they had been ordered from a men's catalogue, and when I gave him my check he asked to see my driver's license. Naomi mounted the beast, and as she sat there it stamped its hooves and flared its agate-colored nostrils. "Thank you, Daddy," she said as she turned and started around the show-ring.

The animal had cost as much as an automobile, and as she paraded it around the ring, her back arched, her high boots pressed into its flanks, I quickly calculated the feed and stable costs on a per-year basis. We had it boarded in a private stable. Like Naomi, the animal turned out to have a dark temperament, and like Naomi's, this temperament was most prominent in regard to its benefactor. Naomi named him Dreamboat, which I did not like. I did not believe that a horse could differentiate among human beings; whenever I approached, however, Dreamboat flared his nostrils and snorted, and whenever I spoke he stamped his hooves. The thought occurred to me that he knew who had written the check for his purchase. On the other hand, whenever Naomi or Rachel or Scheherazade spoke to him, he flicked his tail and bowed his protuberant head, and whenever they approached with oats, he blinked his eyes like a lover. Abba, for his part, took after me and did not seem to notice the beast. For several months Naomi rode every day, and then she began riding a few times per week, and soon after she stopped riding altogether. Dreamboat developed an infection in his leg. Antibiotics were needed, and when these failed, a veterinary surgeon. Up until that time I had thought there was no professional more expensive than a physician. Dreamboat never recovered, and a year later he was taken from his agony.

▎ I shall not mention other examples of the spendthriftery that was a disease in my house. As I have said previously, at one time or another we have dug a pool in our backyard, leased a condominium near the beach at Lake Tahoe, and given to a number of my wife's charities. All the while I had three children in private schools and was afflicted with the standard concerns of any father. Scheherazade had never worked and I needed to think of her security should something happen to me. And after private high school, of course, our children would expect private college.

Therefore, it was with careful consideration that I reacted when, shortly over one month ago, I again had contact with Eugene Peters. I was working at my desk at Farmer, Priebe & Emond when Mrs. Polaris, my secretary, came on the speakerphone to inform me that Mr. Peters was on the line. Naturally this was a surprise, he and I not having spoken in several years, since the evening of our fruitless dinner at the Fairmont Hotel. I organized the papers I was studying, a rather complicated profit-and-loss statement from a sophisticated client, closed the volumes of Tax Code that were on my desk, replaced them in their alphabetical slots on my shelves, returned to my chair, leaned back in it, and answered the call. However, it was not Mr. Peters but Mr. Peters's secretary on the line. "Please hold for Mr. Peters," she said.

The line went quiet and I rang Mrs. Polaris again and asked her to wait on the line for Mr. Peters; then I sat back again in my chair and, resting my eyes on the speaker telephone in front of me, pleasantly noted the cool breeze that was at that moment entering through my window. Finally, after a pause, the telephone chimed, indicating a call transfer, and Mrs. Polaris passed Mr. Peters on to me. "Eugene," I said, picking up the phone, "I'm sorry to make you wait."

"I have a proposition," he said.

I do not need to explain that in the business world one proposition is often nothing more than the camouflage for another, and as I sat back in my chair, noting the details of what he proposed, a pattern took form in my mind. He had called to tell me something rather ridiculous, that he and a group of fellows had arranged to spend a week that January in Scottsdale, Arizona, at a San Francisco Giants fantasy camp. I knew about these fantasy camps from an article in *The Wall Street Journal*, but I asked him questions anyway, because there are times in business when one ought to act as though one is uninformed, and I was well aware that this call was business. I let him tell me that the fantasy camp was an opportunity for athletic men such as ourselves to play live baseball against some of the Giants' stars of the past era, such as Tito Fuentes, Dick Dietz, and Ken Henderson. The food was first-class, Mr. Peters went on, the accommodations were excellent, and business seminars were held in the evenings. One of the fellows had become otherwise engaged, Mr. Peters told me, and the long and the short of it was that a position was now open. Did I want to fill it? He mentioned the cost, close to $4,000 for the week, and I assured him that this was not what mattered to me. I was quick to laugh at this, and told him I would call him in the afternoon after Mrs. Polaris had a moment to consult my schedule.

I hung up and sat thinking. It is phrases like this "group of fellows" that one must be on the lookout for in business, for such a group of fellows can in fact turn out to be a set of industry leaders, chairmen of the board, or senators. It is not like going to the bowling alley with a "group of guys." In fact, what had taken shape in my mind as Mr. Peters and I exchanged jovial barbs about his old inability to hit the curveball and my own occasionally erratic throw to first—although, for the record, my throw is quite reliable—was that in fact he was hoping to use the opportunity at baseball camp to offer me a business proposal.

I don't mind saying that I was a bit agitated at that moment. I went out into the anteroom of my office and stood behind Mrs. Polaris's desk, looking out the window and reviewing the near-misses Mr. Peters and I had had in our dealings. I obviously had made the correct decision the first time he had approached me, for in those days he was an uneducated man with neither the sense nor the appearance for business, and he had not in any reasonable view made analysis of the market. That he succeeded with his venture, indeed, was luck. The second time, he had of course something of a record in the marketplace, and I will not conceal the fact that I was disposed to invest; yet something occurred in our exchange at the Fairmont Hotel that precluded an offer. Although I do not know exactly what it was, I now see the possibility that it was an error to have brought along my wife. It is of no use to think like this, however.

In any case, while I stood at Mrs. Polaris's window now, it seemed perfectly possible that another opportunity was at hand: To wit, I suspected that Mr. Peters was going to approach me at this fantasy camp with another bid for investment. I quickly reviewed in my head my own portfolio, which I had weighted toward bonds in light of the unstable stock market and toward shorter maturities in light of the uncertain future. It seemed once again, I am happy to say, that I could make him a pleasing offer.

And then, of course, I suddenly understood that Mr. Peters had no need for my money. I don't mind saying that I had over the years taken enough interest in his businesses to know that he was heavily capitalized, unencumbered with debt service, and clearly poised for expansion, yet it did not occur to me until that moment, standing at Mrs. Polaris's window, that he wanted me for another reason. Business, of course, is both science and intuition, and this was a moment of intuition.

Mrs. Polaris was typing, and I moved behind her. Because of an architectural quirk, the view from her window runs unobstructed to San Francisco Bay, whereas my own is temporarily obstructed by the back side of a newly built hotel. (Obviously the hotel is not temporary; however, I will be in another office soon.) This hotel has caused quite a stir in this city for its architectural ingenuity, although it can be safely said that any ingenuity is strictly confined to the front quarters of the building; my own view, in back, is limited to the ventilation shafts, to the rows of rather shabby casement windows, already dripping rust stains at their corners, and to the constant flow of beer salesmen hefting their kegs, florists picking among their buckets of blooms, health inspectors in cheap suits, trash collectors with their hats on backward, and butchers, who on Friday mornings converge on the banquet kitchen, carrying pig carcasses over their shoulders like duffel bags.

"Have I neglected something, Mr. Roth?" said Mrs. Polaris.

"Not at all, Ina," I responded.

The fact is that I prefer my own view, full as it is of the suggestive hubbub of commerce, to that of Mrs. Polaris, which is so placid and beautiful that it suggests to me the shame of failed ambition; but to contemplate a question one needs an uninterrupted vista, and that is why I stood at the window of my secretary. Whitecaps were chalking the bay.

"Ina," I said, "would you believe that a grown man would pay four thousand dollars to spend a week with a few baseball players from his childhood?"

"Yes, I would," she said, resuming her typing.

I regarded her. Mrs. Polaris is a matronly woman with neat white hair, plainly coiffed, who gives the distinct impression of having been betrayed. I do not know if this has been by a husband, or by her children, or by another relation I have not imagined, yet in her presence I cannot help thinking that it has been by me. It is not that she says anything, for she does not; it is merely a sense I receive from her.

"To me," I said, "it's ridiculous and a foolish waste of money. If you want to play baseball, go to the park and play. If you want to see professional baseball players, attend a professional game. It's as ridiculous for me to want to play baseball with Willie Mays as it would be for Willie Mays to come in here to prepare his own Schedule Nines."

I had tried not to permit my voice to rise, but I am afraid it had. Mrs. Polaris kept typing. I again had the impression that I had overacted around her, that she had in some way come to expect a rise in my voice or an unpleasant stridor in my bearing. As I have said, however, there is no basis for such a feeling on her part. In the corner of the picture window, a luxury liner had come into view, steaming for the Golden Gate, and when the whole ship had appeared, traversed Mrs. Polaris's segment of window, and disappeared again behind the jamb, I walked around the desk and stood in front of her. I proceeded to address her in a lower voice.

"Could you imagine that?" I said, chuckling. "Willie Mays coming in to prepare his own Schedule Nines?"

"No, I couldn't," she said.

"Ridiculous."

Mrs. Polaris rose from her desk, went to the window, and adjusted the blinds, and as she did so my thoughts turned suddenly to the fact that if I did not spend the $4,000 on baseball for myself, then Scheherazade would spend it on Persian carpets.

"However," I said, "there may be an important business reason for me to attend the camp."

I stood in front of her, a slight smile on my lips, and although I would have preferred her to ask me what that business reason was—for I am not so successful that I cannot feel pleasure from relating my business victories to a willing ear—she did not ask me anything and in fact took her seat again and resumed typing. I went back to my own office. It was a Friday, so I looked into the alley and waited for the butcher trucks to arrive.

That evening when I arrived home, Scheherazade and Naomi were playing backgammon together in our sunroom, on an ivory board that I had never seen before. "Where did that board come from?" I inquired. "And what do the elephants think?"

"What does the gorilla think?" said Naomi, which caused both of them to giggle darkly.

"Well," I said, "you'll never guess who called me today."

Naomi was wearing a radio on her belt, which I had not noticed until she reached to her ears and shifted the speakers.

"You won't believe who called me today."

"Who?" said my wife.

"You'll never guess."

Naomi threw the dice and made her move, and my wife leaned over the board.

"It was Eugene Peters," I said.

Scheherazade looked up. I have not mentioned before that my wife is a beautiful woman who has become only more beautiful as I have known her. Her bone structure is Scandinavian, and although this might imply a harshness to her features, her beauty is softened by the gentle look of her eyes, which appear always to be misted.

"He wants me to go on a vacation with him," I said.

"Oh?"

"Although I had an insight about the business reason that may be involved."

"I wouldn't go," she said.

"I believe I realize why he wants me to come along."

"He's trying to humiliate you."

"Pardon?"

"He's trying to humiliate you and you don't even see it."

"That's ridiculous."

"Remember what happened last time."

At this point I moved back into the kitchen, where I sat down at the table and poured myself a glass of cranberry juice. I should explain what my wife was referring to. She believes that our dinner with Eugene Peters at the Fairmont Hotel was in fact a play on Mr. Peters's part intended to denigrate me in regard to our relative standings in the business world. I have pointed out that this sort of dinner is commonplace in business and can signify any number of intentions, from an entreaty to a reconnaissance to a friendly repast, and that no denigration was intended. She, however, has insisted that Eugene Peters was "pulling my chain." Needless to say I have assured Scheherazade that he was not, although I have not told her my own theory, which involves desserts.

As Scheherazade had made no move to come in from her game of backgammon, I finished my cranberry juice and went upstairs to find Rachel. She was in her bedroom, braiding her hair, and when I entered she came across and hugged me. "Peanut," I said, "you'll never guess who called me today."

"Mr. Peters," she answered immediately. She sat at her vanity and faced me. "I heard you out the window," she said. "What did he want?"

"He wants me to go on vacation with him and I figured out why."

"Why, Daddy?"

"He doesn't want another investment. He's too well capitalized for that. What he wants—" I said. I folded my hands. "What he wants is for our firm to take over his accounting."

It is difficult to describe the pleasure I felt in those first few hours after we had disembarked the airplane at Phoenix and been chauffeured in by van to our accommodations at the fantasy camp. Our rooms were private and luxurious, and their windows looked out over the groomed playing fields to which we would be fanning out in the morning. The hiss and rat-tat of sprinklers filled the air. Not only were we about to play the game whose dearness to my heart I clearly and immediately recalled from my childhood, but I also felt the sudden, heady pleasure of having won the professional respect of Mr. Peters. He was a wealthy and influential man, and it was obvious that he planned to ask me for my services. It is one of the pleasures of life that conscientious study and diligent labor are rewarded in the end.

Swallows darted above the dark fields. On the coffee table sat a vase of fresh flowers and on the nightstand a plate of chocolates. Opening the closet door I found my uniform. It hung from a hanger within a plastic dry-cleaner's bag, and I will describe it. The piping was orange, the number was sewn both on the back and on the shoulders (mine was fifty-nine, which I was not able to identify with any stars of the past), and the carefully scripted Giants emblem arched gently in the traditional manner, so that it would appear level when the uniform was donned. The black stirrup leggings buckled into the knickers, the belt was stitched into the waistband, and the pants contained the classic single pocket, at the left hip, for the hat.

I donned the entire uniform immediately, a fact I am not embarrassed to admit because I know that anyone who has ever worn one will understand the sentimental reasons for doing so, although, of course, we would not be playing until the morning. Indeed, I considered taking a stroll out to the fields at that very moment, for I could smell the new mowings and suddenly felt the childhood urge to ball them in my fingers. However, I assumed that the other men were looking out from their own windows as well, and I decided to stay in. I doffed my uniform and slept soundly.

By daybreak the sprinklers had stopped, and from my room the fields appeared strewn with diamonds. I sat on the sill and contemplated the state of the world, as one often does in such situations. How could I have known that our economy would enter a prolonged and deep recession and that profits at our own firm, which had been robust, would undergo a correction? It stood to reason that Mr. Emond, as the eldest of the principals, would again be weakened in this new footing and that my own advancement might once again be delayed. Profits at Mr. Peters's firm, on the other hand, had remained stable, as his products were low-cost items such as the magnetic oil plug, which in fact reduced the necessity of future high-cost procedures, such as oil changes. The fact was, I realized, gazing over the glistening fields, that he was well positioned and that we were not. I went to my briefcase and removed the documents I had brought, detailed explanations of our services and fees in regards to high-inventory, multiple-point-of-sale businesses such as Mr. Peters's, including several innovations that I am proud of but cannot discuss. Of course, these had been reviewed and approved by Mr. Farmer and Mr. Priebe, whose signatures stood below mine on the penultimate page of the proposal. The entire document had been bound in the imprinted leather portfolio cover that the firm reserved for its more important clients, and I will admit that I felt a certain pride to be carrying it. To wit, I had never made such a large proposal without one of our principals alongside.

Presently the groundkeepers appeared, two Mexican men in white trousers, and my thoughts returned to baseball. They raked the infield briskly, set the bases on their spikes, and then turned their attentions to a section of the right-field fence, which apparently had come loose at an earlier time. As they unscrewed this section and lifted it from its housing, I was pleasantly reminded of the old days of major-league play, when groundkeepers moved the fences in or out depending on the batting strength of the visiting team. It appeared to me that, despite advances in the state of our society, something had been lost in the ensuing years. With a start, I realized I was late for breakfast.

Returning to the task at hand, I decided after brief thought to wear my uniform to the dining area because it seemed to me that most of the other men would do so as well. Thus I donned it, shaved quickly, and went downstairs, where I found breakfast under way. Indeed, I had chosen correctly concerning the uniform, as I now gazed out on the two long tables filled with men similarly dressed. One table wore the home colors and the other the traveling.

My own uniform was home colors, and I was relieved to scan the table and see that Mr. Peters's was as well. One of the men gestured to me and I took the place next to him, which I had not realized was open. The man introduced himself as Randall Forbes, shook my hand forcefully, and mentioned that he too was a friend of Mr. Peters, who now sat across from us. An older man, who I would later discover had been the batting coach for the Cleveland Indians two decades ago, came out from the kitchen and set down in front of me a plate heaped with waffles. I noticed that most of the men were not speaking, so I gestured in a friendly way to Mr. Peters and Mr. Forbes, then rubbed my hands together in a pantomime of hunger and began eating my breakfast.

However, it was not long before I realized the cause for the near silence in the dining area. In fact, only one conversation was taking place, a low affair at our end of the table two seats away from me, and it was not until I had eaten one of the waffles and cut up the second that I glanced over and saw that one of those conversing was none other than Willie Mays.

How can I describe what it was like to eat a Belgian waffle with such a man sitting nearby? Of course, I had expected players like a Dick Dietz or a Tito Fuentes, but now a mere two chairs away from me sat the greatest player of his era and one of the greatest players of all time. Immediately my throat constricted and my mouth became dry. I believe that I finished the waffles in front of me, although I have no memory of doing so. I soon understood that they were talking about the elbow difficulties of the current 49ers quarterback, and I will say that this discussion was enough to make me chuckle, that Willie Mays was talking about football. Of course, why should he not talk about it? Indeed, although it seemed ironic to me, none of the other men returned the small smile I made looking up from my plate.

I shall take a moment to describe Mr. Mays. His hair had begun to gray, and although his face had broadened—there seemed to be a sort of general thickening to his features that spoke perhaps of his recent misfortunes concerning Major League Baseball—he nonetheless moved and spoke with a yawning, feline expansiveness that suggested great strength in reserve. Although he was merely eating a waffle, I can say that his limbs moved like clockwork. That is to say, as though they were attached within him to gears that moved independently. He possessed the unmistakable aura of greatness. I believe that all of us in one way or another were watching his small movements—the way he braced his knife against the inside of his wrist before cutting his waffle or the manner in which he gripped his orange juice at the rim of the glass—and every one of these gestures possessed the clarity of motion one might expect in a juggler, an acrobat, or a magician. Among the men, only Eugene Peters was at ease.

Immediately after breakfast we took to the fields for warm-ups, which began with the group of us running two laps around the entire complex of four baseball diamonds facing one another. Each had dugouts, an overhanging backstop, several rows of bleachers, and the low, curved, asymmetric fence around the outfield. One of the diamonds was surrounded by a larger fan area, fifty or sixty rows of bleachers stretching in a semicircle up to the white Arizona sky, and as we jogged past these seats it seemed to me that we could have been professional players jogging to our positions. I will admit, however, that by the time Mr. Peters and I crossed the last flag in left field and jogged toward home, our breath pounding and our feet lumbering on the grass, I was seized with the idea that I had wasted my money on a foolish dream.

The whole week's endeavor had cost $3,400 in advance, not inclusive of bats, which we brought along ourselves. I personally had purchased three, because, although each one was "indestructible," I remembered that, depending on the humidity and temperature and the limberness of my arms, I sometimes preferred a heavier bat, or one with a more narrow taper. In the style of our current era they were anodized aluminum instead of wood, and of course they were rubberized at the handle rather than taped. Although the money was not important to me, I will note that they cost $45 each.

Other men were gathering at the dugout. These men were financial officers, physicians, and attorneys. One stood peering out from the steps with his foot on top of the low wall the way I remembered my own heroes used to stand—the Alou brothers, Mickey Mantle, Willie Mays himself—although this man probably worked in an office and would be sleeping with a heating pad tonight like the rest of us.

We threw that first day, fielded ground balls, and hit against the old man who ran the camp, a fellow named Corsetti who had pitched two seasons thirty years ago. He was older than we were. I guessed he was almost sixty, and he pitched with the old man's limited, eccentric motion on the mound. He had no leg kick. The arms came together in the glove at chest height and then the ball was on its way. My first at bat, it came faster than I thought, and I swung like a man trying to catch a bird in his bare hands. "Don't hurt yourself," the catcher said through his mask. The old man on the mound threw a curveball next and I fell back out of the box. I heard the catcher snort. But the next pitch I hit on a line into center field. I shall never forget the pop of the bat in my hands. However, I am not too vain to say that after my previous swing I had seen the catcher make a sign with his glove and I believe the pitch I hit might have been lobbed.

In summary, our first day was uneventful, other than the fact that it is of human interest to note how quickly one can become used to the presence of Willie Mays. The first time I tossed a ball to him in the warm-up throws my arm quaked in nervousness, but my throw was a good one and I had no reason to be embarrassed by it. Willie Mays caught it without comment and sent it on to the next player. I suppose the camp needed to be concerned with injuries, and therefore on the first day we ran infield and outfield drills and each man took a turn in the box, but we did not begin actual play.

That night we heard a lecture on the current tax laws. In case anything of value was said I brought my briefcase with me, although I believe some of the other men might have been laughing at this fact. The lecture turned out to be of a basic nature, although the information was reasonably handled and for the most part correct. Afterward we all moved out to the clubhouse lounge, where soda pop and cookies were served and the weekend's teams were posted. Mr. Peters and I were on the same team, as I have noted. He was written in at shortstop and I at third base. This of course was an insult to me, but I was not bothered by it. Various members of the team were introducing themselves to one another, and I did not want to appear slighted at this early juncture. It was bad enough that I was carrying a briefcase. Mr. Peters took off his baseball cap, slapped me on the back with it, and made a comment about it being like old times; of course I had to agree, although I was not sure whether he was referring to our positions in the infield or what we each held in our hands. His mood was expansive, however, and after the cookies we walked back together across the fields to the hotel.

We went into the lounge for a drink. Several of the men had preceded our arrival, joking, as we entered, about "milk and cookies" and the fact that we were "in training," yet at the same time sipping cocktails from the hotel's expensive tumblers. The one thing I have admired about Mr. Peters since we were children is his ease with all sorts of people, and now again I was impressed with how he moved among this group. He shook hands, told a joke here, laughed at one there. It has not eluded me that this has been a key element to his success in business, and perhaps such ease is as important in the final analysis as my own hard work has been.

Shortly, I found myself without conversation, and not knowing what else to do I moved to the window with my drink, where I pretended to stare out at the fields. The room was reflected in the glass, and I used the opportunity to study Mr. Peters's movements among the other players. I do not know whether the men turned to him because of his success in the marketplace or whether his success in the marketplace in fact resulted from the fact that men turned to him, but it was clear that he commanded attention. I myself have never done so. Many of those present in this lounge were successful in their own right, some hugely so, yet Mr. Peters could have spoken to any of them he wished.

However, within a short space of time he left a group he was speaking with, came directly to the window, and stood next to me. "A nice view," he said.

"You see some interesting things from here," I answered.

He commented on the line drive I had hit earlier, and I answered by complimenting him on a double play he had turned, although in truth I thought he had been early on the pivot. We stood looking over the lighted fields, clicking the ice in our tumblers. I had been expecting a business proposal, and this was when it was made.

"Look, Roth," he said, putting his arm around my shoulder, "we're not happy with our bean counters anymore."

I will admit that I had been anticipating more of a cat-and-mouse game than this, and I must say that I was caught unawares. "Yes?" I said.

"Well, I want you to make me a proposal. I want Priebe, Emond to handle our books. Can you do it?"

I looked out the window, trying to appear pensive, although one can imagine the satisfaction I felt at being proved correct in my hypothesis. At this point, of course, I was grateful for the kind of preparatory habits that had resulted in my having access to my briefcase at this moment. I smiled broadly at Mr. Peters, tapped the leather case, and told him I had already prepared exactly such a proposal.

He smiled at me, first humorously, then skeptically, then appreciatively. "Of course, Roth," he said, chuckling and shaking his head. "You've always thought of everything."

The fact was that indeed I always had thought of everything, because this is what an accountant is paid for, and when Mr. Peters suggested that we meet on the evening of the last day of camp to discuss my proposal, I happily agreed. Indeed, I was quite pleased that he wanted to discuss business before we had even returned home.

Although the last day of camp was when the substance of our dealings took place, it is important to relay what occurred in our baseball games before then.

I do not claim to be any more than an average player, but something happened to me in the ensuing days that no doubt will not happen again and that, I admit, had not ever happened to me before. I suppose it began with my sleep in bed that second night. It was deep and slumberous, the type of sleep I had not enjoyed in many years, and when I woke for our first day of play I felt I was a young man again. Our team was nicknamed the Sluggers, and that first morning we played against the Bashers. The Bashers primarily comprised a group of radiologists from a practice in Boulder, Colorado. I do not know how a group of radiologists became so proficient at baseball, yet within two innings they had scattered base hits to every field and gathered a tally of four runs, to none for the Sluggers. Their representative from Major League Baseball was Alan Gallagher, a utility infielder I only vaguely remembered from a number of years back, and our own was one Kent Powell, whom I did not recall at all. Willie Mays, it seemed, would not be playing with us. Naturally this was a disappointment, but I will not dwell on it. Of some interest was the fact that Mr. Gallagher, at his age, could contribute very little to the Bashers' effort and that Mr. Powell could contribute almost nothing to our own. He played first base passably and did not hit at all. The Bashers were led instead by a Dr. Argusian, who some years ago had played baseball for the University of Texas and was now in left field. He scored runs in both the first and second innings and in the outfield caught a ball hit well over his head.

Apparently our own batting order had been chosen randomly, and therefore I did not come to the plate until the third inning. By this time we already had the bearing of a losing team. Mr. Peters had struck out in the number-four position, as had three others of the six men preceding me, and none of our players had reached base. Therefore it was with some trepidation that I entered the batter's box and faced Mr. Corsetti to lead off the third inning. As I said, however, I had slept well, and as I dug in my spikes and loosened the bat on my shoulder, I felt a limberness in my arms and an acuity in my eyes that I had not felt for years. Briefly, I hit the first pitch into left-center field for a double.

Although I was not brought around to score, that inning in the field I made a rather nice play at third base on a ball that had apparently been hit into the hole. Mr. Peters slapped me on the back and Kent Powell paid me a compliment from his position behind me. Furthermore, I noticed afterward that Willie Mays now sat in our dugout and that he had seen the play. Needless to say, I was pleased. Two innings later, I hit a nice ball into right field, and amid the general hubbub from the dugout as I made the turn at first base, I believe I heard the specific praise of Mr. Mays. Although between innings he chatted only with Mr. Peters on our bench, I felt loose of limb and elevated of spirit and did not take notice, although it occurred to me briefly that Willie Mays and Eugene Peters had hobnobbed before.

It would not be inaccurate to say that my play had inspired the Sluggers. Our next turn at the plate produced a run, and in the following inning two more, so that late in the game we trailed by only one run and were in every way a rejuvenated club. In the meantime, Dr. Argusian had matched my feats. In the fourth inning he had made a fine catch of a sinking line drive that ended a brief rally for us, and in the sixth he had hit a ball to the wall in left-center field. It is to new heights that competition naturally lifts us, and in the seventh I myself hit a ball to the same spot. I can only say that some small change seemed to have occurred inside me, some quickening of reflex and sharpening of vision that allowed me to see the pitch as though against a background of black and hit it as though murderous. The ball caromed from my bat and did not dip until the warning track in left field, and by this time I was standing on second base breathing the bracing aroma of infield clay. The game proceeded neck and neck. Our opponents scored a run in the top of the eighth, and we answered with two in the bottom. Willie Mays seemed to be rooting for our side, and as we left the bench that inning tied with the Bashers, he slapped hands with Mr. Peters and spoke general encouragement to us all.

Although Willie Mays said nothing more to me specifically, I believe it is accurate and therefore not immodest to say that by the final inning the game had turned into a contest between Dr. Argusian and me. He had reached base safely four times in four appearances at the plate, and I had made the same percentage in three; he had produced a defensive gem and so had I. I had noticed that in their dugout the men seemed to gather about Dr. Argusian, and although the corollary did not occur in our own, it was easy enough to see why. Willie Mays sat with us through the entire last half of the game, and for all of us, I believe, this was like finding ourselves in a taxicab with the king of England.

Although it strains credibility to recall what happened at the end of that first contest, indeed the final inning unfolded like the glorious dream of a child. We came to the plate in the bottom of the ninth tied with the Bashers, and Eugene Peters led off. Briefly, he reached base on a walk—the first given up by Mr. Corsetti; he was promptly sacrificed to second base, where he remained while the number-six batter struck out swinging and I came to the plate, as luck would have it, with two outs in the bottom of the ninth inning and the winning run in scoring position.

I would like to report that I strode confidently to the batter's box, but what happened in fact was that I suddenly lost my nerve. I tapped my cleats with the bat and noticed with dismay that all the men in our dugout, including Willie Mays, were on their feet. Instead of giving me strength, this sapped it. My stomach felt light and Mr. Corsetti's first pitch broke devilishly so that I could not even bring the bat to stir from my shoulder. A strike was called. It was immediately followed by another, and on the mound I could see a small smile on Mr. Corsetti's face. Behind me the men began to stir. I commenced inexplicably to think of the failures in my life, which seemed to rise before my eyes in a tide of regret and misdecision, so that even as Mr. Corsetti brought his hands together in the glove, I had to step from the batter's box and catch my breath.

Mr. Peters retreated in his lead at second, and I immediately thought of the differences between him and me—that he owned a large and growing business concern, that he had enjoyed his life both then and now, that he moved easily among men, et cetera. Yet I have always been a man of will. I took a breath and even in my weakened state I was able to summon a modicum of courage and take my place again in the box. Across the diamond, Mr. Peters resumed his lead. I have been honest in this portrayal and I will be honest again: Before the last pitch of that game was even thrown, I had decided that I would swing at it, and therefore I cannot say it was anything more than luck that it sprang sharply off my bat up the middle into center field for a single. Mr. Peters crossed the plate and we had won.

The revelry was instant and boisterous, several of the players slapping me on the back, Eugene Peters hugging me across the shoulders, and Willie Mays briefly tousling my hair. Afterward we broke for the showers. Standing among the jets of water, soaping ourselves with the lime-scented lotion provided in large dispensers by the management, the talk was in large measure of my feats. Of course, I enjoyed this but was not altogether comfortable, as I knew my last base hit had been a fluke. When one of the men shook up a soap dispenser as though it were a champagne bottle and said boisterously to me, "To the Most Valuable Player," I nodded gamely but took it upon myself to leave the showers as soon as possible and dress again at my locker.

It was then that Willie Mays entered the room. He passed by Mr. Peters, who had just emerged from the tiled stalls, doffed his cap, and sat down facing me. I greeted him and went about what I was doing, which was folding my uniform and placing it into the team bag with which we had been provided at registration. Several men immediately gathered around us on the benches, and although they appeared to be occupied with combing their hair, restretching their leggings, and fastening their shoes, I knew that they were in fact listening to our conversation.

Willie Mays said, "You had the eye, my friend."

I thanked him.

He said, "You were in the zone."

I thanked him again.

Willie Mays said, "Shoot, you were."

Not certain how to respond to this kind of exchange and believing that he knew what had actually occurred at my last trip to the plate, I was eager to steer the discussion in a slightly different direction. I said, "What do you make of this man's pitching?"

Willie Mays said, "Watch his wrist before he throws—he gives away the curveball."

I said, "I will."

Willie Mays said, "Shoot, you hit the ball, brother."

I ventured, "Shoot, yes."

Willie Mays said, "You creamed that sucker."

I said, "Say, I bet they sock you at tax time."

I do not know why I said this. The smile did not vanish from Willie Mays's face, but it did appear to freeze. At that moment another man passed us on the way from the showers, and Willie Mays held out his open palm for him to slap. In doing so he had turned away from me, and I found myself in the corner of the locker room, gathering my belongings, facing Willie Mays's back yet unable to pass around him and through the door. I sat down again on the bench and, conscious of the eyes of the other men upon me, unpacked my cleats and tapped out the dirt from them onto the concrete floor. For several moments I worked between the cleats with my fingernails, pretending to clean them, and when Willie Mays still had not moved or acknowledged me sitting behind him on the bench, I pretended to be occupied with straightening up the small mess I had created on the floor. I leaned down and gathered up the dirt I had knocked about.

It was Mr. Peters who finally broke the silence. "Jeez," he said in the easy way that made the other men turn to him, "they may sock you, Willie, but I'd give anything to be in your shoes, my friend."

Willie Mays laughed, and in the general agreement that followed I was able to extricate myself from the corner, finish my dressing, and go back to the rooms, where I attempted to take my bearings. I still felt a residue of embarrassment from what had happened, and sitting down at the window I noticed that my hands shook slightly. I looked over the vista and attempted to calm myself. I allowed my mind to wander over the day and my eyes to rest here and there across the fields—on the left-field alley, where my drive had landed in the seventh inning, and on the newly limed foul line, where I had backhanded a sharp ground ball in the fifth. The diamonds had been watered again, and in the setting sun the raked-clay base paths glistened like rivers. Needless to say, I was grateful to Mr. Peters for interceding after what I could now only think of as my "gaffe," yet I was uneasy as to what effect the incident would have on our business dealings, which were yet to take place. That evening I ate alone at a steak restaurant in town.

The next day we played the Bashers again, and although I will not go into great detail, I will indeed say that whatever preternatural strength had been visited upon me the day before returned as miraculously the following morning. Briefly at the plate I went three for five and in the field held my ground without error. To be fair, Eugene Peters also gathered three base hits, although he made a throwing error in the second inning and a fielding in the third. As for Dr. Argusian, he seemed to have lost whatever grace had blessed him earlier and contributed almost nothing to the Bashers' efforts. Again we came from behind to defeat our opponents, and in the clubhouse afterward general hilarity was the order.

This was the end of the weekend, and that evening we ate dinner together with the comradeliness of soldiers and afterward rose at the table to make toasts. As can no doubt be imagined, I myself did not like to speak in such situations, and as one after another of the men stood to deliver good-natured barbs and heartfelt thanks, I grew increasingly uncomfortable in my seat. Finally, to my great relief, Mr. Corsetti rose, went to the podium at the head of the hall, and announced that it was time for the presentation of awards. Now, I should add that it was not until this moment that I considered the possibility that I would be named Most Valuable Player for the weekend.

The awards were given in a lighthearted tone. First Alan Gallagher rose to present the award for "rookie of the year," which went to the oldest player in the group, a former state senator in his seventies who had merely watched the two games while sitting in the dugout in his uniform. This award consisted of Alan Gallagher's own Giants hat, which he proceeded to autograph and present to the venerable old man, who had walked to the podium with a cane. Kent Powell then gave out an autographed Giants shirt for "most improved player," which went to one of the radiologists who had been coming to the camp, apparently, for over a decade.

Then Willie Mays rose. Although he carried with him a pair of black Giants leggings, his bearing was not and could not ever be comedic. He was too great a man. "Say-hey," he said at the microphone as the applause subsided. "These socks are for the Most Valuable Player of the week. They were the ones I wore my last season in the majors." He looked around at us, suddenly at a loss, then glanced down at his hands as the room fell silent. I believe he was near tears.

I did not necessarily expect to win the leggings, as several other players had done well also, and I certainly do not believe in premonitions, yet as Willie Mays stood before us with his head bowed slightly and his hands fidgeting over the leggings, I suddenly understood with certainty that he was in the employ of Mr.

Peters. How my heart sank for a moment. Willie Mays was the greatest player of his era. However, he was of the generation of players who had made their mark before the astronomical salaries of our current stars, and thus I suppose I should not have been surprised that he had to make his own living even in professional retirement. No doubt I would soon be seeing him in a television commercial for automobile parts. "Seeing as he wants to be in my shoes so much," he said softly, "these leggings are for him—Mr. Eugene Peters."

Several of the men looked at me, and although I was grateful for their gesture I nonetheless raised my glass and pantomimed a drink from it as Mr. Peters blushed and rose from the table. At the podium he shook hands with Willie Mays, turned to the crowd, and held up the leggings, one in each hand, like trophies. Here was a man with capital in four western states, a villa at Lake Tahoe, and an enviable position in a shrinking economy, yet he was beaming a sultan's smile because in his hands hung two tubes of limp black cloth that were grayed with age and worn thin at the stirrups. The men applauded and so did I.

After the ceremony a group of us repaired to the lounge, where the talk turned first to Major League Baseball, then to politics, and finally to the economy, which I am not surprised to report was of concern to many present. A consensus was reached concerning downsizing and cost trimming to weather the current crisis, and another round of drinks was ordered by Mr. Peters. At this point Mr. Forbes left for a few minutes, and I could see him down the hall talking to the concierge and then speaking on the desk telephone. He returned, joined the conversation, and a few minutes later the door to the lounge opened and three young women entered.

Mr. Forbes greeted them and waved them to our table, where he provided them with chairs and signaled to the bartender for an order. I rose to be introduced. I am a man with children and it was not until I was standing that I understood what was taking place. From my position above the table I saw that one of them was sitting quite close to Mr. Peters on the red leather bench and was in fact touching him. I wondered briefly whether this kind of behavior was the quid pro quo for the untrammeled success that Eugene Peters had enjoyed, and though I admit that at that moment I felt a bolt of envy, I also understood that without children Eugene Peters would vanish completely from this earth. I excused myself and went outside to the telephone, where I called Scheherazade.

I told her that I missed her, then followed this with a phrase we often used in the early days of our marriage.

"Oh, Abba," she said.

Next I spoke to Naomi, who greeted me suspiciously but then told me about a young man who had taken her to the movies and about a party dress she had recently purchased; Abba came on the line and we spoke about baseball in general terms and our plans to see the Giants at home when I returned; Rachel spoke last and said she missed me. She was eager to hear of my time at camp and quizzed me concerning my at bats, which, needless to say, I found gratifying. We hung up and I returned to my rooms.

I could not imagine what was transpiring downstairs, yet I suspected it would have a bearing on our meetings tomorrow. Perhaps it behooved me to join my colleagues in the sense that a feeling of fraternity is pedimental to the business relationship; perhaps, on the other hand, to stay away would confirm my reputation as a moral force, which of course was integral to the standing of an accountant. I am not unaware that it will perhaps be of disappointment to learn that I indeed stayed in my rooms that evening. I took the proposal documents from my briefcase, read through them once again for accuracy, replaced them in their proper order, and changed for bed.

Sometime after night had descended to its full blackness and the moon had risen in my window, I heard the elevator arrive and boisterous conversation issued from the hallway outside my room. Eugene Peters's voice crowed unmistakably along with the softer intonations of a lady's, and I felt a bolt of distaste for the man who, though successful, spent his days hobnobbing with ballplayers and his nights cavorting with strumpets. To my horror, a knock sounded.

I ignored it at first, but it sounded again and I could hear the two of them in the hallway rustling like raccoons outside a tent. I rose quickly, crossed the room in my pajamas, and opened the door, feigning sleepiness. Eugene Peters stood there, well into his cups, alongside the strumpet, and I will only record the first moments of the conversation to clarify its nature.

"See, Sugar," she said, "you woke the man up."

"Just making sure you're ready for business, eh, Abbot?"

"Indeed I am," I said.

"Please excuse us," she said, pulling on his arm.

"Abba doesn't need to excuse us, I've known him for forty years. Do you, Abba?"

"No, I don't."

"Abba and I are going to make a deal tomorrow, aren't we, Abbot?"

This sort of embarrassment continued for several minutes until the lady, who seemed to be of surprisingly good breeding, succeeded in wrenching him away from my door and steering him down the hall. I climbed back into my bed and was able to dismiss the incident quickly, although it did occur to me that Mr.

Peters was a shrewd negotiator and that this might have been his attempt to establish psychological superiority. Outside my window the sprinklers came on. Again I rose and reviewed the documents.

                       In the morning we had our meeting. I dressed as though for the office, that is, in a neutral suit and striped tie, on the supposition that overgrooming was superior to under, and strolled to Mr. Peters's suite. Mr. Forbes, himself in a similar suit, met me at the door and ushered me into the foyer, which opened onto a second bedroom with a foldout sofa and a dresser, next to which a portable meeting table had been placed. Here I took a seat. I had noticed several more closed doors adjoining the foyer and supposed these led to Mr. Peters's own bedroom and most probably another living room. I noticed no evidence of the lady I had met last night. Although the layout of the suite caused my own rooms to seem puny by comparison, I reflected that in general I prefer small quarters. Mr. Forbes offered me a drink from the bar and I accepted tomato juice. I complimented him on his fielding over the weekend and he nodded. He made no attempt to offer conversation, so I opened my briefcase and pretended to occupy myself with preparation.

     Suddenly Eugene Peters entered from a side door dressed in his bathrobe. He shook my hand, told me that he had one more urgent piece of business to attend to, inquired after my comfort, my tomato juice, et cetera, and left by the same door. Mr. Forbes then entered and rather glumly refilled my glass with tomato juice. He left and I continued reviewing my papers.

     After several minutes I stood and went to the window. The morning sun was shattered in prisms by the blinds, and in the distance I could see a group of men on the grass. I was surprised, I must say, when I realized that these were the new arrivals here to replace us without even a day's interlude. Several of them were throwing the ball around the infield while another took swings on the pitching machine set up alongside the bullpen. The light and the long vista onto the grass reminded me of Fort Bragg, where I had spent a few months at the end of the Korean War. The man hitting on the machine missed most of the pitches or nicked foul pop-ups that flew up behind him and bounced in the rope mesh like birds struggling in a net. It occurred to me that Mr. Peters had worn his bathrobe for a strategic reason, and I doffed my jacket and set it across the dresser.

     At the window the man I was watching suddenly hit a string of low, powerful line drives that sped to the end of the cage and ricocheted off the restraining fence. In a game they would have gone for extra bases. As suddenly as this string began, however, it ended, and he missed four pitches in a row. I was watching this demonstration with some interest. He stepped out of the box and tapped the dirt out of his cleats, but I could see that he was looking to see whether any of the other men had seen his string. On the field beside him they continued their throws. The man put down the bat, switched off the machine, and jogged out to the field. He took a throw from one of the other players. Then he ambled up to the man playing third base and began to chat between the ground balls they were fielding. In a few moments he pointed toward the batting cage, and I moved away from the window.

At this point I heard something that sounded like a burst of giggling followed by another, lower sound, although as soon as it was over I was not sure whether it had come from the fields, from elsewhere in the hotel, or indeed if I had heard it at all. I was beginning to perspire. There was a great deal that made me uncomfortable here, although I shall not go into it. I patted my forehead with my handkerchief, went to the dresser, glanced idly in its mirror, and sat on the foldout sofa beside it. Mr. Peters had been gone several minutes by now and I began to wonder whether he really had another matter to attend to or whether he merely wanted to create the impression for business reasons. Again I checked the contents of my briefcase. I stretched my legs. The drawer to his dresser was slightly open, and without thinking I reached my arm back and drew out what touched my hand, which happened to be a piece of clothing. I do not believe I knew beforehand that it was one of the leggings of Willie Mays.

Yet that is what I now held, and although I suppose I should have replaced it immediately and closed the drawer, I could not help wanting to examine it. Leaning back in the sofa, I held it in my fingers. Though of course it was quite ragged, I do not mind saying that it was beautiful. The elastic top still drew firmly when I stretched it, and the stirrup at the bottom was of a second material—silk, I believe.

Though I knew he had in effect bought these leggings, as I sat there I nonetheless began to have thoughts again about the differences between Mr. Peters and me—that he hobnobbed with ballplayers, that he owned a large and growing business concern, that men of talent and ambition were in his employ, et cetera. I found it difficult to fathom that the lazy scoundrel I knew as a boy was now a captain of industry, and as I sat there with the legging in my hands I tried to remember if our childhoods contained some hint of our futures. At that moment, however, I heard him again in the hall and without thinking I opened my briefcase and dropped his legging into it.

Why did I do this? I cannot say I know. I might as easily have dropped it back into the dresser or simply continued to examine it, which was of course within the bounds of behavior. What troubles me is that my reaction was that of a thief caught red-handed, though of course my whole life had been spent in a profession that as a sidelight prevents exactly such behavior. I had little time to think. I closed the briefcase just as Mr. Peters reentered the room, and this again served to reinforce the dreadful feeling I had that I was acting larcenously, although objectively speaking I do not believe I gave this dread away. Indeed, for a fleeting second I had the bizarre thought that in another life I might indeed have made a competent thief.

Mr. Forbes had come in alongside. The two of them shook hands with me again, and we all took places at the table, Mr. Peters across from me and Mr. Forbes beside. I set the briefcase between us—and again my own behavior surprised me, for one needs not to have read a great many crime novels to know this was exactly the sort of brazen act ubiquitous among the criminal class. It was a feat of discipline that I was able to concentrate on the matter at hand.

I had never been in negotiations with Eugene Peters and I was in fact surprised at the manner in which they began. He had changed his clothing, and now it was only I who was without a suit jacket. Nonetheless he opened by discussing everything other than what we had gathered to discuss. He talked about Willie Mays and the 49ers football team, offered voluble praise for my performance over the weekend, and at one point mentioned that perhaps it was I who had ought to have won the award. Naturally, I was pleased by this and denied vehemently that I deserved it. One can imagine my feelings.

Quite suddenly Mr. Peters slapped the table with both hands, opened his arms expansively, and said, "Well, Abba, let's see it."

I was quite flustered for a moment until I realized that he was referring to the proposal. Without willing the act, I had at some point removed the briefcase from the table and set it on my lap, for that is where I now found it. I nodded and lifted it in front of us again. Mr. Peters smiled. I moved it forward on the cherry table, placed my hands on the latches, then withdrew it to my lap again. He was still smiling, although now something quizzical had entered his expression. I considered opening the case on my lap, but to the side of me stood Mr. Forbes, who I realized was his henchman and would not refrain from peering into it.

I am sure that the reader would have chosen another course of action in this same circumstance, although I am equally sure the reader has not found himself in it. "I'm sorry, Eugene," I said, "but I have no proposal."

"I don't understand," said Mr. Peters.

"Our principals have determined that it would not be in our interest to represent your companies. We no longer wish to solicit your account."

"Pardon me, Abba?"

I hesitated to repeat what I had said, for I was in a dark woods and each moment stepping further into it. As soon as this phrase was spoken, I realized that Mr. Peters might well contact our principals for explanation.

Mr. Forbes had stood and moved a step toward me. "Say that again, fella," he said.

"We are no longer in a position to solicit your account."

"I thought you had the proposals all prepared, Abba."

"Well, I do not."

It is painful and perhaps pointless to recount the remainder of our meeting, or for me to relay how by uttering that single phrase I had destroyed a reputation that had taken me a lifetime to build. He asked me several times to clarify my position, and in each case I was forced to argue against everything I had been working toward over many years.

Of course, it would be less than truthful to claim that I did not consider confession. Indeed, while Mr. Peters formulated several rejoinders to my refusal, I considered opening my briefcase, attempting to cast the whole incident and business refusal as a practical joke, and beginning our negotiations once again. Perhaps this is what I should have done and let the chips fall where they might—it is a tantalizing possibility to consider. However, I did not. Our meeting escalated to threats and culminated in rancor, and in an hour I was on the airplane back to San Francisco.

Naturally I made every effort to put the incident from my mind. I thought of what I would say when Naomi showed me her new dress, and what I would tell Rachel about baseball camp, and as we crossed the snowy peaks of the eastern Sierras I decided that on the way home from the airport I would purchase a small pendant that I knew Scheherazade had been considering. Over San Francisco airport we entered a holding pattern, and it was not until we had circled the southern traverse of the bay, cocking our starboard wing toward the banks of fog in the foothills, that I felt able to consider my situation again. Indeed it seemed that I had irrefutably damaged the progress of my life, all because I had agreed to something I had not even wanted to do. I cursed the day I had decided to attend the camp.

Shortly, I regained hold of myself. The airplane was crossing the northern tip of the bay, and I removed the briefcase from its underseat compartment and moved it to my lap. The man next to me took no notice, and after keeping it there for one complete cycle of our holding pattern, I ventured to open it.

The legging lay across my proposal. Of course it did—where else would it have been?—although I confess that I was surprised to see it. In my mind the events of the preceding hours had taken on a dreamlike quality, and before I opened the case I actually hoped that they had somehow not really occurred. Yet there lay the legging, coiled darkly across my papers. I glanced at my neighbor and brought it up into the air, where I rolled it between my hands, stretched it to and fro in the light of the window, and even smelled it, although the only scent I could discern was that of commercial laundry soap.

Suddenly the thought occurred to me that the man next to me might have believed it to be a woman's stocking. I glanced at him but he did not acknowledge me. I cleared my throat and said, "It's not what you think it is."

"Probably not," he answered.

"It happens to be the legging worn by Willie Mays during his last season in the major leagues."

He turned to me, although I believe he may have been feigning interest. "Where'd you get hold of it?"

"At auction."

He held out his hand to touch it, rubbed it between his fingers like a rug merchant, exaggerated a sigh of impression, then turned back to his work. I was glad to have diverted his suspicions, although I will admit that his indifference jolted me even further, for clearly in my hand lay a piece of thin black cloth for which I had recently traded my career.

On the way home from the airport I bought the pendant for Scheherazade, although, as I acknowledged when I gave it to her, it was smaller than the one on which she had recently had her eye. Nonetheless, when I arrived home she seemed delighted. Rachel rode around the living room on my oxfords and Abba appeared at the back door with a baseball, which we proceeded to throw around in our backyard. Only Naomi had not yet appeared, and when the afternoon began to wane I went upstairs alone to unpack my things.

In the bedroom I set down my valise and briefcase, put on the Toscanini recording of Berlioz's *Romeo and Juliet*, shined my oxfords, and proceeded to hang my shirts and pants and fold my underclothes. I stored the empty valise and sat down on the bed. The string crescendo of the second movement rose to its climax and I went to my briefcase and removed the legging. I placed it in the back of my socks drawer, then removed it and set it underneath our mattress. Presently I retrieved it and hung it on a hanger in the closet, although after a time I took it out again from there and set it next to me on the bed. I thought of Willie Mays in the 1954 World Series, turning away from the plate and sprinting straight back to deep center to catch Vic Wertz's line drive over his shoulder. I thought of him pivoting at the warning track to make the legendary throw that held Al Rosen from advancing to second. I picked up the legging and stretched it in my hands, and I thought of Eugene Peters when he opened the dresser drawer to pack. Of course he would suspect me, although he would have no choice but to suspect Mr. Forbes as well, and without admission there would be no proof. I thought of Willie Mays in the eighth inning on April 30, 1961, hitting his fourth home run in a single game, and in the failing western light of the afternoon my own ambitions seemed suddenly paltry. I knew, and I suppose I had known for quite some time, that I would never make principal at Farmer, Priebe & Emond. The position would no doubt go to a younger man. And although this was a disappointment to me, it was not a great one, for although it is embarrassing, I must acknowledge that within me I have always felt the impulse for uproar and disorder.

This, of course, is a secret I have always kept from my fellow accountants. Indeed, at the office the thought has occurred to me, more often perhaps than I ought to say, that I could just as easily have misadded columns, jumbled figures, and transposed tabulations as performed the careful work that over the years has been my trademark. Sitting on my bedspread I was filled with a strange regret. This is what I had: a beautiful and capricious wife, a brooding daughter and an exuberant one, a son cut from my own cloth, a comfortable house, and a career that had proceeded reasonably well though not exactly as I might have liked. This is what I did not have: mutiny, a life of music, and a future unfounded in the past.

Presently I heard steps on the stairs and I replaced the legging in my briefcase. In a moment the door opened and Naomi entered. She did not greet me but went instead to the window, where she placed herself on the sill and looked out over the yard. I walked over and stood behind her, although I could not discern her mood and was afraid to lay my hands on her shoulders or to speak.

"You seem different, Daddy," she said.

I went to my briefcase and removed the legging. A strange ebullience had taken hold of me. "I stole this," I said.

She turned from the window and regarded me. I sat again on the bed, turned the legging in my hands, and recounted the story as the sun fell lower behind her. Although any man who has ever had girls might understand, others will no doubt think it sad for me to say that up until that moment I believe I had never in my life had the full attention of my daughter. It had grown darker and her eyes, looking closely into my own, shone fiercely.

"I'm glad you did it," she said when I had finished.

I laughed.

"I am," she said.

"Don't be silly," I told her. Evening had descended quickly, and because in the presence of my daughter the darkness was suddenly embarrassing, I went to the desk and switched on the lamp. The bulb is a small one, and standing in its weak light with my daughter behind me I was seized, as I sometimes am, with sadness. I suppose I was wondering, although it is strange for me to admit it, why, of all the lives that might have been mine, I have led the one I have described.

[MAY 1993]

MAGIC

JOHN BARTH

The Remobilization of Jacob Horner

John Barth (1930–   ) began his distinguished career with two short, very readable novels, The Floating Opera and The End of the Road. "The Remobilization of Jacob Horner" is excerpted from the latter book and exhibits Barth's droll command of language as well as his mastery of deep matters of existential philosophy. He went on to write huge books—virtual epics—beginning with The Sot-Weed Factor and Giles Goat Boy; but he also has a collection of very tricky and well-turned stories, Lost in the Funhouse, including many that first appeared in Esquire.

In September it was time to see the Doctor again: I drove out to the Remobilization Farm the morning during the first week of the month. Because the weather was fine, a number of the Doctor's other patients, quite old men and women, were taking the air, seated in their wheelchairs or in the ancient cane chairs along the porch. As usual, they greeted me a little suspiciously with their eyes; visitors of any sort, but particularly of my age, were rare at the farm, and were not welcomed. Ignoring their stony glances, I went inside to pay my respects to Mrs. Dockey, the receptionist-nurse. I found her in consultation with the Doctor himself.

"Good day, Horner," the Doctor beamed.

"Good morning, sir. Good morning, Mrs. Dockey."

That large, masculine woman nodded shortly without speaking—her custom—and the Doctor told me to wait for him in the Progress and Advice Room, which along with the dining room, the kitchen, the reception room, the bathroom, and the Treatment Room, constituted the first floor of the old frame house. Upstairs the partitions between the original bedrooms had been removed to form two dormitories, one for the men and one for the women. The Doctor had his own small bedroom upstairs, too, and there were two bathrooms. I did not know at that time where Mrs. Dockey slept, or whether she slept at the farm at all. She was a most uncommunicative woman.

        I had first met the Doctor quite by chance on the morning of March 17, 1951, in what passes for the grand concourse of the Pennsylvania Railroad Station in Baltimore. It happened to be the day after my twenty-eighth birthday, and I was sitting on one of the benches in the station with my suitcase beside me. I was in an unusual condition: I couldn't move. On the previous day I had checked out of my room in an establishment on St. Paul and 33rd streets owned by the university. I had roomed there since September of the year before when, halfheartedly, I matriculated as a graduate student and began work on the degree that I was scheduled to complete the following June.

But on March 16, my birthday, with my oral examination passed but my master's thesis not even begun, I packed my suitcase and left the room to take a trip somewhere. Because I have learned not to be much interested in causes and biographies, I shall ascribe this romantic move to simple birthday despondency, a phenomenon sufficiently familiar to enough people so that I need not explain it further. Birthday despondency, let us say, had reminded me that I had no self-convincing reason for continuing for a moment longer to do any of the things that I happened to be doing with myself as of seven o'clock on the evening of March 16, 1951. I had thirty dollars and some change in my pocket: when my suitcase was filled I hailed a taxi, went to Pennsylvania Station, and stood in the ticket line.

"Yes?" said the ticket agent when my turn came.

"Ah—this will sound theatrical to you," I said, with some embarrassment, "but I have thirty dollars or so to take a trip on. Would you mind telling me some of the places I could ride to from here for, say, twenty dollars?"

The man showed no surprise at my request. He gave me an understanding if unsympathetic look and consulted some sort of rate scales.

"You can go to Cincinnati, Ohio," he declared. "You can go to Crestline, Ohio. And let's see, now—you can go to Dayton, Ohio. Or Lima, Ohio. That's a nice town. I have some of my wife's people up around Lima, Ohio. Want to go there?"

"Cincinnati, Ohio," I repeated, unconvinced. "Crestline, Ohio; Dayton, Ohio; and Lima, Ohio. Thank you very much. I'll make up my mind and come back."

So I left the ticket window and took a seat on one of the benches in the middle of the concourse to make up my mind. And it was there that I simply ran out of motives, as a car runs out of gas. There was no reason to go to Cincinnati, Ohio. There was no reason to go to Crestline, Ohio. Or Dayton, Ohio; or Lima, Ohio. There was no reason, either, to go back to the apartment hotel, or for that matter to go anywhere. There was no reason to do anything. My eyes, as the German classicist Winckelmann said inaccurately of the eyes of Greek statues, were sightless, gazing on eternity, fixed on ultimacy, and when that is the case there is no reason to do anything—even to change the focus of one's eyes. Which is perhaps why the statues stand still. It is the malady *cosmopsis*, the cosmic view, that afflicted me. When one has it, one is frozen like the bullfrog when the hunter's light strikes him full in the eyes, only with *cosmopsis* there is no hunter, and no quick hand to terminate the moment—there's only the light.

Shortsighted animals all around me hurried in and out of doors leading down to the tracks; trains arrived and departed. Women, children, salesmen, soldiers, and redcaps hurried across the concourse toward immediate destinations, but I sat immobile on the bench. After a while Cincinnati, Crestline, Dayton, and Lima dropped from my mind, and their place was taken by that test-pattern of my consciousness, *Pepsi-Cola hits the spot*, intoned with silent oracularity. But it, too, petered away into the void, and nothing appeared in its stead.

If you look like a vagrant it is difficult to occupy a train-station bench all night, even in a busy terminal, but if you are reasonably well dressed, have a suitcase at your side, and sit erect, policemen and railroad employees will not disturb you. I was sitting in the same place, in the same position, when the sun struck the grimy station windows next morning, and in the nature of the case I suppose I would have remained thus indefinitely, but about nine o'clock a small, dapper fellow in his fifties stepped in front of me and stared directly into my eyes. He was bald, dark-eyed, and dignified, a Negro, and wore a graying mustache and a trim tweed suit to match. The fact that I did not stir even the pupils of my eyes under his gaze is an index to my condition, for ordinarily I find it next to impossible to return the stare of a stranger.

"Weren't you sitting here like this last night?" he asked me sharply. I did not reply. He came close, bent his face down toward mine, and moved an upthrust finger back and forth about two inches from my eyes. But my eyes did not follow his finger. He stepped back and regarded me critically, then snapped his fingers almost on the point of my nose. I blinked involuntarily, although my head did not jerk back.

"Ah," he said, satisfied, and regarded me again. "Does this happen to you often, young man?"

Perhaps because of the brisk assuredness of his voice, the *no* welled up in me like a belch. And I realized as soon as I deliberately held my tongue (there being in the last analysis no reason to answer his question at all) that as of that moment I was artificially prolonging what had been a genuine physical immobility. Not to choose at all is unthinkable: what I had done before was simply choose not to act, since I had been at rest when the situation arose. Now, however, it was harder—"more of a choice," so to speak—to hold my tongue than to croak out something that filled my mouth, and so after a moment I said, "No."

Then, of course, the trance was broken. I was embarrassed, and rose stiffly from the bench to leave.

"Where will you go?" my examiner asked with a smile.

"What?" I frowned at him. "Oh—get a bus home, I guess. See you around."

"Wait." His voice was mild, but entirely commanding. "Won't you have coffee with me? I'm a physician, and I'd be interested in discussing your case."

"I don't have any case," I said awkwardly. "I was just—sitting there for a minute or so."

"No. I saw you there last night at ten o'clock when I came in from New York," the Doctor said. "You were sitting in the same position. You *were* paralyzed, weren't you?"

I laughed. "Well, if you want to call it that; but there's nothing wrong with me. I don't know what came over me."

"Of course you don't, but I do. My specialty is various sorts of physical immobility. You're lucky I came by this morning."

"Oh, you don't understand—"

"I brought you out of it, didn't I?" he said cheerfully. "Here." He took a fifty-cent piece from his pocket and handed it to me and I accepted it before I realized what he'd done. "I can't go into that lounge over there. Go get two cups of coffee for us and we'll sit here a minute and decide what to do."

"No, listen, I—"

"Why not?" He laughed. "Go on, now. I'll wait here."

Why not, indeed?

"I have my own money," I protested lamely, offering him his fifty-cent piece back, but he waved me away and lit a cigar.

"Now, hurry up," he ordered around the cigar. "Move fast, or you might get stuck again. Don't think of anything but the coffee I've asked you to get."

"All right." I turned and walked with dignity toward the lounge, just off the concourse.

"Fast!" The Doctor laughed behind me. I flushed, and quickened my step.

While I waited for the coffee I tried to feel the curiosity about my invalidity and my rescuer that it seemed appropriate I should feel, but I was too weary in mind and body to wonder at anything. I do not mean to suggest that my condition had been unpleasant—it was entirely anesthetic in its advanced stage, and even a little bit pleasant in its inception—but it was fatiguing, as an overlong sleep is fatiguing, and one had the same reluctance to throw it off that one has to get out of bed when one has slept around the clock. Indeed, as the Doctor had warned (it was at this time, not knowing my benefactor's name, that I began to think of him with a capital *D*), to slip back into immobility at the coffee counter would have been extremely easy: I felt my mind begin to settle into rigidity, and only the clerk's peremptory, "Thirty cents, please," brought me back to action—luckily, because the Doctor could not have entered the white lounge to help me. I paid the clerk and took the paper cups of coffee back to the bench.

"Good," the Doctor said. "Sit down."

I hesitated. I was standing directly in front of him.

"Here!" he laughed. "On this side!"

I sat where ordered and we sipped our coffee. I rather expected to be asked questions about myself, but the Doctor ignored me.

"Thanks for the coffee," I said. He glanced at me impassively for a moment, as though I were a hitherto silent parrot who had suddenly blurted a brief piece of nonsense, and then he returned his attention to the crowd in the station.

"I have one or two calls to make before we catch the bus," he announced without looking at me. "Won't take long. I wanted to see if you were still here before I left town."

"What do you mean, catch the bus?"

"You'll have to come over to the farm—my Remobilization Farm near Wicomico—for a day or so, for observation," he explained coldly. "You don't have anything else to do, do you?"

"Well, I should get back to the university, I guess. I'm a student."

"Oh!" He chuckled. "Might as well forget about that for a while. You can come back in a few days if you want to."

"Say, you know, really, I think you must have a misconception about what was wrong with me a while ago. I'm not a paralytic. It's all just silly. I'll explain it to you if you want to hear it."

"No, you needn't bother. No offense intended, but the things you think are important probably aren't even relevant. I'm never very curious about my patients' histories. Rather not hear them, in fact—just clutters things up. It doesn't much matter what caused it anyhow, does it?" He grinned. "My farm's like a nunnery in that respect—I never bother about why my patients come there. Forget about causes; I'm no psychoanalyst."

"But that's what I mean, sir," I explained, laughing uncomfortably. "There's nothing physically wrong with me."

"Except that you couldn't move," the Doctor said. "What's your name?"

"Jacob Horner. I'm a graduate student up at Johns Hopkins—"

"Ah, ah," he warned. "No biography, Jacob Horner." He finished his coffee and stood up. "Come on, now, we'll get a cab. Bring your suitcase along."

"Oh, wait, now!"

"Yes?"

I fumbled for protests: the thing was absurd. "Well—this is absurd."

"Yes. So?"

I hesitated, blinking, wetting my lips.

"Think, think!" the Doctor said brusquely.

My mind raced like a car engine when the clutch is disengaged. There was no answer.

"Well, I—are you sure it's all right?" I asked, not knowing what my question signified.

The Doctor made a short, derisive sound (a sort of "Huf!") and turned away. I shook my head—at the same moment aware that I was watching myself act bewildered—and then fetched up my suitcase and followed after him, out to the line of taxicabs at the curb.

　　　　　　　　　　　　　Thus began my *alliance* with the Doctor.
He stopped first at an establishment on North Howard Street, to order two
wheelchairs, three pairs of crutches, and certain other apparatus for the farm, and
then at a pharmaceutical supply house on South Paca Street, where he also gave
some sort of order. Then we went to the bus terminal and took the bus to the
Eastern Shore. The Doctor's Mercury station wagon was parked at the
Wicomico bus depot; he drove to the little settlement of Vineland, about three
miles south of Wicomico, turned off onto a secondary road, and finally drove up
a long, winding dirt lane to the Remobilization Farm, an aged but white-painted
clapboard house in a clump of oaks on a knoll overlooking a creek. The patients
on the porch, senile men and women, welcomed the Doctor with querulous
enthusiasm, and he returned their greeting. Me they regarded with open suspicion, if not hostility, but the Doctor made no explanation of my presence; for
that matter, I should have been hard put to explain it myself.

　　　Inside, I was introduced to the muscular Mrs. Dockey and taken to the
Progress and Advice Room for my first interview. I waited alone in that clean
room—which, though bare, was not really clinical-looking—for some ten minutes, and then the Doctor entered and took his seat very much in front of me.
He had donned a white medical-looking jacket and appeared entirely official and
competent.

　　　"I'll make a few things clear very quickly, Jacob," he said leaning forward
with his hands on his knees and rolling his cigar around in his mouth between
sentences. "The Farm, as you can see, is designed for the treatment of paralytics.
Most of my patients are old people, but you mustn't infer from that that this is
a nursing home for the aged. Perhaps you noticed when we drove up that my
patients like me. They do. It has happened several times in the past that for one
reason or another I have seen fit to change the location of the farm. Once it was
outside of Troy, New York; another time near Fond du Lac, Wisconsin; another
time near Biloxi, Mississippi. And we've been other places, too. Nearly all the
patients I have on the farm now have been with me at least since Fond du Lac,
and if I should have to move tomorrow to Helena, Montana, or The Rockaways,
most of them would go with me, and not because they haven't anywhere else to
go. But don't think I have an equal love for them. They're just more or less
interesting problems in immobility, for which I find it satisfying to work out
therapies. I tell this to you, but not to them, because your problem is such that
this information is harmless. And for that matter, you've no way of knowing
whether anything I've said or will say is the truth, or just a part of my general

therapy for you. You can't even tell whether your doubt in this matter is an honestly founded doubt or just a part of your treatment: access to the truth, Jacob, even belief that there is such a thing, is itself therapeutic or antitherapeutic, depending on the problem. The reality of your problem is all that you can be sure of."

"Yes, sir."

"Why do you say that?" the Doctor asked.

"Say what?"

" 'Yes, sir.' Why do you say 'Yes, sir'?"

"Oh—I was just acknowledging what you said before."

"Acknowledging the truth of what I said or merely the fact that I said it?"

"Well," I hesitated, flustered. "I don't know, sir."

"You don't know whether to say you were acknowledging the truth of my statements, when actually you weren't, or to say you were simply acknowledging that I said something, at the risk of offending me by the implication that you don't agree with any of it. Eh?"

"Oh, I agree with *some* of it," I assured him.

"What parts of it do you agree with? Which statements?" the Doctor asked.

"I don't know: I guess—" I searched my mind hastily to remember even one thing that he'd said. He regarded my floundering for a minute and then went on as if the interruption hadn't occurred.

"Agapotherapy—devotion therapy—is often useful with older patients," he said. "One of the things that work toward restoring their mobility is devotion to some figure, a doctor or other kind of administrator. It keeps their allegiances from becoming divided. For that reason I'd move the farm occasionally even if other circumstances didn't make it desirable. It does them good to decide to follow me. Agapotherapy is one small therapy in a great number, some consecutive, some simultaneous, which are exercised on the patients. No two patients have the same schedule of therapies, because no two people are ever paralyzed in the same way. The authors of medical textbooks," he added with some contempt, "like everyone else, can reach generality only by ignoring enough particularity. They speak of paralysis, and the treatment of paralytics, as though one read the textbook and then followed the rules for getting paralyzed properly. There is no such thing as *paralysis*, Jacob. There is only paralyzed Jacob Horner. And I don't treat paralysis: I schedule therapies to mobilize John Doe or Jacob Horner, as the case may be. That's why I ignore you when you say you aren't paralyzed like the people out on the porch are paralyzed. I don't treat your paralysis; I treat paralyzed you. Please don't say 'Yes, sir.' "

The urge to acknowledge is an almost irresistible habit, but I managed to sit silent and not even nod.

"There are several things wrong with you, I think. I daresay you don't know the seating capacity of the Cleveland Municipal Stadium, do you?"

"*What?*"

The Doctor did not smile. "You suggest that my question is absurd, when you have no grounds for knowing whether it is or not—you obviously heard me and understood me. Probably you want to delay my learning that you *don't* know the seating capacity of Cleveland Municipal Stadium, since your vanity would be ruffled if the question *weren't* absurd, and even if it were. It makes no difference whether it is or not, Jacob Horner: it's a question asked you by your Doctor. Now, is there any ultimate reason why the Cleveland Stadium shouldn't seat fifty-seven thousand, four hundred, eighty-eight people?"

"None that I can think of." I grinned.

"Don't pretend to be amused. Of course there's not. Is there any reason why it shouldn't seat eighty-eight thousand, four hundred, seventy-five people?"

"No, sir."

"Indeed not. Then as far as Reason is concerned, its seating capacity could be almost anything. Logic will never give you the answer to my question. Only Knowledge of the World will answer it. There's no ultimate reason at all why the Cleveland Stadium should seat exactly seventy-three thousand, eight hundred and eleven people, but it happens that it does. There's no reason in the long run why Italy shouldn't be shaped like a sausage instead of a boot, but that doesn't happen to be the case. *The world is everything that is the case,* and what the case is is not a matter of logic. If you don't simply *know* how many people can sit in the Cleveland Municipal Stadium, you have no real reason for choosing one number over another, assuming you can make a choice at all—do you understand? But if you have some Knowledge of the World you may be able to say, 'Seventy-three thousand, eight hundred and eleven,' just like that. No choice is involved."

"Well," I said, "you'd still have to choose whether to answer the question or not, or whether to answer it correctly, even if you knew the right answer, wouldn't you?"

The Doctor's tranquil stare told me my question was somewhat silly, though it seemed reasonable enough to me.

"One of the things you'll have to do," he said dryly, "is buy a copy of the *World Almanac* for 1951 and begin to study it scrupulously. This is intended as a discipline, and you'll have to pursue it diligently, perhaps for a number of years.

Informational Therapy is one of a number of therapies we'll have to initiate at once."

I shook my head and chuckled genially. "Do all your patients memorize the *World Almanac*, Doctor?"

I might as well not have spoken.

"Mrs. Dockey will show you to your bed," the Doctor said, rising to go. "I'll speak to you again presently." At the door he stopped and added, "One, perhaps two of the older men may attempt familiarities with you at night up in the dormitory. They're on Sexual Therapy. But unless you're accustomed to that sort of thing I don't think you should accept their advances. You should keep your life as uncomplicated as possible, at least for a while. Reject them gently, and they'll go back to each other."

There was little I could say. After a while Mrs. Dockey showed me my bed in the men's dormitory. I was not introduced to my roommates, nor did I introduce myself. In fact, during the three days that I remained at the farm not a dozen words were exchanged between us. When I left they were uniformly glad to see me go.

The Doctor spent two or three one-hour sessions with me each day. He asked me virtually nothing about myself; the conversations consisted mostly of harangues against the medical profession for its stupidity in matters of paralysis, and imputations that my condition was the result of defective character and intelligence.

"You claim to be unable to choose in many situations," he said once. "Well I claim that that inability is only theoretically inherent in situations, when there's no chooser. Given a particular chooser, it's unthinkable. So, since the inability *was* displayed in your case, the fault lies not in the situation but in the fact that there was no chooser. Choosing is existence: to the extent that you don't choose, you don't exist. Now, everything we do must be oriented toward choice and action. It doesn't matter whether this action is more or less reasonable than inaction; the point is that it is its opposite."

"But why should anyone prefer it?" I asked.

"There's no reason why you should prefer it, and no reason why you shouldn't. One is a patient simply because one chooses a condition that only therapy can bring one to, not because one condition is inherently better than another. My therapies for a while will be directed toward making you conscious of your existence. It doesn't matter whether you act constructively or even consistently, so long as you act. It doesn't matter to the case whether your character is admirable or not, so long as you think you have one."

"I don't understand why you should choose to treat anyone, Doctor," I said.

"That's my business, not yours."

And so it went. I was charged, directly or indirectly, with everything from intellectual dishonesty and vanity to nonexistence. If I protested, the Doctor observed that my protests indicated my belief in the truth of his statements. If I only listened glumly, he observed that my glumness indicated my belief in the truth of his statements.

"All right, then," I said at last, giving up. "Everything you say is true. All of it is the truth."

The Doctor listened calmly. "You don't know what you're talking about," he said. "There's no such thing as truth as you conceive it."

These apparently pointless interviews did not constitute my only activity at the farm. Before every meal all the patients were made to perform various calisthenics under the direction of Mrs. Dockey. For the older patients these were usually very simple—perhaps a mere nodding of the head or flexing of the arms—although some of the old folks could execute really surprising feats: one gentleman in his seventies was an excellent rope-climber, and two old ladies turned agile somersaults. For each patient Mrs. Dockey prescribed different activities; my own special prescription was to keep some sort of visible motion going all the time. If nothing else, I was constrained to keep a finger wiggling or a foot tapping, say, during mealtimes, when more involved movements would have made eating difficult. And I was told to rock from side to side in my bed all night long: not an unreasonable request, as it happened, for I did this habitually anyhow, even in my sleep—a habit carried over from childhood.

"Motion! Motion!" the Doctor would say, almost exalted. "You must be always *conscious* of motion!"

There were special diets and, for many patients, special drugs. I learned of Nutritional Therapy, Medicinal Therapy, Surgical Therapy, Dynamic Therapy, Informational Therapy, Conversational Therapy, Sexual Therapy, Devotional Therapy, Occupational and Preoccupational Therapy, Virtue and Vice Therapy, Theotherapy and Atheotherapy—and, later, Mythotherapy, Philosophical Therapy, Scriptotherapy, and many, many other therapies practiced in various combinations and sequences by the patients. Everything, to the Doctor, was either therapeutic, antitherapeutic, or irrelevant. He was a kind of superpragmatist.

At the end of my last session—it had been decided that I was to return to Baltimore experimentally, to see whether and how soon my immobility might recur—the Doctor gave me some parting instructions.

"It would not be well in your particular case to believe in God," he said. "Religion will only make you despondent. But until we work out something for you it will be useful to subscribe to some philosophy. Why don't you read Sartre and become an existentialist? It will keep you moving until we find something more suitable for you. Study the *World Almanac:* it is to be your breviary for a while. Take a day job, preferably factory work, but not so simple that you are able to think coherently while working. Something involving sequential operations would be nice. Go out in the evenings; play cards with people. I don't recommend buying a television set just yet. Exercise frequently. Take long walks, but always to a previously determined destination; and when you get there, walk right home again, briskly. And move out of your present quarters; the association is unhealthy for you. Don't get married or have love affairs yet, even if you aren't courageous enough to hire prostitutes. Above all, act impulsively: don't let yourself get stuck between alternatives, or you're lost. You're not that strong. If the alternatives are side by side, choose the one on the left; if they're consecutive in time, choose the earlier. If neither of these applies, choose the alternative whose name begins with the earlier letter of the alphabet. These are the principles of Sinistrality, Antecedence, and Alphabetical Priority—there are others, and they're arbitrary, but useful. Good-bye."

"Good-bye, Doctor," I said, and prepared to leave.

"If you have another attack and manage to recover from it, contact me as soon as you can. If nothing happens, come back in three months. My services will cost you ten dollars a visit—no charge for this one. I have a limited interest in your case, Jacob, and in the vacuum you have for a self. That *is* your case. Remember, keep moving all the time. Be *engagé*. Join things."

I left, somewhat dazed, and took the bus back to Baltimore. There, out of it all, I had a chance to attempt to decide what I thought of the Doctor, the Remobilization Farm, the endless list of therapies, and my own position. One thing seemed fairly clear: the Doctor was operating either outside the law or on its fringes. Sexual Therapy, to name only one thing, could scarcely be sanctioned by the American Medical Association. This doubtless was the reason for the farm's frequent relocation. It was also apparent that he was a crank—though perhaps not an ineffective one—and one wondered whether he had any sort of license to practice medicine at all. Because—his rationalizations aside—I was so clearly different from his other patients, I could only assume that he had some sort of special interest in my case: perhaps he was a frustrated psychoanalyst. At worst he was some combination of quack and prophet running a semi-legitimate rest home for senile eccentrics; and yet one couldn't easily laugh off his forcefulness, and his insights frequently struck home. As a matter of fact, I was unable to make any judgment one way or the other about him or the farm or the therapies.

A most extraordinary doctor. Although I kept telling myself that I was just going along with the joke, I actually did move to East Chase Street; I took a job as an assembler on the line of the Chevrolet factory out on Broening Highway, where I operated an air wrench that belted leaf springs on the left side of Chevrolet chassis, and I joined the UAW. I read Sartre, but had difficulty deciding how to apply him to specific situations. (How did existentialism help one decide whether to carry one's lunch to work or buy it in the factory cafeteria? I had no head for philosophy.) I played poker with my fellow assemblers, took walks from Chase Street down to the waterfront and back, and attended B movies. Temperamentally I was already pretty much of an atheist most of the time, and the proscription of women was a small burden, for I was not, as a rule, heavily sexed. I applied Sinistrality, Antecedence, and Alphabetical Priority religiously (though in some instances I found it hard to decide which of those devices best fitted the situation). And every quarter for the next two years I drove over to the Remobilization Farm for advice. It would be idle for me to speculate further on why I assented to this curious alliance, which more often than not was insulting to me—I presume that anyone interested in causes will have found plenty to pick from by now in this account.

I left myself sitting in the Progress and Advice Room, I believe, in September of 1953, waiting for the Doctor. My mood on this morning was an unusual one; as a rule I was almost "weatherless" the moment I entered the farmhouse, and I suppose that weatherlessness is the ideal condition for receiving advice, but on this morning, although I felt unemotional, I was not without weather. I felt dry, clear, and competent, for some reason or other—quite sharp and not a bit humble. In meteorological terms, my weather was *sec supérieur*.

"How are you these days, Horner?" the Doctor asked as he entered the room.

"Just fine, Doctor," I replied breezily. "How's yourself?"

The Doctor took his seat, spread his knees, and regarded me critically, not answering my question.

"Have you begun teaching yet?"

"Nope. Start next week. Two sections of grammar and two of composition."

"Ah." He rolled his cigar around in his mouth. He was studying me, not what I said. "You shouldn't be teaching composition."

"Can't have everything," I said cheerfully, stretching my legs out under his chair and clasping my hands behind my head. "It was that or nothing, so I took it."

The Doctor observed the position of my legs and arms.

"Who is this confident fellow you've befriended?" he asked. "One of the other teachers? He's terribly sure of himself!"

I blushed: it occurred to me that I was imitating one of my officemates, an exuberant teacher of history. "Why do you say I'm imitating somebody?"

"I didn't," the Doctor smiled. "I only asked who was the forceful fellow you've obviously met."

"None of your business, sir."

"Oh, my. Very good. It's a pity you can't take over that manner consistently—you'd never need my services again! But you're not stable enough for that yet, Jacob. Besides, you couldn't act like him when you're in his company, could you? Anyway I'm pleased to see you assuming a role. You do it, evidently, in order to face up to me: a character like your friend's would never allow itself to be insulted by some crank with his string of implausible therapies, eh?"

"That's right, Doctor," I said, but much of the fire had gone out of me under his analysis.

"This indicates to me that you're ready for Mythotherapy, since you seem to be already practicing it without knowing it, and therapeutically, too. But it's best you be aware of what you're doing, so that you won't break down through ignorance. Some time ago I told you to become an existentialist. Did you read Sartre?"

"Some things. Frankly I really didn't get to be an existentialist."

"No? Well, no matter now. Mythotherapy is based on two assumptions: that human existence precedes human essence, if either of the two terms really signifies anything; and that a man is free not only to choose his own essence but to change it at will. Those are both good existentialist premises, and whether they're true or false is no concern of us—they're *useful* in your case."

He went on to explain Mythotherapy.

"In life," he said, "there are no essentially major or minor characters. To that extent, all fiction and biography, and most historiography, is a lie. Everyone is necessarily the hero of his own life story. Suppose you're an usher in a wedding. From the groom's viewpoint he's the major character; the others play supporting parts, even the bride. From your viewpoint, though, the wedding is a minor episode in the very interesting history of *your* life, and the bride and groom both are minor figures. What you've done is choose to *play the part* of a minor character: it can be pleasant for you to *pretend to be* less important than you know you are, as Odysseus does when he disguises himself as a swineherd. And every member of the congregation at the wedding sees himself as the major character, condescending to witness the spectacle. So in this sense fiction isn't a lie at all, but a true representation of the distortion that everyone makes of life.

"Now, not only are we the heroes of our own life stories—we're the ones who conceive the story, and give other people the essences of minor characters. But since no man's life story as a rule is ever one story with a coherent plot, we're always reconceiving just the sort of hero we are, and consequently just the sort of minor roles the other people are supposed to play. This is generally true. If any man displays almost the same character day in and day out, all day long, it's either because he has no imagination, like an actor who can play only one role, or because he has an imagination so comprehensive that he sees each particular situation of his life as an episode in some grand overall plot, and can so distort the situations that the same type of hero can deal with them all. But this is most unusual.

"This kind of role-assigning is mythmaking, and when it's done consciously or unconsciously for the purpose of aggrandizing or protecting your ego—and it's probably done for this purpose all the time—it become Mythotherapy. Here's the point: an immobility such as you experienced that time in Penn Station is possible only to a person who for some reason or other has ceased to participate in Mythotherapy. At that time on the bench you were neither a major nor a minor character: you were no character at all. It's because this has happened once that it's necessary for me to explain to you something that comes quite naturally to everyone else. It's like teaching a paralytic how to walk again.

"I've said you're too unstable to play any one part all the time—you're also too unimaginative—so for you these crises had better be met by changing scripts as often as necessary. This should come naturally to you; the important thing for you is to realize what you're doing so you won't get caught without a script, or with the wrong script in a given situation. You did quite well, for example, for a beginner, to walk in here so confidently and almost arrogantly a while ago, and assign me the role of a quack. But you must be able to change masks at once if by some means or other I'm able to make the one you walked in with untenable. Perhaps—I'm just suggesting an offhand possibility—you could change to thinking of me as The Sagacious Old Mentor, a kind of Machiavellian Nestor, say, and yourself as The Ingenuous but Promising Young Protégé, a young Alexander, who someday will put all these teachings into practice and far outshine the master. Do you get the idea? Or—this is repugnant, but it could be used as a last resort—The Silently Indignant Young Man, who tolerates the ravings of a Senile Crank but who will leave this house unsullied by them. I call this repugnant because if you ever used it you'd cut yourself off from much that you haven't learned yet.

"It's extremely important that you learn to assume these masks wholeheartedly. Don't think there's anything behind them: *ego* means *I,* and *I* means *ego,* and the ego by definition is a mask. Where there's no ego—this is you on the bench—there's no *I.* If you sometimes have the feeling that your mask is *insincere*—impossible word!—it's only because one of your masks is incompatible with another. You mustn't put on two at a time. There's a source of conflict; and conflict between masks, like absence of masks, is a source of immobility. The more sharply you can dramatize your situation and define your own role and everybody else's role, the safer you'll be. It doesn't matter in Mythotherapy for paralytics whether your role is major or minor, as long as it's clearly conceived, but in the nature of things it'll normally always be major. Now say something."

I could not.

"Say something!" the Doctor ordered. "Move! Take a role!"

I tried hard to think of one, but I could not.

"Damn you!" the Doctor cried. He kicked back his chair and leaped upon me, throwing me to the floor and pounding me roughly.

"Hey!" I hollered, entirely startled by his attack. "Cut it out! What the hell!" I struggled with him, and being both larger and stronger than he, soon had him off me. We stood facing each other warily, panting from the exertion.

"You watch that stuff!" I said belligerently. "I could make plenty of trouble for you if I wanted to, I'll bet!"

"Anything wrong?" asked Mrs. Dockey, sticking her head into the room. I would not want to tangle with her.

"No, not now." The Doctor smiled, brushing the knees of his white trousers. "A little Pugilistic Therapy for Jacob Horner. No trouble." She closed the door.

"Now, shall we continue our talk?" he asked me, his eyes twinkling. "You were speaking in a manly way about making trouble."

But I was no longer in a mood to go along with the whole ridiculous business. I'd had enough of the old lunatic for this quarter.

"Or perhaps you've had enough of The Old Crank for today, eh?"

"What would the sheriff in Wicomico think of this farm?" I grumbled. "Suppose the police were sent out to investigate Sexual Therapy?"

The Doctor was unruffled by my threats.

"Do you intend to send them?" he asked pleasantly.

"Do you think I wouldn't?"

"I've no idea," he said, still undisturbed.

"Do you dare me to?"

This question, for some reason or other, visibly upset him: he looked at me sharply.

"Indeed I do not," he said at once. "I'm sure you're quite able to do it. I'm sorry if my tactic for mobilizing you just then made you angry. I did it with all good intent. You *were* paralyzed again, you know."

"You and your paralysis!" I sneered.

"You *have* had enough for today, Horner!" the Doctor said. He too was angry now. "Get out! I hope you get paralyzed driving sixty miles an hour on your way home!" He raised his voice. "Get out of here, you damned moron!"

His obviously genuine anger immediately removed mine, which after the first instant had of course been only a novel mask.

"I'm sorry, Doctor," I said. "I won't lose my temper again."

We exchanged smiles.

"Why not?" He laughed. "It's both therapeutic and pleasant to lose your temper in certain situations." He relit his cigar, which had been dropped during our scuffle. "Two interesting things were demonstrated in the past few minutes, Jacob Horner. I can't tell you about them until your next visit. Good-bye, now. Don't forget to pay Mrs. Dockey."

Out he strode, cool as he could be, and a few moments later out strode I: A Trifle Shaken, but Sure of My Strength.

[JULY 1958]

BRUCE JAY FRIEDMAN

Black Angels

Bruce Jay Friedman (1930–   ) is one of Esquire's *most versatile writers, contributing everything from profiles of movie stars (Raquel Welch, in October 1965) to classic stories like "Black Angels." His humorous essays, collected as* The Lonely Guy's Guide to Life, *first appeared in* Esquire, *as did the sequence of Harry Towns stories that later became novels.*

Smothered by debt, his wife and child in flight, Stefano held fast to his old house in the country, a life buoy in a sea of despair. Let him but keep up the house, return to it each day; before long, his wife would come to her senses, fly back to him. Yet he dreaded the approach of spring, which meant large teams of gardeners who would charge him killing prices to keep the place in shape. Cheapest of all had been the Angeluzzi Brothers, who had gotten him off the ground with a two-hundred-and-fifty-dollar cleanup, then followed through with ninety dollars a month for maintenance, April through October, a hundred extra for the leaf-raking fall windup. Meticulous in April, the four Angeluzzis soon began to dog it; for his ninety, Stefano got only a few brisk lawn cuts and a swipe or two at his flower beds. This spring, unable to work, his life in shreds, Stefano held off on the grounds as long as he could. The grass grew to his shins until one day Swansdowne, a next-door neighbor who had won marigold contests, called on another subject, but with much lawn-mowing and fertilizing in his voice. Stefano dialed the Angeluzzis; then, on an impulse, he dropped the phone and reached for the local paper, running his finger along Home Services. A gardener named Please Try Us caught his fancy. He called the number, asked the deep voice at the other end to come by soon and give him an estimate. The following night, a return call came through.

"I have seen and checked out the place," said the voice, the tones heavy, resonant, solid.

"What'll you take for cleanup?" asked Stefano. "We'll start there."

Long pause. Lip smack. Then, "Thutty dollars."

"Which address did you go to? I'm at 42 Spring. Big old place on the corner of Spring and Rooter."

"That's correct. For fertilizing, that'll be eight extra, making thutty-eight."

"Awful lot of work here," said Stefano, confused, tingling with both guilt and relief. "All right, when can you get at it?"

"Tomorrow morning. Eight o'clock."

"You're on."

Stefano watched them arrive the next day, Sunday, a quartet of massive Negroes in two trucks and two sleek private cars. In stifling heat, they worked in checkered shirts and heavy pants, two with fedoras impossibly balanced on the backs of their great shaved heads. Stefano, a free-lance writer of technical manuals, went back to his work, stopping now and then to check the Negroes through the window. How could they possibly make out on thirty-eight dollars, he wondered. Divided four ways it came to nothing. Gas alone for their fleet of cars would kill their nine-fifty each. He'd give them forty-five dollars to salve his conscience, but still, what about their groceries, rent? Late in the afternoon, he ran out with beers for each. "Plenty of leaves, eh?" he said to Cotten, largest of them, the leader, expressionless in dainty steel-rimmed glasses.

"Take about two and a half days," said the Negro.

"I'm giving you forty-five dollars," said Stefano. "What the hell."

The job actually took three full days, two for the cleanup, a third for the lawn and fertilizing the beds. The last day was a bad one for Stefano. Through his window, he watched the black giants trim the lawn, then kneel in winter clothes and lovingly collect what seemed to be each blade of grass so there'd be no mess. He wanted to run out and tell them to do less work; certainly not at those prices. Yet he loved the prices, too. He could take it all out of expense money, not even bother his regular free-lance payments. At the end of the day, he walked up to Cotten, took out his wallet and said, "I'm giving you cash. So you won't have to bother with a check." It had occurred to him that perhaps the Negroes only did cleanups, no maintenance. By doing enough of them, thousands, perhaps they could sneak by, somehow make a living. "What about maintenance?" he asked the head gardener.

The man scratched his ear, shook his head, finally said, "Can't do your place for less than eighteen dollars a month."

"You guys do some work," said Stefano, shivering with glee. "Best I've seen. I think you're too low. I'll give you twenty-two."

The Negroes came back twice a week, turned Stefano's home into a showplace, hacking down dead trees, planting new ones, filling in dead spots, keeping the earth black and loamy. Swansdowne, who usually let Stefano test-run new gardeners and then swooped down to sign them up if they were good, looked on with envy, yet called one day and said, "I would never let a colored guy touch my place."

"They're doing a great job on mine," said Stefano.

Maybe that explains it, he thought. All of the Swansdownes who won't have Negro gardeners. That's why their rates are low. Otherwise, they'd starve. He felt good, a liberal. Why shouldn't he get a slight break on money?

At the end of May, Stefano paid them their twenty-two dollars and distributed four American-cheese sandwiches. The three assistants took them back to a truck where one had mayonnaise. "You guys do other kinds of work?" Stefano asked Cotten, who leaned on a hoe. "What about painting? A house?"

The gardener looked up at Stefano's colonial. "We do," he said.

"How much would you take?" The best estimate on the massive ten-roomer had been seven hundred dollars.

"Fifty-eight dollars," said the huge Negro, neutral in his steel-rims.

"I'll pay for half the paint," said Stefano.

The following day, when Stefano awakened, the four Negroes, on high, buckling ladders, had half the house done, the paint deep brown, rich and gurgling in the sun. Their gardening clothes were spattered with paint. He'd pick up the cleaning bill, thought Stefano. It was only fair.

"It looks great!" he hollered up to Cotten, swaying massively in the wind.

"She'll shape up time we get the fourth coat on."

By mid-June, the four Negroes had cleaned out Stefano's attic for three dollars, waterproofed his basement for another sixteen; an elaborate network of drainage pipes went in for twelve-fifty. One day he came home to find the floors cleaned, sanded, shellacked, his cabinets scrubbed, linen closets dizzying in their cleanliness. Irritated for the first time—I didn't order this—he melted quickly when he saw the bill. A slip on the bread box read: "You owes us $2.80." Loving the breaks he was getting, Stefano threw them bonuses, plenty of sandwiches, all his old sports jackets, venetian blinds that had come out of the attic and books of fairly recent vintage on Nova Scotia tourism. Never in the thick of marriage had his place been so immaculate; cars slowed down to admire his dramatically painted home, his shrubs bursting with fertility. Enter any room; its cleanliness would tear your head off. With all these ridiculously cheap home services going for him, Stefano felt at times his luck had turned. Still, a cloak of loneliness rode his shoulders, aggravation clogged his throat. If only to hate her, he missed his wife, a young, pretty woman, circling the globe with her lover, an assistant director on daytime TV. He saw pictures of her, tumbling with lust, in state-rooms, inns, the backs of small foreign cars. He missed his son, too, a boy of ten, needing braces. God only knows what shockers he was being exposed to. The pair had fled in haste, leaving behind mementos, toys lined up on shelves, dresses spilling out of chests. Aging quickly, his confidence riddled, Stefano failed in his quest for dates with young girls, speechless and uncertain on the phone. What could he do with himself. At these prices, he could keep his home spotless. But would that make everything all right. Would that haul back a disgruntled wife and son. One night, his heart weighing a ton, he returned from an "Over 28" dance to find the burly Negroes winding up their work. Sweating long into the night, they had rigged up an elaborate network of gas lamps, the better to show off a brilliantly laid out thicket of tea roses and dwarf fruit trees. Total cost for the lighting: Five dollars and fifty cents.

"Really lovely," said Stefano, inspecting his grounds, counting out some bills. "Here," he said to the head gardener. "Take another deuce. In my condition, money means nothing." The huge Negro toweled down his forehead, gathered up his equipment. "Hey," said Stefano. "Come on in for a beer. If I don't talk to someone I'll bust."

"Got to get on," said Cotten. "We got work to do."

"Come on, come on," said Stefano. "What can you do at this hour. Give a guy a break."

The Negro shook his head in doubt, then moved massively toward the house, Stefano clapping him on the back in a show of brotherhood.

Inside, Stefano went for flip-top beers. The gardener sat down in the living room, his great bulk caving deeply into the sofa. For a moment, Stefano worried about gardening clothes, Negro ones to boot, in contact with living-room furniture, then figured the hell with it, who'd complain.

"I've got the worst kind of trouble," said Stefano, leaning back on a

Danish modern slat bench. "Sometimes I don't think I'm going to make it through the night. My wife's checked out on me. You probably figured that out already."

The Negro crossed his great legs, sipped his beer. The steel-rimmed glasses had a shimmer to them and Stefano could not make out his eyes.

"She took the kid with her," said Stefano. "That may be the worst part. You don't know what it's like to have a kid tearing around your house for ten years and then not to hear anything. Or maybe you do?" Stefano asked hopefully. "You probably have a lot of trouble of your own."

Silent, the Negro sat forward and shoved a cloth inside his flannel shirt to mop his chest.

"Anyway, I'll be goddamned if I know what to do. Wait around? Pretend she's never coming back? I don't know what in the hell to do with myself. Where do I go from here?"

"How long she gone?" asked the guest, working on the back of his neck now.

"What's that got to do with it?" asked Stefano. "About four months, I guess. Just before you guys came. Oh, I see what you mean. If she hasn't come back in four months, she's probably gone for good. I might as well start building a new life. That's a good point."

The Negro put away the cloth and folded his legs again, crossing his heavy, blunted fingers, arranging them on the point of one knee.

"It just happened out of the clear blue sky," said Stefano. "Oh, why kid around. It was never any good." He told the Negro about their courtship, the false pregnancy, how he had been "forced" to get married. Then he really started in on his wife, the constant primping, the thousands of ways she had made him jealous, the in-laws to support. He let it all come out of him, like air from a tire, talking with heat and fury; until he realized he had been talking nonstop for maybe twenty minutes, half an hour. The Negro listened to him, patiently, not bothering with his beer. Finally, when Stefano sank back to catch his breath, the gardener asked a question: "You think you any good?"

"What do you mean," said Stefano. "Of course I do. Oh, I get what you're driving at. If I thought I was worth anything, I wouldn't let all of this kill me. I'd just kind of brace myself, dig out and really build something fine for myself. Funny how you make just the right remark. It's really amazing. You know, I've done the analysis bit. Never meant a damned thing to me. I've had nice analysts, tough ones, all kinds. But the way you just let me sound off and then asked that one thing. This is going to sound crazy, but what if we just talked this way, couple of times a week. I just sound off and then you come in with the haymaker, the way you just did. Just for fun, what would you charge me? An hour?"

"Fo' hundred," said the Negro.

"Four hundred. That's really a laugh. You must be out of your head. What are you, crazy? Don't you know I was just kidding around?"

The Negro took a sip of beer and rose to leave. "All right, wait a second," said Stefano. "Hold on a minute. Let's just finish up this hour, all right? Then we'll see about other times. This one doesn't count, does it?"

"It do," said the Negro, sinking into the couch and producing pad and pencil.

"That's not really fair, you know," said Stefano. "To count this one. Anyway, we'll see. Maybe we'll try it for a while. That's some price. Where was I? Whew, all that money. To get back to what I was saying, this girl has been a bitch ever since the day I laid eyes on her. You made me see it tonight. In many ways, I think she's a lot like my mom. . . ."

[DECEMBER 1964]

BARRY TARGAN

Harry Belten and the Mendelssohn

Violin Concerto

Barry Targan (1932–   ) was born in Atlantic City, New Jersey, and educated at Rutgers, Chicago, and Brandeis. When he was thirty-four, Targan published in Esquire what longtime fiction editor Rust Hills calls one of the magazine's best-loved stories, "Harry Belten and the Mendelssohn Violin Concerto." That work became the title story of a collection that won the University of Iowa Short Fiction Award in 1975 and was subsequently published by the university press there. Among Targan's other works of fiction are Surviving Adverse Seasons (1980) and Kingdoms (1981).

Alice Belten labored up the thin wooden outer stairway leading to Josephine Goss's tiny apartment above Fulmer's dress shop. She opened the weather-stained door, streamed into the limited sitting room, and cried, "Oh, Josie. I think my Harry's going crazy." From the day thirty-one years before, when Alice and Harry had married, Josephine Goss, Alice's best friend, had suspected that Harry Belten was crazy. Thirty-one years' knowledge of him fed the suspicion. Her friend's announcement came now as no surprise.

"The violin again?" she asked, but as though she knew.

"Yes," Alice said, almost sobbing, "but worse this time, much worse. Oh God!" She put her hands to her head. "Why was I born?"

"Well, what is it?" Josephine asked.

"Oh God," Alice moaned.

"What is it?" Josephine lanced at her.

Alice snapped her head up, to attention. "A concert. He's going to give a concert. He's going to play in front of people."

Josephine slumped a little in her disappointment. "Is that all? He's played in front of people before, the jerk. Do you want some tea?" she asked in a tone which considered the subject changed.

"No, I don't want any tea. Who could drink? Who could eat? It's not the same. This time it's for *real*. Don't you understand?" Alice waved her hands upward. "This time he thinks he's Heifetz. He's renting an orchestra, a hall. He's going to a big city. He's going to advertise. Oh God! Oh God!" She collapsed into the tears she had sought all day.

Josephine revived. "Well I'll be. . . ." She smiled. "So the jerk has finally flipped for real. Where's he getting the money?"

"A mortgage," Alice managed. "A second mortgage." Although not re-lieved, she was calming. "Harry figures it'll cost about three thousand dollars."

"Three thousand dollars!" Josephine shouted. It was more serious than she had thought. "Does he stand to make anything?"

"No."

"No?"

"Nothing."

"Nothing? Nothing? Get a lawyer," she said and she rose to do it.

Harry Belten sold hardware and appliances for Alexander White, whose store was located in the town of Tyler, population four thousand, southwest New York—the Southern Tier. He had worked for Alexander White for thirty-two years, ever since he came up from the Appalachian coal country of western Pennsylvania on his way to Buffalo and saw the little sign in the general-store window advertising for a clerk. Harry had had the usual young-man dreams of life in the big city, but he had come up in the Depression. He had figured quickly on that distant afternoon that a sure job in Tyler was better than a possible soup line in Buffalo, so he stopped and he stayed. Within a year he had married Alice Miller, the young waitress and cashier at what was then Mosely's filling station, bus depot, and restaurant—the only one in Tyler. Two years later Alice was pregnant and gave birth in a hot August to a son, Jackson (after Andrew Jackson, a childhood hero of Harry's). Two years after that Harry started to pay for a house. That was in 1939. He didn't have the down payment, but in 1939, in or around Tyler, a bank had to take some risk if it wanted to do any business at all. And Harry Belten, after six years in

Tyler and at the same job, was considered by all to be, and in fact was, reliable.

His life had closed in upon him quickly. But, he sometimes reflected, he would not have arranged it to be anything other than what it was.

In 1941 Harry Belten bought a violin and began to learn to play it. Once a week, on Sunday afternoon, he would take the short bus ride over to neighboring Chamsford to Miss Houghton, a retired schoolteacher who gave music lessons to an occasional pupil. A couple of jokes were made about it in Tyler at the time, but the war was starting and all interest went there. Alice was pregnant again, and in 1942 gave birth to a daughter, Jane. Harry started working part time in a ball-bearing factory in Buffalo. He drove up with four other men from Tyler three times a week. Mr. White didn't object, for there wasn't much to sell in the hardware line anymore, and besides, it was patriotic. Through it all Harry practiced the violin. Hardly anyone knew and no one cared, except maybe Josephine Goss, who never tired of remembering that Harry's violin playing and the Second World War started together.

"Harry," Alexander White called out from his little cubbyhole office in the back of the store, "could you come back here a minute please?"

"Right away, Alex," Harry answered. He took eighty cents out of a dollar for nails, handed the customer his change, and walked to the back of the store. "Keep an eye on the front," he said to Martin Bollard, who was stacking paint cans, as he passed him. While not technically a manager—besides himself and White there were only two others—Harry was by far the senior clerk. Frequently he would open and close the store, and more than once, when the boss took a vacation or had an operation, he had run the entire business, from ordering stock to making the bank deposits and ledger entries. Over the accumulating years White had sometimes reminded himself that you don't find a Harry Belten every day of the week or around some corner.

Harry squeezed into the office and sat down in the old ladderback chair. "What can I do for you, Alex?"

"Oh, nothing . . . nothing," the older man said. He was looking at a household-supplies catalog on the desk, thumbing through it. After a few seconds he said, "You know these new ceramic-lined garbage pails? You think we should try a gross?"

"Too many," Harry said. "We don't sell a gross of pails in a year."

"Yeah, yeah. That's right, Harry. It was just that the discount looked so good." He thumbed the catalog some more. "Harry," he started again, "yesterday at lunch down at Kiwanis I heard a couple of guys saying you was going to give a violin concert?"

"Yes sir, Alex. That's correct. As a matter of fact," he continued, "I'd been meaning to talk to you about it." Harry rushed on into his own interest and with an assurance that left his employer out. He made it all seem so "done," so finished, so accomplished. "You see, I figure I'll need a year to get ready, to really get ready. I mean I know all the fingerings and bowings of the pieces I'll be playing. But what I need is *polish*. So I've contacted a teacher—you know, a really top professional teacher. And, well, my lessons are on Monday afternoons starting in a month. The end of April that is." Alexander White looked sideways and up at Harry.

"Harry," he said slowly, smilingly, "the store isn't closed on Mondays. It's closed on Wednesday afternoons. Can't you take your lessons on Wednesday?"

"No," Harry said. "Karnovsky is busy on Wednesday. Maybe," he offered, "we could close the store on Monday and open on Wednesday instead?" White gave a slight start at such a suggestion. "Anyway, I've got to have off Monday afternoons. Without pay, of course." Alexander White shook his hand in front of his eyes and smiled again.

"Harry, when did you say the concert was? In a year, right? And you said just now that you knew all the fingers and bows?"

"Fingerings and bowings," Harry corrected.

"Fingerings and bowings. Yeah. You said so yourself all you need was polish. Okay. Good! But Harry, why a *year?* I mean how much polish do you need for Tyler anyway?"

"Oh," Harry said, "the concert isn't going to be in Tyler. Oh no sir." Harry was igniting. It was something that Alexander White did not behold easily: this fifty-one-year-old man—his slightly crumpled face, the two deep thrusts of baldness on his head, the darkening and sagging flesh beneath the eyes—beginning to burn, to be lustrous. "This isn't going to be like with the quartet that time or like with Tingle on the piano. No sir, Alex. This is *it!* I'm giving the concert in Oswego."

"Uuuh," White grunted as though he had been poked sharply above the stomach.

"I'm renting the Oswego Symphony Orchestra—two days for rehearsals, one day for the performance," Harry continued.

"Uuuh. Aaah," White grunted and wheezed again, nodding, his eyes wincing and watering a little.

"Are you okay, Alex?" Harry asked.

"Harry!" Martin Bollard shouted from the front of the store. It meant that there were customers waiting.

"Be right there," Harry shouted back. He stood to leave and started to squeeze his way out. "And I'm renting the auditorium there," he said over his shoulder and was gone back to work.

"Eeeh. Uuuh," White grunted in conclusion, his breath escaping him. The corners of his mouth turned down. He had blanched and the color had not come back. He said softly to himself, "Then it's true," and waited as if for refutation from a spirit more benign than Harry's demonic one. "But Harry," he rose up, "you're not that kind of fiddler!"

"Mr. Belten, in all candor, you are not a concert-caliber violinist." Karnovsky was speaking. His English was perfect, tempered by a soft, prewar Viennese lilt which could bring delicate memories of music and a time past. Harry had just finished playing a Spanish dance by Sarasate. He put his violin down on top of the piano and turned to the old, gentle man. It was the first time Karnovsky had heard him play.

"I know," Harry said. "I know. But I don't want to be a concert violinist. All I want to do is to give this one concert." Somewhere Karnovsky sighed. Harry went on. "I know all the notes for all the pieces I'm going to play, all the fingerings and bowings. What I need now is polish."

"Mr. Belten, what you need is . . ." But Karnovsky did not finish. "Mr. Belten, there is more to concertizing than all the notes, all the fingerings and bowings. There is a certain . . ." And again he did not finish. "Mr. Belten, have you ever heard Heifetz? Milstein? Stern? Either on records or live?" Harry nodded. "Well that, Mr. Belten, that kind of polish you aren't . . . I'm not able to give you." Karnovsky ended, embarrassed by his special exertion. He was a small man, bald and portly. His eyebrows flickered with every nuance of meaning or emotion, either when he spoke or when he played. He stood now before Harry, slightly red, his eyes wide. Harry soothed him.

"Ah, Mr. Karnovsky, that kind of playing no man can give to another. I don't ask so much from you. Just listen and suggest. Do to me what you would do to a good fiddler." Karnovsky could not look at him longer this way. He turned around.

"What do you propose to play for your concert, Mr. Belten?" Suspicions began to rise in Karnovsky's mind.

"I thought I'd start with the Vivaldi Concerto in A Minor." Karnovsky nodded. "Then Chausson's *Poème*, then the two Beethoven romances, then something by Sarasate. . . ." Karnovsky's head continued to bob. "And finish up with the Mendelssohn." Karnovsky could not help it. He spun around on Harry.

"The *Mendelssohn?*"

"Yes."

"The Mendelssohn? The Mendelssohn Violin Concerto? You are going to play the Mendelssohn? You know the Mendelssohn?"

"Yes," Harry said. "Yes. Yes." He was himself excited by the excitement of the older man, but in a different way.

"How do you know the Mendelssohn?" Karnovsky asked him. His tone was tougher. A fool was a fool, but music was music. Some claims you don't make. Some things you don't say.

"I've studied it," Harry answered.

"How long?" Karnovsky probed. "With whom?"

"Eighteen years. With myself. Ever since I learned how to play in all the positions, I've worked on the Mendelssohn. Every day a little bit. Phrase by phrase. No matter what I practiced, I always saved a little time for the Mendelssohn. I thought the last forty measures of the third movement would kill me. It took me four and a half years." Harry looked up at Karnovsky, but that innocent man had staggered back to the piano bench and collapsed. "It's taken a long time," Harry smiled. No matter what else, he was enjoying talking about music.

"Eighteen *years?*" Karnovsky croaked from behind the piano.

"Eighteen years," Harry reaffirmed, "and now I'm almost ready." *But is the world?* Karnovsky thought to himself. His own wryness softened him toward this strange and earnest man.

"It's fifteen dollars an hour, you know," he tried finally.

"Right," Harry said. Karnovsky fumbled in his pocket and withdrew a white Life Saver. He rubbed it in his fingers and then flipped it like a coin in the air. He caught it in his hand and put it into his mouth. Outside, March rain slicked the grimy streets.

"Okay," he muttered. "Like we agreed before you . . . when we spoke . . . on the . . ." The eyebrows fluttered. "Go," he said. "Get the fiddle. We begin." Harry obeyed.

"Then you're really going through with it?" Alice asked.

"Of course," Harry said, swallowing quickly the last of his Jell-O. He pushed his chair back and stood up.

"Where are you going?" Alice asked.

"I've got something Karnovsky showed me that I want to work on. It's

terrific." He smiled. "Already I'm learning stuff I never dreamed of." He started
to leave.

"Harry," Alice said, getting up too, "first let's talk a little, huh?"

"Okay," he said, "talk."

"Come into the living room," she said, and walked into it. Harry followed.
They both sat down on the sofa. Alice said, "Harry, tell me. Why are you doing
it?"

"Doing what?" he asked.

"Throwing three thousand bucks out the window, is what," Alice said, her
voice beginning to rise, partly in offended surprise at his question, at his
innocence.

"What are you talking about, 'throw out the window'? What kind of talk
is that? Is lessons from Louis Karnovsky throwing money away? Is performing
the Mendelssohn Violin Concerto with a full, professional orchestra behind you
throwing money away? What are you talking about? Drinking! That's throwing
money away. Gambling! That's throwing money away. But the Mendelssohn
Violin Concerto? Jeezzz," he concluded turning away his head, not without
impatience.

Alice sat there trying to put it together. Something had gotten confused,
switched around. It had all seemed so obvious at first. But now it was she who
seemed under attack. *What had drinking to do with anything?* she wondered. *Who
was doing what wrong?* She gave it up to try another way.

"Do you remember when you and the other guys played together and
sometimes put on a show . . . concert . . . in the Grange Hall?"

Harry smiled and then laughed. "Yeah," he said. "Boy, were we a lousy
string quartet." But it was a pleasant memory and an important one, and it
released him from both his excitement and his scorn.

Shortly after the war some gust of chance, bred out of the new mobility
enforced upon the land, brought to Tyler a cellist in the form of a traveling
salesman. His name was Fred Miller and he represented a company which sold
electric milking machines, their necessary supporting equipment, and other dairy
sundries. It was not the first merchandise Fred Miller had hawked across America; it proved not to be the last—only one more item of an endless linkage of
products which seemed to gain their reality more from such as he than from their
own actual application. Who, after all, can believe in the abstraction of an electric
milking machine, of plastic dolls, of suppositories, of Idaho? But Fred Miller was
real, full of some American juice that pumped vitality into whatever he touched.
And he had brought his cello with him.

After they played, over beer and sandwiches, Fred Miller would tell them about America and about music. "Once," he would begin, "when I was selling automobile accessories [or brushes or aluminum storm windows or animal food] in Denver, one night after supper I was outside the hotel when looking up the street I saw on the movie marquee, instead of the usual announcement of 'Fair star in a country far,' the single word 'Francescatti.' " (The other three would look at each other knowingly.) "Of course, I hurried to the theater." And then he would take them through the music, through the performance, piece by piece, gesture by gesture, play by play.

"And there he was, not more than twenty bars away from his entrance, big as life and cool as day, wiping his hands on his handkerchief, that forty-grand Strad sticking out from under his chin. *And then he starts to mess with the bow.* Yep. He's got both hands on the bow tightening the hairs. It's a bar to go. It's two beats away. You're sure he's missed it and *wham.* Faster than the speed of light he's whacked that old bow down on the cleanest harmonic A you've ever heard, and it's off to the races, playing triple stops all the way and never missing nothing. Hand me a beer, will you, Harry?" And only then would the three of them breathe.

There was the one about when Milstein lost his bow and it almost stabbed a lady in the eighth row. Or the Heifetz one, where he didn't move anything but his fingers and his bow arm, not even his eyes, through the entire Beethoven Concerto. There was Stern and Rosand and Oistrakh and Fuchs and Ricci and Piatigorsky and Feuermann and Rose and the Juilliard and the Hungarian and the Budapest and Koussevitsky and Toscanini and Ormandy and the gossip and the feuds and the apocryphal. All of music came to Tyler on those Thursday nights mixed gloriously with the exotic names of Seattle and Madison and Butte and Tucson and with the rubber, steel, plastic, and edible works of all our hands and days.

One Tuesday Fred Miller came into the hardware store to tell Harry that he was leaving. The electric-milking-machine business hadn't made it and he was off to Chicago to pick up a new line. There wasn't even time for a farewell performance. For a few weeks after, Harry, Tingle, and the reconstructed viola player from Bath had tried some improvised trios, but the spirit had gone out of the thing. Harry would sometimes play to Tingle's piano accompaniment or to Music Minus One records. But mostly he played alone.

"Harry," Alice broke in upon him gently, for she sensed where he had been, "Harry, all I'm trying to say is that for people who don't have a lot of money, three thousand dollars is a lot of money to spend . . . on anything!"

"I'll say," Harry agreed, getting up. "I'll be five years at least paying this thing off." He walked away to the room at the back of the house in which he had practiced for twenty-four years. Alice sat, miserable in her dumbness, frustrated and frightened. Something was catching and pulling at her which she couldn't understand. What was she worried about? When he had spent the eight hundred dollars on the new violin, she had not flinched. She had taken the six hundred dollars of hi-fi equipment in her wifely stride, indeed, had come to like it. All their married life they had lived in genteel debt. She looked then as she had in other anxious times for reference and stability to the bedrock of her life, but what she found there only defeated her further: the children were grown and married, the boy, even, had gone to college; all the insurance and the pension plans were paid to date; the second mortgage on the house—which would pay for all of this concertizing—would only push back the final ownership slightly, for the house, on a thirty-year mortgage to begin with, had only four more years to go. The impedimenta of existence were under control.

As Alice sat in the midst of this, the phone rang. She rose to answer it. What was the problem? Was there a problem? Whose problem? It was all so hard. Alice could have wept.

"Hello, Alice." It was Josephine Goss.

"Yes."

"I've been talking to the lawyer." Josephine sounded excited in the way people do who act after obliterating ages of inaction have taught them to forget the taste—giddy, high-pitched, trying to outrun the end of it. "He says you can't do anything legal to stop Harry unless he really is crazy, and if he really is crazy, you've got to be able to prove it."

"So?" Alice said, bracing for the lash of her friend's attitude her questions always earned.

"*So?* So you got to get him to a psychiatrist, so that's what." All at once Alice was deeply frightened, only to discover in the center of her fear the finest speck of relief. Terrible as it was to contemplate, was this the answer? Was this why nothing made sense with Harry anymore? Was he really mad?

From the back of the house Harry's violin sounded above it all.

Harry came out of the storeroom with an armload of brooms.

"Well, if it ain't Pangini himself," Billy Rostend shouted out.

"Paganini," Harry corrected him, laughing, "the greatest of them all." He put the brooms down. "What can I do for you, Billy?"

"I came for some more of that off-white caulking compound I bought last week. But what I'd really like is to know what is all this about you giving a concert in Oswego. You really going to leave all us poor people and become a big star?"

"Not a chance," Harry said. "How many tubes do you want?"

"Eight. But no kidding, Harry, what's the story?" Alexander White put down the hatchet he had been using to break open nail kegs to listen. The shy, ubiquitous Tingle, a frequent visitor to the store, slipped quietly behind a rack of wooden handles for picks and axes. Martin Bollard and Mrs. George Preble, who had been talking closely and earnestly about an electric toaster at the front of the store, paused at the loudness of Billy's voice and at the question too. There were many in Tyler who wanted to know the story.

"No story," Harry answered him. "I've got this feeling, you see, that I've always wanted to give a real, big-time concert. And now I'm going to do it. That's all. It's that simple." He had been figuring on a pad. "That'll be three twelve, Billy. Do you want a bag?" Billy became conspiratorial. He dropped his voice to a whisper, but it was sharp and whistling.

"Come on, Harry, what gives?" It was more a command than a question, the kind of thing living for three decades in a small town permits, where any sense of secret is affront.

"It's nothing more than what I just told you, Billy. It's something I've always wanted to do, and now I'm going to do it."

"Yeah!" Billy spat at him. "Well, I'll believe that when I believe a lot of other things." He scooped up the tubes of caulking and slammed out of the store. Mrs. George Preble followed, either unnerved by the encounter or bent on gossip, without buying the toaster. Harry looked at Martin Bollard and shrugged his shoulders, but what could Martin say, who also wanted answers to the question Billy had asked. Only the wraithlike Tingle, glancing quickly about himself twice, looked at Harry, smiled, and then was gone.

"Harry, could I see you a minute," Alexander White called to him.

In back, in the little office, White explained to Harry that "it" was all over the town, indeed, all over the entire area of the county that had contact with Tyler. He explained to Harry that business was a "funny thing" and that people were "fickle." He explained that if a man didn't like you he would drive (county roads being so good now) ten miles out of his way to do his business elsewhere. After more than thirty years people didn't distinguish between Harry Belten and White's Hardware. What Harry did reflected on the business. And what Harry was doing, whatever it was, wasn't good for it. Harry listened carefully and attentively, as he always had. In thirty-two years he had never sassed the boss

or had a cross word with him. He wasn't going to start now. Whatever was
bugging Alexander White and the town of Tyler was something they were going
to have to learn to live with until April 28, eight months away.

"Yes, sir," Harry said. After almost a minute, when Alexander White
didn't say anything more, Harry went back to work. And Alexander White went
back to opening nail kegs, smashing vigorously and repeatedly at the lids,
splintering them beyond necessity.

                    When Harry came into Karnovsky's stu-
dio and said hello, Karnovsky's expressive eyebrows pumped up and down four
times before he said a thing. The gray-and-yellow sallowness of the old man's
skin took on an illusory undercast of healthy pink from the blood that had risen.

"Mr. Belton, from the beginning I have felt strangely about our relationship. I never minced words. I told you from the beginning that you didn't have
it to be a concert violinist. That the idea of you concertizing, beginning to
concertize, you, a man your age, was . . . was . . . *crazy!*" Harry had never seen
the gentle Karnovsky sputter before. It affected him deeply. "But okay, I
thought," Karnovsky continued, "so who cares. So a man from the Southern
Tier wants to put on a performance with the local high-school orchestra or
something. So okay, I thought. So who cares." He was using his arms to form
his accusation the way that a conductor forms a symphony. Karnovsky brought
his orchestra to a climax. "But now I find that you have engaged the Oswego
Symphony Orchestra and are going to perform in . . . in public! *You are doing
this thing for real!*" Not in years, perhaps never before, had Karnovsky shouted
so loudly. The sound of his reaching voice surprised him, shocked him, and he
fell silent, but he continued to look at Harry, his eyebrows bouncing.

After a moment Harry asked, "Am I committing some crime? What is this
terrible thing I am about to do?"

Karnovsky hadn't thought about it in those terms. Six weeks earlier he had
told Bronson, his stuffy colleague at the university where he was Professor of
Violin, about Harry. A frustrated Heifetz, he had called him. He had also used
the word "nut," but gently and with humor. So it was that when at lunch that
very day, Bronson had told him that his Harry Belten had hired a professional
orchestra and had rented a hall in the middle of the downtown of a large city,
Karnovsky felt unjustly sinned against, like the man who wakens belatedly to the
fact that "the joke's on him." He considered, and reasonably, the effect that this
might have upon his reputation. To be linked with this mad venture was not

something you could easily explain away to the musical world. And Karnovsky had a reputation big enough to be shot at by the droning snipers who, living only off of wakes, do what they can to bring them about. Finally, there was the central offense of his musicianship. After fifty-five years of experience as performer and teacher, he knew what Harry's performance would sound like. It wouldn't be unbearably bad, but it didn't belong where Harry was intent on putting it. Maybe, he thought, that would be the best approach.

"Mr. Belten, the musicians will laugh at you. Anyone in your audience—if you even have an audience—who has heard a professional play the Mendelssohn will laugh at you."

"So." Harry shrugged it off. "What's so terrible about that? They laughed at you once."

"What?" Karnovsky started. "What are you talking about?"

"In 1942, when you played the Schoenberg Violin Concerto for the first time in Chicago. Worse than laugh at you, they booed and shouted and hissed, even. And one lady threw her pocketbook and it hit you on the knee. I read about it all in *Grant's History of Music Since 1930.*"

Who could help but be softened? Karnovsky smiled. "Believe me, that performance I'll never forget. Still, in Italy in 1939, in Milan, it was worse. Three guys in the audience tried to get up on the stage, to kill me I guess, at least from the way they were screaming and shaking their fists. Thank God there were some police there. I was touring with the Schoenberg Concerto then, so I guess they had heard about the trouble it was causing and that's why the police were there." He was warming to his memory and smiling broadly now. *It is a good thing*, he thought, *to have a big, good thing to remember.*

"So what's the difference?" Harry asked.

"What?" Karnovsky came back to the room slowly.

"They laughed at you. They'll laugh at me. What's the difference?"

Repentantly softened, Karnovsky gently said, "It wasn't me they were laughing at, it was the music." He looked away from Harry. "With you it will be you."

"Oh, of course," Harry agreed. "What I meant was what is the difference to the performer?" Harry really wanted to know. "Does the performer take the cheers for himself but leave the boos for the composer? In Italy they were going to kill *you*, not Schoenberg."

Karnovsky had moved to the large window and looked out, his back to Harry. March had turned to May. He heard Harry unzip the canvas cover of his violin case.

"No lesson," he said without turning. He heard Harry zip the case closed again. "Next week," he whispered, but Harry heard and left. Karnovsky stood before the window a long time. Auer had Heifetz, he thought. Kneisel had Fuchs. And I got Harry Belten.

"You're home early," Alice called out.

"Yeah. It's too hot to sell, too hot to buy. White closed up early." He had the evening paper under his arm and in his hand the mail.

"Oh, the mail," Alice said. "I forgot to get it. Anything?"

Harry was looking. He saw a letter addressed to him from the Oswego Symphony, opened it and read.

"Ha!" he shouted, flinging his hand upward.

"What is it?" Alice came over to him.

"It's from the Oswego Symphony. They want to cancel the agreement. They say they didn't know I was going to use the orchestra to give my own public performance." Harry hit the letter with his fist. "They want out. Listen." Harry read from the letter.

". . . given the peculiar nature of the circumstances surrounding your engagement of the orchestra and considering that it is a civically sponsored organization which must consider the feelings and needs both present and future of the community, I am sure that you will be sensitive to the position in which we find ourselves. It has taken many years to establish in the minds and hearts of our people here a sense of respect and trust in the orchestra, and while this is not to say that your intended performance would violate that trust, yet it must be obvious to you that it would perhaps severely qualify it. It goes without saying that upon receipt of the contract, your check will be returned at once along with a cash consideration of fifty dollars for whatever inconvenience this will have involved you in."

Somewhere in the middle of the first ponderous sentence, Alice had gotten lost. "Harry," she asked, "what does it mean?"

"Wait," Harry said as he read the letter again. And then he laughed, splendidly and loud. "It means," he gasped out to her, "that they are offering me my first chance to make money from the violin—by *not* playing." He roared. "Well, the hell with them!" he shouted up at the ceiling. "A contract is a contract. We play!" And he thundered off to his music room to write a letter saying so.

"Harry," Alice called after him. "Harry," she trailed off. But he was gone. She had meant to tell him that the children were coming that night for supper.

And she had meant to tell him that Tingle had quietly left at the front door that morning a bundle of large maroon-and-black posters announcing the debut of Harry Belten in Oswego. But, then, it seemed that it was not important to tell him, that until all of this was settled one way or another she would not be able to tell what was important or what was not. Under her flaming flesh, she felt heavy, sodden, cold.

Throughout supper he regaled them with his excitement. Although neither of his children had become musicians, Jackson had learned the piano and Jane the violin. But once past high school they had left their instruments and their skill in that inevitable pile of lost things heaped up by the newer and for a time more attractive urgencies. College had engulfed the boy, marriage and babies the girl. As children they had made their music and had even liked it, but the vital whip of love had never struck them. Still, they had lived too long in that house and with that man not to be sympathetic to his joy. It was, then, wrenchingly difficult when, after supper, after the ice cream on the summer porch which he and his father had built, Jackson told his father that everyone was concerned by what they thought was Harry's strange behavior. Would he consent to be examined?

"Examined?" Harry asked.

"By a doctor," his son answered.

The daughter looked away.

"What's the matter?" Harry looked around surprised. "I feel fine."

"By a different kind of doctor, Dad."

"Oh," Harry said, and quickly understood. "By a . . . uh . . . a psychiatrist?"

"Yes." Jackson's voice hurried on to add, to adjust, to soften. "Dad . . . it's not that we . . ."

But Harry cut him off. "Okay," he said.

They all turned and leaned toward him as though they expected him to fall down.

"Daddy?" his daughter began, putting her hand out to him. She didn't think that he had understood. She wanted him to be certain that he understood what was implied. But he forestalled her, them.

"It's okay," he said, nodding. "I understand. A psychiatrist. Make the arrangements." And then, to help them out of their confused silence and their embarrassment, he said, "Look. I really may be nuts or something, but not," he added, "the way everybody thinks." And with the confidence of a man who knows a thing or two about his own madness, he kissed them all good night and went to bed.

By the middle of September all kinds of arrangements had been made or remained to be made. First of all, there was the Oswego Symphony. A series of letters between Mr. Arthur Stennis, manager of the orchestra, and Harry had accomplished nothing. It was finally suggested that Harry meet with the Board of Directors personally. A date, Tuesday afternoon, September 21, was set. Then there was the psychiatrist. For convenience, an appointment had been made for Tuesday morning. The psychiatrist was in Rochester. Harry's plan was to have his lesson as usual Monday afternoon, sleep over in Buffalo, drive to Rochester and the psychiatrist the following morning, and then on to Oswego and the Board of the Symphony in the afternoon; home that night and back to work on Wednesday. That was the way he explained it to Alexander White at the store.

After lunch on the 20th of September Harry prepared to enter upon his quest. He knew it was off to a battle that he went, so he girded himself and planned. And it was the first time he would be sleeping away from home without his wife since he took his son camping fourteen years before. He was enjoying the excitement.

"Is everything in the suitcase?" he asked Alice.

"Yes," she said.

"Are you sure?"

"Yes, yes. I've checked it a dozen times." She held up the list and read it off. "Toothbrush, shaving, underwear, shirt, handkerchief."

"Tie?"

"Tie."

"Okay," he said. "Tonight I'll call you from the Lake View Hotel and tomorrow after the doctor I'll call you too. I won't call after the meeting. I'll just drive right home." He picked up the suitcase and walked toward the door. "Wish me luck," he said.

"Oh, Harry," Alice called and ran to him. She kissed him very hard on his cheek and hugged him to her. "Good luck," she said.

Harry smiled at the irony. "With whom?" he asked.

"With . . . with all of them," she said, laughing and squeezing his arm.

At the door he picked up his violin case and, hoisting it under his arm in exaggerated imitation of an old-time movie gangster, turned and sprayed the room. "Rat-a-tat-tat."

They both laughed. Harry kissed his wife and left the house, his weapon ready in his hand.

The psychiatrist was fat and reddish, his freckles still numerous and prominent. He sat behind an expensive-looking desklike table and smoked a large, curved pipe. Harry thought that he looked like a nice man.

"Good morning, Mr. Belten," he said, gesturing for Harry to be seated. "Please, be comfortable."

"That pipe smells wonderful," Harry said. The doctor wrote on a legal-size yellow pad on the desk. "Did you write that down?" Harry asked.

The doctor looked up and smiled. "Not exactly. I wrote down something about what you said."

"Oh," Harry nodded.

"Mr. Belten, do you know why you're here?" the psychiatrist asked.

"Certainly," Harry answered. "For you to see if I'm crazy."

"Not exactly. In fact, not at all." The word "crazy" made the doctor's ears redden. "Your family felt that your behavior in the past six months exhibited a definite break with your behavior patterns of the past and felt that, with your consent, an examination now would be useful in determining any potential developments of an aberrated nature. Are you laughing?" he asked Harry, a bit put off.

"I was just thinking, my family felt that, all that?"

The doctor laughed too.

"Doctor, do you know why my family felt whatever it was you said they felt and wanted me examined? I'll tell you. One: Because they can't understand why I want to give this big, public concert. Two: Because it's costing me three thousand dollars, which for me is a lot of money. And three: Because my wife's best friend, who has always disliked me for no good reason, put the bug into my wife."

"Suppose you tell me about it," the doctor said.

Although not certain what the doctor meant by "it," Harry told him plenty. He told him about Alexander White and the hardware business and about Tyler, about Fred Miller and about Miss Houghton, the old violin teacher, and about Karnovsky, the new one, and about the teachers in between. He told him about Josephine Goss and about his children, about his wife and about the gentle Tingle and about when he bought the new violin. It took a long time to tell all the things that Harry was telling. The doctor was writing rapidly.

"Are you writing down things about that too?" Harry asked.

The doctor paused and looked up at Harry. "Do you want to see what I'm writing?" he asked.

"No," Harry said. "I trust you."

The doctor leaned forward. "Good," he said. "Now, what do you mean by 'trust me'?"

"I mean," Harry answered, "that you'll see I'm not craz . . . not . . . ah . . ." He gave it up with a shrug. ". . . *crazy* and that you'll tell my family that and they'll feel better and won't try to stop me from giving the concert."

The doctor leaned back heavily. His pipe had gone out. "Mr. Belten, I can tell you right now that you're not *crazy*—as you put it—and that I have nothing to do with stopping you from giving your concert. Even if I thought you were *crazy* I couldn't stop you. It would have to go through the courts, there would have to be a trial . . ."

"Fine," Harry interrupted. He stood up. "Just tell them that nothing's wrong with me."

"I didn't say that," the doctor said.

Harry sat down. "What do you mean?" he asked.

"Well." The doctor lit his pipe at length. "Sometimes people can be 'sane' and still 'have something wrong with them.' " He was uncomfortable with Harry's phrasing but decided to use it for the sake of clarity. "By helping the individual to find out what that thing is, we help him to lead a . . . a . . . *happier* life."

"Oh, I get it." Harry brightened. "We find out why I want to give the concert so that when I do give it I'll enjoy it even more?"

"Not exactly." The doctor smiled, but something in what Harry had said lurked dangerously over him. He stiffened slightly as he said, "By finding out why you want to give it maybe we discover that it isn't so important after all, that maybe, finally, you don't really need to give it, that you would be just as happy, maybe happier, by *not* giving it." He continued, his pipe steaming, "There are all kinds of possibilities. It might easily be that your apparent compulsion to give this concert is in reality a way of striking back at the subconscious frustrations of a small life, a way of grasping out for some of the excitement, some of the thrill that you never had."

"Sure," Harry said. "Now that you put it that way, I can see where it could be that too." Harry smiled. "That's pretty good." The doctor smiled. "Still, I don't see where that means that I *shouldn't* have the thrill, the excitement of giving the concert. Maybe after the concert I won't have any more—what did you call them—'subconscious frustrations.' Maybe the best thing for me *is* to give the concert."

There was a long silence. The doctor let his pipe go out and stared at Harry. At last he said, "Why not?"

It didn't take the Board, or more precisely, Mr. Arthur Stennis, manager of the orchestra and secretary to the Board, more than ten minutes to come to the point. To wit: even though they (he) had executed a contract with one Harry Belten, the Board felt that the reputation of the orchestra had to be protected and that there were sufficient grounds to charge misrepresentation on his part and take the whole thing to court if necessary, which action could cost Harry Belten a small fortune. Why didn't he take their generous offer (now up to two hundred dollars) for returning the contract and forget the whole thing?

"Because," Harry explained again, "I don't want the money. I want to give a concert with a professional orchestra." But that simple answer, which had alienated others, did not aid him here.

He looked around him at the other eight members of the Board. Five were women, all older than Harry, all looking identical in their rinsed-gray hair and in those graceless clothes designed to capture women in their age. They all wore rimless glasses and peered out at Harry, silently, flatly, properly. No help there, he thought. There was the conductor, Morgenstern, a good minor-leaguer. He had said nothing and had not even looked at Harry from the time both had entered the room. Next to him was the treasurer, elected to the Board but, Harry knew, strictly a hired hand. He would take no opposite side. Finally there was Mr. Stanley Knox, eighty-three years old and one of the wealthier men in Oswego, improbably but defiantly present. Although Harry had never seen this ancient man before that afternoon, he knew instinctively that he knew him well. Stanley Knox wore the high-button boot of the past. The too-large check of his unlikely shirt, the width of his tie, the white, green-lined workman's suspenders which Harry glimpsed under the Montgomery Ward suit marked Stanley Knox for what he basically was: for all that counted, just one more of Harry's customers. He had dealt with Stanley Knoxes for more than thirty years. Had he learned anything in all that time that would matter now? Yes.

"It isn't fair," Harry said.

"It might not seem fair to you," Stennis countered, "but would it be fair to the people of Oswego?" He looked around the table in that kind of bowing gesture which suggested that he spoke for them all.

But Harry pursued. "You start by being fair one man at a time." He paused for that to work. Then he continued. "But *besides* me," he said, waving himself out of the picture, "it isn't fair to the musicians. You talk about the good of the orchestra, but you take bread out of the musicians' mouths. Do you think *they* would mind playing with me?"

"What does each man lose?" Stanley Knox asked of anyone. His eyes were rheumy and his teeth chattered in his head.

"For two rehearsals and the performance, between thirty and forty dollars a man," Harry answered.

Stanley Knox looked at Stennis. "Hee, hee," he began. His head lolled for a moment and then straightened. "That's a lot of money for a man to lose."

"Mr. Knox," Stennis explained in the tone affected for the young and the senile, "the thirty dollars lost now could mean much more to the individual members of the orchestra in the years to come. The thirty dollars now should be looked at as an investment in the future, a future of faith and trust that the Oswego Symphony will bring to its people the *best* in music *all* of the time." He said the last looking, glaring, at Harry.

The old man leaned forward in his chair, shaking, and said, "Forty bucks now is forty bucks now." His spittle flew around him. He slapped his open palm down upon the sleek conference table. And then he asked Stennis, "Have you ever heard him play?" Stennis told him no. "Then how do you know he's so bad?" The old ladies, who had been watching either Harry or Stanley Knox, now turned to Stennis. It was the first sign that Harry had a chance.

Then Stennis said, too prissily, too impatiently, "Because at fifty-one years of age you *don't* start a career as a concert violinist. You *don't* start giving concerts."

But that was exactly the wrong thing to say.

"Get your fiddle and play for us," the old man said to Harry. Harry got up and walked to the back of the room where his violin case rested on a table. He took the violin out of the case. Behind him he could hear Stennis squawk:

"Mr. Knox. This is *still* a Board meeting and we are *still* subject to the rules of parliamentary procedure."

"Shut up, Stennis," Stanley Knox said. Harry came forward and played. After he finished a pleasant little minuet of Haydn's he saw the old ladies smiling.

"Very nice," Stanley Knox said.

Stennis interrupted him, feverishly. "But Haydn minuets don't prove anything. My twelve-year-old *daughter* can play that, for God's sake."

Stanley Knox paid him no heed. "Do you know 'Turkey in the Straw'?"

Harry nodded and played. Stennis was frantic. As Harry finished, he stood up. "Mr. Knox. I must insist on order." He looked around him for support, and, much as they were enjoying the music, the old ladies nodded, reluctantly, in agreement—Board business was, after all, Board business.

But Stanley Knox slapped the table for his own order. "Quiet," he commanded. "Let the boy play. Play 'The Fiddler's Contest,' " he ordered Harry.

"*Mr. Knox!*" Stennis shouted.

"*Quiet!*" Knox shouted back. "Let the boy play."

Harry played.

Stennis hit his hand to his head and rushed noisily from the room.

One by one the old ladies tiptoed out, and then the treasurer left, and then Morgenstern, who walked by Harry and neither looked at him nor smiled nor frowned. Harry played on.

"Let the boy play," Stanley Knox roared, pounding the table. "Let the boy play."

By the time Alexander White ate lunch on Monday, April 24, Harry was halfway to Buffalo and his last lesson with Karnovsky. "Well, this is the week," he had cheerfully observed for White that morning. "It sure is," his wearied boss had replied. Although it was spring and the busier time of the year in the hardware business, he had suggested that Harry take off Tuesday as well as the other three and a half days of the week. Harry had objected that he didn't mind working Tuesday. "I know," White told him. "It's me. I object. Go. Get this thing over with." So Harry went. Now Alexander White sat in the Tyler Arms coffee shop—restaurant on Route 39 eating a chicken-salad sandwich. It was two in the afternoon, but he couldn't have gotten away sooner. Louis Bertrand came into the shop and walked over to where Alexander White was sitting.

"Mind if I join you, Alex?" he asked.

"No, no. Sit down," White said, gesturing to the seat opposite him. But even before Bertrand had settled creakingly down into the cane chair, White regretted it.

"So Harry's gone and left you," he observed lightly.

For a fact, White thought, everything travels fast in a small town. "No, no. He had three and a half days off so I gave him the fourth too. Let him get it out of his system. Thank God when this week is over." He went to bite into the other half of his sandwich but found that he didn't want it. He sipped at his coffee several times. Thank God when this week is over, he thought.

"But will it be over? Will he get it out of his system?"

"What? What do you mean? You don't think he's going to become a musician, do you? A gypsy?" With his voice Alexander White turned the idea down. He knew his man.

"Why not?" Louis Bertrand asked.

"*Why not? Why not?* Because a man lives and works in a place all his life, he doesn't just like that leave it. Because . . . because he likes it here, the people, his job and everything. And besides, he couldn't afford it even if he wanted to."

"Couldn't he?"

In all the weeks, in all the months that Alexander White had been engulfed and upset by the impinging consequences of Harry's action, he had never been frightened because he had never imagined conclusions more complex than the return to normal which he expected to take place after the concert. But now, for the first time, he imagined more largely.

"What does that mean?" he asked Louis Bertrand steadily and hard.

"I don't say it means anything." He looked away from White over to where George Latham, owner of the Tyler Arms, was sitting drinking coffee. He raised his voice to attract an ally. There had been something in Alexander White's tone. "But when a clerk starts spending three thousand bucks on nothing and takes off a week just like that and buys fancy violins, well . . ." George Latham had come over and so had George Smiter, who had just entered. Bertrand looked up at them.

"Well *what?*" White demanded.

"Now take it easy, Alex," George Latham soothed him. "Lou didn't mean anything."

"*The hell he didn't.* Are you accusing Harry of something? Are you saying he's been stealing from me?" No one had said it and none of them thought that it was so, but anger breeds its kind, and mystery compounds it. It wasn't long before they were all arguing heatedly, not to prove a point but to attack an enigma. All except Alexander White, who found out that in thirty-two years men could be honest and loyal and even courageous, and that in the face of that exciting truth violin concerts or what have you for whatever reasons didn't matter much. Uncertain of Harry's compelling vision, unnerved by the ardor of his dream, certain only of the quality of the man and what that demanded of himself, he defended Harry and his concert stoutly. He was surprised to hear the things he was saying, surprised that he was saying them. But he felt freed and good.

In the Green Room Karnovsky paced incessantly.

"Relax," Harry said to him. Karnovsky looked up to see if it was a joke. Harry was tuning his violin.

"I'm relaxed," he said. "I'm relaxed. Here. Give me that," he commanded Harry and grabbed the violin away from him. He began to tune it himself, but it was in tune. He gave it back to Harry. "And don't forget, in the *tutti* in the second movement of the Vivaldi, you have got to come up *over* the orchestra, *over* it."

An electrician knocked at the door. "How do you want the house lights?" he asked Harry.

"What?" Harry said, turning to Karnovsky.

"Halfway," Karnovsky said to the electrician, who left. "Never play in a dark house," he explained to Harry. "You should always be able to see them or else you'll forget that they're there and then the music will die. But don't look at them," he rushed to add.

Harry laughed. "Okay," he said. Then he heard the merest sound of applause. The conductor had taken his place. Harry moved for the door.

"Good luck," Karnovsky said from back in the room.

"Thanks," Harry said. And then, turning, he asked, "You care?"

"I care," Karnovsky said slowly. "I care."

In the great auditorium, built to seat some five thousand, scattered even beyond random were, here and there, a hundred twenty-seven people. Most had come from Tyler, but at least thirty were people who would come to hear a live performance, especially a live performance of the Mendelssohn, anywhere, anytime. In their time they had experienced much. But what, they wondered this night as Morgenstern mounted the podium, was this? Certainly it was Morgenstern and indeed that was the orchestra and there, walking gaily out upon the stage, was a man with a violin in his hand. The house lights were sinking, as in all the concerts of the past. But where were the people? What was going on? Some four or five, unnerved by the hallucinated spectacle, stood up and raced out of the auditorium. But it was only after Harry had been playing (the Vivaldi) for three or four minutes, had wandered for ten measures until he and the orchestra agreed upon the tempo, had come in flat on two successive entrances, and had scratched loudly once, that the others—the strangers—began to get nervous. Now a fine anxiety sprang up in them. Their minds raced over the familiar grounds of their expectations—the orchestra, the conductor, the hall, the music—but nothing held together and no equation that they could imagine explained anything. One woman felt in herself the faint scurryings of hysteria, the flutters of demonic laughter, but she struggled out of the hall in time. Among the other strangers there was much nudging of neighbors and shrugs of unknowing. Then, each reassured that he was not alone in whatever mad thing it was that was happening, they sank down into the wonder of it all. And Harry got, if not good, better.

He played through the rest of the first half of the concert pleasantly enough and without incident.

There was no intermission. The time for the Mendelssohn had come.

The Mendelssohn Concerto in E minor for Violin and Orchestra, Op. 64, was completed September 16, 1844, and was first performed by the celebrated virtuoso Ferdinand David in Leipzig, March 13, 1845. From its first performance and ever after it was and is greatly received in its glory. Every major violinist since David has lived long enough to perform it well. And of concerti for the violin it is preeminent, for it combines a great display of violin technique with lyric magnificence, holding the possibilities of ordered sound at once beyond and above satisfying description. Nowhere in all the vast world of violin literature does the instrument so perfectly emerge as a disciple of itself. No one performs the Mendelssohn Violin Concerto publicly without entering into, at least touching upon, its tradition.

After a measure and a half, the violin and the orchestra engage each other and stay, throughout the piece, deeply involved in the other's fate. But the music is for the violin, after all, so it is important that the violinist establish at once his mastery over the orchestra, determine in his entrance the tempo and the dynamic pattern that the orchestra must bow to. This Harry did. But he did not do much more. Playing with a reasonable precision and, even, polish; with, even, a certain technical assurance which allowed his tone to bloom, he played well enough but not grandly. As he concluded the first movement he thought to himself, with neither chagrin nor surprise, "Well, Belten. You're no Heifetz," and at the end of the lovely, melancholy second movement, "You're no Oistrakh, either." It was really just as he expected it would be. He was enjoying it immensely.

In the Mendelssohn Violin Concerto there are no pauses between the three movements. Part of the greatness of the piece lies in its extraordinary sense of continuity, in its terrific pressure of building, in its tightening, mounting pace (even the cadenza is made an integral part of the overall development). Because there are no pauses and because of the length of the piece and because of the great physical stress put upon the instrument by the demands of the music, there is an increased possibility for one of the strings to lose that exact and critical degree of tautness which gives it—and all the notes played upon it—the correct pitch. If such a thing happens, then the entire harmonic sense of the music is thrown into jeopardy.

Deep into the third movement, at the end of the recapitulation in the new key, Morgenstern heard it happen. He glanced quickly over at Harry. And Glickman, the concertmaster, heard it. He glanced up at Morgenstern. And Karnovsky heard it too. In the many times that he himself had performed the

Mendelssohn, this same thing had happened to him only two terrible times. He remembered them like nightmares, perfectly. There was only one thing to do. The performer must adjust his fingering of the notes played on the weakened string. In effect, he must play all the notes on that one string slightly off, slightly wrong, while playing the notes on all the other three strings correctly. Karnovsky tightened in his seat while his fingers twitched with the frustrated knowledge that he could not give to Harry up on the stage. He was suffocating in his black rage at the injustice about to overtake this good man. That the years of absurd dreaming, the months of aching practice should be cast away by the failure of a miserable piece of gut strangled Karnovsky almost to the point of fainting.

Even before Morgenstern had looked at him (and with the first real emotion Harry had seen on that man's face), Harry had heard the pitch drop on the D string. Only his motor responses formed out of his eighteen years of love carried him through the next three speeding measures as terror exploded in him. He had time to think two things: *I know what should be done,* and *Do it.* He did it. It almost worked.

Harry Belten played the worst finale to the Mendelssohn Violin Concerto probably ever played with a real orchestra and before the public, any public. But it was still recognizably the Mendelssohn, it was not too badly out of tune, and if he was missing here and there on the incredibly difficult adjustments to the flatted D string, there were many places where he wasn't missing at all. Besides Karnovsky, Morgenstern, and Glickman, nobody in the tiny audience in the Coliseum knew what was going on. What they knew was what they heard: to most, sounds which could not help but excite; to the more knowledgeable, a poor performance of a great piece of music. But what Karnovsky knew made him almost weep in his pride and in his joy. And then, in that wonder-filled conclusion, violin and orchestra welded themselves together in an affirming shout of splendor and success. The Mendelssohn Concerto in E minor for Violin and Orchestra, Op. 64, was over.

In all his life Harry did not remember shaking as he was shaking now as Morgenstern and then the concertmaster grasped his hand in the traditional gesture made at concert's end. His sweat was thick upon them. He turned, smiling, to the world. Out of the great silence someone clapped. One clap. It rang like a shot through the empty hall, ricocheting from high beam to vacant seat and back. And then another clap. And then a clapping, an uncoordinated, hesitant buzz of sound rising up into the half gloom of the hollow dome. Then someone shouted out, "Hey, Harry. That was terrific."

"Yeah," fourteen rows back a voice agreed, "terrific." Two on either distant side of the auditorium whistled shrilly their appreciation. Someone pounded his feet. Joe Lombardy remembered a picture he had seen on TV once where after a concert they had shouted *bravo*.

"Bravo," he shouted. He was on his feet, waving to the stage. "Hey, Harry. Bravo." He looked around him to bring in the others. "Bravo," he shouted again. Other joined, almost chanting: "Bravo. Bravo. Bravo. Bravo." And the sounds flew upward like sparks from fire glowing and dying in the dark.

"Encore," Joe Lombardy, remembering more, shouted out. "Encore," he screamed, pleased with himself. "Encore," he knifed through the thinly spread tumult.

"Encore," the others yelled. "Encore. Encore." What there was there of Tyler cheered.

Alice Belten, sitting between her two children, holding their hands, her eyes full, laughing, was at ease. She looked up at the man on the stage. He threw her a kiss. And she kissed him back.

Then Harry Belten tuned his violin, placed it under his chin, and played his encore. And then he played another one.

[JULY 1966]

GABRIEL GARCÍA MÁRQUEZ

Blacamán the Good, Vendor of

Miracles

TRANSLATED FROM THE SPANISH BY GREGORY RABASSA

A native of Colombia, Gabriel García Márque₹ (1928–   ) worked as a newspaper man for fifteen years before turning to his own writing full-time in 1965. His fourth novel, One Hundred Years of Solitude, *is perhaps the most important Hispanic novel since* Don Quixote. *It is also the foremost example of so-called magical realism. To critics who knocked the book for ignoring the social and political realities his earlier novels had addressed, the novelist replied that "reality includes what men dream and imagine as well as what they pay for tomatoes." "Blacamán the Good, Vendor of Miracles," which* Esquire *published in January 1972, is written in the fantastic vein of* One Hundred Years. *García Márque₹ won the Nobel Prize for Literature in 1982.*

From the first Sunday I saw him he reminded me of a bullring mule, with his white suspenders that were backstitched with gold thread, his rings with colored stones on every finger, and his braids of jingle bells, standing on a table by the docks of Santa María del Darién in the middle of the flasks of specifics and herbs of consolation that he prepared himself and hawked through the towns along the Caribbean with his wounded shout, except that at that time he wasn't trying to sell any of that Indian mess but was asking them to bring him a real snake so that he could demonstrate on his own flesh an antidote he had invented, the only infallible one, ladies and gentlemen, for the bites of serpents, tarantulas, and centipedes, plus all manner of poisonous mammal. Someone who seemed quite impressed by his determination managed to get a bushmaster of the worst kind somewhere and brought it to him in a bottle, the snake that starts by poisoning the respiration, and he uncorked it with such eagerness that we all thought he was going to eat it, but as soon as the creature felt itself free it jumped out of the bottle and struck him on the neck, leaving him right then and there without any wind for his oratory and with barely enough time to take the antidote, and the vest-pocket pharmacist tumbled down into the crowd and rolled about on the ground, his huge body wasted away as if he had nothing inside of it, but laughing all the while with all of his gold teeth. The hubbub was so great that a cruiser from the north that had been docked there for twenty years on a goodwill mission declared a quarantine so that the snake poison wouldn't get on board, and the people who were sanctifying Palm Sunday came out of church with their blessed palms, because no one wanted to miss the show of the poisoned man, who had already begun to puff up with the air of death and was twice as fat as he'd been before, giving off a froth of gall through his mouth and panting through his pores, but still laughing with so much life that the jingle bells tinkled all over his body. The swelling snapped the laces of his leggings and the seams of his clothes, his fingers grew purple from the pressure of the rings, he turned the color of venison in brine and from his rear end came a hint of the last moments of death, so that everyone who had seen a person bitten by a snake knew that he was rotting away before dying and that he would be so crumbled up that they'd have to pick him up with a shovel to put him into a sack, but they also thought that even in his sawdust state he'd keep on laughing. It was so incredible that the marines came up on deck to take colored pictures of him with long-distance lenses, but the women who'd come out of church blocked their intentions by covering the dying man with a blanket and laying blessed palms on top of him, some because they didn't want the soldiers to profane the body with their Adventist instruments, others because they were afraid to continue looking at that idolater who was ready to die dying with laughter, and others because in that way perhaps his soul at least would not be poisoned. Everybody had given him up for dead when he pushed aside the palms with one arm, still half-dazed and not completely recovered from the bad moment he'd had, but he set the table up again without anyone's help, climbed on it like a crab once more, and there he was again, shouting that his antidote was nothing but the hand of God in a bottle, as we had all seen with our own eyes, but it only cost two *cuartillos* because he hadn't invented it as an item for sale but for the good of all humanity, and as soon as he said that, ladies and gentlemen, I only ask you not to crowd around, there's enough for everybody.

They crowded around, of course, and they did well to do so, because in the end there wasn't enough for everybody. Even the admiral from the cruiser bought a bottle, convinced by him that it was also good for the poisoned bullets of anarchists, and the sailors weren't satisfied with just taking colored pictures of him up on the table, pictures they had been unable to take of him dead, but they had him signing autographs until his arm was twisted with cramps. It was getting to be night and only the most perplexed of us were left by the docks when with his eyes he searched for someone with the look of an idiot to help him put the bottles away, and naturally he spotted me. It was like the look of destiny, not just mine, but his too, for that was more than a century ago and we both remember it as if it had been last Sunday. What happened was that we were putting his circus drugstore into that trunk with purple straps that looked more like a scholar's casket, when he must have noticed some light inside of me that he hadn't seen in me before, because he asked me in a surly way who are you, and I answered that I was an orphan on both sides whose papa hadn't died, and he gave out with laughter that was louder than what he had given with the poison and then he asked me what do you do for a living, and I answered that I didn't do anything except stay alive, because nothing else was worth the trouble, and still weeping with laughter he asked me what science in the world do you most want to learn, and that was the only time I answered the truth without any fooling, I wanted to be a fortune-teller, and then he didn't laugh again but told me as if thinking out loud that I didn't need much for that because I already had the hardest thing to learn, which was my face of an idiot. That same night he spoke to my father and for one *real* and two *cuartillos* and a deck of cards that foretold adultery he bought me forevermore.

That was what Blacamán was like, Blacamán the Bad, because I'm Blacamán the Good. He was capable of convincing an astronomer that the month of February was nothing but a herd of invisible elephants, but when his good luck turned on him he became a heart-deep brute. In his days of glory he had been an embalmer of viceroys, and they say that he gave them faces with such authority that for many years they went on governing better than when they were alive, and that no one dared bury them until he gave them back their dead-man look, but his prestige was ruined by the invention of an endless chess game that drove a chaplain mad and brought on two illustrious suicides, and so he was on the decline, from an interpreter of dreams to a birthday hypnotist, from an extractor of molars by suggestion to a marketplace healer; therefore, at the time we met, people were already looking at him askance, even the freebooters. We drifted along with our trick stand and life was an eternal uncertainty as we tried to sell escape suppositories that turned smugglers transparent, furtive drops that baptized wives threw into the soup to instill the fear of God in Dutch husbands, and anything you might want to buy of your own free will, ladies and gentlemen, because this isn't a command, it's advice, and, after all, happiness isn't an obligation either. Nevertheless, as much as we died with laughter at his witticisms, the truth is that it was quite hard for us to manage enough to eat, and his last hope was founded on my vocation as a fortune-teller. He shut me up in the sepulchral trunk disguised as a Japanese and bound with starboard chains so that I could attempt to foretell what I could while he disemboweled the grammar book looking for the best way to convince the world of my new science, and here, ladies and gentlemen, you have this child tormented by Ezequiel's glow-worms, and those of you who've been standing there with faces of disbelief, let's see if you dare ask him when you're going to die, but I was never able even to guess what day it was at that time, so he gave up on me as a soothsayer because the drowsiness of digestion disturbs your prediction gland, and after whacking me over the head for good luck, he decided to take me to my father and get his money back. But at that time he happened to find a practical application for the electricity of suffering, and he set about building a sewing machine that ran connected by cupping glasses to the part of the body where there was a pain. Since I spent the night moaning over the whacks he'd given me to conjure away misfortune, he had to keep me on as the one who could test his invention, and so our return was delayed and he was getting back his good humor until the machine worked so well that it not only sewed better than a novice nun but also embroidered birds or astromelias according to the position and intensity of the pain. That was what we were up to, convinced of our triumph over bad luck, when the news reached us that in Philadelphia the commander of the cruiser had tried to repeat the experiment with the antidote and that he'd been changed into a glob of admiral jelly in front of his staff.

He didn't laugh again for a long time. We fled through Indian passes and the more lost we became the clearer the news reached us that the marines had invaded the country under the pretext of exterminating yellow fever and were going about beheading every inveterate or eventual potter they found in their path, and not only the natives, out of precaution, but also the Chinese, for distraction, the Negroes, from habit, and the Hindus, because they were snake charmers, and then they wiped out the flora and fauna and all the mineral wealth they were able to because their specialists in our affairs had taught them that the people along the Caribbean had the ability to change their nature in order to confuse gringos. I couldn't understand where that fury came from or why we were so frightened until we found ourselves safe and sound in the eternal winds of La Guajira, and only then did he have the courage to confess to me that his antidote was nothing but rhubarb and turpentine and that he'd paid a drifter two *cuartillos* to bring him that bushmaster with all the poison gone. We stayed in the ruins of a colonial mission, deluded by the hope that some smugglers would pass, because they were men to be trusted and the only ones capable of venturing out under the mercurial sun of those salt flats. At first we ate smoked salamanders and flowers from the ruins and we still had enough spirit to laugh when we tried to eat his boiled leggings, but finally we even ate the water cobwebs from the cisterns and only then did we realize how much we missed the world. Since I didn't know of any recourse against death at that time, I simply lay down to wait for it where it would hurt me least, while he was delirious remembering a woman who was so tender that she could pass through walls just by sighing, but that contrived recollection was also a trick of his genius to fool death with lovesickness. Still, at the moment we should have died, he came to me more alive than ever and spent the whole night watching over my agony, thinking with such great strength that I still haven't been able to tell whether what was whistling through the ruins was the wind or his thoughts, and before dawn he told me with the same voice and the same determination of past times that now he knew the truth, that I was the one who had twisted up his luck again, so get your pants ready, because the same way as you twisted it up for me, you're going to straighten it out.

That was when I lost the little affection I had for him. He took off the last rags I had on, rolled me up in some barbed wire, rubbed rock salt on the sores, put me in brine from my own waters, and hung me by the ankles for the sun to flay me, and he kept on shouting that all that mortification wasn't enough to pacify his persecutors. Finally he threw me to rot in my own misery inside the penance dungeon where the colonial missionaries regenerated heretics, and with the perfidy of a ventriloquist, which he still had more than enough of, he began to imitate the voices of edible animals, the noise of ripe beets, and the sound of fresh springs so as to torture me with the illusion I was dying of indigence in the midst of paradise. When the smugglers finally supplied him, he came down to the dungeon to give me something to eat so that I wouldn't die, but then he made me pay for that charity by pulling out my nails with pliers and filing my teeth down with a grindstone, and my only consolation was the wish that life would give me time and the good fortune to be quit of so much infamy with even worse martyrdoms. I myself was surprised that I could resist the plague of my own putrefaction and he kept throwing the leftovers of his meals onto me and tossed pieces of rotten lizards and hawks into the corners so that the air of the dungeon would end up poisoning me. I don't know how much time had passed when he brought me the carcass of a rabbit in order to show me that he preferred throwing it away to rot rather than giving it to me to eat, but my patience only went so far and all I had left was rancor, so I grabbed the rabbit by the ears and flung it against the wall with the illusion that it was he and not the animal that was going to explode, and then it happened, as if in a dream. The rabbit not only revived with a squeal of fright, but came back to my hands, hopping through the air.

That was how my great life began. Since then I've gone through the world drawing the fever out of malaria victims for two pesos, visioning blind men for four-fifty, draining the water from dropsy victims for eighteen, putting cripples back together for twenty pesos if they were that way from birth, for twenty-two if they were that way because of an accident or a brawl, for twenty-five if they were that way because of wars, earthquakes, infantry landings, or any other kind of public calamity, taking care of the common sick at wholesale according to a special arrangement, madmen according to their theme, children at half price, and idiots out of gratitude, and who dares say that I'm not a philanthropist, ladies and gentlemen, and now, yes, sir, commandant of the twentieth fleet, order your boys to take down the barricades and let suffering humanity pass, lepers to the left, epileptics to the right, cripples where they won't get in the way, and there in the back the least urgent cases, only please don't crowd in on me because then I won't be responsible if the sicknesses get all mixed up and people are cured of what they don't have, and keep the music playing until the brass boils, and the rockets firing until the angels burn, and the liquor flowing until ideas are killed, and bring on the wenches and the acrobats, the butchers and the photographers, and all at my expense, ladies and gentlemen, for her ends the evil fame of the Blacamáns and the universal tumult starts. That's how I go along putting them to sleep with the techniques of a congressman in case my judgment fails and some turn out worse on me than they were before. The only thing I don't do is revive the dead, because as soon as they open their eyes they're murderous with rage at the one who disturbed their state, and when it's all done, those who don't commit suicide die again of disillusionment. At first I was pursued by a group of wise men investigating the legality of my industry, and when they were convinced, they threatened me with the hell of Simon Magus and recommended a life of penitence so that I could get to be a saint, but I answered them, with no disrespect for their authority, that it was precisely along those lines that I had started. The truth is that I'd gain nothing by being a saint after being dead, an artist is what I am, and the only thing I want is to be alive so I can keep going along at donkey level in this six-cylinder touring car I bought from the marines' consul, with this Trinidadian chauffeur who was a baritone in the New Orleans pirates' opera, with my genuine silk shirts, my oriental lotions, my topaz teeth, my flat straw hat, and my bicolored buttons, sleeping without an alarm clock, dancing with beauty queens, and leaving them hallucinated with my dictionary rhetoric, and with no flutter in my spleen if some Ash Wednesday my faculties wither away, because in order to go on with this life of a minister, all I need is my idiot face, and I have more than enough with the string of shops I own from here to beyond the sunset, where the same tourists who used to go around collecting from us through the admiral, now go stumbling after my autographed pictures, almanacs with my love poetry, medals with my profile, bits of my clothing, and all of that without the glorious plague of spending all day and all night sculptured in equestrian marble and shat on by swallows like the fathers of our country.

It's a pity that Blacamán the Bad can't repeat this story so that people will see that there's nothing invented in it. That last time anyone saw him in this world he'd lost even the studs of his former splendor, and his soul was a shambles and his bones in disorder from the rigors of the desert, but he still had enough jingle bells left to reappear that Sunday on the docks of Santa María del Darién with his eternal sepulchral trunk, except that this time he wasn't trying to sell any antidotes, but was asking in a voice cracking with emotion for the marines to shoot him in a public spectacle so that he could demonstrate on his own flesh the life-restoring properties of this supernatural creature, ladies and gentlemen, and even though you have more than enough right not to believe me after suffering so long from my tricks as a deceiver and falsifier, I swear on the bones of my mother that this proof today is nothing from the other world, merely the humble truth, and in case you have any doubts left, notice that I'm not laughing now the way I used to, but holding back a desire to cry. How convincing he must have been, unbuttoning his shirt, his eyes drowning with tears, and giving himself mule kicks on his heart to indicate the best place for death, and yet the marines didn't dare shoot, out of fear that the Sunday crowd would discover their loss of prestige. Someone who may not have forgotten the Blacamanipulations of past times managed, no one knew how, to get and bring him in a can enough barbasco roots to bring to the surface all the *corvinas* in the Caribbean, and he opened it with great desire, as if he really was going to eat them, and, indeed, he did eat them, ladies and gentlemen, but please don't be moved or pray for the repose of my soul, because this death is nothing but a visit. That time he was so honest that he didn't break into operatic death rattles, but got off the table like a crab, looked on the ground for the most worthy place to lie down after some hesitation, and from there he looked at me as he would have at a mother and exhaled his last breath in his own arms, still holding back his tears of a man, all twisted up by the tetanus of eternity. That was the only time, of course, that my science failed me. I put him in that trunk of premonitory size where there was room for him laid out. I had a requiem mass sung for him which cost me fifty-four peso doubloons, because the officiant was dressed in gold and there were also three seated bishops. I had the mausoleum of an emperor built for him on a hill exposed to the best seaside weather, with a chapel just for him and an iron plaque on which there was written in Gothic capitals here lies Blacamán the Dead, badly called the Bad, deceiver of marines and the victim of science, and when those honors were sufficient for me to do justice to his virtues, I began to get my revenge for his infamy, and then I revived him inside the armored tomb and left him there rolling about in horror. That was long before the fire ants devoured Santa María del Darién, but the mausoleum is still intact on the hill in the shadow of the dragons that climb up to sleep in the Atlantic winds, and every time I pass through here I bring him an automobile load of roses and my heart pains with pity for his virtues, but then I put my ear to the plaque to hear him weeping in the ruins of the crumbling trunk, and if by chance he has died again, I bring him back to life once more, for the beauty of the punishment is that he will keep on living in his tomb as long as I'm alive, that is, forever.

[JANUARY 1972]

WILLIAM KOTZWINKLE

Horse Badorties Goes Out

William Kotzwinkle's novel The Fan Man *is surely one of the oddest books ever written, as will be apparent from the excerpt reprinted here, "Horse Badorties Goes Out," with its unnerving litany of "dorky, dorky, dorky, dorky . . ."—a masterpiece of the genre that was briefly known as the New Fiction, an offshoot of the antifiction movement of the early 1970s. Kotzwinkle (1938–) himself went on, if not to fame then certainly to fortune, as the man who novelized the movie* E.T.

I am all alone in my pad, man, my piled-up-to-the-ceiling-with-junk pad. Piled with sheet music, piled with garbage bags bursting with rubbish, piled with unnameable flecks of putrefied wretchedness in grease. My pad, my own little Lower East Side Horse Badorties pad.

I just woke up, man. Horse Badorties just woke up and is crawling around in the sea of abominated filth, man, which he calls home. Walking through the rooms of my pad, man, from which I shall select my wardrobe for the day. Here, stuffed in a trash basket, is a pair of incredibly wrinkled-up muck-pants. And here, man, beneath a pile of wet newspapers is a shirt, man, with one sleeve. All I need now, man, is a tie, and here is a perfectly good rubber Japanese toy snake, man, which I can easily form into an acceptable knot.

SPAGHETTI! MAN! Now I remember. That is why I have arisen from my cesspool bed, man, because of the growlings of my stomach. It is time for breakfast, man. But first I must make a telephone call to Alaska.

Must find telephone. Important deal in the making. Looking around for telephone, man. And here is an electric extension cord, man, which will serve perfectly as a belt to hold up my falling-down Horse Badorties pants, simply by running the cord through the belt loops and plugging it together.

Looking through the shambles wreckage busted chair old sardine can with a roach in it, empty piña-colada bottle, gummy something on the wall, broken egg on the floor, some kind of coffee grounds sprinkled around. What's this under here, man?

It's the sink, man. I have found the sink. Wait a second, man . . . it is not the sink but my Horse Badorties easy chair piled with dirty dishes. I must sit down here and rest, man, I'm so tired from getting out of bed. Throw dishes onto the floor, crash break shatter. Sink down into the damp cushions, some kind of fungus on the armrest, possibility of smoking it.

I'm in my little Horse Badorties pad, man, looking around. It's the nicest pad I ever had, man, and I'm getting another one just like it down the hall. Two pads, man. The rent will be high but it's not so bad if you don't pay it. And with two pads, man, I will have room to rehearse the Love Chorus, man, and we will sing our holy music and record it on my battery-powered portable falling-apart Japanese tape recorder with the corroded worn-out batteries, man. How wonderful, man.

Sitting in chair, staring at wall, where paint is peeling off and jelly is dripping and hundreds of telephone numbers are written. I must make a telephone call immediately, man, that is a MUST.

Sitting in chair, staring at wall. Unable to move, man, feeling the dark heavy curtain of impassable numbness settling on me, man.

Falling back to sleep, head nodding down to chest, arm falling off side of chair. I've found the phone, man. It was right beside me all the time, man, and I am holding it up, man, and there is margarine in the dial holes. This, man, is definitely my telephone.

". . . hello? . . . hello, man, this is Horse Badorties . . . right, man, I'm putting together a little deal, man. Acapulco artichoke hearts, man, lovely stuff . . . came across the Colorado River on a raft, man, it's a little damp, but other than that . . . can you hold on a second, man, I think I hear somebody trying to break through the window. . . ."

I cannot speak a moment longer, man, without something to eat. I am weak from hunger, man, and must hunt for my refrigerator through sucked oranges, dead wood, old iron, scum-peel. Here it is, man, with the garbage table wedged against it. Tip the table, man, Horse Badorties is starving.

Some kind of mysterious vegetable, man, is sitting in the refrigerator, shriveled, filthy, covered with fungus, a rotten something, man, and it is my breakfast.

Rather than eat it, man, I will return to my bed of pain. I will go back to my bed, man, if I can locate my bed. It's through this door and back in here somewhere, man. I must get some more sleep, I realize that now. I cannot function, cannot move forward, man, until I have retreated into sleep.

Crawling, man, over the bureau drawers which are bursting with old rags and my used-sock collection, and slipping down, man, catching a piece of the bed, man, where I can relax upon a pile of books old pail some rocks floating around. Slipping onto my yellow smeared still mortified ripped wax-paper scummy sheets, man. And the last thing I do, man, before I sleep, is turn on my battery-powered hand-held Japanese fan. The humming note it makes, man, the sweet and constant melodic droning lulls me to sleep, man, where I will dream symphonies, man, and wake up with a stiff neck.

Horse Badorties waking up again, man. Man, what planet am I on? I seem to be contained in some weird primeval hideous grease. Wait a second, man, this is my Horse Badorties pillowcase. I am alive and well in my own Horse Badorties abominable life.

Time to get up, to get out. Get up, man, you've got to get up and go out into the day and bring fifteen-year-old chicks into your life.

I'm moving my Horse Badorties feet, man, getting my stuff together, collecting the various precious contents of my pad, man, which I MUST take along with me. I have the Japanese fan in my hand, man, and I am marching forward through my rubbish heap. Cooling myself, man, on a hot summer morning or afternoon, one of the two.

Over to the window, man, which looks far out over the rooftops to a distant tower, where the time is showing four o'clock in the afternoon. Late, man. I've got to get out of the pad or I will circle around in it again, uncovering lost treasures and I will get hung up and stuck here all day.

Here is my satchel, man. Now I must stuff it with essential items for survival on the street: sheet music, fan, alarm clock, tape recorder. The only final and further object which must be packed in my survival satchel is the Korean ear-flap cap in case I happen to hear Puerto Rican music along the way.

There are countless thousands of other things in these rooms, man, I should take along with me, in case of emergency, and since it is summertime, I MUST take my overcoat. I have a powerful intuition it will come in handy.

Many other things, man, would I like to jam in my satchel. All of it, man, I want to take it all with me, and that is why I must, after getting a last drink of water, get out of here.

Roaches scurrying over the gigantic pile of caked and stuck-together greasy dishes in my Horse Badorties sink. The water is not yet cold enough. I'm going to let the water run here, man, for a second, while it gets cold. Don't let me forget to turn it off.

I've got everything I need, man. Everything I could possibly want for a few hours on the street is already in my satchel. If it gets much heavier, man, I won't be able to carry it.

"I'm turning on the tape recorder, man, to record the sound of the door closing as I go out of my pad. It is the sound of liberation, man, from my compulsion to delay over and over again my departure . . . wait just a second, man, I forgot to make sure if there's one last thing I wanted to take."

Back into pad once more, man. Did I forget to do anything, take anything? There is just one thing and that is to change my shoes, man, removing these plastic Japanese shoes which kill my feet, because here, man, is a Chinese gum rubber canvas shoe for easy Horse Badorties walking. Where is the other one, man? Here it is, man, with some kind of soggy wet beans, man, sprouting inside it. I can't disturb nature's harmony, man, I'll have to wear two different shoes, man, one yellow plastic Japanese, the other red canvas Chinese, and my walking, man, will be hopelessly unbalanced. I'd better not go out at all, man.

Look, man, you have to go out. Once you go outside, man, you can always buy a fresh pair of Lower East Side Ukrainian cardboard bedroom slippers. Let's go, man, out the door, everything is cool.

Out the door again, man, and down the steps, down the steps, down . . . one . . . two . . . three flights of stairs. . . .

Jesus, man, I forgot my walkie-talkies. I've gone down three flights of steps, man. And I am turning around and going back up them again.

I am climbing back up the stairs because, though I am tired and falling apart, I cannot be without my walkie-talkies, man. Common sense, man.

"It is miraculous, man. I am making a special tape-recorded announcement of this miracle, man, so that I will never forget this moment of superb unconscious intuition. Ostensibly, man, I returned for my walkie-talkies, but actually it was my unconscious mind luring me back, man, because I left the door to my pad wide open. Anyone might have stepped in and carried away the valuable precious contents of my pad, man. And so I am back in the scrap heap, man, the wretched tumbled-down strewn-about everything of my pad, man, and I am seeing a further miracle, man. It is the miracle of the water in the sink, man, which I left running. Man, do you realize that if I had not returned here for my walkie-talkies, I would have flooded the pad, creating tidal waves among my roaches, and also on the roaches who live downstairs with the twenty-six Puerto Rican chickens? A catastrophe has been averted, man. And what is more, now the water is almost cold, man. It just needs to run a few more minutes, man, and I can have my drink of water."

But first, man, I see that I forgot to take my moon-lute, man, hanging here inside the stove. The moon-lute, man, the weirdest instrument on earth, man. Looks like a Chinese frying pan, man, and I am the only one in the Occidental world who would dare to play it, man, as it sounds like a Chinaman falling down a flight of stairs. Which reminds me, man, I'd better get out of this pad, man, and down the stairs. I'm going, man, I'm on the way, out of the door. I am closing up the pad, man, without further notice.

No, man, on second thought, I am not closing up my pad, man, I am returning to it once again for the last time, man, to make a single telephone call to my junkman, man, who is going to sell me a perfectly good used diving bell with a crack in it, man. It will only take the smallest part of a moment, man, for me to handle this important piece of business.

My telephone, man, how wonderful to get back to my telephone again, linking myself once more to the outer world.

"Hello, man . . . there's a shipment of organic carrots on the way, man, are you interested in a few bunches. . . ."

"Hello, man, will you get out your *I Ching*, man, and look up this hexagram I just threw, number 51, nine in the fourth place, what is it . . . *shock is mired?* Right, man, I'm hip, I lost my school bus in a swamp. . . ."

"Hello, baby, this is Horse Badorties . . . sing this note for me will you, baby, I need to have my tympanic cavity blown out: *Boooooooooooooooooooooop!*"

"Hello, Mother, this is Horse. Did I, by any chance, on my last visit, leave a small container of vitamin C tablets, little white tablets in an unmarked bottle . . . yes, I did? Good, I'll be up to get them soon, man, but don't under any circumstances take one of them."

"Hello, man, Horse Badorties here . . . listen, man, I'm sorry I didn't get over to your pad with the Swiss chard, man, but I was unavoidably derailed for three days, man. I was walking along, man, and I saw these kids, man, in the street, playing with a a *dead rat,* man. I had to go back to my pad to get a shovel and bury it, man. You understand, man, kids must not be imprinted with such things. Look, man, I'll be over soon, I'll be there at . . . hold on a second, man, just a second. . . ."

"Hello, man . . . this is Horse Badorties, I've got a deal cooking, man . . . stop shouting, man . . . right, man, now I remember—I already have your bread, that is, man, I had your bread until today, man, when a strange thing happened, man, which you will find hard to believe . . . don't go away, man, I'll call you back in five minutes."

". . . hello? . . . hello, man, Horse Badorties here, man. Man, I'm sorry I didn't get over to you with the tomato surprise, man, but dig, a very strange thing happened, man. I was walking in Van Cortlandt Park, man, and suddenly I saw this airplane overhead, man, running out of gas. The cat was circling low, man, looking for a place to land. I had to guide him in, man, for a forced landing, man, and it took quite a long time, which is why I'll be late getting to your pad, man. . . ."

". . . hello, man, listen, man, I've been having fantastically precognitive dreams lately, man, I am digging the future every night, and last night I had a definite signal, man, that the flying saucers are about to land. That's right, man, I wouldn't kid you, and dig, man, I am getting everyone I know to come up to the roof of my pad, man, to watch the saucers land, as there is a possibility I'll be carried away, man, into the sky and taken to another planet. . . ."

Tired, man, I am getting so tired telephoning. I will just close my eyes for a brief nap, man. I have trained myself through the years, man, to close my eyes and sleep for exactly ten minutes, man, no more no less, and wake up perfectly refreshed.

It is morning, Horse Badorties, what a wonderful sunshining morning, wait a second, man, it is afternoon, I overslept. I must hurry, man, *Horse Badorties must go out!*

No, no, it's dorky day again!

"Dorky dorky . . ."

(Dorky day again, man, and I am stumbling around my pad, repeating over and over):

". . . dorky dorky dorky dorky dorky dorky dorky dorky . . ."

(Constant repetition of the word *dorky* cleans out my consciousness, man, gets rid of all the rubble and cobwebs piled up there. It is absolutely necessary for me to do this once a month and today is dorky day):

". . . dorky dorky dorky dorky dorky dorky dorky dorky . . ."

(There is a knock at the door, man, go answer it.)

". . . dorky dorky dorky dorky dorky dorky dorky . . ."

(It is a knapsack blond chick, man! I wave her in but I cannot stop my dorky now.)

". . . dorky dorky dorky dorky dorky dorky dorky dorky . . ."

"I got a VD shot."

". . . dorky dorky dorky dorky dorky dorky dorky dorky . . ."

"I tried hitchhiking out through the Lincoln Tunnel and the cops stopped me."

". . . dorky dorky dorky dorky dorky dorky dorky dorky . . ."

"I figured maybe I should stay in the city a while longer. I thought it must be a sign."

". . . dorky dorky dorky dorky dorky dorky dorky dorky . . ."

"What's going on, man, what's all this dorky?"

". . . dorky dorky dorky dorky dorky dorky dorky dorky . . ."

"I brought some breakfast . . . some bread and jelly."

". . . dorky dorky dorky dorky dorky dorky dorky dorky dorky dorky dorky dorky dorky dorky dorky dorky dorky dorky . . ."

"Christ, man, knock it off, will you?"

". . . dorky dorky dorky dorky dorky dorky dorky dorky dorky dorky dorky dorky dorky dorky dorky dorky dorky dorky . . ."

"You're driving me up the wall, man."

". . . dorky dorky dorky dorky dorky dorky dorky dorky . . ."

(Another knock at the door, man. It always happens on dorky day. It is a saxophone player, man.)

". . . dorky dorky dorky dorky dorky dorky dorky dorky . . ."

"How's it going, Horse?"

". . . dorky dorky dorky dorky dorky dorky dorky dorky . . ."

"What's up with Horse, baby?"

". . . dorky dorky dorky dorky dorky dorky dorky dorky . . ."

"I don't know. He was like this when I got here."

". . . dorky dorky dorky dorky dorky dorky dorky dorky dorky dorky dorky dorky dorky dorky dorky . . ."

"Hey, Horse, what's all this dorky, man?"

". . . dorky dorky dorky dorky dorky dorky dorky dorky . . ."

"I have some bread and jelly in my knapsack. Do you want some?"

". . . dorky dorky dorky dorky dorky dorky dorky dorky dorky dorky dorky dorky dorky dorky dorky dorky dorky dorky . . ."

"What is it, raspberry?"

". . . dorky dorky dorky dorky dorky dorky dorky . . ."

"Strawberry."

". . . dorky dorky dorky dorky dorky dorky dorky dorky . . ."

"Hey, Horse, man, knock it off, man, and we'll play some music."

". . . dorky dorky dorky dorky dorky dorky dorky dorky dorky dorky dorky dorky dorky dorky dorky dorky dorky . . ."

"He won't answer you. I know he won't answer you."

". . . dorky dorky dorky dorky dorky dorky dorky dorky . . ."

"I think maybe he's composin' some kind of song, baby."

". . . dorky dorky dorky dorky dorky dorky dorky dorky . . ."

"I thought I might stay here for a while, but I can't stay here, not with all this dorky."

". . . dorky dorky dorky dorky dorky dorky dorky dorky dorky dorky dorky dorky dorky dorky dorky dorky dorky dorky . . ."

"Dig, baby, you can stay with me if you want. My pad's just around the corner."

". . . dorky dorky dorky dorky dorky dorky dorky dorky dorky . . ."

"Can we go there right now? I can't take any more of this dorky."

". . . dorky dorky dorky dorky dorky dorky dorky dorky dorky . . ."

"Sure, baby, let's go."

". . . dorky dorky dorky dorky dorky dorky dorky dorky dorky dorky dorky dorky dorky . . ."

"Do you think . . . he'll be all right?"

". . . dorky dorky dorky dorky . . ."

"Yeah, he just has to work it on out. Come on, baby, let's go. So long, man, take it easy with your dorky."

". . . dorky . . ."

Dorky day, man, has changed my life, I see that now. Because now that it is the day after dorky day, I have a clear picture of what I must do with my life. I must, man, and this is absolute necessity, *Horse Badorties must go out!* The time, man, has come to get out of the pad NOW, man, right now!

Okay, man, I am going straight out the door, without breakfast, without looking around, without further ado. I will be in actual sunlight, man, walking along. Man, I must be straightening out my life, I must be shaping up, man.

Have I forgotten anything?

Sunglasses, tape recorder, fan, umbrella, satchel, used tea bag, disgusting blobular something, my tire pump, man, and this medicinal herb from the Himalayas, the leaves of which bloom only once in a thousand years and I have a shipment of it waiting for me in a subway tunnel, go Horse, go man, out into the real world.

Wait a second, man, I've got to smoke a few of these dandelion stalks to accelerate my brain waves. However, before I make that important step, I must use the stopped-up toilet, man, down which someone flushed a Turkish bath mat by mistake. How wonderful, man, to attend to vital bodily needs before anything else. I should be out buying a dogsled, man, but first I must rearrange my piles of completely disordered everything imaginable, so I can find the toilet. That is a *must* man.

And then I'll go out.

[SEPTEMBER 1973]

RAY BRADBURY

The Illustrated Man

Ray Bradbury (1920–) has written twenty-seven books of fiction, plays, and essays, including Fahrenheit 451 *and* Something Wicked This Way Comes. *"The Illustrated Man" was three years in the writing and entailed fifty thousand words of rewriting until the author struck upon his "Pet Milk" conclusion. "You'll understand what I mean," Bradbury explained in* Esquire's *July 1950 issue, "if you examine a Pet Milk can with its picture of a cow coming out of a can on which there is a picture of a cow coming out of a can on which there is a picture of a cow coming out of a can . . ."*

"Hey, the Illustrated Man!"

A calliope screamed, and Mr. William Philippus Phelps stood, arms folded, high on the summer-night platform, a crowd unto himself.

He was an entire civilization. In the Main Country, his chest, the Vasties lived—nipple-eyed dragons swirling over his fleshpot, his almost feminine breasts. His navel was the mouth of a slit-eyed monster—an obscene, in-sucked mouth, toothless as a witch. And there were secret caves where Darklings lurked, his armpits, adrip with slow subterranean liquors, where the Darklings, eyes jealously ablaze, peered out through rank creeper and hanging vine.

Mr. William Philippus Phelps leered down from his freak platform with a thousand peacock eyes. Across the sawdust meadow he saw his wife, Lisabeth, far away, ripping tickets in half, staring at the silver belt buckles of passing men.

Mr. William Philippus Phelps's hands were tattooed roses. At the sight of his wife's interest, the roses shriveled, as with the passing of sunlight.

A year before, when he had led Lisabeth to the marriage bureau to watch her work her name in ink, slowly, on the form, his skin had been pure and white and clean. He glanced down at himself in sudden horror. Now he was like a great painted canvas, shaken in the night wind! How had it happened? Where had it all begun?

It had started with the arguments, and then the flesh, and then the pictures. They had fought deep into the summer nights, she like a brass trumpet forever blaring at him. And he had gone out to eat five thousand steaming hot dogs, ten million hamburgers, and a forest of green onions, and to drink vast red seas of orange juice. Peppermint candy formed his brontosaur bones, the hamburgers shaped his balloon flesh, and strawberry pop pumped in and out of his heart valves sickeningly, until he weighed three hundred pounds.

"William Philippus Phelps," Lisabeth said to him in the eleventh month of their marriage, "you're dumb and fat."

That was the day the carnival boss handed him the blue envelope. "Sorry, Phelps. You're no good to me with all that gut on you."

"Wasn't I always your best tent man, boss?"

"Once. Not anymore. Now you sit, you don't get the work out."

"Let me be your Fat Man."

"I *got* a Fat Man. Dime a dozen." The boss eyed him up and down. "Tell you what, though. We ain't had a Tattooed Man since Gallery Smith died last year. . . ."

That had been a month ago. Four short weeks. From someone, he had learned of a tattoo artist far out in the rolling Wisconsin country, an old woman, they said, who knew her trade. If he took the dirt road and turned right at the river and then left . . .

He had walked out across a yellow meadow, which was crisp from the sun. Red flowers blew and bent in the wind as he walked, and he came to the old shack, which looked as if it had stood in a million rains.

Inside the door was a silent, bare room, and in the center of the bare room sat an ancient woman.

Her eyes were stitched with red resin-thread. Her nose was sealed with black wax-twine. Her ears were sewn, too, as if a darning-needle dragonfly had stitched all her senses shut. She sat, not moving, in the vacant room. Dust lay in a yellow flour all about, unfootprinted in many weeks; if she had moved it would have shown, but she had not moved. Her hands touched each other like thin, rusted instruments. Her feet were naked and obscene as rain rubbers, and near them sat vials of tattoo milk—red, lightning-blue, brown, cat-yellow. She was a thing sewn tight into whispers and silence.

Only her mouth moved, unsewn: "Come in. Sit down. I'm lonely here."

He did not obey.

"You came for the pictures," she said in a high voice. "I have a picture to show you, first."

She tapped a blind finger to her thrust-out palm. "See!" she cried.

It was a tattoo-portrait of William Philippus Phelps.

"Me!" he said.

Her cry stopped him at the door. "Don't run."

He held to the edges of the door, his back to her. "That's me, that's me on your hand!"

"It's been there fifty years." She stroked it like a cat, over and over.

He turned. "It's an *old* tattoo." He drew slowly nearer. He edged forward and bent to blink at it. He put out a trembling finger to brush the picture. "Old. That's impossible! You don't know *me*. I don't know *you*. Your eyes, all sewed shut."

"I've been waiting for you," she said. "And many people." She displayed her arms and legs, like the spindles of an antique chair. "I have pictures on me of people who have already come here to see me. And there are other pictures of other people who are coming to see me in the next one hundred years. And you, you have come."

"How do you know it's me? You can't see!"

"You *feel* like the lions, the elephants, and the tigers, to me. Unbutton your shirt. You need me. Don't be afraid. My needles are as clean as a doctor's fingers. When I'm finished with illustrating you, I'll wait for someone else to walk along out here and find me. And someday, a hundred summers from now, perhaps, I'll just go lie down in the forest under some white mushrooms, and in the spring you won't find anything but a small blue cornflower. . . ."

He began to unbutton his sleeves.

"I know the Deep Past and the Clear Present and the even Deeper Future," she whispered, eyes knotted into blindness, face lifted to this unseen man. "It is on my flesh. I will paint it on yours, too. You will be the only *real* Illustrated Man in the universe. I'll give you special pictures you will never forget. Pictures of the Future on your skin."

She pricked him with a needle.

He ran back to the carnival that night in a drunken terror and elation. Oh, how quickly the old dust-witch had stitched him with color and design. At the end of a long afternoon of being bitten by a silver snake, his body was alive with portraiture. He looked as if he had dropped and been crushed between the steel rollers of a print press, and come out like an incredible rotogravure. He was clothed in a garment of trolls and scarlet dinosaurs.

"Look!" he cried to Lisabeth. She glanced up from her cosmetic table as he tore his shirt away. He stood in the naked bulb-light of their car-trailer, expanding his impossible chest. Here, the Tremblies, half-maiden, half-goat, leaping when his biceps flexed. Here, the Country of Lost Souls, his chins. In so many accordion pleats of fat, numerous small scorpions, beetles, and mice were crushed, held, hid, darting into view, vanishing, as he raised or lowered his chins.

"My God," said Lisabeth. "My husband's a freak."

She ran from the trailer and he was left alone to pose before the mirror. Why had he done it? To have a job, yes, but, most of all, to cover the fat that had larded itself impossibly over his bones. To hide the fat under a layer of color and fantasy, to hide it from his wife, but most of all from himself.

He thought of the old woman's last words. She had needled him two *special* tattoos, one on his chest, another for his back, which she would not let him see. She covered each with cloth and adhesive.

"You are not to look at these two," she had said.

"Why?"

"Later, you may look. The Future is in these pictures. You can't look now or it may spoil them. They are not quite finished. I put ink on your flesh and the sweat of you forms the rest of the picture, the Future—your sweat and your thought." Her empty mouth grinned. "Next Saturday night, you may advertise! The Big Unveiling! Come see the Illustrated Man unveil his picture! You can make money in that way. You can charge admission to the Unveiling, like to an Art Gallery. Tell them you have a picture that even *you* never have seen, that *nobody* has seen yet. The most unusual picture ever painted. Almost alive. And it tells the Future. Roll the drums and blow the trumpets. And you can stand there and unveil at the Big Unveiling."

"That's a good idea," he said.

"But only unveil the picture on your chest," she said. "That is first. You must save the picture on your back, under the adhesive, for the following week. Understand?"

"How much do I owe you?"

"Nothing," she said. "If you walk with these pictures on you, I will be repaid with my own satisfaction. I will sit here for the next two weeks and think how clever my pictures are, for I make them to fit each man himself and what is inside him. Now, walk out of this house and never come back. Good-bye."

"**H**ey! The Big Unveiling!"

The red signs blew in the night wind: NO ORDINARY TATTOOED MAN! THIS ONE IS "ILLUSTRATED"! GREATER THAN MICHELANGELO! TONIGHT! ADMISSION 10 CENTS!

Now the hour had come. Saturday night, the crowd stirring their animal feet in the hot sawdust.

"In one minute—" the carny boss pointed his cardboard megaphone—"in the tent immediately to my rear, we will unveil the Mysterious Portrait upon the Illustrated Man's chest! Next Saturday night, the same hour, same location, we'll unveil the Picture upon the Illustrated Man's *back!* Bring your friends!"

There was a stuttering roll of drums.

Mr. William Philippus Phelps jumped back and vanished; the crowd poured into the tent, and, once inside, found him reestablished upon another platform, the band brassing out a jig-time melody.

He looked for his wife and saw her, lost in the crowd, like a stranger, come to watch a freakish thing, a look of contemptuous curiosity upon her face. For, after all, he was her husband, and this was a thing she didn't know about him herself. It gave him a feeling of great height and warmness and light to find himself the center of the jangling universe, the carnival world, for one night. Even the other freaks—the Skeleton, the Seal Boy, the Yoga, the Magician, and the Balloon—were scattered through the crowd.

"Ladies and gentlemen, the great moment!"

A trumpet flourish, a hum of drumsticks on tight cowhide.

Mr. William Philippus Phelps let his cape fall. Dinosaurs, trolls, and half-women-half-snakes writhed on his skin in the stark light.

Ah, murmured the crowd, for surely there had never been a tattooed man like this! The beast eyes seemed to take red fire and blue fire, blinking and twisting. The roses on his fingers seemed to expel a sweet pink bouquet. The tyrannosaurus rex reared up along his leg, and the sound of the brass trumpet in the hot tent heavens was a prehistoric cry from the red monster throat. Mr. William Philippus Phelps was a museum jolted to life. Fish swam in seas of electric-blue ink. Fountains sparkled under yellow suns. Ancient buildings stood in meadows of harvest wheat. Rockets burned across spaces of muscle and flesh. The slightest inhalation of his breath threatened to make chaos of the entire printed universe. He seemed afire, the creatures flinching from the flame, drawing back from the great heat of his pride, as he expanded under the audience's rapt contemplation.

The carny boss laid his fingers to the adhesive. The audience rushed forward, silent in the oven vastness of the night tent.

"You ain't seen nothing yet!" cried the carny boss.

The adhesive ripped free.

There was an instant in which nothing happened. An instant in which the Illustrated Man thought that the Unveiling was a terrible and irrevocable failure.

But then the audience gave a low moan.

The carny boss drew back, his eyes fixed.

Far out at the edge of the crowd, a woman, after a moment, began to cry, began to sob, and did not stop.

Slowly, the Illustrated Man looked down at his naked chest and stomach.

The thing that he saw made the roses on his hands discolor and die. All of his creatures seemed to wither, turn inward, shrivel with the arctic coldness that pumped from his heart outward to freeze and destroy them. He stood trembling. His hands floated up to touch that incredible picture, which lived, moved and shivered with life. It was like gazing into a small room, seeing a thing of someone else's life, so intimate, so impossible that one could not believe and one could not long stand to watch without turning away.

It was a picture of his wife, Lisabeth, and himself.

And he was killing her.

Before the eyes of a thousand people in a dark tent in the center of a black-forested Wisconsin land, he was killing his wife.

His great flowered hands were upon her throat, and her face was turning dark and he killed her and he killed her and did not ever in the next minute stop killing her. It was real. While the crowd watched, she died, and he turned very sick. He was about to fall straight down into the crowd. The tent whirled like a monster bat wing, flapping grotesquely. The last thing he heard was a woman, sobbing, far out on the shore of the silent crowd.

And the crying woman was Lisabeth, his wife.

In the night, his bed was moist with perspiration. The carnival sounds had melted away, and his wife, in her own bed, was quiet now, too. He fumbled with his chest. The adhesive was smooth. They had made him put it back.

He had fainted. When he revived, the carny boss had yelled at him, "Why didn't you *say* what that picture was like?"

"I didn't know, I didn't," said the Illustrated Man.

"Good God!" said the boss. "Scare hell outa everyone. Scared hell outa Lizzie, scared hell outa me. Christ, where'd you *get* that damn tattoo?" He shuddered. "Apologize to Lizzie, now."

His wife stood over him.

"I'm sorry, Lisabeth," he said, weakly, his eyes closed. "I didn't know."

"You did it on purpose," she said. "To scare me."

"I'm sorry."

"Either it goes or I go," she said.

"Lisabeth."

"You heard me. That picture comes off or I quit this show."

"Yeah, Phil," said the boss. "That's how it is."

"Did you lose money? Did the crowd demand refunds?"

"It ain't the money, Phil. For that matter, once the word got around, hundreds of people wanted in. But I'm runnin' a clean show. That tattoo comes off! Was this your idea of a practical joke, Phil?"

He turned in the warm bed. No, not a joke. Not a joke at all. He had been as terrified as anyone. Not a joke. That little old dust-witch, what had she *done* to him and how had she done it? Had she put the picture there? No; she had said that the picture was unfinished, and that he himself, with his thoughts and his perspiration, would finish it. Well, he had done the job all right.

But what, if anything, was the significance? He didn't want to kill anyone. He didn't want to kill Lisabeth. Why should such a silly picture burn here on his flesh in the dark?

He crawled his fingers softly, cautiously down to touch the quivering place where the hidden portrait lay. He pressed tight, and the temperature of that spot was enormous. He could almost feel that little evil picture killing and killing and killing all through the night.

I don't wish to kill her, he thought, insistently, looking over at her bed. And then, five minutes later, he whispered aloud: "Or *do* I?"

"What?" she cried, awake.

"Nothing," he said, after a pause. "Go to sleep."

T he man bent forward, a buzzing instrument in his hand. "This costs five bucks an inch. Costs more to peel tattoos off than put 'em on. Okay, jerk the adhesive."

The Illustrated Man obeyed.

The skin man sat back. "Christ! No wonder you want that off! That's ghastly. *I* don't even want to look at it." He flicked his machine. "Ready? This won't hurt."

The carny boss stood in the tent flap, watching. After five minutes, the skin man changed the instrument head, cursing. Ten minutes later he scraped his chair back and scratched his head. Half an hour passed and he got up, told Mr. William Philippus Phelps to dress, and packed his kit.

"Wait a minute," said the carny boss. "You ain't done the job."

"And I ain't going to," said the skin man.

"I'm paying good money. What's wrong?"

"Nothing, except that damn picture just won't come off. Damn thing must go right down to the bone."

"You're crazy."

"Mister, I'm in business thirty years and never seen a tattoo like this. An inch deep, if it's anything."

"But I've got to get it off!" cried the Illustrated Man.

The skin man shook his head. "Only one way to get rid of that."

"How?"

"Take a knife and cut off your chest. You won't live long, but the picture'll be gone."

"Come back here!"

But the skin man walked away.

They could hear the big Sunday-night crowd, waiting.

"That's a big crowd," said the Illustrated Man.

"But they ain't going to see what they came to see," said the carny boss. "You ain't going out there, except with the adhesive. Hold still now, I'm curious about this *other* picture, on your back. We might be able to give 'em an Unveiling on this one instead."

"She said it wouldn't be ready for a week or so. The old woman said it would take time to set, make a pattern."

There was a soft ripping as the carny boss pulled aside a flap of white tape on the Illustrated Man's spine.

"What do you see?" gasped Mr. Phelps, bent over.

The carny boss replaced the tape. "Buster, as a Tattooed Man, you're a washout, ain't you? Why'd you let that old dame fix you up this way?"

"I didn't know who she was."

"She sure cheated you on this one. No design to it. Nothing. No picture at all."

"It'll come clear. You wait and see."

The boss laughed. "Okay. Come on. We'll show the crowd part of you, anyway."

They walked out into an explosion of brassy music.

He stood monstrous in the middle of the night, putting out his hands like a blind man to balance himself in a world now tilted, now rushing, now threatening to spin him over and down into the mirror before which he raised his hands. Upon the flat, dimly lighted table top were peroxides, acids, silver razors, and squares of sandpaper. He took each of them in turn. He soaked the vicious tattoo upon his chest, he scraped at it. He worked steadily for an hour.

He was aware, suddenly, that someone stood in the trailer door behind him. It was three in the morning. There was a faint odor of beer. She had come home from town. He heard her slow breathing. He did not turn. "Lisabeth?" he said.

"You'd better get rid of it," she said, watching his hands move the sandpaper. She stepped into the trailer.

"I didn't want the picture this way," he said.

"You did," she said. "You planned it."

"I didn't."

"I know you," she said. "Oh, I know you hate me. Well, that's nothing. I hate you, I've hated you a long time now. Good God, when you started putting on the fat, you think anyone could love you then? I could teach you some things about hate. Why don't you ask me?"

"Leave me alone," he said.

"In front of that crowd, making a spectacle out of me!"

"I didn't know what was under the tape."

She walked around the table, hands fitted to her hips, talking to the beds, the walls, the table, talking it all out of her. And he thought: *Or did I know? Who made this picture, me or the witch? Who formed it? How? Do I really want her dead? No! And yet. . . .* He watched his wife draw nearer, nearer, he saw the ropy strings of her throat vibrate to her shouting. This and this and *this* was wrong with him! That and that and *that* was unspeakable about him! He was a liar, a schemer, a fat, lazy, ugly man, a child. Did he think he could compete with the carny boss or the tent-peggers? Did he think he was sylphine and graceful, did he think he was a framed El Greco? Da Vinci, huh! Michelangelo, my eye! She brayed. She showed her teeth. "Well, you can't scare me into staying with someone I don't want touching me with their slobby paws!" she finished, triumphantly.

"Lisabeth," he said.

"Don't Lisabeth me!" she shrieked. "I know your plan. You had that picture put on to scare me. You thought I wouldn't *dare* leave you. Well!"

"Next Saturday night, the Second Unveiling," he said. "You'll be proud of me."

"Proud! You're silly and pitiful. God, you're like a whale. You ever see a beached whale? I saw one when I was a kid. There it was, and they came and shot it. Some lifeguards shot it. Jesus, a whale!"

"Lisabeth."

"I'm leaving, that's all, and getting a divorce."

"Don't."

"And I'm marrying a man, not a fat woman—that's what you are, so much fat on you there ain't no sex!"

"You can't leave me," he said.

"Just watch!"

"I love you," he said.

"Oh," she said. "Go look at your pictures."

He reached out.

"Keep your hands off," she said.

"Lisabeth."

"Don't come near. You turn my stomach."

"Lisabeth."

All the eyes of his body seemed to fire, all the snakes to move, all the monsters to seethe, all the mouths to widen and rage. He moved toward her—not like a man, but a crowd.

He felt the great blooded reservoir of orangeade pump through him now, the sluice of cola and rich lemon pop pulse in sickening sweet anger through his wrists, his legs, his heart. All of it, the oceans of mustard and relish and all the million drinks he had drowned himself in the last year were aboil; his face was the color of a steamed beef. And the pink roses of his hands became those hungry, carnivorous flowers kept long years in tepid jungle and now let free to find their way on the night air before him.

He gathered her to him, like a great beast gathering in a struggling animal. It was a frantic gesture of love, quickening and demanding, which, as she struggled, hardened to another thing. She beat and clawed at the picture on his chest.

"You've got to love me, Lisabeth."

"Let go!" she screamed. She beat at the picture that burned under her fists. She slashed at it with her fingernails.

"Oh, Lisabeth," he said, his hands moving up her arms.

"I'll scream," she said, seeing his eyes.

"Lisabeth." The hand moved up to her shoulders, to her neck. "Don't go away."

"Help!" she screamed. The blood ran from the picture on his chest.

He put his fingers about her neck and squeezed.

She was a calliope cut in mid-shriek.

Outside, the grass rustled. There was the sound of running feet.

Mr. William Philippus Phelps opened the trailer door and stepped out.

They were waiting for him. Skeleton, Midget, Balloon, Yoga, Electra, Popeye, Seal Boy. The freaks, waiting in the middle of the night, in the dry grass.

He walked toward them. He moved with a feeling that he must get away; these people would understand nothing, they were not thinking people. And because he did not flee, because he only walked, balanced, stunned, between the tents, slowly, the freaks moved to let him pass. They watched him, because their watching guaranteed that he would not escape. He walked out across the black meadow, moths fluttering in his face. He walked steadily as long as he was visible, not knowing where he was going. They watched him go, and then they turned and all of them shuffled to the silent car-trailer together and pushed the door slowly wide. . . .

The Illustrated Man walked steadily in the dry meadows beyond the town.

"He went that way!" a faint voice cried. Flashlights bobbled over the hills. There were dim shapes, running.

Mr. William Philippus Phelps waved to them. He was tired. He wanted only to be found now. He was tired of running away. He waved again.

"There he is!" The flashlights changed directions. "Come on! We'll get the bastard!"

When it was time, the Illustrated Man ran again. He was careful to run slowly. He deliberately fell down twice. Looking back, he saw the tent stakes they held in their hands.

He ran toward a far crossroads lantern, where all the summer night seemed to gather; merry-go-rounds of fireflies whirling, crickets moving their song toward that light, everything rushing, as if by some midnight attraction, toward that one high-hung lantern—the Illustrated Man first, the others close at his heels.

As he reached the light and passed a few yards under and beyond it, he did not need to look back. On the road ahead, in silhouette, he saw the upraised tent stakes sweep violently up, up, and then *down!*

A minute passed.

In the country ravines, the crickets sang. The freaks stood over the sprawled Illustrated Man, holding their tent stakes loosely.

Finally they rolled him over on his stomach. Blood ran from his mouth.

They ripped the adhesive from his back. They stared down for a long moment at the freshly revealed picture. Someone whispered. Someone else swore, softly. The Thin Man pushed back and walked away and was sick. Another and another of the freaks stared, their mouths trembling, and moved away, leaving the Illustrated Man on the deserted road, the blood running from his mouth.

In the dim light, the unveiled Illustration was easily seen.

It showed a crowd of freaks bending over a dying fat man on a dark and lonely road, looking at a tattoo on his back which illustrated a crowd of freaks bending over a dying fat man on a . . .

[OCTOBER 1973]

BARRY HANNAH

Return to Return

In the seventies, Esquire published the Mississippi-born-and-bred Barry Hannah's (1942–   ) stories nearly as quickly as he could write them. In fact, one report, perhaps somewhat apocryphal, has Hannah rapidly scrawling with crayon a few words per page on an enormous artist's pad, bundling up the result, and mailing the whole thing off to the magazine, where the distinctive manuscript was immediately set in print. All of Hannah's seventies Esquire stories were collected in his masterful collection Airships (1978), for which he was awarded the Arnold Gingrich Prize for Short Fiction, an honor that was given only once.

They used to call French Edward the happiest man on the court, and the prettiest. The crowds hated to see him beaten. Women anguished to conceive of his departure from a tournament. Once, when Edward lost a dreadfully long match at Forest Hills, an old man in the audience roared with sobs, then female voices joined his. It was like seeing the death of Mercutio or Hamlet, going down with a resigned smile.

Dr. Levaster drove the Lincoln. It was rusty and the valves stuck. On the rear floorboard two rainpools sloshed, disturbing the mosquitoes that rode the beer cans. The other day Dr. Levaster became forty. His hair was thin, his eyes swollen beneath the sunglasses, his ears small and red. Yet he was not monstrous. He seemed, though, to have just retreated from conflict. The man with him was two years younger, curly passionate hair, face dashed with sun. His name was French Edward, the tennis pro.

A mosquito flew from one of the beer cans and bit French Edward before it was taken out by the draft. Edward became remarkably angry, slapping his neck, turning around in the seat, rising and peering down on the cans in the back, reaching over and smacking at them. Then he fell over the seat head down into the puddles and clawed in the water. Dr. Levaster slowed the Lincoln and drove into the grass off the highway.

"Here now, here now! Moan, moan!" Dr. Levaster had given up profanity when he turned forty, formerly having been known as the filthiest-mouthed citizen of Louisiana or Mississippi. He opened the back door and dragged Edward out into the sedge. "You mule." He slapped Edward overvigorously, continuing beyond the therapeutic moment.

"He got me again . . . I thought. He. Doctor Word," said Edward.

"A bug. Mule, who do you think would be riding in the back of my car? How much do you have left, anything?"

"It's clear. A bug. It felt just like what he was doing."

"He's dead. Drowned."

"They never found him."

"He can't walk on water."

"I did."

"You just think you did." Dr. Levaster looked in the back seat. "One of your rackets is in the water, got wet. The strings are ruined."

"I'm all right," French Edward said.

"You'd better be. I'm not taking you one mile more if we don't get some clarity. Where are we?"

"Outside New York City."

"Where, more exactly?"

"New Jersey. The Garden State."

At his three-room place over the spaghetti store on Eighty-ninth, Baby Levaster, M.D., discovered teenagers living. He knew two of them. They had broken in the door but had otherwise respected his quarters, washed the dishes, swept, even revived his houseplants. They were diligent little street people. They claimed they knew by intuition he was coming back to the city and wanted to clean up for him. Two of them thought they might have gonorrhea. Dr. Levaster got his bag and jabbed ten million units of penicillin in them. Then French Edward came up the stairs with the baggage and rackets and went to the back.

"Dear God! He's, oh. Oh, he looks like *love!*" said Carina. She wore steep-heeled sandals and clocked about nineteen on the age scale. The others hung back, her friends. Levaster knew her well. She had shared his sheets, and, in nightmares of remorse, he had shared her body, waking with drastic regret, feeling as soiled and soilsome as the city itself.

"Are you still the mind, him the body?" Carina asked.

"Now more than ever. I'd say he now has about an eighth of the head he was given," Levaster said.

"What happened?"

"He drowned. And then he lived," Levaster said.

"Well, he looks happy."

"I am happy," said French Edward, coming back to the room. "Whose thing is this? You children break in Baby's apartment and, not only that, you carry firearms. I don't like any kind of gun. Who are these hoodlums you're talking to, Baby?" Edward was carrying a double-barreled .410 shotgun/pistol; the handle was of cherrywood and silver vines embossed the length of the barrels.

"I'll take that," said Dr. Levaster, since it was his. It was his Central Park nighttime gun. The shells that went with it were loaded with popcorn. He ran the teenagers out of his apartment, and when he returned, Edward was asleep on the couch, the sweet peace of the athlete beaming through his twisted curls.

"I've never slept like that," Levaster said to Carina, who had remained. "Nor will I ever."

"I saw him on teevee once. It was a match in Boston, I think. I didn't care a rat's prick about tennis. But when I saw him, that face and in his shorts, wow. I told everybody to come here and watch this man."

"He won that one," Dr. Levaster said.

Levaster and Carina took a cab to Central Park. It was raining, which gave a congruous fashion to Levaster's raincoat, wherein, at the left breast pocket, the shotgun/pistol hung in a cunning leather holster. Levaster swooned in the close nostalgia of the city. Everything was so exquisitely true and forthright. Not only was the vicious city there, but he, a meddlesome worthless loud failure from Vicksburg, was jammed amok in the viciousness himself, a willing lout in a nightmare. He stroked Carina's thigh, rather enjoying her distaste.

They entered the park under a light broken by vandals. She came close to him near the dark hedges. What with the inconsequential introversion of his youth, in which he had not honed any skill but only squatted in derision of everything in Vicksburg, Levaster had missed the Southern hunting experience. This was more sporting, bait for muggers. They might have their own pistols, etc. He signaled Carina to lie on the grass and make with her act.

"Oh, I'm coming, I'm coming! And I'm so rich, rich, rich! Only money could make me come like this!"

The rain had stopped and a moon was pouring through the leaves. Two stout bums, one with a beer-can opener in his hand, circled out of the bush and edged in on Carina. The armed bum made a threatening jab. In a small tenor voice, Levaster protested.

"Please! We're only visitors here! Don't take our money! Don't tell my wife!" They came toward Levaster, who was speaking. "Do you fellows know Jesus? The Prince of Peace?" When they were six feet away, he shot them both in the thigh, whimpering, "Glory be! Sorry! Goodness. Oh, wasn't that *loud!*"

After the accosters had stumbled away, astounded at being alive, Levaster sank into the usual fit of contrition. He removed his sunglasses. He seemed wracked by the advantage of new vision. It was the first natural light he had seen since leaving French Edward's house in Covington, across the bridge from New Orleans.

They took a cab back and passed by French Edward, asleep again. He had taken off his trousers and shirt, appeared to have shucked them off in the wild impatience of his sleep, like an infant, and the lithe clusters of his muscles rose and fell with his breathing. Carina sat on the bed with Levaster. He removed his raincoat and everything else. Over his spread-collar shirt was printed a sort of Confederate flag as drawn by a three-year-old with a sludge brush. Levaster wore it to Elaine's to provoke fights but was ignored and never even got to buy a writer or actor a drink. Undressed, it was seen how oversized his head was and how foolishly outsized his sex, hanging large and purple, a slain ogre. Undressed, Levaster seemed more like a mutinous gland than a whole male figure. He jumped up and down on his bed, using it for a trampoline. Carina was appalled.

"I'm the worst, the awfullest!" he said. Carina gathered her bag and edged to the door. She said she was leaving. As he pounced on the bed, he saw her kneeling next to the couch with her hand on Edward's wrist. "Hands off!" Levaster screamed. "No body without the mind! Besides, he's married. A New Orleans woman wears his ring!" Jump, jump! "She makes you look like a chimney sweep. You chimney sweep!" Levaster bounced as Carina left.

He fell on the bed and moiled two minutes before going into black sleep. He dreamed. He dreamed about his own estranged wife, a crazy in Arizona who sent him photographs of herself with her hair cut shorter in every picture. She had a crew cut and was riding a horse out front of a cactus field in the last one. She thought hair interfered with rationality. Now she was happy, having become ugly as a rock. Levaster did not dream about himself and French Edward, although the dream lay on him like the bricks of a hysterical mansion.

In high school, Baby Levaster was the best tennis player. He was small but devious and could run and get the ball like a terrier. Dr. Word coached the college team. Dr. Word was a professor of botany and was suspected as the town queer. Word drew up close to the boys, holding them to show them the full backhand and forehand of tennis, snuggled up to their bodies and worked them like puppets as large as he was. Rumorers said Dr. Word got a thrill from the rear closeness to his players. But his team won the regional championship.

Dr. Word tried to coach Baby Levaster, but Levaster resisted being touched and handled like a big puppet and had heard Word was a queer. What he had heard was true—until a few months before French Edward came onto the courts.

Dr. Word first saw French Edward in a junior-high football game; the boy moved like a genius, finding all the openings, sprinting away from all the other boys on the field. French was the quarterback. He ran for a touchdown nearly every time the ball was centered to him, whenever the play was busted. The only thing that held him back was passing and handing off. Otherwise, he scored, or almost did. An absurd clutter of bodies would be gnashing behind him on the field. It was then that Dr. Word saw French's mother, Olive, sitting in the bleachers, looking calm, auburn-haired, and handsome. From then on Dr. Word was queer no more. Mrs. Edward was a secretary for the P.E. department, and Dr. Word was bald-headed and virile, suave with the grace of his Ph.D. from Michigan State, obtained years ago but still appropriating him some charm as an exotic scholar. Three weeks of tender words and French's mother was his, in any shadow of Word's choosing.

Curious and flaming like a pubescent, he caressed her on back roads and in the darkened basement of the gym, their trysts protected by his repute as a queer or, at the outside, an oyster. Her husband—a man turned lopsided and cycloptic by sports mania—never discovered them. It was her son, French Edward, who did, walking into his own home wearing sneakers and thus unheard—and unwitting—to discover them coiled infamously. Mr. Edward was away as an uninvited delegate to a rules-review board meeting of the Southeastern Conference in Mobile. French was not seen. He crawled under the bed of his room and slept so as to gather the episode into a dream that would vanish when he awoke. What he dreamed was exactly what he had just seen, with the addition that he was present in her room, practicing his strokes with ball and racket, using a great mirror as a backboard, while on the bed his mother and this man groaned in approval, a monstrous twin-headed nude spectator.

Because by that time Word had taken French Edward over and made him quite a tennis player. French could beat Baby Levaster and all the college aces. At eighteen, he was a large angel-bodied tyrant of the court, who drove tennis balls through, outside, beyond, and over the reach of any challenger Dr. Word could dig up. The only one who could give French Edward a match was Word himself, who was sixty and could run and knew the few faults French had, such as disbelieving Dr. Word could keep racing after the balls and knocking them back, French then knocking the odd ball ten feet out of court in an expression of sheer wonder. Furthermore, French had a tendency to soft-serve players he disliked, perhaps an unthinking gesture of derision or perhaps a self-inflicted handicap, to punish himself for ill will. For French's love of the game was so intense he did not want it fouled by personal uglinesses. He had never liked Dr. Word, even as he learned from him. He had never liked Word's closeness, nor his manufactured British or Boston accent, nor the zeal of his interest in him, which French supposed surpassed that of mere coach. For instance, Dr. Word would every now and then give French Edward a *pinch*, a hard, affectionate little nip of the fingers.

And now French Edward was swollen with hatred of the man, the degree of which had no name. It was expelled on the second day of August, hottest day of the year. He called up Word for a match. Not practice, French said. A match. Dr. Word would have played with him in the rain. At the net, he pinched French as they took the balls out of the can. French knocked his hand away and lost games deliberately to keep the match going. Word glowed with a perilous self-congratulation for staying in there; French had fooled Word into thinking he was playing even with him. French pretended to fail in the heat, knocking slow balls from corner to corner, easing over a drop shot to watch the old man ramble up for it. French himself was tiring in the disguise of his ruse when the old devil keeled over, falling out in the alley with his racket clattering away. Dr. Word did not move, though the concrete must have been burning him. French had hoped for a heart attack. Word mumbled that he was cold and couldn't see anything. He asked French to get help.

"No. Buck up. Run it out. Nothing wrong with you," said French.

"Is that you, French, my son?"

"I ain't your son. You might treat my mother like I was, but I ain't. I saw you."

"A doctor. Out of the cold. I need medical help," Dr. Word said.

"I got another idea. Why don't you kick the bucket?"

"Help."

"Go on. Die. It's easy."

When French got home, he discovered his mother escaping the heat in a tub of cold water. Their house was an unprosperous and unlevel connection of boxes. No door of any room shut properly. He heard her sloshing the water on herself. His father was up at Dick Lee's grocery watching the Cardinals on the television. French walked in on her. Her body lay underwater up to her neck.

"Your romance has been terminated," he said.

"French?" She grabbed a towel off the rack and pulled it in the water over her.

"He's blind. He can't even find his way to the house anymore."

"This was a sin, you to look at me!" Mrs. Edward cried.

"Maybe so," French said, "but I've looked before, when you had company."

              French left home for Baton Rouge, on the bounty of the scholarship Dr. Word had hustled for him through the athletic department at Louisiana State. French swore never to return. His father was a fool, his mother a lewd traitor, his mentor a snake from the blind side, the river a brown ditch of bile, his town a hill range of ashes and gloomy souvenirs of the Great Moment in Vicksburg. His days at college were numbered. Like that of most natural athletes, half French Edward's mind was taken over by a sort of tidal barbarous desert where men ran and struggled, grappling, hitting, cursing as some fell into the sands of defeat. The only professor he liked was one who spoke of "muscular thought." The professor said he was sick and tired of thought that sat on its ass and vapored around the room for the benefit of limp-wrists and their whiskey.

As for Dr. Word, he stumbled from clinic to clinic, guided by his brother Wilbur, veteran of Korea and colossal military boredoms all over the globe, before resettling in Vicksburg on the avant-garde of ennui.

Baby Levaster saw the pair in Charity Hospital when he was a med student at Tulane. Word's arm was still curled up with stroke and he had only a sort of quarter vision in one eye. His voice was frightful, like that of a man in a cave of wasps. Levaster was stunned by seeing Dr. Word in New Orleans. He hid in a closet, but Word had already recognized him. Brother Wilbur flung the door open, illuminating Levaster demurring under a bale of puke sheets.

"Our boy won the Southern!" shouted Word. "He's the real thing, more than I ever thought!"

"Who are you talking about?" said Baby Levaster. The volume of the man had blown Levaster's eyebrows out of order.

"Well, French! French Edward! He won the Southern tournament in Mobile!"

Levaster looked to Wilbur for some mediator in this loudness. Wilbur cut away to the water fountain. He acted deaf.

"And the Davis Cup!" Word screamed. "He held up America in the Davis Cup! Don't you read the papers? Then he went to Wimbledon!"

"French went to Wimbledon?"

"Yes! Made the quarterfinals!"

A nurse and a man in white came up to crush the noise from Word. Levaster went back into the closet and shut the door. Then he peeped out, seeing Word and his brother small in the corridor, Word limping slightly to the left, proceeding with a roll and capitulation. The stroke had wrecked him from brain to ankles, had fouled the centers that prevent screaming. Levaster heard Word bleating a quarter mile down the corridor.

Baby Levaster read in *The Times-Pica-yune* that French was resident pro at the Metairie Club, that French was representing the club in a tournament. Levaster hated med school. He hated the sight of pain and blood, and by this time he had become a thin, weak, balding drunkard of a very disagreeable order, even to himself. He dragged himself from one peak of cowardice to the next and began wearing sunglasses, and when he saw French Edward fend off Aussie, Wop, Frog, Brit, and Hun in defending the pride of the Metairie Club, Levaster's body left him and was gathered into the body of French. He had never seen anything so handsome as French Edward. He had never before witnessed a man as happy and winsome in his occupation. Edward moved as if certain animal secrets were known to him. He originated a new, dangerous tennis, taking the ball into his racket with a muscular patience; then one heard the sweet crack, heard the singing ball, and hung cold with a little terror at the speed and the smart violent arc it made into the green. French was by then wearing spectacles. His coiled hair, the color of a kind of charred gold, blazed with sweat. On his lips was the charmed smile of the seraphim. Something of the priest and the brute mingled, perhaps warred, in his expression. Baby Levaster, who had no culture, could not place the line of beauty that French Edward descended from, but finally remembered a photograph of the David statue he'd seen in an old encyclopedia. French Edward looked like that.

When French Edward won, Levaster heard a louder, baleful, unclublike bravo from the gallery. It was Dr. Word. Levaster watched Word fight through the crowd toward French. The man was crazed with partisanship. Levaster, wanting to get close to the person of French himself, three-quarters drunk on gin he'd poured into the iced Cokes from the stand, saw Word reach for French's buttock and give it a pinch. French turned, hate in his eye. He said something quick and corrosive to Word. All the smiles around them turned to straight mouths of concern. Dr. Word looked harmless, a tanned old fellow wearing a beige beret.

"You ought to be dead," said French.

"As graceful, powerful an exhibition of the grandest game as your old coach would ever hope to see! I saw some of the old tricks I taught you! Oh, son, son!" Dr. Word screamed.

Everyone knew he was ill then.

"Go home," said French, looking very soonly sorry as he said it.

"You come home and see us!" Word bellowed, and left.

French's woman, Cecilia Emile, put her head on his chest. She was short, bosomy, and pregnant, a Franco-Italian blessed with a fine large nose, the arrogance of which few men forgot. Next came her hair, a black field of delight. French had found her at L.S.U. They married almost on the spot. Her father was Fat Tim Emile, a low-key monopolist in pinball and wrestling concessions in New Orleans—filthy rich. Levaster did not know this. He stared at the strained hot eyes of French, having surrendered his body to the man, and French saw him.

"Baby Levaster? Is it you? From Vicksburg? You look terrible."

"But you, you . . ." Levaster tripped on a tape and fell into the green clay around Edward's sneakers. ". . . are beauty . . . my youth memory elegant, forever!"

The Edwards took Levaster home to Covington, across the bridge. The Edwards lived in a great glassy house with a pool in back and tall pines hanging over.

French was sad. He said, "She still carries it on with him. They meet out in the Civil War park at night and go to it in those marble houses. One of my old high-school sweethearts saw them and wrote me about it. She wrote it to hurt me, and it did hurt me."

"That old fart Word? Impossible. He's too goddamn loud to carry on any secret rendezvous, for one thing. You could hear the bastard sigh from a half mile off."

"My mother accepts him for what he is."

"That man is destroyed by stroke."

"I know. I gave it to him. She doesn't care. She takes the limping and the bad arm and the hollering. He got under her skin."

"I remember her," Baby Levaster said. "Some handsome woman, auburn hair with a few gray ends. Forgive me, but I had teen-age dreams about her myself. I always thought she was waiting for a romance, living on the hope of something out there, something. . . ."

"Don't leave me, Baby. I need your mind with me. Somebody from the hometown. Somebody who knows."

"I used to whip your little ass at tennis," Levaster said.

"Yes." French smiled. "You barely moved and I was running all over the court. You just stood there and knocked them everywhere like I was hitting into a fan."

They became fast friends. Baby Levaster became an intern. He arrived sober at the funeral of the Edwards' newborn son and saw the tiny black grave its coffin went into behind the Catholic chapel. He looked over to mourners at the fringe. There were Dr. Word and his brother Wilbur under a mimosa, lingering off fifty feet from the rest. Word held his beret to his heart. Levaster was very glad that French never saw Word. They all heard a loud voice, but Word was on the other side of the hill by then, bellowing his sympathetic distress to Wilbur, and the Edwards could not see him.

"Whose voice was that?" asked French.

"Just a voice," said Levaster.

"Whose? Don't I know it? It makes me sick." French turned back to Cecilia, covered with a black veil, her handkerchief pressed to lips. Her child had been born with dysfunction of the involuntary muscles. Her eyes rose toward the hot null blue of the sky. French supported her. His gaze was angrier. It penetrated to the careless heart of nature, right in there to its sullen riot.

On the other side of the cemetery, Dr. Word closed the door of the car. Wilbur drove. Loyal to his brother to the end, almost deaf from the pitch of his voice, Wilbur wheeled the car with veteran patience. Dr. Word wiped his head and held the beret to his chest.

"Ah, Wilbur! They were so unlucky! Nowhere could there be a handsomer couple! They had every right to expect a little Odysseus! Ah, to see doubt and sorrow cloud the faces of those young lovers! Bereft of hope, philosophy!"

Wilbur reached under the seat for the pint of philosophy he had developed since his tour of Korea. It was cognac. The brotherly high music came, tasting of burnt plums, revealing the faces of old officer friends to him.

"James," he said. "I think after this . . . that this is the moment, now, to break it off with Olive—forever. Unless you want to see more doubt and sorrow cloud the face of your young friend."

Word's reply was curiously quiet.

"We cannot do what we cannot do. If she will not end it—and she will not—I cannot. Too deep a sense of joy, Wilbur. The whole quality of my life determined by it."

"Ah, Jimmy," Wilbur said, "you were just too long a queer. The first piece you found had to be permanent. She ain't Cleopatra. If you'd just've started early, nailing the odd twat like the rest of us. . . ."

"I don't want old soldier's reason! No reason! I will not suffer that contamination! Though I love you!"

Dr. Word was hollering again. Wilbur drove them back to Vicksburg.

Cecilia was too frightened to have another child after she lost the first one. Her body would not carry one longer than a month. She was constantly pregnant for a while, and then she stopped conceiving. She began doing watercolors, the faintest violets and greens. French Edward took up the clarinet. Baby Levaster saw it: they were attempting to become art people. Cecilia was pitiful. French went beyond that into dreadfulness; ruesome honks poured from his horn. How wrong and unfortunate that they should have taken their grief into art, thought Levaster. It made them fools who were cut from glory's cloth, who were charmed darlings of the sun.

"What do you think?" asked French, after he'd hacked a little ditty from Mozart into a hundred froggish leavings.

"Yes," Dr. Levaster said. "I think I'll look through some of Cissy's pictures now."

"You didn't like it," French said, downcast, even angry.

"When are you going to get into another tournament? Why sit around here revealing your scabs to me and the neighbors? You need to get out and hit the ball."

French left, walked out, smoldering and spiteful. Baby Levaster remained there. He knocked on Cecilia's door. She was at her spattered art desk working over a watercolor, her bare back to Levaster, her hair lying thick to the small of it, and below, her naked heels. Her efforts were thumbtacked around from ceiling to molding, arresting one with their meek awkward redundancies, things so demure they resisted making an image against the retina. They were not even clouds; rather, the pale ghosts of clouds: the advent of stains, hardly noticeable against paper.

"I can't turn around, but hello," said Cecilia.

"What are all these about?"

"What do you think?"

"I don't know . . . smudges? The vagueness of all things?"

"They aren't things. They're emotions."

"You mean hate, fear, desire, envy?"

"Yes. And triumph and despair." She pointed.

"This is subtle. They look the same," Levaster said.

"I know. I'm a nihilist."

"You aren't any such thing."

"Oh? Why not?"

"Because you've combed your hair. You wanted me to come in here and discover that you're a nihilist," Levaster said.

"Nihilists can comb their hair." She bit her lip, pouting.

"I'd like to see your chest. That's art."

"You toilet. Leave us alone."

"Maybe if you *are* art, Cissy, you shouldn't try to *do* art."

"You want me to be just a decoration?"

"Yes," Levaster said. "A decoration of the air. Decoration is more important than art."

"Is that what you learned in med school? That's dumb." She turned around. "A boob is a boob is a boob."

Dr. Levaster fainted.

At the River Oaks Club in Houston, French played again. The old happiness came back to him, a delight that seemed to feed off his grace. The sunburned Levaster held French's towel for him, resined French's racket handles, and coached him on the weaknesses of the opponents, which is unsportsmanly, untennislike, and all but illegal. A Spaniard Edward was creaming complained, and they threw Levaster off the court and back to the stands. He watched French work the court, roving back and forth, touching the ball with a deft chip, knocking the cooties off it, serving as if firing a curved musket across the net, the Spaniard falling distraught. And throughout, French's smile, widening and widening until it was just this side of loony. Here was a man truly at play, thought Levaster, at one with the pleasant rectangle of the court, at home, in his own field, something *peaceful* in the violent sweep of his racket. A certain slow anomalous serenity invested French Edward's motion. The thought of this parched Levaster.

"Christ, for a drink!" he said out loud.

"Here, son. Cold brandy." The man Levaster sat next to brought out a pint from the ice in a Styrofoam box. French chugged it—exquisite!—then almost spat up the boon as he noticed the fellow on the far side of the brandy man. It was Dr. Word. The man beside Levaster was Wilbur. Word's noble cranium glinted under the sun. His voice had modulated.

"Ah, ah, my boy! An arc of genius," Word whispered as they saw French lay a disguised lob thirty feet from the Spaniard. "He's learned the lob, Wilbur! Our boy has it all now!" Word's voice went on in soft screaming. He seemed to be seeing keenly out of the left eye. The right was covered by eyelid, the muscles there having finally surrendered. So, Levaster thought, this is what the stroke finally left him.

"How's Vicksburg?" Levaster asked Wilbur.

"Nothing explosive, Doctor. Kudzu and the usual erosion."

"What say you try to keep Professor Word away from French until he does his bit in the tournament. A lot depends on his making the finals here."

"I'm afraid the professor's carrying a letter on him from Olive to French. That's why he's not hollering. He's got the letter. It's supposed to say everything."

"But don't let French see him till it's over. And could I hit the brandy again?" Levaster said.

"Of course," said Wilbur. "One man can't drink the amount I brought over. Tennis bores the shit out of me."

In the finals, Edward met Whitney Humble, a tall man from South Africa whose image and manner refuted the usual notion of the tennis star. He was pale, spindly, hairy, with the posture of a derelict. He spat phlegm on the court and picked his nose between serves. Humble appeared to be splitting the contest between one against his opponent and another against the excrescence of his own person. Some in the gallery suspected he served a wet ball. Playing as if with exasperated distaste for the next movement this game had dragged him to, Humble was nevertheless there when the ball came and knocked everything back with either speed or a snarling spin. The voice of Dr. Word came cheering, bellowing for French. Humble identified the bald head in the audience that had hurrahed his error at the net. He served a line drive into the gallery that hit Word square in his good eye.

"Fault!" said the judge. The crowd was horrified.

Humble placed his high-crawling second serve to French.

Levaster saw little of the remaining match. Under the bleachers, where they had dragged Word, Levaster and Wilbur attended to the great black peach that was growing around Word's good eye. With ice and a handkerchief, they abated the swelling, and then all three men returned to their seats. Dr. Word could see out of a black slit of his optic cavity, see French win in a sequel of preposterous dives at the net. Levaster's body fled away from his bones and gathered on the muscles of French Edward. The crowd was screaming over the victory. Nowhere, nowhere, would they ever see again such a clear win of beauty over smut.

Fat Tim, Cecilia's father, would be happy and put five thousand in French's bank if French won this tournament, and Fat Tim would pay Levaster one thousand, as promised, for getting French back on the track of fame. Fat Tim Emile, thumbing those greasy accounts of his concessions, saw French as the family knight, a jouster among grandees, a champion in the whitest sport of all, a game Fat Tim viewed as a species of cunning highbrowism under glass. So he paid French simply for being himself, for wearing white, for symbolizing the pedigree Fat Tim was without, being himself a sweaty dago, a tubby with smudged shirt cuffs and phlebitis. "Get our boy back winning. I want to read his name in the paper," said Fat Tim. "I will," said Levaster.

So I did, thought Levaster. French won.

Dr. Levaster saw Dr. Word crowding up, getting swarmed out to the side by all the little club bitches and fuzzchins with programs for autographing in hand. Word fought back in, however, approaching French from the back.

Levaster saw Word pinch French and heard Word bellow something hearty. By the time Levaster reached the court, the altercation had spread through the crowd. A letter lay in the clay dust, and Word, holding up his hand to ameliorate, was backing out of sight, his good eye but a glint in a cracked bruise, the lid falling gruesome.

"Baby! Baby!" called French, the voice baffled. Levaster reached him. "He pinched me!" French screamed. "He got me right there, really hard!"

Levaster picked up the letter and collected the rackets, then led French straight to the car. No shower, no street clothes.

My Dearest French,
This is your mother Olive writing in case you have forgotten what my handwriting looks like. You have lost your baby son and I have thought of you these months. Now I ask you to think of me. I lost my grown son years ago. You know when, and you know the sin which is old history. I do not want to lose you, my darling. You are such a strange handsomely made boy I would forget you were mine until I remembered you fed at my breast and I changed your diapers. When I saw you wearing new glasses at your wedding if I looked funny it was because I wanted to touch your eyes under them they changed you even more. But I knew you didn't want me anywhere near you. Your bride Cissy was charming as well as stunning and I'm deeply glad her father is well-off and you don't have to work for a living if you don't want to. Your father tried to play for a living or get near where there was athletics but it didn't work as smoothly for him. It drove him crazy, to be truthful. He was lost for a week in February until James Word, the bearer of this letter, found him at the college baseball field throwing an old wet football at home plate. He had been sleeping in the dugout and eating nothing but these dextrose and salt tablets. I didn't write you this before because you were being an expectant father and then the loss of your child. Maybe you get all your sports drive from your father. But can you see how awfully difficult it was to live with him? Certain other things have happened before, I never told you about. He refereed a high-school football game between Natchez and Vicksburg and when it was tight at the end he threw a block on a Natchez player. We love him, French, but he has been away from us a long time.
    So I fell in love with James Word. Don't worry, your father

*still knows nothing. That is sort of proof where his mind is, in a
way. Your father has not even wanted "relations" with me in years.
He said he was saving himself up. He was in a poker game with
some coaches at the college but they threw him out for cheating.
James tried to arrange a tennis doubles game with me and your
father against another couple, but your father tried to hit it so hard
when it came to him that he knocked them over into the service
station and etc. so we had no more balls.*

*The reason I sent this by James is because I thought if it was
right from his hand you would see that it was not just a nasty
slipping-around thing between us but a thing of the heart. His stroke
has left him blind in one eye and without sure control of his voice.
But he loves you. And he loves me. I believe God is with us too.
Please take us all together and let's smile again. I am crying as I
write this. But maybe that's not fair to mention that. James has
mentioned taking us all, your father included, on a vacation to Padre
Island in Texas, him paying all the expenses. Can't you please say
yes and make everything happy?*

Love,
Mother

"It was his fingers pinching me," whined French. "He pinched me all the
time when he was coaching me."

Levaster said, "And if he hadn't coached you, you wouldn't be anything
at all, would you? You'd be selling storm fencing in Vicksburg, wouldn't you?
You'd never have pumped that snatch or had the swimming pool."

Back at his clinic, Levaster slept on a
plastic couch in the waiting room. The nurse woke him up. He was so lonely
and horny that he proposed to her, though he'd never had a clear picture of her
face. Months ago he'd called her into his office. He'd had an erection for four days
without rest.

"Can you make anything of this, Louise? Get the *Merck Manual*. Severe
hardship even to walk." She had been charming. But when he moved to her leg,
clasping on it like a spaniel on the hot, she denied him, and he had since
considered her a woman of principle.

She accepted his proposal. They married. Her parents, strong Methodists

living somewhere out in New Mexico, appeared at the wedding. They stood in
a corner, leaning inward like a pair of sculling oars. Levaster's mother came, too,
talking about the weather and her new shoes. Someone mistook her for nothing
in one of the chairs and sat on her lap. French was best man. Cecilia was there,
a dress of lime sherbet and titties, black hair laid back with gemlike roses at the
temples. She made Levaster's bride look like something dumped out of a ship,
a swathed burial at sea. Cecilia's beauty was unfair to all women. Furthermore,
Levaster himself, compared to French (nugget-cheeked in a tux), was no beau
of the ball. He was balding, waxen, all sweat, a small man with bad posture to
boot.

Levaster expected to lean on the tough inner goodness of his bride, Louise.
He wanted his life bathed and rectified. They resumed their life as doctor and
nurse at the alley clinic, where Levaster undercharged the bums, winos, hustlers,
hookers, artists, and the occasional wayward debutante, becoming something of
an expert on pneumonia, herpes, potassium famine and other diseases of the
street. He leaned on the tough inner goodness of Louise, leaning and leaning,
prone, supine, baby-opossum position. Levaster played tennis, he swam in the
Edwards' pool, he stuck to beer and wine. In the last whole surge of his life, he
won a set from French at the Metairie Club. This act caused Dr. Levaster a hernia
and a frightful depletion of something untold in his cells, the rare *it* of life, the
balm that washes and assures the brain happiness is around the corner. Levaster
lost this sense for three months. He became a creature of the barbarous moment;
he had lost patience. Now he cursed his patients and treated them as malingering
clutter. He drank straight from a flask of rye laced with cocaine, swearing to the
sick about the abominations they had wreaked on themselves. At nights Levaster
wore an oversized black sombrero and forced Louise into awkward and nameless
desecrations. And when they were over, he called her an idiot, a puppet. Then
one morning the hopeful clarity of the mind returned to him. He believed again
in sun and grass and the affable complicity of the human race. But where was his
wife? He wanted to lean on her inner goodness some more. Her plain face, her
fine muscular pale legs, where were they? Louise was gone. She had typed a note.
"One more week of this and you'd have taken us to the bottom of hell. I used
to be a weak but good person. Now I am strong and evil. I hope you're satisfied.
Good-bye."

At the clinic, his patients were afraid of him. The freeloaders and gutter
cowboys shuddered. What will it be, Doc? "French. It was French Edward who
. . . took it away from me. It cost me. I suppose I wanted to defeat beauty, the
outrage of the natural, the glibness of the God-favored. All in that one set of

tennis. Ladies and gentlemen, the physician has been sick and he apologizes." He coughed, dry in the throat. "It cost me my wife, but I am open for business." They swarmed him with the astounded love of sinners for a fallen angel. Levaster was nursed by whores. A rummy with a crutch fetched him coffee. Something, someone, in a sputum-colored blanket, functioned as receptionist.

At last he was home. He lived in a room of the clinic. On his thirty-fourth birthday, they almost killed him with a party and congratulations. The Edwards came. Early in the morning French found Levaster gasping over his fifth Cuban cigar on the roof of the clinic. The sky over New Orleans was a glorious blank pink.

"We're getting older, Baby."

"You're still all right, French. You had all the moves at Forest Hills. Some bad luck, three bad calls. But still the crowd's darling. You could've beat Jesus at Wimbledon."

"I always liked to play better than to win," said French.

"I always liked to win better than to play," said Levaster.

"But, Baby, I never played. First it was my father, then Word. I don't know what kind of player I would be like if I truly *played* when I play."

"But you smile when you play."

"I love the game, on theory. And I admire myself."

"You fool a lot of people. We thought you were happy."

"I am. I feel like I'm doing something nearly as well as it could ever be done. But it's not play. It's slavery."

"A slave to your talent."

"And to the idea of tennis. But, Baby, when I die I don't want my last thought to be a tennis court. You've got people you've cured of disease to think about. They're down there giving you a party. Here I am, thirty-two."

"I'm thirty-four. So what?"

"I want you to tell me, give me something to think about. You've done it before, but now I want something big." French pointed to the sky.

"I won't do that. Don't you understand that the main reason you're a star is the perfect mental desert you're able to maintain between your ears for hours and hours? You memorize the court and the memory sinks straight to your muscles, because there is nothing else in there to cloud the vision."

"Are you calling me stupid?"

"No. But a wild psychic desert. I'm sure it works for artists as well as jocks."

"You mean," said French, "I can't have a thought?"

"You could have one, but it wouldn't live for very long. Like most athletes, you'll go straight from glory to senility with no interlude of thought. I love you," Levaster said.

French said, "I love you, Baby."

Dr. Levaster could no longer bear the flood of respect and affection spilling from the growing horde at the clinic. *The Times-Picayune* had an article about his work among the down-and-out. It was as if Levaster had to eat a tremendous barge of candy every day. The affection and esteem bore hard on a man convinced he was worthless. He had a hundred thousand in the bank. No longer could he resist. He bought a Lincoln demonstrator, shut the clinic, and drove to New York, carrying the double-barreled .410 shotgun/pistol with cherrywood handle paid to him in lieu of fee. He sifted into Elaine's, drunk, Southern and insulting, but was ignored. By the time Levaster had been directed to a sullen playwright, some target frailer than he, on whom he could pour the black beaker of his hatred of art, the movement of the crowd would change and Levaster would be swept away to a group of new enemies. Idlers, armchairers, martini wags, curators of the great empty museums (themselves), he called them. Not one of them could hold a candle to Willum Faulkner, Levaster shouted, having never read a page of the man. He drove his Lincoln everywhere, reveling in the hate and avarice of the city, disappearing into it with a shout of ecstasy.

Then Dr. Levaster met V.T., the Yugoslav sensation, drinking a beer at Elaine's with a noted sportswriter. Forest Hills was to begin the next day. Levaster approved of V.T. Heroic bitterness informed V.T.'s face and he dressed in bad taste, a suit with padded shoulders, narrow tie, pointy shoes.

"Who did you draw first round?" asked Levaster.

"Freench Edwaird," V.T. said.

"Edward won't get around your serve if you're hitting it," said the sportswriter. V.T.'s serve had been clocked at 170 m.p.h. at Wimbledon.

"Ees always who find the beeg rhythm. You find the beeg rhythm or you play on luck."

"If you beat Edward tomorrow," Levaster said, "I will eat your suit."

But the two men had turned away and never heard.

He took the Lincoln out to the West Side Tennis Club and tore his sweater clambering over a fence. He slept in a blanket he had brought with him, out of the dew, under the bleachers. When morning came, Levaster found the right court. The grass was sparkling. It was a heavy minor classic in the realm of tennis. The crowd loved French Edward and V.T., the both of them. When Edward hit one from behind the back for a winner off an unseen overhead smash from V.T., the crowd screamed. V.T. was in his rhythm and knocking his serve in at 160 m.p.h. The crowd adored this, too. French, who had always had a big, very adequate serve, took up the velocity of it to match the great bullet of V.T. At the end, they were men fielding nothing but white blurs against each other. Edward won.

For a half second the crowd was quiet. They had never imagined the ball could be kept in play at such stupendous speed. Then they roared. French Edward leaped over the net. Levaster swooned. His head sailed and joined the head of French Edward, rolled and tossed in the ale-colored curls. Then Levaster saw Dr. Word run out onto the grass, his bellowing lost in the crowd's bellowing. The old man, whose beret had fallen off on the churned service court, put his hand on French's back. Word looked frail, liver spots on his forearms, his scalp speckled and lined. Levaster saw French turn in anger. Then the both of them were overrun by a whirlpool of well-groomed tennis children and mothers and men who rode trains to work, half of their mental life revolving around improvement of the backhand. Levaster wished for his elegant pistol. He left, picking fights with those who looked askance at his blanket.

        A few years passed and Levaster was almost forty. He opened the clinic in New Orleans again. Then he closed it and returned to New York. Now Levaster admitted that he languished when French Edward was out of his vision. A hollow inconsequence filled his acts, good or evil, whenever Edward was not near. He flew with Edward to France, to Madrid, to Prague. He lay angry and mordant with hangover on hotel beds as French Edward worked out on the terrible physical schedule Levaster had prescribed— miles of running, sit-ups, swimming, shadowboxing.

Edward was hardly ever beaten in an early round, but he was fading in the third and fourth day of tournaments now. He had become a spoiler against high seeds in early rounds, though never a winner. His style was greatly admired. A Portuguese writer called him "the New Orleans ace who will not surrender his youth." The Prague paper advocated him as "the dangerous happy cavalier"; Madrid said, "He fights windmills, but, viewing his style, we are convinced his contests matter." Yes, thought Levaster, this style must run its full lustrous route. It cannot throw in the towel until there is the last humiliation, something neither one of us can take.

Then it occurred to Levaster. French had never been humiliated in a match. He had lost, but he had never been humiliated. Not in a single match, not a single game. The handsome head had never bowed, the rusting gold of French Edward's curls stayed high in the sun. He remained the sage and brute that he was when he was nineteen. There was still the occasional winner off his racket that could never have been predicted by the scholars of the game. Levaster felt his soul rise in the applause for this. In Mexico City, there was a standing ovation for the most uncanny movement ever seen on the court. El Niño de Merida smacked down an overhead that bounced high and out of play over the backstop. But Edward had climbed the fence to field it, legs and one arm in the wire, racket hand free for the half second it took to strike the ball back, underhanded. The ball took a boomerang arc to the other side and notched the corner of the ad court. My Christ, thought Levaster, as the Mexicans screamed, he climbed the fence and never lost style.

When they returned from this trip, Levaster read in the paper about an open tournament at Vicksburg. Whitney Humble had already been signed up. The prize money was two thousand dollars, singles winner take all. They called it the Delta Open.

"I know Word has something to do with this. Nobody in Vicksburg ever gave a damn about tennis but him, you Baby, and me," French Edward said.

"You should let the home folks finally see you. Your image would do wonders for the place," said Levaster. "They've read about you. Now they want to see you. Why not? I've been wanting to go back and put a headmarker on my mother's grave, though it would be false to what she was. I've got all this money hanging around. I get sentimental, guilty. Don't you ever?"

"Yes," French Edward said.

They went back to Vicksburg. On the second day of the tournament, they got a call at the Holiday Inn. Fat Tim Emile had died. Nobody had known he was dying but him. He had written a short letter full of pride and appreciation to Cecilia and French, thanking French for his association with the family and for valiant contests in the tennis world. Fat Tim left them two hundred thousand and insisted on nobody giving any ceremony. He wanted his remaining body to go straight to the Tulane med school. "This body," he wrote, "it was fat maybe, but I was proud of it. Those young doctors-to-be, like Baby Levaster, might find something new in me. I was scared all my life and stayed honest. I never hurt another man or woman, that I know of. When I made money, I started eating well. Baby Levaster warned me. I guess I've died of success."

"My poor Cecilia," said French.

"Cissy is fine," said Levaster. "She said for you to finish the tournament." So he did.

           Levaster looked on in a delirium of sober nostalgia. Through the trees, in a slit of the bluffs, he could see the river. French's mother and father sat together and watched their son. Dr. Word, near eighty, was a linesman. They are old people, thought Levaster, looking at the Edwards. And him, Word, he's a goddamned *relic*. A spry relic. Younger brother Wilbur was not there because he was dead.

Whitney Humble and French Edward met in the finals. Humble had aged gruesomely, too, Levaster saw, and knew it was from fighting it out in small tournaments for almost two decades, earning bus fare and tiny fame in newspapers from Alabama to Idaho. But Humble still wanted to play. The color of a dead perch, thinner in the calf, Humble smoked cigarettes between ad games. All his equipment was gray and dirty, even his racket. He could not run much anymore. Some teeth were busted out.

A wild crowd of Vicksburg people, greasers and their pregnant brides from the mobile homes included, met to cheer French. Humble did not have a fan. He was hacking up phlegm and coughing out lengths of it, catching it on his shirt, a tort even those for the underdog could not abide. The greasers felt lifted to some estate of taste by Humble.

It was a long and sparkling match. Humble won.

Humble took the check and the sterling platter, hurled the platter outside the fence and into the trees, then slumped off. The image of tennis was ruined for years in Vicksburg.

           Dr. Word and the Edwards meet French on the court. Levaster sees Word lift an old crabby arm to French's shoulder, sees French wince. Mr. Edward says he has to hurry to his job. He wears a comical uniform and cap. His job is checking vegetable produce at the bridge house of the river so that boll weevils will not enter Mississippi from Louisiana.

Levaster looks into the eyes of Mrs. Edward. Yes, he decides, she still loves
Word; her eyes touch him like fingers, and perhaps he still cuts it, and perhaps
they rendezvous out in the Civil War cemetery so he won't have far to fall when
he explodes with fornication, the old infantryman of lust.

"Mother," says French, "let's all meet at the bridge house."

Levaster sees the desperate light in French's eye.

"Don't you, don't you!" says Levaster afterward, driving the Lincoln.

"I've got to. It'll clear the trash. I can't live if Word's still in it."

"He's nothing but bones," says Levaster. "He's done for."

"She still loves him," says French.

They all gather at the bridge house, and French tells his father that his wife
has been cheating on him for twenty years, and brings up his hands, and begins
crying, and points to Word. Mr. Edward looks at Word, then back to his son.
He is terribly concerned. He asks Word to leave the little hut for a second,
apologizing to Word. He asks Olive to come stand by him and puts his arm over
his wife's shoulders.

"Son," he whispers, "Jimmy Word, friend to us and steady as a brick to
us, is a homosexual. Look out there, what you've done to him. He's running."

Then they are all strung out on the walkway of the bridge, Levaster
marveling at how swift old Word is, for Word is out there nearing the middle
of the bridge, Mrs. Edward next, fifty yards behind, French passing his mother,
gaining on Word. Levaster is running, too. He, too, passes Olive, who has given
out and is leaning on the rail. Levaster sees Word mount the rail and balance on
it like a gymnast. He puts on a burst of speed and catches up with French, who
has stopped running and is walking toward Word cautiously, his hand on the rail.

"Just close your eyes, son. I'll be gone," Word says, looking negligible as
a spirit in his smart tennis jacket and beret. He trembles on the rail. Below Word
is the sheen of the river, the evening sun lying over it down there, low reds
flashing on the brown water.

That's a hundred feet down there, Levaster thinks. When he looks up,
French has gotten up on the rail and is balancing himself, moving step by step
toward Word.

"Don't," say Levaster and Word together.

French, the natural, is walking on the rail with the ease of an avenue
hustler. He has found his purchase: this sport is nothing.

"Son! No closer!" bawls Word.

"I'm not your son. I'm bringing you back, old bastard."

They meet. French seems to be trying to pick up Word in an infant position, arm under legs. Word's beret falls off and floats, puffed out, into the deep hole over the river. French has him, has him wrestled into the shape of a fetus. Then Word gives a kick and Olive screams, and the two men fall backward into the red air and down. Levaster watches them coil together in the drop.

There is a great deal of time until they hit. At the end, Edward flings the old suicide off and hits the river in a nice straight-legged jump. Word hits the water flat as a board. Levaster thinks he hears the sound of Word's back breaking.

The river is shallow here, with strong devious currents. Nothing comes up. By the time the patrol gets out, there is no hope. Then Levaster, standing in a boat, spots French, sitting under a willow a half mile downriver from the bridge. French has drowned and broken one leg, but has crawled out of the river by instinct. His brain is already choked.

French Edward stares at the rescue boat as if it is a turtle with vermin gesturing toward him, Levaster and Olive making their cries of discovery.

Carina, Levaster's teen-ager, woke him up. She handed him a cold beer and a Dexedrine. At first Levaster did not understand. Then he knew that the sun had come up again, seeing the grainy abominable light on the alley through the window. This was New York. Who was this child? Why was he naked on the sheets?

Ah, Carina.

"Will you marry me, Carina?" Levaster said.

"Before I saw your friend, I might have," she said.

French Edward came into the room, fully dressed, hair wet from a shower.

"Where do I run, Baby?" he said.

Levaster told him to run around the block fifty times.

"He does everything you tell him," said Carina.

"Of course he does. Fry me some eggs, you dumb twat."

As the eggs and bacon were sizzling, Levaster came into the kitchen in his Taiwan bathrobe, the huge black sombrero on his head. He had oiled and loaded the .410 shotgun/pistol.

"Put two more eggs on for French. He's really hungry after he runs."

Carina broke two more eggs.

"He's so magnificent," she said. "How much of his brain does he really have left?"

"Enough," Levaster said.

Levaster drove them to New Hampshire, to Bretton Woods. He saw Laver and Ashe approach French Edward in the lobby of the inn. They wanted to shake hands with French, but he did not recognize them. French stood there with hands down, looking ahead into the wall.

The next day Levaster took French out to the court for his first match. He put the Japanese Huta into his hand. It was a funny manganese-and-fiberglass racket with a split throat. The Huta firm had paid French ten thousand to use it on the circuit just before he drowned in the river. French had never hit with it before.

French was looking dull. Levaster struck him a hard blow against the heart. French started and gave a sudden happy regard to the court.

"I'm here," said French.

"You're damned right. Don't let us down."

Edward played better than he had in years. He was going against an Indian twenty years his junior. The boy had a serve and a wicked deceptive blast off his backhand. The crowd loved the Indian. The boy was polite and beautiful. But then French Edward had him at match point on his serve.

Edward threw the ball up.

"Hit it, *hit*. My life, hit it," whispered Levaster.

[OCTOBER 1975]

Human Moments in World War III

Don DeLillo (1936–   ) has contributed two remarkable short stories to Esquire: "Human Moments in World War III," which appeared in 1983, and "In the Men's Room of the Sixteenth Century," which dates back to 1971. Excerpts from his novel Libra, about the assassination of John F. Kennedy, were published in two consecutive issues in 1988; Esquire also ran an excerpt from his most recent novel, Mao II, which won the PEN/Faulkner Award in 1991.

A note about Vollmer. He no longer describes the earth as a library globe or a map that has come alive, as a cosmic eye staring into deep space. This last was his most ambitious fling at imagery. The war has changed the way he sees the earth. The earth is land and water, the dwelling place of mortal men, in elevated dictionary terms. He doesn't see it anymore (storm-spiraled, sea-bright, breathing heat and haze and color) as an occasion for picturesque language, for easeful play or speculation.

At two hundred and twenty kilometers we see ship wakes and the larger airports. Icebergs, lightning bolts, sand dunes. I point out lava flows and cold-core eddies. That silver ribbon off the Irish coast, I tell him, is an oil slick.

This is my third orbital mission, Vollmer's first. He is an engineering genius, a communications and weapons genius, and maybe other kinds of genius as well. As mission specialist I'm content to be in charge. (The word "specialist," in the peculiar usage of Colorado Command, refers here to someone who does not specialize.) Our spacecraft is designed primarily to gather intelligence. The refinement of the quantum burn technique enables us to make frequent adjustments of orbit without firing rockets every time. We swing out into high wide trajectories, the whole earth as our psychic light, to inspect unmanned and possibly hostile satellites. We orbit tightly, snugly, take intimate looks at surface activities in untraveled places.

The banning of nuclear weapons has made the world safe for war.

I try not to think big thoughts or submit to rambling abstractions. But the urge sometimes comes over me. Earth orbit puts men into philosophical temper. How can we help it? We see the planet complete, we have a privileged vista. In our attempts to be equal to the experience, we tend to meditate importantly on subjects like the human condition. It makes a man feel *universal*, floating over the continents, seeing the rim of the world, a line as clear as a compass arc, knowing it is just a turning of the bend to Atlantic twilight, to sediment plumes and kelp beds, an island chain glowing in the dusky sea.

I tell myself it is only scenery. I want to think of our life here as ordinary, as a housekeeping arrangement, an unlikely but workable setup caused by a housing shortage or spring floods in the valley.

Vollmer does the systems checklist and goes to his hammock to rest. He is twenty-three years old, a boy with a longish head and close-cropped hair. He talks about northern Minnesota as he removes the objects in his personal preference kit, placing them on an adjacent Velcro surface for tender inspection. I have a 1901 silver dollar in my personal preference kit. Little else of note. Vollmer has graduation pictures, bottle caps, small stones from his backyard. I don't know whether he chose these items himself or whether they were pressed on him by parents who feared that his life in space would be lacking in human moments.

Our hammocks are human moments, I suppose, although I don't know whether Colorado Command planned it that way. We eat hot dogs and almond crunch bars and apply lip balm as part of the pre-sleep checklist. We wear slippers at the firing panel. Vollmer's football jersey is a human moment. Outsized, purple-and-white, of polyester mesh, bearing the number 79, a big man's number, a prime of no particular distinction, it makes him look stoop-shouldered, abnormally long-framed.

"I still get depressed on Sundays," he says.

"Do we have Sundays here?"

"No, but they have them there and I still feel them. I always know when it's Sunday."

"Why do you get depressed?"

"The slowness of Sundays. Something about the glare, the smell of warm grass, the church service, the relatives visiting in nice clothes. The whole day kind of lasts forever."

"I didn't like Sundays either."

"They were slow but not lazy-slow. They were long and hot, or long and cold. In summer my grandmother made lemonade. There was a routine. The whole day was kind of set up beforehand and the routine almost never changed. Orbital routine is different. It's satisfying. It gives our time a shape and substance. Those Sundays were shapeless despite the fact you knew what was coming, who was coming, what we'd all say. You knew the first words out of the mouth of each person before anyone spoke. I was the only kid in the group. People were happy to see me. I used to want to hide."

"What's wrong with lemonade?" I ask.

A battle management satellite, unmanned, reports high-energy laser activity in orbital sector Dolores. We take out our laser kits and study them for half an hour. The beaming procedure is complex and because the panel operates on joint control only we must rehearse the sets of established measures with the utmost care.

A note about the earth. The earth is the preserve of day and night. It contains a sane and balanced variation, a natural waking and sleeping, or so it seems to someone deprived of this tidal effect.

This is why Vollmer's remark about Sundays in Minnesota struck me as interesting. He still feels, or claims he feels, or thinks he feels, that inherently earthbound rhythm.

To men at this remove, it is as though things exist in their particular physical form in order to reveal the hidden simplicity of some powerful mathematical truth. The earth reveals to us the simple awesome beauty of day and night. It is there to contain and incorporate these conceptual events.

Vollmer in his shorts and suction clogs resembles a high-school swimmer, all but hairless, an unfinished man not aware he is open to cruel scrutiny, not aware he is without devices, standing with arms folded in a place of echoing voices and chlorine fumes. There is something stupid in the sound of his voice. It is too direct, a deep voice from high in the mouth, well back in the mouth, slightly insistent, a little loud. Vollmer has never said a stupid thing in my presence. It is just his voice that is stupid, a grave and naked bass, a voice without inflection or breath.

We are not cramped here. The flight deck and crew quarters are thoughtfully designed. Food is fair to good. There are books, videocassettes, news and music. We do the manual checklists, the oral checklists, the simulated firings with no sign of boredom or carelessness. If anything, we are getting better at our tasks all the time. The only danger is conversation.

I try to keep our conversations on an everyday plane. I make it a point to talk about small things, routine things. This makes sense to me. It seems a sound tactic, under the circumstances, to restrict our talk to familiar topics, minor matters. I want to build a structure of the commonplace. But Vollmer has a tendency to bring up enormous subjects. He wants to talk about war and the weapons of war. He wants to discuss global strategies, global aggressions. I tell him now that he has stopped describing the earth as a cosmic eye, he wants to see it as a game board or computer model. He looks at me plain-faced and tries to get me in a theoretical argument: selection space-based attacks versus long-drawn-out well-modulated land-sea-air engagements. He quotes experts, mentions sources. What am I supposed to say? He will suggest that people are disappointed in the war. The war is dragging into its third week. There is a sense in which it is worn out, played out. He gathers this from the news broadcasts we periodically receive. Something in the announcer's voice hints at a letdown, a fatigue, a faint bitterness about—*something*. Vollmer is probably right about this. I've heard it myself in the tone of the broadcaster's voice, in the voice of Colorado Command, despite the fact that our news is censored, that they are not telling us things they feel we shouldn't know, in our special situation, our exposed and sensitive position. In his direct and stupid-sounding and uncannily perceptive way, young Vollmer says that people are not enjoying this war to the same extent that people have always enjoyed and nourished themselves on war, as a heightening, a periodic intensity. What I object to in Vollmer is that he often shares my deep-reaching and most reluctantly held convictions. Coming from that mild face, in that earnest resonant run-on voice, these ideas unnerve and worry me as they never do when they remain unspoken. Vollmer's candor exposes something painful.

It is not too early in the war to discern nostalgic references to earlier wars. All wars refer back. Ships, planes, entire operations are named after ancient battles, simpler weapons, what we perceive as conflicts of nobler intent. This recon-interceptor is called Tomahawk II. When I sit at the firing panel I look at a photograph of Vollmer's granddad when he was a young man in sagging khakis and a shallow helmet, standing in a bare field, a rifle strapped to his shoulder. This is a human moment and it reminds me that war, among other things, is a form of longing.

We dock with the command station, take on food, exchange videocassettes. The war is going well, they tell us, although it isn't likely they know much more than we do.

Then we separate.

The maneuver is flawless and I am feeling happy and satisfied, having resumed human contact with the nearest form of the outside world, having traded quips and manly insults, traded voices, traded news and rumors—buzzes, rumbles, scuttlebutt. We stow our supplies of broccoli and apple cider and fruit cocktail and butterscotch pudding. I feel a homey emotion, putting away the colorfully packaged goods, a sensation of prosperous well-being, the consumer's solid comfort.

Volmer's T-shirt bears the word *Inscription*.

"People had hoped to be caught up in something bigger than themselves," he says. "They thought it would be a shared crisis. They would feel a sense of shared purpose, shared destiny. Like a snowstorm that blankets a large city—but lasting months, lasting years, carrying everyone along, creating fellow-feeling where there was only suspicion and fear. Strangers talking to each other, meals by candlelight when the power fails. The war would ennoble everything we say and do. What was impersonal would become personal. What was solitary would be shared. But what happens when the sense of shared crisis begins to dwindle much sooner than anyone expected? We begin to think the feeling lasts longer in snowstorms."

A note about selective noise. Forty-eight hours ago I was monitoring data on the mission console when a voice broke in on my report to Colorado Command. The voice was unenhanced, heavy with static. I checked my headset, checked the switches and lights. Seconds later the command signal resumed and I heard our flight dynamics officer ask me to switch to the redundant sense frequencer. I did this but it only caused the weak voice to return, a voice that carried with it a strange and unspecifiable poignancy. I seemed somehow to recognize it. I don't mean I knew who was speaking. It was the tone I recognized, the touching quality of some half-remembered and tender event, even through the static, the sonic mist.

In any case, Colorado Command resumed transmission in a matter of seconds.

"We have a deviate, Tomahawk."

"We copy. There's a voice."

"We have gross oscillation here."

"There's some interference. I have gone redundant but I'm not sure it's helping."

"We are clearing an outframe to locate source."

"Thank you, Colorado."

"It is probably just selective noise. You are negative red on the step-function quad."

"It was a voice," I told them.

"We have just received an affirm on selective noise."

"I could hear words, in English."

"We copy selective noise."

"Someone was talking, Colorado."

"What do you think selective noise is?"

"I don't know what it is."

"You are getting a spill from one of the unmanneds."

"If it's an unmanned, how could it be sending a voice?"

"It is not a voice as such, Tomahawk. It is selective noise. We have some real firm telemetry on that."

"It sounded like a voice."

"It is supposed to sound like a voice. But it is not a voice as such. It is enhanced."

"It sounded unenhanced. It sounded human in all sorts of ways."

"It is signals and they are spilling from geosynchronous orbit. This is your deviate. You are getting voice codes from twenty-two thousand miles. It is basically a weather report. We will correct, Tomahawk. In the meantime, advise you stay redundant."

About ten hours later Vollmer heard the voice. Then he heard two or three other voices. They were people speaking, people in conversation. He gestured to me as he listened, pointed to the headset, then raised his shoulders, held his hands apart to indicate surprise and bafflement. In the swarming noise (as he said later), it wasn't easy to get the drift of what people were saying. The static was frequent, the references were somewhat elusive, but Vollmer mentioned how intensely affecting these voices were, even when the signals were at their weakest. One thing he did know: it wasn't selective noise. A quality of purest, sweetest sadness issued from remote space. He wasn't sure but he thought there was also a background noise integral to the conversation. Laughter. The sound of people laughing.

In other transmissions we've been able to recognize theme music, an announcer's introduction, wisecracks and bursts of applause, commercials for products whose long-lost brand names evoke the golden antiquity of great cities buried in sand and river silt.

Somehow we are picking up signals from radio programs of forty, fifty, sixty years ago.

Our current task is to collect imagery data on troop deployment. Vollmer surrounds his Hasselblad, engrossed in some microadjustment. There is a seaward bulge of stratocumulus. Sunglint and littoral drift. I see blooms of plankton in a blue of such Persian richness it seems an animal rapture, a color-change to express some form of intuitive delight. As the surface features unfurl, I list them aloud by name. It is the only game I play in space, reciting the earth-names, the nomenclature of contour and structure. Glacial scour, moraine debris. Shatter-coning at the edge of a multi-ring impact site. A resurgent caldera, a mass of castellated rimrock. Over the sand seas now. Parabolic dunes, star dunes, straight dunes with radial crests. The emptier the land, the more luminous and precise the names for its features. Vollmer says the thing science does best is name the features of the world.

He has degrees in science and technology. He was a scholarship winner, an honors student, a research assistant. He ran science projects, read technical papers in the deep-pitched earnest voice that rolls off the roof of his mouth. As mission specialist (generalist), I sometimes resent his nonscientific perceptions, the glimmerings of maturity and balanced judgment. I am beginning to feel slightly preempted. I want him to stick to systems, onboard guidance, data parameters. His human insights make me nervous.

"I'm happy," he says.

These words are delivered with matter-of-fact finality and the simple statement affects me powerfully. It frightens me in fact. What does he mean he's happy? Isn't happiness totally outside our frame of reference? How can he think it is possible to be happy here? I want to say to him, "This is just a housekeeping arrangement, a series of more or less routine tasks. Attend to your tasks, do your testing, run through your checklists." I want to say, "Forget the measure of our vision, the sweep of things, the war itself, the terrible death. Forget the overarching night, the stars as static points, as mathematical fields. Forget the cosmic solitude, the upwelling awe and dread."

I want to say, "Happiness is not a fact of this experience, at least not to the extent that one is bold enough to speak of it."

Laser technology contains a core of foreboding and myth. It is a clean sort of lethal package we are dealing with, a well-behaved beam of photons, an engineered coherence, but we approach the weapon with our minds full of ancient warnings and fears. (There ought to be a term for this ironic condition: primitive fear of the weapons we are advanced enough to design and produce.) Maybe this is why the project managers were ordered to work out a firing procedure that depends on the coordinated actions of two men—two temperaments, two souls—operating the controls together. Fear of the power of light, the pure stuff of the universe.

A single dark mind in a moment of inspiration might think it liberating to fling a concentrated beam at some lumbering humpbacked Boeing making its commercial rounds at thirty thousand feet.

Vollmer and I approach the firing panel. The panel is designed in such a way that the joint operators must sit back to back. The reason for this, although Colorado Command never specifically said so, is to keep us from seeing each other's face. Colorado wants to be sure that weapons personnel in particular are not influenced by each other's tics and perturbations. We are back to back, therefore, harnessed in our seats, ready to begin. Vollmer in his purple-and-white jersey, his fleeced pad-abouts.

This is only a test.

I start the playback. At the sound of a prerecorded voice command, we each insert a modal key in its proper slot. Together we count down from five and then turn the keys one-quarter left. This puts the system in what is called an open-minded mode. We count down from three. The enhanced voice says, *You are open-minded now.*

Vollmer speaks into his voiceprint analyzer.

"This is code B for bluegrass. Request voice identity clearance."

We count down from five and then speak into our voiceprint analyzers. We say whatever comes into our heads. The point is simply to produce a voiceprint that matches the print in the memory bank. This ensures that the men at the panel are the same men authorized to be there when the system is in an open-minded mode.

This is what comes into my head: "I am standing at the corner of Fourth and Main, where thousands are dead of unknown causes, their scorched bodies piled in the street."

We count down from three. The enhanced voice says, *You are cleared to proceed to lock-in position.*

We turn our modal keys half right. I activate the logic chip and study the numbers on my screen. Vollmer disengages voiceprint and puts us in voice circuit rapport with the onboard computer's sensing mesh. We could down from five. The enhanced voice says, *You are locked in now.*

"Random factor seven," I say. "Problem seven. Solution seven."

Vollmer says, "Give me an acronym."

"BROWN, for Bearing Radius Oh White Nine."

My color-spec lights up brown. The numbers on my display screen read 2, 18, 15, 23, 14. These are the alphanumeric values of the letters in the acronym BROWN as they appear in unit succession.

The logic-gate opens. The enhanced voice says, *You are logical now.*

As we move from one step to the next, as the colors, numbers, characters, lights and auditory signals indicate that we are proceeding correctly, a growing satisfaction passes through me—the pleasure of elite and secret skills, a life in which every breath is governed by specific rules, by patterns, codes, controls. I try to keep the results of the operation out of my mind, the whole point of it, the outcome of these sequences of precise and esoteric steps. But often I fail. I let the image in, I think the thought, I even say the word at times. This is confusing, of course. I feel tricked. My pleasure feels betrayed, as if it had a life of its own, a childlike or intelligent-animal existence independent of the man at the firing panel.

We count down from five. Vollmer releases the lever that unwinds the systems-purging disk. My pulse marker shows green at three-second intervals. We count down from three. We turn the modal keys three-quarters right. I activate the beam sequencer. We turn the keys one-quarter right. We count down from three. Bluegrass music plays over the squawk box. The enhanced voice says, *You are moded to fire now.*

We study our world map kits.

"Don't you sometimes feel a power in you?" Vollmer says. "An extreme state of good health, sort of. An *arrogant* healthiness. That's it. You are feeling so good you begin thinking you're a little superior to other people. A kind of life-strength. An optimism about yourself that you generate almost at the expense of others. Don't you sometimes feel this?"

(Yes, as a matter of fact.)

"There's probably a German word for it. But the point I want to make is that this powerful feeling is so—I don't know—*delicate*. That's it. One day you feel it, the next day you are suddenly puny and doomed. A single little thing goes wrong, you feel doomed, you feel utterly weak and defeated and unable to act powerfully or even sensibly. Everyone else is lucky, you are unlucky, hapless, sad, ineffectual and doomed."

(Yes, yes.)

By chance we are over the Missouri River now, looking toward the Red Lakes of Minnesota. I watch Vollmer go through his map kit, trying to match the two worlds. This is a deep and mysterious happiness, to confirm the accuracy of a map. He seems immensely satisfied. He keeps saying, *"That's it, that's it."*

Vollmer talks about childhood. In orbit he has begun to think about his early years for the first time. He is surprised at the power of these memories. As he speaks he keeps his head turned to the window. Minnesota is a human moment. Upper Red Lake, Lower Red Lake. He clearly feels he can see himself there.

"Kids don't take walks," he says. "They don't sunbathe or sit on the porch."

He seems to be saying that children's lives are too well supplied to accommodate the spells of reinforced being that the rest of us depend on. A deft enough thought but not to be pursued. It is time to prepare for a quantum burn.

We listen to the old radio shows. Light flares and spreads across the blue-banded edge, sunrise, sunset, the urban grids in shadow. A man and woman trade well-timed remarks, light, pointed, bantering. There is a sweetness in the tenor voice of the young man singing, a simple vigor that time and distance and random noise have enveloped in eloquence and yearning. Every sound, every lilt of strings has this veneer of age. Vollmer says he remembers these programs, although of course he has never heard them before. What odd happenstance, what flourish or grace of the laws of physics, enables us to pick up these signals? Traveled voices, chambered and dense. At times they have the detached and surreal quality of aural hallucination, voices in attic rooms, the complaints of dead relatives. But the sound effects are full of urgency and verve. Cars turn dangerous corners, crisp gunfire fills the night. It was, it is, wartime. Wartime for Duz and Grape-Nuts Flakes. Comedians make fun of the way the enemy talks. We hear hysterical mock German, moonshine Japanese. The cities are in light, the listening millions, fed, met comfortably in drowsy rooms, at war, as the night comes softly down. Vollmer says he recalls specific moments, the comic inflections, the announcer's fat-man laughter. He recalls individual voices rising from the laughter of the studio audience, the cackle of a St. Louis businessman, the brassy wail of a high-shouldered blonde, just arrived in California, where women wear their hair this year in aromatic bales.

Vollmer drifts across the wardroom, up-side-down, eating an almond crunch.

He sometimes floats free of his hammock, sleeping in a fetal crouch, bumping into walls, adhering to a corner of the ceiling grid.

"Give me a minute to think of the name," he says in his sleep.

He says he dreams of vertical spaces from which he looks, as a boy, at—*something*. My dreams are the heavy kind, the kind that are hard to wake from, to rise out of. They are strong enough to pull me back down, dense enough to leave me with a heavy head, a drugged and bloated feeling. There are episodes of faceless gratification, vaguely disturbing.

"It's almost unbelievable when you think of it, how they live there in all that ice and sand and mountainous wilderness. Look at it," he says. "Huge barren deserts, huge oceans. How do they endure all those terrible things? The floods alone. The earthquakes alone make it crazy to live there. Look at those fault systems. They're so big, there's so many of them. The volcanic eruptions alone. What could be more frightening than a volcanic eruption? How do they endure avalanches, year after year, with numbing regularity? It's hard to believe people live there. The floods alone. You can see whole huge discolored areas, all flooded out, washed out. How do they survive, where do they go? Look at the cloud buildups. Look at that swirling storm center. What about the people who live in the path of a storm like that? It must be packing incredible winds. The lightning alone. People exposed on beaches, near trees and telephone poles. Look at the cities with their spangled lights spreading in all directions. Try to imagine the crime and violence. Look at the smoke pall hanging low. What does that mean in terms of respiratory disorders? It's crazy. Who would live there? The deserts, how they encroach. Every year they claim more and more arable land. How enormous those snow-fields are. Look at the massive storm fronts over the ocean. There are ships down there, small craft some of them. Try to imagine the waves, the rocking. The hurricanes alone. The tidal waves. Look at those coastal communities exposed to tidal waves. What could be more frightening than a tidal wave? But they live there, they stay there. Where could they go?"

           I want to talk to him about calorie intake, the effectiveness of the earplugs and nasal decongestants. The earplugs are human moments. The apple cider and the broccoli are human moments. Vollmer himself is a human moment, never more so than when he forgets there is a war.

The close-cropped hair and longish head. The mild blue eyes that bulge slightly. The protuberant eyes of long-bodied people with stooped shoulders. The long hands and wrists. The mild face. The easy face of a handyman in a panel truck that has an extension ladder fixed to the roof and a scuffed license plate, green and white, with the state motto beneath the digits. That kind of face.

He offers to give me a haircut. What an interesting thing a haircut is, when you think of it. Before the war there were time slots reserved for such activities. Houston not only had everything scheduled well in advance but constantly monitored us for whatever meager feedback might result. We were wired, taped, scanned, diagnosed, and metered. We were men in space, objects worthy of the most scrupulous care, the deepest sentiments and anxieties.

Now there is a war. Nobody cares about my hair, what I eat, how I feel about the spacecraft's decor, and it is not Houston but Colorado we are in touch with. We are no longer delicate biological specimens adrift in an alien environment. The enemy can kill us with its photons, its mesons, its charged particles faster than any calcium deficiency or trouble of the inner ear, faster than any dusting of micrometeoroids. The emotions have changed. We've stopped being candidates for an embarrassing demise, the kind of mistake or unforeseen event that tends to make a nation grope for the appropriate response. As men in war we can be certain, dying, that we will arouse uncomplicated sorrows, the open and dependable feelings that grateful nations count on to embellish the simplest ceremony.

A note about the universe. Vollmer is on the verge of deciding that our planet is alone in harboring intelligent life. We are an accident and we happened only once. (What a remark to make, in egg-shaped orbit, to someone who doesn't want to discuss the larger questions.) He feels this way because of the war.

The war, he says, will bring about an end to the idea that the universe swarms, as they say, with life. Other astronauts have looked past the star-points and imagined infinite possibility, grape-clustered worlds teeming with higher forms. But this was before the war. Our view is changing even now, his and mine, he says, as we drift across the firmament.

Is Vollmer saying that cosmic optimism is a luxury reserved for periods between world wars? Do we project our current failure and despair out toward the star clouds, the endless night? After all, he says, where are they? If they exist, why has there been no sign, not one, not any, not a single indication that serious people might cling to, not a whisper, a radio pulse, a shadow? The war tells us it is foolish to believe.

Our dialogues with Colorado Command are beginning to sound like computer-generated teatime chat. Vollmer tolerates Colorado's jargon only to a point. He is critical of their more debased locutions and doesn't mind letting them know. Why, then, if I agree with his views on this matter, am I becoming irritated by his complaints? Is he too young to champion the language? Does he have the experience, the professional standing, to scold our flight dynamics officer, our conceptual paradigm officer, our status consultants on waste-management systems and evasion-related zonal options? Or is it something else completely, something unrelated to Colorado Command and our communications with them? Is it the sound of his voice? Is it just his *voice* that is driving me crazy?

Vollmer has entered a strange phase. He spends all his time at the window now, looking down at the earth. He says little or nothing. He simply wants to look, do nothing but look. The oceans, the continents, the archipelagos. We are configured in what is called a cross-orbit series and there is no repetition from one swing around the earth to the next. He sits there looking. He takes meals at the window, does checklists at the window, barely glancing at the instruction sheets as we pass over tropical storms, over grass fires and major ranges. I keep waiting for him to return to his prewar habit of using quaint phrases to describe the earth. It's a beach ball, a sun-ripened fruit. But he simply looks out the window, eating almond crunches, the wrappers floating away. The view clearly fills his consciousness. It is powerful enough to silence him, to still the voice that rolls off the roof of his mouth, to leave him turned in the seat, twisted uncomfortably for hours at a time.

The view is endlessly fulfilling. It is like the answer to a lifetime of questions and vague cravings. It satisfies every childlike curiosity, every muted desire, whatever there is in him of the scientist, the poet, the primitive seer, the watcher of fire and shooting stars, whatever obsessions eat at the night side of his mind, whatever sweet and dreamy yearning he has ever felt for nameless places faraway, whatever earth-sense he possesses, the neural pulse of some wilder awareness, a sympathy for beasts, whatever belief in an immanent vital force, the Lord of Creation, whatever secret harboring of the idea of human oneness, whatever wishfulness and simplehearted hope, whatever of too much and not enough, all at once and little by little, whatever burning urge to escape responsibility and routine, escape his own overspecialization, the circumscribed and inward-spiraling self, whatever remnants of his boyish longing to fly, his dreams of strange spaces and eerie heights, his fantasies of happy death, whatever indolent and sybaritic leanings, lotus-eater, smoker of grasses and herbs, blue-eyed gazer into space—all these are satisfied, all collected and massed in that living body, the sight he sees from the window.

"It is just so interesting," he says at last. "The colors and all."

The colors and all.

[JULY 1983]

LOUISE ERDRICH

Fleur

Louise Erdrich (1954–   ) grew up in North Dakota near the Turtle Mountain (Chippewa) Reservation, where her grandfather was the tribal chairman. She graduated from Dartmouth College in 1976 and went on to study at the Johns Hopkins Writing Seminars. Love Medicine, her first novel, won numerous awards, including the National Book Critics Circle Award for the best work of fiction in 1984. She lives in New Hampshire with her husband, Michael Dorris, with whom she often collaborates. The novelist Anne Tyler, writing in Esquire, has applauded "the grace with which [Erdrich] slips from realistic to mythic and back again," a quality clearly visible in "Fleur," which won a National Magazine Award for fiction in 1987.

The first time she drowned in the cold and glassy waters of Lake Turcot, Fleur Pillager was only a girl. Two men saw the boat tip, saw her struggle in the waves. They rowed over to the place she went down, and jumped in. When they dragged her over the gunwales, she was cold to the touch and stiff, so they slapped her face, shook her by the heels, worked her arms back and forth, and pounded her back until she coughed up lake water. She shivered all over like a dog, then took a breath. But it wasn't long afterward that those two men disappeared. The first wandered off, and the other, Jean Hat, got himself run over by a cart.

It went to show, my grandma said. It figured to her, all right. By saving Fleur Pillager, those two men had lost themselves.

The next time she fell in the lake, Fleur Pillager was twenty years old and no one touched her. She washed onshore, her skin a dull dead gray, but when George Many Women bent to look closer, he saw her chest move. Then her eyes spun open, sharp black riprock, and she looked at him. "You'll take my place," she hissed. Everybody scattered and left her there, so no one knows how she dragged herself home. Soon after that we noticed Many Women changed, grew afraid, wouldn't leave his house, and would not be forced to go near water. For his caution, he lived until the day that his sons brought him a new tin bathtub. Then the first time he used the tub he slipped, got knocked out, and breathed water while his wife stood in the other room frying breakfast.

Men stayed clear of Fleur Pillager after the second drowning. Even though she was good-looking, nobody dared to court her because it was clear that Misshepeshu, the waterman, the monster, wanted her for himself. He's a devil, that one, love-hungry with desire and maddened for the touch of young girls, the strong and daring especially, the ones like Fleur.

Our mothers warn us that we'll think he's handsome, for he appears with green eyes, copper skin, a mouth tender as a child's. But if you fall into his arms, he sprouts horns, fangs, claws, fins. His feet are joined as one and his skin, brass scales, rings to the touch. You're fascinated, cannot move. He casts a shell necklace at your feet, weeps gleaming chips that harden into mica on your breasts. He holds you under. Then he takes the body of a lion or a fat brown worm. He's made of gold. He's made of beach moss. He's a thing of dry foam, a thing of death by drowning, the death a Chippewa cannot survive.

Unless you are Fleur Pillager. We all knew she couldn't swim. After the first time, we thought she'd never go back to Lake Turcot. We thought she'd keep to herself, live quiet, stop killing men off by drowning in the lake. After the first time, we thought she'd keep the good ways. But then, after the second drowning, we knew that we were dealing with something much more serious. She was haywire, out of control. She messed with evil, laughed at the old women's advice, and dressed like a man. She got herself into some half-forgotten medicine, studied ways we shouldn't talk about. Some say she kept the finger of a child in her pocket and a powder of unborn rabbits in a leather thong around her neck. She laid the heart of an owl on her tongue so she could see at night, and went out, hunting, not even in her own body. We know for sure because the next morning, in the snow or dust, we followed the tracks of her bare feet and saw where they changed, where the claws sprang out, the pad broadened and pressed into the dirt. By night we heard her chuffing cough, the bear cough. By day her silence and the wide grin she threw to bring down our guard made us frightened. Some thought that Fleur Pillager should be driven off the reservation, but not a single person who spoke like this had the nerve. And finally, when people were just about to get together and throw her out, she left on her own and didn't come back all summer. That's what this story is about.

During that summer, when she lived a few miles south in Argus, things happened. She almost destroyed that town.

When she got down to Argus in the year of 1920, it was just a small grid of six streets on either side of the railroad depot. There were two elevators, one central, the other a few miles west. Two stores competed for the trade of the three hundred citizens, and three churches quarreled with one another for their souls. There was a frame building for Lutherans, a heavy brick one for Episcopalians, and a long narrow shingled Catholic church. This last had a tall slender steeple, twice as high as any building or tree.

No doubt, across the low, flat wheat, watching from the road as she came near Argus on foot, Fleur saw that steeple rise, a shadow thin as a needle. Maybe in that raw space it drew her the way a lone tree draws lightning. Maybe, in the end, the Catholics are to blame. For if she hadn't seen that sign of pride, that slim prayer, that marker, maybe she would have kept walking.

But Fleur Pillager turned, and the first place she went once she came into town was to the back door of the priest's residence attached to the landmark church. She didn't go there for a handout, although she got that, but to ask for work. She got that too, or the town got her. It's hard to tell which came out worse, her or the men or the town, although the upshot of it all was that Fleur lived.

The four men who worked at the butcher's had carved up about a thousand carcasses between them, maybe half of that steers and the other half pigs, sheep, and game animals like deer, elk, and bear. That's not even mentioning the chickens, which were beyond counting. Pete Kozka owned the place, and employed Lily Veddar, Tor Grunewald, and my stepfather, Dutch James, who had brought my mother down from the reservation the year before she disappointed him by dying. Dutch took me out of school to take her place. I kept house half the time and worked the other in the butcher shop, sweeping floors, putting sawdust down, running a hambone across the street to a customer's bean pot or a package of sausage to the corner. I was a good one to have around because until they needed me, I was invisible. I blended into the stained brown walls, a skinny, big-nosed girl with staring eyes. Because I could fade into a corner or squeeze beneath a shelf, I knew everything, what the men said when no one was around, and what they did to Fleur.

Kozka's Meats served farmers for a fifty-mile area, both to slaughter, for it had a stock pen and chute, and to cure the meat by smoking it or spicing it in sausage. The storage locker was a marvel, made of many thicknesses of brick, earth insulation, and Minnesota timber, lined inside with sawdust and vast blocks of ice cut from Lake Turcot, hauled down from home each winter by horse and sledge.

A ramshackle board building, part slaughterhouse, part store, was fixed to the low, thick square of the lockers. That's where Fleur worked. Kozka hired her for her strength. She could lift a haunch or carry a pole of sausages without stumbling, and she soon learned cutting from Pete's wife, a string-thin blonde who chain-smoked and handled the razor-sharp knives with nerveless precision, slicing close to her stained fingers. Fleur and Fritzie Kozka worked afternoons, wrapping their cuts in paper, and Fleur hauled the packages to the lockers. The meat was left outside the heavy oak doors that were only opened at 5:00 each afternoon, before the men ate supper.

Sometimes Dutch, Tor, and Lily ate at the lockers, and when they did I stayed too, cleaned floors, restoked the fires in the front smokehouses, while the men sat around the squat cast-iron stove spearing slats of herring onto hardtack bread. They played long games of poker or cribbage on a board made from the planed end of a salt crate. They talked and I listened, although there wasn't much to hear since almost nothing ever happened in Argus. Tor was married, Dutch had lost my mother, and Lily read circulars. They mainly discussed about the auctions to come, equipment, or women.

Every so often, Pete Kozka came out front to make a whist, leaving Fritzie to smoke cigarettes and fry raised doughnuts in the back room. He sat and played a few rounds but kept his thoughts to himself. Fritzie did not tolerate him talking behind her back, and the one book he read was the New Testament. If he said something, it concerned weather or a surplus of sheep stomachs, a ham that smoked green or the markets for corn and wheat. He had a good-luck talisman, the opal-white lens of a cow's eye. Playing cards, he rubbed it between his fingers. That soft sound and the slap of cards was about the only conversation.

Fleur finally gave them a subject.

Her cheeks were wide and flat, her hands large, chapped, muscular. Fleur's shoulders were broad as beams, her hips fishlike, slippery, narrow. An old green dress clung to her waist, worn thin where she sat. Her braids were thick like the tails of animals, and swung against her when she moved, deliberately, slowly in her work, held in and half-tamed, but only half. I could tell, but the others never saw. They never looked into her sly brown eyes or noticed her teeth, strong and curved and very white. Her legs were bare, and since she padded around in beadwork moccasins they never saw that her fifth toes were missing. They never knew she'd drowned. They were blinded, they were stupid, they only saw her in the flesh.

And yet it wasn't just that she was a Chippewa, or even that she was a woman, it wasn't that she was good-looking or even that she was alone that made their brains hum. It was how she played cards.

Women didn't usually play with men, so the evening that Fleur drew a chair up to the men's table without being so much as asked, there was a shock of surprise.

"What's this," said Lily. He was fat, with a snake's cold pale eyes and precious skin, smooth and lily-white, which is how he got his name. Lily had a dog, a stumpy mean little bull of a thing with a belly drum-tight from eating pork rinds. The dog liked to play cards just like Lily, and straddled his barrel thighs through games of stud, rum poker, vingt-un. The dog snapped at Fleur's arm that first night, but cringed back, its snarl frozen, when she took her place.

"I thought," she said, her voice soft and stroking, "you might deal me in."

There was a space between the heavy bin of spiced flour and the wall where I just fit. I hunkered down there, kept my eyes open, saw her black hair swing over the chair, her feet solid on the wood floor. I couldn't see up on the table where the cards slapped down, so after they were deep in their game I raised myself up in the shadows, and crouched on a sill of wood.

I watched Fleur's hands stack and ruffle, divide the cards, spill them to each player in a blur, rake them up and shuffle again. Tor, short and scrappy, shut one eye and squinted the other at Fleur. Dutch screwed his lips around a wet cigar.

"Gotta see a man," he mumbled, getting up to go out back to the privy. The others broke, put their cards down, and Fleur sat alone in the lamplight that glowed in a sheen across the push of her breasts. I watched her closely, then she paid me a beam of notice for the first time. She turned, looked straight at me, and grinned the white wolf grin a Pillager turns on its victims, except that she wasn't after me.

"Pauline there," she said, "how much money you got?"

We'd all been paid for the week that day. Eight cents was in my pocket.

"Stake me," she said, holding out her long fingers. I put the coins in her palm and then I melted back to nothing, part of the walls and tables. It was a long time before I understood that the men would not have seen me no matter what I did, how I moved. I wasn't anything like Fleur. My dress hung loose and my back was already curved, an old woman's. Work had roughened me, reading made my eyes sore, caring for my mother before she died had hardened my face. I was not much to look at, so they never saw me.

When the men came back and sat around the table, they had drawn together. They shot each other small glances, stuck their tongues in their cheeks, burst out laughing at odd moments, to rattle Fleur. But she never minded. They played their vingt-un, staying even as Fleur slowly gained. Those pennies I had given her drew nickels and attracted dimes until there was a small pile in front of her.

Then she hooked them with five-card draw, nothing wild. She dealt, discarded, drew, and then she sighed and her cards gave a little shiver. Tor's eye gleamed, and Dutch straightened in his seat.

"I'll pay to see that hand," said Lily Veddar.

Fleur showed, and she had nothing there, nothing at all.

Tor's thin smile cracked open, and he threw his hand in too.

"Well, we know one thing," he said, leaning back in his chair, "the squaw can't bluff."

With that I lowered myself into a mound of swept sawdust and slept. I woke up during the night, but none of them had moved yet, so I couldn't either. Still later, the men must have gone out again, or Fritzie come out to break the game, because I was lifted, soothed, cradled in a woman's arms and rocked so quiet that I kept my eyes shut while Fleur rolled me into a closet of grimy ledgers, oiled paper, balls of string, and thick files that fit beneath me like a mattress.

The game went on after work the next evening. I got my eight cents back five times over, and Fleur kept the rest of the dollar she'd won for a stake. This time they didn't play so late, but they played regular, and then kept going at it night after night. They played poker now, or variations, for one week straight, and each time Fleur won exactly one dollar, no more and no less, too consistent for luck.

By this time, Lily and the other men were so lit with suspense that they got Pete to join the game with them. They concentrated, the fat dog sitting tense in Lily Veddar's lap, Tor suspicious, Dutch stroking his huge square brow, Pete steady. It wasn't that Fleur won that hooked them in so, because she lost hands too. It was rather that she never had a freak hand or even anything above a straight. She only took on her low cards, which didn't sit right. By chance, Fleur should have gotten a full or flush by now. The irritating thing was she beat with pairs and never bluffed, because she couldn't, and still she ended up each night with exactly one dollar. Lily couldn't believe, first of all, that a woman could be smart enough to play cards, but even if she was, that she would then be stupid enough to cheat for a dollar a night. By day I watched him turn the problem over, his hard white face dull, small fingers probing at his knuckles, until he finally thought he had Fleur figured out as a bit-time player, caution her game. Raising the stakes would throw her.

More than anything now, he wanted Fleur to come away with something but a dollar. Two bits less or ten more, the sum didn't matter, just so he broke her streak.

Night after night she played, won her dollar, and left to stay in a place that just Fritzie and I knew about. Fleur bathed in the slaughtering tub, then slept in the unused brick smokehouse behind the lockers, a windowless place tarred on the inside with scorched fats. When I brushed against her skin I noticed that she smelled of the walls, rich and woody, slightly burnt. Since that night she put me in the closet I was no longer afraid of her, but followed her close, stayed with her, became her moving shadow that the men never noticed, the shadow that could have saved her.

August, the month that bears fruit, closed around the shop, and Pet and Fritzie left for Minnesota to escape the heat. Night by night, running, Fleur had won thirty dollars, and only Pete's presence had kept Lily at bay. But Pete was gone now, and one payday, with the heat so bad no one could move but Fleur, the men sat and played and waited while she finished work. The cards sweat, limp in their fingers, the table was slick with grease, and even the walls were warm to the touch. The air was motionless. Fleur was in the next room boiling heads.

Her green dress, drenched, wrapped her like a transparent sheet. A skin of lakeweed. Black snarls of veining clung to her arms. Her braids were loose, half-unraveled, tied behind her neck in a thick loop. She stood in steam, turning skulls through a vat with a wooden paddle. When scraps boiled to the surface, she bent with a round tin sieve and scooped them out. She'd filled two dishpans.

"Ain't that enough now?" called Lily. "We're waiting." The stump of a dog trembled in his lap, alive with rage. It never smelled me or noticed me above Fleur's smoky skin. The air was heavy in my corner, and pressed me down. Fleur sat with them.

"Now what do you say?" Lily asked the dog. It barked. That was the signal for the real game to start.

"Let's up the ante," said Lily, who had been stalking this night all month. He had a roll of money in his pocket. Fleur had five bills in her dress. The men had each saved their full pay.

"Ante a dollar then," said Fleur, and pitched hers in. She lost, but they let her scrape along, cent by cent. And then she won some. She played unevenly, as if chance was all she had. She reeled them in. The game went on. The dog was stiff now, poised on Lily's knees, a ball of vicious muscle with its yellow eyes slit in concentration. It gave advice, seemed to sniff the lay of Fleur's cards, twitched and nudged. Fleur was up, then down, saved by a scratch. Tor dealt seven cards, three down. The pot grew, round by round, until it held all the money. Nobody folded. Then it all rode on one last card and they went silent. Fleur picked hers up and blew a long breath. The heat lowered like a bell. Her card shook, but she stayed in.

Lily smiled and took the dog's head tenderly between his palms.

"Say, Fatso," he said, crooning the words, "you reckon that girl's bluffing?"

The dog whined and Lily laughed. "Me too," he said, "let's show." He swept his bills and coins into the pot and then they turned their cards over.

Lily looked once, looked again, then he squeezed the dog up like a fist of dough and slammed it on the table.

Fleur threw her arms out and drew the money over, grinning that same wolf grin that she'd used on me, the grin that had them. She jammed the bills in her dress, scooped the coins up in waxed white paper that she tied with string.

"Let's go another round," said Lily, his voice choked with burrs. But Fleur opened her mouth and yawned, then walked out back to gather slops for the one big hog that was waiting in the stock pen to be killed.

The men sat still as rocks, their hands spread on the oiled wood table. Dutch had chewed his cigar to damp shreds, Tor's eye was dull. Lily's gaze was the only one to follow Fleur. I didn't move. I felt them gathering, saw my stepfather's veins, the ones in his forehead that stood out in anger. The dog had rolled off the table and curled in a knot below the counter, where none of the men could touch it.

Lily rose and stepped out back to the closet of ledgers where Pete kept his private stock. He brought back a bottle, uncorked and tipped it between his fingers. The lump in his throat moved, then he passed it on. They drank, quickly felt the whiskey's fire, and planned with their eyes things they couldn't say out loud.

When they left, I followed. I hid out back in the clutter of broken boards and chicken crates beside the stock pen, where they waited. Fleur could not be seen at first, and then the moon broke and showed her, slipping cautiously along the rough board chute with a bucket in her hand. Her hair fell, wild and coarse, to her waist, and her dress was a floating patch in the dark. She made a pig-calling sound, rang the tin pail lightly against the wood, froze suspiciously. But too late. In the sound of the ring Lily moved, fat and nimble, stepped right behind Fleur and put out his creamy hands. At his first touch, she whirled and doused him with the bucket of sour slops. He pushed her against the big fence and the package of coins split, went clinking and jumping, winked against the wood. Fleur rolled over once and vanished in the yard.

The moon fell behind a curtain of ragged clouds, and Lily followed into the dark muck. But he tripped, pitched over the huge flank of the pig, who lay mired to the snout, heavily snoring. I sprang out of the weeds and climbed the side of the pen, stuck like glue. I saw the sow rise to her neat, knobby knees, gain her balance, and sway, curious, as Lily stumbled forward. Fleur had backed into the angle of rough wood just beyond, and when Lily tried to jostle past, the sow tipped up on her hind legs and struck, quick and hard as a snake. She plunged her head into Lily's thick side and snatched a mouthful of his shirt. She lunged again, caught him lower, so that he grunted in pained surprise. He seemed to ponder, breathing deep. Then he launched his huge body in a swimmer's dive.

The sow screamed as his body smacked over hers. She rolled, striking out with her knife-sharp hooves, and Lily gathered himself upon her, took her foot-long face by the ears and scraped her snout and cheeks against the trestles of the pen. He hurled the sow's tight skull against an iron post, but instead of knocking her dead, he merely woke her from her dream.

She reared, shrieked, drew him with her so that they posed standing upright. They bowed jerkily to each other, as if to begin. Then his arms swung and flailed. She sank her black fangs into his shoulder, clasping him, dancing him forward and backward through the pen. Their steps picked up pace, went wild. The two dipped as one, box-stepped, tripped each other. She ran her split foot through his hair. He grabbed her kinked tail. They went down and came up, the same shape and then the same color, until the men couldn't tell one from the other in that light and Fleur was able to launch herself over the gates, swing down, hit gravel.

The men saw, yelled, and chased her at a dead run to the smokehouse. And Lily too, once the sow gave up in disgust and freed him. That is where I should have gone to Fleur, saved her, thrown myself on Dutch. But I went stiff with fear and couldn't unlatch myself from the trestles or move at all. I closed my eyes and put my head in my arms, tried to hide, so there is nothing to describe but what I couldn't block out, Fleur's hoarse breath, so loud it filled me, her cry in the old language, and my name repeated over and over among the words.

The heat was still dense the next morning when I came back to work. Fleur was gone but the men were there, slack-faced, hung over. Lily was paler and softer than ever, as if his flesh had steamed on his bones. They smoked, took pulls off a bottle. It wasn't noon yet. I worked awhile, waiting shop and sharpening steel. But I was sick, I was smothered, I was sweating so hard that my hands slipped on the knives, and I wiped my fingers clean of the greasy touch of the customers' coins. Lily opened his mouth and roared once, not in anger. There was no meaning to the sound. His boxer dog, sprawled limp beside his foot, never lifted its head. Nor did the other men.

They didn't notice when I stepped outside, hoping for a clear breath. And then I forgot them because I knew that we were all balanced, ready to tip, to fly, to be crushed as soon as the weather broke. The sky was so low that I felt the weight of it like a yoke. Clouds hung down, witch teats, a tornado's green-brown cones, and as I watched one flicked out and became a delicate probing thumb. Even as I picked up my heels and ran back inside, the wind blew suddenly, cold, and then came rain.

Inside, the men had disappeared already and the whole place was trembling as if a huge hand was pinched at the rafters, shaking it. I ran straight through, screaming for Dutch or for any of them, and then I stopped at the heavy doors of the lockers, where they had surely taken shelter. I stood there a moment. Everything went still. Then I heard a cry building in the wind, faint at first, a whistle and then a shrill scream that tore through the walls and gathered around me, spoke plain so I understood that I should move, put my arms out, and slam down the great iron bar that fit across the hasp and lock.

Outside, the wind was stronger, like a hand held against me. I struggled forward. The bushes tossed, the awnings flapped off storefronts, the rails of porches rattled. The odd cloud became a fat snout that nosed along the earth and sniffled, jabbed, picked at things, sucked them up, blew them apart, rooted around as if it was following a certain scent, then stopped behind me at the butcher shop and bored down like a drill.

I went flying, landed somewhere in a ball. When I opened my eyes and looked, stranger things were happening.

A herd of cattle flew through the air like giant birds, dropping dung, their mouths opened in stunned bellows. A candle, still lighted, blew past, and tables, napkins, garden tools, a whole school of drifting eyeglasses, jackets on hangers, hams, a checkerboard, a lampshade, and at last the sow from behind the lockers, on the run, her hooves a blur, set free, swooping, diving, screaming as everything in Argus fell apart and got turned upside down, smashed, and thoroughly wrecked.

Days passed before the town went looking for the men. They were bachelors, after all, except for Tor, whose wife had suffered a blow to the head that made her forgetful. Everyone was occupied with digging out, in high relief because even though the Catholic steeple had been torn off like a peaked cap and sent across five fields, those huddled in the cellar were unhurt. Walls had fallen, windows were demolished, but the stores were intact and so were the bankers and shop owners who had taken refuge in their safes or beneath their cash registers. It was a fair-minded disaster, no one could be said to have suffered much more than the next, at least not until Fritzie and Pete came home.

Of all the businesses in Argus, Kozka's Meats had suffered worst. The boards of the front building had been split to kindling, piled in a huge pyramid, and the shop equipment was blasted far and wide. Pete paced off the distance the iron bathtub had been flung—a hundred feet. The glass candy case went fifty, and landed without so much as a cracked pane. There were other surprises as well, for the back rooms where Fritzie and Pete lived were undisturbed. Fritzie said the dust still coated her china figures, and upon her kitchen table, in the ashtray, perched the last cigarette she'd put out in haste. She lit it up and finished it, looking through the window. From there, she could see that the old smokehouse Fleur had slept in was crushed to a reddish sand and the stockpens were completely torn apart, the rails stacked helter-skelter. Fritzie asked for Fleur. People shrugged. Then she asked about the others and, suddenly, the town understood that three men were missing.

There was a rally of help, a gathering of shovels and volunteers. We passed boards from hand to hand, stacked them, uncovered what lay beneath the pile of jagged splinters. The lockers, full of the meat that was Pete and Fritzie's investment, slowly came into sight, still intact. When enough room was made for a man to stand on the roof, there were calls, a general urge to hack through and see what lay below. But Fritzie shouted that she wouldn't allow it because the meat would spoil. And so the work continued, board by board, until at last the heavy oak doors of the freezer were revealed and people pressed to the entry. Everyone wanted to be the first, but since it was my stepfather lost, I was let go in when Pete and Fritzie wedged through into the sudden icy air.

Pete scraped a match on his boot, lit the lamp Fritzie held, and then the three of us stood still in its circle. Light glared off the skinned and hanging carcasses, the crates of wrapped sausages, the bright and cloudy blocks of lake ice, pure as winter. The cold bit into us, pleasant at first, then numbing. We must have stood there a couple of minutes before we saw the men, or more rightly, the humps of fur, the iced and shaggy hides they wore, the bearskins they had taken down and wrapped around themselves. We stepped closer and tilted the lantern beneath the flaps of fur into their faces. The dog was there, perched among them, heavy as a doorstop. The three had hunched around a barrel where the game was still laid out, and a dead lantern and an empty bottle, too. But they had thrown down their last hands and hunkered tight, clutching one another, knuckles raw from beating at the door they had also attacked with hooks. Frost stars gleamed off their eyelashes and the stubble of their beards. Their faces were set in concentration, mouths open as if to speak some careful thought, some agreement they'd come to in each other's arms.

Power travels in the bloodlines, handed out before birth. It comes down through the hands, which in the Pillagers were strong and knotted, big, spidery, and rough, with sensitive fingertips good at dealing cards. It comes through the eyes, too, belligerent, darkest brown, the eyes of those in the bear clan, impolite as they gaze directly at a person.

In my dreams, I look straight back at Fleur, at the men. I am no longer the watcher on the dark sill, the skinny girl.

The blood draws us back, as if it runs through a vein of earth. I've come home and, except for talking to my cousins, live a quiet life. Fleur lives quiet too, down on Lake Turcot with her boat. Some say she's married to the waterman, Misshepeshu, or that she's living in shame with white men or windigos, or that she's killed them all. I'm about the only one here who ever goes to visit her. Last winter, I went to help out in her cabin when she bore the child, whose green eyes and skin the color of an old penny made more talk, as no one could decide if the child was mixed blood or what, fathered in a smokehouse, or by a man with brass scales, or by the lake. The girl is bold, smiling in her sleep, as if she knows what people wonder, as if she hears the old men talk, turning the story over. It comes up different every time and has no ending, no beginning. They get the middle wrong too. They only know that they don't know anything.

MARK RICHARD

Strays

Mark Richard (1955–   ) grew up in Texas and Virginia. As a boy
he contracted polio and spent much of his convalescence reading. At
thirteen, he was reputed to be the youngest disc jockey in America,
presiding over his own radio show in Franklin, Virginia. He attended
Washington and Lee University and then went off to sea for three years,
working on ocean-going trawlers, coastal steamers, and small fishing
boats. At the time that "Strays" was published in Esquire, Richard and
a friend had been doing a less-than-thriving business in mail-order hams.
The story was reprinted in Best American Short Stories, as well as in
his collection, The Ice at the Bottom of the World, which won the
PEN/Hemingway Award for first work of fiction in 1990. His first
novel, Fishboy, was published in 1993.

At night stray dogs come up underneath
our house to lick our leaking pipes. Beneath my brother and my's room we hear
them coughing and growling, scratching their ratted backs against the boards
beneath our beds. We lie awake listening, my brother thinking of names to name
the one he is setting out to catch. Salute and Topboy are high on his list.

I tell my brother these dogs are wild and cowering. A bare-heeled stomp
on the floor off our beds sends them scuttling spine-bowed out the crawl space

beneath our open window. Sometimes when my brother is quick he leans out and touches one slipping away.

Our father has meant to put the screens back on the windows for spring. He has even hauled them out of the storage shed and stacked them in the drive. He lays them one by one over sawhorses to tack in the frames tighter and weave patches against mosquitoes. This is what he means to do, but our mother that morning pulls all the preserves off the shelves onto the floor, sticks my brother and my's Easter Sunday drawings in her mouth, and leaves the house on through the fields cleared the week before for corn.

Uncle Trash is our nearest relative with a car, and our mother has a good half-day head start on our father when Uncle Trash arrives. Uncle Trash runs his car up the drive in a big speed splitting all the screens stacked there from their frames. There is an exploded chicken in the grill of Uncle Trash's car. They don't even turn it off as Uncle Trash slides out and our father gets behind the wheel backing back over the screens setting out in search of our mother.

Uncle Trash finds out that he has left his bottle under the seat of his car. He goes in our kitchen pulling out all the shelves our mother missed. Then he is in the towel box in the hall, looking, pulling out stuff in stacks. He is in our parents' room opening short doors. He is in the storage shed opening and sniffing a mason jar of gasoline for the power mower. Uncle Trash comes up and asks, Which way is it to town for a drink? I point up the road and he sets off saying, Don't y'all burn the house down.

My brother and I hang out in the side yard doing handstands until dark. We catch handfuls of lightning bugs and smear bright yellow on our shirts. It is late. I wash our feet and put us to bed. We wait for somebody to come back home but nobody ever does. Lucky for me when my brother begins to whine for our mother the stray dogs show up under the house and he starts making up lists of new names for them, soothing himself to sleep.

Hungry, we wake up to something sounding in the kitchen not like our mother fixing us anything to eat. It is Uncle Trash throwing up and spitting blood into the pump-handled sink. I ask him did he have an accident and he sends my brother upstairs for Merthiolate and Q-Tips. His face is angled out from his head on one side, so that sided eye is shut. His good eye waters wiggling loose teeth with cut-up fingers. Uncle Trash says he had an accident all right. He says he was up in a card game and then he was real up in a card game, so up he bet his car, accidentally forgetting that our father had driven off with it in search of our mother. Uncle Trash said the man who won the card game went ahead and beat up Uncle Trash on purpose anyway.

All day Uncle Trash sleeps in our parents' room. We can hear him snoring from the front yard where my brother and I dig in the dirt with spoons making roadbeds and highways for my tin-metal trucks. In the evening Uncle Trash comes down in one of our father's shirts, dirty, but cleaner than the one he had gotten beat up in. We then have banana sandwiches for supper and Uncle Trash asks do we have a deck of cards in the house. He says he wants to see do his tooth-cut fingers still flex enough to work. I have to tell him how our mother disallows all card playing in the house but that my brother has a pack of Old Maid somewhere in the toy box. While my brother goes out to look I brag at how I always beat him out, leaving him the Old Maid, and Uncle Trash says, Oh yeah? and digs around in his pocket for a nickel he puts on the table. He says we'll play a nickel a game and I go into my brother and my's room to get the Band-Aid box of nickels and dimes I sometimes short from the collection plate on Sunday.

Uncle Trash is making painful faces flexing his red-painted fingers around the Old Maid deck of circus-star cards, but he still shuffles, cuts, and deals a three-way hand one-handed, and not much longer I lose my Band-Aid box of money and all the tin-metal trucks of mine out in the front yard. He makes me go out and get them and put them on his side of the table. My brother loses a set of bowling pins and a stuffed beagle. In two more hands we stack up our winter boots and coats with hoods on Uncle Trash's side of the table. In the last hand my brother and I step out of our shorts and underdrawers while Uncle Trash smiles and says, And now, gentlemen, if you please, the shirts off y'all's backs.

Uncle Trash rakes everything my brother and I own into the pillowcases off our beds and says let that be a lesson to me. He is off through the front porch leaving us buck naked across the table, his last words as he goes up the road shoulder-slinging his loot, Don't y'all burn the house down.

I am burning hot at Uncle Trash, then I am burning hot at our father for leaving us with him to look for our mother, and then I am burning hot at my mother for running off through the fields leaving me with my brother, and then I am burning hot at my brother who is starting to cry. There is only one thing left to do and that is to take all we still have left that we own and throw it at my brother, and I do, and Old Maid cards explode on his face setting him off on a really good red-face howl.

I tell my brother that making so much noise will keep the stray dogs away and he believes it, and then I start to believe it when it gets later than usual, past the crickets and into a long moon over the trees, but they finally do come after my brother finally falls asleep, so I just wait until I know there are several beneath the bed boards scratching their rat-matted backs and growling, and I stomp on the floor, what is my favorite part about the dogs, watching them scatter in a hundred directions and then seeing them one by one collect in a pack at the edge of the field near the trees.

I n the morning right off I recognize the bicycle coming wobble-wheeling into the front yard. It's the one the boy outside Cuts uses to run lunches and ice water to the pulpwood truck Mr. Cuts has working cutover timber on the edge of town. The colored boy that usually drives it snaps bottle caps off his fingers at my brother and I when we go to Cuts with our mother to make groceries. We have to wait outside by the kerosene pump, out by the papered-over lean-to shed, the pop-crate place where the men sit around and Uncle Trash does his card work now. White people generally don't go into Cuts unless they have to buy on credit.

We at school know Mr. and Mrs. Cuts come from a family that eats children. There is a red metal tree with plastic-wrapped toys in the window and a long candy counter case inside to lure you in. Mr. and Mrs. Cuts have no children of their own. They ate them during a hard winter and salted the rest down for sandwiches the colored boy runs out to the pulpwood crew at noon. I count colored children going in to buy some candy to see how many make it back out, but generally our mother is ready to go home way before I can tell. Our credit at Cuts is short.

The front tire catches in one of our tin-metal truck's underground tunnel tracks and Uncle Trash takes a spill. The cut crate bolted to the bicycle handle-bars spills out brown paper packages sealed with electrical tape into the yard along with a case of Champale and a box of cigars. Uncle Trash is down where he falls. He lays asleep all day under the tree in the yard moving just to crawl back into the wandering shade.

We have for supper sirloins, Champale, and cigars. Uncle Trash teaches how to cross our legs up on the table after dinner but says he'll go ahead and leave my brother and my's cigars unlit. There is no outlook for our toys and my Band-Aid can of nickels and dimes, checking all the packages, even checking twice again the cut crate bolted on the front of the bicycle. Uncle Trash shows us a headstand on the table drinking a bottle of Champale, then he stands in the

sink and sings "Gather My Far-flung Thoughts Together." My brother and I
chomp our cigars and clap, but in our hearts we are low and lonesome.

Don't y'all burn down the house, says Uncle Trash pedaling out the yard
to Cuts. My brother leans out our window with a rope coil and scraps strung
on strings. He is in a greasy-finger sleep when the strings slither like white snakes
off our bed and over the sill into the fields out back.

There's July corn and no word from our
parents. Uncle Trash doesn't remember the Fourth of July or the Fourth of July
parade. Uncle Trash bunches cattails in the fenders of his bicycle and clips our
Old Maid cards in the spokes and follows the fire engine through town with my
brother and I in the front cut-out crate throwing penny candy to the crowds.
What are you trying to be, the colored men at Cuts ask us when we end up there.
I spot a tin-metal truck of mine broken by the Cuts' front step. Foolish, says
Uncle Trash.

Uncle Trash doesn't remember winning Mrs. Cuts in a game for a day to
come out and clean the house and us in the bargain. She pushes the furniture
around with a broom and calls us abominations. There's a bucket of soap to wash
our heads and a jar of sour-smelling cream for our infected bites. Fleas from
under the house and mosquitoes through the windows. The screens are rusty
squares in the driveway dirt. Uncle Trash leaves her his razor opened as long as
my arm. She comes after my brother and I with it to cut our hair, she says. We
know better. My brother dives under the house and I am up a tree. Uncle Trash
doesn't remember July, but when we tell him about it he says he thinks July was
probably a good idea at the time.

It is August with the brown twisted corn
in the fields next to the house. There is word from our parents. They are in the
state capital. One of them has been in jail. I try to decide which. Uncle Trash
is still promising screens. We get from Cuts bug spray instead.

I wake up in the middle of a night. My brother floats through the window.
Out in the yard he and a stray have each other on the end of a rope. He reels
her in and I make the tackle. Already I feel the fleas leave her rag-matted coat
and crawl over my arms and up my neck. We spray her down with a whole can
of bug spray until her coat lathers like soap. My brother gets some matches to
burn a tick like a grape out of her ear. The touch of the match covers her like

a blue-flame sweater. She's a fireball shooting beneath the house. By the time Uncle Trash and the rest of town get there the fire warden says the house is Fully Involved.

In the morning our parents drive past where our house used to be. They go by again until they recognize the yard. Uncle Trash is trying to bring my brother out of the trance he is in by showing him how some card tricks work on the left-standing steps of the stoop. Uncle Trash shows Jack-Away, Queen in the Whorehouse, and No Money Down. Our father says for Uncle Trash to stand up so he can knock him down. Uncle Trash says he deserves that one. Our father knocks him down again and tells him not to get up. If you get up I'll kill you, our father says.

Uncle Trash crawls on all fours across our yard out to the road. Good-bye, Uncle Trash, I say. Good-bye, men, Uncle Trash says. Don't y'all burn the house down, he says and I say, We won't.

During the knocking down nobody notices our mother. She is a flat-footed running rustle through the corn all burned up by the summer sun.

[JULY 1988]

Acknowledgments

Grateful acknowledgment is made to the following for permission to reprint copyrighted material:

Georges Borchardt, Inc.: "My Mother's Lover," by Vince Passaro. Copyright © 1992 by Vince Passaro. "I Look Out for Ed Wolfe," from *Criers and Kibitzers, Kibitzers and Criers* by Stanley Elkin. Copyright © 1962 by Stanley Elkin. "Heart of a Champion," from *Descent of Man and Other Stories* by T. Coraghessan Boyle. Copyright © 1974 by T. Coraghessan Boyle.

Curtis Brown Ltd.: "August Afternoon," by Erskine Caldwell. Copyright © 1933, 1961 by Erskine Caldwell.

Cayuse Press: "The Quarterback Speaks to His God," from *The Quarterback Speaks to His God* by Herbert Wilner. Copyright © 1987 by Nancy Wilner.

Don Congdon Associates, Inc.: "The Illustrated Man," by Ray Bradbury. Copyright © 1950 by Esquire, Inc.; renewal copyright © 1977 by Ray Bradbury.

Darhansoff & Verrill Literary Agency: "Return to Return," from *Airships* by Barry Hannah. Copyright © 1978 by Barry Hannah.

Donadio & Ashworth, Inc.: "Black Angels," by Bruce Jay Friedman. Copyright © 1964 by Bruce Jay Friedman.

Louise Erdrich: "Fleur," by Louise Erdrich. Copyright © 1986 by Louise Erdrich.

Farrar, Straus & Giroux, Inc.: "Parker's Back," from *Everything That Rises Must Converge* by Flannery O'Connor. Copyright © 1965 by the Estate of Mary Flannery O'Connor. "Steady Hands at Seattle General," from *Jesus' Son* by Denis Johnson. Copyright © 1992 by Denis Johnson.

Arthur B. Green: "The Eighty-Yard Run," by Irwin Shaw. Copyright © 1940, 1968 by Irwin Shaw.

Maxine Groffsky Literary Agency: "Accountant," by Ethan Canin. Copyright © 1988 by Ethan Canin.